Pamela Belle lives in Wiltshire with her husband, Steve, and two sons, Hugh and Patrick. She is the author of eight historical novels including *Wintercombe*, *Herald of Joy*, *A Falling Star*, and *Treason's Gift*. *Blood Imperial* is the final part of a fantasy trilogy begun with *The Silver City* and continued with *The Wolf Within*.

Also by Pamela Belle in Pan Books

The Silver City
The Wolf Within

BLOOD IMPERIAL

PAMELA BELLE

PAN BOOKS

First published 1996 by Pan Books
an imprint of Macmillan Publishers Ltd
25 Eccleston Place London SW1W 9NF
and Basingstoke

Associated companies throughout the world

ISBN 0 330 34789 6

Copyright © Pamela Belle 1996

The right of Pamela Belle to be identified as the
author of this work has been asserted by her in accordance
with the Copyright, Designs and Patents Act 1988.

All rights reserved. No part of this publication may be
reproduced, stored in or introduced into a retrieval system, or
transmitted, in any form, or by any means (electronic, mechanical,
photocopying, recording or otherwise) without the prior written
permission of the publisher. Any person who does any unauthorized
act in relation to this publication may be liable to criminal
prosecution and civil claims for damages.

1 3 5 7 9 8 6 4 2

A CIP catalogue record for this book is available from
the British Library.

Typeset by Parker Typesetting Service, Leicester
Printed by Mackays of Chatham plc, Chatham, Kent

This book is sold subject to the condition that it shall not,
by way of trade or otherwise, be lent, re-sold, hired out,
or otherwise circulated without the publisher's prior consent
in any form of binding or cover other than that in which
it is published and without a similar condition including this
condition being imposed on the subsequent purchaser.

For Sam,
because behind every working mother
is another woman,
looking after her children

The Imperial Family of Toktel'yi, showing male and some female members

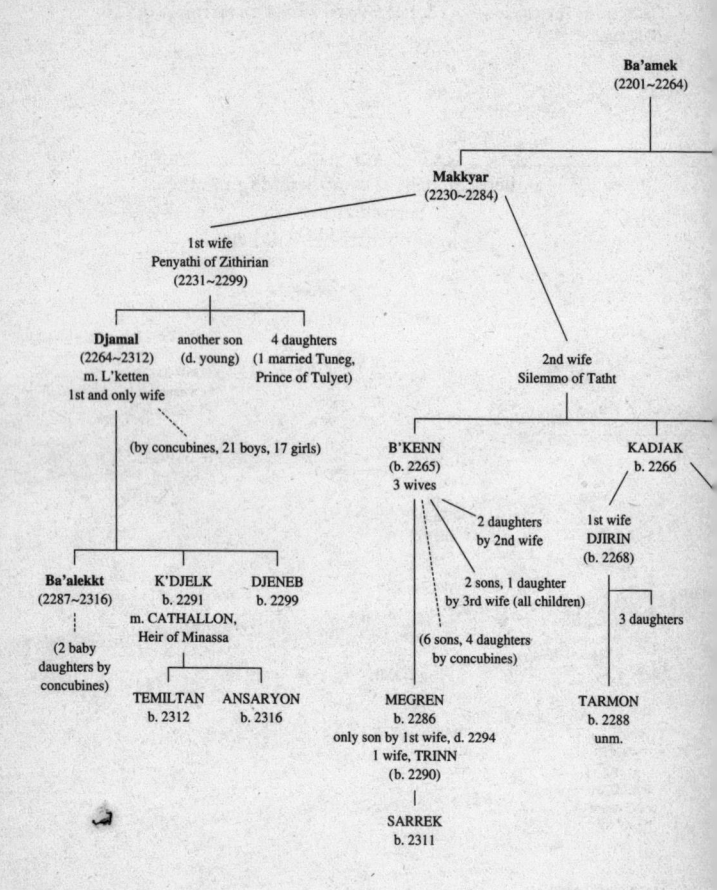

Ba'amek (2201~2264)
└── **Makkyar** (2230~2284)
    ├── 1st wife: Penyathi of Zithirian (2231~2299)
    │   ├── **Djamal** (2264~2312) m. L'ketten, 1st and only wife
    │   │   │ (by concubines, 21 boys, 17 girls)
    │   │   ├── **Ba'alekkt** (2287~2316)
    │   │   │   ⋮ (2 baby daughters by concubines)
    │   │   ├── **K'DJELK** b. 2291 m. CATHALLON, Heir of Minassa
    │   │   │   ├── TEMILTAN b. 2312
    │   │   │   └── ANSARYON b. 2316
    │   │   └── **DJENEB** b. 2299
    │   ├── another son (d. young)
    │   └── 4 daughters (1 married Tuneg, Prince of Tulyet)
    └── 2nd wife: Silemmo of Tatht
        ├── **B'KENN** (b. 2265) 3 wives
        │   ├── 2 daughters by 2nd wife
        │   ├── 2 sons, 1 daughter by 3rd wife (all children)
        │   ├── (6 sons, 4 daughters by concubines)
        │   └── **MEGREN** b. 2286, only son by 1st wife, d. 2294
        │   1 wife, TRINN (b. 2290)
        │   └── **SARREK** b. 2311
        └── **KADJAK** b. 2266
            └── 1st wife DJIRIN (b. 2268)
                ├── 3 daughters
                └── **TARMON** b. 2288 unm.

Emperors are shown in **bold**.

Those alive at the start of the book are shown in CAPITALS.

Dates are in Toktel'yan years, counted from the start of the first Emperor Akkatanat's reign.

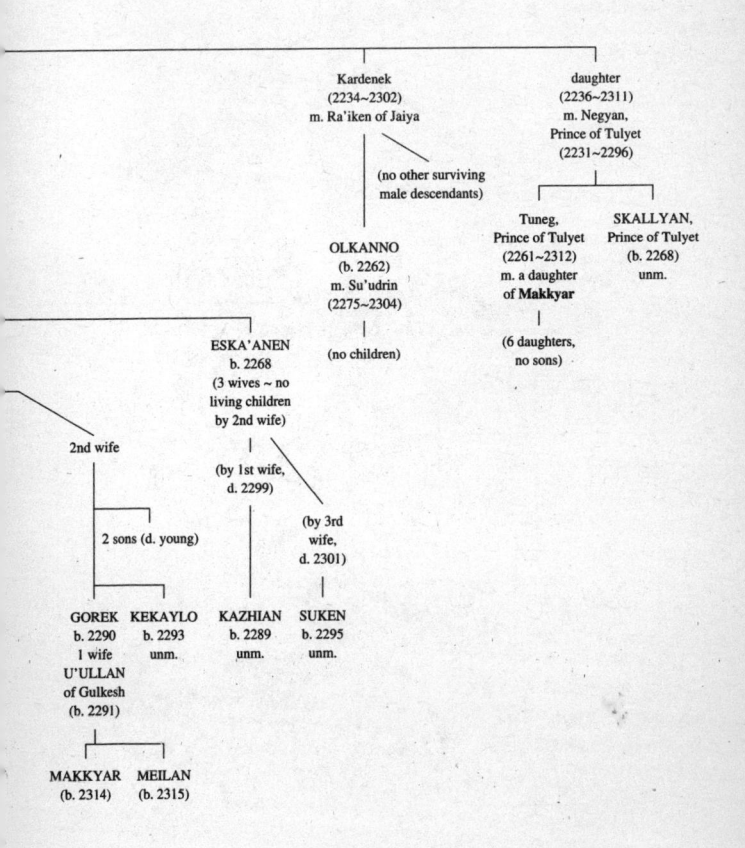

```
                                        Kardenek              daughter
                                        (2234~2302)           (2236~2311)
                                        m. Ra'iken of Jaiya   m. Negyan,
                                                              Prince of Tulyet
                                                              (2231~2296)
                                            (no other surviving
                                             male descendants)
                                                                    Tuneg,              SKALLYAN,
                                        OLKANNO                     Prince of Tulyet    Prince of Tulyet
                                        (b. 2262)                   (2261~2312)         (b. 2268)
                                        m. Su'udrin                 m. a daughter       unm.
                                        (2275~2304)                 of Makkyar
                        ESKA'ANEN                                       |
                        b. 2268         (no children)               (6 daughters,
                        (3 wives ~ no                                 no sons)
                        living children
                        by 2nd wife)
                            |
2nd wife                (by 1st wife,
                         d. 2299)
                                     (by 3rd
        2 sons (d. young)             wife,
                                      d. 2301)

GOREK   KEKAYLO    KAZHIAN   SUKEN
b. 2290 b. 2293    b. 2289   b. 2295
1 wife  unm.       unm.      unm.
U'ULLAN
of Gulkesh
(b. 2291)

MAKKYAR   MEILAN
(b. 2314) (b. 2315)
```

PROLOGUE

Even in Minassa, bordering the Empire, black faces were obviously rare.

Al'Kalyek, once Court Sorcerer to two Emperors of Toktel'yi, was beginning to find the stares and whispered comments rather tiresome. He had been tramping this hot, dusty road for more than a day, under the burning sun of High Summer, and he was in no mood to be patient with the rude, unabashed curiosity of the few people he met on the road. He felt old, sad, shaken to the core by a grief he had never expected, and as exhausted as if he had lived twice his seventy years. He wanted to weep, or rage, or scream his anguish to the oblivious sky. Instead, he plodded doggedly onwards, intent only on reaching his journey's end.

It came sooner than he had expected. A cloud of dust, moving rapidly towards him on the long straight road ahead, proved to be a patrol of barbarian riders, both men and women, some twenty strong. They surrounded him, and in polite but firm Zithiriani, a language he understood very well, suggested that he continue in their company.

There was no point whatsoever in argument. Glad of the opportunity to rest his aching feet, Al'Kalyek was hoisted on to a handsome horse that was obviously used to carrying sorcerers, for apart from a swish of the tail it made no objection to his presence on its back. Then he was escorted on, rather more rapidly than he wished, towards the camp of the Kings of Zithirian and Minassa.

His captors were Tanathi, of course. Men and women were all clad in dyed leather tunics and trousers, their plaited hair chiming with golden talismans, and woven with bright braid and ribbons. Everywhere, on both animals and riders, there was the gleam of bullion. Tanathi horseflesh was prized throughout the known world, and barbarians were notorious lovers of gold. Their leader, a tall, lean man with red hair and a face that Al'Kalyek thought he recognized, was wearing enough jewels and precious metalwork to buy a Toktel'yan town. He asked his name of the young woman riding on his left, and she grinned. 'Abreth, High Chieftan of all the ten clans of of the Tanathi. His sister is Queen of Zithirian.'

That explained the familiarity of the face. 'Is Queen Halthris with her husband?'

'Oh, no,' said the woman, looking surprised. 'No, she is in – in a secret place, with her younger children. Didn't you know? You are a sorcerer, aren't you?'

'Yes,' Al'Kalyek said drily. 'But sorcerers don't know everything.'

The Tanathi woman gave him a rather scornful look, as if his power had been exposed as the poor fraudulent shadow which he himself now knew it to be, and fell silent. Al'Kalyek concentrated on keeping in the saddle. Like most wealthy Toktel'yans – and all sorcerers – he usually travelled by boat, wagon or litter rather than on horseback, and balancing on top of this high and spirited beast was not easy.

The combined armies of Zithirian and Minassa lay between the road and the looping course of the river Kefirinn, some thirty miles north of the border. Al'Kalyek, staring at the multitude of tents and soldiers sprawled across a mile or more of summer-dry meadow, calculated that there might be more than fifty thousand men here. It was a puny number when compared with the overwhelming strength of the Toktel'yan Army, the finest troops in the known world, but still a vast and heroic effort from two small, scattered kingdoms. Such a terrible threat to life and freedom had obviously been a very powerful motive.

The Kings' tent, distinguished by the royal banners drooping from the poles before it on this hot, airless late afternoon, had been pitched close to the river. Al'Kalyek looked at the smooth, endless flow of brown water, and felt a renewed surge of sorrow. The Kefirinn had so nearly ended his own life, and the Emperor of Toktel'yi, entombed in his heavy steel armour, had sunk without trace beneath that calmly innocent surface.

And so had the man who had killed him: and thus was the world changed, and the prophecy fulfilled.

The Kings of Zithirian and Minassa were waiting for him. They sat together in the dim, stuffy gloom of the tent, cooled by a huge fan of woven leaves and grass that waved above them with no discernible cause. Al'Kalyek could not detect the use of sorcery, though, and he remembered that King Temiltan had a considerable reputation as a maker of ingenious devices.

The ruler of Minassa was over seventy now, a short, narrow, stringy man whose air of vigour and determination took years off his actual age. Beside him, in an identical folding campaign chair with no trappings of royalty, sat his sister's son, the King of Zithirian, who was nearly three decades younger.

Al'Kalyek had met Ansaryon on his various visits to Toktel'yi, and knew him well. Indeed, one of the main reasons why he had dreaded the late Emperor's planned attack on the northern cities was his aversion to making war on a man he liked and admired. He performed the brief obeisance which the King preferred, and lifted his gaze to the younger man's face.

It was pale and haggard, and deep lines were engraved between his fair brows and around his mouth. Then he smiled and stood up, holding out his hands. 'Al'Kalyek, my old friend – you are most welcome.'

They embraced, and then the old man said sadly, 'And I am glad to see you – but I wish with all my heart that I had different news.'

There was a brief silence. The sorcerer looked into the King's haunted silver-grey eyes, and saw that Ansaryon already knew much of what had happened yesterday – only yesterday! – in Tamat.

He said slowly, 'How much have you heard – or seen?'

Ansaryon was particularly skilled in the use of the scrying-bowl, one of the most difficult arts for an aspiring sorcerer to master. His mouth twisted. 'Enough. Too much. I know that Ba'alekkt is dead, leaving no single heir. I know that the invasion has been halted – and given the likelihood of a struggle over the succession to the Onyx Throne, we will probably be safe at least for the rest of this year, if not for several to come. You need no sorcery to recognize that.' He paused, and added at last, his voice strained with grief, 'And I know – I know that my son is dead.'

'Do you know how he died?'

'Yes,' said Ansaryon with difficulty, and his remarkable eyes closed for a moment, as if to shut out a vision too painful to bear. 'I was watching in the bowl. I saw him bound a prisoner in the boat, and I saw him vanish beneath the Kefirinn with Ba'alekkt. And though I watched and waited, and prayed to all the gods of earth and sky, I did not see him again.'

'He killed Ba'alekkt,' Al'Kalyek told him softly. 'I was in the boat too, as you must have seen. He was hurt, badly hurt, from the beatings he had received. I did not think he had any strength left, and neither did Ba'alekkt. But I felt his power, at the last. He tipped up the boat, and the Emperor sank like the stone of evil he was, and drowned. He will lie there forever within the Kefirinn's embrace, weighted down with all that splendid, useless armour that he was so proud of – but it proved to be his doom and not his salvation. And the river took Bron too.'

'Did – are you certain?'

'Yes,' said Al'Kalyek heavily. 'Yes, I am sure. I searched for him, when I reached the bank. I could find no trace of his life or his spirit. He was weak, and bound hand and foot. He used the last of his power to upset the boat – he had none left to save himself.'

'He was taken by the Kefirinn once before, and survived,' Ansaryon said, as if he could not bear to abandon all possible traces of hope. 'But then, the Wolf saved him – the demon which lurked in his soul.'

'I could discern no such creature within him,' Al'Kalyek said. 'And I made contact with his mind several times. I would have known if it was there – at the end, he was in no state to hide such a thing from me.'

Ansaryon drew a deep, harsh breath. 'Did he know he would die, when he overturned the boat?'

'I am certain of it. But he accepted his fate. He must have thought that it was a price worth the paying, to save Zithirian and Minassa from slaughter and destruction.'

'Perhaps.' The King's face was distorted with anguish. Temiltan cast him a swift, sympathetic glance, and then rose and left the tent without a word.

'I was often with him, in his last days,' Al'Kalyek said. 'He was a young man, but already marked with greatness. It is a tragedy for the world that he is dead so soon, with all his vast potential unfulfilled.'

'And yet he was also my son,' Ansaryon whispered. 'No more and no less than that – my son. And now he is gone for ever. Tell me everything, Al'Kalyek – everything you know. My mind is open to you, if that will help.'

The sun rolled red down to the horizon of the distant steppes, as the old sorcerer, sparing the King nothing, related in words and in thought-linked pictures how the young man called Bron, once Bronnayak, had come to Tamat to kill the Emperor. He had failed, been captured, beaten, escaped with Al'Kalyek's help, was captured again, and had finally drowned beside his victim in the deep waters of the Kefirinn on the borders of the Empire. But Bron's sacrifice had ensured that Ba'alekkt would never, despite all his long-cherished plans, set foot on Minassan soil.

It was a lengthy tale, and grim, but the old man persevered, ignoring the pain of his own grief and guilt and regret. It was almost dark when he finished, and he was glad that the gloom made it impossible to see Ansaryon's face. The King had the reputation of a reserved, unemotional man, but Al'Kalyek knew now how great was the pain he was holding in check. He thought of Bron, of the terrible waste of his power and his future. So much life, so great a gift: if he had known what was to happen to Ansaryon's son, he would gladly have sacrificed himself in his stead.

'Thank you, Al'Kalyek.' Ansaryon's voice was almost unrecognizable. 'You are supposed to be our enemy – it must have taken some courage to come here. I shall always be grateful to you.'

'I have never been your enemy,' the sorcerer pointed out. 'Ba'alekkt was that – and he is better dead.'

'I know. In a month, or several, or a year, we will be able to take the longer view, beyond our own personal sorrow. Bron saved us, and he also saved Toktel'yi from an Emperor who was a cruel and vicious tyrant. But as long as I live I shall wish that it could have happened another way. It need not have been like this. And now he is gone, and freedom is our only legacy of him.'

'That is hardly a negligible inheritance,' Al'Kalyek pointed out. 'But he may have left us something more tangible, after all.'

The brief pause was suddenly full of hope. Ansaryon said sharply, 'What do you mean?'

'Your son had a woman, whom he loved. She may be carrying his child. And I know where she is.'

There was a much longer silence. When he spoke again, the King's voice was hesitant, unbelieving. 'His *child*? Are you sure? How do you know of this?'

'I saw her, when I entered his mind. His spirit had found her. I had met her once before, on Tekkt, after she had tried and failed to assassinate Ba'alekkt. He rescued her then, and they took a ship. I don't know where they went – to Jo'ami, possibly, or another island in the Archipelago. That was nearly half a year before he appeared in Tamat. But when I saw her in his dream a few days ago, I am certain she was in Kerenth.'

'Tell me about her. What is her name?'

'She is called Mallaso. She is from Penya, and was enslaved as a child. In Toktel'yi, she was a concubine and then a dancer. She is very beautiful. She is also a woman of great courage, and intelligence, and determination. Whatever her history, she was worthy of his love, and he of hers. And when I saw her, she was pregnant.'

'Bron's son,' Ansaryon said softly, caressingly, as if he already held the child in his arms. Al'Kalyek said nothing of the alternative, unpalatable possibility, which had just slithered into his mind, that the Penyan woman's baby might instead be Ba'alekkt's.

It was unlikely. Despite his paraded, vaunted appetites, his legions of conquests and concubines, the Emperor had produced only two acknowledged but illegitimate offspring. The old sorcerer uttered a silent prayer to Kaylo, Lord of Life, that the seed sown within the woman Mallaso had indeed been planted by Bron, to carry his gift onward into the future.

'You say she is in Kereneth. Al'Kalyek, my friend – do you know where?'

'Not exactly, but she should be easy to locate.'

'Will you find her for me?'

He had expected that. He wanted to find her too. She would also wish to know what had happened to Bron. From the little he had learned of her, she deserved no less.

And besides, there was the child.

If his theories were correct, it might well have inherited Bron's gift. Even if it possessed only half his power, it would be the greatest sorcerer in the known world. It would carry the flame of a new hope, and a new kind of magic, untainted by the drug that gave Al'Kalyek and all other mages their power, and also kept them alive. Such a vast potential would need training, guidance, help: and Al'Kalyek nourished the hope that he might be asked to provide it.

'I will, if you wish,' the old man said, bowing his white head in acceptance. 'But why . . . ?'

'If she is carrying my grandson, then she should come to us in Zithirian. Halthris and I would welcome her – she would be a loved and honoured member of our family. Even if she wishes to stay in Kereneth, she should know that if she ever needs help, or shelter, there is a home for her with us.'

'She may not want it. She is a proud woman, fiercely independent. She may well reject your offer.'

'That isn't the point,' Ansaryon said wearily. 'The point is to *ask*. I will be sad if she refuses, but perhaps she will not – or maybe one day she will change her mind. Whatever she may decide, I would like her to know that we will always care for her, and the child.'

'I understand. And I will go, gladly. It will take a long time – I have no desire to travel through the Empire, so I will have to take a considerable detour round its borders. But I have had enough of serving Emperors. Let them fight and argue amongst themselves – I'll take no further part in it. And when I have found Mallaso, I shall go home to Onnak, and live with my brother and his family, in peaceful retirement.'

'A wise decision,' Ansaryon said, his dry tone sounding almost normal. 'Which Vessel of the Blood Imperial do you think they will choose?'

'I have no idea. Ba'alekkt had three uncles, Djamal's half-brothers, and they all have grown sons, most of them as bad as Ba'alekkt, if not worse. There is only one who has both the character and the ability to make a good Emperor – and so he probably won't be the one chosen.'

'And he is?'

'Megren, son of B'kenn.'

'He's in the Army, isn't he?'

'Yes – he is a Ta-K'taren, a Ten-Thousand Commander, though he's still only thirty. He's extremely capable, and Sekkenet thinks very highly of him. But if he's as honest and genuine as his reputation, he won't want to be Emperor.'

'I didn't think I wanted to be King,' Ansaryon pointed out. 'But in the end, the lure of power proved too great. The temptation to put right your predecessor's mistakes is overwhelming, but it is more difficult to avoid becoming as bad as the tyrant you replace.'

'You still possess the love of your people, though.'

'So it seems – but many of them have never liked or trusted my sorcery, which is why I use it as little and as discreetly as possible. My sons and daughters all seem to have some natural ability, though, so perhaps one day magic will be as acceptable in Zithirian as it is in Toktel'yi.' He moved, and Al'Kalyek could just discern the glimmer of his smile. 'Shall we have some light, and refreshments? I have been a most discourteous host, offering you nothing, not even a cup of water, and you have had a long hard journey.'

Within moments, the darkness had been banished, first by a ball of pure white glowing witchfire, then by a collection of lanterns and lamps. Servants brought food, rather plainer fare than the rich spicy dishes of Toktel'yi, and some very good Hailyan wine. Temiltan returned with his son Cathallon, Heir of Minassa, a pleasant but rather colourless young man who was married to K'djelk, elder of the late Emperor's two sisters. And far into the night, they talked about Toktel'yi, of what might now happen, and what they themselves would do.

The immediate threat of invasion had died with Ba'alekkt, but Ansaryon and Temiltan had no intention of disbanding their soldiers until the Imperial Army was no longer mustered menacingly on the border at Tamat. Messages had already been sent by pigeon to Minassa and Zithirian, to tell the people the glad news, but neither King wanted to take any chances. Bron's sacrifice had saved them, but the next Emperor, whoever he proved to be, might share Ba'alekkt's rapacious and aggressive intentions.

Al'Kalyek was quick to assure them that they were unlikely to be attacked in the near, perhaps even the far, future. 'The Imperial Council has the task of deciding who the next Emperor will be. Of course, where son follows father, it's a pure formality – and also, as is alas common practice in the Empire, Councillors will have been bribed or threatened or bullied into making their choice. There has not been a disputed succession for two hundred years, but the precedents are clear. The strongest, the most feared, the most wealthy, will win the greatest support, regardless of his virtues or vices. Men have cheated, lied and murdered to occupy the Onyx Throne. Knowing the probable contenders as I do, I cannot suppose that this occasion will be any different. And it may take days, months even, before one candidate surpasses the others.'

'You are a Councillor,' said Temiltan. 'Whom would you choose?'

'Megren,' Al'Kalyek told him, without hesitation. 'But he will never be Emperor. He hates corruption and brutality. He is unique in his family – an honest man. Who is *likely* to succeed? I do not know. It could be Kadjak, second of Ba'alekkt's three uncles. He has vast wealth, and he will not trouble anyone. Or Eska'anen, the youngest. Ba'alekkt made him Governor of Sabrek, and he is a very pleasant man with a rather unpleasant reputation. He is also, I would imagine, extremely ambitious. Both he and his nephew are capable of gathering the necessary support. But the Army's choice is also important, and they would certainly want Megren. He is much loved by the troops, and Sekkenet will back him.' He smiled. 'But this matter no longer concerns me. I have left Toktel'yi, I have resigned my post. The next Emperor, whoever he is, will have to find another Court Sorcerer. I, my friends, am going home to Onnak.'

First, of course, he would visit Kerenth, to find Mallaso. But Ansaryon had asked him to say nothing about Bron's woman, or her child, to Temiltan and Cathallon, and Al'Kalyek had agreed. Her name was known in Toktel'yi, and she had been wanted, was probably still wanted, for her failed attempt to murder Ba'alekkt. The fewer people who knew of her existence, the place of her refuge, or about her precious child, the better.

He had told them that he was no longer interested in the labyrinthine complexities of Toktel'yan politics. But he could not help wondering, as he lowered himself on to the uncomfortable camp-bed in the tent they had hastily cleared for him, what was happening, now, in Tamat.

PART ONE
OPENING RITES

CHAPTER ONE

'You are the obvious choice. The only choice – the only man capable of cleaning up this festering snake-pit of an Empire.'

It was unlike Sekkenet, General-in-Chief of the Imperial Army, to reveal his real feelings so vehemently. His younger companion glanced at him, and smiled. 'You flatter me, sir. I would not know where to begin.'

'You do not usually deprecate yourself, Megren son of B'kenn,' said his Commander. 'You have a very keen sense of your abilities. This is a chance you must seize. Empires do not always lie in a man's grasp for the taking.'

Megren looked around him. They were standing on the south bank of the Kefirinn, just outside the walls of Tamat. Behind them, people went about their business along the river road, or laboured in the broad, fertile, irrigated fields that spread around the city: but no one was within earshot, a very necessary precaution in a land where even the most unlikely bystander could be a paid informer.

Sekkenet waited. He was a wiry grizzled man in his sixties, with a face as tough and crackled as a walnut shell. Like his companion, he was bare-headed, and his sparse locks, close-cropped for comfort under a helmet, were ruffled lightly by the river breeze. In contrast Megren, though the same height, looked menacingly muscular, and his thick, black hair bristled aggressively upwards from his scalp.

'I'm not cut out to be Emperor,' said the younger man at last. 'As you're always pointing out, I'm too honest.'

'After half-a-dozen venal or vicious tyrants, an honest man would make a refreshing change,' Sekkenet said. 'You could do it. You'd have the support of the Army. You would be by far the most popular candidate.'

'I don't want to occupy the Onyx Throne by force. I may be popular with the soldiers, but what do ordinary people know of me? Nothing!'

Sekkenet made a dismissive gesture. 'And they count for nothing, too. Any Emperor worthy of the name must gain the support of the Army, and of the Council. And for you, the battle's three parts won.'

Megren gave him a frowning glance. 'Who? Who would support me, on the Council?'

'I would, for a start. Al'Kalyek, if he ever returns. Bekkul, the Shipmaster. The Governors of Ukkan and Lai'is – and Balki, of course. That's six out of thirty already. You can't tell me that all the rest are your sworn enemies.'

'Perhaps not – but not many of them are my friends, either. And as I've told you until I'm sick of it – I will *not* resort to bribery, or force. If the Lord of Life wishes me to become Emperor, so be it – but not by corrupt means, or foul play.'

Sekkenet sighed. Megren was an extremely competent soldier, and his unique standards of personal integrity had made him universally beloved amongst the men under his command, but such a high-minded moral stance had not endeared him to those for whom bribery and blackmail were a principal source of wealth. It was normal practice in Toktel'yi. From the moment of birth, attended by a midwife who had probably been persuaded by a handful of gold to leave another woman's bedside, through schooldays eased by judicious payments to tutors, compulsory service in an army where preferential treatment could be bought, to a comfortable and lucrative government post obtained by well-placed backhanders, and finally to a pyre lit by the most important priests of Olyak that grieving relatives could buy, the life of a wealthy citizen was smoothed and embellished by the liberal outlay – and acceptance – of large amounts of money. Megren had achieved his present command entirely on merit, having refused to use his father's riches to further his career. Sekkenet, who had also risen to pre-eminence by his own efforts, but from a starting-point far more humble than this grandson of Emperor Makkyar, admired the young man's stance, while privately admitting to himself that scruples in public life could be extremely tiresome.

'I'd like to know what Trinn thinks.'

And so could uxorial devotion. Megren's wife came from Balki, and her family was neither rich nor powerful. He had met her while garrisoned there, and married her for love. Most Toktel'yan men didn't think women had any views on political matters, let alone bother to listen to them. Sekkenet, who would rather have jumped off a cliff than ask his various wives and concubines for their opinions, suppressed his irritation. 'That'll take too long.'

'A day each way, as the pigeon flies – and I've got half-a-dozen with me. I've sent her some birds from the Tamat pigeon-house, too. I could have her reply by the evening after next.'

'Kaylo's bones!' Sekkenet cried in exasperation. '*You* have to make the decision, and make it *now*! Do you want the Onyx Throne or don't you? Yes or no?'

There was a long silence. Megren stared out across the rolling, mud-brown water in which, only two days previously, his cousin the Emperor Ba'alekkt had drowned. Beyond the river, the distant fields and low hills were Minassan. This was the northern border of the Empire, and behind them, three hundred miles as the pigeon flew, lay the shores of the Southern Sea, eight hundred miles from west to east. In between stretched the nine provinces, producing wealth without end, full of people without number: and beyond, the islands of the K'tali Archipelago, so various and so many that no one had ever counted them.

All that had been Ba'alekkt's. And now, it would be seized by whichever Vessel of the Blood Imperial could prove himself the strongest, the fittest, the most desperate and greedy for the vast rewards, the most heedless of the terrible risks. Successful candidates for the Onyx Throne often had a somewhat jaundiced view of their unluckier rivals, and the price of failure could be high.

Sekkenet knew that Megren was thinking of his wife and young son. He was probably wondering, too, if a public denial that he had any desire to be Emperor would protect them. All the other possible candidates were close members of his own family: his father, uncles, cousins. In the murderous world of Toktel'yan power politics, that only increased the dangers. And Sekkenet hoped that Megren knew, as he himself knew very well, the identity of his most lethal relations.

But such vast riches, such absolute and unimaginable power, represented a temptation so great that not even an honest man could resist for long. Megren smiled reluctantly at the General, standing patiently by his side. 'Very well. You have persuaded me. When the Council meets this afternoon, you may speak in my support.'

The Emperors of Toktel'yi had ruled with the assistance of a Council for many hundreds of years, ever since their dominions grew too large to be easily governed by one man, however able, efficient and energetic. Indeed, recent times had seen a succession of Emperors conspicuous for their indolence and love of pleasure. Ba'alekkt, though even more vicious and depraved than his immediate ancestors, had been popular because his youth and vigorous aggression promised a return of past Imperial glories. But even he had leaned heavily on his

Council, leaving its thirty members to carry out the tedious daily business of government, while he dallied with his concubines and worked out grandiose schemes to enlarge the boundaries of the Empire. And his Council, mindful that Ba'alekkt had murdered most of their predecessors at the notorious Council of Poison as soon as he had ascended the throne, had been extremely careful not to antagonize him. The late Emperor had possessed very hasty and brutal notions of justice, and Sekkenet counted himself fortunate to have survived so long.

For over two hundred years, the Imperial succession had passed undisputed from father to chosen son. Sometimes Emperors had died a little before their appointed time, hastened to the pyre by eager heirs, and sometimes disappointed and aggrieved rivals had had to be swiftly eliminated. But Ba'alekkt, secure in the immortality of youth, had left no sons, no brothers, and no indication of whom, amongst his more distant relatives, he wished to follow him. So the Council would have to choose their next Emperor from the dozen or so remaining adult male Vessels of the Blood Imperial.

Sekkenet didn't have much faith in his twenty-nine colleagues. This disparate collection of Governors, Ministers of State, military chiefs, and the Archpriests of Olyak, God of Death, and his twin Kaylo, Lord of Life, had not been chosen by Ba'alekkt for their powers of independent thought. He reckoned that he might muster at best half a score of backers for Megren, but many of those would probably change their minds at the first sniff of an unfavourable wind. Not for the first time over the past two days, he wished for the calm wisdom of his friend Al'Kalyek. But although the old sorcerer had survived the accident that had drowned Ba'alekkt, he appeared to have turned his back on the Empire, and defected to Minassa and Zithirian.

There were times when Sekkenet could not blame him: and also times when he could begin to glimpse, through the fog of fear and confusion and uncertainty, the brighter, cleaner future that an Emperor such as Megren might bring.

So he arrayed himself in his ceremonial uniform, the clanking bronze plates weighing down his shoulders and the tall plumed helmet making his neck ache, and with a substantial escort marched out of the vast camp to the Governor's Residence in Tamat, where the most crucial Council meeting in two hundred years was about to start.

By now, two days after Ba'alekkt's death, allegiances would have been bought, supporters gathered, bribes passed, threats made. Looking round at the other men as he seated himself on the soft low cushions,

Sekkenet felt the same quickening of the heart that sharpened his mind on the field of battle. The game had begun, and if he lost, both he and Megren would probably pay with their lives.

The unofficial leader of the Council was Ikko, Governor of the City of Toktel'yi and the heartland province around it. He was, however, no more than a figurehead, an elderly and pompous man with unrealistic ideas of his own importance, who had been chosen by Ba'alekkt purely for his administrative abilities. He looked unusually nervous today, and Sekkenet, glancing at the lean, elegant figure beside him, could guess why.

Eska'anen, Governor of Sabrek, was the youngest and most able of the late Emperor's three uncles. He was a dignified and handsome man, with a distinguished strand of grey in his immaculately groomed hair, and a pleasant, courteous manner. Sekkenet, who knew him mainly by reputation, suspected that his cultivated affability concealed a cold and brazen core. Certainly the people of Sabrek, the second richest province of the Empire, regarded him with a mixture of fear and respect, a typically Toktel'yan ambiguity. Strong ruthless men were much admired by many citizens, who appreciated the commercial advantages of a peaceful and stable government.

As the only Vessel of the Blood Imperial present, Eska'anen opened the proceedings. He had a rich, attractive voice, and his words were well chosen and concise. Sekkenet observed the glazed, fawning expressions of many of his colleagues with secret and cynical derision. Eska'anen had obviously been busy in the last few days, but his accession to the Onyx Throne was not entirely a foregone conclusion.

His eulogy on the late and lamented Emperor ended, the Governor of Sabrek paused. Sekkenet wished desperately for Al'Kalyek's presence beside him, for the old mage's reassuring glance and quiet wisdom. And apart from Megren, there was no one else in all of Tamat whom he could trust.

'And so I come, with heavy but hopeful heart, to the real purpose of this meeting.' Eska'anen said. 'Not for more than two hundred years, since the untimely death of the Emperor Mennekaylo, has the succession to the Onyx Throne been in doubt. At that time, the Council made the final decision, after prolonged and careful consideration, and offered the Empire to his cousin Akketta'an. We shall follow that time-honoured precedent, with due reverence and respect for the importance of our task. It is our duty to discover, in the course of our deliberations, the man whose strength and wisdom, maturity and intelligence, character and ability, make him the most suitable to assume the glorious title of One Hundredth Emperor of Toktel'yi.' He coughed briefly. 'The first step is to name all the possible candidates for your consideration. They must of course be Vessels of the Blood Imperial, that has flowed unbroken through the veins of our Emperors since the first of them, Akkatanat. They must also be male, adult, and of sound mind. And because I myself am one of these Vessels, I must of necessity be listed too. I will therefore ask my esteemed friend and colleague Councillor Ikko, Governor of Toktel'yi, to place the names before you.'

Ikko stood, clearing his throat nervously, a long piece of thick charsh paper in his hand. 'I thank you, Lord Eska'anan, for your kind words. The list I have prepared contains only the names of male and legitimate descendants of Makkyar, ninety-seventh Emperor, as it seems most likely that one of their number will succeed to the dignity of the Onyx Throne. I will make no comment on their characters, nor upon their suitability for our purpose – I will merely enumerate all those who are eligible under Toktel'yan law.

B'kenn, son of Makkyar.

Kadjak, son of Makkyar.

Eska'anen, son of Makkyar.

Megren, son of B'kenn.

Tarmon, son of Kadjak.

Kekaylo, son of Kadjak – although as he is dedicated to the Lord of Life, his eligibility is in grave doubt.

Gorek, son of Kadjak.

Kazhian, son of Eska'anen.

Suken, son of Eska'anen.'

He glanced round the ring of Councillors. 'These are the nine names from which we must choose. Each has his own merits, each his own supporters. It will be our task to decide whom we wish to be Emperor. May I begin by asking if any of you have a preference?'

Hands were slowly raised. With a feeling of righteous determination, Sekkenet lifted his own. No going back now – the first spears had been cast. And in a situation where there was no single obvious candidate, there was bound to be confusion, changes of mind, shifts of allegiance.

One by one, the Councillors stated their chosen contenders, and their reasons for their decisions, and Ikko dutifully recorded every detail. Sekkenet, listening and watching the proceedings closely, saw that there was definitely no clear winner. Megren had his own support, and that of four others. Eska'anen was nominated by seven, including the man the General most feared and hated, the sinister, cruel and devious Spymaster Olkanno, who himself had Imperial blood, being the son of Makkyar's brother. Eska'anen's brother Kadjak, reputedly the richest man in the Empire, was also mentioned several times. There were three Councillors who backed Megren's father, B'kenn, presumably on the grounds that his indolence was such that no one would be in any danger from him. And a lone voice, that of the very unpleasant Governor of Mynak, spoke in favour of Kadjak's eldest son Tarmon.

Sekkenet remembered Tarmon from the young man's five years of compulsory military service. He had bribed his inferiors to perform his duties, which was usual. What had curdled Sekkenet's blood was his unsavoury habit of raping any handsome young soldier who took his fancy. Several had killed themselves, or died in suspicious circumstances, but Tarmon, wallowing in the huge heaps of his father's inexhaustible wealth, had literally got away with murder. He had all the viciousness and depravity of Ba'alekkt, without any of his energy and ability. Sekkenet shuddered inwardly. Anyone, even the flabby and mediocre B'kenn, would be preferable to Tarmon.

There were still eight Councillors undecided, and those whose choice proved unpopular could be induced to change their minds. Ikko and Eska'anen whispered together for a few moments, while the rest waited expectantly. Then the Governor of Sabrek rose, his smile, like a snake's, showing his long glistening teeth. 'I thank you, friends, for your suggestions, and for your honesty. Ikko has set it all down, and the scribes will make a copy for each of you, so that you may peruse the list at your leisure. Perhaps, on second thoughts, some of you may wish to revise your decisions. Perhaps your eyes have been opened by our discussions, so that you now see new virtues, new possibilities, in a man you might not otherwise have considered. But it is plain from what we have heard today that no one can yet attract the support of a clear majority. Obviously, we need a consensus. I therefore propose that we take a further vote in four days' time – and that if there is still no agreement, we choose again from only those two or three men who have won most support. Are you all in favour?'

With greater or lesser degrees of enthusiasm, the Council gave him their assent.

'I thank you, friends and colleagues, for your patience. This is a task of the highest importance, and we must not rush hastily into a decision we might afterwards regret. And now I come to the other matter I wish to raise at this meeting.' Eska'anen looked round at the

Council, and his gaze lingered fractionally longer on Sekkenet, sitting almost opposite. 'The disbanding of the Army.'

The Imperial Army, nearly two hundred thousand strong, had been camped outside Tamat for nearly a month, and the countryside for miles around had been picked bare to feed them. Now, with the prospect of fighting vanished, they were bored and quarrelsome. Only that morning, Sekkenet had ordered the execution of a promising young Hundred-Commander who had killed a comrade in some drunken brawl over a whore. He loathed the necessity of such punishments, and he was well aware, listening to Eska'anen's logical, reasonable, persuasive arguments, that sending the regiments back to their home provinces was the most sensible course, before too many of them died of drink, or disease, or in stupid, pointless squabbles.

But that wasn't why Eska'anen wanted to disband them. Sekkenet knew, as surely as he knew that the sun set in the west, the real reason why the Governor of Sabrek needed them out of the way.

The Army, almost to a man, would back Megren for the Onyx Throne. And the presence, not five miles from this very room, of nearly two hundred thousand of the finest troops in the known world would undoubtedly persuade most Councillors to support Megren too, once they realized what the soldiers wanted. Armies had made Emperors before. And Megren, despite his refusal to use force, knew that their loyalty, in such overwhelming numbers, would make his succession a certainty.

'May I speak, Lord Eska'anen?' Sekkenet was on his feet almost before the other man had finished. 'In my view, this would be a most unwise course. Lacking the services of a competent sorcerer, we have no idea of what the Kings of Minassa and Zithirian plan to do. By now, they must surely know of our late Emperor's tragic death. Is it not likely that they will seize the opportunity to launch a surprise attack, if they see the border unprotected? King Ansaryon is himself a sorcerer, skilled in scrying. He may have the assistance of our former colleague, Al'Kalyek. He will certainly be aware of our every move, and he may well be tempted to eliminate any further threat to his kingdom by attacking us. After all, Tamat was ruled by his family, not so long ago. He might wish to take it back, and slaughter all of us in the process.'

'Al'Kalyek is a renegade and a traitor,' said the Governor of Tamat, pale under his swarthy skin. 'And everyone knows that two sorcerers can greatly increase their power by uniting it. Sekkenet is right, we are in considerable danger. And where can we find another sorcerer of the same calibre in a hurry?'

'They certainly don't grow on date-palms,' muttered the Archpriest of Kaylo.

Other voices were raised in agreement, and Sekkenet sat back, satisfied. Toktel'yans, reared on treachery, cunning and ruthlessness, could always be relied upon to see ambush behind every tree. It was why the Spymaster was such an important Imperial Minister: and even Olkanno was nodding. Eska'anen did not protest as almost all the council disagreed with his suggestion, but he glanced around the table from time to time, a narrow smile tucked into his thin lips, and the General knew that he had not conceded defeat.

He thought of his soldiers, their temper and their potential for danger. Now the Army lay like a slumbering tiger outside Tamat, apparently oblivious to the deliberations of the Council.

But if Eska'anen dared to pull the tiger's tail . . .

He wasn't meant to be there. All the slaves had been sent out on various errands simultaneously, and every member of the household knew what that meant: a visitor not intended to be seen, words too dangerous to be overheard. And for anyone caught spying, the punishment would be swift, and terminal.

But the youngest houseboy had been paid to listen, and he still cherished dreams of buying his freedom with the money he earned from eavesdropping. So he left without his basket, and came back for it. There would be no one left in the house to challenge him, save for his master Eska'anen and his mystery guest: and with luck, the two of them would be so intent on their nefarious conversation that they wouldn't notice the slight, subtle sounds indicating that they were not, after all, alone in the house.

Eska'anen's money and rank had given him the means to rent a villa in a prime position on the outskirts of Tamat, well away from the crowded central streets. The house was hidden from the road by a high brick wall, and the gardens sloped down to the river and its own private landing-stage. The mysterious visitor had almost certainly arrived by boat, and now he was being entertained in Eska'anen's bedchamber, a spacious room on the upper floor, overlooking the Kefirinn on one side and the central quadrangle on the other.

A flight of stairs led up to a covered walkway all round the courtyard. The boy slid up them as lightly and noiselessly as a shadow, confident that there was no one else around to see him. It was the middle of the morning, and the High Summer sun baked the whitewashed mudbrick walls and painted the wooden columns with flat swabs of merciless and brilliant light.

The window-grilles were shut, and he didn't dare peer through. But he could hear quite well, even crouched beneath the sill, his heart thumping with fear and excitement, and his brief tunic, the yellow of Eska'anen's household livery, blotched dark brown and dripping with sweat.

'It is a beginning. A beginning, no more. There is still much to be done.'

He didn't recognize the voice. It was soft and sweet, like a woman's or a eunuch's, yet essentially masculine. And the sound of it, lingering, caressing, menacing, raised the hairs on his head.

'Too much.' Eska'anen's usually pleasant and affable tones had vanished. 'That fool Sekkenet! As if the northern kings would dare mount an unprovoked attack on the Empire!'

'Maybe he is not such a fool. Maybe he realized what your motives were.'

'Whether he did or not, we'll have to get rid of him. If we don't, that self-righteous nephew of mine will be Emperor before the month ends, and you and I, my friend, will be finished.'

'Not necessarily.'

'I disagree. He's too fastidious even to fart, let alone employ anyone like you. You'll be sent off to twiddle your thumbs on some barren rock in the Scatterlings until you wither in the sun. Is that the sort of living death you crave? I know I don't.'

'Megren trusts you. You are his beloved uncle.'

'Then he's a fool as well as a prig. *Trust no one* – he should have sucked that in with his nurse's milk. Well, we'll have to get rid of him too.'

'Not here. Not while the Army is still in camp. They love him, poor simple soldiers that they are. If he dies suspiciously, they'll want someone to blame, and someone to punish. And you will be the chief suspect. You and Megren are the only candidates actually present in Tamat. Naturally they'll think you had something to do with it.'

'So how do we get rid of him?'

'Persuade him to leave Tamat. Family reasons, perhaps, calling him home at once. And once he's back in Ukkan, we can kill him. You'd still be here, three hundred miles away, and obviously innocent. I have a dozen men trained to make murder look like accident, and poison resemble the consequences of eating bad fish. Leave it to me, my friend, and neither Sekkenet nor Megren will trouble you further.'

'You are very generous.' Eska'anen had returned to his usual urbane and amiable manner. 'May I ask you why you are so eager to put your mind and your resources at my disposal?'

'I know where the sun shines brightest. In my opinion, you are the man most likely to become what we need – a strong Emperor who will not – how shall I put it? – rock the boat too much.'

Eska'anen chuckled. 'I thought you lacked a sense of humour, my friend.'

'I do. I merely repeat what my most promising agent said of you. He was the man who found Ba'alekkt's assassin. One day, if he continues to show such promise, he may inherit my mantle. In the meantime, I shall make full use of his talents.'

'In Ukkan?'

'Yes, I think certainly in Ukkan. He is subtle, skilled, ruthless – and very ambitious. But you know him, Lord Eska'anen – he is Arkun, the slave-born son of your first wife's brother.'

'Ah. Of course. I hope that he proves more loyal and reliable than the rest of that untrustworthy breed.'

'I trust no one, but if I did, I would trust him. He has bitter childhood memories to drive him onward. We rich Toktel'yans, my friend, have had our lives too easy. I find my best men have a very similar history to Arkun's. They all possess a burning desire to be revenged on the world, and no scruples about how they do it.'

'That hardly explains you,' Eska'anen pointed out. 'You were born in a golden cradle.'

'So were you. We are aberrations, my friend – exceptions to the rule. And that is what makes us so dangerous. Look at your brothers. B'kenn is a weak idle fool out of Djamal's stupid mould, and Kadjak thinks of nothing but feeding his belly and counting his money. They will not want the Onyx Throne.'

'But their sons do.'

'Yes. Megren is obviously much more formidable than his father. As for Tarmon – well, if he becomes Emperor we might as well all troop down to Olyak's domain tomorrow. Kekaylo's a priest, and likes the life too much to want to leave it, even if he could. And Gorek . . . Gorek is Kadjak's favourite. What he does not want or need for himself, he might well desire for his most beloved son.'

'The game grows complicated. We may have to dispose of them all.'

'Then, if necessary, we will. We have the cunning, and the resources. And what of your own sons? What will be their wishes?'

'Kazhian . . .' Eska'anen made a noise of contempt. 'I abandoned him to his fate long since. He is wilful, irresponsible, rebellious – he should have drowned in that wreck three years ago.'

'I forget what happened. Refresh my memory.'

'I thought you made it your business to know such things. It was his first command – a two-banker, one of the old type, the *Spear of Vengeance*. He thought he'd show off his seamanship and take the short route into Lai'is Harbour. Stuffed full of drink and khlar, probably. The tide was too low and she hit a rock and sank, with the loss of more than half her crew. Unfortunately, Kazhian was one of the survivors. That should have been the end of his career, but he must have bribed that old fool of a Shipmaster, because he was given a courier ship not long afterwards.'

'I take it then that if you attain the Onyx Throne, you do not intend to make him Emperor-in-Waiting?'

'Kazhian has forfeited all rights he may have thought he possessed. Suken is my heir.' Eska'anen's voice softened suddenly. '*He* is everything a man could want in a son – obedient, loyal, dutiful, intelligent.'

'Yes – he will go far, even if he never leaves my Ministry for greater things. In the four years he has been in my employ, I have had cause to commend him highly. He is most diligent and assiduous in every task he is set. You spent your money wisely when you bought him out of Army service and placed him with me.'

Outside, the boy crouched, trembling. He knew the identity of his master's guest now, and it terrified him. If he was discovered, they would show him no mercy. But if he could slink away undetected, with the most important information safe in his head, then his future looked bright. He could sell his knowledge for a great deal of money, and buy his freedom.

Under his cautious feet, a wooden board creaked softly. By chance, he had missed it earlier. Now, the betraying sound seemed horrifyingly loud in the hot, silent air. The voices stopped, and he shrank against the rough-cast wall, praying to Kaylo that neither man would look out.

The Lord of Life was not listening. The door opened, and Eska'anen's voice hissed like a cobra's. 'There he is!'

The boy, impelled by terror, sprang to his feet and fled. He had almost reached the stairs when something crashed into the back of his head, and he fell.

Eska'anen and his companion watched as the houseboy's body rolled lazily down from step to step, to finish in an undignified sprawl at the foot.

'There will always be a traitor,' observed Oklanno, the Imperial Spymaster, with his bland, empty smile. 'Next time we meet, my friend, it had better be in absolute secrecy. Too much is at stake to risk discovery – even by vermin such as that.'

'I thank you.' Eska'anen was breathing fast, his usual suave composure upset. 'I had no idea you were so skilled in the use of such things. What are they?'

'These?' Olkanno held out his chubby pink palm. Covering his hand was a bronze disc, edged with five razor-sharp points. 'They are Ma'alkwen throwing-stars. As you have seen, they are silent, and very effective. There is little blood, and the boy was dead before he hit the first step.'

They walked down the stairs and stared reflectively at the huddled corpse. 'The river will take him,' Eska'anen said. 'There can be no pyre for such traitors.'

'As there was none for Ba'alekkt – or his assassin.'

'Good riddance to both of them. The invasion was a madman's dream – it would inevitably have come to grief. So that sorcerer has saved a great deal of time and money, not to mention lives. Still, undoubtedly the world is a safer place without him.'

'Undoubtedly.' Olkanno smiled again, and bent to wrench the throwing-star from the dead slave's skull. 'Not such a tragedy, either for the Empire or for us, my friend. Death has many uses.'

Eska'anen was silent. It had begun: the first killing in his careful, devious, ruthless plan to become Emperor. And he wondered, with calm curiosity, how many more would die before he achieved his ambition.

CHAPTER TWO

'The General is sick!'

'The Old Man is ill!'

'They say he's dying!'

The word fled round the huge camp with the speed of the worst news. The troops loved Sekkenet. For twenty years he had commanded the mighty Toktel'yan Army, with vigorous efficiency and scrupulous fairness. Hardened career soldiers, veterans with thirty years of experience in all the most restless corners of the Empire from Tulyet to Djebb, Tatht to Penya, wept on the shoulders of bewildered young conscripts only a few months into their compulsory five years' service. And a vast, silent, stricken crowd gathered around the General's plain canvas tent and waited, in hope and terror, for tidings of recovery, or death.

Inside, it was stiflingly hot, and despite the increasingly desperate efforts of Sekkenet's bodyslaves, the stench was appalling. The General had been laid low by the bowel fever, so common in the camp. Many did recover, but this seemed to be a particularly virulent attack, and the Court Healer, summoned in haste from Tamat, had examined the commander, shaken his head, and privately admitted that there was no hope. Sekkenet's robust constitution meant that death might be kept at bay for a day, perhaps two days longer. But inevitably, sooner or later, he would succumb.

Megren sat at his side whenever his military duties would permit. He had served under the General for twelve years, and their relationship was firmly founded in mutual liking, respect and admiration. But now, when he needed him most, his friend and mentor was dying.

A high fever racked Sekkenet's lean frame. Sweat washed from him in stinking tides, and he had lost all control of his body's functions. In his agonized delirium, he talked endlessly – sometimes to his wives, his concubines or his children, but most often to invisible subordinates, ordering them to sharpen their weapons, polish their armour, march in step. And Megren listened, his face like a rock to mask his sorrow, and bathed the old man's brow, and unhappily tried to assess the consequences that would follow on Sekkenet's death.

He knew that without the General's persuasive support, he would lack the heart to continue as a candidate for the Onyx Throne. He would much rather take Sekkenet's place as General-in-Chief, but no Emperor would tolerate a popular Vessel of the Blood Imperial in a position of such dangerous power. Probably Enmek, the deputy commander, would be chosen. He was a good soldier, but dour, unimaginative and politically inexperienced. And he, or someone else, would have to decide whether to disband the Army now, or keep it here in Tamat until the next Emperor was chosen.

Megren closed his eyes. For the thousandth time he wished for Trinn: for her calm, rational, sensible advice, her gentle hands, her dark skin and exuberant hair, so much at odds with her serene and dignified public pose, so characteristic of her liveliness in private. He had met her eight years ago, while on garrison duty on Balki, most barren and inhospitable island of the Archipelago, famous for its stone quarries, its sour wine, and the allegedly uncouth sexual practices of its inhabitants. Like his comrades, he had laughed and mocked their backward ignorance: and then he had met Trinn.

Her father was a farmer who supplied the troops. She had had no idea that the short, brusque, awkward young man paying shy court to her was a Vessel of the Blood Imperial. When she did at last find out from one of his men, she had refused at first to believe it. Grandsons of Emperors didn't get posted to this unpopular backwater, or live austerely in barracks with the other soldiers: they did their compulsory service in luxurious idleness on Tekkt, or in Mynak, or Ukkan, paying the less fortunate to do their more onerous duties and bribing their superiors to turn a blind eye.

But Megren, obviously, was very different. And he had married her, swept her off to his father's palatial villa near Ukkan, and showered her with love and luxury. Trinn had always been level-headed, despite her smiles and laughter: she knew that his wealth didn't matter. What counted was his deep and passionate devotion.

He had been away from her for far too long – they hadn't seen each other since the end of the rainy season, which they had spent together at Ukkan.

'Megren!'

Sekkenet's voice had diminished to a croaking whisper. A hot, claw-like hand reached out to grasp his arm. Staring into the sunken, blood-shot eyes, he realized that for the first time in several days, his General's mind was lucid. A dart of brief hope pierced him. Surely this was a sign of recovery.

'Megren – listen.' The hand feebly pulled him closer. The younger man glanced round. The slaves stood respectfully at a distance, but he waved them away, and they filed obediently out of the tent.

'Danger – mortal danger!' The General struggled for breath, coughed, and gasped out the words. 'Throne – don't – try for – the Throne!'

'It's all right,' Megren assured him. 'I've already decided not to.'

'Tell – tell them—'

Another fit of coughing racked Sekkenet's shrunken frame. His eyes bulged, and his fingers clutched frantically at Megren's arm. Then a huge shudder convulsed him, the air rattled in his throat, and he fell back on to the bed.

It was all over. Numb, disbelieving, Megren saw that his arm was marked and bloody where the dying man's nails had clawed through his skin in his final agony. As he had so often done before for dead comrades, he closed the staring eyes. Then he bowed his head and tried to utter the prayers of Olyak, to speed the departing soul to that Hall which his conduct in life best merited. For children, the brightest and lightest: for the irredeemably evil, the dark cells of torment, far below the earth. Like most people, Sekkenet would dwell for all eternity somewhere between the two.

'And may we one day meet again,' Megren said aloud, to his commander's fleeing shade, and rose stiffly to his feet. He did not want to think any more about the implications of Sekkenet's sudden death, or ponder the significance of his last words. Stunned by the force of his grief, he walked out of the tent.

His face must have betrayed the truth to the waiting soldiers, for at once a great groaning wail burst from several hundred throats, as if all hope were ended. Megren paused reluctantly, recognizing that he must speak to them, but not knowing what to say or how to say it.

'Sir!' It was Sekkenet's chief bodyslave, his eyes filled with tears. 'Sir, Lord Megren, is he dead?'

'Yes, he is dead – his soul is now facing Olyak's judgment.' Megren brushed a hand across his own eyes. 'See to him – make all the necessary arrangements. I will send word to his family in Toktel'yi.'

The soldiers made way for him, their sorrow open and extravagant. And behind him, somewhere amidst the jostling, anguished crowd, a voice shouted, 'Megren for Emperor!'

At once the cry was taken up a thousandfold. He had to acknowledge them, so he turned and waved. They wanted him to lead them, but he was only a Ten-Thousand Commander, not a General, and only one of many Vessels of the Blood Imperial. And the warning in Sekkenet's last words had assumed a vast significance in his mind.

Back in the blessed solitude of his tent, he sent his slaves away and lay face down on his bed, his face buried in the cushions as if he could shut out the world, and deny the choice he had made only a few days previously, and now wished most desperately that he had not.

In an Empire so vast, so reliant on bureaucracy to keep it running smoothly and efficiently, good communications were of vital importance. Rivers were used for transport wherever possible: in their absence, roads took travellers and goods from province to province. The poor walked, the rich rode in elaborate covered wagons, or litters around towns and cities. Toktel'yans were not great horsemen, and the Army had only one regiment of cavalry, permanently stationed on the extreme western borders of the Empire to deal with mounted raiders from the steppes. There was a system of fast government and military couriers, who carried official letters, packages and documents, but for the swiftest spread of messages and information, pigeons were used.

Each city and town of any size had a pigeon-house, to which its own birds would return when released. Of course, it always kept stock of captive pigeons from other places, to carry messages away. For a fee, a traveller could hire half-a-dozen birds in his home town, and take them with him on his journey to keep in touch with business associates or his family while he was away. So important was this system that it was a capital offence to kill a pigeon: and there was a proverb, 'rare as hawks in Toktel'yi', for birds of prey had almost been eliminated from the Empire's skies to ensure that the vital messengers could fly unmolested.

Already they had carried the news of Ba'alekkt's death to every town in the Empire. Now, the seven scribes of the Tamat pigeon-house used their tiny, delicate writing to describe the demise of General Sekkenet on minute squares of thin charsh paper. Then, the Fliers, the highly skilled men who bred, trained and looked after the pigeons, folded their messages over and over again and tied one round each of the birds' slender pink legs before releasing them. They would fly to all the large towns up to two hundred miles away, and the Fliers there, seeing the red paper, would know that this was an urgent message, to be passed on everywhere within their region. Using this method, the entire Empire could be covered within three days.

All messages carried by the public birds, however, were read by Olkanno's spies as a matter of course. He had a Flier in his pay in every official pigeon-house in the Empire. So for privacy and convenience, Megren had brought his own birds with him from Ukkan, kept ready, bright-eyed and cooing, in his tent. He had already written to Trinn, telling her in detail about the recent momentous events. Her answer would, of course, have to come via the pigeon-house in Tamat – the birds were trained to find a place, not a person – but his wife, despite her humble origins, had quickly grasped the realities of Toktel'yan politics, and was always as discreet as necessary.

But when the bird arrived from Ukkan, it did not carry a message from Trinn. It was from the senior of his father's two surviving wives, and brought urgent news.

Megren had been attending Sekkenet's pyre. It was his task, by common agreement, to set the flame to the mound of pitch-soaked wood on which his friend, comrade and commander lay. The fire had roared up eagerly, consuming the mortal remains of the man who had cast him to the leopards and then abandoned him. And Megren, looking into the heart of the blaze, knew that death might await him too, if he was not very careful. Anyone who desired the Onyx Throne would sweep everything out of his path to reach it. And he, Megren, was still in the way.

For there seemed to be no going back. His name had been put forward, he had supporters on the Council – though when they next met, he was certain that some, if not all, would have changed their allegiance. But the Army stood behind him and around him in the pyre field near the camp, a vast, grief-stricken, angry throng, certain that the sudden death of their beloved General was suspicious, unsure where to place the blame. Megren had grave doubts himself, but he still could not quite believe that Sekkenet had not, after all, died of bowel fever. Who would benefit from the General's permanent absence? And in any case, a public accusation would probably lead to the slaughter of innocent men.

Unhappily conscious of his own indecision – he was never so hesitant on the field of battle, but somehow everything seemed much simpler when he was fighting – Megren accepted the sympathy of Sekkenet's other friends and comrades. No one mentioned their suspicions, if they had any, that the General had been helped on his way to Olyak's Halls. In such a public place, even the most innocuous statement might be misheard or twisted, to be used against the speaker by some informer at a future date. And with every expression of grief, Megren's own sense of loss and confusion and doubt grew harder to bear, like a lump of stone lodged in his heart.

He returned at last to his tent, a little after sunset, and found a messenger from the Tamat pigeon-house waiting for him, with a piece of paper coloured red in his hands.

Red for desperate urgency, danger, death. Suddenly certain that catastrophe had befallen his wife or his son, Megren snatched the scrap and unrolled it with shaking fingers.

Thanks to the Lord of Life, it was not Trinn or Sarrek who was dying, but his father, B'kenn. And his presence was needed at home.

Guiltily, Megren felt a lightening of his burden. He must return to Ukkan at once. For at least a month, perhaps even longer, he would not have to resist the growing, vast, inexorable pressure of his soldiers, urging him to seize the throne without waiting to be asked. He would see Trinn. He could ask her what to do. And he would be able to think clearly again.

Almost cheerfully, he called his slaves, and ordered them to begin packing.

The New Palace lay half a mile from the sea, well away from the noisome stink and foul waterways of Toktel'yi. Within its high surrounding wall, its gardens and courtyards were thickly planted with fragrant flowers and aromatic herbs, and the air was full of sweet scents and fine music and the endless cool trickle of water from innumerable fountains. A quarter of the building's vast area was set apart for the Imperial women: mothers, wives, daughters, sisters, concubines. And only in the guarded privacy of their own quarters could they cast off their veils.

The ninety-eighth Emperor, known throughout his dominions as Djamal the Indolent, had had fifty concubines, and nearly forty children by them. With his only wife, L'ketten of Tekkt, he had produced Ba'alekkt, the eldest, and two girls. Female offspring, though despised, did have some dynastic uses, and the elder, K'djelk, had been married to Cathallon, Heir of Minassa, and was now the mother of a small son, with another baby due at any time.

Djeneb was eight years younger than K'djelk, the pretty one, who had found a handsome young prince, love and happiness. Djeneb, spotty and plain and heavily saddled with puppy-fat, had been betrothed to the elderly and notoriously unsavoury Prince of Tulyet.

She had hated Ba'alekkt for his masculine arrogance, for the casual, callous spite with which he had arranged her miserable future. As a very small child, she had worshipped her splendid brother, until he had killed her kitten because it had scratched him. He had mocked her tears, and he had laughed at her ever since. And when the white Imperial pigeon had brought the news of his death, something dark and savage inside her had laughed in response.

And it meant, too, that perhaps she wouldn't have to marry the Prince of Tulyet after all.

The other women, of course, wept and wailed for days, even the ones whom Ba'alekkt had beaten and abused. Djeneb refused to join them, but she was not so foolish as to make her delight public. Instead, she cultivated an air of silent suffering, and the elderly concubines who had serviced her father gossiped admiringly about her Imperial dignity and her commendable self-control.

Trust no one. Confide in no one. Reveal nothing. These were the maxims which she had tried to obey, ever since she had left childhood and entered the devious, complicated, dangerous world of Palace life. She was an Emperor's daughter, an Emperor's sister, but the power of the Blood Imperial would not save her if the next incumbent of the Onyx Throne decided to dispose of all possible present or future rivals. A woman had never ruled Toktel'yi, but her sons could.

Or he might marry her. Being a dynastic bargaining counter was a fate far preferable to marrying the ghastly Prince of Tulyet, whose blood was too dilute to make him eligible. Djeneb pondered all the likely candidates for the throne.

Of course, being a despised woman, she had very little direct knowledge of them, although the Women's Quarters were always a hive of gossip. But she had met some on formal Court occasions, and had peered at them through her shrouding veil. Her uncle B'kenn was fat and jolly. Her uncle Kadjak was even fatter, and laden with gold and perfume. Her uncle Eska'anen was thin and dignified and had a very pleasant manner, but she had never liked the coldness of his eyes. And all his wives were dead, two of them in suspicious circumstances.

That wasn't unusual. There were much nastier rumours about Olkanno, the Spymaster, and if Djeneb had been told that he ate fried babies for breakfast, she would have believed it without question. But although he was also her cousin, the son of Emperor Makkyar's younger brother, he was not, fortunately, a candidate for the Onyx Throne.

And her younger cousins? Megren was much admired, but he was notoriously and exclusively faithful to his only wife. Tarmon was apparently a depraved pervert who liked raping children. Kekaylo was a priest. No one had anything, good or bad, to say about Gorek. Suken worked for Olkanno, and that was all she needed to know about him.

And Kazhian had a reputation as a troublemaker so full of khlar he couldn't steer his ship straight.

It was not a very inspiring or edifying list. The only one she might consider as a husband wouldn't be interested in her. And a couple of them were probably almost as bad as the Prince of Tulyet.

'Lady!' Ga'agen, her Head Eunuch, stood in the doorway. He was more slender than most of his kind, with a lazy, sleek air, like a pampered cat. He had attended L'ketten, her mother, and if she trusted anyone in this nest of cobras, she trusted him.

'His Highness Skallyan, Prince of Tulyet, has come to offer his condolences on the sad loss of your dear brother,' said Ga'agen.

'Oh, no!' Djeneb thumped her fist on the cushion in a sudden fury. It was as if her thought had conjured him up, the very last person in all the world whom she wished to see.

'Alas, yes, lady,' the eunuch said sympathetically. Not for the first time, Djeneb wondered just how much he knew of her complex inward thoughts, and the turmoil in her head. But at least he had been the only witness of her betraying outburst. She thanked the Lord of Life that his deputy, Umyet, who was almost certainly one of Olkanno's spies, had not been hanging around her this morning.

'Lady? You should change your gown to something more appropriate.'

Djeneb looked down at her plain blue cotton dress, flowing kindly over the folds and bulges of her body. She would have to put on some jewellery, too, and a veil. Her bodyslaves would fuss over her as if she was a coy and beautiful maiden meeting her handsome young bridegroom. And the reality was so painfully, miserably different that she almost stamped her foot in frustration and anger.

'Very well,' she said at last. 'But you will have to tell him to wait until I am ready to receive him.'

'Certainly, lady.' Ga'agen made obeisance and withdrew, shutting the door gently behind him.

It was nearly an hour by the water-clock before Djeneb was arrayed as befitted her rank. A silken gown of Imperial scarlet, the most expensive dye, trailed on the tiled floor behind her, the hem richly embroidered in turquoise and gold. Rings weighed down every finger, and she wore a delicate pendant in the shape of a hawk, wings outstretched, that had been the mark of Blood Imperial since the days of Akkatanat, the first Emperor of Toktel'yi. And the gauze veil which concealed her plain, blunt features was secured with a circlet of twisted gold, studded with rubies.

The Prince of Tulyet's eyes glistened as she swept into her reception chamber. He seemed to be under the impression that she was a beauty, like her elder sister. For a mad moment she longed to cast off her veil and reveal her unlovely face, so inappropriate for an Emperor's daughter. He would surely not want her once he knew what she looked like.

But of course he would. He wanted the wagonload of gold and jewels, the chests of spices, the lands in Mynak and Sabrek, and the seventeen entire islands in the Scatterlings that comprised her dowry. If she had a hunchback and only half her wits, instead of being too plain, too tall and much too clever for Toktel'yan tastes, he would still want her dowry — but not *her*.

She sat down on the gilded chair, a carved wooden copy of the famous Onyx Throne, symbol of Imperial rule. Ga'agen and her eunuchs stood around her, with two of her women, but she had never felt more alone. The Emperor's harem was not a place for deep friendships, and she was so much younger than Ba'alekkt and K'djelk that she had always been their baby sister, to be teased, pampered, humoured, played with, but never treated as an equal. She had thirty-eight half-siblings, the offspring of Djamal by his numerous concubines, but most of them were also considerably older.

So she was used to keeping her true self, her fierceness, her anger, her frustration, locked away. She was an Emperor's daughter, an Emperor's sister, perhaps one day an Emperor's wife. And pride stiffened her back and kept her strong voice level and firm as she addressed Skallyan, Prince of Tulyet. 'Greetings to you, noble cousin.'

The Toktel'yan habit of assassinating those Vessels of the Blood Imperial who were inconveniently vigorous, able, popular and attractive, had unfortunately ensured that the survivors were men like Skallyan, nonentities too stupid, timid or inadequate to present much of a threat. The previous Prince, his brother Tuneg, had been eliminated by Ba'alekkt at the infamous Council of Poison. Skallyan had indeed proved the willing tool that the Emperor desired, but at a price. The people of Tulyet were a hardy, independent and bloodthirsty race, given to death-feuds and banditry amongst their inhospitable mountains, and looked upon their new Prince with utter contempt, as a puppet of the loathed Emperors, who had long ago imposed their rule upon the peninsula with usual Toktel'yan efficiency and brutality. The three-year reign of Prince Skallyan II had so far been characterized by rebellion, lawlessness and acts of extreme violence against anyone regarded as an Imperial stooge. It had taken several regiments of the Army to restore order, and a precarious peace had been imposed at the point of sword and spear. But even Skallyan must surely be aware that the news of Ba'alekkt's death would probably provoke a fresh resurgence of trouble, particularly since most of the garrison were still in Tamat.

He was fifty, and looked older. The lines of his face had sagged downwards into gloomy folds, and his flabby belly, unkindly revealed by the soft silk of his expensive robe, seemed to have dropped in sympathy. As he launched into a long-winded, pompous and falsely sorrowful speech regretting the sudden and dreadful death of the late Emperor, her beloved brother, Dejneb was seized with a terrible urge to laugh, and to tell him, in words even he would understand, why Ba'alekkt's end was an occasion for gladness.

She didn't, of course. She sat on the hard, uncomfortable throne, as rigid as gold, and let her mind wander. Escape – oh, if only she could escape this room, this Palace, this city . . .

But she had never in her life travelled beyond the city's boundary. She thought of the horse races run on the shore near the Palace, and the feel of the salt wind in her veil, speaking of freedom.

K'djelk had found freedom, of a sort, in Minassa. Her letters spoke of a kind husband, an adorable son, a likeable father-in-law and a Palace where everyone in the land could come and go at will, and where the people treated her as an equal, with genuine liking and respect. K'djelk had embraced the customs of her new home with enthusiasm, and wrote in glowing terms of her new life. Djeneb had always liked her sister, but envy, sharp and corrosive as quicklime, was rapidly eroding her better nature.

'Lady?'

The Prince's querulous, indignant voice brought her back to dismal reality. She said hastily, 'I thank you for your kind words, most gracious cousin. You have been of great comfort to me in my grief.'

'I am so glad, dear lady. And now, I must ask you to ensure that our next words are private.'

It was a foolish request, of course, for nothing said in the Palace could ever be kept private. But although she was theoretically above him in rank – an Emperor's daughter, whereas he was merely an Emperor's grandson, and moreover through the female line – his gender gave him the right to issue this thinly disguised order, and have it obeyed. In the Women's Quarters, Djeneb ruled. Outside, she was just another chattel, a gaming piece, a plaything, a possession of men.

With a vicious snap of her fingers, she dismissed her attendants. A tiny gesture of one hand told Ga'agen to listen at the door. She didn't think Skallyan would rape or murder her, but she didn't trust him.

As soon as they were alone, the Prince scuttled closer. He had one leg slightly shorter than the other, and a peculiar, uneven gait. He stood so near that she could smell what he had eaten last – something heavily laden with aniseed and garlic – and see the grey sprouting hairs in his nose and ears.

'Dearest lady – we must marry at once!'

His words were so unexpected that Djeneb, despite all her training, could not hide her astonishment. For the first time in her life, she was grateful for the privacy of her veil. She hastily composed her features and her voice, and said mildly, 'There seems no need for such haste, gracious Prince. With my poor brother hardly dead—'

'But that is precisely the reason why we must hurry! There are several contenders for the Onyx Throne, and not all are benevolent. Married to me, you would be safe.'

'Are you suggesting that I am in danger inside the Palace?' Djeneb demanded in her most formidable voice.

She was glad to see that Skallyan looked alarmed. He shook his head so that his grey, greasy curls waved lankly round the small bald patch in the centre. 'Of course not, dearest lady – of course not. But out of my sincere affection and regard for you, I feel it is best if our marriage takes place as soon as possible.'

In case someone else marries me first, Djeneb thought. She said, 'Have the other members of the Council returned from Tamat yet? In the absence of an Emperor, their permission will surely be necessary before any ceremony is performed.'

'It has already been granted,' said Skallyan, with a ready smile that convinced her that he was lying. He must have sneaked back from Tamat before his colleagues, and hoped to make her his wife before any of them realized what he planned. And although he was an unpleasant and mediocre man, he was still a Prince, possessing the wealth, power and influence conferred by his rank. This time tomorrow, she would be on a ship bound for Tulyet, and once secured within one of his mountain fortresses, it would take an army to retrieve her. Not that anyone would bother, even for the daughter of an Emperor, for women could only be married once, and so her usefulness would be ended. People would gossip about the scandal, sigh with envy at the thought of all her dowry wasted on the undeserving and underhand Prince, and then forget about her. And she would be trapped in Tulyet, enduring Skallyan's marital rape until she gave him an heir, and then neglected.

She had known for years that it was her destiny, of course, but she had always placed it in the distant future. To have her fate knocking so imminently on her door was horribly unpleasant.

'This – this is unexpectedly sudden,' said Djeneb, trying to keep herself calm. 'I – I do not think I am yet ready, gracious cousin, for such an immediate ceremony.'

'Nonsense,' said Skallyan, and a new, impatient note had displaced his earlier tones of wheedling flattery. 'You have no choice in the matter, dearest lady. Permission has been granted. The Priests of Kaylo expect our presence at the Temple this evening. My own galley is moored at the Palace Dock, ready to transport us to Tulyet.' He moved closer, and reached out to touch her hand: it took all her pride and self-control not to shrink away. 'In a few hours, my dear Lady Djeneb, you will be my wife, in ceremony and in fact. Our union was your dear brother's fondest wish. He spoke to me many times of the perfect match we would make, and of how well we would be suited. I have been looking forward to this day for three years, dear Lady Djeneb, and I will not allow you to disappoint me now.' And his hand moved upwards to linger over her breast, greedily assessing its ripeness.

'Leave.' Djeneb stood up abruptly, and swiped his fingers away.

'Lady?' He stared at her in pained astonishment. 'Lady, this is hardly proper—'

'Neither is your behaviour. I am not a beast at market, to be squeezed and pawed and poked,' said Djeneb, her fury boiling over at last. 'If I am to marry you, whether it is today or next month or next year, I demand to be treated with due respect. Do you understand me, *gracious* Prince?'

He was almost a handspan shorter than she was, and he couldn't have looked more surprised if she'd turned into a leopard. Then his toothy grimace of a smile broke out, and he took a couple of steps backwards. 'Of course I do, dear lady. You are naturally overwrought with grief for your brother. But the best remedy for bereavement is a new life, new surroundings. Trust me, dear lady. I hold your welfare very close to my heart.' He made a perfunctory obeisance, and stepped back again. 'I will return this evening, never fear, at an hour before sunset. Be ready and waiting for me, my dear bride.'

Still smiling ingratiatingly, he left: and Djeneb, giving way to the full force of her rage, ripped her veil from her head and hurled the gold circlet at the door which her prospective husband had just closed behind him.

The act of violence calmed her. She retrieved it as her attendants hurried in, and smiled reassuringly at their anxious, puzzled faces. 'It seems that I am to be married this evening, and will voyage to Tulyet immediately afterwards, so we have much to do. Emelis and Dalmu, begin packing my favourite clothes and my jewels. I will come to oversee you in few moments. There is a great deal to arrange and we must be quick. Ga'agen? Come with me.'

There was a place in the central garden of the Women's Quarters, where the noise of the fountain meant that they would not be overheard. Ignoring the spray of fine cool water drifting over her beautiful gown, Djeneb turned to face her Chief Eunuch. 'What can I do?' she cried in despair. 'I *can't* marry him, Ga'agen – I *can't*. And the very fact he wants it done so quickly is certain proof that he hasn't got the Council's permission. By the time they return, it will be too late – I'll be half-way to Tulyet.'

The eunuch studied her thoughtfully. 'You could refuse.'

'He would carry me off by force. He has men, money, a ship. The Imperial Guard is in Tamat – Ba'alekkt only left me a dozen, he obviously didn't think I was in need of much protection.' Her voice twisted bitterly. 'Skallyan will drag me off to the Temple under cover of darkness, bribe the priests to ignore my protests, and then hustle me on board his galley and set sail before anyone can help. If they *want* to help me.'

'I want to help you, lady,' said Ga'agen, and his unnaturally smooth face was stiff with distress. 'But unless you leave the Palace, I do not see how you can avoid this marriage. And after all, it is what your brother wanted.'

'To Olyak's lowest Hall with my brother!' Djeneb cried furiously. 'He wanted to make me unhappy, so he betrothed me to that loathsome gobbet of slime. I'm *glad* he's dead, Ga'agen – I'm *glad*. And if leaving the Palace is the only way I can escape Skallyan's clutches, then that's what I'll do.'

There was a short, shocked silence. Ga'agen said miserably, 'But lady, I did not mean to suggest – Vessels of the Blood Imperial do not run away like common criminals.'

'But common criminals aren't usually forced into marriage with repellent slugs like Skallyan,' Djeneb pointed out vehemently. 'Shall I tell you what I think, Ga'agen? I think that the Council are planning to marry me to someone else, and the Prince knows it. That's why he's in such a hurry. If I can only hide for a few days, long enough for the Council to return, then I won't have to marry him.'

'They may want you to marry someone even worse,' said the eunuch.

'*No one* could possibly be worse than the Prince of Tulyet! I *won't* marry him, and if you don't help me, Ga'agen,' Djeneb said, dropping her voice to a whisper, 'then I shall kill myself.'

His face blenched in horror. 'No, lady – for all the affection that is between us, no, I beg you, not that – why, I held your hand when you took your first steps! I taught you to read and write!'

'And you comforted me when my mother died,' Djeneb said, bitterly regretting her hasty words. There were tears in her eyes, and her face felt hot with guilt. 'Oh, Ga'agen, I'm sorry – I would never do such a terrible thing. But help me, please help me – I can't marry that man.'

Her contrition, and her obvious desperation, had at last pierced his resistance: Ga'agen's soft heart was notorious. He nodded reluctantly. 'Very well, Lady Djenn – if you are truly determined to do this, than I will help you.'

His use of her old childish pet-name made her tears spill over, and she hugged him gratefully. 'Oh, Ga'agen, thank you – thank you! I'll see you well rewarded when all this is over.'

'The only reward I want is your happiness, lady,' said the old eunuch, and smiled at her sadly.

When the Prince of Tulyet, arrayed in the splendid traditional green and gold of the bridegroom, presented himself at the Imperial Palace at the appointed hour, he found to his fury that his bride's attendants refused to let him in. In vain he shouted, he beat on the door with his fists, he argued, persuaded, cajoled, threatened. In the end, he summoned his own men, and told them to use force. They objected, for entering the Women's Quarters without authority was punishable by death.

'I'm not asking you to rape all the women!' Skallyan shouted. 'I just want you to break the door down!'

In the end, they obliged, but only after he had promised them enough gold Imperials to buy a village. They watched with lively curiosity as he stormed into the forbidden apartments, pushing Djeneb's shrieking attendants aside.

She wasn't there. Unable to believe it, he searched over and over in scented bathrooms, in tiled halls, in cool night gardens. Not one of the screaming, fluttering, protesting, hastily veiled concubines had the sturdy build and unusual height of his intended bride. And in the end, well after midnight, he had to admit defeat.

Humiliatingly, he had been outwitted by a gaggle of women and eunuchs.

CHAPTER THREE

The docks of Toktel'yi spread for a mile or more along both banks of the main channel of the river Kefirinn, two or three miles from the sea. Apart from the months of the winter rains, over a hundred ships might be tied up there, from all over the known world. Bulky traders from the Archipelago; lumbering Gulkeshi craft with peculiar rigs; graceful Kerentan ships, mostly owned and worked by women; sleek, shallow-draughted river boats, that plied up and down the Kefirinn, bringing gold and furs and embroidered silks from Zithirian, the exquisite and delicate pottery of Minassa, yellow Hailyan wine, valuable timber from Lelyent. And out from Toktel'yi would go the produce of the Empire: oils and spices, charsh paper, bales of cotton, bars of iron, bags of delicate beads and precious stones. It was said that every dwelling in the known world contained at least one item that had been traded at these wharves.

The Toktel'yan Navy had its own length of quayside, where the swift deadly galleys, rowed by slaves, could take on provisions, wait for orders, or undergo minor repairs. These berths were heavily guarded, in case any rowers should be tempted to escape into the anonymous, foetid, teeming ring of slums, water lanes and tenements that fed on the wealthy centre of Toktel'yi like a fungus.

But the courier ships, light, small, fast, relied upon their crowded sails to spin them across the waters of the Southern Sea, and all their crews were free men. So if the naval berths were full, they were allowed to moor amongst the cargo vessels, dwarfed by the towering sides of traders from Balki or Annatal.

There was only one courier here now, for most were at sea, carrying the confirmation of the Emperor's death to the far-flung islands of the Archipelago. But the *Wind of Morning* had been sent to Tekkt, only two days' voyage away at the most, and she had returned that afternoon. She lay dark and silent, save for the coloured lanterns hung at bow and stern, for most of her crew had seized the opportunity to go ashore for the night of carousing in the numerous dockside taverns and brothels.

A man walked casually down the line of sleeping ships. He was alone, for despite the lateness of the hour the docks were patrolled by the City Guard, and thus comparatively safe at least until the curfew. He wore a black hooded cloak over his long robe, but no other details of his appearance were visible in the gloom.

He stopped by the *Wind of Morning* and glanced up at her prow, where her name was carved in gilded letters above the Imperial monogram of Djamal, in whose reign she had been built. Then he walked up the boarding plank.

The sailor whose losing throw of the dice had put him on guard duty was dozing against the gunwale, a flask at his side. The man paused, studying him, and then crept past him with cat-like stealth. Once on the deck, he stopped again, waiting until he was sure that the watchman still slept. Then he made his way aft.

In common with every other ship, the Captain's cabin lay below the stern deck, where damage from enemy rams was least likely to occur. The uninvited visitor climbed down the ladder, passed two other doors, and tapped softly on the one at the end.

The significant noises on the other side ceased abruptly. A voice, deep and pleasant but sharp with annoyance, said, 'Go away, Lekken, unless the ship's on fire.'

'It's urgent.'

'Bugger off.'

'No.'

There was a curse, a woman's giggle, footsteps. The door was wrenched open, and the *Wind of Morning*'s Captain stood splendidly and rampantly naked in the entrance, his black hair coiling in riotous curls to his shoulders like a woman's, and his brown skin sleek and shiny with sweat. 'You're not Lekken,' he said.

'Correct. Tell the woman to go.'

The Captain's wide mouth curved in a contemptuous sneer as he studied the intruder. 'Why should I?'

'You know why. Get rid of her.'

For a moment longer the Captain's eyes, green as a panther's, held the other man's in defiance. Then he made a gesture of disgust and turned to the woman, still sprawled voluptuously on the mattress within. 'Get dressed and go.'

She was obviously Gulkeshi, with the big build and muddy complexion of her people, but unexpectedly handsome. Eyeing the stranger warily, she slithered into her thin gown, tucked the coin the Captain tossed her between her ample breasts, and flounced past him. The hooded man watched until she had vanished up the ladder, and then walked into the cabin, shutting the door behind him.

'So – what in Olyak's name do you want? Or should I say, in Olkanno's name?'

The other man did not reply. He glanced round at the small, chaotic cabin: the mattress on the floor under a heap of tangled bedding; the narrow shelf that doubled as a table, cluttered with dirty cups and plates; the small iron-bound clothes chest in the corner; and the single lantern, hung from a hook in the low, beamed ceiling. Then he looked again at the man who presided over this squalor. His hair was much longer than Toktel'yan fashion, an array of rings glinted in both ears, and his hard, muscular body indicated that, most unusually for a Navy Captain, he was not afraid to work his own ship. A Fabrizi pirate could be similarly described, but this man was unmistakably Toktel'yan, with the proud, high-boned features often seen on those Vessels of the Blood Imperial who had not run to fat.

'My Lord Kazhian,' said the Spymaster's agent softly. 'You have a ship. I have need of one.'

Eska'anen's disowned, disgraced, disreputable son stared back at him, his green eyes sharp. Then he laughed. 'I know you! Take that ridiculous garment off, and let me see if I'm right.'

For a moment, the tall man stood still. Then, with an ironic flourish, he pulled the hood back, revealing reddish hair and a nose the shape of a hawk's beak. 'Your cousin Arkun,' he said. 'Remember me?'

'I doubt I could ever forget.' Kazhian bent to pick up his discarded tunic, and pulled it over his head. He indicated the mattress. 'I won't apologize for being rude. Your sort deserve anyone's contempt, and get it too seldom. What in Olyak's name possessed you to work for that poisonous viper?'

'You didn't always swear by the Lord of Death.'

'Why not?' Kazhian's deep, pleasant voice was deceptively casual. 'I've given him enough lives, after all. And when I last saw you, you hadn't sold your soul. Wine? It's Hailyan.'

It was pure and fragrant, the colour of Zithiriani gold, and came in a Minassan goblet of exquisite form, badly chipped on the rim. Arkun sat down on a corner of the mattress, and surveyed his host. 'I am surprised that Olyak has not yet claimed you. Do you always speak with such dangerous freedom?'

'Why not? The only reason I'm alive is because my father hasn't got round to killing me yet.' Kazhian poured himself an overflowing quantity of wine, and took a gulp of it. 'Did you know that he murdered my mother?'

The red-haired man looked up at him. Slowly, he shook his head.

'I thought she'd died of a fever. I was only ten, after all. And once she was gone, no one ever mentioned her again. I was the only proof she'd ever existed. I know now that there had always been rumours about what had happened – but no one said anything to me, presumably on my father's orders.'

'Then how did you find out?'

'He told me himself. When I returned home after the *Spear of Vengeance* sank. He called me a drug-riddled incompetent.' Kazhian's mouth twisted briefly. 'I called him a domineering tyrant. Then he said, *"I should have had you poisoned like your mother."*'

There was a brief, horrible silence. Arkun stared down at his hands. He said quietly, 'She didn't deserve that. She didn't deserve marriage to Eska'anen, let alone death at his hands. She was always kind to me when I was a child – the only one of my father's household who was. I was fifteen when she died, but I wept when I heard the news.'

'My mother – your aunt. I don't know why he killed her. Perhaps she stood up to him once too often. Or maybe Suken's mother had something to do with it – she was still alive then. She was never happy to be junior wife, and she was always his favourite, even though she was a nasty, vindictive bitch.'

'As is Suken. I come across him frequently.'

'Do you? What a pleasure. As you can imagine, there's absolutely no love lost between us – and my father adores him.' Kazhian finished the wine and walked over to the long shelf. He picked up a wooden pipe with a short, curved stem, and tipped some of the powdery contents of a small silver box into the bowl. Arkun watched as he lit it with a roll of paper from the lantern. 'Aren't you worried about setting the ship on fire?'

'No.' Kazhian sat down cross-legged on the mattress beside his cousin, and inhaled deeply. The fumes of the narcotic drug khlar began to seep into the air, and Arkun coughed.

'Don't worry,' Kazhian added with a wry sideways glance. 'I've learned my lesson – I only smoke when off-duty. And unlike that filthy stuff sorcerers take, it's not addictive. I'll have a clear head tomorrow, I promise you.'

'Just as well. You'll sail for Ukkan with the morning tide.'

The younger man's eyes, already dilating with the effects of the drug, widened in unguarded surprise. '*Ukkan?* Oh, no, I won't. My orders are to stay in Toktel'yi.'

'My orders override them. And as you know, only an Emperor can dictate to the Spymaster.'

'There is no Emperor.' Kazhian stared at his cousin, the bastard his mother's brother had engendered on a Fabrizi slave, and let his disgust fill his face. 'So Olkanno thinks he can do as he likes. What unspeakable crime "*for the greater good of the Empire*" has he told you to commit?'

Arkun's harsh face, moulded by the bones of his mother's people and by the hardships and bitterness and humiliations of his childhood, did not move. 'If I ignored our old ties of blood and friendship, I could have your tongue torn out for that.'

'Then tear it out.' Kazhian's voice dropped to a savage, contemptuous whisper. 'Do you remember telling me, once, how you wanted to change the world? It was the summer after my mother died, and I'd just been sent to Tulyet. You said that you wanted an end to slavery and injustice, poverty and cruelty. We sat on the wall above your father's courtyard, and I hung on every word. I believed you – I saw that people *should* try for it, even if they were bound to fail. And although I've done much to be ashamed of, at least I haven't betrayed that dream – *your* dream, Arkun the hypocrite!'

'That's a trifle inconsistent, coming from you.' Arkun's face was pale with anger. 'Kazhian the idealist – a Captain in the Imperial Navy, stuffed so full of khlar he kills half his men in a shipwreck a child could have avoided – and most of them galley-slaves marked by his own whip! So let's hear no more about hypocrisy, cousin, because you're as guilty as I am. And as you weren't born in slavery, you haven't my excuse.'

The pause was thick with hostility. Kazhian's mouth tightened. 'And if I refuse to take you to Ukkan?'

'Then Olkanno will certainly hear of it. There is no other courier ship in port, and I must be there as soon as possible. And once my master knows you have defied him, he will need no further excuse. You may be a Vessel of the Blood Imperial, but that will not save you from being lost overboard, or knifed in a brothel. And few will think your fate undeserved.'

'And none will weep for me,' said Kazhian softly. 'So – if I am forced to obey your orders – may I know why you are going there, in such furtive haste?'

'No,' Arkun said. 'Nor may any of your crew know our destination, either, until after we have set sail. And my presence on the ship must be kept hidden. If word gets out, Olkanno will not hesitate to lay the blame at your feet. Where does the whore live?'

'It will take too long to find her.'

'Now, perhaps. But it is only a matter of time. Don't look so squeamish, Kazhian son of Eska'anen.' Arkun's voice was silky with menace. 'Do you understand? This is an errand of utmost secrecy. If I am discovered before I leave the ship at Ukkan, then you and all your men will die. Small vessels like this are often lost in a summer storm.'

Kazhian's eyes flared green, and Arkun knew that if his cousin had had a knife in his hand, he would have used it. He held the younger man's gaze with his own, silently urging him to see sense.

At last, Kazhian made an explosive noise of bitter disgust, and sprang to his feet as if he could no longer endure to be so close to the kinsman whom he had once admired, and liked, and trusted.

'If I have no choice, then I must do it,' he said. 'But for my crew's sake, not mine. Tell me, Arkun – does my compliance really buy our lives? Or is mass murder in your orders anyway, however discreet and obedient I am? Perhaps Eska'anen has decided to get rid of me at last, and Olkanno always was very fond of killing two birds with one arrow.'

The other man continued to survey him, but something in his face had altered. Kazhian swore softly, bitterly. 'That's it, isn't it! We take you to Ukkan, for Olyak alone knows what hideous purpose, and you ensure that once we've dropped you off we are never seen again. How very convenient! Olkanno knows his latest plot won't be betrayed – Eska'anen's troublesome black sheep is eliminated – and I'm no longer around to remind you of a time when you were a human being like the rest of us.'

'I do still have a conscience,' Arkun said.

'Do you? You work for Olkanno – you can't. Oh, how I despise you,' Kazhian said wearily. 'Even more than I despise myself. Go on, get out – you can have the passenger cabin on the starboard side, it's full of junk and rubbish, and the ceiling leaks when the decks are awash, so there's no danger that anyone will want to use it. I'll get you food and water for the voyage, and you can lock yourself in.'

'Thank you,' Arkun said. He got to his feet, his face still calm, though paler under the onslaught of Kazhian's vicious words. 'How long?'

'If we have a following wind, which isn't likely at this time of year, a day and a night without stopping. My weather-worker's fairly competent, though. Realistically, if we sail in the morning, we should reach Ukkan on the evening of the day after next. Is that soon enough for you?'

'It might be,' said Arkun, ignoring the other man's sneer. 'Tell your sorcerer to increase his dose of Annatal.' He stood still for a moment, as if about to say something else, and then turned and went out, closing the cabin door quietly behind him.

Alone again at last, the *Wind of Morning*'s Captain turned and rammed his clenched fist into the panelling. It was Onnak ironwood, and absolutely unyielding. With a savage curse, he sucked his bruised and bleeding knuckles, and wondered why his father should hate him so much.

From Eska'anen's point of view, it was understandable. He wanted a son exactly like himself – pleasant, charming, treacherous, devious, ruthless. He wanted a snake like Suken. And neither on Kazhian nor on his unfortunate Tulyettan mother, both outspoken, strong-willed and rebellious, had he wasted any love, or liking, or respect.

Well, the loathing was mutual. Just now, the urge to kill Arkun had almost overwhelmed him, even though it would inevitably, sooner or later, be followed by his own death. The same force, ten times stronger, had once compelled him to attack his father. But Eska'anen had yelled for his guard, and they had beaten Kazhian half senseless and slung him out into the street as if he were a beggar or a criminal.

The memory, three years old, still had the power to sear his soul. He had thought it locked away, until Arkun reminded him.

The door opened without the courtesy of a knock. His cousin stood there, his bony face still impassive. 'There is something you should see. Come.'

Deliberately, he had given his unwelcome guest the nastiest hole on board. The tiny cabin was filled with things either broken or unwanted, the mattress had sprouted green fungi during the last rainy season and smelt appalling, and there was hardly room to lie down.

But despite these obvious disadvantages, it was already occupied. The lantern, held high, revealed that the rubbish had been rearranged to make a hiding-place, tucked into the curving side of the ship. And there, crouched awkwardly in the limited space, was a woman.

Kazhian drew in his breath sharply. She was veiled, so unlikely to be a whore. He could see little of her, but the gauzy cloth covering her face was sucking in and out rapidly with the force of her breathing.

'Did you know about this?' Arkun's voice held that quality of menace which made his cousin want to retch, or do murder.

'No, I did not. What are you going to do with her? Stick a knife into her and throw her overboard?'

'You won't find it easy,' said the woman. She must be terrified, but her voice was low, and surprisingly firm.

'Who are you?' Kazhian asked. He was a handspan shorter than

Arkun, so he did not have to bend his neck under the low deck beams. It gave him a small but distinct advantage over the agent. He added pleasantly, 'Don't be alarmed, lady. I at least have no intention of hurting you. I'd merely like to know what you are doing on my ship.'

'Are you the Captain?'

'I have that honour, yes.' Kazhian glanced at Arkun, whose face was fierce enough to frighten the dead, and gave her his most charming smile. 'You must have cramp if you've been cooped up there for a while. Why don't you come out and stretch your legs?'

'Not if he's going to knife me,' said the woman. 'I've got a knife too, and I'll use it.'

'He won't,' Kazhian told her, with a significant glare at Arkun. 'I know he bears a passing resemblance to one of Olyak's messengers, but he's as harmless as a kitten really.'

'He doesn't look it,' said the woman.

'I'll vouch for him. I've known him for at least an hour.' Kazhian pushed past his cousin and squatted down so that he was on the stowaway's level. It usually worked with dogs: hopefully, it would reassure her too. He added, very gently, 'Why are you here?'

The woman drew a long, harsh breath. 'I've run away from home,' she said, a most unsubmissive defiance in her voice.

His long experience of whores had accustomed Kazhian to assertive females, but ladies were supposed to be meek, feminine and compliant – especially when alone with two completely strange men. And this one was certainly of good family: no whore would bother with a veil, and her loose gown, though a plain and unadorned dark blue, was made of fine, expensive cotton.

'Did you? Why was that?' Kazhian enquired, his thick brows raised and a look of sudden mischief curving the corners of his mouth. She was so refreshingly fierce, and determined, and brave.

'Don't laugh at me,' the woman warned, suddenly sounding very young. 'They – they wanted me to marry someone loathsome.'

'So did my father, but I didn't run away. I just told him what he could do with his fat ugly suggestion.'

'Men can do that,' said the girl resentfully. 'We can't. We're just supposed to put up with it. Anyway, my – my parents are – are away, and this man, the horrible one, tried to marry me by force. He knew they'd changed their minds and he wanted to be sure of me before they returned. So I ran away. And you can't send me home because I won't tell you where home is!'

Silence. Kazhian wondered when his crew would start to trickle back, and what he could do with this second uninvited and unwanted guest. She'd be almost as much of a menace as Arkun, especially if there was an enraged prospective husband searching for her, and perhaps a father as well.

Of course, he could always let the agent knife her and throw her overboard. The Kefirinn was infested with corpses, few of whom had met a natural end, and one more wouldn't be noticed. Bloated, stinking and unrecognizable, she'd be hooked out by the scavenger boats in two or three days, and burned on the public pyre with all the other anonymous flotsam and jetsam of this huge, corrupt and lethal city. The ashes were sold for fertilizer.

'I only need somewhere to hide for a few days,' said the woman, her voice beginning to show signs of stress. 'Just until the – until my parents come back. I'll never mention you, I swear on Kaylo's life. I'll just creep away when no one's looking and go back home. I can pay you for my keep.'

'What with?'

'This.' The stowaway pulled a ring from one of her brown, stubby fingers and held it out.

Kazhian took it curiously. Long ago, before some ingenious Toktel'yan had discovered the secret of making charsh paper, all writing had been done with a metal or reed stylus on tablets of wax or clay, and every wealthy householder had had a signing ring like this, carved with his family's device, to impress on important documents or letters.

It was very heavy, made of the rare reddish gold once produced by one small mine in Tulyet, that had run out nearly a thousand years previously. Kazhian looked at the crude, archaic workmanship. The design seemed to be a bird of some sort, wings outstretched . . .

He laughed, with sudden and genuine amusement, and flipped the ring in the air, catching it left-handed. 'That was a mistake, my dear – a very big mistake indeed. You've given it to one of the few people who would recognize it. But of course, if you've been kept shut up in the Women's Quarters all your life, you can't be expected to know who I am, can you?'

'Who are you?' the girl asked thinly.

'What's more to the point, who are *you*? We've landed a rare fish here, my friend,' he added, glancing at Arkun. 'And I don't think you'll want to stick a knife in her once you realize her identity.' He reached forward and hauled her, unresisting, out of her hiding-place. She was exactly his height, far too tall for a woman, and her decorously voluminous gown could not disguise the heaviness of her body.

'Well, who is she?' Arkun demanded.

Kazhian smiled, showing uneven white teeth. 'May I present to you, kinsman, another of my cousins – my father's brother's youngest daughter – the Lady Djeneb, Vessel of the Blood Imperial.' And with a swift, ruthless gesture, he dragged the veil from her head.

She was not at all beautiful. Her brows were too thick, her nose blunt and prominent, her mouth much wider and fuller than the prim little orifice that was considered ideal. It was shameful to have her face revealed to strangers, but although she flushed, she returned their interested gaze with stubborn defiance in her large hazel eyes.

'At a guess, the Prince of Tulyet has tried to claim his bride somewhat prematurely,' said Kazhian. 'Am I right? I'm not surprised you ran away. I find him utterly loathsome too, and I'm not in danger of being married to him.'

'My brother – the late Emperor – betrothed me to him,' Djeneb said. Strangely, though her face felt cold and naked without the veil, she was no longer frightened, at least of Kazhian. It must be Kazhian – he was the only one of her Imperial cousins to command a ship, and his unconventional and wholly disreputable appearance fitted exactly with all the gossip about him. Silently, furiously, she cursed her own stupidity. If she'd only thought to look at the name of the ship, she'd have walked straight past. But her escort, one of the younger eunuchs, had suggested it. There had seemed to be no one on board save for the slumbering watchman, and it had been wonderfully easy to creep past him unnoticed and find this dank, uncomfortable but apparently secure hiding-place.

And now, after barely an hour, she had been discovered by these two very different men. Kazhian had the reputation of a desperate rogue who'd sink his ship or sell his grandmother for a pipe of khlar, but she sensed intuitively that he genuinely sympathized with her plight, for he was a rebel too.

But the other man, the tall one with the hair and nose of a Fabrizi pirate and a mouth like a steel trap, was altogether more frightening. He certainly looked like one of Olyak's messengers, and she wondered apprehensively if he was in fact one of the Spymaster's minions. And if so, it was certainly possible that he would want to kill her.

But surely not now he knew who she was. And so perhaps giving Kazhian her Imperial signing-ring had actually saved her life.

'So did the Prince really try to carry you off?' Kazhian asked, his green eyes glinting.

'Yes. He tried to force me into marriage today. He said he had the Council's permission, but I'm certain he hadn't – or why do it in such haste, and whisk me off to Tulyet afterwards?'

'You're probably right,' said her cousin thoughtfully, a frown between his thick, slanting brows. 'So, you reckon the Council want to marry you to someone else?'

'Yes, I'm sure of it. And whoever he might be, he can't possibly be worse than Skallyan.'

'He could – he might be me,' Kazhian pointed out, grinning. 'Or he might be my brother Suken. Personally, I'd rather marry a cobra. Well, I myself am perfectly happy to keep you here. We sail with the morning tide, so once we're at sea you'll be quite safe from the Prince until we reach our destination – which is supposed to be secret, but is certainly not, you'll be relieved to learn, Tulyet. Then if you like you can go back to Toktel'yi and marry this other person, whoever he is. Or you can disappear.' He smiled at her wickedly. 'I won't tell anyone about you if you don't want me to.'

'I don't know.' This unexpected friendliness and understanding had almost dismantled Djeneb's composure. 'I'll – I'll think about it.'

'You've got at least a day and a night to make up your mind. Meanwhile, you can have my cabin. Don't worry, I won't try anything. Raping Vessels of the Blood Imperial is not my style, whatever my father says. Our voyage is urgent, and no one will think it strange if I spend most of the time on deck. And my cabin is always kept private. You'll be quite safe from discovery.'

'Thank you,' said Djeneb, keeping calm with a supreme effort.

'Not at all. Any enemy of Skallyan's is a friend of mine,' said Kazhian cheerfully. 'Go and make yourself comfortable before the crew come back. If I need sleep, I'll borrow someone's hammock. There's still some wine in the jug, and bread too, if it hasn't gone stale. I'll make sure you have enough fresh food to last the voyage. Go on, go – you look dead on your feet.'

Djeneb stayed where she was. She indicated Arkun, standing silently behind the Captain. 'What about him?'

'Forget you've seen him, and he'll forget he's seen you. He won't dare lay a finger on you, anyway – or he'll have me to reckon with, as well as the Council and all your uncles.'

'Thank you,' Djeneb said, and fled before her exhaustion and relief could finally dissolve into tears.

Kazhian waited until he heard his cabin door shut behind her. Then he said softly, 'If you even think about harming her, I'll kill you with my bare hands.'

'I wouldn't dream of it,' Arkun said grimly. 'She's far too valuable. If necessary, I'll take charge of her at Ukkan.'

'And if she doesn't want to go back to Toktel'yi?'

'Her wishes have nothing to do with it,' said the agent. 'She is at the bidding of the Council, and the future Emperor, whoever he may be. She is right, the betrothal to the Prince has been cancelled. It is possible that a greater match is in prospect, one more worthy of her.'

'It would be kinder to let her vanish,' Kazhian said. 'She's like me – too pig-headed for her own good. In Kereneth, perhaps, she would be happy. In Toktel'yi, whoever she marries, she'll be miserable.'

Arkun shrugged. 'So what? Only the priests of the Lord of Life are granted absolute pleasure. The rest of us are bound by duty, or poverty, or in her case the constraints of birth and gender. I am not happy. Nor are you. So why should she have any right to be?'

Kazhian stared at him. Finally, with a snort of contempt, he pushed roughly past and slammed the door shut on his repellent cousin. *One day, I swear I shall kill him . . .*

There were unfamiliar sounds coming from his cabin. Startled out of his fury, he knocked on the door and opened it.

The Lady Djeneb, far from weeping or sinking into an exhausted slumber, had pulled her sleeves up, tucked the hem of her gown into the rolled-up veil tied round her waist, and was energetically clearing up the mess.

For once bereft of speech, Kazhian stared at her. Unabashed, she stared back. 'This place is a pigsty! How can you live like this?'

'I manage,' he told her, grinning. 'But I shouldn't bother. Make it too neat and tidy and they'll realize I've got a woman in here.'

'I don't suppose the one you had in here earlier would care much, as long as the bed was soft,' said Djeneb acidly. She dumped an armful of dirty garments into the open clothes-chest, and slammed the lid shut. 'But I do.'

Kazhian laughed aloud. 'You'd have eaten Skallyan for breakfast! How did you come to be on my ship?'

Djeneb gave him a wary glance. Instinctively, she knew he was her friend, but the long years of seclusion in the Women's Quarters had taught her to doubt all men. At last she said, 'I left the Palace this afternoon. The Prince had said he'd be back at sunset, to take me to the Temple to be married. So I put on my plainest clothes, and one of the young eunuchs came with me, so I wasn't in any danger. Stowing away on a ship was his suggestion — we couldn't think of anywhere safe in the City. It's not too far from the Palace to the docks, and I was sure Skallyan wouldn't dream of looking for me here. And if the ship took me away from Toktel'yi, even better.' Her warm hazel eyes, disturbingly similar to Ba'alekkt's, gazed earnestly into his. 'Perhaps I will . . . disappear.'

'You'd find it difficult now. The man who discovered you is indeed one of Olkanno's agents. You might as well try to get rid of a leech. And I'm not sure even I could outwit him.'

'You could kill him.'

'I could. But Olkanno would know I'd done it. And there are very few people who've managed to evade his vengeance. If I went to Ma'alkwen, perhaps . . . but even there, I'd be seeing a knife in every hand. Why not accept your fate?'

'If I had, the Prince of Tulyet would now be raping me,' said Djeneb bluntly. 'At least I've escaped that.'

'I'm glad. You deserve better. So tell me — why the *Wind of Morning*? Why not some other ship?'

'Kerenek — the eunuch — suggested it. She looked deserted, and the watchman was asleep. He waited until I was safely on board, and then he went back to the Palace.'

'You didn't want him to come with you?'

Djeneb frowned. 'I thought I did — but then I decided I didn't really like the idea of being cooped up with him, perhaps for weeks. And when I told him to leave me, he was quite happy about it — I thought he'd need a lot of persuading, but he went off as meek as a lamb.'

'Perhaps he's one of Olkanno's agents too. Perhaps your presence here isn't coincidence,' Kazhian said grimly. 'I may be imagining plots where none exist, but people who take everything at face value don't last very long in Toktel'yi, do they?'

Looking suddenly sick, Djeneb slowly shook her head.

'Don't worry. Whatever happens to me, or the ship, you'll be safe. Arkun will see to that. You're a prize far too precious for the Prince of Tulyet — or for me, come to that. So sleep well, and pleasant dreams, and enjoy your brief hours of freedom.'

His hand was on the door-latch before she spoke, her voice uncharacteristically diffident. 'Kazhian?'

'Yes?'

'Why don't *you* try for the Onyx Throne?'

He laughed, the green eyes brilliant with amusement. 'Me? I'd rather face a dozen Fabrizi pirate ships, or sail through a storm on a disintegrating raft – and I'd have more chance of survival, too. Come on, Djeneb, look at me – I'm hardly fit to command a humble courier ship, let alone an Empire.'

'You undervalue yourself,' she said with stubborn perspicacity.

'Perhaps I do – but no one else does,' Kazhian pointed out. 'It's a great pity you were born female, Djeneb – you'd have made a remarkable Emperor.'

'Don't mock me,' she said angrily. 'I've had enough of false flattery.'

'If you can't tell an honest compliment from flattery, then I was wrong,' Kazhian told her. 'Goodnight, cousin – and I apologize in advance for the fleas and bed-bugs!'

Once more alone, Djeneb flopped down on to the stained, scratchy mattress, and brushed a few stray unwelcome tears from her eyes. In this unpromising, unexpected place she had encountered sympathy, liking, perhaps even genuine admiration – and from a handsome, confident and capable man of the world.

Why had she asked him about the Onyx Throne? Because she had been deluded by a brief, stupid, adolescent dream, in which they were married and worked together, as equal partners, to bring a little justice to the wide, populous and often resentful lands under Toktel'yi's rule.

A woman, equal to a man? As impossible as a bird flying backwards, or rain falling in the Ma'al Desert.

With a muffled sob of self-annoyance and self-pity, Djeneb rolled over, buried her face in the pillow, and tried to sleep.

CHAPTER FOUR

The pyre, soaked in pitch, flared up with roaring intensity, and the mourners who ringed it took several involuntary steps back. Alone, the dead man's eldest son stayed dangerously close to the heat of the flames, staring steadily as the corpse was consumed. Only when it was no longer visible did he turn and walk away to join his wife.

By Toktel'yan custom, women were not supposed to attend adult male funerals, but Trinn came from Balki, and the ways of the island's Imperial conquerors lay very lightly over the old habits of a stubborn, hardy and independent people. She said nothing as Megren stood beside her, but clasped his hand briefly in hers before bowing her head in the conventional attitude of grief.

They waited until the pyre had collapsed into glowing ashes, and the smoke no longer disfigured the deep blue summer sky. The black-robed priests of Olyak chanted, as they had throughout the ceremony, the ritual words which would accompany B'kenn, son of Makkyar, Vessel of the Blood Imperial, to whichever Hall the Lord of Death had assigned him.

As her father-in-law, though greedy and slothful, had also been good-natured and generous, Trinn hoped that his soul now resided in one of the lighter and more pleasant rooms in Death's House. She shivered, although it was so warm that she was sweating under her light gown and transparent veil. She had been fond of him, and he had not deserved such an end. The Healer had blamed a batch of bad oysters for the mysterious illness which had killed, in addition to B'kenn, one of his wives and two concubines. Certainly, people died that way every summer, slain by unwise overindulgence in Ukkan's favourite delicacy. But B'kenn had lingered in agony for days, threshing so violently that he had had to be tied down to his bed. His death had been almost a relief, ending his sufferings at last. And the shrouded figure on the pyre had been a drained and diminished husk of Megren's fat, cheerful father: at the end, B'kenn had lost more than half his bulk.

Poison. No one had mentioned it openly yet, but the word hung in the air of the household as if it had been shouted aloud, and the slaves wore hunted, frightened expressions. Someone had administered it. Someone was guilty. And anyone with inconvenient knowledge, or a memory too acute for safety, might be struck down next.

At the head of the mourners, Megren and Trinn rode back in litters to Megren's father's villa on the outskirts of Ukkan. It commanded a wonderful view of the broad estuary below the city, and in the twenty-five years of his residence there, B'kenn had filled it with exquisite sculptures and antiquities from all over the Empire, and beyond. Even the slaves' quarters were pleasant and comfortable, and they were treated with far more consideration than most in Toktel'yi: which made the fact that one of them might have poisoned their master all the more shocking and incomprehensible.

As was the custom, a funeral feast of huge proportions was laid out in the Reception Hall. B'kenn had a marvellous cook, and the food was delicious, the wine excellent and free-flowing. Most of Ukkan's provincial aristocracy seemed to be present, and Trinn, whose realistic mind might have been called cynical in a man, suspected that many were there for reasons of gluttony, rather than out of respect for B'kenn.

She left the gathering and returned to the Women's Quarters, where her father-in-law's surviving wife and two concubines were consoling themselves with a slightly smaller feast. Later, Megren would come to her, and in her small, beautiful room they would make love, for the first time since his hasty return from Tamat. He had been at B'kenn's bedside day and night, and she knew that the grief and stress displayed in his haggard face and haunted eyes could best be exorcized in her bed.

And then she must tell him, plainly and bluntly as few Toktel'yan women ever spoke to their husbands, what he must do next.

It had long been dark when the familiar soft double knock finally arrived on her door. Trinn was sitting before her mirror while her bodyslave finished the last of the scores of tiny gold-sheathed plaits in which her hair was usually dressed, after Balki custom. The glinting tubes of yellow metal contrasted richly with her deep brown skin, and took up echoes in the flowing gold and crimson silk of her gown. Trinn smiled, dismissed the slave, and spoke softly. 'Come in, my husband.'

She had loved him from the moment she had first seen him, and she loved him now, after eight years of marriage, and one son living, two more dead in infancy. And in return this splendid, powerful, popular, admired man, the choice of most people for the Onyx Throne, adored her to the exclusion of all other women, and depended on her love, her advice and support. She was rooted deep in his soul, as he was in hers, and if either of them were to die, the other would be utterly bereft.

She rose to greet him, and they embraced tightly and silently. Talking could wait until later. Now, physical comfort was what they both needed, above all else.

It was even better than usual, the pleasure surely heightened by his long absence. Afterwards, Trinn lay with her head on his shoulder, trying to banish the tempting, insidious waves of sleep, and rehearsing in her mind what she would say. Even Megren, fairest and most honest of men, must be approached carefully on such a momentous subject as this.

At last she said softly, 'What will you do now?'

'Sleep, I hope,' Megren said drowsily. 'Oh, how I have missed you, beloved. Have you missed me?'

'You know I have – and so has Sarrek. He's hardly seen you since you arrived.'

'I've had other things on my mind,' said Megren sadly. 'But I'll take him out sailing with the oyster-fishers tomorrow – he enjoys that.'

Trinn took a deep breath. 'Do you think it *was* the oysters?'

Megren moved his head to look at her. 'You were here when it started. Do you?'

'The only people who were affected were the only ones to eat the oysters. So it *looks* as if that was the cause. But it would have been easy enough to inject them with poison. Everyone knows that B'kenn is – was – very fond of them. If someone wanted to kill him, and wasn't too particular about who else died, it would be an excellent method. And I think that's what happened.'

Megren drew a deep breath. 'But why? Why kill him? He never harmed anyone in his life – unlike most members of my family.'

'I know,' said Trinn, hearing the grief in his voice. 'But he was a Vessel of the Blood Imperial. That alone made him a candidate for the Onyx Throne.'

'He did have one or two supporters on the Council, but no one could seriously believe that he wanted it, surely?'

'His blood itself might be a threat, to a rival whose own claim is perhaps inferior. And there is another possible reason why someone would want to kill him. Perhaps it was done to lure you here.'

Megren sat up and stared down at her, shock expelling the drowsiness from his face and voice. 'You mean – to kill me too?'

'Perhaps,' said Trinn, aware that her voice was unsteady. 'Perhaps they wouldn't dare try to do anything while you were still with the

Army. Or – or maybe they – whoever they are – just wanted to get you out of the way for a while. If B'kenn hadn't fallen ill, wouldn't you now probably be Emperor?'

Megren looked stunned and horrified. Obviously he had been so anxious about his father that the possibility had never entered his head. Like most men of integrity, he was alarmingly unaware of just how ruthless and devious possible enemies could be. And a Vessel of the Blood Imperial, especially one as able and popular as Megren, would have a great many enemies, most of them his kin.

'I don't know,' he said at last. 'But unlikely. Sekkenet persuaded me to let him support my claim at the Council, but there were several other candidates too.'

'Who were they?'

'Eska'anen. Kadjak. Three spoke for B'kenn, and one man apparently wanted Tarmon, Lord of Life alone knows why. There was no clear favourite. Eska'anen had the most votes, then me, then Kadjak. And I can't see Kadjak using poison, can you? He's so rich he doesn't need to – he can just shower everyone with gold.'

'Which is probably why he has so much support. And on the whole,' said Trinn drily, 'considering all the options, I prefer bribery to murder, don't you?'

Megren was frowning. 'Eska'anen has a reputation for ruthlessness in Sabrek. But surely he wouldn't poison his own brother?'

'Why not? He murdered two wives.'

'That was just an unfounded rumour.'

Come on, beloved. Wake up. THINK, for our lives and Sarrek's depend on it. Aloud, she said, 'Forget who might be behind it, for a moment. Let's consider how to keep ourselves safe. The poisoner might have orders to strike again, at you. So you make it difficult. Get the slave you like least to be your taster.'

'I can't do that!'

'If there *is* a poisoner, the taster will be perfectly safe. So will you. An assassin wouldn't risk discovery just to kill a slave. Once they know you're suspicious, they'll back off.'

'And then they'll find another method. Trinn, beloved, if there is someone who wants to kill me, he or she will succeed eventually. You know that as well as I do. Short of going into exile, there's no escape.'

'Then you tell everyone, loudly, clearly and publicly, so that all your uncles and cousins can understand, that you have no desire for the Onyx Throne. Not now, and not ever.'

Nothing stirred in the hot, lamp-lit room, save for the light flickering on Trinn's golden hair-ornaments. Then Megren sighed harshly, and ran his fingers through his bristly hair, making it stand up like a crest on his scalp. His brown eyes were dark with distress and bewilderment. 'Why, beloved?'

'For Sarrek. For your two young brothers. For me, and our love and our life together. If there is a poisoner at work, then whoever directs him, or her, is a master of ruthlessness and cunning. We cannot possibly defeat them at their own game without making ourselves as bad as they are, or worse. I love and admire you so much – I know that you would be the Emperor that Toktel'yi has been waiting for, for many years. But it isn't worth risking your life, and your family's lives. Not unless you plan to take the Onyx Throne by force.'

Megren's face was bleak. 'I refuse to walk through blood to obtain it. And using the Army would almost certainly mean many deaths. This Empire is rotten, it needs a man of honesty, yes, but also one who is completely ruthless. Someone prepared to cut the canker out, if necessary. Sekkenet persuaded me that I was that man. I had my doubts at the time, but I suppressed them. Now that he is dead—'

'*Sekkenet* is dead?'

'Yes, didn't I tell you? I returned from his pyre to find the message about B'kenn.'

'What did he die of?'

'A bowel fever. It's very common in the camp.'

'So it may be, but didn't it occur to you that his death was very convenient for whoever might want you out of the running? As was B'kenn's. Separately, I might just believe that they died naturally,' said Trinn vehemently. 'So close together, it's surely no coincidence. And logically, you must be next – *unless* you renounce all claim to the Onyx Throne, as soon as possible.'

'Perhaps you are right,' Megren said at last, his eyes haunted.

Oh, thank Kaylo, Trinn cried in her heart with relief. She said softly, 'Then you do not wish to become Emperor?'

'I love you, and Sarrek, more than anything else. Not for all the riches of the known world would I put you in danger. So – you have won, beloved. It may not make us safe, even so. But I will send a message to the Council by pigeon at dawn tomorrow, and follow it up with a detailed letter.' He gave a harsh, regretful sigh. 'I was tempted. Sorely tempted, and for the best of reasons. But I can see you are right.'

'Oh, I am so glad,' Trinn whispered, tears in her eyes. 'My own dear love, how I am glad.'

They slept in each other's arms, exhausted by the effort of making such a fateful decision. And she prayed to Kaylo, before sleep carried her away, that Megren's public renunciation of the Onyx Throne would be enough to keep them all safe.

Crowding on all her sails, her long slender masts seeming hardly strong enough to bear such a great weight of spars and canvas, the *Wind of Morning* left Toktel'yi with the first tide and fled westwards towards Ukkan like an outlaw – or like a runaway bride.

When Kazhian had time to think about it, which was fortunately seldom, he could appreciate the absurdity and the irony of his situation. He was carrying two illicit passengers, both of whom he must keep hidden from his crew, on pain of death: one the plain, forceful, clever girl who was also the only unmarried Imperial Daughter left in Toktel'yi, and therefore a potential bargaining piece of great value: and the other his bastard cousin, his boyhood friend, who was almost certainly under orders to kill him and all his crew, once the mission was ended, so that it could remain for ever a secret.

Kazhian had packed a fair amount of living into his twenty-seven years, but he had no intention of dying just yet. As one part of his mind gave orders, assessed the weather-worker's predictions, and plotted the ship's course, the other was working out, with the quick sharp logic that even considerable quantities of khlar had never been enough to diffuse, exactly what Arkun was going to do when they reached their destination.

It must be connected with the various candidates for the Onyx Throne. Kazhian's own father was one of them. And knowing Eska'anen as he did, he knew also that he would eliminate every possible rival, if necessary.

B'kenn, Eska'anen's oldest surviving brother, lived in Ukkan. If Arkun had orders to murder him, Kazhian could understand the need for secrecy and haste. And the agent probably wouldn't restrict himself to B'kenn. His wives, concubines, children, daughter-in-law and grandson all shared that luxurious pink villa above the estuary. Kazhian wondered what method would be used. If he were Arkun, intent on covering his tracks at all costs, he'd knife them all in their beds, and then set the place alight.

If he were Arkun. He was not, but he might have been. His father had devoted all the years of Kazhian's childhood to the production of a callous, ruthless and cunning politician, just like himself. He'd failed because his elder son had inherited his mother's Tulyettan rebelliousness in full measure. But he'd succeeded with Suken, his only son by his beloved third wife, whose untimely death had been quite natural, and mourned only by her husband. Suken, with his hooded, cobra eyes, his sly smile, his delight in cruelty.

Kazhian consigned his half-brother to Olyak's nethermost Halls, and turned his thoughts to Djeneb. At present she was probably sitting on his unsavoury mattress, reading. Like most unmarried men of his rank, he had little adult experience of high-born women, who were invariably kept in close seclusion until, and usually after, their wedding day. Her bluntness had initially surprised him, as had her courage and her determination. Great ladies were supposed to be timid, obedient, refined and feminine. Djeneb, greatest of all, was none of these things. She hadn't succumbed to terror. She had tidied and cleaned his squalid cabin, a heroic and self-imposed task which he had, most ungratefully, rewarded with mockery. And she had found his small store of books – a copy of *Imperial Histories*, a dog-eared sailing manual, a volume of *Issan's Plays* and a collection of poetry and song – and had devoured them eagerly, even the sailing manual, which was barely legible under all the corrections, comments and additions which he had made in his vile, left-handed scrawl.

Well, at least she'd escaped the Prince of Tulyet. But if his suspicions were correct, another bridegroom was being chosen for her, at this very moment.

She had told him that nothing could be worse than Skallyan. He felt a touch of real, painful pity for her innocence. For he knew who could. And as Suken's wife, she could expect nothing but grief, and an early pyre.

He couldn't bludgeon his brain into further thought. The demands of the voyage, the orders he must give, the constant attention to wind and tide, the stink of Annatal as his tame sorcerer kept his powers stoked high and the weather under control, left little room for anything else in his mind. With a silent curse on the rest of his family, in all its most unpleasant ramifications, he climbed up the rigging to the stork's nest, just below the top of the mainmast.

The boy on lookout duty was surprised to see him. 'Lord Kazhian?'

'You can go down,' he told the child, a happy, intelligent youngster with sharp eyes and an intense and touching love for the sea. Like all the rest of the *Wind of Morning*'s crew, he'd be dead in a few days' time if Arkun obeyed Olkanno's orders.

Unless the agent could be persuaded otherwise. Or unless Kazhian could outwit him. And as his ship sailed on towards Ukkan, he began to see how it might be done.

*

As the sun fell towards the distant horizon, thirty-two hours after leaving Toktel'yi, the *Wind of Morning* entered the estuary below Ukkan.

It had been a swift passage, considering the weather. Out in the Archipelago, far to the south, an unusually vicious summer storm was brewing, and the ship's weather-worker, a flamboyant young sorcerer from Tatht, had exerted a great deal of power just to keep the outriding winds at bay. Unfortunately, other mages on other ships were also trying to influence the weather. A small hurricane might be batted to and fro across hundreds of miles of the Southern Sea as weather-workers fought to control it. A big storm would simply be too much for them. And Kazhian's sorcerer had told him that the storm massing north of Balki was the worst he had encountered for years.

Another piece in his plan, to be slotted in its place like a Kal-Gan puzzle. Kazhian watched as the *Wind of Morning* dropped anchor in the roads below Ukkan. The natural wind had died away, and the evening air was heavy and still, laden with the smell of the marshes fringing the shores of the estuary. At this point, the channel was three miles wide, but he could clearly see the tiny figures of the workers, still toiling in the salt-pans that provided much of the province's wealth.

At his orders, a flag was run up the mainmast. It was yellow, with a red border, and signalled to the flotilla of small provision boats and tenders putting out from Ukkan that the *Wind of Morning* did not require their services. The crew eyed it with dismay, and Kazhian heard some grumbling, but ignored it. He wanted all his men on board tonight, sober and ready for any eventuality.

There was no hint in the southern sky of the storm lurking beyond the horizon. Kazhian looked round at the tranquil loveliness of the estuary, and then beckoned to his mate, Ozgan, a freed Gulkeshi whose surliness was – just – outweighed by his competence as a sailor. 'Give the men their supper. There's no need to set a watch, but have the skiff lowered and make it fast to the stern. I'm going below for a while.'

'Yes, Lord Kazhian.' Ozgan's dark eyes registered no emotion or dissent, but his Captain knew what he was thinking. Without further word, he turned and climbed the ladder down to the stern cabins, taking care to make enough noise to warn Djeneb.

As he had expected, though, she was so engrossed in her book – it was the *Histories* – that she hardly acknowledged his entrance. 'We've anchored,' Kazhian told her softly.

The girl on the mattress grunted in reply, and didn't lift her eyes from the page. Suddenly exasperated, he bent and pulled the book out of her grasp. 'I said, we've landed.'

'I heard you,' Djeneb answered with obvious annoyance. She reached out for it, but Kazhian tossed it into the corner, behind his clothes-chest. 'You can go back to it later. *Listen* to me, lady – this is important.'

Wrenched from the heroic and comfortingly distant world of the Empire's glorious past, Djeneb stared up at him. 'What's going to happen?'

'I don't know. Not for certain. But we've reached Ukkan, and anchored in the roads. The city is about three miles upstream. I've ordered the skiff to be lowered. Do you still want to disappear?'

Faced with the awful significance of an imminent decision, Djeneb had gone grey under her brown skin. 'Yes. No. I don't know! I *want* to, but . . .'

'Yes?' he prompted gently.

'I'm frightened of the consequences,' she said, doggedly honest. 'Arkun didn't kill me because he found out who I was. I don't think I want to be murdered because other people haven't.'

'Even if it means that you'll be bundled back to Toktel'yi and married off?'

'As long as it isn't to Skallyan, I don't mind. I am a Vessel of the Blood Imperial, and I must marry where I am told. My sister was lucky – she found love. I've never expected as much,' Djeneb said flatly. 'And nothing could be worse than that slimy lump of rancid tallow pawing at me.'

He didn't have the heart, or the courage, to tell her otherwise. He said softly, 'Then when Arkun goes ashore, once it's dark, he will take you with him. Are you prepared for that? You will be quite safe – his master wants you alive and well.'

She nodded grimly.

'Then good luck, Lady Djeneb, and may the Lord of Life have you in his keeping always,' said Kazhian, and gave her the two hands of friendship. 'Goodbye, brave cousin.'

'Goodbye,' she said, and despite all her efforts, her voice shook. 'And thank you, Lord Kazhian, for – for being so kind.'

'"*A pleasure too great to be told*",' he said, quoting from a famous poem. And with a courageous smile, she capped it. '"*Till this limitless world shall grow old*", I shall always remember you and your kindness. Thank you.'

He left quickly, before her tears could betray her pride, and stood for a moment outside Arkun's door. Then, with a bitter smile, he lifted the latch and went in.

His other, less high-born cousin was sitting amidst the rubbish. His cloak lay over his shoulders, and his reddish hair glinted copper in the dim light from the small, filthy porthole above his head. Kazhian kicked the door shut and said, 'I take it you're leaving at nightfall?'

'Yes. The moon rises just before the dead hour. I want to be in Ukkan before then.'

'Will you take the Lady Djeneb with you?'

The agent smiled. 'So she has seen sense after all. A lady of some courage.'

'She hasn't any other option, and she's got the intelligence to realize it. So what will you do with her? Dump her in the Deputy Governor's lap?'

'The fewer people who know about her escapade, the better. I will arrange for her to be taken quietly back to Toktel'yi. No word need ever get out. She doesn't concern you any longer.'

'Perhaps not. But the manner of my death does. Hasn't it occurred to you that there's one of you and thirty of us?'

'Of course,' said Arkun. 'But you will be pleased to learn that you were wrong. You are free to sail back to Toktel'yi in the morning. My business in Ukkan will detain me for some time, and I no longer require your services.'

His cousin studied him, searching for the truth. The agent's face, well prepared, gave absolutely nothing away. Kazhian had the disturbing sense that he was floundering in quicksand, with no one to help him out. The fate of thirty people, or fifty, depended on what he did now. And he wasn't sure, at this moment of ultimate trial, whether he was capable of carrying the burden alone.

Well, he must, because no one else could. Years ago, he'd been famous for his recklessness and daring. The dreadful end of the *Spear of Vengeance* had quenched his fire, but he had nothing left to lose now. And at least he might regain a little of his drowned self-respect.

With his sudden, brilliant smile, he dropped down on the horrible mattress beside his cousin, and pulled a box of khlar from the pouch at his belt. 'Share a pipe with me? For old times' sake?'

Arkun's brown eyes surveyed the drug with narrow contempt. 'No. But if you want to stupefy yourself, go ahead.'

'With pleasure,' said Kazhian, his eyes glinting green, and began to fill his pipe.

*

Darkness settled over the *Wind of Morning* at her quiet, lonely anchorage. There were no other ships moored so far down the estuary, and the empty water around her lapped softly against her planking as the tide turned. She swung round like a stately dancer, pulling at her anchor line, and the little skiff clinging to her gracefully slanting stern came too, almost invisible in the starlight.

Arkun rose to his feet and surveyed the man sprawled against the cracked cooking-pot. His head lolling back, his eyes glazed, and the empty pipe dangling from lax fingers, his cousin gave no indication that he had even noticed the agent's movement. Arkun bent and flicked his fingers in front of Kazhian's face. He stirred and muttered something, then relapsed into his drug-induced stupor.

With a curious smile, compounded of regret and contempt, the red-haired man left the tiny compartment which had been his hiding-place for nearly two days, and entered the stern cabin.

Djeneb was waiting for him, her veil once more hiding her face. 'Are you going?'

'Yes,' Arkun said briefly. 'Come with me, lady.'

She rose gracelessly to her feet, her bundle in her hand. The veil sucked in and out suddenly. 'Where is Lord Kazhian?'

'He's doped himself to the eyeballs on khlar.' Arkun held out his hand for the bundle. 'There's no one on watch, but don't make a sound.'

'I know,' said the Imperial Daughter pointedly. 'Or you'll knife me.'

Arkun stared at her for a moment. Invisible behind her anonymous veil, she could be frightened, or miserable, or defiant, and his inability to read her thoughts was disturbing. 'If it means that we might be discovered, then I will,' he told her. 'You are a valuable commodity, lady, but there are limits on your worth.'

As he had hoped, she followed him as silently and obediently as a shadow, out on to the narrow gallery that surrounded the ship's stern. A rope ladder hung down to the boat below. Arkun descended it first, then put out a steadying hand as Djeneb, slow and determined, climbed over the rail and followed him down, the skirts of her gown trailing over her feet. The crew were singing some raucous chorus up on deck. With any luck, they would not be seen: and if they were, any observer would think that Kazhian was venturing shorewards on some private and nefarious purpose of his own.

Kazhian. He'd had a mind once, and a wild, carefree spirit that nothing, neither his father's beatings nor the stern discipline of the Navy, had been able to obliterate. And now all that potential had gone to waste in a murky cloud of khlar fumes, because of a tragic shipwreck and Eska'anen's brutally casual disclosure of his first wife's fate.

Arkun did not usually indulge in regret. He untied the rope, shipped the oars, and began to row himself and Djeneb upstream, with the rising tide, towards Ukkan.

A while later, Kazhian moved. Arkun had blown out the lamp, and the darkness around him was intense, impenetrable, and reeking of khlar.

He sat up, swallowing as the familiar nausea began to rise. He'd overdone it, but that couldn't be helped now. And at least Arkun had been convinced.

So was I, thought Kazhian grimly. He fumbled in the blackness, found the pitcher of water that he'd noticed earlier, and poured half down his throat and the rest over his head.

That helped to disperse the fumes, but not entirely. Cursing Arkun, Eska'anen, and all other Vessels of the Blood Imperial, particularly himself, Kazhian struggled to his feet and found the door at the third attempt.

Outside, everything was quiet, save for the crew singing. They'd got on to 'Flower of Balki', which had eighty-seven verses in its full, unexpurgated form, and each one cruder and more inventive than the last. He listened intently. Sixty-two to go. Plenty of time.

There was a lamp still lit in his empty cabin. Dim as it was, it dazzled him, and the pain inside his head increased. He ignored it, and stepped through the open door on to the gallery.

No boat lay below, but he thought he could see it, far away over the water. Yes: that sudden glimmer was surely the splash of oars.

So the agent was beyond earshot, and under the impression that Kazhian would lie in a drugged stupor until morning. With grim satisfaction, he climbed down the rope ladder and lowered himself carefully, silently, into the river.

The coolness of it helped to revive him. He took a deep breath, and began to swim towards the distant, southward shore.

CHAPTER FIVE

Trinn had seen the courier ship arrive. She was so beautiful, with her mass of pure white canvas like vast wings, gently swollen with the last of the dying breeze. She swooped gracefully up the estuary, and Sarrek, who had spent all morning out on the river with his father and the oyster-fishers, stood beside his mother, eagerly pointing out every shiver of the sails, every subtle manoeuvre, every felicitous line of the narrow, shapely hull, built for lightness and speed.

Beautiful, and deadly. She felt renewed stirrings of dread as she watched the lovely ship drop anchor, just only below their vantage-point on the highest terrace of the villa's extensive gardens. The last of her kind to reach Ukkan had brought confirmation of the Emperor's death. Did this one also bear grievous news? Did she carry someone who would be the means of Trinn's death, and her husband's, and her son's? Or was she after all as blithe and innocent as she appeared?

Sarrek prattled on, while Trinn watched the ship's sails furl. The sun had almost reached the hills behind her, and its last light, golden and mellow, shone on the marshes fringing the other side of the estuary. *Lifegiver*, Trinn prayed in silent despair. *Lifegiver, grant long life to my son. If Megren and I are doomed, so be it – but keep Sarrek safe!*

'Mama?' The child's voice was suddenly doubtful. 'Mama, what is it?'

'Nothing, sweetheart,' Trinn said fiercely, and clasped him to her side. 'Nothing at all. Let's go in and find your father. It must be time for supper.'

She couldn't discuss the possible significance of the courier ship's arrival in front of the slaves, but she mentioned it in passing, as they ate. Megren gave her a quick glance, and said lightly, 'Good. If it's heading back to Toktel'yi tomorrow, it can carry my letter to the Council, announcing that I have withdrawn from candidacy to the Onyx Throne.'

Trinn saw the widened eyes of the men and women who served them, the indrawn breaths and exchanged glances. The timing of his revelation made sense – if one of them had murdered B'kenn, they now knew there would be no need to kill Megren. She said, 'You'd best take a boat out in the morning, beloved, and speak to the Captain.'

'I'll certainly do that,' Megren said, and turned to admonish Sarrek, sitting beside him, for some minor breach of table manners.

He came very late to her bed that night, when despite all her fears she had almost fallen asleep. 'I've been checking the walls and doors,' he said, in answer to her drowsy question. 'We can't be too careful. I haven't made my announcement public here in Ukkan yet, have I? I've only sent a pigeon to Toktel'yi.'

'You've told Pekkrem,' Trinn pointed out. The province's Governor, a member of the Council by right of office, was away in Tamat, but his deputy was an inveterate gossip, who could be relied upon to spread such choice titbits of news all round the city, and far beyond it.

'Even Pekkrem's grapevine can't reach everywhere instantly. I've doubled the guard, and set all the dogs loose. Unless an intruder is invisible and can fly, we'll be safe.' He kissed her, and she pulled him into her warm embrace.

Much, much later, a sudden cacophony of barks yanked Trinn from sleep. The lamp was still alight, and she sat up, her heart thudding. Megren leapt from the bed, pulling on his tunic. He took his sword from its scabbard by the bed, and gave her a quick, reassuring smile. 'I'll go and see what's up. Probably just a wild animal in the garden.'

When he had gone, Trinn dressed in haste, took her small, silver-shafted dagger from under her pillow, and ran first for Sarrek's room, on the other side of the courtyard.

He hadn't even woken. She stared down, her throat taut with love and fear, at his dark curls, the soft roundness of his face, and the long black lashes lying on his cheeks. So bright, so precious, so beloved. She told his attendants to guard him with their lives, and hurried in search of her husband.

Megren and half-a-dozen of his personal guard were standing in a tight group in the entrance courtyard. As Trinn entered, the gate leading to the terraced gardens banged open, and more soldiers burst in, dragging someone between them. Shouting threats and abuse, they hurled him face down on the flagstones at their master's feet, and stood with their swords pointing menacingly at the intruder's back.

Trinn gazed at him with horrified curiosity. He wore a short, belted tunic, like a sailor's. It was soaking wet, and a puddle was growing around the man's prone body. One of the guards handed a dagger over to Megren. 'We found this on him, sir. Reckon he'd have murdered us all in our beds. He didn't half put up a fight when we grabbed him!'

Their captive moved, and at once several sharp weapons jabbed at him. Megren held up his hand. 'Stop. Stand back, and let him get up. He can't possibly do any harm now, and I'd very much like to hear how he came to be in my garden at this hour, and carrying a knife. Well? Come on, up, and let's hear what you have to say.'

The intruder rolled over cautiously, and sat up, rubbing his head. He had taken quite a beating: his jaw was bruised, his nose and mouth leaked blood, and he had the beginnings of an impressive black eye. He said with considerable exasperation, 'What's the matter, cousin? Don't you recognize me?'

Megren stared, and so did Trinn. Long, wet, tangled black hair; earrings; and, most distinctive of all, eyes as green as the balefire that hung over the night marshes. 'Kazhian,' said Megren at last, in some amazement. 'What in Kaylo's name are you doing here?'

'Just paying you a courtesy visit, as I was in the area,' said the intruder, fingering his split lip gingerly. 'Could you kindly tell those ill-mannered brutish guards of yours that when I ask them to take me to their master, I want to be escorted with some dignity and respect.'

'He fought like a tiger when I grabbed him, sir!' the leader of the guards cried indignantly. 'How was I to know he was who he said he was? He could have been another assassin for all I knew!'

'Aye,' said his deputy. 'And better safe than dead, that's always your watchword, ain't it, sir?'

Kazhian broke in urgently. '*Another* assassin? What's been happening here?'

There was a short, pregnant pause. Then Megren said, 'My father, Lord B'kenn, died two days ago. It could have been poison. That is why I am here, and not in Tamat.'

Kazhian took a deep breath. 'I see. Well, if you'd be so good, cousin, as to act the host – I could do with a cup or two of wine, and a change of clothing. Then perhaps one or two of your late father's concubines? They'd probably appreciate some company.'

Megren's bristling brows snapped together. He gestured to the guards. 'Back to your posts. You did well. As you say, much better safe than dead. In fact, I think you were probably too gentle, even if he is a Vessel of the Blood Imperial. These days, you can't be too careful. Dismiss!'

The soldiers saluted and filed out. Round the colonnaded perimeter of the courtyard, Trinn could see the wary, curious faces of the household, woken by the noise. She said, 'We may not wish to supply all your requirements, cousin, but at least you may share a jug of wine in my husband's quarters. Megren?'

'Yes,' said her husband, still glaring at Kazhian. 'Yes. Come with me, Lord Kazhian. My wife will attend to your wounds shortly.'

Within a few moments, the courtyard was empty. Trinn sent her steward to fetch wine and food, and then returned to her own room, where she kept the medicines and salves which she used for minor damage: major injuries were the responsibility of their Healer. She selected a bag of clean rags to mop up the blood, a bowl of water, and an ointment that was effective but notoriously stinging. Then she hurried back to Megren's rooms, which lay beside the Women's Quarters.

She had never met Kazhian before, but, in common with most of the Empire, she had heard a great deal about his exploits – as a dashing and daring Captain, as a womanizer, as a drug-taker. Many wealthy young men indulged in khlar, but not to the levels of excess that Kazhian was rumoured to reach. And he was Eska'anen's elder son. Admittedly, his father was supposed to have disowned him, but that might be a ploy to lull suspicion. Even now, Megren might be in danger—

She burst into his reception chamber, and found their uninvited guest sprawled calmly with his feet up on a couch, already changed into one of Megren's spare tunics, and a cup of wine in his hand.

His host, quite undamaged, was pouring another for himself. 'Ah, Trinn. Do you want some?'

'Yes,' she said fervently, and took a good swig of cool, reviving Hailyan. After the alarms of the past half-hour, she felt she needed it.

Although she must still keep a clear head. What if Kazhian wanted to murder them both? And her beloved, foolish, trusting Megren had given him back his dagger.

'It's all right,' said Kazhian, his deep voice amused. 'I haven't come to kill you. But I've come to warn you about someone else who might.'

'Tell us everything you know,' said Megren, sitting down on the cushions in front of him.

Kazhian talked. He had a pleasant voice, and a dry, cheerful, extravagant mode of speech which at first disguised the full import of what he said.

'You had the Lady Djeneb on board?' Megren said in astonishment.

'As large as – or larger than – life. She's a formidable young woman.' Kazhian put his wine-cup down and surveyed his host. 'But for the moment, she doesn't matter. She's safe, now and for the immediate future. It's you I'm worried about. I'm certain Arkun has come to kill you.'

'Why?' Trinn demanded. 'If he's one of Olkanno's agents – does *Olkanno* want the Onyx Throne?'

'Well, he's a Vessel of the Blood Imperial too, though he's only descended from Makkyar's brother, not Makkyar himself. But as far as I know, he has no intention of becoming Emperor. On the other hand, he is very friendly with my father – though very few people know of it.'

'Eska'anen,' said Megren softly. 'And he was in Tamat when Sekkenet died. So was Olkanno.'

'Why would they want to kill poor Sekkenet?' Trinn asked, though she suspected she had already guessed the answer.

'Because he nominated and supported me. Because he commanded the Army. Because he was an honest man. Because he wanted to keep the Army in Tamat to ensure that the Council chose me for Emperor – a threat of force, even if they never left the camp. It's difficult to argue with nearly two hundred thousand soldiers. But I don't think,' Megren said wearily, running a hand through his upright hair, 'that your father needs a reason. Or B'kenn would still be alive. He was no threat to anyone.'

'But they used him to lure you here,' Kazhian pointed out. 'There would be plenty of time and opportunity for Eska'anen and Olkanno to arrange for one of your slaves who was in their pay to administer the poison. So you leave the Army's protection to come home, where they can kill you too, at their convenience. And any other Vessel of the Blood Imperial here as well. How many wives and children did your father have?'

'He has one wife still alive – my own mother died many years ago, and the other was killed by the same poison, as well as two of the concubines. There are five legitimate children apart from myself, the eldest fourteen and the youngest hardly more than a baby. There are also two young daughters by concubines here – all the others are adult, and gone. And my own son Sarrek, of course – he's five.'

'But if they see your branch of the family as a threat to Eska'anen's ambition, they'll have no qualms about wiping you out wholesale, even the baby,' said Kazhian. 'You're well guarded, I admit. But sooner or later, unless you turn the place into a fortress, Arkun will find a way in.'

'But I have sent a message to the Council saying that I no longer wish to be a candidate for the Throne,' Megren said. 'If Eska'anen does not know that now, he will tomorrow.'

'I doubt it'll make any difference. Most people still want you for Emperor, whatever you say. My father doesn't like rivals. But it's my guess that whatever he and Olkanno have planned, it will be made to look like an accident. Or why keep Arkun's mission so secret?'

'It's all pure conjecture, of course,' Megren said. The lamplight cast unflattering shadows across his bony face, making it look much older and harsher. 'But when my family is threatened, I have no alternative but to do my best to save them. How can I do it?'

'That's for you to decide,' Kazhian told him bluntly. 'I just came here to warn you. And if you should meet Arkun in your travels, kindly don't tell him you've seen me. It took me two days to persuade him not to kill me and my crew.'

As he finished speaking, something sailed gently in through the grille of the terrace window, and landed with a soft thud on the floor.

It was black, and cylindrical, and smoking. Suddenly flames burst from one end, setting fire to the cushions. Megren leapt up, shouting something. As Kazhian yelled and ran towards him, a flash of light shot through the air and thumped into flesh.

It had been meant for Megren, but his cousin had got in the way. The small, black-fletched dart jutted from Kazhian's shoulder. Trinn had seen such weapons before – boys on the islands blew them from a tube, to bring down birds. And sometimes they were poisoned.

Kazhian didn't seem to notice it. 'Get down, you idiots!' he yelled, and pushed Megren and Trinn to the floor. She heard herself scream, stopped the sound and her panic by stuffing her hand into her mouth, and began to crawl through the thickening smoke towards the door. Someone grabbed her and pulled her in the opposite direction. Coughing and choking, she was dragged briskly into the clean air of the tiny courtyard at the centre of Megren's apartments.

'Arkun,' said Kazhian concisely. The dart was still in his shoulder, and Trinn unceremoniously wrenched it out. A rush of dark blood followed, and he swore and clamped his hand to the wound. 'What did you do that for?'

'It could be poisoned,' Trinn said. She stuck the evil little weapon point down in a tub of flowers. Curiously, despite their desperate danger, she felt suddenly quite calm and detached, as if all this were happening to someone else, in a story. 'Megren? Thank Kaylo you're safe! What do we do now?'

'We let them think you're all dead,' Kazhian said. 'Let the villa burn. Take the women and children out, and down to the river. If we can get you on to my ship, you'll be safe.'

'I'd rather stay and fight the bastard,' said Trinn's husband grimly. 'Those stupid guards must have been blind!'

'Or dead, more likely. Olkanno's agents are all trained to be lethal, silent and virtually invisible. They probably didn't see a thing.' Kazhian surveyed them, and gave a gesture of annoyance. 'Come on – we can't stand here talking all night! By the sound of it, more fires have been started. Go and get all the others of your family. Is there a door leading into the river side of the gardens?'

'Yes – from the Women's Quarters,' said Trinn.

'How will I recognize which one from the outside?'

'There's a big orange tree growing in a white tub just beside it.'

'Good. I'll go into the garden. When I'm sure it's safe, I'll whistle once, count to ten, and whistle again. Come out at the second signal.'

'You can't,' Trinn said. 'You're hurt – you might—'

'Be poisoned? I think I'd know by now if I was. Get moving, you halfwits, before you're burnt to a crisp!'

It was like a bad dream, a frantic, terrifying conjuration of the dreadful Horses of the Night. The beautiful villa was ablaze, every room on the landward side well alight. Fortunately none of them were sleeping chambers, but the smoke was already filling the courtyards and colonnades, menacing and deadly. As she ran at Megren's side, Trinn could sense the assassin, the sinister Arkun, silent, deadly, lurking outside with his darts and arrows and throwing-stars, waiting until the villa's terrified occupants fled in panic to the darkness outside, to be picked off callously, one by one . . .

Don't think about it. The Women's Quarters were in uproar, screaming women and children and eunuchs and slaves running to and fro like beheaded geese. B'kenn's youngest child, barely walking, sat in the middle of the courtyard, wailing in terror as the adults rushed past her. 'For Kaylo's sake!' Megren bawled. '*Stop!* Stop, all of you, and listen!'

Somehow, his strong soldier's voice penetrated the pandemonium. The people, sobbing, clung together in clumps like curdled cream, their terrified faces turned towards him, begging him to save them.

'There is at least one assassin outside,' her husband said. 'He has no interest in killing slaves or servants. If you are not one of my blood, I suggest you leave now, all together, by the front entrance. I hereby give all who are still slaves their freedom, and call on free and unfree to witness it. The others—' He beckoned to his father's remaining wife, and the two concubines. 'There is a good chance of saving you. Are all the children here?'

They were, including Sarrek. Terrified into silent obedience, they and their mothers hurried through the smoke-filled villa, led by Megren and shepherded by Trinn. And she wondered, with bowel-clutching fear, how Kazhian could do the impossible: or whether he was already dead.

The Captain of the *Wind of Morning* crouched beneath a potted and bushy shrub on the topmost terrace of the villa's gardens, and wondered with astonished amusement if he had gone mad.

It had been lunacy enough agreeing to take the Lady Djeneb to Ukkan. It had certainly been crazy not to throw Arkun overboard during the voyage, and hang the consequences. It had been the height of insanity to warn the villa's occupants of the probably imminent attempt on their lives. And although the risk had been entirely justified, in the process he had smoked far too much khlar, swum a mile, climbed up a hillside, unsuccessfully fought burly guards, and been hit by a K'tali dart. Fortunately, it was his right shoulder, so that a wound which would have crippled most men was no more, yet, than a painful inconvenience to him. But he was beginning to regret the bravado with which he had assured Trinn that it wasn't poisoned. Certainly he was feeling dangerously light-headed, although that could be the effect of losing a lot of blood.

Ignoring it, he hefted the dagger in his left hand and peered through the darkness. He could hear the screams of the villa's inhabitants above the intensifying roar of the flames. Ironically, his unscheduled arrival in the villa's garden must have presented an ideal opportunity for Arkun and his accomplices to gain entrance unnoticed, while the guards were busy taking their captive to Megren. And the assassins hadn't wasted their time. Kazhian had already found the corpses of two of the dogs, presumably fed poisoned meat. And just behind him lay one of his cousin's soldiers in a sticky pool of blood, his throat cut.

He listened intently, separating the distant pandemonium from closer sounds, the breeze in the leaves around him, the incessant crickets, the call of a Nightsinger, discordantly sweet. There was someone in front of him, creeping with extreme stealth along the terrace: he heard a tiny scrabble as gravel moved briefly under soft soles. And it was unlikely to be one of the guards: if any were still alive, they'd be inside the villa, fighting the flames.

Using sound and intuition to guide him, Kazhian slunk up to the assassin. He could see only a black shape, crouched next to the low terrace wall, but he struck unerringly in the place his father's master-at-arms had shown him, long ago. Olkanno's minions were not the only ones trained to kill in silence.

The man grunted once, and fell sprawling. Kazhian jerked the dagger out and struck again to make sure. He heard the agent's last breath leave his body, and knelt down, feeling for a pulse. There was none, and blood, warm and wet, seemed to be everywhere.

Clumsily one-handed, he heaved his victim over. The moon wasn't up yet, but there was enough light from the fire to see that the face was not Arkun's.

As he had suspected, his cousin must have borrowed the Ukkan Governor's team of highly trained, lethally skilled assassins. And against them, one wounded man, with a dagger.

Another sound plucked at his ears. He glanced up and saw a dark shape, clear against the paler wall of the villa, in the act of throwing something through a window. As flames erupted within, Kazhian killed him.

He had now accounted for two, but neither of them was Arkun, and he didn't know whether to be glad or sorry. He crawled along the grassy edge of the gravel, aware that if he stood up he would, like his last victim, present a perfect target. Where in Olyak's name was that door?

Fortunately, there didn't seem to be any more agents on this part of the terrace. He lifted his head cautiously, and saw a large white tub directly in front of him, with a substantial tree growing in it. Praying that this was the orange, Kazhian crept silently into its shelter, and listened again.

Nothing. He peered above the tub. There was the door, closed, blank, apparently unwatched. Further along, flames shot into the sky as part of the villa's roof collapsed, and the screaming intensified.

Very softly, Kazhian whistled, and waited. No sound, no movement. His dagger at the ready, he signalled again.

As arranged, the door opened, and Megren's distinctive, bristly head appeared cautiously round it.

'All clear!' Kazhian hissed, and jabbed the point of his dagger in the direction of the river. 'I'll guard your back – get them going, as quickly as you can – and for the love of Kaylo, *go quietly!*'

One by one, the fleeing women and children scurried into the garden. He counted them. The wife, and Trinn, and two concubines. A couple of Megren's guards, who had managed to escape the assassins. And the children, eight of them, some whimpering and sobbing in terror, others bravely silent. They ran stumbling down the steps to the lower terraces, Megren leading them, the guards flanking them and Trinn bringing up the rear, the smallest child in her arms.

Of course, there was no chance that they could escape the attention of any agent left in the garden. Something whispered past Kazhian, still on the upper terrace, and one of the concubines screamed and fell. The group's impetus faltered, but Trinn gave a cry of desperation and pushed at those immediately in front of her. 'Move, hurry, don't stop – *run*!'

Kazhian ran too, but in the other direction. The arrow, or dart, had come from his right, and he had just caught the archer's movement as he ducked out of sight. He sprinted softly along the grass verge, his dagger ready.

A dark figure rose up to meet him. He saw the flash of a knife, and parried. The blades clashed violently, and both weapons were wrenched from their owners' hands. Disarmed, Kazhian launched himself at his adversary's throat.

It was Arkun. He could sense his bastard cousin's presence within the soft black assassin's garments, and fury lent power to his hands. They rolled over and over on the gravel, struggling fiercely. Kazhian knew that he must kill soon, for exhaustion and loss of blood were sapping his stamina, and Arkun was bigger than he was and probably stronger. But every heartbeat longer that he could fight meant that Megren and his family were closer to safety.

He got a grip on the agent's neck, and squeezed tightly, ignoring the other man's wild thrashing and frantic gasps for air. Arkun's hands beat at his face, and then a finger jabbed into his eye. Kazhian jerked involuntarily backwards, loosening his grip. And then his cousin hurled himself on top of him, grasped his overlong hair and smashed his head back on to the stones beneath.

The fight was over. Breathing hard through his bruised throat, Arkun sat back on his heels. The moon had risen at last, and he could see one of the daggers lying only a stride away on the gravel. He leaned over, retrieved it and held it above Kazhian, ready to strike down into the unconscious man's heart.

And he could not do it. He had killed so often he had long ago lost count, he had slain men and women and children without compunction or compassion, and fixed his eyes not on their pleading faces but on the rewards that his devotion to duty would bring. Wealth: rank: power: and above all the respect and fear of of those who would otherwise have despised him, the landless, moneyless bastard son of a Fabrizi slave and a Tulyettan merchant.

Once, Kazhian had not despised him. Kazhian kept his contempt for those who had earned it. And Kazhian's mother, as spirited, contrary and wilfully rebellious as her only son, had been kind to the child Arkun, whose own mother had died when he was very young. He had loved her. And she had been sent away from him into a miserable marriage to Eska'anen, who had eventually murdered her.

And who had ordered the deaths of Megren and all his family, along with Kazhian?

Eska'anen. Not Olkanno, who served Emperors but who had no desire to become one himself. Not Olkanno, his own master, but Eska'anen, Governor of Sabrek, father of Kazhian and the repellent Suken, and quite likely to become the Hundredth Emperor of Toktel'yi.

Without any thought in his head beyond regret, and self-loathing, and rage, without any regard for the consequences, Arkun stumbled to his feet, the dagger still in his hand, and without a backward glance walked away from the man he had been ordered to kill.

The villa was ablaze from end to end. In the leaping red light, he could see the corpses of dogs, guards and assassins strewn along the terrace. He must be the only agent left alive: Kazhian had slain the two stationed on this side of the house, and the four on the other had all fallen victim to the guards, or to Arkun himself. Olkanno had told him to leave no accomplice alive to tell the tale: and if he dragged the bodies into the burning villa, no one would realize that the charred, unrecognizable corpses did not belong to Megren's household.

But several had escaped, thanks to Kazhian. And if they included Megren, or his son, or either of his two young half-brothers, then Olkanno would not readily forgive Arkun's failure.

Suddenly regretting his brief lapse into compassion, he turned back, and saw that Kazhian had gone.

CHAPTER SIX

Megren knew the marshes along the Ukkan estuary as well as he knew the contours of his wife's face: every narrow track through the reeds, every dyke, every mudhole, every salt-pan, whether still in use or long since abandoned. He led his shivering, terrified, weeping family through the tall, sheltering rushes, pausing every so often to listen for sounds of pursuit.

There were none: and no sign of Kazhian, either. Megren knew that he was probably dead, and felt the beginning of a real and surprising grief. He had always doubted his cousin, and scorned his flamboyant self-indulgence. Now, owing him his life and the lives of those he loved, he saw too late that he had been guilty of prejudice and misjudgement.

It was too late for Kazhian, but not for Trinn, or Sarrek, or the other women and children. Grateful beyond words for the gift of their safety, Megren halted at the edge of the reeds and peered through.

The tide was coming in fast. An expanse of soft, squelchy mud, some twenty paces across, lay between him and the gently encroaching river. He knew, from past and unpleasant experience, that it was almost bottomless, and impossible to negotiate unless wearing the special broad mudshoes that the fishermen used. But just to his left lay a narrow creek, winding in through the reeds. Already, the water was creeping up it. And at its head, tied firmly to a stake, old D'naygan kept his boat.

If they were to reach Kazhian's ship, moored tantalizingly in the middle of the estuary and nearly a mile offshore, they'd have to take the boat, and it wasn't big enough to hold all of them: some would have to swim. The risk was considerable, but Megren knew it represented their only chance of escape. He turned back to his family. 'Follow me – and hurry!'

The Lord of Life, and luck, was watching over them. D'naygan had left not only his boat, but someone's marsh-raft, tied to its stern. Made from bundles of reeds, it was completely unsuitable for use on open water, even the comparatively calm estuary, but they had no choice.

Quietly, carefully, boat and raft were launched with their precious cargo. The children, Megren and the guards were packed into the little boat, while Trinn balanced precariously with the remaining wife and concubine on the raft. The men poled the two craft down the narrow winding creek, working with silent, intense determination against the rising tide, and emerged at last on to the river.

Trinn looked back. From here, she could see her home burning, a huge pyre of leaping flame and boiling, turbulent smoke pouring into the night sky. She and Megren and Sarrek had escaped that fate at least, but what lay ahead of them?

She bowed her head, overcome with grief for the violent, catastrophic end to her lovely, peaceful, happy life: for the beautiful villa that had been the harbour of all her joy; for the men and women who had died in the blaze, or at the hands of the assassins; and for the grim uncertainty of their future.

But above all she mourned Kazhian, who had saved their lives at the expense of his own.

The sailors on the *Wind of Morning*, alerted by Megren's hail, at first refused to let them on board. They lined the gunwale, peering suspiciously down at the approaching craft, and Trinn, fiercely wiping her face with the corner of her torn and filthy sleeve, saw moonlight and lamplight glinting on arrows nocked and spears held ready.

'Where's Lord Kazhian?' their spokesman demanded. 'He's the one who gives the orders around here.'

'He ain't in his cabin,' said another sailor, arriving at the rail. 'And how are we to know these folks ain't planning to take over the ship?'

'I told you,' said Trinn's husband, his patience shredded. 'I am Lord Megren, son of B'kenn, and I and these members of my family have just escaped murder by the skin of our teeth, and with the assistance of Lord Kazhian. He offered us refuge on his ship.'

'Well, where is he, then?'

'He's probably dead,' said Megren wearily. 'If he is, then he sacrificed his life to save us. But in the name of the Life Giver, let us on board before these boats sink under us! What possible danger can we be to you?'

'Don't be so obtuse, Ozgan.' It was a new voice, affected, casual, dismissive. 'Look at them. He's right – a boatload of women and children is hardly likely to seize the ship, after all. If I were you, I'd hoist them all on board before Lord Kazhian gets back and chops you up for shark-bait. And besides, there are two naval galleys less than a mile away, and heading straight for us.'

His intervention tipped the balance. Swearing under his breath, Ozgan shouted his orders. The fishing-boat touched the *Wind of Morning*'s side, and rope ladders were flung down. Megren and the two guards held the flimsy craft steady as the older children scrambled up to safety: the younger ones were pulled up precariously in a basket. Then it was the turn of the three women on the raft. Trinn was the last to leave. She kicked at the waterlogged bundles of reeds that had borne her away from Ukkan, and death, and pulled herself swiftly up the ladder.

The sailors were staring at them as if they couldn't believe the flotsam which had landed on their deck. Trinn saw Sarrek, his nose running, trying not to cry. Then he flung himself into her arms, and burst into tears.

As she comforted him, she was remotely aware, amid the sorrow and relief, that the bustle around her had acquired new purpose. A sailor brushed past her, yelling, to join a group of his colleagues hauling on a rope. With a creak of effort, the huge mainyard began to rise up the mast, unfurling the broad white sail below it.

A sudden vision assaulted Trinn's mind. She saw a man stumbling down to the water's edge, calling in vain as his ship drew up her anchor and swung downstream, the offshore night breeze filling her sails. Gripped with a sudden, irrational terror, she struggled to her feet and grabbed the nearest member of the crew.

It was the man who'd persuaded Ozgan to take them on board. From his long, voluminous embroidered robes and studied air of exotic mystery, she guessed he must be Kazhian's sorcerer, who had the task of influencing wind, wave and weather in the ship's favour. She said urgently, 'Are we going? We mustn't – we'll leave him behind!'

'Who?' the sorcerer demanded swiftly. 'Lord Kazhian?'

'Yes – I think so. He's there in the marshes, I can *feel* him!' Trinn cried. 'Please get them to wait!'

Thanks to the Lord of Life, he took her seriously. He shouted at Ozgan, who was standing by the steersman, and then ran down the deck. Trinn saw him speaking forcefully to the sailor, and his vehement gestures. She turned and peered across the dark water to the marshes, featureless and shadowy, below the burning villa on its hillside. There was no sound, no movement, and she began to think she had imagined it. But within her ordinary, sensible, rational mind, the feeling remained, so strong that she could visualize him. Kazhian was out there. He was being pursued. And if they left him behind, after all he had done for them, she would never forgive herself for the betrayal.

'Lady!' Ozgan stood in front of her, breathing hard. 'You heard what the sorcerer said – there are two navy galleys coming downriver towards us. If we don't weigh anchor now, we'll be a sitting target for their rams. You can't possibly see anything in those marshes, not from here, and in the dark—'

'He's there,' Trinn said doggedly, detesting the note of patronizing contempt in the man's voice. 'I *know* he's there. He'll be killed if we leave him.'

'And we'll all be killed if we stay here any longer,' said the Gulkeshi bluntly. 'Lord Kazhian wouldn't want to see all his efforts wasted, even if it meant his own death. Which I doubt – he's a sly fox, is our Captain, and he's got himself out of much tighter corners than this.'

'If you weigh anchor, then I'll jump overboard,' said Trinn desperately. 'And you won't be able to leave *me* behind.'

'She's right,' said the sorcerer suddenly. 'I sense him too. Lower the boat, Ozgan.'

'I can't,' said the mate, with a sneer. 'It's gone, remember? All we've got is that leaky little fisher this lot arrived in.'

'Then that'll have to do.' The sorcerer glanced up at the moonlit sky, then upstream. 'There's just enough time. If I have to, I'll raise a wind to get us out of this, well ahead of the rams. Don't weigh anchor until I tell you – or Lord Kazhian does. Understand?'

The Gulkeshi scowled at him. 'In Lord Kazhian's absence, *I'm* in charge.'

'Is that why you don't want him rescued? Perhaps you're planning a voyage to Gulkesh.'

With an incoherent yell of rage, the mate swung his fist at the sorcerer. He side-stepped neatly, and gestured. Ozgan fell to the deck as if struck down by an invisible hammer, and lay still.

'No one to weigh anchor until I give the word. Got it?' The sorcerer glared round at the frightened, astonished sailors and fugitives, and collected a harvest of nods. 'Good.' And he turned and strode swiftly to the side of the ship where D'naygan's fishing-boat was tied. He hitched up his robes, soared over the rail, and floated gracefully down into the little craft. Trinn felt her skin prickle. Like all Toktel'yans, she was accustomed to sorcery, but it still had the power to impress and disturb her.

With all the rest on board the courier ship, she watched and waited as the sorcerer raised the boat's patched, inadequate sail without using his hands, and filled it with a wind that was not of the air.

'Mama, where's he going?' asked Sarrek, who was standing beside her.

'To save Lord Kazhian,' Trinn told him, and prayed to the Life Giver that she was right. She knelt by the port rail, staring out across the water. Megren crouched down too, and put his arms around his wife and his son.

Out on the river, Sargenay, sorcerer of Tatht, was likewise praying to the Lord of Life. He had no doubt that he would find his Captain, dead or alive, and pick him up. But it was rather less certain whether they would get back to the *Wind of Morning* before the naval galleys arrived.

His magewind swelled the little boat's single triangular sail, and she skimmed over the dim water. Sargenay used his enhanced senses to peer forward into the gloom ahead, focusing on the unlit marshes rather than the blazing villa above and behind them.

He had hardly believed Trinn – women weren't meant to have powers of sorcery, and nor was anyone who hadn't taken Annatal and undergone the seven years of rigorous training in the Highest Art. But a brief acquaintance, half a year ago, with a man whose vast powers were entirely natural and inborn, had radically broadened and opened Sargenay's mind. And the lady's certainty had persuaded him to look for himself.

Someone was running through the marshes. He caught a glimpse of the man's aura, and recoiled from its bitterness, rage and self-loathing. It wasn't Kazhian. He closed his eyes, letting the boat sail itself, and searched for his Captain.

He was there, just ahead in the water, but so weak that the fury of his pursuer, though much further away, had almost obliterated his presence. Sargenay leaped to his feet, and hurried forward to the bow, 'Lord Kazhian! Kazhian, where are you?'

A feeble splashing was his answer. Sorcery guided the boat and sped her on a slightly different course, then halted her as if she had been anchored. Sargenay bent over the gunwale and reached out a hand to the dark, struggling shape being swept upstream by the inexorable force of the tide.

Fingers cold as death touched his, and clung on. Using all the power of his training and skill, Sargenay drew his Captain up the side of the boat, and heaved him on board.

At any rate he was still alive. That was all the sorcerer had time to find out. He left Kazhian gasping in the bottom of the boat, and concentrated on turning the little craft around.

The galleys were coming, sent by Arkun to destroy the *Wind of*

Morning and her Captain. He could see them, away to his left, two long dark menacing shapes slicing through the water, the white splash of the oars clearly visible. Sargenay gathered all his power, and poured it into the fishing-boat's sail. The vessel leaped forward, scudding over the quiet river like a skimmed stone. Sargenay cupped his hands round his mouth and yelled at the top of his voice, 'Raise the anchor!'

The *Wind of Morning*'s huge mainsail was already set, and flapping white and impotent in the darkness. For a moment, Sargenay thought they hadn't heard him, and gathered breath to call again. Then, unmistakable across the water, came the grate and clank of the chain in the windlass, and the chant of the sailors as they worked.

With a prayer of thanks, Sargenay altered the boat's course to intercept the courier ship. Slowly, she was beginning to move, backwards and upstream with the tide at first. Then, as the sail filled, she started to push against the steady torrent of incoming water.

The galleys were working with the tide too, but with fifty oars apiece to help them, instead of a small and fickle breeze. Sargenay closed his eyes again and summoned up the last burst of extra effort that might make the difference between continued life or an unpleasant, premature and violent death.

Kazhian was muttering something, but Sargenay ignored him. The fishing-boat shot up to the *Wind of Morning*, executed a perfect and graceful turn to starboard, and kept pace with the bigger ship, nuzzling her flank like a new lamb, as she gathered way.

'Have you got him?' Megren called down anxiously.

'Yes.' Sargenay didn't know how long he could continue to use his sorcery for three or four things at once, and any disturbance to his concentration was dangerous. 'Throw me a rope – I'll tie it round him and you can haul him up.'

Trinn watched, her heart thumping hard inside her ribs, as Kazhian's dark, dripping body was dragged over the rail by a dozen willing hands, her husband's amongst them. Sargenay followed, but showed no concern for the man he had rescued. Instead, she saw him lean over the gunwale and gesture downwards. As the *Wind of Morning* sped south-east, towards the sea, D'naygan's empty fishing-boat, powered by a less natural wind, left the bigger vessel's side, altered course, and sailed back up the estuary, directly into the path of the pursuing galleys.

Those sailors and fugitives who were watching gave a cheer as the two Navy ships took evasive action too hastily. Clear over the water came distant yells of alarm, angry shouts, and the crunch of colliding wood. 'That's sorted 'em good and proper,' someone said with satisfaction.

'Sargenay?'

It was Kazhian. He sat on the deck in a pool of water, his hair streaming. In the lamplight he looked ghastly, the black shadows accentuating the hollows of his face and the bruises and other injuries that Megren's guards had inflicted. But at least he was alive.

'Sargenay! Come here, you miserable weather-worker!'

Trinn hid a smile. The sorcerer strode back down the deck, dusting his hands, and stood over his Captain with an indignant swirl of his robes. 'Yes, Lord Kazhian?'

'Thought that'd make you take notice. Thank you. You saved my life – I couldn't have swum for much longer.'

'You should thank the Lady Trinn as well. She persuaded me to search for you.'

'Then I thank you too,' Kazhian said, turning towards her with a pale imitation of his usual flashy smile. 'I am in your debt, lady.'

'It's cancelled. You saved us, remember.'

'Good. I don't like owing anyone anything.' The *Wind of Morning*'s Captain looked up at his sorcerer and his mate, now recovered from Sargenay's blow of sorcery. They were standing next to one another, but their mutual hostility was obvious. 'Ozgan. When we finally get clear of this bloody estuary, set a course due south.'

There was a short silence, filled with the smack of wood against water as the ship beat against the tide. Ozgan said, 'Haven't you forgotten the storm, sir? The wizard here said it lay between Ukkan and Balki, and that's due south of us.'

'Exactly. I hadn't forgotten. Set a course due south.'

'But sir! Lord Kazhian! You must be—'

The Gulkeshi broke off. His Captain struggled to his feet and stood, swaying with exhaustion, one hand clenched on Megren's shoulder for support. 'Mad?' Kazhian finished helpfully. 'No. I'm sure even Sargenay can steer us through. And I'm sure even you can ensure we don't sink. Use the brains you were born with, if you can. Balki will shelter Lord Megren and his family. The galleys won't follow us through a storm, and if we leave some wreckage for them, they won't look any further. And if I find you've countermanded my orders in my absence, I'll feed you to the sharks myself. Understand?'

Green eyes blazed into brown. Ozgan's gaze dropped. 'Yes, sir. I understand.'

'In your absence?' Megren demanded. 'Where are you going?'

'Below,' said Kazhian concisely. 'I want to lie down before I fall down. It's more comfortable that way. Do you have to have *everything* spelt out for you?' He withdrew his hand from his cousin's shoulder and walked, with stubborn determination, towards the hatchway. At the top, he turned. 'You're all big boys and girls now – sort out the sleeping arrangements for yourselves. Oh, and Ozgan?'

The mate stood as straight as the mast above him. 'Yes, sir?'

'It might be an idea to batten down the hatches and secure loose objects on deck. Tomorrow could be a little rough.'

And with a smile and a wave, he disappeared down the ladder, leaving his crew and passengers staring blankly after him.

Megren assumed command of the fugitives. As the discomfited Ozgan issued his orders, Trinn's husband ushered the huddle of women and children to the forward companionway. The *Wind of Morning*, being a courier ship, often carried passengers on official business, and there were several comfortable cabins set aside for their use.

By the time the children had been settled and soothed, the courier ship had reached the open sea. Trinn stood on the vessel's smooth, moonlit deck, listening to the different sound of the waves, and feeling her increasingly lively pitch and toss as she plunged through the water. They were safe: now, they were safe. But not for much longer, if Ozgan were to be believed.

On the whole, she thought that she would rather drown than be murdered by Arkun, or any other of Olkanno's agents.

She stared for a long time at the impenetrable darkness ahead, that might shield them or destroy them. Then she walked to the stern, where Sargenay and the Gulkeshi sat in mutual antipathy, a spear's length apart.

'Yes, Lady Trinn, what can I do for you?' The sorcerer got to his feet, smiling charmingly, and made elaborate obeisance. Ozgan's look of disgust was comical.

'Can you spare yourself for a while?'

'Of course he can,' the mate growled into his shaggy beard. 'It's a natural wind.'

Sargenay sent him a look of purest contempt. 'I never know when my Art may be needed.'

'It could be needed now,' Trinn told him. 'Have you any skill as a Healer?'

The sorcerer stared at her, eyebrows archly raised. The contrast between the brisk efficiency he had showed earlier and this studied affectedness might in other circumstances have amused her. But now she had no space for laughter.

'My dear lady, of course I am – it is part of our training,' he said. 'But in my own way, I can perhaps claim some extra ability.'

'He mended Durkel's ingrowing toenail for him,' Ozgan muttered scornfully. 'That's about his level.'

'Pay no attention to him,' said Trinn hastily, seeing Sargenay's indignant expression. 'Come with me.'

She led the sorcerer to the stern hatchway, and paused at the top. Ozgan was staring at her in horror. 'You can't go down there without his say-so,' he said. 'That's Captain's quarters, lady, and private.'

'Oh, go bugger yourself, you plank-brained wanker,' said Sargenay courteously, and followed Trinn down the ladder.

At the foot, she turned to the sorcerer. 'He got a K'tali dart in his shoulder. It might be poisoned. I know he doesn't want anyone to fuss, but if we don't he could be dead by morning.'

Sargenay's face was suddenly very serious. 'If that is so, he may be beyond my power to Heal, lady.'

'Even if it is, at least we'll have tried to help him. And after all your efforts, and his, it would be a shame if he died.'

'I agree,' said Sargenay lightly. 'We don't want him giving up his spirit now, do we? Apart from the waste, it leaves that rat Ozgan in command, and we'll all be stuck in Gulkesh.'

'Oh, shut up,' said Trinn impatiently, and rapped on the Captain's door.

There was no reply. Fearing the worst, she opened it cautiously and peered round, wondering if she was about to face Kazhian's rage at this unauthorized intrusion.

'Lord of Life!' said Sargenay in amazement. 'He must have had a woman in here – it's clean and tidy!'

Trinn ignored him, and walked to the mattress. Kazhian lay on it face down, unmoving. The long, curling hair was tangled and matted with blood, and there were plentiful stains of it on his borrowed tunic. Suddenly afraid, she knelt and searched for a pulse. It was not strong, and his skin was cold and clammy.

'He needs help,' she told the sorcerer, who was crouching beside her. 'Can you do anything?'

'I don't know.' Sargenay had once more shed his elaborate manner. 'But we've got to keep him alive. I don't trust that bone-headed Gulkeshi not to betray you, or sell you into slavery, or dump you all overboard. And Ozgan's sure that Kazhian will wreck the ship, like he thinks he did before.'

'And did he?'

'No. Eska'anen paid the steersman,' said Sargenay grimly. 'It's a wonder Kazhian is as normal as he is, given his parentage. Go and get some water and clean cloths, lady, and I'll try to find out the extent of the damage.'

Trinn filled a deep wooden bowl from the jug on the shelf, and rummaged in the clothes-chest. When she returned to the mattress, Kazhian was lying on his back, his eyes closed and his hands at his sides. Sargenay sat beside him, a look of intense and frowning concentration on his face. As she knelt down, he glanced at her and smiled. 'The dart was indeed poisoned, lady, but fortunately its effects were weak, and they are rapidly wearing off now. He is exhausted, though, his face is badly bruised, he's been hit on the back of the head and he's lost a lot of blood from that wound in his shoulder.'

'Quite a fair description,' said Kazhian, his eyes still closed. 'Add to that two generous pipefuls of khlar, and you'll understand why I don't feel up to arguing with Ozgan at this precise moment.'

'I should think again,' Sargenay said softly. 'I'm certain he's planning to take over the ship.'

Explosively, Kazhian sat up. 'What in Olyak's name – oh, Lord of Life, I think I'm going to be sick.'

Trinn hastily thrust the bowl at him. When he'd finished, she emptied it over the stern gallery rail and poured him a cup of wine, which seemed to be the only liquid left in the cabin. Kazhian sipped it cautiously. He looked even worse, his skin greyish-green under the deep sailor's tan, and he was shivering. She pulled a blanket out of the clothes-chest, and tucked it round him. He gave her a wry grin. 'I've heard many things about you, Lady Trinn, but none of them remotely match up to the reality.'

'Thank you,' she said. 'But I'm just being sensible. It'll do none of us any good if you succumb to a fever.'

'I won't. Sargenay's a Healer. Sargenay can patch me up. And then I'm going to feed Ozgan to the sharks, piece by piece.'

'That's fine by me,' said the sorcerer. 'But don't overtax yourself, Lord Kazhian. We need you to get us through that storm.'

'If I can.' The green eyes were suddenly bleak. 'It's a desperate throw, weather-worker. If it comes off, then the lady here and her husband are safe from my father and Olkanno's minions, for a while at least. But if it doesn't – if the winds and seas defeat us – then we'll be dead after all.'

And Trinn, staring at him, knew that he thought their chances of survival were slender indeed.

CHAPTER
SEVEN

Olkanno surveyed his most ruthless, efficient and obedient servant. Something was wrong. Something had marked the man, and blunted his edge. His plans depended on the use of one agent, as sharp and deadly as a knife in the dark, and as secret. If he couldn't rely on Arkun any more, there was no one else to take his place.

He said softly, 'Show me the proof that they are dead.'

'The galleys found a quantity of wreckage, sir. Including this.'

It was a short piece of planking, about the length of Arkun's arm, and painted. Olkanno realized that the white marks formed part of the ship's name.

'Only you and I understand the significance of this, sir,' said Arkun. 'We alone know that Megren and his family did not die in the fire, but escaped on Kazhian's ship. In the end, though, the result has been the same. Thanks to the storm, disaster has been averted. Everyone will continue to think that Megren and his family died in that fire, and that Kazhian went down with his ship. We know differently, of course, but at least Megren will not appear on Balki or in Gulkesh. So my mistakes at Ukkan do not matter, fortunately.'

'No,' said Olkanno, regarding his agent thoughtfully. 'It is well for you, Arkun, that they do not. But you will not make such errors again. I sent you to kill Megren and his family, and Kazhian as well. I thought that you hated him for the humiliations of your birth and childhood. I did not expect you to let him escape in a moment of sentimental compassion. Such lapses are dangerous in an agent. Any more, and you will cease to enjoy my favour and protection, do you understand?'

'Yes, sir,' said Arkun.

Olkanno's soft, impermeable gaze rested speculatively on the red-haired man's face. 'Good. You are the best I have, and I would not want to lose you. Certainly, you did well to remove the Lady Djeneb from the Prince of Tulyet's clutches. Putting her on Kazhian's ship was a masterstroke.'

'Thank you, sir. The eunuch must deserve some credit, too. But the lady's own strength of character was also important. She is unusually independent and spirited.'

'Well, Suken should soon change that. And once she's given him a son, her usefulness will be ended. Wife-murder runs in that branch of the family.' Olkanno smiled. 'I expect you've heard the gossip.'

'I have.'

'For once, it was correct. Well, we have safely disposed of Megren and B'kenn, and we have eliminated Kazhian. Only Kadjak and his family now block Lord Eska'anen's rightful path to the Onyx Throne. What unfortunate accidents have you in mind for them?'

'Too many accidents,' Arkun pointed out, 'can begin to look like more than unfortunate coincidence.'

'Really? A bad oyster could arrive on anyone's plate – and villas burn down all the time. What shall we arrange for Kadjak and his sons?'

'Tarmon should be easy enough. Most people are surprised he's still alive.'

'I know. How much debauchery does it take to kill a man? I'll leave him to you,' Olkanno said. 'You can prove to me that you are still my most reliable, ruthless and efficient agent. I don't care about the details. You can use whatever means you like, and you needn't even make it look accidental. A fight over a gambling debt or a catamite? An adulterated batch of khlar? A jealous woman? Use your limitless imagination.'

'I will,' said Arkun thoughtfully. He had never met Tarmon, but from what he'd heard, Olkanno's assessment of him was correct. He preferred not to know his victims personally. It was easy to arrange the death of a stranger: not so simple to drive a knife into the heart of a man whom he had known, and liked, when they were boys. He had obeyed a fleeting impulse of compassion, and spared Kazhian's life. That had been the height of folly: he was in danger of becoming soft, and soft agents didn't last long.

'So I can rely on you, Arkun,' Olkanno said.

'Have no fear, sir. Tarmon is as good as dead – and I have the added reward of knowing that few people will regret his premature departure to Olyak's lowest Hall.'

'Excellent.' Olkanno smiled with smooth menace. 'You have a good chance to justify my leniency, Arkun, and redeem yourself. Perform as competently as you have in the past, and you will be handsomely rewarded. I shall expect to hear the news of Tarmon's death shortly. You may go.'

The agent bowed, and left the room. Beneath his formal robe, he was sweating with relief. It had been a close-run thing. He had not lied to Olkanno, but neither had he told his master the entire truth. And if he ever revealed how much he grieved for Kazhian, his life would be worth as much as a handful of dirt.

He *was* getting soft. He must mend his ways. And certainly he would enjoy devising a suitable end for the repellent Tarmon, whose death would surely be mourned by no one in all the known world.

The Empire, though lacking a head, ran fairly smoothly under its army of bureaucrats. Many Councillors saw no particular reason why the appointment of the new Emperor should be hurried. True, the unfortunate death of Megren had somewhat reduced the field of candidates, but there was still no clear leader. Eska'anen had attracted those who wished for a strong and capable ruler, but his brother Kadjak was spreading his incalculable wealth with stunning generosity in his efforts to win support for his favourite son, Gorek. And even those who secretly doubted the wisdom of putting an untried young man on the Onyx Throne were vociferous in his favour with a few bags of Kadjak's gold in their grasp.

It was a hidden, delicate game. None of the Councillors were naïve enough to believe that the deaths of Sekkenet, B'kenn and Megren were either natural or coincidental. They looked cautiously over their shoulders and felt their way gingerly towards agreement. There had not been an actual war over a disputed succession for over a thousand years. Instead, the Toktel'yans had reduced the less wasteful and destructive methods of conspiracy, bribery and political murder to a very fine art. But the penalty for backing, or being, the losing candidate might very well be death.

Kadjak, third son of the Emperor Makkyar, was not afraid for himself. Only a few months previously, his Healer had told him that unless he immediately and drastically moderated his prodigious intake of food and drink, he would be dead within a year. Kadjak had no intention of obeying these instructions, and had dismissed the Healer because, as he told his senior wife, Djirin, he didn't want to see the man's smug face saying '*I told you so*' in attendance at his deathbed.

Djirin knew better than to object. As a good Toktel'yan wife, from one of the Empire's most ancient and wealthy families, she must submit to her husband in all things, and she was not averse to becoming a rich widow, for her beloved only son Tarmon would never try to rule her life. But when the Onyx Throne had fallen suddenly and unexpectedly vacant, she had felt it her duty to remind her husband that their son was a Vessel of the Blood Imperial, and therefore entitled to fill it.

So she had invited him to her luxurious suite within the Women's Quarters of his palatial villa, for a private supper. She was well aware that Kadjak, vast and chronically short of breath, had long since ceased to function sexually, but she knew what would please him most. Mountains of spiced almond rice tottered in huge bowls next to plates of expensive delicacies from the Archipelago: doves' breasts marinated in honey, sweet-smelling exotic fruits, heaps of the slender, tangy kaymon roots that were more costly, weight for weight, than bars of gold, iced fruit drinks and jugs of the finest vintage of Hailyan wine. Djirin had picked delicately at the choicest morsels, and watched her husband shovel down enough food to feed most households for two or three days. When his mood had changed from greed to satisfied fulfilment, she could gently broach the question of Tarmon's claim to the throne.

Kadjak belched loudly and comfortably, and patted his enormous belly. 'A beautiful meal, my dear wife. Give my compliments to the cook.'

'I shall, husband. And I accept your praise, too, on my own behalf. The fried sandmice in butter pastry were made with my own hands.'

'Were they, indeed? You still have a remarkably light touch, my dear, after all these years.' Kadjak leaned across the heaped cushions and patted his senior wife's shoulder indulgently. Even at close on fifty, she was still a fine-looking woman, and her figure was as slender as a girl's. 'A shame that you have fed me so well that I cannot contemplate enjoying your touch in other areas.' He smiled at her with wistful regret.

Djirin didn't regret it. Although, like all well-born Toktel'yan women, she had received a formal and entirely theoretical training in the erotic arts before her marriage, sex had never interested her. All her love, her passion, her energy had been poured into Tarmon, her first-born and her only son: her daughters had never enjoyed a fraction of such attention. From earliest infancy, she had given him everything: his every whim had been indulged, his lapses rewarded with uncritical excuses, and his most obnoxious transgressions completely ignored. And if Kadjak's health was too poor to allow him to claim the Onyx Throne, she had no intention of letting such a wonderful opportunity evade her adored son's fingers.

'I understand that you have no desire to be Emperor?' she enquired, fluttering her painted eyelashes.

'None whatsoever,' said Kadjak. 'My life is more than comfortable, and may well end soon anyway, if that Healer is right. I have no intention of giving anything up for the distant prospect of ruling the Empire. Why should I? I have everything I have ever desired, and besides, Emperors have to work. Even Djamal attended Council meetings and made some decisions. Beyond me at my time of life, my dear.'

'Then . . . if you are *absolutely* certain that you do not want it for yourself – what about your son?'

Kadjak stared at her. Djirin's naked and partisan devotion to Tarmon had in his own opinion ruined the boy. He owed her much – after all, her dowry had formed the substantial foundation of his immeasurable wealth – but he had never really liked her, and he detested Tarmon, who had inherited both his father's greed and his mother's ill-nature in full measure.

'Gorek might indeed be a good choice,' he said, deliberately misunderstanding her. 'He's young, pleasant, hard-working.'

'I didn't mean Gorek.' Djirin hastily muted her angry hiss to a more compliant tone. 'I meant, of course, our first-born – your eldest and most gifted son, Tarmon.'

Gifted in excess, perversion and depravity, thought Kadjak. Even in Toktel'yi, Tarmon's gluttonous pursuit of pleasure had caused comment. Once his tastes had become apparent, his father had bought a villa for him on the other side of the city, where he could sink into catastrophic self-indulgence out of his sight. Gossip informed Kadjak that Tarmon had a retinue of a dozen concubines, and as many catamites; that he consumed vast and expensive quantities of khlar; that his tame sorcerer constructed obscene Illusions for the entertainment of himself and his guests; and that when all these and other diversions bored him, he sent out his slaves to buy young boys and girls from the slums. It was whispered that after he had gratified his lusts, the children were thrown into the Kefirinn. And Kadjak could believe it.

But he had never made any attempt to condemn his eldest son's activities. Kadjak's own life was dedicated purely to ensuring his own comfort, and it would be a great deal less pleasant if he aroused Djirin's hostility by trying to thwart her precious boy.

'Surely Tarmon would not be interested,' he said cautiously. 'His unique . . . talents hardly lie in the field of politics.'

'Of course he'll be interested.' Djirin snapped. '*You* may be at the end of your life, husband, but he is at the beginning of his. No young man of his gifts could possibly ignore such a glorious and beckoning future. I want you to use your wealth, dearest, to persuade your friends on the Council to give him their support. I hear the Governor of Mynak has already spoken in his favour.'

Kadjak had heard it too, with disbelief, and privately thought that the Governor must be mad. But despite his desire for a quiet end to his life, he knew that the time had come to make a stand against Djirin, if only for the sake of the Empire. He said pleasantly, 'If Tarmon truly wants to be a candidate, then of course I will use my influence to support him. But to be fair, I must also give equal help to Gorek, should he also wish to become Emperor.'

'*Gorek?*' Djirin's ingratiating mask slipped, briefly, to reveal the vindictive and unpleasant woman lurking behind it. 'That stupid nonentity would be a disaster!'

'You may think so, dear wife, and you are of course entitled to your opinion, although perhaps you should not express it quite so forcefully,' Kadjak said mildly. 'I, however, happen to disagree with you. In any case, I have decided. What I spend on Tarmon, I shall also spend on Gorek. It is that, or nothing.'

And with a brief glance of savage resentment before she lowered her eyes in submission, Djirin had to accept her defeat.

The company at Tarmon's villa was celebrating his favourite concubine's birthday, and his dining-hall was packed with guests, intent only on enjoying themselves to the full at someone else's expense. In one corner, a traditional quartet played energetically on djarleks, flute and hand-cymbals, but their music was completely overwhelmed by the noise of the revellers. Tarmon's cronies had earlier watched a troupe of male and female dancers, whose minimally clad bodies had performed intricate and obscene gyrations for their amusement and arousal, and had then joined the proceedings already in full swing around the room. The cloying reek of khlar had replaced almost all the air, the tenth cask of choice wine had been broached, and everywhere Tarmon looked there was naked, sweating flesh pressed shamelessly against naked, sweating flesh. It was a very good party – one of his best.

Curiously, though, he seemed to have temporarily lost his enthusiasm. Normally he'd be on his fourth or fifth woman by now, but tonight he'd only managed it once. The girl had been the most gorgeous of the dancers, agile, supple and extraordinarily draining, so perhaps that was the reason. She had covered herself with sweet oils, and invited him to lick them off. His loins tingled at the memory, but failed to rise. He looked around for her, but she had vanished, probably with one of his guests.

Well, there were plenty more to choose from. Determined to enjoy himself, Tarmon beckoned to the beautiful boy he'd been eyeing all evening. With a practised, promising smile, the catamite walked over, and without a word began to use his hands in a most unusual and delightful way.

It was a very good party. The rising sun illuminated the villa, and the men and women lying sprawled in drugged and drunken slumber in the courtyards, in the halls, in the bedrooms, in the dining-room. The stench of stale khlar and fresh vomit made the slaves, approaching reluctantly with buckets and brooms, gag in revulsion. As the guests, one by one or two by two, staggered to their feet and departed, the man in charge of the cleaning noticed that one of them, lying on the cushions by the fountain, had not stirred. Suddenly uneasy, he went over to investigate.

It was Tarmon. His robe pulled up around his waist, his mouth open and filled with vomit, he was not a very edifying sight. And he was, moreover, quite dead.

With the usual blistering speed of good news masquerading as bad, everyone in Toktel'yi had heard of Tarmon's sudden demise before sunset. Few were surprised: those who immersed themselves in depravity with such enthusiasm generally succumbed to over-indulgence sooner or later. Some commented, with sympathy, on the bad luck presently afflicting the Vessels of the Blood Imperial. Others, more circumspect, took care to keep their suspicions to themselves. And a few rash individuals laid secret bets with their friends on who would be next.

In the Women's Quarters of Kadjak's villa, Djirin howled and screamed with grief and rage. One of her slaves lay dead, slain by an antique marble sculpture which her mistress had thrown at her. Several more had been injured as they tried to restrain her. In desperation, the Head Eunuch had sent a message to her eldest daughter Inneken, who lived nearby: and eventually, after much persuasion, Djirin at last grew calm enough to drink the sedative potion prepared by Kadjak's Healer.

Even within his own family, his mother was Tarmon's only mourner. Inneken had loathed him ever since he had tried to force himself on her when he was twelve and she was ten, and her sisters had suffered similar experiences. Kadjak detested him. His half-brother

Kekaylo had also been the object of Tarmon's attentions, and still had the scars to prove it. And his other half-brother, Gorek, who had been terrified of him in childhood, felt nothing but gladness and relief at the death of his chief rival.

On the morning after Tarmon's abrupt departure to Olyak's Halls, the male members of his family gathered with his cronies at the pyre. Kadjak arrived in a litter borne by eight puffing slaves, rather than the more usual four, and exuded an air of cheerful affability that seemed singularly inappropriate at the funeral of his eldest son. It was noticeable, too, that none of the motley assortment of profligate young aristocrats, painted catamites, khlar sellers, gamblers, adventurers and other examples of Toktel'yan low-life who formed the bulk of Tarmon's friends looked particularly downcast either. Most of them had been sponging off him for years, but they had probably spent much of the previous day looting his villa of everything valuable. And there were plenty more wealthy, spoilt and decadent young men waiting to be fleeced.

Gorek looked around at the company and allowed himself a smug smile. None of *his* friends looked like the dregs of the city. *His* friends were like him, young and respectable, with wives and families, eager to make a favourable impression on the world. If they went to brothels or enjoyed catamites or smoked khlar, they did so discreetly.

He let his mind wander further. There was no reason now why he shouldn't succeed to the Onyx Throne. His father had spread his money with a lavish hand. Now that Tarmon was dead, it could all be spent on him.

'Hallo, brother.'

It was Kekaylo. Three years younger than Gorek, he had been dedicated since birth to the service of the Lord of Life, and had entered the priesthood at the age of eighteen, when other, less fortunate young men began their compulsory five years of military service. The brothers both favoured their mother, who came from Annatal, and were very alike, with dark skin and short, curling hair.

'Greetings,' said Gorek, smiling. 'You look well.'

'I am well,' said Kekaylo, beaming. His already considerable belly strained against his gorgeous silk robe, dyed in splashes of every colour of the rainbow and more, and his ceremonial smiling mask, gilded and studded with jewels, hung from his plump fingers. 'You have lost a little weight, Gorek. Isn't U'ullan feeding you?'

'She's put me on a diet,' said his brother gloomily. 'No sweetmeats, no butter, no oil, no rice. She says she doesn't want me to get as fat as Father.'

'You're henpecked,' said Kekaylo, with the good humour born of having a troupe of concubines to cater for every whim. 'How is Father taking it?'

'Very well – though of course Tarmon wasn't exactly his favourite. Djirin, as you can imagine, is less happy.'

'I never liked her,' Kekaylo said. 'She makes Mother's life a misery. Now, if Olyak could be persuaded to take her as well . . .'

'Not a chance. He'll let her live as long as possible. Can't you imagine it? She'd be forever nagging him to move Tarmon up a few Halls, and grant him undeserved special privileges. No, I bet you she outlives us all.'

'Done,' said Kekaylo. 'The only trouble is, you won't collect.' He glanced round and lowered his voice to a whisper. 'And another thing. With Tarmon out of the way, what's to stop you being Emperor now, eh? I can't – priests aren't allowed to sit on the Onyx Throne.'

'There's only Eska'anen,' Gorek said. 'And who'd vote for him? One son dead and the other a repellent piece of reptilian slime, and a few cobwebs lurking in *his* cupboards, beyond a doubt. Whereas I am upright, young, respectable, with a growing family – I'll found a dynasty that Toktel'yi can be proud of.'

'If I were on the Council, I'd certainly vote for you,' Kekaylo said.

'You might be yet. The post of Archpriest is in the Emperor's gift, remember. And old Gemmek can't have much longer to go.'

'He's sixty-nine, whereas I am only twenty-three. Young for the post, I admit, but not impossibly so.' His eyes gleamed greedily. 'I have already been persuading him that you would make a better Emperor than Eska'anen – he's sure to vote for you.'

Riding home in his litter, Gorek reflected with satisfaction on the glowing prospect before him. U'ullan was right: he deserved to be Emperor. He had explained to her that she would not be Empress: unlike Gulkeshi women, the females of Toktel'yi took no part in public life or politics. Her duty was to support him, comfort him, serve him, and bear his children. Little Makkyar – the Imperial name now seemed appropriately prophetic – was two and a half, and his sister Meilan had just celebrated her first birthday. It was time for another. The more sons he and U'ullan could produce, the less chance there would be of any more succession crises in the future. If necessary, he could take a second wife, or even a third . . .

Gorek lay back on the cushions of his curtained palanquin, and surveyed his rosy prospects with closed eyes and a blissful smile.

*

The Councillors, viewing the fast-diminishing number of candidates with some alarm, voted at their next meeting to delay the election of the Emperor for half a month more. Their instinct for self-preservation being uppermost, they were well aware that the longer the vital decision was delayed, the greater was the chance that the choice would be made for them, and they would not risk rousing the antagonism of the victor.

It seemed increasingly likely that Eska'anen would succeed to the throne. Despite the lure of Kadjak's gold, and the prospect of a young, comparatively sane, comparatively moral Emperor, most of the Councillors knew that Gorek was not the sort to dispose of his opponents wholesale. In the past three months, five adult male Vessels of the Blood Imperial had died suddenly. Individually, all the deaths had a plausible explanation. Collectively, the hand of a murderer was obvious. And no one thought it was likely to be Gorek. Indeed, the prevailing opinion, secretly whispered from Councillor to Councillor, was that Gorek would be wise to take himself and his family on an extended visit to his in-laws in Gulkesh.

And embedded securely and invisibly in his household, waiting for the ideal moment, Olkanno's agent bided his time.

In the event, he proved unnecessary. The day after Tarmon's funeral, a splendid palanquin, heavily curtained and draped in mourning black silk, was carried to the crumbling pile of the Old Palace, in the heart of the ancient city, from which Olkanno directed his army of agents and informers. A woman, copiously shrouded in voluminous robes and veils, was assisted from the litter by her eunuchs, and escorted within the building. And a few moments later the Spymaster himself, successfully concealing his astonished delight behind a façade of courteous interest, was receiving the Lady Djirin, senior wife of Kadjak son of Makkyar, in his private office.

Cushions were brought, and trays of food and drink offered, but Djirin waved them away. She said in a voice hoarse from weeping, 'I will not stay. I have come to see you, Lord Olkanno, for one reason alone. I wish to denounce to you the murderers of my beloved only son Tarmon!'

Olkanno stared at her. He said at last, '*Murderers?* You think that Lord Tarmon was *murdered*, Lady Djirin? Whatever gives you that idea?'

'I *know* it!' Djirin cried. 'And what's more, I know who ordered it – my husband's second son, Gorek. He's been jealous of poor Tarmon since they were children, and now he's killed him!'

'But why now, Lady Djirin?' Olkanno asked. He leaned back

against his cushions, his fat fingers tented in front of him, his blandly curious gaze concealing the fact that he knew the answer very well.

'Because Gorek wants the Onyx Throne, of course,' Djirin snapped. Even in the throes of mourning, she could not keep up the display of tragic bereavement for very long. 'So he had Tarmon murdered.'

'Have you any proof? Do you know how?'

'I don't need proof, it's obvious to a blind man! Who else would want to murder my poor dear darling?'

Olkanno suspected that the list would have run into thousands, but said nothing.

'As to *how* . . . well, you're the Spymaster, Lord Olkanno, you must know about such things . . . some poison, surely.'

'You do not think, as everyone else seems to think, that his death was the inevitable result of – of certain excesses?'

'I certainly do not!' Djirin cried indignantly. 'Wicked people with nothing better to do have always spread foul malicious gossip about my poor darling. He was no worse than many, and a lot better than some. It's all evil rumours.' Her voice trembled. 'He would have made such a splendid Emperor – he had such plans . . . all gone . . . such a waste . . .'

Olkanno waited with apparently sympathetic patience while the grieving woman sobbed into a handkerchief behind her veil. When the sounds of weeping had diminished, he said kindly, 'So what do you want me to do, Lady Djirin?'

'I want you to bring his murderers to justice! Gorek and his Gulkeshi bitch of a wife! They're guilty and they should die for it!'

'But there is no proof, Lady Djirin. You said so yourself. A mother's natural suspicion is not enough. Even I require proof, before I can act.'

'Then find some,' she cried vehemently. 'It shouldn't be too difficult. That stupid smug self-righteous lump of lard must have left some clues.' She leaned forward, the intensity of her gaze obvious even through the veil. 'Find it, Olkanno. Find what's necessary to have them executed.' Her voice became self-consciously flattering. 'A man of your talents and resources should have no trouble – whereas I, a weak and suffering old woman . . .'

You're about as weak as an iron bar, Olkanno thought grimly. He smiled, and said aloud, 'I will do my best, Lady Djirin. But first, you must understand, I shall need some . . . assistance. Informers have to be . . . encouraged to tell their stories.'

'Of course.' Djirin clapped her hands. At once the door swung open and two of her eunuchs staggered in, carrying a small box between them. They dropped it on the floor with a dull thud, and Olkanno heard the soft, seductive jingling of a great many coins.

'I have come prepared,' said Tarmon's mother. 'My husband has vast riches.'

'Have you considered, lady – forgive me if this suggestion is offensive to you – have you considered that he too might be implicated in your son's death?'

Djirin became very still, as if she had only just realized this, although it had probably already occurred to her. At last, she said, with touching dismay, 'Oh – oh, yes, he might. Lord Kadjak has always harboured an unreasonable and irrational dislike for poor Tarmon. Gorek is his favourite. And he has been told by his Healer that his heart is failing. Perhaps he wishes to ensure before he dies that Gorek will become Emperor.'

'Never mind, lady,' said Olkanno comfortingly. 'I shall discover the full truth, never fear, and it will be done very discreetly. If your husband is innocent, he need never know of your suspicions. And if he is guilty . . .'

He paused, and his black eyes were like chips of obsidian.

'If he is guilty, then he will die a murderer's death, and his son with him.'

On the second day of the ninth month of the Toktel'yan Year 2316, the Imperial Council met at last to decide who would henceforth occupy the Onyx Throne.

Of the nine Vessels of the Blood Imperial mentioned at their first gathering after Ba'alekkt's death, most had now been eliminated. Kekaylo, as a consecrated priest, could never be Emperor: and fortunately for him, it was considered extremely unwise to risk eternal bad luck by killing an acolyte of the Lord of Life. Kadjak had announced that because of his poor health, he did not wish to be considered: however, he urged the Council to give full consideration to the eminent suitability of his son Gorek. Suken had also issued a public statement declaring his wholehearted support for his father Eska'anen. And all the others – B'kenn, Megren, Kazhian and Tarmon – were dead.

Gorek or Eska'anen. Eska'anen or Gorek. The outwardly affable, inwardly ruthless Governor of Sabrek, an experienced and capable ruler, a wily and devious politician, a man still comparatively young – not yet fifty – and yet with a son already adult. Or the untried twenty-six-year-old with no experience of public office, and no reputation, either good or bad, save as a nonentity.

The Palace had a forlorn air, empty and echoing. As was the custom, many of the slaves had been sold after Ba'alekkt's death, for a successor would usually import members of his own household. Even in the Women's Quarters, the Lady Djeneb had dismissed all her brother's concubines on her return from her escapade, and waited to learn what her own future would bring. She would almost certainly be the reward for whoever won the throne. Gorek's second wife; Eska'anen's fourth; Suken's first. None of the options were attractive, but at least they were all much better then Skallyan. And she, the daughter and sister of Emperors, was simply too valuable to be wasted on the elderly and incompetent ruler of Toktel'yi's inhospitable dependent Princedom.

The twenty-nine Councillors met in their usual chamber in the Palace. One by one, the assorted Governors, Ministers, Archpriests and other holders of high office took their places, nodding at each other in courteous greeting that could be genuine, or feigned. An air of tense speculation and excitement fizzed in the echoing tiled room. Despite all the intense intrigue, manipulation, persuasion, bribery and blackmail which had filled their lives for the past two and a half months, few felt they could confidently guess the outcome. And only two men knew for a certainty who would be offered the Onyx Throne at the climax of the meeting.

The aspiring candidates were seated on either side of Ikko, Governor of Toktel'yi. Eska'anen was immaculately dressed in a long summer tunic of soft beige silk, tastefully and discreetly embroidered. Its elegant and flattering simplicity enhanced his natural air of dignified distinction. Most Councillors found it easy to imagine such a man as their Emperor. Whatever his secrets, he would not disgrace two thousand years of Imperial history by lapsing into coarseness or vulgarity.

In contrast, Gorek had laden his portly figure with lavish tokens of his family's wealth. Rings gleamed on every finger, and his long tunic was dyed in scarlet, its neckline picked out in gold thread and a clashing assortment of different-coloured gems. His hair had been cut in the most fashionable style, very short at the back and longer at the front, and several stray curls had flopped down over his forehead, which was dripping with sweat. More than one Councillor noted the unfavourable contrast with his coolly impressive uncle, and resolved to ignore the temptation of Kadjak's bribes. What did it matter, in the end, how many of his rivals Eska'anen had eliminated in order to obtain power? After Djamal's indolence and Ba'alekkt's brief but violent reign, the higher echelons of Toktel'yan society longed for an Emperor who would enhance the dignity of the Onyx Throne and rule firmly without upsetting the traditional order. The wits in the taverns and kuldi-houses had decided that Gorek couldn't run twenty paces, let alone a country. Looking at his pudgy, perspiring person, the aptness of the joke was immediately obvious.

As Ikko rose to begin the proceedings, Olkanno lifted his hand. 'My friends and colleagues – before we commence our all-important duty, may I beg your patience for a moment or two? I wish to introduce to you someone whose words will bear heavily on the decision we are about to make. I ask you to listen and act upon these words, for the future of our glorious Empire depends on you. My friends, Lady Djirin, wife of Lord Kadjak.'

All around the table there were gasps of astonishment and disapproval. Not since the reign of the boy Emperor Ka'akell, whose mother had briefly acted as Regent, had a woman attended any Council meeting.

The door opened, and a black-clad, shrouded figure strode briskly in. As Olkanno had hoped, neither tradition nor open male hostility was sufficient to deflect Djirin from her obsessive desire for revenge. With a fine sense of the dramatic, she walked round the table until she stood opposite Gorek and Eska'anen, her black robe swirling over the tiled floor.

For a moment there was absolute silence and the Councillors stared at her in astonished bewilderment. Then Djirin flung our her hand. 'Traitor!' she cried. 'Murderer! Assassin! I denounce you, loathsome spawn of evil, for the slaughter of my poor innocent son Tarmon!'

For an instant, some thought she meant Eska'anen. Then the incredulous Councillors realized that her bony finger was stabbing straight at the plump figure of Gorek.

Under his tan, Kadjak's son had gone grey with shock. His mouth opened and closed like a landed fish, and a stutter of protest emerged. 'But – but—'

'The Lady Djirin is quite correct.' Olkanno said smoothly. 'Such was her grief at the loss of her beloved only son that she overcame her natural feminine weakness and modesty, and conveyed her suspicions directly to me. Fortunately, I was able to use my own methods and resources to confirm the dreadful, unbelievable truth. Yes, my friends and colleagues – the man sitting here before us, hopeful of occupying the highest summit of power and prestige in all the known world, is a fratricide who arranged the murder of his own brother in order to strengthen his claim to the throne!'

'It – it's lies!' Gorek cried frantically, finding his voice at last. 'She's mad, she's lying, I swear it! I never killed Tarmon! He killed himself with his own filthy habits!'

'*You* are the liar, Lord Gorek.' Olkanno's voice was sticky with menace. '*You* are the liar – and I have proof of it.' He picked up a piece of paper, closely written on both sides. 'This is the sworn statement of a dancing girl by the name of Hettekar. She states that you paid her a hundred gold Imperials to kill Tarmon.'

'I don't *know* any dancing girls!' Gorek screamed. 'She's lying, she's lying!'

'He did not die a natural death. He died of poison, added at your suggestion to the sweet oils with which she had covered her body.' Olkanno paused just long enough for the other Councillors to imagine and savour the idea. 'Then she invited him to lick them off. Within the hour, he was dead.'

Djirin gave a howl of grief and buried her veiled face in her hands. Olkanno snapped his fingers, and two eunuchs emerged from the anteroom to usher her out, her usefulness ended.

As the sounds of her sobbing died away, the Spymaster looked round at the transfixed Councillors. 'He denies his guilt, yet I have proof. Proof comprised of a mother's unerring instincts, and of a testimony sworn and signed. Proof also in the motive for such a foul and unnatural crime. Gorek feared that his brother would be a dangerous rival for the Onyx Throne. Jealousy, too, played its part, for Gorek has always enjoyed his father's favour, and wished that he, and not Tarmon, was the eldest son.'

'It's not true,' Gorek was repeating, over and over again, as if the words alone could protect him.

'And therein lies a further tragedy. Lord Kadjak is in poor health, but I understand that he encouraged his second son's rivalry with Lord Tarmon. He may even have suggested murder. I have no proof of that, although many of the household slaves have conveyed their suspicions to me. I do know, however, that Gorek's Gulkeshi wife U'ullan undoubtedly shares his guilt. She has encouraged his ambitions and urged him to commit this most vile of crimes!'

'No!' Gorek shouted. 'No – you're lying – it's all lies – don't believe him, for Kaylo's sake don't believe him!'

'Lord Gorek.' Ikko's voice cut through the noise. 'We have all heard these very grave accusations against you. There is proof of them. Have you any answer to these charges?'

'He's lying!' Gorek wailed. 'He's lying – it isn't true – I didn't kill Tarmon, I didn't!'

'I speak only the truth,' Olkanno said calmly. 'I have no reason to lie. *I* am not a candidate for the Onyx Throne. *I* have nothing to gain from denouncing you – although I have no wish to see a man who can cold-bloodedly commit such a heinous crime achieve supreme power over us all. Lord Gorek, will you go quietly into custody? Or will you continue to abuse your dignity with this unseemly and pointless exhibition?'

But Gorek had been gripped by panic. Long after the soldiers of the Imperial Guard had dragged him away, the shocked, stunned Councillors could hear his howls of protest diminishing into the distance.

'I suggest his immediate execution,' Olkanno said at last. 'And that of his wife, of course. As for Lord Kadjak, perhaps he could be removed to some secluded island, where he can reflect for the remainder of his life on the folly of misplaced ambition. And he may have his grandchildren to keep him company. The Lady Djirin, of course, in the absence of other heirs, will inherit her husband's wealth. I think that is a most satisfactory outcome, and I am sure you will agree with me.'

All round the table, the Councillors were nodding their heads with a mixture of terror and relief.

A few moments later, they had unanimously offered Eska'anen the Onyx Throne.

PART TWO
HIDDEN POWER

CHAPTER
EIGHT

The land of Kereth, lying between Tatht, the easternmost province of the Empire, and the inland Kerentan Sea, was blessed above all others with peace, fertility and wealth. For this was the sacred country of Sarraliss, the Mother Goddess, worshipped as a minor deity by the Toktel'yans but revered all over the rest of the known world as the Lady of Earth, the Lady of Harvest, the Lady of Plenty.

To many Toktel'yans, the idea of a land ruled by women was at best ridiculous, at worst an abomination. But Kerenth, under her line of hereditary Queens, had nestled comfortably around the western shores of the Kerentan Sea for several thousands of years. Protected by the Goddess, she had no need of armies or conquests. Her women tilled the sacred earth, and wove the marvellous silk which was exported all over the known world. The men tended the humble, industrious worms who spun the silk, and built and mended roads and bridges, houses and barns, and their children, beloved and healthy, played in the mulberry groves and learned from their mothers that women were naturally superior to men.

Some visitors found it very hard to accept Kerentan ways. Toktel'yans in particular could not get used to the fact that women, far from being powerless and feeble chattels, controlled their lives, their sexuality and their men. And they were deceived, too, by the lush, lovely, smiling countryside, sunlit and serene. Like everywhere else along the shores of the Southern Sea, conventional sorcery was used in Kerenth, but with some reluctance and mistrust. A far deeper, older, more powerful magic lay dark and fierce within the land itself, the gift of Sarraliss, and channelled through her priestesses for the benefit of everyone. The Lady was savage in protection of her own land and people, the last left in the world now that Tatht and Penya had both fallen to the Empire. Twice in the past hundred years, her aggressive neighbour had tried to invade Kerenth, and twice the Imperial Army had been repelled by the curse of the Goddess, with dreadful loss of life from disease or tempest.

Al'Kalyek, once Court Sorcerer to the most belligerent Emperor of recent times, harboured a healthy respect for all deities, and had no intention of attracting any more interest than was inevitable, given the lively curiosity of the Kerentan people. It was a characteristic that had served them well in the past, for the art of smelting metal had been discovered here first, nearly two thousand years previously, as well as the unique and valuable properties of silk.

As the gifts conferred by Annatal were still regarded with suspicion, Al'Kalyek took his drug discreetly, and kept his power to himself. He had travelled a very long distance, and he was old, and tired. Instinct told him that there was no hurry. He no longer cared if the Toktel'yans murdered each other in pursuit of the Onyx Throne, until there was not a single Vessel of the Blood Imperial left alive. His oath of loyalty had died with Ba'alekkt, and his spirit with Bron. All he wanted was to find the Penyan woman who had been the young sorcerer's lover, to see her child, and to tell her what had happened to its father. He would also inform her of Ansaryon's offer of shelter, though from the little he knew, or could guess, of the woman called Mallaso, she would not even consider accepting it. And when his duty was done, he would take ship for Onnak, and the home and family he had not seen for fifty years.

He had left Minassa a month after High Summer, when it was clear that war no longer threatened. The Toktel'yan Army, outside Tamat, had been sent back to the provinces, and the Northern soldiers had also gone home. People had begun to talk about the future with confidence, knowing that there would be no invasion. And in Toktel'yi, the Council were discussing the succession.

The Empire had survived a series of more or less useless sloths and madmen on the Onyx Throne. It would probably survive a few months without any incumbent at all. Al'Kalyek had heard of his friend Sekkenet's death with sorrow and suspicion: then, just before he left Minassa, of Megren's hasty departure for Ukkan. There was a hand at work, and he did not need to be a sorcerer to guess whose.

But it didn't concern him now. All that mattered was the finding of the woman Mallaso. And then he could go home.

So he took a boat down the Kefirinn to the borders of the Empire, and then, on an old placid mule immune to any odour of sorcery, and leading a sturdy nag to carry his supplies, he began the long trek eastwards. As far as his colleagues on the Council were concerned, he was a renegade and a deserter. The new Emperor, whoever he might be, would appoint another Court Sorcerer, and Al'Kalyek very much hoped that he would be forgotten.

It was after Year-turn by the time he reached the edge of Kerenth, after a journey that had lasted over a thousand miles, mostly across the rolling, uninhabited hills between the Empire and the bleak steppe land to the north. He had only seen one group of people, a hunting party over the border from Djebb, and had given them a very wide berth. He drank from streams, ate the dried and preserved food carried by his packhorse, and let the wilderness sink its peace into his battered, unhappy soul.

After all that time alone, it was a shock to see human faces again, and even more of a shock to see that half of them were female. Al'Kalyek had never visited Kerenth before, although like most educated Toktel'yans he had an adequate command of its language, history and customs, and the sight of so many bare-faced women unsettled him. In Toktel'yi, they ventured out seldom, and heavily shrouded in veils: only children and harlots exposed their features in public. But here, women strode along the highways in their practical, calf-length dresses, tall, sunburnt, strong and confident, and worked cheerfully in the bountiful fields, easing their toil with songs and chants. They might almost have been a different species from the pampered, submissive, secluded ladies of Toktel'yi.

Al'Kalyek scolded himself for a fool. Everyone knew what Kerenth was like: its very name meant 'land of women'. He should not be so disturbed by the reality. But it took him several days, and many miles, before he could feel relaxed in this strange and very different country.

He had no idea where Mallaso could be found. But in Bron's dream, or vision, she had been standing in a field of sesame, surrounded by low, gentle hills. Al'Kalyek had some knowledge of Kerenth's geography, and knew that such a place was most likely to be found in the south of the country, near the city of Kerenth itself.

If she was still there, and if she had not died in childbirth. By now, the baby must have been born. Every night, the old sorcerer sent his mind in search of Bron's child, but in vain. His power must be waning: certainly, compared to that remarkable young man's, it was weak indeed. Or perhaps the elemental magic steeped into the rock and soil of this land had drowned his paltry, acquired and masculine skill. He did not know. He knew only that he was old, and tired, and that Kerenth in winter was warm, but rather wet: and above all that his chances of finding the Penyan woman were much more slender than he had ever imagined.

Kerenth was not a small country, and it contained many, many people. True, black-skinned women seemed rare, but as he rode south, he saw more and more who looked like her. And he did not want to draw attention to himself by asking too many prying questions, which might also put her in danger. For only a year ago she had tried, and failed, to assassinate Ba'alekkt, and the late Emperor had vowed to track her down. Even in Kerenth, the Spymaster would have agents, and if Al'Kalyek began to enquire indiscreetly about a woman from Penya named Mallaso, he might inadvertently lead some murderous spy straight to her and her precious child.

So he was careful, and cautious. He had already concocted a story to account for his presence here and satisfy the Kerentans' notorious curiosity. To every questioner in every inn he explained that he was a Toktel'yan scholar, called Kaylen (in actual fact his brother's name), and that he was travelling through Kerenth gathering material for a book about the country and its inhabitants.

As he had hoped, his listeners were invariably charmed and flattered. If he had really been planning such a project, he would have had to spend a year and more committing all their information to paper. He learned far more than he had ever wanted about Kerentan customs, history, geography, politics, and even building methods. On one all too memorable evening he was regaled by a burly builder with the details of the usual plumbing and sanitary arrangements (far superior, he had to admit, to Toktel'yi's) to be found in every Kerentan villa. And he began to ask about the crops grown in each region. Orchard fruits – plums, apricots, pears, peaches, almonds – flourished in the cooler hills and valleys of the north, around Sarquaina, mixed with broad fields of wheat, or sky-blue flax, or vegetables. Further south, around Kerenth City and the shores of the Southern Sea, there were tropical grains such as millet, sesame or rice, legumes, date-palms, citrus fruits. And everywhere he saw the groves of mulberry trees on which fed the grubs who spun the silk that was the chief source of Kerenth's wealth.

And the further Al'Kalyek journeyed into this strange place, the better he liked it. He liked the richness of the land and the prosperity of the people: though they all worked hard, he had seen no one in rags, no abject poverty, no beggars. The children were happy and healthy, although they were allowed an alarming amount of freedom compared to their counterparts in the Empire. At first he answered their astonishingly direct questions reluctantly, thinking them bad-mannered. Later, though, as the warmth and generosity of the Kerentans began to soften his reserve, he found himself chattering to adults and children alike as if he had known them all his life.

The new year had reached its second month when he arrived in the city of Kerenth, perched on its clifftop above the Southern Sea. It was a dramatic site, the crowded painted stone houses jostling on the edge of the world, looking out over the blue ocean towards Penya. And the Royal Palace, home to Inrai'a, Queen of Kerenth, stood at the highest point of all, crowning the city below.

Inrai'a was reputedly capricious, beautiful and self-willed, and Bron had once been her Consort. She had another now, some handsome young man who had given her the heir she craved. Al'Kalyek had no intention of going anywhere near her, for fear of reopening old wounds.

The city was full of Penyan refugees. The island of Mallaso's birth was the greatest and most wealthy of all the many, many islands, large and small, barren and fertile, in the K'tali Archipelago. Like Kerenth, it had been dedicated to the Goddess, and Sarraliss had laid her blessings thickly over the terraced hills, the lush valleys, the orchards and palms and brilliant flowers. It did not possess Onnak's valuable spices and ironwood, nor Annatal's precious drug: its wealth lay in its rich soil, its colourful and dazzling beauty, and its clear turquoise waters, teeming with fish. Until almost twenty years ago, the Emperor Djamal, seeking easy glory and affronted by Penya's situation as the last independent island in the Archipelago, had decided to add it to his dominions.

The fighting had been long, and very bitter. Thousands died, and thousands of children were enslaved and taken to Toktel'yi, Mallaso amongst them. Some, mostly young, unwed adults, stayed behind, hiding in the rugged central mountains, to carry on a heroic and futile struggle against overwhelming odds, while their homes and lands were taken over by Toktel'yan immigrants. Finally, Djamal, needing a suitable toy for his aggressive only son and heir, had sent Ba'alekkt to subdue the island once and for all. And in three terrible, bloody years, the Emperor-in-Waiting had wiped out almost all remaining resistance, leaving a pall of smoke hanging evilly over the destruction.

But now Ba'alekkt was dead, and there was a new mood of hope amongst the refugees. Al'Kalyek, dark-skinned like most Penyans, was stopped several times as he plodded wearily through the steep, winding streets of the city, and addressed in their language. It was a sing-song dialect of Kerentan, and also owed some of its grammar and intonation to Onnak, Penya's southern neighbour. He found that he could understand most of what they said, which was curiously encouraging. He did not ask anyone directly about Mallaso, though, but merely requested directions to a cheap and respectable inn.

The Silkworm stood down by the harbour, a crowded inlet encircled by the cliffs on which most of the city stood, and protected from stormy seas by a long mole jutting out into the water. The inn's landlady was Penyan, and so were most of her guests, some of whom seemed to be long-term residents. Al'Kalyek made no secret of his nationality, but took care to let everyone know that he was a native of Onnak, and therefore almost one of them. Certainly Garrenden, the inn's owner, accepted her slightly unusual guest with friendly courtesy. Some of her other customers, however, were rather more suspicious, and Al'Kalyek was aware of sidelong looks and whispered conversations whenever he ate in the Silkworm's communal dining-hall. He behaved with perfect and smiling decorum, asked no questions, and kept his eyes and ears open. He could not blame those who assumed he was a spy: in their place, he would have thought the same.

But he could wait. Sooner or later he would find Mallaso. And meanwhile, there was the city of Kerenth to explore, with its gracious public buildings and splendid Temple of Sarraliss, its picturesque houses and lovely gardens and steep, narrow, flower-hung streets. He was an old man, but fit and strong for his age, and he walked, and looked, and listened.

And at last, from scraps of overheard conversation, from apparently trivial questioning and logical consideration of the answers, he found the information he had been seeking for so long.

To the west of Kerenth City, the cliffs slumped lower into the sea, and the hills behind them grew more gentle. Meandering small rivers idled towards the ocean, watering the fields through which they flowed. All this part of the country was intensively farmed, and its produce fed the people in cities and towns all over the south. Here, as in the rest of Kerenth, and much of the Empire as well, the villa was the centre of rural life. Each main building, rambling round several courtyards, was home to an extended family and its workers and dependants, living in cheerful communality. Unlike Toktel'yi, however, there were no slaves in Kerenth, only men and women working freely and willingly for hire. And the head of the household was almost always a woman, owner of property inherited through the female line.

The villa called Twin Waters lay, as its name implied, at the junction of two rivers, about fifteen miles west of Kerenth City, and five miles from the sea. The estate was not particularly large, but the soil was good and the land very productive. It was owned by a woman called Vanaina, who had Penyan connections, and over the years many refugees from the island had made their way to her home, assured of sympathetic and generous treatment. Some soon returned to Kerenth City, to join those fugitives who were planning to drive the Toktel'yans out: others stayed, to live and work and raise their children in this lovely, sheltered place, a haven of tranquillity after the slaughter and destruction from which they had fled.

On the twenty-fifth day of the third month of the year 2317, Al'Kalyek rode up the long, winding, tree-lined road that led to Twin Waters. It was late in the afternoon, and the sun had just emerged after a brief shower of warm soft rain. He had been grateful for the refreshing moisture, washing the gritty dust from his skin and his clothes. Spring, a season not much noticed in Toktel'yi or Onnak, was a time of especial beauty in Kerenth. Yellow light glinted on the puddles and on the drenched trees beside the road, and Al'Kalyek shaded his eyes and wondered if he would find Mallaso here.

There were women working in the fields, ploughing or planting. They looked up curiously as the old man plodded past on his mule, and then returned to their work. Many of them were black-skinned, but none carried a young baby.

A group of children ran up to him, preceded by a couple of the big yellow dogs common in southern Kerenth. Al'Kalyek eyed their sharp fangs and raised hackles with considerable doubt. No animal liked sorcery, or sorcerers, although in Toktel'yi many horses and beasts of burden were trained to ignore it. But the biggest and oldest of the children, a dark-haired girl of eleven or twelve, yelled at them to lie down, an order obeyed with instant and impressive effect.

'Can I help you, sir?' she enquired courteously. She looked as if she might be at least partly Penyan, as did most of the other children.

'I am seeking an old friend,' Al'Kalyek explained in his careful, correct Kerentan. 'She is a woman of Penyan birth, named Mallaso, and she has recently borne a child. I was told that she might be at a villa called Twin Waters. Is this the right place?'

'It is,' the girl said, frowning. 'But there is no one of that name here.'

'Tipeya has a new baby,' said one of the smaller children. 'And she's from Penya.'

'My friend may be calling herself by another name,' Al'Kalyek said. 'She is tall and slender, with fine features and hair cut very short. She was once a dancer, and moves with much grace.'

The girl frowned deeper, staring up at him with suspicious eyes. Then she turned and said something that he did not catch. One of the little ones turned and sprinted back down the road to the villa, some two hundred paces away and half-hidden by the trees.

'Please wait here,' said the girl. 'Ilyenno has gone to fetch Vanaina. She owns the villa, and she will be able to help you.'

Al'Kalyek silently cursed himself for his failure to foresee this. Of course it was likely that Mallaso would be going under an alias, just as he was, for fear of Toktel'yan spies. And if she was indeed this woman Tipeya, she would certainly refuse to see him if she found out his real identity. In her eyes, he would still be part of the hated Empire, a minion of the man she had tried to kill. And she would think that he had come to harm her and the child . . .

Sure that he would be denied the chance to see her after all this time, he closed his eyes in despair, feeling suddenly exhausted. Perhaps they would be kind enough to give him a cup or two of water before they sent him packing.

'What do you want?'

The voice was brisk, but not hostile. Al'Kalyek looked up and saw a woman surveying him. She wore the belted calf-length dress of working Kerentan women, and her hands were covered in earth. From her greying, untidy hair and weathered face, she appeared to be in her fifties, and a lifetime of experience lay in the shrewdness of her gaze.

'I am seeking a friend,' he said, praying that she would understand that he was no threat. 'Her name is Mallaso, but she may have changed it. She has borne a child, I think in the last three or four months. I have been looking for her for more than half a year, and I heard something in the city which led me to hope that she might be here.'

'There is no one called Mallaso in my villa,' said Vanaina. 'Who are you, old man?'

'A friend. A friend of the baby's father. I have travelled many miles to bring her news of him. If she is here, I beg you, let me see her.'

'I repeat – there is no one called Mallaso living here,' said Vanaina sternly.

'But, Grandmama, Tipeya's had a baby!' one of the smaller children said with an air of self-righteousness.

'Indeed she has, but her name is not Mallaso. And even if it were, she has asked me for privacy.' Vanaina shrugged. 'And as she is my guest, I must respect her wishes. There is only one man whom she wants to see – and you are certainly not the person she described.'

'He is of average height and slender build, with hair the colour of bleached flax, and eyes as dark as my own,' Al'Kalyek told her. As she stared at him in surprise, he added, 'That man is the baby's father. I have seen him – I have news of him. I have come in friendship. Please, at least tell her that I am here. Let her decide if she wishes to see me.'

Vanaina frowned at him. She said at last, 'Very well. Since you seem to be speaking the truth, I will do as you suggest. Follow me, please.' And she turned and strode back towards the villa.

The children and the dogs escorted him. The mule plodded wearily along, and Al'Kalyek flexed his stiff, aching back. He had not ridden for two months, and his eagerness to find Mallaso had tempted him to be too ambitious. If she refused to see him, he would have to ride all the way back to the Silkworm before nightfall, for he could hardly ask Vanaina for a bed.

The rambling villa was built round a central courtyard, reached through tall gates. The children took his mule off to the stables, and Al'Kalyek hobbled painfully into a small room set aside for visitors. There was a jug of water, a basin for washing, comfortable chairs, and a bowl of fresh and delicious fruit. He drank thirstily, and was sampling one of the peaches when Vanaina returned.

'Tipeya is happy to see you,' she said with a friendly smile that was in complete contrast to her earlier manner. 'She is in the nursery courtyard with her baby. I will take you to her.'

His heart suddenly pounding with anticipation, Al'Kalyek struggled to his feet and followed her into the bright, hot heart of the villa, a broad quadrangle graced by a central fountain. Climbing plants rioted up and over a charmingly rustic wooden colonnade around the perimeter, and there were seats and benches in the shade beneath, but they were empty. Vanaina led him on, through a series of rooms that seemed impenetrably dark after the brilliance outside, and into another, much smaller courtyard.

A tree grew in the middle, laying a circle of cool black shade around it: and on a cushioned, high-backed wooden seat under the spreading branches a woman sat, suckling a child at her breast.

Al'Kalyek paused for a moment to compose himself. He had come so far for this meeting: he had placed all his hopes for the future upon it, and upon the baby. And now he was here, he had no idea what he would say to the woman whom he had last seen a half-naked prisoner in Ba'alekkt's winter palace on Tekkt.

Vanaina was looking at him enquiringly. Then she gave him a smile of encouragement, and went back into the house.

The woman under the tree glanced up from her child. She smiled in recognition, and said softly, in Toktel'yan, 'Welcome, Al'Kalyek.'

After so many months it was surprisingly good to hear the sound of his own language. He walked forward into the wonderful cool of the shade. As his eyes adjusted to the lessening of light, he saw that she was not so thin as he remembered, and her face glowed with happiness and fulfilment. He said softly, so as not to disturb the feeding baby, 'I have spent a long time searching for you. I bring news for you – news of him.'

Mallaso's dark gaze never wavered. 'I know what you are going to tell me. I know that he is dead. He died with Ba'alekkt.'

Remembering that last, terrible moment of self-sacrifice, Al'Kalyek nodded. 'Yes. But how did you know?'

'We heard that the Emperor had drowned in the Kefirinn, leading the invasion force into Minassa. It was assumed to have been a tragic accident – there was no mention of any assassin. But he spoke to me.' She paused, and Al'Kalyek sensed the depths of her grief. 'He spoke inside my head, just before he died. He said, *"Think of me, when you cherish our child."*' Her smile was full of sadness, and also of hope. 'And I do. It was the best and greatest gift that he could ever have given me, and he knew it. Now I have the baby, and despite his death I am happier than I have ever been, since I was a girl on Penya.' Her arm cradled the small suckling bundle with tender devotion. 'Can you understand that, even though you are a man?'

The old man smiled at the dry tone of her voice. 'Yes,' he said. 'I think I can. May I see the baby?'

For a moment she hesitated. He sensed her protective wariness, and added, 'I will be very careful.'

'I know you will,' Mallaso told him. 'I would have asked Vanaina to turn you away if I did not trust you. Bron always spoke of you with great respect, and so did an old friend of mine, who was also a sorcerer. And I remember that you walked away in disgust, that night on Tekkt, when Olkanno and Ba'alekkt . . .'

For the first time, her voice faltered. She looked down at the child, and added in a whisper, 'I failed. If I had succeeded, Bron would still be alive. It's the only thing I regret.'

'I failed too,' he said gently. 'I tried to help him kill Ba'alekkt, but it wasn't enough. If I had had more courage – if I had been less of a hypocrite, less willing to let him take the risks that my own cowardice would not allow me to take—'

He broke off, and spread his hands helplessly. 'Believe me, if blame is to be apportioned, then I must take the whole of it.'

'But that isn't why you have come,' she said, her dark face calm now. 'You are here to see me, and the baby. You can look now, if you like.'

Al'Kalyek stepped forward hesitantly, almost reverently, and gazed down. The child was much lighter in complexion than Mallaso, and the wisps of black hair were already beginning to curl. Dark eyes stared up at him in apparent wonder. He could see no sign at all of Bron in the plump little face, and wondered, not for the first time, if this scrap of life, so greatly cherished, was in fact Ba'alekkt's child, conceived on the night that Mallaso had tried to kill him.

'When – when was the birth?' he asked.

'On the last day of the eleventh month,' Mallaso said with a smile. 'So she is nearly four months old.'

A girl. Al'Kalyek felt a grievous pang of disappointment. Women in Toktel'yi were forbidden to practise sorcery. It was different, of course, here in Kerenth, where the Priestesses commanded the power of the Goddess. But he had taken it for granted that Bron's child would be male, equipped by right and nature to change and mould the sorcery of Toktel'yi into the shape of renewed greatness. How could a woman, lacking any rights or status, do this within the Empire?

'Are you disappointed?'

Startled, Al'Kalyek stared at the woman. He wondered if she was one of those who had a limited amount of inborn sensitivity. He had found several of them in Toktel'yi, and Bron's own family seemed to be full of natural sorcerers. And if he was right, then would the child, inheriting her mother's gift as well as her father's, be blessed with more than a feeble shadow of Bron's vast powers?

'I am glad she is a girl,' Mallaso went on. 'For she is less likely to be coveted by those who might wish to use her, and try to exploit a gift which she might not possess.'

'I don't want to exploit her!' Al'Kalyek cried indignantly, although his conscience told him that exploitation was exactly what he had intended, however much he might try to disguise it in fine words and altruistic phrases.

'No?' said Mallaso, and her dark eyes narrowed. The baby snuffled softly in her arms, her mouth hazy with milk, sleep slinking into her face. 'But everyone wanted to use Bron for their own purposes, so why not her? Looking back, I realize now that even I used him – I wanted a child to replace the one that I had lost. But never, ever, for any power that she might have.' Her voice became defiant. 'In fact, I hope there is no sorcery in her at all – not a trace, not a drop. I saw the burden that Bron carried – I saw the dark side of his power. In the end, it led him to his death. And I don't want that for Kiyu – I want her to be an ordinary, happy, laughing little girl, with a normal child's sorrows and a normal child's fears. When she cries, I want it to be because she has hurt her knee or lost her toy, not because her soul is tormented by powers she cannot understand. So don't look at her like that, Al'Kalyek – don't tell me if she has any gift – for her sake I hope she hasn't, and I don't want to know if she has!'

She stopped, shaken by the force of her feelings. The infant stirred and whimpered, as if reacting to the angry vehemence in her mother's voice. Al'Kalyek watched her regain her self-control with a determined effort. He admired her strength and courage, while thinking that her words were too optimistic. If the child had inherited any of Bron's power, it would be impossible to hide or ignore. One day, three or five or seven years hence, Mallaso might be compelled to acknowledge that her child was far from normal.

But it was much too soon to tell. A baby so young would still be trying to make sense of the world around her, learning to control and interpret her senses, muscles, limbs. The youngest child in whom he had discerned native sorcery had been four years old.

He said, quietly and calmly, 'Kiyu. Is that a Penyan name?'

Mallaso shook her head, and her long gold earrings, in the shape of interlaced serpents, clinked softly. 'No. It's from Jo'ami.'

As she must have known, her mention of the legendary island of sorcerers astonished Al'Kalyek. 'Jo'ami? You were on *Jo'ami*?'

'Bron and I sailed there when we escaped from Tekkt,' Mallaso told him. And as the baby slept, and the sun drifted down towards the horizon of the day, she told him about the enchanted place, far to the south of the Archipelago, where sorcery had been born.

He listened, and asked questions. Mallaso, who had spent less than half a month on the island, answered him as best she could. Once, she shook her head, smiling, and said, 'No, I can't tell you, but Bron would know.' Then she stopped, her hand to her mouth, caught by sudden and painful memory.

'Do you forget, sometimes, that he is dead?' Al'Kalyek asked her. 'Do you never think that he might still perhaps be alive? After all, he had survived other disasters before.'

'I know – but then, he still had the Wolf in his heart,' Mallaso said. 'In Jo'ami, he and the sorcerers drove it out. As a result, his powers became much greater, because he was freed of the fear of becoming a demon. The Wolf wanted him to use his power to kill and destroy. When it fled, he could do what he wished. But in return, he had become vulnerable – he could be killed, because the Wolf would no longer be there to save him. And even so, he went back to Toktel'yi, to assassinate Ba'alekkt.' She looked up at him. 'You were there, at the end. Can you tell me what happened?'

The old man, with sadness flowering afresh in his heart, gave her the story of Bron's last days in Tamat, but he spared her, as he had not spared Ansaryon, the most unpleasant details.

'He is surely dead, and his bones lie in the Kefirinn,' he said at last. 'I sought his spirit, but it had fled. And to the end of my days, I shall regret, most bitterly, that I did not help him. Between us, we could have slain Ba'alekkt. But I did not want to endanger myself, and I did not want to break my vows. I adhered to the letter of the Rules, but not to their spirit. And so I betrayed him, and he died. The world was changed, but it was not enough, for me or for him. And he, not I, paid the price.'

'You *betrayed* him?'

'Not in reality – but in my heart I did. I let him die,' Al'Kalyek said, and at last the grief that had torn at him for nine long months ripped apart his composure, and he wept.

Mallaso, her arms encumbered with the sleeping baby, watched him as he sobbed, a slight frown of doubt, or pity, between her strongly marked brows. But she made no move to comfort him.

It grew dark under the tree, and the air was soft and warm, filled with the perfume of the flowers and the obsessive harping of the crickets. Voices rose in the distance, doors banged, lights were lit. The girl who had spoken to Al'Kalyek on the road came running into the courtyard. 'Tipeya! There you are! Vanaina wants to know if your friend will be staying, so Arra can make up one of the guest beds.'

Across the old man's bowed, desolate head, Mallaso smiled at the girl. 'Yes, S'raya. Tell Vanaina he will stay.'

Mallaso woke to the soft sound of Kiyu's gurgles, and stretched luxuriously before reaching for her daughter, who was snuggled warmly beside her. After the first difficult months, full of broken sleep and fretful days, the baby had settled down and now usually only woke once in the night for a feed. And how she had grown! The crumpled bluish slippery scrap that Mallaso had at last expelled from her body with so much pain and effort, four months ago, had miraculously transformed herself into a strong-willed but delightful individual, demanding, playful, annoying, fun. She was as golden as the little brown bird for whom she had been named, and Mallaso hoped that one day her song would be as lovely, and her movements as graceful.

But although she wanted the best of life for her daughter – the love, security and companionship that had been so brutally wrenched from herself in childhood – in her heart was the knowledge that it didn't matter how Kiyu turned out. Beautiful or ugly, clever or foolish, good or bad, whatever she was, Mallaso would love her always, unconditionally and for ever.

And beside her feelings for this small, determined creature now greedily sucking at her breast, all her memories of the baby's father, and the brief, wild, terrifying months of their friendship had faded like cloth left too long in the sun. Looking back, she was not even sure if she had loved Bron. He loved her: he had told her so, in that last, strange communication.

She had been working in the fields, on a bright High Summer day, when the inside of her head had begun to tingle in a disturbing and peculiar way. She had cried out, and dropped her hoe: and his voice had sounded in her mind like a memory, although he had never said the words to her aloud.

I love you. Think of me, when you cherish our child.

And she did. She was grateful beyond all measure for his gift, guilty for everything she had never told him, stricken with grief for his fate. But she had Kiyu: and however great her sorrow, she could not be sad for long at the sight of her daughter's dark eyes gazing raptly up at her face, or her enchantingly dimpled smile, or the delightful sound of her laughter.

She leaned back against the cushions, listening to the dawn birdsong and the muted but unmistakable sounds of a waking and busy household. Vanaina had been very kind. Her mother had been a Penyan merchant who had settled in Kerenth, so she was always happy to help refugees. But she had not only given Mallaso work, and a secure home for herself and her baby, she had put her in touch with the leaders of Penya-in-exile, and had even managed to find someone who had known her family. The meeting had been a deeply moving and emotional experience for Mallaso. Insubstantial and unreliable memory had been her only, her desperately hoarded link with the past, through all the bitter years of slavery and beyond. To speak with a woman who had been one of her mother's closest friends, and who had known her as an untouched, undamaged child, at long last confirmed her own identity, the sense of self that she had guarded for so long. Only then had she finally been able to slough off the shrouding skin of the Toktel'yan Mallaso, to reveal the Penyan woman, strong, confident, free and above all happy and secure in herself, that she had never dared to hope she might become.

And now Al'Kalyek had found her, and she did not know what he would do. She had no fear that the would try to take Kiyu away from her, or that he would betray her to the Toktel'yan authorities, who might still be hunting her. With Ba'alekkt dead, she did not think even Olkanno would bother to look for her, but it would be unwise to underestimate the Spymaster's tenacity or vindictiveness. And so, as Bron had suggested, in Kerenth she had called herself by her mother's name, Tipeya.

But despite all her care, Al'Kalyek had managed to discover her refuge, and she didn't feel safe here any more. For where he led, others might follow, despite all his good intentions. And although if she had been alone she would have disregarded any hypothetical danger, for Kiyu's sake she could not afford to take even the smallest risk.

She dressed, and bound the baby to her back, as all women did in Kerenth, and went in search of him.

He was already sitting in the communal dining-hall, taking the usual breakfast of bread and cheese and fruit as if he had been living on a Kerentan farm all his life. Mallaso helped herself to her own food, and sat down beside him on the bench. 'Good morning. I trust you slept well?'

'I did indeed, I thank you.' Al'Kalyek took a sip of citrus juice and smiled at her. 'You have been very kind.'

'The kindness is Vanaina's. She always keeps a bed for guests and travellers.' Mallaso studied the old man's face, graven with the deep sad lines of age, of Annatal, of exhaustion and distress, and said softly, 'We must talk again, privately. Have you enough energy for a stroll? Not a long one, I promise.'

'I can find some,' said Al'Kalyek.

When they had finished eating, they left the villa and walked along the larger of the two rivers which gave the place its name. A little way upstream there was a wooden bridge for the convenience of Vanaina's small herd of dairy cattle, which was often pastured in the meadows beyond. Mallaso walked out to the middle and leaned on the rail, looking down at the sliding clear water beneath. 'The fish have grown quite large here – the children give them titbits so that they'll be fat and easy to catch. Watch.'

A small school of brown carp drifted lazily into their view. With a flash of silver scales and drops of water, one of them leapt for a surface-skimming insect, and the spiralling ripples broke their reflections into chaotic fragments of colour. Two children were herding the cattle, at the far end of the meadow, but there was no one else in sight.

'You wished to talk?' Al'Kalyek prompted her gently, amidst the peaceful silence.

'I did – but I don't know how to begin,' Mallaso said ruefully. 'I know what I want to say, and to ask, but I can't find any words that won't seem discourteous.'

'Then perhaps I can help you. Would you like me to leave?'

Mallaso glanced at him, and smiled. 'I don't know. I honestly don't know. But I am worried that you may somehow have given away my whereabouts to . . .'

'To Olkanno's agents? I doubt it very much. I have been extremely careful. And besides, there is a new Emperor now, and I think the Spymaster will have other fish to fry.'

'You think? Or you hope?'

'A little of both, perhaps. Emperor Eska'anen has a considerable reputation for ruthlessness and efficiency.'

'I know. I was Toktel'yan, remember, until fourteen months ago.'

'Of course. He has made Olkanno his Chief Minister, and someone else is Spymaster – a man called Arkun, one of Olkanno's protégés. He has no special desire to find you – he may not even know of your existence. Ba'alekkt is dead, and I think that Eska'anen and Olkanno are too busy with their own affairs to worry about one stray failed assassin – especially since they both have very good reasons for wishing you had succeeded.'

Despite herself, Mallaso laughed, and the baby on her back stirred. 'I hope – I very much hope you are right. But I shall have to leave Twin Waters, even so.'

'Why? Surely it is your home now.'

'No. Penya is my only true home. And for Kiyu's sake, I cannot risk the smallest danger. I know some people in the city, they'll take me in.'

'I'm sorry,' said Al'Kalyek. 'If I had realized – I did not intend to uproot you from a place where you have been so happy. I can understand your fears, though I cannot believe that you and the baby are in any real danger.'

'But I can't take the risk,' Mallaso repeated, softly and vehemently. 'I cannot take the risk, for Kiyu's sake.'

'If you wanted, I could stay, and protect you. Then you would not have to leave.'

The silence was only broken by the sound of the insects in the hot grass on the river bank, and by the distant lowing of the cattle. The baby whimpered suddenly, and began to squirm within her bindings. Finally, Mallaso said wryly, 'Do you think I need protection, then?'

'No,' said Al'Kalyek frankly. 'I think you are quite safe from Toktel'yi. But I am unhappy that you feel you must leave this lovely place. So if you agree, if you would like to stay here, then I will stay too, for a while, before I go on to Onnak.'

'Onnak?'

'It is where I was born, and my brother and his children and grandchildren live there still. I have long cherished a dream of ending my days there in peaceful retirement. Certainly I have no desire whatsoever to return to Toktel'yi. I would as soon walk into a nest of vipers – which would probably be safer.'

Mallaso considered the options. The thought of leaving Twin Waters and going back to Kerenth did not really appeal to her, although she would probably feel more secure in the anonymity of the city. She had lived here for almost a year now, and she liked the place and the people. They had made her welcome, and she thought of them, and particularly Vanaina's Penyan cousin Ammenna and her daughter S'raya, as her friends. Al'Kalyek's offer was extremely tempting, but would Vanaina agree, especially if she discovered who he really was?

But he had called himself by a pseudonym, for the name of Al'Kalyek, Court Sorcerer to two Emperors, was famous all along the shores of the Southern Sea and throughout the Archipelago. If they were careful, Vanaina need never know the true identity of Mallaso's friend.

She didn't like deceiving her hostess, but she very much wanted to stay – and she would certainly feel safer under a sorcerer's protection.

'I have plenty of money,' he said. 'I'm too old to work for my keep, and besides, I feel that this land is not very friendly towards my kind of sorcery. But I will gladly pay.'

'Vanaina would not take your money. She is wealthy enough already, and she is kind and generous. If she agrees, then I would like you to stay here for a while – at least until I am sure no one has followed you.'

'I am very glad.' The old man's dark face cracked into a broad smile. 'So very glad. I wish to see Onnak again, of course, but I have spent most of the past year travelling, and I would like to rest for a while. But before we go to see Vanaina, there is one more thing. I told you yesterday that I spoke with Ansaryon, the King of Zithirian and Bron's father. I did not have the chance to tell you his message to you, which he asked me to carry. He said that you and your child will always be welcome in Zithirian – that you would be a loved and honoured member of his family. "*Even if she wishes to stay in Kerenth*", he told me, "*she should know that if she ever needs help, or shelter, there is a place for her with us.*"'

'That is kind of him,' Mallaso said. 'But as I'm sure you realize, I must stay here. One day, Penya will be free – and I want to help the other refugees, once Kiyu is a little older.'

'The day may come sooner than you think. Have you heard the latest news? The city was buzzing with it yesterday. Apparently Djebb is in revolt.'

'Djebb is always in revolt. It's famous for rebellion.'

'I know, but this time it seems to be more serious. The gap between Emperors allowed the discontented to gather support and make preparations. There were also rumours that some regiments of the Provincial Army were involved. The deaths of General Sekkenet and Lord Megren have caused a great deal of ill-feeling, and the soldiers blame Eska'anen.'

'Are they right?'

'Undoubtedly. Megren was a good man, and his troops loved him. They would have declared him Emperor if he had not been killed. Eska'anen probably eliminated him with Olkanno's help.' He stared bleakly into the clear water. 'If I had not happened to swim to the Minassan bank, when Bron's last act of sorcery flung us into the Kefirinn, I would probably now be dead. Such a small twist of fate, to be the saving of my life.'

'So would Eska'anen have had you murdered too?'

'Naturally. He knows I hate and abhor evil men like himself, and Olkanno. Sekkenet felt the same, which is probably why he died. I grieve for the Empire, for Eska'anen may turn out to be worse in the end than Ba'alekkt, deranged and vicious though he was. And it seems that many people feel the same. Where Djebb leads, others may follow. Including Penya.'

'I hope so,' Mallaso said softly, her face suddenly aflame with the power of her belief. 'I *know* so. I want Kiyu to walk there, safe and free, before she is grown.'

'If the Army is no longer loyal to the Emperor, the island may find itself undefended,' Al'Kalyek told her. 'There is nothing certain, of course, but I am sure of one thing – I would not want to be in Eska'anen's shoes now, not for all the gold in Zithirian.'

CHAPTER
NINE

'But why not, Father?'

The hundredth Emperor of Toktel'yi gazed at his younger son. His distinguished, handsome face wore an expression of paternal indulgence, but his eyes were implacable. 'Because I say not. You are still only twenty-two. If you had done your service in the army, you would have another year to go. Stay at the Ministry for a while longer. You will learn a great deal of value.'

'At my age, Ba'alekkt was commanding the army on Penya,' Suken smiled wheedlingly. 'If he could be given such responsibility, when he was Emperor-in-Waiting, why can't I?'

A great many conflicting thoughts chased through Eska'anen's head as he looked at his last, and favourite son. Suken's mother had been the only one of his three wives to have died a natural death – unfortunately, after just seven years of marriage. The boy had been brought up by eunuchs and concubines, until Eska'anen, won over by the child's spoilt charm and flattering adoration, had taken over his education. In pleasant contrast to his rebellious and unsatisfactory half-brother, Kazhian, Suken had been gratifyingly obedient and eager to please. And although he had already learned to get his own way by subtlety and deceit, Eska'anen encouraged him, knowing that such skills would serve the boy well in adult life.

So he had moulded his son in his own image, teaching him to smile and to be pleasant to all the world, while plotting its downfall behind its back. He had also noticed Suken's propensity for cruelty, manifested in the torture and mutilation of small animals, and did nothing to curb it. Compassion and kindness were hardly qualities appropriate to a Vessel of the Blood Imperial: and even then, years previously, Eska'anen had secretly cherished the hope that one day, he or his beloved son would become Emperor.

And now, luck, careful planning and extreme ruthlessness had combined to set Eska'anen on the Onyx Throne, and his son obviously expected to share in his father's good fortune.

It was not what Eska'anen wanted. Suken was not like Ba'alekkt, whose father had prudently given him Penya to play with in order to keep him away from Toktel'yi and the temptation to arrange his accession rather earlier than would have happened naturally. Suken was devoted to his father, and he was hard-working and clever. Before he had relinquished the post of Spymaster to become Eska'anen's Chief Minister, Olkanno had written an excellent report on his young protégé. Words and phrases such as 'industrious', 'calculating and devious', 'shows great aptitude for such work', glowed in Eska'anen's memory. The boy was a natural, and he would learn a great deal more about the Empire helping to run its network of spies and informers, than idling round the Palace all day, dallying with concubines and getting into trouble. A Toktel'yan proverb stated that empty hands made empty minds, and Eska'anen had no intention of allowing Suken to waste his talents, however much he wanted to share in the trappings of Imperial power.

It was apparent, however, that Suken had other ideas. 'Please, Father,' he repeated, still wearing the ingratiating smile that had won him so many favours as a child. 'I'm so bored at the Spy Ministry – all that paperwork! I want to rule my own life, Father, not be at everyone's beck and call. They still treat me like a baby, and Arkun's far worse than Olkanno – he won't let me do anything!'

Eska'anen ignored the unattractively petulant note in his son's voice. 'That is hardly true – you are exaggerating. You have more responsibility now than you ever had under Olkanno. The agents of two provinces have been placed under your control. At your age, that is a considerable achievement.'

'I don't like Arkun,' Suken complained. 'He watches me all the time – he's always telling me what to do. Why don't you get rid of him, Father?'

'I have no intention of getting rid of him. Olkanno recommended him most highly for the post. I know he is of very inferior birth, but such men are always hungry for success and material reward – they are easy to control. He owes me everything, and so I am assured of his loyalty – as I hope I am of yours.'

Suken stared indignantly at his father. 'Of course I am loyal – I'm your son! But why won't you let me *prove* it? Give me something to do, Father, *please* – a province, or an island even, one of the Scatterlings, or Tekkt – nothing much ever happens on Tekkt, it would be a good place for me to start. Or let me attend Council meetings, or launch a ship, or anything – just don't let me rot in that miserable hole, pushing a reed-pen all day!'

His voice had risen with frustrated anger. Eska'anen frowned at the unwise and unseemly display of emotion. 'Quiet, boy. You are not some dockside whore, arguing with a customer. You are Emperor-in-Waiting, and you should behave at all times with dignity, decorum and restraint. Understand me?'

Suken's face had darkened sulkily. 'Ba'alekkt didn't behave like that!'

'And Ba'alekkt is dead, as a result of letting his instincts overrule his judgement. You must stay in control of yourself, Suken, or you will allow yourself to be exploited. Work hard, and in a year or two I may be able to find a better place for you. Think of your future, boy, and strive towards it. What you do now will stand you in good stead when you come to rule a Province – and, later, the Empire. And if you do as I say, you will be able to set up your own household soon, and start your dynasty.'

It took a moment or two for Suken to realize what he meant. 'A dynasty? Then you have found a wife for me?'

'Certainly I have. You will marry the Lady Djeneb.'

His son frowned. 'Djeneb? That fat lump of tallow? Why can't I marry someone else?'

'There isn't anyone else of comparable blood. None of the northern princesses are old enough. All B'kenn's daughters are either already married, or died in that fire.'

'What a pity,' said Suken silkily.

Eska'anen stared at the slender, graceful young man sitting opposite him on the heaped cushions. He had assumed he knew the boy through and through – every useful vice, every inconvenient virtue, every quirk of thought and strand of motivation. And now that unmistakable note of menace in Suken's voice took him aback, as if a pampered pet had suddenly turned and snarled a warning. He had taught his son to be devious, secretive, cunning and callous, and now he wondered with alarm if the boy had absorbed the lesson too well.

He took care to let none of this show on his face. 'Kadjak has three daughters, but two of them are married, and the third is betrothed.'

'Betrothals can be unmade. After all, Djeneb is no longer engaged to the Prince of Tulyet, is she? Why not let him marry her after all, and give me Tarmon's sister?'

'Because Djeneb is the daughter of one Emperor and the sister of another. Aska'at is only the daughter of a banished traitor. You deserve better than her. and once you have produced a couple of legitimate heirs, you can take other wives, and as many concubines as you want.'

'I don't want to marry her,' Suken repeated sullenly.

'It doesn't matter what she looks like,' Eska'anen pointed out, with fraying patience. What had got into the boy? He was usually so amenable. Becoming Emperor-in-Waiting had obviously given him all these unsuitable ideas.

'It doesn't matter if she's as ugly as a sea-hag or as stupid as a mule!' he added. 'That isn't the point. The point is that you marry her, and impregnate her. Once you have your heir, you can do what you like. Have a hundred concubines or six wives, if you choose. Arrange for her death, if you really can't stand the thought of being married to her any longer. But my future grandsons will need her blood in their veins, or their claim to the Onyx Throne won't be any better than anyone else's.'

Suken's eyes lowered. He toyed with his wine-cup, and gestured to a slave to fill it. Once more, Eska'anen was uneasily conscious of standing on the brink of an abyss. What was his son really thinking? Was his parade of loyalty and obedience all a pretence?

The thought was so appalling that he slammed a mental door shut on the horror. Not Suken, his favourite, his darling, his hope for the future. Suken was a good son, who had always been a credit to him.

'Send the slaves out, Father,' said the young man softly. 'I have something to tell you.'

That was another sign of his inexperience, despite the thoroughness of Olkanno's training. There was no better way to ensure that someone listened at the door. Eska'anen sighed, and gestured. One by one, the slaves filed out. He beckoned to Suken, and his son, with a look of bewilderment, crossed over to the pile of cushions on which the Emperor was sitting.

'Here. No, not there – close enough to hear me whisper. Haven't you the brains you were born with, boy? Never let the slaves know that what you say is too important for their ears. There are plenty of other ways.'

'I am sorry, Father,' said Suken, after a brief pause.

'Good. Remember it. You have a great deal still to learn, it seems. Now, what was it you wanted to tell me? And take good care to shield your mouth with your hand, and whisper.'

Obediently, Suken leaned forward, and his voice was hardly more than a breath in the quiet room. 'I saw a report today, from Balki. Arkun didn't intend me to know of it, but I have a friend in his office who promised to tell me if there was anything of interest.'

Suken had no friends: his informant had probably been coerced or blackmailed. Eska'anen nodded approvingly. 'Go on.'

'There are rumours all over the island, apparently. The agent couldn't confirm them, but they are spread widely enough to be worrying, or he wouldn't have bothered to report them.'

'Rumours? What rumours?'

Suken waited just long enough for maximum dramatic effect, and then hissed, 'Kazhian is supposed to be alive!'

He had the supreme satisfaction of seeing his father dumbfounded. Eska'anen gaped in disbelief, and then shook his head in denial. 'No. No, he can't be. His ship was lost with all hands in the great storm last year.'

'That's not what they're saying on Balki. They're saying he survived.'

'There was wreckage. Olkanno showed me himself.' Again, Eska'anen felt as if he were floundering. He was the most powerful man in the known world, and yet this potentially vital information had not reached him.

'Not enough to be certain the ship was sunk. And don't you think it was more than coincidence, that part of the nameboard was found?' Suken, aware that he had his father at a disadvantage, pressed on. 'And there's more. They're saying some of Megren's family aren't dead either.'

This time, Eska'anen could not control his horror. '*What?*'

'Hush,' said Suken. 'The slaves might hear you.' He smiled. 'What's the story we all heard? Megren and every member of his family sadly perish in a fire at their villa. How very tragic. How very convenient – for you. And quite coincidentally, Kazhian's ship is sunk with all hands a couple of days later. But that's not what I've heard. The tale I've pieced together is very, very different.'

Eska'anen felt chilled to his bones' marrow. Suken looked as if he were enjoying his father's discomfiture. He went on, his voice creamy with self-satisfaction. 'Arkun was sent to kill Megren. He sailed on Kazhian's ship – with instructions to kill Kazhian as well, once the deed was done. But somehow, he botched it. Kazhian managed to warn Megren, and he and his family escaped on Kazhian's ship. The charred bodies found in the burnt-out villa were in fact the slaves.'

'Why did Olkanno not tell me any of this?' Eska'anen demanded.

'Perhaps he felt it unnecessary to trouble you,' said Suken reassuringly. 'After all, the ship had apparently sunk, so Megren and Kazhian were dead anyway. Why complicate the matter further? And perhaps also,' he added pointedly, 'he did not wish to cast any shadow on Arkun's reputation. If you had known of this, you might have been less willing to make him Spymaster. And Olkanno very much wanted his own creature to succeed him. I ask myself why, if Arkun is not in fact the perfect agent. Is his loyalty perhaps first to Olkanno, rather than to the Emperor he has sworn to serve?'

Eska'anen felt like a man who has bitten into a piece of luscious-looking fruit, only to find it heaving with maggots. Fury at being outwitted struggled with alarm and horror. For months, he had glowed with the satisfaction of knowing that Kazhian's flesh and bones were feeding the fish at last. And now it seemed that he might be alive after all – and Olkanno knew of it, and had not told him.

For an instant he contemplated having his Chief Minister executed, but unfortunately he still needed him. Djebb was in revolt, and if some of the more restless islands and provinces were not to follow suit, he needed Olkanno's ruthlessness, his contacts and his expertise to sniff out the earliest signs of rebellion and stamp on them, hard and fast.

'Are you all right, Father?' Suken's voice was full of apparently genuine concern, but Eska'anen knew that he could no longer rely on his son's devotion. With an effort, he brought himself sternly under control, and nodded brusquely. 'Yes. Yes, of course I am. What has Arkun done about these rumours?'

'A ship sailed for Balki this morning. I understand that an assassin was on board.'

'I won't believe that rogue is dead until I turn the knife in his heart myself,' Eska'anen said softly. 'Lord of Death, how many times do I have to order him killed?'

'I want to see him dead too, Father,' Suken reminded him. 'After all, if he is still alive, he can claim to be Emperor-in-Waiting.'

'I disowned him years ago. You are my appointed heir. Everyone knows it.'

'No, they do not, Father. Not while you hide me away from true responsibility – as if you were ashamed of me—'

'No!' Eska'anen roared. 'No, no, *no* – I have told you a hundred times, boy, do you never listen? You're as bad as your wretched brother! Now get out, quick, before I forget myself!'

Suken, as swift and slippery as an eel, was already half-way to the door. He paused and smiled at his father, and Eska'anen knew he had not imagined the contemptuous menace in the young man's eyes. 'What price Imperial dignity and decorum now, Father?'

Alone at last, Eska'anen felt sick. He gulped down a cup of wine, and tried to employ his usual clear, pitiless logic to analyse what he had just learned.

Kazhian didn't really matter, of course. He was a reprobate, a good-for-nothing, a thorn in his father's side, always insolent and disobedient, perverse, incorrigible, unmanageable: the derogatory adjectives paraded through his mind, along with a memory of his son's face, the mocking green eyes and sneering mouth. He had always loathed Kazhian, and he wanted him dead as much as Suken did, but he was an irrelevance. Eska'anen was sure that his elder son had no desire to become Emperor, no interest in politics, no intention of doing anything save indulge his vices and create mischief. Despite Suken's fears, he wasn't a threat.

Unlike Megren. If Megren was alive, he could become the focus for rebellion. Megren *had* wanted the Onyx Throne. True, he had apparently changed his mind shortly before the fire, but Eska'anen did not believe he had really meant it. If Megren had survived, and knew that his uncle had ordered his murder, he would want revenge. Although he was reputedly a man of integrity who would be above such base urges, Eska'anen had never had any faith in public probity. Beneath the posture of decency, Megren would be as corrupt, venal and merciless as any other Vessel of the Blood Imperial.

Eska'anen waited until his hands were steady and the tide of anger had washed away. Then, he sent for his Spymaster.

The sea was as blue and flat as a Minassan plate. Not a touch of wind lightened the still, heavy air. On the southern horizon the rocky, dangerous coast of Balki was no more than a brown serration against the shimmering sky.

Captain Karrek was in no particular hurry. He didn't like Balki, which was hot, bare, inhospitable and full of surly natives and execrable wine. Unfortunately, his passenger had a bewildering urge to reach the island as soon as possible. Something to do with outsmarting a trading rival, he'd said, but Captain Karrek didn't believe him. After thirty years plying between Toktel'yi and the Archipelago, he knew the Spymaster's agents when he saw them. It was something to do with the prickle on his skin and the vulnerable itch between his shoulder-blades.

So in deference to his passenger's request, he had ordered his weather-worker to raise a wind, and the tubby, capacious *Sea Urchin*, loaded with timber, cotton and silk, skimmed over the calm waters of the Southern Sea with much more speed and grace than she usually displayed. Inexorably, the jagged and unlovely outline of Balki grew nearer.

With the magewind propelling and steering the ship, there was little for the Captain to do, and he was dozing under the stern-deck awning when the look-out's raucous yell wrenched him from a pleasant dream involving several concubines. 'Sail on the port bow! A mile ahead, and closing fast!'

Annoyed, Karrek sat up and bellowed, 'So what?'

'She's set a course straight at us, sir!'

Beside him, the agent was looking watchful and wary. More than anything else, that made the Captain suspicious. With a speed and agility unusual in a man of his years, he sprinted to the port rail and stared at the approaching ship.

Of course, she was also driven by sorcery, but at a far swifter rate. Her sails, patched unpainted canvas, swelled out before her masts, and her bow-wave curved thick and creamy as she cut remorselessly through the water. Karrek stared at her in horror. The *Sea Urchin* was small and slow, her crew virtually unarmed save for a few bows and spears. And the other ship had '*pirate*' written all over her, as clearly as if the letters had been painted across her sails.

It couldn't be a pirate, surely. Local sea robbers infested certain parts of the Scatterlings, and Fabrizis sometimes raided Annatal or even Onnak: but not here, not between Tekkt and Balki, in an area regularly patrolled by the Toktel'yan Navy precisely to keep raiders away.

In appalled disbelief, Karrek watched the inexorable approach of his fate. He thought of his precious cargo, valuable but much too bulky to interest a pirate. He also remembered his passenger's luggage, which had included a wooden box, iron-bound, locked, and far too heavy for its size.

Resistance would be futile, and they had no hope of outrunning their attackers. Captain Karrek gave the order to heave to. Then, with his crew crowded along the rail, he watched with unwilling admiration as the pirate swooped close, came about, and kissed his old tub's bulging sides as sweetly as if she had been some fair and delicate maiden.

The raider's deck was crowded with ferocious-looking men, all carrying swords or daggers. Karrek noted the squad of archers at bow and stern, and knew that he had been right to surrender. At least they had a chance of survival, although their lives now depended on the pirate Captain's mercy. And compassionate men did not generally take to sea robbery.

The man who leaped lightly from ship to ship, ignoring the narrow but lethal gap between them, did not inspire Karrek with much hope for his future well-being. Unlike his crew, who by the look of them came from every land and island between Fabriz and Ma'alkwen, the pirate Captain was unmistakably an aristocratic Toktel'yan. Unusually, however, he wore a brief sailor's tunic, with a curved Ma'alkwen sword and a gold-hilted dagger stuck into the belt, and his curling black hair was very long and tied loosely back with a strip of bright red rag. He stood on the merchant ship's white scrubbed deck, surveying her crew, while behind him the rest of the pirates swarmed over the rail like a tide of cockroaches, eager for plunder.

Captain Karrek approached the man who now held his life in his keeping, his hands turned palm-up before him to show that he was unarmed. He halted a few paces away, just out of reach of that wicked blue-steel sword, and said formally, 'I surrender myself to you, with my ship and my men, and beg for your mercy.'

'If you behave yourselves, you'll have it,' said the pirate, and grinned, showing white, uneven teeth, with a gap between the front pair at the top.

Behind him, Karrek heard the agent suck in his breath, perhaps in recognition. The Captain said curiously, 'Who are you?'

'My men call me the Madman,' said the pirate. He drew his sword and tossed it lightly in the air, caught it left-handed as it spiralled towards the deck, and brandished it with swift and menacing grace. Several of the robbers sniggered, and Karrek took an involuntary step backwards.

The man stuck the sword back into his belt, and began instead to fiddle with the gold hilt of his dagger. 'What's your cargo?'

Karrek said hastily, 'Seasoned timber from Lelyent. Cotton from Kannt. Silk from Tatht and Kerenth.'

'Really? Is that all? Search it,' the pirate said over his shoulder. 'Any gold, silver, jewels and spices up on the deck. Annatal too – leave his sorcerer a day's worth. Weapons as well, and we could do with some decent wine. And hurry – we haven't got all afternoon. U'ugar, round up the crew and guard them. How many men do you command, Captain?'

'Eighteen. And one passenger.'

'A passenger? Where is he?'

Karrek looked round. Without surprise, he saw that the mysterious man had vanished. A moment's thought told him that if the pirates found the money-box, the agent would have to be killed, or he'd report back to his master, and Karrek would probably be knifed in some dark alley somewhere. That was what usually happened to anyone who incurred the Spymaster's displeasure, however undeserved.

'A tall dark man with a scar on his hand,' he said. 'One of Olyak's messengers, I think. You might find his cabin worth a search.'

The pirate gave him a wide, flashing smile. The numerous rings in his ears glittered in the sunlight as he laughed. 'Oh, might we? Come on, men – I smell the tang of gold!'

Herded into a huddle with the rest of his crew, Karrek watched and listened as the robbers wrenched up the hatches and streamed down into the hold. Silently, he prayed to Kaylo, who dispensed good luck, that they wouldn't damage his cloth, wouldn't kill anyone – except the agent – and wouldn't take anything – except the agent's money-box. He knew, of course, that the pirates would probably loot his ship and then burn or scuttle her with all hands. But somehow, he still hoped that they might be spared.

In what seemed like a frighteningly short time, the pirate Captain appeared again in front of Karrek. He held the dagger in his left hand, but the blade was still clean of blood. He said briefly, 'There's no sign of that agent – though we've found his strong-box. I wonder whom he was planning to kill?'

'I don't ask unnecessary questions,' said Karrek, eyeing the knife, which was of Gulkeshi make and decorated with a pattern of allegedly magical runes. 'He told me he was a trader, and he paid me well. I had no reason to refuse him passage.'

'But you had a very good idea what he might really be,' the pirate pointed out. 'Don't look so worried, Captain. In your place I'd have done likewise. Refusing one of the Spymaster's agents has the same effect as refusing to breathe. Where do you suppose he is? And you know, don't you, that we'd better find him, or there'll be no point in letting you go.'

'Let us go?' said Karrek, hoarse with relief.

'Yes. I may be a pirate,' said the Toktel'yan, with that wide, untrustworthy smile. 'But unlike most members of my family, I don't enjoy killing for the sake of it. Now, have you any hiding places on your ship? Secret compartments, cubby-holes, that sort of thing?'

Karrek opened his mouth to deny it. A dark shape plunged to the deck in front of him, arm raised to strike. He saw the dagger flash, and instinctively quailed. The blow, however, was not meant for him.

Quicker than thought, the pirate whipped his sword from his belt. There was a sickening sound, somewhere between a thud and a squelch, as the thin blade sliced into the agent's body. With a gurgling moan, he collapsed in a bleeding heap, almost at Karrek's feet.

'We forgot to look upwards,' said the pirate, and grinned ruefully.

'Good thing my reactions are quick.' He walked forward and rested the point of his sword on the dying man's chest. 'Who were you paid to kill, spy? Was it me, by any chance?'

The agent's face was grey and distorted with pain, but his answer came clearly. 'You amongst others, Lord Kazhian.'

Kazhian, the drowned and unregretted son of the new Emperor. Karrek stared at him in astonishment. 'But you're supposed to be dead.'

'Reports have exaggerated. I am, as you can see, still alive, and I intend to remain so. Unlike this unsavoury sample of villainy. Who's your master now? Is Olkanno still spinning his web like a fat and venomous spider?'

The agent was dying fast, but he could still laugh. 'No. He's Chief Minister. Arkun is the new Spymaster.'

'Arkun.' Kazhian's face was quietly reflective, hiding any stronger emotion. 'Well, he's risen far and fast, hasn't he? But you, my friend, will rise no more.' He pressed hard on the sword. As the blade went in, the agent choked, writhed convulsively, and became still.

'That'll keep the sharks happy,' said Kazhian. 'If you and your men behave themselves, Captain, he's all they'll get today. Throw him overboard!'

Two of the pirates heaved the bloodstained corpse over the side. Their Captain turned to survey the disappointingly small collection of valuables that his men had discovered during their search. The dead agent's strong-box was easily the most significant item. If it did contain money, though, it was plunder well worth taking.

Karrek watched as the haul was transferred to the pirate vessel by its cheerfully chanting crew. He still couldn't quite believe that he, his men and his ship were all going to survive this experience. Silently, he gave thanks for the agent's presence. If he and his box hadn't been on board, then Kazhian would probably have sunk them out of pique. Outlawed pirates, even pirates who were the sons of Emperors, couldn't afford to be squeamish. And he had killed the agent with no compunction whatsoever.

'You're a lucky man, Captain. I caught you on one of my good days.'

'Yes, Lord Kazhian. I am very grateful.'

The pirate surveyed him, his eyes narrowed and his brown hand resting lightly on the hilt of his sword. 'It would appear that rumours of my continued existence have reached Toktel'yi. You may add to the tales, if you like. Swear that I killed that agent with my bare hands, and then fed him piece by piece to my tame sharks. And then perhaps my father will come after me himself.'

'Your father, Lord Kazhian? But—'

'Yes, my father the Emperor can't wait to see me dead.' Kazhian's long, mobile mouth twisted suddenly with bitterness. 'But not, I can assure you, half as much as I want *him* dead. Tell him that, Captain, if you ever meet him!'

He turned and leaped across to his own craft with casual agility. Karrek watched as he waved in farewell. Pushed apart by poles, the two vessels lay briefly idle in the blue, clear water. Then the pirate ship's sails filled, her bow turned, and slowly, gently, she began to move away from the *Sea Urchin*, still becalmed.

With unbounded relief and gratitude, Karrek uttered a thankful prayer to Kaylo, Lord of Life and Luck, and then set about returning his ship to something approaching her normal working condition, or they wouldn't reach Balki by nightfall.

'Enough gold to bribe half the island, from the Governor downwards.'

The strong-box had proved resistant to Kazhian's subtler attempts to open it, and in the end he'd called for an axe. The coins, bright new-minted Imperials, lay in a yellow stream over the deck, a feast for the eyes of his crew, gathered greedily round. Their Captain bent and picked one up. It bore an unpleasantly accurate image of his father's head and shoulders. He stared with loathing at the familiar patrician profile, and then flipped the piece back on to the heap. 'Zendeq? Count it. Divide it by thirty-five. Then I'll check it. And remember, I know all the tricks, and all the possible hiding-places, even the most unlikely ones. If necessary, I'll search them personally.'

Several pirates laughed. Zendeq, a huge Fabrizi with a gold chain between nose and lip and many Imperials' worth of bullion attached to other parts of his anatomy, laughed too, entirely without rancour. Kazhian had chosen him for the task precisely because, unusually for a Fabrizi, he was honest, good-natured, and too big to be threatened.

He watched as the thirty-five columns of coins grew to a finger's length each, and smiled. So far, piracy had proved to be a very profitable solution to the problems that had faced him after his rescue of Megren and his family.

Nine months previously, he had taken the biggest gamble of his life when he had told Sargenay to steer the *Wind of Morning* straight into the black heart of the storm. The little courier ship, with her crew and passengers, had survived the howling winds and the monstrous waves, though with the loss of the mainmast and everything not nailed down to the deck. Under a single tattered mizzen-sail, she had struggled through the tempest towards Balki, her abused timbers leaking with every pitch and roll of the huge seas beneath her. And then, seized in the grip of the fierce Archipelagian tide that his exhausted weather-worker had been powerless to influence, she had been driven broadside on to the rocks known as the Dragon's Teeth, just off Balki's northern coast.

The mizzen-mast had collapsed, killing several members of the crew, and Megren. Many more had drowned as they tried to swim to the safety of the shore. There had been only a dozen survivors, amongst them Kazhian, Sargenay, and Megren's wife Trinn and his son Sarrek.

They had struggled ashore half-drowned, battered by the waves and the rocks, and found that their desperate fight for life had provided an interesting spectacle for a large group of surly, uncooperative Balkians.

Kazhian, close to collapse, had begged them to help. They stared at him sullenly. Then Trinn began to shout at them in the uncouth local dialect. With reluctance, they pushed a small skiff into the sea and began to search for survivors. Three of Kadjak's daughters were saved, and five members of the crew. Some women brought blankets, and carts arrived to take them to the nearest farm.

If it had not been for Trinn, Kazhian was certain that the Balkians would have left them to die of cold on the beach, while they plundered the wreck. But although she must have been distraught at Megren's tragic death, so close to safety, Trinn did not show it. Instead, she poured all her considerable energy into haranguing her reluctant countrymen, and they grudgingly obeyed her.

Kazhian could remember very little of his first month on Balki. Trying to ensure that the *Wind of Morning* survived the tempest, he had ignored the injuries he had received at B'kenn's villa, and exhaustion, coupled with the guilt he felt for the deaths of Megren and his crew, had weakened him further. Trinn's nursing skills and Sargenay's powers of Healing had been stretched to their limits, and his weather-worker told him afterwards that he had been certain that Kazhian would die. And indeed, such had been his despair in the first dreadful days after the wreck, that he had wanted Olyak to take him at last.

Olyak had not obliged: and slowly, painfully, Kazhian had recovered. Trinn had told him, with a brave smile that did not reach her unhappy eyes, that she did not blame him for Megren's death, or for the loss of Kadjak's wife, concubine and four children who had also perished with the *Wind of Morning*. And Kazhian did not have the heart to tell her that her words made no difference, for he would always blame himself.

But as he regained his strength, his black mood had lightened. At least, despite Arkun, despite the storm, despite the notorious Balki coast, he had saved Trinn and her son and three of B'kenn's children. His actions had made a difference. And with any luck, thanks to the pieces of wood and the nameboard that he had thrown into the sea before they were engulfed by the storm, the Toktel'yans would assume that the *Wind of Morning* had sunk with all hands.

Balki was the most backward and neglected of all the major islands in the Archipelago. It was supposed to have more goats than people, and Balkian men were popularly assumed, in more sophisticated places, to be a bunch of half-witted sheep-shaggers. The Governor was a mediocre time-server addicted to ral, the raw, fiery and sometimes lethal spirit distilled in every farmhouse. The garrison was largely made up of men sent to Balki as a punishment for incompetence, or because they couldn't afford to bribe their way to a more congenial posting, and the natives were hostile, obstreperous and insular.

As a result, no one in authority was told about the end of the *Wind of Morning*. Debris from the wreck was collected, like all driftwood, for fuel and building materials. Within two days, the beach where the survivors had staggered ashore was as white and pristine as it had been at the creation of the world. The people who had watched them were all sworn to secrecy, won over by the fact that Trinn was a native of the island, and also by the delightful prospect of outsmarting the hatred Toktel'yans.

So their presence on Balki had remained a secret, right up to the turn of the year. It was a time of celebration and over-indulgence, and the subsistence farmers on this part of the island took it in turns to host the festival. Over the five days of the holiday, hundreds of men, women and children journeyed from holding to holding, to drink and feast and dance.

The farm which had sheltered the survivors was owned by a small, ancient man called Hetten. He had a stooped back, arthritic joints and a command of invective that advancing years had not withered, but he was a cousin of Trinn's brother-in-law, and happy to give them refuge for a while. Soon after the wreck, one of his sons had carried a message to Trinn's father, who owned a more substantial estate in the most fertile part of the island, to tell him that his daughter and grandson were safe: and once it had become apparent that Kazhian would live, she had taken Sarrek and Megren's three young half-sisters, and gone back to her family.

The tedious process of convalescence kept Kazhian indoors for much too long: he craved action, any occupation for his quick, restless mind. As he regained his health and strength, he found some satisfaction working on the bare, scrubby land along this barren coast, helping to repair stone walls, herd cattle, and build a barn. It was hard, laborious toil, but it got him fit again, and kept him busy. And it gave him some opportunity to think about his future.

Despite the long feud with his father, Kazhian had enjoyed a gilded upbringing. Doors opened wide indeed for Vessels of the Blood Imperial, and a brilliant career in the Toktel'yan Navy had seemed a certainty. Even after the disastrous wreck of the *Spear of Vengeance*, which had effectively ended any further chance of commanding a fighting ship, he had been given the *Wind of Morning*. Not everyone was prepared to listen to Eska'anen's spiteful denunciations of his elder son, and Kazhian had impressed his superiors with his seamanship, intelligence and flair. The little courier ship carried no glory and no prestige, but Kazhian knew that he was lucky to have her.

But now he had her no longer. His father was Emperor, and his father wanted him dead. So he was effectively outlawed, with no more than the clothes he stood up in, the gold on his hands and in his ears, and the contents of his money-belt, which he had prudently saved from the wreck. And now that Trinn had gone back to her father, he couldn't rely on Hetten's generosity for much longer.

Five of his crew had survived, and they had stayed with him, out of loyalty or cowardice. So had Sargenay, although he at least was capable of making a good living with his skills as a sorcerer and Healer. And Kazhian, though grateful to his weather-worker, who had now saved his life twice, was not sure whether to be glad or sorry.

At first, the man's languid, affected manner had irritated him, even though he knew that Sargenay was unusually good at his job. He didn't ask why he had left an apparently successful practice in Toktel'yi for the much less comfortable and much less prestigious life of a weather-worker: he was certain he wouldn't like the answer. But gradually, a rather precarious affinity had grown up between them, and Kazhian had begun to treat Sargenay with the casual, affectionate derision which he reserved for his friends.

He knew, of course, that the sorcerer was not interested in women, and he knew also, if he was honest with himself, that Sargenay wanted rather more than friendship. Kazhian had attracted several men in his life, as well as women, and he knew that look of desire when he saw it. And because he had come to like the weather-worker, he hoped that he would settle for less.

The farm buildings had been decorated for the festival, with faded coloured banners and bunches of dried flowers, and the long trestle tables in Hetten's big barn were laden with food. Sargenay sat in the centre of the stone floor, his patched and tattered robes arranged artistically round him, performing a series of Illusions for the delight of a crowd of children. Exotic beasts paraded, fought, flew and pranced before their fascinated eyes, and the applause when the last one faded was unrestrained and enthusiastic.

'If I must prostitute my Art,' said Sargenay, brushing the dust and chaff from his garments with an elegantly disdainful hand, 'then I do prefer an appreciative audience.' He smiled at Kazhian, and counted the coins in his hand. 'This should buy our keep for a few more days. I've got some ral – do you want to share it with me?'

They found a space in a corner, and settled down comfortably on a seat made of straw bales and grain sacks. The ral went down very quickly, and Kazhian bought another flask. He would have given half his gold for a pipe of khlar, but all his supplies had been lost with the *Wind of Morning*, and there seemed to be none at all on Balki.

'So,' he said to Sargenay, when the second flask was almost empty. 'What do we do now?'

'Now? I know what I'd like to do with that luscious boy over there,' said the sorcerer wistfully. 'But Balkians aren't as enlightened and tolerant as the rest of the Empire.'

'Exactly. Why bother with humans when you've got all those nice tempting goats?'

Sargenay snorted with laughter. 'Don't let them hear you call them sheep-shaggers. They're very sensitive about it.'

'I wouldn't dream of it,' said Kazhian, grinning. He felt reckless, carefree, powerful, as if the future, so recently grim and uncertain, now seemed to beckon enticingly, wide and free and open. There was a girl, tall and dark and pretty, who had already sent him several significant looks. He had been celibate for much too long, and the thought of a woman in his arms was almost as intoxicating as the ral.

'She's eyeing you again,' Sargenay said, watching the girl. 'It's funny, she reminds me of someone I used to know.'

'A woman? I didn't think you were interested.'

'I'm not – not for sex – but this one was a friend,' said Sargenay, and a look of sorrow suffused his smooth, handsome face. 'A dear friend – a very dear friend. She was like the sister I never had.'

'What happened to her?' Kazhian asked curiously.

Sargenay brushed a hand over his eyes. 'Dead,' he said sadly. 'I imagine she must be, anyway. Ba'alekkt would never have let her live.'

Kazhian swallowed a crude remark and waited. This seemed to be the heart of the mystery surrounding the sorcerer.

'She tried to kill him, you see,' Sargenay said at last. 'On Tekkt, a year ago.'

'I heard about that,' Kazhian said, taking a generous swig of ral. 'But she escaped, didn't she? Wasn't she a tavern-keeper in the Old City?'

'She ran the Golden Djarlek,' Sargenay said. He glanced at his companion. 'Don't tell anyone this, will you? Olkanno has a long memory. Even though Ba'alekkt's dead now, my name is probably still on some list.'

'Whichever list yours is on, mine's certainly at the top, and underlined in triplicate,' Kazhian reminded him grimly. 'So that's why you turned to weather-working, is it? I wondered.'

'It had something to do with it,' Sargenay admitted. He sighed, and took the ral. 'You've finished it. Come on, let's get really drunk. Every time I think of Mallaso, I want to weep.'

'Well, don't think about her,' Kazhian said brutally. 'Think instead about what we're going to do with ourselves. Hetten wants us gone, that's obvious.' He stood up, swaying slightly, and held out his hand. 'If we want any more ral, we'll need some of your cash.'

'Bloody pirate,' Sargenay grumbled, struggling to his feet and kicking at his extravagant and hampering robes. 'Use your own money – I bought the last one.'

Kazhian was staring at him, his face suddenly alight with inspiration. 'Sod the ral. That's what we'll do.'

'Do what?' Sargenay's face was full of bleary bewilderment.

'Turn pirate. Just think of it, my ragged old tame weather-worker – gold for the taking, a life of excitement and freedom, and the chance to seriously annoy the Emperor. Couldn't be better. What d'you say?'

'Sounds fine.' Sargenay waved at the ral-seller. 'Only one problem. We haven't got a ship, remember?'

'Don't be such a spoil-sport,' said Kazhian, his smile huge with drunken delight. 'You're talking to the best, the most daring, the wiliest Captain in all the Southern Seas. No ship? A trifling inconvenience. There's bound to be several to choose from in Balki Port. We can plan it tomorrow. In the meantime, I'm going to celebrate.'

'How?' Sargenay was trying to find the right coins for the ral-seller.

'What d'you think, weather-worker? I'm going to find that girl.'

The rest of the day had passed in a very pleasant blur of self-indulgence, but Kazhian would always remember, with absolute clarity, the moment when he had chosen his new career. Kaylo had been smiling on him then, and the Lord of Life had been good to him ever since. In Balki Port, he had recruited a motley crew of villains and criminals that would have frightened the life out of an orthodox Toktel'yan Captain, and stolen the *Sea Serpent*, a lovely Annatal spice trader built for lightness and speed, with ridiculous ease. They had been living off the proceeds of piracy for three months now, and the contents of the agent's strong-box should ensure his men's loyalty for some time to come.

Yes, life on the whole was sweet. And if the Emperor chanced to hear of his elder son's new vocation, with any luck it would bring on a fatal seizure.

Smiling, Kazhian ordered the steersman to set course for the secluded bay that was their usual base, with a village nearby where he and his crew could spend some of their profits on women and ral.

CHAPTER TEN

'I regret, Imperial Majesty, that there is no doubt of it whatsoever. Your son Kazhian is alive.'

Eska'anen glared at his Spymaster, and Arkun gazed imperturbably back. Physically, he could not have been more different from his short, plump predecessor, being tall and thin, with red hair and a hawk's nose, but the air of contained menace was very similar.

'Tell me,' said the Emperor through gritted teeth. 'Tell me exactly what happened.'

'Hearing of the rumours that Kazhian had survived, I despatched an agent to investigate and, if the stories proved to be true, to kill him. He was one of my best men, well-prepared and well-funded. I did not anticipate any difficulty.'

'But?'

'But by an unlucky coincidence, the ship on which he was a passenger was taken by pirates off Balki. Their Captain was your son. There is no doubt about it – the description was specific. He had long curling hair and green eyes, there were many rings in his ears, and he used his left hand in preference to his right.'

'So the son of a bitch is alive,' said Eska'anen viciously.

'Unfortunately, he killed my agent as the man was attempting to carry out my orders, and the money was stolen. The Captain and crew were released, together with their vessel and its cargo, and reported to the Governor of Balki, who relayed the information to me.'

'So Kazhian left them alive to tell the tale? How very foolish of him. Still, I shall ensure that his curious omission is swiftly rectified.' Eska'anen smiled. 'So – what is your remedy for this sorry state of affairs?'

'Kazhian appears to be operating from Balki. As you know, its coastline is very rocky and dangerous to shipping. He will have local knowledge, and local assistance – Balkians are notoriously unhelpful and resistant to proper authority. I suggest a squadron of galleys, backed up by about ten thousand extra soldiers, and considerable reserves of cash. He's clever, but not so clever that he can evade capture indefinitely.'

'I can't spare the men,' Eska'anen said. 'Even now, twenty-five thousand are on their way to Djebb.' He rose to his feet and glared at Arkun. 'In any case, you are extraordinarily profligate. An entire squadron, to capture one small ship? A thousand soldiers, to hunt for one man?'

'Any less would be a waste of time and effort. If you really want to seize your son, you must do it with overwhelming force, or you will be a laughing-stock – especially if he eludes you.'

Eska'anen, so conscious of his Imperial dignity, did not like the prospect at all. He said bitterly, 'He's as wily and slippery as a snake. He has already escaped us once, and I do not intend to give him the chance to do so again. Very well, Spymaster. You may have your squadron and your ships.'

'Thank you, Imperial Majesty,' Arkun said, and made obeisance with considerable relief. The Emperor was peculiarly blind where his two sons were concerned, discerning imaginary virtues in Suken, while treating Kazhian's very real abilities with dismissive contempt. And all because he had hated one mother and loved the other – as far as Eska'anen could love anyone.

Arkun suspected that if his Imperial master despatched his entire fleet and fifty thousand soldiers to Balki, Kazhian would still evade them. With his talent for outrageous impudence, he would probably sail back to Toktel'yi while they were fruitlessly searching the island, and set fire to the Palace. An involuntary smile twitched his mouth at the thought, and he admonished himself severely. The childhood bonds between him and his cousin must be severed, or he would be guilty of neglecting his duty. He should forget the liking and companionship which had illuminated that long ago summer, and pursue Kazhian with as much vigour and ruthlessness as if he were indeed the vicious and depraved criminal of Eska'anen's warped paternal imagination.

When Arkun had left, the squat, unprepossessing figure of his predecessor slid round the screen in the corner of the Imperial audience chamber. Olkanno's dark, chubby face was thoughtful as he addressed the Emperor. 'Imperial Majesty, before we discuss the Prince of Tulyet, may I make a suggestion regarding your son?'

'Kazhian?' Eska'anen's mouth was set in a thin grim line. 'The only suggestion you may make is as to the manner of his death. I spend many hours debating the precise method I shall use to kill him, when I finally get my hands on him.'

'Imperial Majesty, do you think that perhaps, out of your natural feelings of parternal disappointment, you have invested Kazhian with an importance he does not actually possess?'

There was a chilly silence. Eska'anen gazed with cold hostility at his Chief Minister. 'Explain yourself.'

'He is a renegade and an outlaw. By all means put a price on his head – Balki is so poor and backward that a hundred gold Imperials should suffice. But it might be unwise to overreact to this incident. What real harm can one man do? Arkun is wrong – you would be better off sending those ships and men to Tatht. The Governor there is very worried.'

'I know. I have read his reports.' Eska'anen chewed his lip, and Olkanno's opaque observant eyes noted the tiny lapse in his usually rigid self-control. 'But in my opinion, he is a timorous fool. Those stories and rumours are all nonsense, fairy tales to incite the credulous. Of course there will be no increase in taxes.'

'Yet,' Olkanno said softly. 'But Ba'alekkt's lunatic invasion preparations swallowed up an alarming proportion of your Treasury, Imperial Majesty. If you are to contain the rebellion in Djebb, you will need to buy back the loyalty of the defecting soldiers, and increase the pay of the rest of the Army, to ensure that they do not mutiny as well. If you waste time, money and men in what will probably be a very public wild goose chase all over Balki, you risk losing valuable prestige and respect, as well as depleting the Treasury still further. Send a couple of galleys and half-a-dozen agents. Put a price on his head, as large as you like. But don't let him make a fool of you, Imperial Majesty. The scoundrel is not worth the risk.'

'And what if he wants to be Emperor-in-Waiting?'

'Only the Emperor has the right to appoint his official heir,' Olkanno reminded him. 'And Kazhian has hardly shown much interest in the prospect. Besides, he knows that you will never name him. Your younger son holds the only place in your heart.'

'Yes,' said Eska'anen, but his voice did not soften as it usually did when speaking of Suken. 'Yes, he does. But he is too young for such responsibility. He must wait until he is ready.'

'I agree, Imperial Majesty. He is doing as well under Arkun's direction as he did under mine – even better, if reports are true. In a year or two, he will be ripe for promotion as befits his great rank.'

'That's exactly what I told him,' Eska'anen said. 'Unfortunately, he did not agree. He wishes to enjoy all the trappings of his status – his own Palace, retinue, even a Governorship. But in my opinion, he is too young and untried for such a position.'

'But of course, like any youth of vigour and ability, he is impatient.' Olkanno's smile was indulgent. 'Well, I can understand his enthusiasm. And I am sure, Imperial Majesty, that you would prefer him to show such encouraging signs of an independent spirit, rather than feebly agreeing to every suggestion. It is an indication of his inward strength – and weak men do not make good Emperors.'

'As my brother Djamal's mediocre career amply demonstrated,' said Eska'anen. He sighed heavily. 'But I must confess that Suken has been a little disappointing lately. For instance, he told me that he does not wish to marry Djeneb.'

'I hope that you told him in detail about all the advantages to him of such a match.'

'I did indeed. I refused to listen to his arguments – which in any case were extremely trivial. It is not her looks that count, it's her blood. And if he marries her, then no one else can.'

A Toktel'yan man could take as many wives or concubines as he wished, or could afford, and cast them out with impunity if they displeased him. A wife, however, was forbidden to desert or divorce her husband, and even if he died, she could not marry again. Once wed to Suken, Djeneb's Imperial blood would only benefit Eska'anen's descendants.

'But he can wait for a while,' said the Emperor. 'There is no hurry. The girl is only just eighteen, and apparently good breeding stock.' He glanced up at his Chief Minister, 'You mentioned the Prince of Tulyet, did you not?'

'I did, Imperial Majesty. It has come to my notice that he has been threatening to spread scandalous stories about the Lady Djeneb – stories that will seriously damage her reputation, if they ever become current in Toktel'yi.'

'Stories? What stories?'

'That she ran away from the Palace, last year, rather than marry him.'

'Is that true?'

'It is true that he tried to seize her and force her into marriage. Fortunately, one of my agents in her household was able to assist her to escape. You were still in Tamat, but I did not think that you would wish her to be wasted on that stupid lout.'

'I certainly do not. Well? Go on.'

'Arkun, who was engaged on another business, discovered her hiding-place quite by chance, and was able to escort her back to the Palace before word could spread. Naturally, strenuous efforts were made to ensure that there was no whisper of scandal. But of course the

Prince of Tulyet is harder to silence than a few talkative eunuchs and slave-girls. Or so he thinks.'

'He is mistaken. So why is he only threatening to spread these malicious rumours?'

'He still wishes to marry her. He has informed me that if he does not obtain your permission, he will tell all Toktel'yi that she was with a lover – thus ensuring that Suken, or anyone else, will be unable to marry her.'

'If she is still a virgin, that can be proved.'

'Of course it can, Imperial Majesty. But although I am certain that the Lady Djeneb is still untouched, it would be easier, and quicker, and altogether much more satisfactory, to get rid of the Prince of Tulyet.'

'And he has no heirs. His brother left only daughters. Tulyet could be formally annexed to the Empire.'

'My thinking precisely, Imperial Majesty.' Olkanno smiled broadly. 'And Skallyan is no longer young. There will be no surprise if he dies during a drinking bout, or after a heavy session in the bath-house. Vessels of the Blood Imperial do not, alas, seem to live as long as other, lesser men – a life of excess and debauchery usually takes its toll sooner rather than later.'

Eska'anen, whose private habits were rigorously under control, smiled in response. 'I shall leave it to you, Olkanno. You are very skilled at such matters. I could not wish for a better assistant – you are my right-hand man, and you can be assured that your devotion to my service will not go unrewarded.'

'Your Imperial Majesty is too kind to this humble servant,' Olkanno murmured, with pleased deference. 'And if I may be so presumptuous – your son, Suken – perhaps a private word from a trusted and respected mentor in the ear of a confused but essentially loyal and dutiful son will do much to heal any breach.'

A memory of Suken, his expression just short of a sneer, rose to haunt Eska'anen. If his favourite, his beloved, his *only* son turned against him, then all the pomp and power of the Onyx Throne was merely a hollow mockery. The boy had been insolent, but perhaps Olkanno, whom he revered, could persuade him to see reason.

'Of course – an excellent idea,' he said, and smiled at his Chief Minister with hope and gratitude. 'And meanwhile, I think I will honour the Lady Djeneb with a visit. It is time her future was made plain to her, and her obedience ensured.'

*

Djeneb knew that if her life did not change soon, she would go mad. She did not care if her situation changed for the better, or even grew worse, so long as it *changed*. And yet she could see no end, no end at all, to this grey fog of tedium and petty repression that throttled her endless, identical days.

She could see now that her brief foray out into the real world, the world outside the Women's Quarters, had been risky, foolhardy and terrifying in its potential for disaster. But she could not regret her escape. If she had stayed, she would now be married to Skallyan, or, more likely, condemned at the age of eighteen to a lifelong, barren and lonely widowhood. Centuries ago, women in Toktel'yi had thrown themselves on to their dead husbands' pyres rather than live on in a dim and humiliating limbo, forbidden to remarry and treated with callous contempt. Some, of course, especially if they had children, could find contentment. But Djeneb knew that she, too, would have killed herself rather than endure such an existence for perhaps thirty or forty years.

At least she still had hope, the hope that soon she would marry, and exchange one stifling prison for another. But always, at the back of her mind, was the feel of a ship's graceful dance through the waves, the brush of wind on her skin and the sounds of the sea: and a man's eyes, gazing at her with unaccustomed admiration and respect.

She thought about Kazhian constantly: she could not help it. And when she heard about his death in the great storm, she refused to believe it. He had seemed so alive, so full of vitality that he had thrummed with it like a djarlek string. She could recall every detail of his appearance, and every word he had said to her. And the twists of fate seemed bitter indeed, for if he had not been estranged from his father, he would now be Emperor-in-Waiting – and therefore, her most likely husband.

But if he hadn't rebelled, he would not have been Kazhian. Instead, she would almost certainly marry Suken. And she hoped that he would prove to be at least a little like his half-brother.

No one, though, came to her with marriage plans. The Women's Quarters were guarded day and night, presumably to prevent Skallyan carrying her off – or to stop her escaping again. Even the little excursions which had once brightened her days – trips on the river in the Imperial Barge, attending the horse races on the beach, frivolous shopping in the Old City – had stopped altogether. And, worst of all, her household, many of whom had known her since childhood, had been replaced by Eska'anen on his accession. The people around her now were strangers, who treated her with polite but distant courtesy, and her loneliness was absolute.

So when her new Chief Eunuch informed her, with much fussing and bowing and rubbing of hands, that the Emperor himself was to visit her in person, this very afternoon, what a wonderful event, what a tremendous honour, she felt a huge and joyful lifting of her heart. At last, this must be the news for which she had been waiting. For why else would Eska'anen bother to come, except to tell her that she would be married?

So, with the help of her ladies, twittering and bustling and chattering around her like a flock of bright birds, she dressed herself with extraordinary care. A bath in sweet-scented water was followed by a relaxing massage with aromatic oils. Her face was painted, with great care, to emphasize her best features, her lustrous eyes and full red lips, for the Emperor might wish to see her unveiled. From the scores of gowns hanging in her closet, she chose the richest, in a deep red silk, woven through with gold. She had been so miserable, over the past months, that she had lost a considerable amount of weight, and though she was still far from slender, the clinging garment emphasized her voluptuous curves. The woman she saw in the mirror hardly conformed to Toktel'yan ideals. But she was none the less startlingly seductive.

So it was with a new sense of hope and self-assurance that she entered her private reception chamber, where once she had received Skallyan, and made graceful obeisance to her uncle the Emperor.

Eska'anen had met Djeneb only rarely, on public and ceremonial occasions, and he remembered her as a veiled, clumsily overweight figure. Surprised out of his usual urbane equanimity, he stared at the buxom, enticing woman kneeling before him with growing desire. He had never been particularly interested in sex: his three wives had been acquired for financial, dynastic and political reasons, and since the untimely death of Suken's mother he had only kept a couple of concubines, resorting to them more out of habit than need. Like every other feeling, he had always managed to keep his physical urges under control, and to find this girl exciting his loins was at once disturbing and strangely invigorating.

'Get up, my dear,' he said, in the deep, pleasant voice that was, disconcertingly, so similar to Kazhian's. 'Put back your veil.'

Her heart thumping, Djeneb rose to her feet. Kazhian had exposed her face, and she had endured it with defiant aplomb, but this was different. Her future depended on the Emperor's reaction. Either he would marry her to Suken, giving her prestige, status, a purpose, children: or she would be left here to rot until she died in a morass of boredom.

With broad, trembling hands, she pulled off the gold-embroidered veil, and stood with eyes cast modestly down, too nervous to watch his reaction.

The silence dragged on. Eska'anen gazed at the sweeping dark lashes, the blunt nose, the full, slightly drooping mouth. He wanted her, more than he had wanted any woman for years. If it had not been for the guards, the courtiers, the circle of watching eunuchs, he would have been tempted to take her then and there on the floor of her reception chamber. And the sense of astonishment was almost as overwhelming as his sudden lust. Why, out of all women, did he desire this one? His concubines were slender, fragile creatures with tiny hands and feet and pretty, dainty faces. By comparison, Djeneb was as coarse as a peasant.

Then he realized that she reminded him of Hannek, his beloved third wife, Suken's mother. She too had been plump and shapely, and she had also been as gratifyingly ardent in bed as any paid whore, with one crucial difference – her pleasure had been genuine. And if Djeneb was the same . . .

He would marry her himself. The stunning power and simplicity of the idea amazed him. Suken did not want her: indeed, his defiance of his father's wish had been the main cause of the rift between them. Well, he would let Suken pick another wife: there were plenty of aristocratic young ladies to choose from. The eldest of Skallyan's six nieces was nearly ready for marriage, and she was supposed to be pretty. Suken could marry her, take the title of Prince of Tulyet, found his dynasty, and thus be reconciled to his father. Eska'anen would find unlooked-for pleasure late in life, with the Lady Djeneb. She was his niece, but that was no bar to marriage under Toktel'yan law. And if she bore him sons, Suken would still be Emperor-in-Waiting, but Eska'anen's line would be safe in case anything happened to his heir.

The more he thought about it, the more appropriate and felicitous the idea seemed. He had prepared a little speech, telling Djeneb that she was intended for his son: instead, he said quietly, 'My dear lady – you should know that, within a few days, you will become my wife.'

Djeneb's head jerked up. Her eyes wide and dark with shock, she stared at him. '*Your* wife? But I thought—'

'I have not enjoyed the company and comfort of a wife for sixteen years. It is too long. I have decided to take another – and my choice, Lady Djeneb, has fallen on *you*.'

All round the room, she could hear gasps and murmurs of

amazement. Djeneb swallowed convulsively, and tried to shake her wayward emotions into obedience. It was so unexpected – so astonishing – so *appalling* . . .

He was old. Handsome, certainly, for his age, his face bearing, now that she was searching for it, more than a passing resemblance to Kazhian. But he lacked entirely the warmth, the humour, the irrepressible spontaneity and high spirits that had been his elder son's most attractive qualities. This man was ruthless and calculating, and his eyes were as cold and hard as stones. She'd heard the gossip about the fate of his first two wives, and fear flooded her. She was too inexperienced to realize that, ironically, for the first time for many years, Eska'anen had succumbed to impulse.

If she had married Suken, she would have escaped the stifling formality of the Palace, its petty rituals, its smothering luxury. She had imagined making a pleasant home with her new husband, having some say in running the household, a little freedom . . .

And instead, she would become an old man's wife, another appendage, walled up within the confines of the Imperial Women's Quarters, until his death. And since he was nearly three times her age, she would probably outlive him by thirty years or more – unless he tired of her, and had her discreetly murdered.

But she had no choice. This time, she couldn't run away from the golden cage awaiting her. She was the daughter and sister of Emperors. The Blood Imperial ran thick and strong in her veins: more potently, indeed, than in Eska'anen's. And so her pride spoke clearly to the man who wanted her, although she would never, until the Southern Sea boiled dry, want him.

'I am greatly honoured, Imperial Majesty. And I will gladly consent to be your wife.'

'*What?*' Suken stared at his former master in horror. '*He's* going to marry her? But he ordered *me* to marry her!'

'Although you did not wish to, so his Imperial Majesty informed me. But when he went to tell her the glad news, the sight of her beauty overwhelmed him.' Olkanno shook his head. 'He is a man in love.'

Suken made a derisive noise. 'My father has never loved anyone but himself. He makes a great display of paternal affection, but it's a complete sham. He's got all the feelings of a Delta Crocodile.' He paused, and then said softly, 'Did you say that the Lady Djeneb is . . . *beautiful*?'

Aware with satisfaction that his prey had seized the bait, Olkanno began to reel him in. 'Yes. he asked her to unveil. She is not as ugly as we have all assumed. In fact, she . . . how shall I put it? She gives promise of being a devoted and very ardent wife.'

'I see.' Suken's eyes glistened, and he licked his lips. 'And my cold fish of a father wants this hot property to warm his bed, does he? Well, I won't have it. He promised her to me, and by Kaylo's bones I'll have her!'

'Your father is the Emperor,' Olkanno reminded him. 'It is not for you to decide.'

'Oh, isn't it? I shall be Emperor myself one day – and if he doesn't watch out, it'll be sooner than he thinks!'

Olkanno's dark eyes gleamed. 'That is a very rash statement, if I may say so, Lord Suken. You are tottering on the brink of treason. If anyone should overhear—'

'He won't do anything to me,' Suken said scornfully. 'I'm the Emperor-in-Waiting. Even if Kazhian *is* alive, I'm his favourite son – his *only* son. Kill me, and his dynasty dies with him.'

'But not if he marries the Lady Djeneb. Your father is fit and healthy. He does not indulge in immoderate eating or drinking. He could well live for another twenty, even thirty years. His new wife might give him half-a-dozen sons from which to choose a new heir – and you will be left out in the dark.'

Suken's handsome face became suffused with rage and fear. 'He wouldn't! He loves me! I'm his favourite!'

'But as you yourself have just pointed out, His Imperial Majesty is a cold-blooded and devious man who has already arranged the deaths of half-a-dozen rivals in order to ascend the Onyx Throne. Only this morning, the Prince of Tulyet died suddenly and tragically of a seizure – and it was not, despite appearances, a natural death. Why should your father shrink from murdering you, if he considers you a danger? And once he is married to the Lady Djeneb, and breeding a new clutch of sons, your position grows less and less secure.'

Suken's eyes narrowed. 'Then there is only one solution, I must kill him before he kills me. And if I do it before the wedding, then I can have the Lady Djeneb for myself.'

'My thoughts exactly,' said Olkanno approvingly. 'It has long been my opinion that you are far more suited to wield the highest power than your father is. He is restricted by narrow cunning and self-interest – whereas you, Lord Suken, have intelligence, ability and breadth of vision – all qualities that will ensure that you become one of the greatest rulers this Empire has ever known.'

He saw in the young man's glistening eyes that he was both foolish and greedy enough to take the bait. And with carefully concealed satisfaction, he began to tell Suken exactly what he must do, to ensure he would soon occupy the Onyx Throne.

'You son wishes to see you, Imperial Majesty.'

Eska'anen gazed at his chief usher with annoyance. 'What, now? I am busy.' He indicated the pile of papers in front of him, all decrees and orders which required his signature to be effective under Toktel'yan law.

'He is outside, Imperial Majesty, and he is most insistent.'

The Emperor sighed, and put his pen back in the gold ink-pot. 'Very well. Send him in.'

As the usher bowed and went out, Eska'anen thought, with a pang of grief, how greatly his feelings for his beloved son had been changed, and in such a terrifyingly short space of time. Only a few days previously, the news of Suken's arrival would have enlivened his day. Now, however, he was dreading the next few moments, for not only did he mistrust his son, he also feared him.

The boy's familiar, slender figure slid elegantly round the door. He had dressed very handsomely, in a long dark green silk tunic with gold embroidery, and he carried a small packet in one hand. He made the humblest form of obeisance, and Eska'anen surveyed him with dawning hope. This was not the argumentative, petulant boy who had flounced out of his presence a few days ago: this was the old, dear Suken, properly respectful and obedient.

'I have come to apologize to you, Father,' he said. 'I was disrespectful and ungrateful when we last met, and I have felt much guilt and remorse ever since.' His dark eyes met Eska'anen's, and the Emperor saw that they were liquid with tears. 'Please forgive me, dear Father? I could not bear it if – if I had lost your affection for ever.'

'Oh, my dear boy.' Overwhelmed with delight and relief, Eska'anen rose from his desk and held out his hands in reconciliation. 'Of course I forgive you. I was overbearing, and over-hasty – the fault was not entirely yours. Sit down, and take some wine. There is still some of last year's Hailyan, and it was a very fine vintage.'

'Thank you, Father,' said Suken. Hesitatingly, he proffered the package. 'I have brought you a small gift – a very unworthy token of my repentance.'

Eska'anen smiled as he took it. 'You are very kind, dear boy. What is it?'

'A ship docked this morning from Onnak, with a cargo of spices. I know how you like to flavour your wine, and so I asked the Captain to make up this recipe specially. It is not much, but . . .'

'Perfect,' said Eska'anen, charmed. 'How thoughtful, Suken – how very thoughtful of you. Although I do not think this Hailyan needs such embellishment.'

'Oh,' said Suken, and his face drooped like a disappointed child's. At once, Eska'anen clapped him affectionately on the shoulder. 'But on this occasion, I shall make an exception. Menlekko?'

The usher appeared from outside. 'Yes, Imperial Majesty?'

'I want a jug of the Hailyan and two goblets. My son and I have several things to celebrate.'

'Certainly, Imperial Majesty,' said Menlekko, and withdrew.

'Several things, Father?' Suken enquired.

'Yes. I have decided that you need not after all marry the Lady Djeneb. The late and unlamented Prince of Tulyet has several nieces. The eldest is supposed to be a beauty, if that's what you're after, and she is a Vessel of the Blood Imperial twice over, through her mother, who was my half-sister, as well as her grandmother, who was my aunt. And even better, by marrying her you can assume the title of Prince of Tulyet, so you may have your province to govern after all. How will that suit you?'

'Oh, Father.' Suken's face was full of gratitude and relief. 'I don't know what to say – how very kind – thank you, Father, thank you.'

'And as the Lady Djeneb cannot remain single, I have decided to marry her myself.'

'But she's so young, Father! She's younger than me.'

'That does not matter. I have decided that I need the company and comfort of a wife. You will be occupied with your own bride, after all, and in Tulyet for long periods. The Lady Djeneb is young, certainly, but older women are invariably already wed, or widowed.' He studied his son, suddenly remembering how Suken, as a child, would always want a toy as soon as Kazhian picked it up. 'You do not mind?'

Suken's smile seemed quite genuine. 'No, Father. I am glad for you, and I hope you will both be very happy.'

A knock announced the return of the usher, bearing a tray with two Minassan goblets of exquisite fragility, the white glazed clay turned so thin that light could be seen through it. He poured wine from a matching jug, bowed, and went out.

'Your spices, Father,' said Suken, indicating the unopened packet.

'Of course. How could I forget?' The Emperor carefully

unwrapped the soft white paper and folded back the edges. A small hump of ground spice, flecked grey and white and brown, lay in the centre.

'Cinnamon, Father – mace, allspice, dried ginger root and cloves. Did I remember correctly? Oh, and just a pinch of cardamom.'

Eska'anen beamed with delight. 'You did, dear boy, you certainly did.' He leaned forward and sniffed delicately. 'And mixed in just the right proportions, too, otherwise the cardamom tends to overpower everything else.'

'The Captain said that he will make up some more,' Suken told him. 'It's not cheap, but I think it's well worth the trouble and expense.'

'You only have your Ministry salary, of course,' Eska'anen said. 'I have made you no extra allowance. Well, if you are going to be married, all that must change. A Prince of Tulyet cannot appear mean.'

'Indeed not, Father. And I would like to be able to afford clothes befitting my new status.'

His earlier doubts completely forgotten, the Emperor smiled at his son, and carefully lifted the paper. He tipped the entire mound of spices into the nearest goblet, and stirred it with a little paperknife of carved ivory. Once more, he inhaled the aroma, and then lifted his cup. 'Drink with me, dear boy, to our reconciliation and to our future.'

'To the future,' said Suken fervently, and swallowed his wine in two gulps.

Eska'anen drank more slowly, savouring the spicy fragrance. It completely drowned the delicate taste of the Hailyan, but he did not mind. The gift was a symbol of his son's sincere penitence, and the ruination of a few mouthfuls of fine wine did not matter.

He drained it to the last drop, and poured in more wine to absorb the last gritty specks at the bottom. It had a slightly unusual taste, he thought, but the tingle on his tongue was not unpleasant, just unexpected. He coughed, and a little bile came up. The tingle turned suddenly into a burn, scorching his throat as if he had swallowed fire.

Then, Eska'anen knew. Even as he coughed again and again, and clawed at his seared mouth, he saw his son's expression change from polite concern to gloating delight, and the agony of this last, most terrible betrayal was more dreadful even than the pain of the poison. He tried to speak, but nothing emerged save a ghastly, raucous crowing sound as his breath rasped in his throat.

'A taste of your own medicine, Father,' said Suken, and chuckled gleefully. 'How many have you poisoned over the years? A score? Several score? Hundreds? Olyak's Halls must be full of your victims –

and now you're going to join them. And no one will know it was me.' He picked up the paper which had contained the spice, screwed it up into a ball, and tossed it into the pile of discarded rubbish in the corner. 'They'll think you've had a seizure, like the Prince of Tulyet. It was Olkanno's idea – clever of him, eh?' He bent over his father as he struggled to breathe, his lips already turning blue. 'The poison won't leave a trace. Everyone knows I'm your favourite, your only son. Why should anyone suspect me? And it doesn't matter anyway – in a few minutes I'll be the new Emperor, and then no one can touch me.'

With a wild, frantic effort, Eska'anen made a grab for his son's tunic. Suken hastily stepped back, and his father toppled to the floor and lay writhing and cawing, pink froth gathering at the corners of his gaping mouth.

'Die, won't you?' Suken hissed viciously. 'Die, you stupid old fool – it's no more than you deserve.'

The door opened with a crash. He whipped round and saw the usher's white, horrified face. Behind him stood a dozen soldiers of the Imperial Guard, their swords drawn. And with them, blandly menacing, the plump and familiar figure of Olkanno.

Eska'anen saw him. Perhaps he realized the full extent of his Chief Minister's malevolent design, or perhaps, in his last paroxysm, he hoped only for revenge. He pointed a shaking finger, and incoherent syllables stuttered hoarsely from his mouth. 'Su – Su – poi – poi—'

'On behalf of His Imperial Majesty,' Olkanno said loudly, 'I arrest you, Lord Suken, for the attempted murder of your father. Seize him.'

The soldiers pushed into the room, stepping over the Emperor's jerking body. 'No!' Suken wailed. 'No! *No!*' And in a fury he flung himself at Olkanno, who was standing just inside the door.

As briskly and efficiently as a butcher slaughtering a pig, one of the Guards swept his sword up in a swift, flashing arc. Suken screamed, staring in horror at the blood and entrails spilling from his ripped belly. Then, with another, more final blow, the soldier sliced the head from his body.

Olkanno had been careful to keep well clear of the mess. He negotiated the body of Eska'anen, who was still twitching, his blue robe sprayed with his son's blood, and bent over Suken. 'I warned you that he would resist arrest. You did well, Terreken.'

'Thank you, sir!' The guardsman who had dealt the first blow hastily wiped his weapon on the dead man's tunic, and saluted with a clash of bronze armour.

'I shall ensure your promotion. At least the murderer has been justly punished for his crime, even if he has escaped official execution. May he linger in Olyak's lowest Halls, until the end of time! Usher?'

The slave, green with shock and horror, crept reluctantly forward, averting his eyes from the corpses.

'See that this mess is cleared up. The late Emperor's body is to be treated with all possible respect and reverence. As for that—' He indicted the mutilated remains of Suken. 'As for that, have it carried to the public pyre tomorrow, with criers to tell all the people what he did. Go now.'

'Yes, sir.' The usher bowed hastily and scurried out. A moment later came the sound of anguished retching.

'The room stinks like a slaughter-house,' Olkanno observed. He turned, and stepped delicately back to the door, drawing the hem of his gown away from the lake of blood around Suken's corpse. 'Guard it until the men come to clear it up. Meanwhile, I shall convene an emergency meeting of the Council at once.'

By the time that all the Councillors present in the city had received Olkanno's summons, the dreadful news had already poured through the Palace itself, and was surging like a flood tide through the streets and alleys and water-lanes of Toktel'yi. The Emperor was dead, poisoned by his own son. And Suken too had been killed resisting arrest, while his father lay dying at his feet.

Djeneb heard it, and through her horror and amazement, amidst the ritual wailing of her women, her mind kept working. And she knew now who had choreographed this long and murderous dance of death, for he was the only one left alive when the music finally stopped.

So she displayed no surprise when the news came, late in the afternoon, that the Council had proclaimed Olkanno, son of Kardenek, son of Ba'amek, the hundred and first Emperor of Toktel'yi. There had been no dissenting voices, for there was no other adult male Vessel of the Blood Imperial left alive in all the Empire, save only for the renegade Kazhian and the priest Kekaylo. And the Councillors, like everyone else, knew what Olkanno was. If they had not believed the sinister tales about him during his years as Spymaster, the convoluted cunning and extreme ruthlessness that he had used to seize the Onyx Throne were more than sufficient to terrify them into abject compliance.

So they made him Emperor, and secretly trembled for their own futures, and for the fate of the Empire. To a man who had arranged the cold-blooded murders of at least seven of his close relatives, no life would be sacrosanct.

Djeneb could not think of what lay in front of her. Events moved so fast that she could hardly believe that she was not to marry Eska'anen, even as the smoke from his funeral pyre shrouded the furnace blue of the sky. A clear glaze, like the lacquer which Lelyentan craftsmen painted on their exquisite wooden furniture, seemed to have formed a protective carapace round her mind, through which she could see, and speak, but could not feel.

So she showed no emotion when Olkanno came to her, in the splendid formal robes of an Emperor, and told her that in three days they would be married in the Temple of Kaylo. She knew his reputation for cruelty: she knew the gossip about the dreadful fate of his first wife. But somehow she seemed to be immune to the fear that should have infected her like poison, as she listened to his smooth words and watched his empty, chilling smile.

For how could she bear to consider her future, without being overtaken by terror and madness?

CHAPTER
ELEVEN

The summer of the year 2317 was unusually hot and dry, even for Toktel'yi. The Kefirinn sank lower into the mudbanks, and marsh fever and other, more lethal pestilences stalked through the narrow, squalid water-lanes of the city. Every day the public pyre burned hundreds of diseased, malnourished corpses, polluting the air for several miles downwind. The poor continued their daily struggle for survival, as they had always done. Events in the Palace did not concern them, save as a source of gossip and speculation that briefly enlivened their desperate days. But the rich, those who had a stake in the complicated web of bureaucracy, bribes, trade and conspiracy upon which the Empire was built, drew in their horns, made discreet provision for their families if the worst should happen, and eyed the new Emperor with nervous and wary respect.

Further away, in the provinces and on the islands of the Archipelago, the people seemed at first indifferent to the accession of the third incumbent of the Onyx Throne in a year. After long years of comparative peace within the bounds of the Empire, such a rapid turnover of rulers would surely have little effect on the cement of greed, fear, habit and apathy that had bound its constituent parts together for so long.

But just as a landslide may start with a few trickling grains of sand, so did a few apparently unconnected and trivial incidents threaten the impossible.

It had already begun, in Djebb. The huge, remote province on the north-eastern boundary of the Empire had always been obstinately inclined towards independence. Its conquest, more than a hundred and fifty years previously, had been unusually protracted, and savage even by Toktel'yan standards. The Army had taken nearly ten years to subdue the population, and another six to catch their King, who had not unnaturally objected strongly to the occupation of his realm. Even now, the citizens of Djebb were notoriously stubborn and difficult to rule, and their Governors were attacked and even murdered with monotonous regularity.

For close on three months, while Ba'alekkt's successor was being chosen, the present Governor had been absent. His deputy was weak and ineffectual, and the province had effectively been left to its own devices. Malcontents who harboured a grudge, on their own and their ancestors' behalf, against the Toktel'yans, began to spread rumours thick as weeds. The new Emperor would raise taxes to exorbitant levels, the Army would lay the land waste, and children would be enslaved while their parents were slaughtered . . .

The province's soldiers began the rebellion in earnest. Summarily sent home after the demise of Sekkenet, they had been deeply suspicious about the true cause of their beloved General's death, and an unfortunate delay in distributing their pay had proved to be the match to the pyre. They mutinied, killed several unpopular officers, besieged the deputy Governor in his residence, and called upon the people to join them. And the people, beset by fear and rumour, obeyed.

But something else, too, had begun to seep through the resentful citizens of Djebb, shadowy at first, but swiftly gaining strength and substance. A dream: a dream of freedom, a belief that one day, very soon, the overlords who ruled them, oppressed them, taxed them, surrounded them with petty restrictions and regulations, and punished them with ferocity if they transgressed, would be swept away, and Djebb would once more become an independent land, and governed by its own people rather than the corrupt and venal minion of some remote, oblivious and authoritarian Emperor, hundreds of miles away.

Men talked in taverns and kuldi-houses, comparing notes. And they told each other of the dreams that, strangely, almost everyone seemed to have experienced. Some left almost no trace in the waking mind, save as a sense of hope and a desire for freedom, but others remembered, in detail as bright and vivid as if it had been reality, the final expulsion of the hated Toktel'yans. They spoke of a banner painted like a streaming torrent of flame, and a presence – not a man, not a woman, but some shadowy figure holding the bright pennant high above them, and urging the people on to victory. And they called this nebulous leader the Flamebearer, the bringer of hope.

During the last two months of his brief reign, Eska'anen had despatched soldiers to Djebb, men from other provinces who did not owe any secret allegiance to the treasonous, illusory ideal of freedom. They were resisted, abused, attacked. The capital city became a battleground, the Toktel'yans struggling to retake it street by street, or desperately fighting to hold the little they had gained. The men of Djebb, dour, sullen, stubborn, led by the renegade troops and inflamed by a dream, kept them at bay all through a beautiful, flowering spring. On Eska'anen's desk, the day of his assassination, had lain yet another report from the leader of his soldiers, begging for more men and more money, and carrying the smell of his frustration and despair between every line.

The news of Olkanno's accession did not terrify the rebels of Djebb into submission: indeed, it only strengthened their resolve. After all, a man so cruel and devious could hardly expect to command either their loyalty or their obedience. And their dreams still contained the ghostly image of the Flamebearer, who would lead them out of Imperial darkness and into the brilliance of a free and glorious future.

Like a forest fire, or a subtle, infectious plague, the rumours spread. They seeped southwards, into Tatht, another province added to the Empire fairly recently. There, the elderly could remember their grandparents' terrible tales of the conquest of their land, which once, like its neighbour Kereneth, had been dedicated to the Goddess. People talked about their dreams, compared what they had seen in their sleep, and discussed the meaning of such strange marvels. Once more, amongst every street-corner gathering, or through the fields like a summer wind, the name of the Flamebearer began to be whispered, a harbinger of hope. And the new Emperor, who offered no hope at all, was universally loathed and reviled.

On Balki, no one dreamed of mysterious leaders, or vague yet attainable ideas of liberty. But the news of Eska'anen's murder was greeted with typically Balkian satisfaction, sour and cynical. No one danced in the streets, but there was a general and pervasive mood of pleasure in his downfall.

Sargenay had assumed that Kazhian would have more reason than anyone else to rejoice in the deaths of his father and brother. He was not, therefore, surprised to find his Captain in his cabin, sinking a jug of the thin, sour, potent Balki wine. But the look in his green eyes puzzled the sorcerer.

'I thought you hated him,' he said in bewilderment.

'I do – did.' Kazhian had already finished one jug, and his speech, always undisciplined and inclined to wildness, was beginning to escape his control. 'Have some – there's plenty, the cask's only just been broached.'

Sargenay took the fine Minassan goblet, plundered from their last capture, without much enthusiasm. Their next prize would have to be a wine-ship carrying good Hailyan – he'd even settle for a few barrels of Djebban, if the rebellion hadn't put paid to its wine-making industry.

This vinegary stuff did a man's gut no good at all, and Kazhian's capacity for it was beginning to worry him.

In the half-year since they had stolen that Annatal spice trader, renamed her the *Sea Serpent*, and turned pirate, his initial hopes of a sexual relationship with his Captain had gradually withered away. He knew now, realistically, that they would never be lovers, for Kazhian's preference for women was as strong as Sargenay's for men. He had still cherished a dream, though, that they might soon enjoy a close and long-lasting friendship.

But it was difficult, however subtly and carefully he tried, to sneak his way past Kazhian's apparently light-hearted and irresponsibly carefree façade. It *was* only a façade: he knew, with a sorcerer's sensitivity, that unknown depths lurked beneath the smiling surface, the cheerful wit and the friendly camaraderie, like the sweetly deceptive calm of the Southern Sea before a storm. But Kazhian had never revealed his soul to anyone: instead, over the long months hovering around the Balkian coast, dodging Navy patrols and chasing merchant ships, he had retreated more and more within himself, laughing and joking with his crew but withdrawing alone to his cabin every night, to drink and brood.

This was the first occasion since that Year-Turn festival that he'd offered Sargenay a drink, and the sorcerer had no intention of wasting the opportunity. He sat down on his Captain's untidy mattress, and sipped the wine with considerable caution.

'The best Balki has to offer,' said Kazhian derisively. 'We'd better make sure the next ship we take is carrying a cargo of Hailyan.'

'I was thinking exactly the same myself.' Sargenay repressed a shudder as the unappetizing liquid set his teeth on edge. If this didn't give him indigestion later, he was a Balki fishwife. 'But you surely can't regret Suken's death,' he added casually. If Kazhian thought he was probing, he'd retreat into his shell faster than a hermit crab.

'Oh, Suken.' Kazhian laughed, and swallowed the rest of his wine. 'He got what he deserved. My guess is that Olkanno persuaded him to murder my – the Emperor, and gave him time and place and method in minute detail. And of course the stupid bastard didn't have the brains to do anything other than what he was told. So he was caught with the sword in his hand.'

'I thought Eska'anen was poisoned – so they said.'

'Poison, sword – whatever Suken used, they're both still dead.' Kazhian stared at the lamp flame, his eyes hooded so that Sargenay could not read them. 'Ironic, isn't it? Suken was always his favourite –

so obedient, so eager to please, so devoted. Whereas I could do nothing right. He loathed me, always did. But it was Suken who killed him for greed, in cold blood.'

He paused, still gazing at the lamp. Sargenay waited knowing that he had never been closer to the darkness in the other man's soul.

'I never realized what Eska'anen was like,' Kazhian said suddenly, his voice quiet and reflective, as if he were thinking aloud. 'All my childhood, I looked up to him. My mother hated him, but she never – she never taught me to hate. She made me think for myself, and form my own opinions. Perhaps she knew that if I could win my father's affection, I would be safe – as she was not. When she . . . when she died, I had no idea that he'd arranged it. She just fell ill, and died. So I tried to turn to him for comfort, and he made his dislike very obvious. Suken was only four, and a spoilt little brat, but he was Eska'anen's favourite even then. And his mother hated me too, because she saw me as a threat to her precious Suken. So I was packed off to my mother's family in Tulyet, as if my father could not bear the sight of me. I thought that he blamed me for her death.' His mouth twisted bitterly. 'Stupid, wasn't I? That was when I still thought the face he showed the world was real. Later, as soon as I was old enough, he bought me an officer's place on a Navy galley. He wouldn't have done it if he'd realized how much I wanted it – ever since going to Tulyet, I'd wanted to be a sailor. If he'd known, he'd have had me pen-pushing in some office.'

'Like Suken.'

'Ah, but that was what Suken wanted. And whatever Suken desired, he could have. Nothing was too good for him. He even wanted to be my father's heir.'

'And when Suken came of age,' Sargenay said reflectively, swirling the blood-red wine around the cup, 'Eska'anen decided to give him that as well.'

Kazhian glanced up sharply. 'What do you mean?'

There was a tense pause. Sargenay made a languid, deprecating gesture. 'Nothing, nothing at all. Forget it.'

'Sod that. What do you mean, "*decided to give him that as well*"?'

The sorcerer sighed. 'I'm sorry. It hadn't occurred to me that you did not know.'

'Didn't know what? Come on, weather-worker. I'm grown up now. I'm a big boy. I can take it.'

'The sinking of the *Spear of Vengeance* was nothing to do with you. Your father paid the steersman to put her on the rocks.'

This time, the silence was absolute. The *Sea Serpent*, anchored in the shelter of a deserted cove, heaved rhythmically in the gentle swell, her timbers creaking in time with the movement beneath her.

'Where did you hear that?' Kazhian's usually agreeable, flippant voice was hoarse and strained.

'It's not gossip, I know it for a fact. I had a lover who was the steersman's cousin.'

'And once again I was the last to know.' Kazhian laughed suddenly. 'Don't look so terrified, wizard. It's the best news I've had in years.'

The sorcerer stared at him in wary surprise. 'Why?'

'You may find this hard to believe, but it is a crippling burden on the conscience to think that your own incompetence caused fifty deaths,' said Kazhian, with exaggeratedly polite patience. 'So when you discover, three or four years later, that you were quite innocent, and that all the blame can be justifiably piled on the head of the person you hate most – well, it brings a certain sense of relief.'

'*Were* you drunk, or drugged?'

'I'd smoked some khlar before we set sail. Not much, but I was never sure that it wasn't the reason.'

'And now you know it was not.'

'Now I know . . . Lord of Life, I could do with a pipe!' He smiled at Sargenay, with dazzling brilliance, and the sorcerer's heart, already snared and yearning, missed a beat. 'Thank you, weather-worker. I was feeling low – beset by too many unpleasant memories.'

'And learning that your father deliberately organized your disgrace – that he might even have wanted you dead – that *isn't* unpleasant?'

'Like I said – it's always good to be able to shift the blame. I can accept that my father was one of the nastier Vessels of the Blood Imperial,' Kazhian said. 'I've had several years to come to terms with it. And now he's dead, the future looks . . . different.'

'Safer,' Sargenay pointed out. 'I shouldn't think Olkanno will waste very much time and money pursuing you.'

'I hope he won't – although I'm the last remaining candidate for the Onyx Throne, after all.'

'Do you want it?'

Kazhian looked genuinely surprised. 'No. No, I never have. All I've ever wanted is the freedom to do what I choose – and good company, good wine, and a hot and willing woman.' He grinned. 'And the *Sea Serpent* is a little short of the last two items at present. No, I don't want to live in that huge gold and marble cage of a Palace, with the terror of poison always at the back of my mind, and endless Council meetings and bureaucracy. I don't want to lead armies or invade harmless peaceful neighbours. And least of all do I want the likes of Arkun whispering slyly and corruptingly in my ear.' He glanced at the sorcerer. 'But Megren seemed to want it – sane and sensible though he appeared to be.'

'His wife didn't. And she wielded the power in that family, despite convention.'

'A remarkable woman, Trinn. She was absolutely devoted to him, and yet she's coped with his death remarkably well. Did you know he left her pregnant? She has a baby daughter, now, as well as young Sarrek. Let's hope Olkanno doesn't find out that *they're* still alive.'

'He may suspect it. But he might be satisfied with Megren's death. And if Trinn and her children go on living quietly and anonymously up in the hills, rumours that they're alive will just be rumours.'

'She won't have any wild ideas of claiming the Onyx Throne for her son, anyway. Good luck to her. More wine?'

'Er – I haven't finished the first cup yet.'

'A connoisseur, eh?' said Kazhian, with his sly, teasing grin. 'Never mind. I'll get you some Hailyan, weather-worker – a shame you can't check their cargoes before we go to the trouble of attacking them.'

'I knew someone once who could have done that,' said Sargenay reminiscently. 'Another sorcerer – but, gods, what power. I stopped him killing someone once – he'd have fried the man's heart in his own blood. And yet to look at him, you'd have thought him quite harmless – and as beautiful as a brothel boy.'

'Yours?' Kazhian enquired, with raised eyebrows.

'No such luck, alas. He took off with my friend, the girl I was telling you about at the Year-Turn festival, the tavern-keeper, Mallaso. Olyak alone knows what happened to him – I never heard. He's probably dead as well, though. Power like that can't be hidden long. If only . . .' Sargenay gave himself a little slap on the wrist, and smiled ruefully. 'But it's no use yearning after the unobtainable.'

Kazhian smiled back, and filled his wine-cup. He said softly, 'There is one person whom I pity most in all this.'

'Who is that?'

'Djeneb.'

'Djeneb? Why?'

'Think, weather-worker. Would *you* like to be married to Olkanno?'

'I see what you mean,' said Sargenay, after a pause. 'Let's hope she can poison him at the first opportunity. By all accounts, she's capable of it.'

'Oh, yes – but unlikely to succeed. Pure venom runs in that repellent man's veins already. Lord of Life alone knows what their children will be like.'

'Well, let's hope they never have any,' said Sargenay grimly, and swallowed the rest of the wine with a shiver that was not entirely due to its sourness.

The Lady Djeneb, only living wife of the Emperor of Toktel'yi, dug her nails into the palms of her hands so tightly that they drew blood, and clamped her teeth shut on a scream.

She had thought nothing could equal the experience of her first night with Olkanno. She had not expected pleasure, but she had at least hoped to be treated with courtesy and respect. After all, her birth was several degrees higher than his, and he had surely married her for the extra prestige her Blood Imperial would confer on his children.

But she had not imagined that he would want to inflict pain on her. He had used his hands quite calmly and deliberately, seeking out those places where even the lightest pressure would cause agony, and where the marks he made would not show. And it was only when, sobbing, she had begged him to stop, that he had taken her as briefly and brutally as a dockside labourer with a cheap whore.

Afterwards, trying to control her tears, bitterly ashamed of her weakness, she had realized that he could not have sex with her until he had hurt her to screaming point. And the knowledge terrified her. How many more nights of subtle, exquisite torture would she have to endure?

Once, in her vanished and foolish innocence, she had thought that no husband could possibly be worse than the Prince of Tulyet. And now she would gladly have welcomed his stinking breath and balding head, in place of the smooth, plump, sinister man whose cold-blooded and deliberate cruelty ruled her life.

And as for her dreams of Kazhian, they now seemed as ridiculous and naïve as a simpleton's.

Olkanno thrust his hand into her again, hard, and she willed herself not to give in, not to cry out, for if she did, her screams would only incite his lust. She felt as if his fingers were ripping her apart: the agony shrieked like a knife. In despair, she drew on the inner core of independence, of rebellion, the fighting spirit that had once sustained her against the casual malevolence of her brother Ba'alekkt, and shrank deep inside her mind, trying to keep inviolate the self that Olkanno could never touch, never defile, never destroy.

With an exclamation of disgust, he flung himself off the bed and began to dress. She had no idea where he was going, or what he would do: as long as he left her alone, she did not care. But she prayed, with silent misery, to the Goddess, who watched over all women, even the abused, oppressed, ill-treated women of Toktel'yi, that she would be able to keep herself from surrender. For only then could she be sure that she would never bear his child.

He left without a word. In all the endless days – nearly two months now – of their marriage, he had only spoken to her once, when exchanging vows at the wedding ceremony. He treated her like an object, save that an object was not expected to feel pain, or beg for mercy.

Alone at last, Djeneb pulled the sheet over her ravaged bleeding body. She did not know how much longer she could endure this. She had already thought of killing herself, but Olyak was said to loathe suicides, preferring to choose the hour of death himself, and Djeneb could not face, yet, an eternity in the lowest Halls of torment. She knew, though, that one day even that fate might seem preferable to the horror of being Olkanno's wife.

Or she could give in, and scream and writhe and weep and beg as her tortured body urged her to do. Then at last his flaccid manhood would rise in response, and he would feverishly ram it into her over and over again, trying to impregnate her with the son he so desperately wanted . . .

Not yet. She would not be defeated, not yet, not so soon.

The next night, she waited for him to come to her. All day, she had been practising her mind's withdrawal, in prayer and meditation. She had eaten nothing, and she felt light-headed and remote. When the eunuchs appeared, she stared at them, stupid with fatigue and fear and hunger, and tried to understand what they wanted.

They had their orders. Her slaves dressed her in a gown that was not hers, made of a diaphanous silk that concubines often wore, with a thick veil that must conceal all the details of her face, for she could see very little through it. Then she was led out of the Women's Quarters, and into her husband's private apartments.

The room to which they took her was small and bare. The only piece of furniture was a long, narrow wooden table, with leather straps nailed to it at each end. Staring at it through the stifling veil, Djeneb felt a growing and terrible horror. She turned, and saw Olkanno enter, accompanied by two soldiers and the Spymaster.

Then she knew what he planned, and screamed. Ignoring her, the soldiers grabbed her arms and dragged her on to the table. They tied her wrists and ankles with the straps, and at a word from the Emperor, went out.

'Who is she?' Arkun asked. 'What has she done, Imperial Majesty?'

'She is merely one of my concubines,' said Olkanno blandly. 'Unfortunately, she has been less than enthusiastic in her work, and needs to be taught a lesson.'

Rigid with terror, Djeneb waited. Olkanno bent over her, smiling. 'I thought you would like to witness the proceedings, Arkun. Many people enjoy such things. I know that I would, in your position.'

The Spymaster's voice did not sound particularly eager. 'I expect I will, Imperial Majesty.'

'Good,' said Olkanno. 'Look at her. That voluptuous body is wasted on her. Does she excite you? You'd be disappointed if she were yours, I can tell you. Well, let us see if we can obtain some response.'

'Imperial Majesty, is this necessary? Why not just dismiss her? To end up in some squalid brothel will surely be punishment enough.'

'Squeamish, Arkun? That is not like you. She is my concubine, and I will do as I please with her. And now, can you pass me my instruments? Thank you.'

After all, the pain was not so bad as she had feared. The humiliation was worst: the knowledge that Arkun was there, watching, as the supposed concubine was delicately stroked and pierced with knives of hideous sharpness, that would leave little trace save for the agony they inflicted. Djeneb wanted to cry out, to scream that she was the Emperor's wife, not some low-born concubine, but she knew that if she revealed her identity to Arkun, she would ensure his death as well as her own. Even in Toktel'yi, there were some things that were beyond all decency, and this was surely one.

Then, when she could no longer suppress her sobs of pain, he climbed on to the table and raped her, with even more viciousness than usual. Her body jerked at each thrust, and the heavy veil fell on the floor.

Arkun had seen her face on Kazhian's ship. He knew who she was: she heard his soft intake of breath. Olkanno, thrusting brutally towards his climax, noticed nothing. He finished with a grunt, and heaved himself off her.

'No beauty, is she?' he said, with dismissive contempt. He did not seem perturbed that she was unveiled, and Djeneb realized that he had not considered the possibility that Arkun might have recognized her.

'She certainly is not now,' said the Spymaster, and she wondered if she was imagining the subtle note of pity in his voice. Arkun was a creature of death, one of Olyak's minions, and he had surely never felt compassion for anyone in his life.

'She deserved all she got,' Olkanno said. 'She's lucky to have her life. Release her.'

She heard him move to the door and call for the soldiers. Arkun began to untie her. His face came into her field of vision. It was no longer cold and impassive: she saw that his brown eyes burned with anger. Then, quite unexpectedly, he smiled at her, and in response to this unsought, unlooked-for sympathy, she felt tears dribbling into her hair.

'Take her back to the Women's Quarters,' said the Emperor. 'And do not bother to be too gentle.'

The men dragged her off the table. She wanted to walk, to display even in this extremity the rags of the pride that had sustained her in the face of extreme horror. But she managed only a few steps before the merciful darkness overwhelmed her, and for the first time in her life, she fainted.

She woke in her own bed, and found that her first and only emotion was utter despair, that she was still alive and must endure.

'Lady?'

It was not Olkanno's voice. Her husband had never called her anything, had never spoken to her as one human being to another. And the sound of gentle kindness in a man's voice was enough to dismantle her mind entirely. She turned her face into the pillow and wept.

Someone gave her a soothing drink, and she slept, dreamed of Olkanno, and woke screaming. Inside her head there was only pain, and confusion: the boundaries between reality and nightmare had been thrust aside by his cold-blooded savagery. She fought with her attendants, thinking that they came to drag her away to be raped and tortured again. Even their concerned, urgent female voices could not soothe her, for what had been done to her was more horrific than any imagining.

But there came at last a time when, exhausted, she lay staring at the magnificent painted ceiling above her bed, with the fresco of dancing cranes symbolizing love and fidelity, and knew who and where she was.

Her body no longer hurt. She tested every muscle, just the tiniest movements, and found that although she felt utterly weak and drained, her tiredness was uninterrupted by pain. And she was hungry. She thought of new bread and fresh fruit, and her stomach grumbled hopefully.

'Lady!' Are you awake?'

It was Tezna, one of her bodyslaves. She was Fabrizi, but her hair was brown and her eyes a pleasant dark blue. She leaned over and touched Djeneb's forehead. 'Thanks to the Lord of Life, no more fever!'

'Fever?'

'Yes, lady – you have been very ill. We despaired of your life,' the girl stood by the bed, an expression of genuine concern on her face. 'Oh, lady – you had a child, you carried a child within you, and you lost it.'

'A child?' Djeneb stared up at the slave in bewilderment. 'But I didn't know – surely—'

'There was no doubt, lady. And you were so ill, you nearly died. We all lit candles for your life, lady, in the Palace Temple, and we prayed so hard for you – and you lived.'

'I wish I had not.' She should not have spoken the words aloud, for the girl was certainly an informer. But she was too weak to regret it. And then, with amazement, she saw that Tezna's eyes were full of tears.

'Oh, lady, you shouldn't say such things,' the girl said softly. 'We all wished so much for you to live.'

'Why?' Djeneb whispered. 'Why should I want to live? What is there for me in my life, save for more pain, more misery, more despair?' Tears were pouring from her own eyes, but she could not care.

'Listen, lady, please.' Tezna knelt by the bed, and clasped Djeneb's hand. Her fingers were warm and gentle. 'I know – we all know what he did. There isn't one of us who doesn't feel disgusted by it. We all want to help you, lady. We are yours, not his – even Kedrain, whom he pays to spy on you, is on your side now.'

'And you?' Djeneb asked. 'Who pays you?'

Tezna lowered her gaze. She had very long dark lashes, and a nose that was only slightly aquiline. She said at last, 'The Spymaster, lady. But compared to that monster Olkanno, he is a good man.'

He had smiled at her as she lay on the torture table, and he had let her see his compassion. Even so, she shook her head. 'No, he is not. Please, Tezna, do not trust him.'

'I don't,' said the girl. 'I trust no one in this nest of vipers, lady – except you. For you are as much his slave as I am – despite your silken sheets and splendid gowns. And you are more to be pitied, for we have each other. But you are quite alone.'

'No,' Djeneb whispered. 'No, I am not – not now.' And she smiled, with hesitant gratitude, at the slave who held her hand.

Later, when Tezna had gone to get her some food, she knew that she had been foolish. It was surely madness to confide in a bodyslave, especially one who had admitted that she was in the pay of the Spymaster. But she could not help it. The apparently genuine offer of sympathy, concern and friendship, after all her suffering, was so wonderful that her heart could not resist it, however much her head might warn her of the dangers. She had been alone, and so lonely, for such a very long time.

Tezna brought her a savoury and nourishing soup, sweet soft white bread, still warm from the oven, and bright oranges and apricots that shone like lamps in the darkening room. Djeneb ate carefully, afraid that her hunger would soon turn to nausea. But it did not, and a steaming, refreshing cup of kuldi completed her revival. She lay back on the pillows and rang her bell.

'It's all right, lady,' Tezna said, when she had cleared the bowls on to a tray. 'You husband will not come to you again – not tonight, not tomorrow night, not for a very long time. The Healer told him that if he wished for healthy sons, he must let you recover. You have lain here for nearly half a month, lady. Even Olkanno thought you would die. And the Healer, thanks be to Kaylo, is a brave man. He told the Emperor to leave you alone, until past Year-Turn at least.'

More than five months. Five months to rebuild her body and her mind. Five months of freedom, within this elaborate and luxurious cage. And then Olkanno would clamp his fetters on her once more, and try, doubtless with renewed urgency, to break her stubborn spirit, so that he could force another child on her.

A child engendered by Olkanno would be a monster. He would take it away from her and rear it to be as cruel and cunning and evil as himself. She felt sick with horror at the thought. 'No Tezna, no – I can't face him again – I can't!'

'But a lot can happen between now and then. And next time, it may be different. The Healer told him to be more gentle. He said his treatment of you had caused you to lose the child. Oh, how I wish you had heard him, lady – I wish you had seen the Emperor's face!'

'I must speak with the Healer,' Djeneb said urgently. 'I must thank him, with all my heart. Send for him now, Tezna.'

The girl's long, long lashes drooped. She said very quietly, 'I am afraid I cannot, lady. Once it was clear you would live, he left the Palace, and has not returned.'

Djeneb knew what Tezna was implying, and knew too that it was entirely probable that the man had been murdered for his impudence, or because he knew too much. And she had such cause to be grateful to him, for he had saved her life and her sanity, and given her the chance to rebuild her ruined existence.

'Who was he?' she asked, her voice shivery with sorrow. 'I don't remember anything except the nightmares. Was it Akhan'tar?'

'No, lady. If you recall, Akhan'tar was dismissed by Eska'anen, along with all the other members of your original household. I do not know where this man came from. He was quite young, for a healer, but his hair was white. He said his name was Galken.'

With one consonant changed, the word meant 'hope'. He had given her that, at the price of his own future. And she would never be able to thank him, until they met at last in Olyak's Halls.

Once more, Djeneb wept, for the unknown fate of a man whom she had never met: and Tezna embraced her, sharing her grief.

CHAPTER
TWELVE

In Kerenth, the news of Olkanno's accession to the Onyx Throne had barely disturbed the unchanging, peaceful depths of the land's life. Work continued in the fields, for the crops were growing, there was fruit to be picked, orchards to be tended. And at the villa known as Twin Waters, Kiyu, seven months old, had learned to crawl.

Now that Vanaina's farm was so busy, Mallaso joined the labouring gangs of women. Sometimes she took the baby with her, bound on her back with a huge triangle of stout blue cotton: sometimes she left Kiyu with Ammenna's daughter S'raya, or in the care of Al'Kalyek. As men were forbidden to till the Goddess's sacred soil, he could not work in the fields, but he had more than earned his keep with his skills as a Healer.

For Mallaso, whose first child, Grayna, had died whilst in the care of foster-parents, it was agony at first to give over this new, most precious child to others, even it if was only for an hour or two. But she knew she must do it, for she should repay at least a little of the enormous debt she owed to Vanaina's kindness and hospitality. And Kiyu was a sociable baby, generous with her smiles and laughter, and possessed of an enchantingly cheeky grin that revealed two small, perfect teeth in her lower gum. Everyone at Twin Waters loved her, and S'raya was her devoted slave.

One evening, Mallaso returned to the villa with the other women, hot and dusty after several hours hoeing millet. Two strange horses were being led away, and there was an unusual bustle in the central courtyard, excitement buzzing in the warm air. S'raya ran up, bursting with news. 'It's Essyan! Essyan is here!'

Mallaso's heart gave a lurch, and she gasped. After all this time, all these years, how could she have forgotten? But so peaceful and pleasant was her life at Twin Waters, so entrancing her child, that for months she had hardly given the past a thought. Al'Kalyek had brought back memories of Bron and of her life in Toktel'yi. And now the mere name of the leader of the Penyans-in-exile reminded her painfully of that lovely, mountainous isle: the rich turquoise sea surrounding it: the brilliance and fragrance of the flowers: the white houses above the harbour, as sharp against the deep green hills as if they had been cut from new paper: and above all, her father's wisdom, her brothers' jokes and the low, gentle laughter of her mother.

All gone now, crushed by the Empire, its people slaughtered, or enslaved, or fled. Essyan, who had been a member of the Penyan government before the invasion, was by common consent the leader of those, many thousands in number, who had sought refuge in Kerenth or in its sister land of Katho. He lived in the city, and worked tirelessly for the day when Penya might once more be free.

Although he was Vanaina's distant cousin, Essyan had not visited her farm during the time that Mallaso had lived there. Hastily washing the dust from her hands and face at the water-trough, she thought of the recent news – the rebellion in Djebb, the change of Emperor, serious disturbances in Tatht and Tulyet – and wondered, with sudden hope, whether Essyan was here for more than just a courtesy visit.

Al'Kalyek was coming over, Kiyu in his arms. The child's plump face broke into a delighted grin at the sight of her mother, and she kicked her feet and held out her hands. Mallaso swept her daughter into a joyous embrace, feeling her solid warmth nestling against her, the sweet baby smell, the burrowing movements of her head as she sought the breast. Her love for Kiyu seemed so overpowering, so exclusive, so much more important than the fate of one island, one nation, one displaced and grieving people. And she doubted that Essyan would understand such feelings: by all accounts, he was a stern man, unemotional and intellectual, and completely single-minded in his determination to return to Penya in freedom.

She found a bench under the arbour, and sat down to let Kiyu suckle. The baby was partly weaned, but both she and her mother enjoyed these moments of intimacy so much that Mallaso was loath to give them up, even though her time in the fields was restricted as a result.

'Has she been good?' she asked the old sorcerer.

'Of course,' said Al'Kalyek, smiling with great fondness at the child. During the months that he had lived at Twin Waters, he had come to love Kiyu dearly, though he, a typical Toktel'yan, had not been in such close contact with a baby since leaving Onnak fifty years previously. He had had some misgivings about taking charge of her, but her entrancing charm had won him over, and he was touched by Mallaso's trust in him.

But in all this time, he still had no answers to the question he had come so far to ask. Had she inherited any of her father's colossal, astonishing power?

He had gazed so often into her merry dark eyes, studied her golden-brown face and chubby infant features, sought for a glimmer of raw, untaught sorcery around her. Attempting to link his thoughts to hers might have told him the truth, but he knew very well the damage that his invasion of her immature, elemental mind might do. If she did possess some of Bron's power, she would show some sign of it, sooner or later. And if she was not an embryo sorcerer, he did not mind. For already he doted on her, as if she was the grand-daughter he never had.

He gave Mallaso a brief description of what Kiyu had done during the few hours that she had been out of her mother's care, but the Penyan woman did not give his words her usual attention. As soon as he had finished, she said, 'I understand Essyan has arrived. Have you seen him?'

Al'Kalyek gave her a long, considered look. 'Yes,' he said. 'He arrived just before you did, with a companion. Gemain, I believe his name is. They are talking to Vanaina at this moment. They did not say why they are here, but there has been no shortage of ideas.'

'I don't doubt it.' Mallaso said. She leaned back against one of the round posts of the arbour, cradling the suckling baby in her arms. 'And I can guess, too. Olkanno is Emperor and no one likes it. The thought of that sinister, repulsive man wielding such power is terrifying.'

'It certainly is. I have known him for a very long time. There have been many ruthless Emperors, many of whom were devious, or power-crazed, idle, depraved or vicious. But I cannot think of another, in all the Empire's history, with such a relish for cruelty, such a terrible delight in torture and mutilation. I pity poor Lady Djeneb, married to such a man. Her life with him will never be less than torment.'

Mallaso was silent, remembering the man who had once, on Tekkt, contemplated torturing her. The look of greedy expectation on his face still haunted her dreams, and her mind sickened at the memory of it. To speak of him in the presence of Kiyu, so bright and fresh and innocent, seemed peculiarly horrible.

Within her arms, her daughter struggled suddenly, lost the nipple, and uttered a sharp wail. Mallaso cuddled her close, soothing her with soft endearments, and eventually the baby settled into a light, milky doze.

'Perhaps it would be better not to discuss such things when she is with us,' Al'Kalyek said softly.

Mallaso glanced up at him, suddenly afraid. For if Kiyu had indeed sensed her horror, if her reaction had not been caused by wind or discomfort or the arrival of another tooth, then she must have inherited some of Bron's power. And her mother still clung to the hope that the baby would possess only the precious, everyday, ordinary gifts of a normal child, and that she would never suffer the crippling burden of pain, responsibility and guilt that Bron's power had bestowed on him.

She said with spurious confidence, 'Just a touch of wind, that's all.'

'I expect so,' said Al'Kalyek, but she could discern a subtle tone of doubt in his voice. 'Anyway, let us continue our discussion in more general terms. Olkanno is greatly feared, of course, throughout the Empire, but he is also greatly hated. All the known world now understands the nature of his menace. And perhaps events in Djebb have shown even the most timid that when the people are united, they have a good chance of success.'

'We were united in Penya, and the Toktel'yans defeated us even so.'

'Yes – but you were unprepared, unsuspecting, and faced by overwhelming odds. In Djebb, even the soldiers have rebelled. And they are still gaining ground, apparently. The Emperor will have to send many more troops to have any chance of defeating them. And if he does, he will leave other provinces poorly defended. Tatht and Tulyet are already in turmoil.'

'Tulyet has always been lawless and full of bandits,' Mallaso pointed out, but she knew that her objections could be answered, that there was a new wind, a fresh spirit of hope and freedom scenting the stale air of the Empire.

'Precisely. But in Tulyet lie the iron mines on which the Emperor depends, for weapons and armour. And all but one of them are now in rebel hands. The murder of their last Prince has given them a bitter sense of grievance. Olkanno is cunning and devious, certainly, but he does not understand the workings of human nature. He thinks that everyone can be cowed and terrified into submission. He cannot see that many normal and sensible people can be pushed and goaded beyond fear and beyond reason, into open revolt. That is what has happened in Djebb, and Tulyet. It will soon happen in Tatht, too.'

'How do you know all this?' Mallaso asked, for the news filtering through to Vanaina's farm was usually very vague.

'I am, after all, a sorcerer,' Al'Kalyek reminded her, with his dry dignity. 'In the privacy of my chamber, I practise the scrying arts – you know what they are?'

'Of course. My good friend Sargenay was a sorcerer – he came from Tatht, incidentally. He often used to talk about his art.' She smiled with wistful and reminiscent affection. 'I wish I knew what had happened to him. I hope he managed to escape Ba'alekkt's vengeance.'

'I never heard that a sorcerer was among those of your associates whom he executed. So perhaps he did.'

'I hope so. None of them deserved such a fate.' She paused, her face suddenly sad. 'Nor did Bron. And though he killed Ba'alekkt, the world hasn't changed, has it? The prophecy they mentioned in Jo'ami said that because of him, the world would change. But the Empire just goes on and on, for ever and ever.'

'Nothing can last for ever,' Al'Kalyek said softly. 'There will come a time when even Toktel'yi no longer exists. And it may be sooner than you think. Like a fine house built on a swamp, the Empire is not so strong as it seems. And Bron's act did have very significant consequences. If he had not killed the Emperor, the northern cities would have been invaded. And moreover, Eska'anen would not have taken Ba'alekkt's place, thus giving Olkanno a perfect opportunity to clear a path to the Onyx Throne without throwing suspicion on himself. Now, of course, everyone knows that he must have been responsible for the murders of all his rivals – but he is the Emperor, and therefore above the law, for he *is* the law.'

'Mallaso?' It was Vanaina, striding briskly over to them, looking more than usually untidy, her grey hair unbrushed. 'Have you heard that Essyan's here, with his son? He'll speak to us after supper, on a very important matter, so make sure you're there, won't you? S'raya can look after the baby.' She glanced at Al'Kalyek. 'And you too, of course, Healer Kaylen.'

Mallaso wondered, guiltily, what her friend would say if she knew that she was harbouring an Imperial sorcerer under her roof. She had welcomed him and trusted him for Mallaso's sake, but such an important representative of the enemy would hardly be acceptable. But it was too late for honesty now: Vanaina would be grievously hurt and angered by the deception.

'Thank you,' the old man said, with a smile. 'I shall be delighted to attend.'

The communal dining-hall was unusually crowded that evening. Everyone had taken care to arrive early, rather than trailing in at any time during the hour that food was served. Nearly forty men, women and children lived and worked at Twin Waters, and every adult was present. Mallaso had secured a place at the table next to Vanaina's, and she studied the two Penyans with interest. Essyan was in his sixties, a tall, thin, rather stooping man with grizzled hair and a severe mouth. He looked like a proficient but uncomfortable leader, someone who would not tolerate inefficiency, laziness, or anything less than complete loyalty to the cause. And she knew that her own allegiance to Penyan freedom would be less than perfect in his eyes, for she had Kiyu to cherish and protect.

The meal ended much sooner than usual: no one wanted to linger over their food while Essyan waited impatiently, his plate already clean and his fingers tapping on the table. When everyone had finished, he rose, and at once the whole room dropped into an expectant silence.

The Penyan looked round at the gathering, no hint of a smile on his face. 'My friends – I thank you for your patience and your support. And I have come here to tell you that there is hope, hope more real and bright than for many years, ever since the Enemy stole our homeland from us, and murdered so many of our friends and families.' He paused, and the fifteen women and eleven men stared at him with faith and trust written clear on almost every face.

'I bring news that may seem unimportant in Toktel'yi, but is momentous indeed to us. As you all know, there has been rebellion in Djebb, which both the past and present Emperors have been unable to crush – indeed, the entire province has now apparently almost escaped Imperial control, with the few troops still loyal to Olkanno besieged with the Governor in his Residence. Regaining Djebb will require a full-scale war, and an enormous outlay of resources. And now there is considerable trouble in Tatht. The Deputy Governor has been murdered, and rioting has broken out in the streets. And to help contain it, the Emperor has ordered that the bulk of the Penyan garrison be transferred to Tatht City. A fleet of Navy transports is already ferrying them over. In a few days' time, only a thousand soldiers will be left on the island.'

There was a collective gasp of delight and amazement, followed by an outbreak of cheering. Two elderly women embraced each other, weeping, and Mallaso felt tears washing her own eyes. At last, at last, there was a real chance of recapturing Penya.

'A thousand Toktel'yan soldiers are, of course, still a formidable obstacle. But I am reliably informed that their morale is low, and discipline weak. The whole army has never really recovered from the murders of General Sekkenet and Lord Megren, and they know that Olkanno is responsible for those crimes. They owe him no allegiance, and I do not think that they will put up much of a fight – especially if we offer them free quarter and a passage to Tatht, where they may join whichever side they please.'

He paused to sip from a cup of water, while his audience watched him avidly, and then continued.

'You know, my friends, that I do not have a reputation for reckless optimism. For nearly twenty years, I have worked in exile for the restoration of freedom to Penya the Blessed. I have seen our homes defiled and destroyed by the Enemy, our children enslaved, our people murdered, our leaders hunted down and exterminated like animals. There are still perhaps several hundred of our people left on Penya, who will emerge from their hiding-places as soon as we set foot on the island. All of us who have survived have lived on hope, and on the generosity and kindness of our friends and neighbours here in Kerenth. In the city, and in the towns and villages as far as Skathak and Sarquaina, I and my comrades have spoken to nearly eight thousand men and women who have promised to join the invasion force. Our weapons will be makeshift, for there are few swordsmiths here in peaceful Kerenth. But we fight for our homes, for justice, for freedom, and the righteousness of our cause will give us overwhelming strength. Between us and those brave few still on Penya, we will drive the Enemy into the sea! Are you with us?'

'Yes!' shouted Vanaina's people, with one voice and whole hearts, and Mallaso's cry was as loud as the rest.

Essyan waited until the noise had died away. Then he raised his hand for absolute quiet, and was instantly obeyed.

'I know that some of you have dependants. I am well aware that words spoken in the heat of the moment may be regretted later. I do not wish to coerce, nor even to persuade. I want only those who can offer every shred of their heart, soul and body to our cause. And there will always be room for those who do not wish to fight. In such a large enterprise, we need people to help organize the provision of ships, money, weapons and supplies. Those people will be unsung heroes, but heroes none the less. And for the rest of your lives, you can all take pride in the knowledge that your efforts, however small they might seem at the time, will have contributed to the liberation of Penya.'

Mallaso felt her blood stirring, her heart rising. Why should she stay here, in comfort and idleness, while others worked so hard and at such risk for the freedom she longed for? She could not use Kiyu as an excuse for inaction. And even if she did not fight, because of her daughter, Essyan had given her an alternative.

'We must move soon,' he was saying. 'This opportunity will not last for ever. But there is a new mood, a new tide, beginning to surge through the Empire. Djebb has almost gone. Tatht and Tulyet may be next. Terebis, too is restless. The Emperor can crush one rebellion at a time. He cannot possibly hope to subdue them all simultaneously, especially if he is unable to rely on the allegiance of his troops. If we take Penya now, we can hold it for our children, and our children's children, and for all time to come. The world is changing, my friends, my comrades. The hour of freedom is at hand. Will you be part of this, with me?'

And once more, with tears and with joy, they shouted their fervent assent.

Apart from Vanaina and her immediate family, the people of Twin Waters were almost entirely Penyan. Chattering with febrile excitement, they queued to give their names to Gemain, who had paper and pen in front of him. Mallaso wondered guiltily how the farm would manage without them. But Vanaina would surely be able to recruit more workers to replace those who had gone to Penya. Jobs on well-run estates were always in demand.

She glanced at Al'Kalyek. He was gazing thoughtfully into space, but he turned and smiled at her. 'And what will you do?' he enquired, although he must already have guessed her answer.

'I will go to Kerenth,' she told him. 'I can't stand by and watch. I don't want to fight, though – Kiyu needs me, and I need her. But as Essyan said, there are many other ways I can help.' She took a deep breath, aware that her body was trembling with hope, and terror – terror that despite their leader's confident words, their venture would end in failure and disaster. 'What will you do? Will you join us? Or will you return to Onnak?'

'I think so,' the old man said at last. 'I never intended to stay in Kerenth for ever. It is plain now that you are in no danger, either from Olkanno or from anyone else. In the city, you and Kiyu will certainly be safe without my protection.' He smiled at her, with warm affection. 'But I shall miss you, Mallaso of Penya – and I shall miss the baby, too. Whatever her heritage, she is a delightful child.'

'So you still do not know whether – whether she is different?'

'Not for certain, no. She is still so very young, and her mind is unformed. She does show some signs of sensitivity, as she did in the courtyard earlier – but so might an ordinary baby. No, I cannot tell yet. Enjoy her, Mallaso, love her and cherish her. Whether she carries power or not, she is a rare and precious gift.'

'I know,' Mallaso said softly. The queue in front of Gemain had almost disappeared, and she rose to her feet, touching the old man's hand for an instant. 'Thank you. You have been such a good friend to both of us.'

'And you to me,' said Al'Kalyek.

He watched as she gave her name to Essyan's son, and talked with him. They were speaking Penyan, and she smiled and gestured gracefully, more animated than he had ever seen her before. Despite her long years in Toktel'yi, it was very obvious that the childhood on Penya had shaped her capacity for joy, just as slavery had hardened and strengthened her. With such qualities added to her cool, sculptured beauty and dancer's grace, she was a very formidable young woman. And one day soon, she would surely find a man – perhaps even Gemain, who was looking at her with frank admiration – as worthy of her as Bron had been.

So the world had changed, and was still changing. It had not all been for nothing, after all. The familiar sensations of sadness and regret seeped once more into Al'Kalyek's mind. He wished that Bron could have lived to see his lover so fulfilled, to take pleasure in the joyous gift of his daughter, and to help shape the new and different age that was beginning at last to emerge from the old.

Mallaso returned to the table, smiling broadly. 'I've arranged it all,' she said, sitting down again next to the old sorcerer. 'Gemain has offered us rooms in Essyan's house in the city, and he wants me to help with the financial side of the operation. Apparently they have contributions flowing in from all over Kerenth, and need someone to keep track of it – and not spend too much.' She grinned. 'And of course, when I ran the Golden Djarlek, I learned how to do that sort of thing as part of the business. I've helped Vanaina do her accounts, too. Ammenna and S'raya are going as well, so there'll be someone familiar to look after Kiyu. And we leave tomorrow. Do you want to come with us? Is it too soon?'

'No – I have very little to pack. There must be ships plying between Kerenth and Onnak, and I'll book a passage home.' He smiled ruefully. 'I expect my brother and his family have long since given me up for dead. I hope they won't be too shocked when I arrive at their door.'

'I expect they'll be delighted,' Mallaso said. She looked round at the plain, familiar room, the whitewashed plaster, the beamed and boarded ceiling, the long counter where food was laid out, the tables and benches, the embroidered silk hanging from Zithirian, Vanaina's most precious possession, decorating the wall opposite the door. 'I shall be sad to leave, and so perhaps will Kiyu – we've made many good friends here. But most of them are coming with us tomorrow. Essyan wants to attack as soon as possible, before the Emperor has time to send the soldiers back. Though from what Gemain was saying, the trouble in Tatht is so serious that he'll need every man of the Penyan garrison just to stop it spreading to the rest of the province.' She paused, and then said curiously, 'Have you ever heard of someone called the Flamebearer?'

Al'Kalyek sensed a sudden prickling in his skin as she spoke the word in its Toktel'yan form, Makkenekken: a disturbance in the air, an omen of great importance, but whether of hope or of doom, he had not the gift of prophecy to tell. He shook his head. 'No, I have not – but the name has a significant resonance, somehow. Who, or what, is it?'

'No one knows – man, woman, god, spirit, it could be any one of them. But Gemain said that in Djebb, they talk of the Flamebearer who will lead them to freedom. He, or she, or it, appeared in their dreams, and inspired them to rebellion. And now they are speaking of this person in Tatht, too, almost as a god.'

'I see. And does this Flamebearer haunt everyone's dreams?'

'Almost everyone's, I think. He is not in mine, though – yet.'

'But your eyes are already open to the hope of freedom,' Al'Kalyek pointed out. 'The people of Djebb and Tatht probably needed more help.'

'But from whom?' Mallaso asked in bewilderment. 'Who can enter or control dreams? Only a god – or a sorcerer.'

'Not a single sorcerer – he would not have the power. But mages can join together, you know.' Al'Kalyek was looking very thoughtful. 'There is a School of Wizards in Terebis. They have always been loyal to the Emperors, and indeed their last Principal, T'lekko, was intended by Ba'alekkt to replace me. But perhaps they are not so devoted to Olkanno.'

'There is another school of sorcerers,' Mallaso said. 'They are much further away, but probably much more powerful, and I don't think Sé Mo-Tarmé would miss any opportunity to manipulate events to her liking. She isn't evil, but she hates Toktel'yi. She wanted Bron to kill Ba'alekkt because she thought that the Empire would disintegrate in the struggle to find a successor. And if she decided that Olkanno was looking too secure on the Onyx Throne, she would certainly want to help push him off it.'

'Jo'ami,' Al'Kalyek said musingly. 'I still cannot quite believe that you have walked on its soil, for to us it is almost a legend, a myth. And the idea of female sorcerers . . . even their leader is a woman.' He shook his head wryly. 'Do you really think they would have the power to enter so many dreams, at such a distance?'

'I'm not sure. Bron knew much more about their capabilities than I do. But I am certain that by combining their forces, they keep the fire-mountain beneath them asleep. That must take some power. And they tested Bron, when we first arrived – tested him almost to the point of destruction. He was stronger than they were, though, and stronger then the Wolf too, with their help. I would think that Jo'ami is far more likely to be responsible for the Flamebearer rumours than the sorcerers of Terebis.'

'You are probably right,' said Al'Kalyek. 'And if so, then you and your people owe them a great debt.'

Mallaso smiled. 'I was frightened of Sé Mo-Tarmé. I was certain that she wanted to harm me, and Kiyu. I think now that I was wrong, but she did want to keep me on Jo'ami, so that my child, Bron's child, could be taught, and made safe, and exploited for their benefit. But he arranged my escape on a Kerentan ship, and so I came here.'

Vanaina was approaching again. 'Mallaso, would you be very kind and favour us with a display of your dancing? After such wonderful news, I think we need a celebration. Tuyaiya and Maneg will provide the music, and everyone is going through to the courtyard. Will you come?'

She had danced for Ba'alekkt, and never since. But she would dance now for Penya, and the promise of freedom. 'Of course,' said Mallaso, smiling, and she and Al'Kalyek followed Vanaina out of the room.

Far, far to the south and west of Kerenth, Jo'ami shimmered in the heat below a high tropical sun. Around the conical fire-mountain at the island's heart, the lushly forested slopes, the terraced fields full of the red-berried plant that yielded the precious sorcerer's drug, the still blue waters of the Haven, the white sails of the fishing fleet, all hung in the idle air as if they had been painted in brilliant colours on the wall of the world.

In the long, rambling, mostly unoccupied building which housed the remaining mages and their apprentices, the High Sorcerer of Jo'ami was studying her silver scrying bowl. All around stood her chief acolytes, their robes in bright and various colours, dazzlingly at odds with the dull green of their leader. They were very still, their eyes wide and empty as they focused and joined their power and skill to hers, so that a small, vivid image could be brought across six hundred miles of land and ocean, to be set sharp and clear in the dark surface of the ink.

A cavalcade was travelling along a dusty road. There were men, women and children, some riding horses or mules, most on foot. They did not trudge wearily, however, but strode out with hope and confidence and smiling faces. Scrying brought no sound, but it was obvious that several were singing. One man on horseback was playing a reed flute, while a woman walking beside him beat time with her hand on a small flat drum.

Sé Mo-Tarmé's lips moved too. She watched as the people passed, and let her breath out in a long exhalation of triumph. There, walking beside the old man on the mule, was the tall, elegant black woman whom she had last seen in the flesh here, in the School of Wizards, a year and a half previously.

So where was the child? The woman called Mallaso carried a bundle slung over her back, but there was no baby inside it. Had it died? If it had, Sé Mo-Tarmé did not know whether to be glad, that the possible threat to Jo'ami was ended, or sorry, that such a potential of power had been wasted.

The old man had it, in a basket fastened to his saddle-bow. She could just see the curling hair and the soft, sleeping face. She knew already that it was a girl, but its sex made no difference to the High Sorcerer. The prejudiced Toktel'yans might believe that women were incapable of practising sorcery – indeed, that no female could do anything apart from giving pleasure to men – but she, the most powerful mage in the known world, was living proof that they were utterly and disastrously wrong.

She did not speak. At such a vast distance, the link was very tenuous, and any disturbance to the concentration of her acolytes would risk destroying the image. And she wanted very much to know where they were going, the Penyan woman and her sorcerer friend and her precious, dangerous child.

Sweat broke out on Sé Mo-Tarmé's forehead. A few moments more would suffice. She called on her inmost reserves of power, although such an effort would reduce her to abject exhaustion for days. This long-distance scrying could be done only at infrequent intervals, for it always drained her and her acolytes of their strength and energy. It had taken her many months of searching to locate Mallaso in Kerenth, and she had managed to find her only a few times since. But she knew all the vital facts: the existence and sex of her child, the inconvenient and unexplained presence of the Toktel'yan sorcerer, and now the fact that they had all left the farm where Mallaso had lived for so long, and were going . . . where?

She closed her eyes briefly and managed to move the viewpoint a little, to look ahead. At once, she saw the clustered houses and buildings on the steep hills above the Southern Sea, and knew that their destination was Kereneth City.

The picture wavered. One of the younger sorcerers uttered a soft sigh and fell in a faint to the floor. At once the image vanished, and Sé Mo-Tarmé cursed inwardly. It would be five or six days before she could attempt to scry again.

But at least she knew that Mallaso had left her farm, and travelled to the city. From the look of the bundles and baggage that she and her companions were carrying, the move was permanent. So perhaps at last the Penyans were planning to retake their island. And in that case, Sé Mo-Tarmé must move quickly. She did not want the child to fall into Toktel'yan hands, for that would be far, far worse than her death.

But the presence of the old sorcerer posed a considerable problem. She knew who he was, and she respected his power. While he stayed close to Mallaso and the baby, they would be protected. Of course, the mages of Jo'ami together were far stronger than he was, but he would still be able to warn the woman of possible danger.

She chewed her lip thoughtfully, weighing risk against risk. It did not take very long: after all, she had made the decision long ago, when she had tried to keep Mallaso in Jo'ami against her will. She would defy the prophecy, defy Bron, and make Mallaso's daughter an instrument to be used by Jo'ami, rather than against it.

She turned, and began to tell her acolytes what she planned.

PART THREE

DARK ENCHANTMENT

CHAPTER
THIRTEEN

Essyan lived in a large villa occupying a prime site in the most favoured part of Kerenth City, high on the cliffs and close to the Palace. Mallaso never discovered exactly how many people lived and worked there, but guessed that it must be over a hundred. It was a maze of rooms, wings, suites and courtyards and gardens, on two and sometimes three floors, and with the invasion now so close, the place bristled with news and talk and hope.

Mallaso and her daughter shared a room with Ammenna and S'raya on the ground floor, on a courtyard apparently set aside for families. It was tiny, and barely furnished, but they had never needed much: food and a bed for herself and Kiyu satisfied all her physical requirements, and the prospect of working directly, at long last, to liberate Penya certainly occupied her mind.

S'raya, of course, looked after the baby while she and Ammenna spent a large part of each day in Essyan's strong-room on the top floor of the house. Even though only a bird could have entered it from the outside, the windows were closely barred with iron, and there was just one set of keys, carried by Essyan himself, to the treble-locked door. Under Gemain's direction, the contents of four large, immovably heavy chests had to be counted, weighed and recorded, and S'raya worked with Ammenna, taking turns with several other pairs of men and women, one to number, the other to write it down. The amount of gold, silver and jewels donated to the cause was astonishing. But nearly fifty thousand Penyan exiles lived in Kerenth or in the city itself, and many of these refugees had escaped with much of their wealth, or had prospered in exile.

Most of Penya's riches, though, had been garnered from her fertile soil – wine, oil, fruit, essences and spices, nuts and raisins – and had been exported all over the known world. Gemain's talk of wrecked vineyards, orchards hacked down for firewood and houses wantonly destroyed was heartbreaking, and aroused Mallaso to bitter, futile anger. What was the point of such devastation? The native population had already fled, and few of the Toktel'yan immigrants had been able to make much of a living there. Ba'alekkt had behaved like a spoilt child who preferred to break a disputed toy, rather than let a rival have possession of it.

Although her days were very full, she missed Al'Kalyek. He had found a ship in harbour which was about to sail for Onnak, and was now on his way back to his beloved homeland, south of Penya. Kiyu missed him too, and looked for him every morning. She was fretful at first in these new surroundings, but S'raya kept her occupied, and Mallaso was able to work without worrying about her daughter.

The amount of logistic organization involved in this enterprise was astonishing. Of course, such a huge invasion force could not just step into the first passing ship and sail for Penya. Transports had to be hired, each one capable of ferrying hundreds of men and women, with their equipment and supplies, across the Southern Sea. Weapons had to be bought or made, provisions stockpiled, tents purchased. They were not attacking a desert, but the Toktel'yan garrison would probably have left little food or shelter in the ruined towns or in the neglected, depopulated countryside. At first Mallaso, carefully counting and recording, had thought such a vast amount of money excessive. Now, she wondered if it could possibly be enough for what they needed. But Essyan and his son seemed very confident, and she knew that they were receiving considerable help from the Queen of Kerenth, as well as from the Penyan refugees.

She had seen the Queen a few times in the city, and had observed her curiously, remembering that Bron had once been her Consort. The haughty, beautiful, imperious face of Inrai'a certainly resembled the wilful and passionate woman of his description. But the Queen had another Consort now, and a baby daughter to ensure the succession. Mallaso wondered if she had ever heard that Bron had, in fact, survived his sacrificial leap from the cliffs. She doubted it, for his story was complicated and obscure, clouded by aliases and apparently impossible escapes. Even she, who had shared his life for a few months, knew very little of what had happened to him before and after their friendship. If Al'Kalyek had not found her, she would never have learned the full truth about his death.

One night, sleeping warm in her bed, Kiyu cuddled in her arms as always, Mallaso dreamed of Bron for the first time. She saw him walking through a vast bleak landscape of moorland or steppe, striding through long grass amidst a cloud of dancing brown and russet butterflies, while above him a bright and cloudy sky rushed along with the wind. The image was so vivid that she called his name, and began to run. But just as in the forest on Jo'ami, the stones and grass under and around her feet seemed to be conspiring against her. She fell again and again, increasingly exhausted, and shouted to him in desperation. But he drew inexorably and effortlessly away from her, until at last she stopped, knowing that it was hopeless.

And then he turned, and although he was so far away that she could hardly see his face, she heard his voice as clearly as if he was standing next to her. 'Oh, Mallaso, no – no, you can't follow. It was never meant to be for ever. Stay where you belong – stay where you are needed. She needs you – look after her, for I cannot guard her now.'

She woke on a sob of grief, bewildered by his words. Kiyu stirred and whimpered, and Mallaso drew her close, staring into the dark. Of course, he was dead, so she could not follow him. And their love was not destined to be for ever. For a little while, their paths had converged, that was all. He was dead, and although she would always remember him with affection and sorrow, she no longer needed him. She had Kiyu to look after, as he had told her, and work to do.

But in the morning, she found the memory of that sleeping encounter curiously comforting, for it seemed that somehow he must still watch over her, from Olyak's Halls. True, that bare upland, with its own harsh and unfamiliar beauty, bore very little resemblance to the dwellings of the dead, as described by the Lord of Death's priests. But Bron came from the north, and perhaps his beliefs, and his afterlife, were different.

Three months after her arrival, the invasion fleet was almost ready to sail. Nearly nine thousand refugees packed every available room in the city and all the towns and villages around. Fifty ships of all sizes, from fishing-boats to bulky traders capable of carrying several hundred people (although in considerable discomfort), crowded the outer anchorages in the harbour, and a flotilla of smaller craft transported weapons and supplies to them from the docks. Essyan had somehow managed to obtain enough swords, daggers and spears to give each of his volunteers at least one serviceable weapon. Three of the huge chests were now empty, and the fourth only about half full.

Diligently and accurately, Mallaso and Ammenna had doled out expenses to the Penyans, and recorded everything in the huge leather-bound ledger which Essyan had supplied. In the evenings, the villa would be full of music and talk: Mallaso listened to songs which she had heard as a child, but remembered only vaguely, and learned the dances of Penya, full of grace and vitality, from women who had performed them as adults. Wondering, delighted, she realized that the

Penyans-in-exile had kept their rich culture and customs alive through all the long and bitter years of banishment, as vibrantly and as completely as if they had never left the island. In Toktel'yi, she had thought that her homeland had been destroyed for ever. Now, she knew that if Essyan succeeded, a new Penya would rise like the firebird from its own ashes, renewed and invigorated, and perhaps even greater than before. For they were all acutely aware of the preciousness and fragility of what they had thought lost for ever, and would strive always to preserve and protect the land if it was restored to them.

Kiyu was a year old now, and taking her first steps, holding on to her mother's hand. Mallaso hoped that soon she would walk on the white soft sand of Penya Harbour, her rightful home.

The three months of preparation had been rather longer than Essyan had wanted, or expected, but although he chafed impatiently at the delay, his own meticulous caution was largely to blame. He had insisted on planning everything himself, down to the last detail, and although his care should ensure that the invasion itself would progress with smooth efficiency, Mallaso more than once had to stop herself from reminding him that two missing barrels of salt fish would not inevitably mean the failure of the entire operation.

But Essyan was not the type of man whose judgement could be questioned. Mallaso had been too young to remember him before the Toktel'yan attack on Penya. Perhaps he had not been so stern and forbidding: perhaps he had even smiled occasionally. She herself had faced Ba'alekkt's fury with pride and courage, and was not afraid of Essyan, but did not want to cause disagreement. The refugees were a remarkably united and enthusiastic group, and she still felt herself to be an outsider. After all, she had only been part of the team for a few months, and to utter any word of complaint seemed ungrateful, even disloyal.

At least, though, the delay was not disastrous. The disturbances in Tatht had now erupted into outright rebellion, and by all accounts Olkanno, who had only occupied the Onyx Throne for five months, had his hands full trying to extinguish the flames of revolt in three provinces simultaneously. He could not afford to let Tatht and Tulyet go the same way as Djebb, which was now to all intents and purposes beyond Imperial control. Half a month before the provisional date agreed by Essyan and his chief officers for the invasion of Penya, half the remaining garrison, five hundred men, were despatched to help their beleaguered comrades on the mainland.

Mallaso found herself sorely tempted. She knew, of course, that she could not risk going with the invasion force. If she were killed, her beloved daughter would be left an orphan, too young to remember her. But it was extraordinarily difficult to accept that others, less tied, less cautious, were hazarding their lives on her behalf. She wanted to share in the excitement, the comradeship and the glory, but it was not possible. And moreover Essyan, who was well aware of her circumstances, would be adamant. Her child must take priority, and no blame or stigma would be attached to her if she was not part of that first brave band.

Still, she took Kiyu down to the harbour every evening, to watch the preparations. It was a long way from Essyan's villa, but she had a little money, earned from Vanaina, and sometimes hired a donkey-sled back up the steep hill. And the baby loved the bustle of the waterfront, the smaller ships tied up at the quayside, the larger vessels anchored out in the bay, and the constant traffic to and fro of skiffs, fishing boats and huge flat-bottomed ferry barges, wind-driven by a single square sail and steered by poles pushed into the soft sand and mud below Kerenth Bay. Sometimes S'raya accompanied them, and held Kiyu while Mallaso helped to load supplies for the waiting invasion ships. But mostly, mother and child came alone.

One warm afternoon in the last month of the year, the Kerentan trader *Lady Inrai'a* dropped anchor in the harbour. It was so crowded with shipping that only space in the deeper and less sheltered waters outside the mole was available, but she did not have the shallow draught needed to thread her way through the mass of moored craft to the quayside below the cliffs.

Beygan, her Master, was one of the few male sea-captains in Kerenth, and also one of the poorest, with a single, rather shabby and elderly ship, a heap of debts and no particular scruples about whom he carried and where he sailed. The Jo'ami trade, which entailed a long, perilous but usually profitable voyage, was usually undertaken by a comparatively small elite, and he had incurred the wrath of several captains by daring to join them. He needed the money, though, and when he had unloaded his cargo of wine and silk at the Wizard's Isle, and found the High Sorcerer herself asking for passage back to Kerenth, he had accepted with an enthusiasm that most of his compatriots, suspicious of drug-driven sorcery, would never have shown.

It was not just Sé Mo-Tarmé, either – four of her acolytes were coming too. Their demands for cabin space were so outrageous that he'd have no room for any return cargo, apart from a few boxes of

Annatal, but they paid so handsomely, in the gold Imperials that were good currency all over the known world, that he could not complain. And at least with that number of sorcerers aboard, he'd have a good fair following wind all the way back to Kerenth, and no fear of pirates, storms, rocks or sea-monsters.

And so it had proved. After the easiest and most uneventful voyage in his entire sailing career, although it was supposed to be the height of the hurricane season, the *Lady Inrai'a* dropped anchor outside the mile-long mole protecting Kerenth harbour, and Beygan let out a sigh of relief. They had arrived safely. He'd earned his money. Now he just had to take on fresh food and water while the sorcerers did whatever urgent business they'd come to Kerenth for, and then they would sail back to Jo'ami. It would be hard work, but his debts would be paid, and he'd even have a little left over. The *Lady Inrai'a* needed a new suit of sails, and one or two seams could do with caulking before she encountered another storm.

In her cramped cabin below the high stern deck, Sé Mo-Tarmé gazed intently into her scrying bowl. At last the wretched ship was at rest: it had proved extraordinarily difficult to focus her concentration when being heaved up and down by unruly waves, and although the weather had been good, she had suffered the humiliation of sea-sickness. Since Healing was not a branch of the High Art taught on Jo'ami, she had been forced to endure it. Fortunately, two of her acolytes were from Fabriz, and therefore immune to such weakness. Their skill, not hers, had steered the *Lady Inrai'a* while she had been incapacitated, and provided the steady breeze to propel her around the southern coast of Onnak, and due north to Kerenth.

Her four companions knew about the old prophecy, which foretold that Bron's 'legacy' would destroy Jo'ami. The words of the ancient soothsayer were ambiguous and obscure, but the High Sorcerer's interpretation of them seemed to convince the others, and in any case few of them would have dared to question their leader's decision. And her remedy for the problem was stark in its simplicity. 'The child is a threat. Therefore, remove it.'

Seeing the shock on their faces, she had explained that she did not intend to harm Bron's daughter. She merely wanted, for the sake of the power the baby must carry, and her consequent potential for harm, to take her back to Jo'ami, to be brought up on the island, and trained for sorcery.

'And her mother?' her kinswoman, Gen Lul-Tarmé, had enquired, with a look in her eyes that the High Sorcerer did not like.

'Her mother has no interest in magic. She detests the very idea that her daughter might possess power. She told me so herself. Obviously, she is not fit to rear such a child.'

There had been some shuffling of feet, and use of thoughtlink. Sé Mo-Tarmé had glared at the possible doubters. 'May I remind you that it is the fate of our beloved island, and of sorcery itself, that is at stake? We cannot afford to be lenient. The woman Mallaso is of no account. The child is all-important. She is young, and she will soon forget her mother. We are not monsters – we will treat her with kindness, as one of our own. Indeed, as she was conceived on Jo'ami, she *is* one of our own. Now, are there any further objections? Remember, our island, our entire existence, is in peril.'

There had been no more dissent, and Sé Mo-Tarmé and her four acolytes had embarked on the *Lady Inrai'a*. The vessel was hardly ideal, but it was the first Kerentan ship to reach Jo'ami after the High Sorcerer had finally decided to abduct Kiyu, and she wanted no further delay. There was every chance that the Penyan woman would join the invasion force, and in the confusion and fighting the child could be harmed, or lost. Sé Mo-Tarmé had no intention of letting such a valuable prize fall into enemy hands.

She had tried to keep track of Mallaso through her scrying bowl, but sea-sickness had overwhelmed her power, and the images, usually so clear and bright, had become shadowy and obscure. But now the ship was at anchor in Kerenth harbour, and the sea beneath her no longer heaved and tossed like an angry whale. With relief, Sé Mo-Tarmé was able at last to bend all her formidable will upon the black ink within the silver bowl.

So close to the one she sought, she had no need of assistance, and she was quite alone, her door locked against inconvenient intrusion. She closed her eyes and chanted the mantras of concentration, followed by the charm of finding, and her quarry's name, repeated over and over again. And when she looked down at the bowl, Mallaso was reflected within it, her child in her arms.

The speed and ease of her success took even the High Sorcerer by surprise. She gasped, and a triumphant smile spread across her lined face. For her prey was actually standing on the quayside. If she went up on deck, she would see them.

There was no time to waste. This stunning stroke of fortune was a sign that Kaylo was smiling on them, and it would be extremely bad luck not to take immediate advantage of it. Sé Mo-Tarmé checked the image, then abandoned her bowl and swept out of her cabin in search of her companions.

They were all on deck, gazing at Kereth City, piled on its cliff, as if they were country bumpkins from some remote rock in the Scatterlings who'd never seen more than three houses together before. The High Sorcerer strode up to them, her face shining with the power of her purpose. 'They are here, now, on the quayside. There may not be another such opportunity. We must strike at once, or risk failure.'

'But we've only just arrived,' one of the younger acolytes objected.

'We are not here on a pleasure trip, Amzaren. We are here on a mission of paramount importance. *Everything* must be subservient to the taking of that child – *everything*. Captain Beygan? Where's that Captain?'

He hurried up, his face pale with anxiety. 'Yes, Most Wise? How can I be of service?'

'You may lower a boat at once. I and my companions are going ashore. We will return as soon as our aim is achieved – it will not take very long. And the moment we step back on board, you will weigh anchor and head back to Jo'ami.'

Beygan's unshaven, rather prominent jaw dropped in horrified disbelief. '*What?* But – but we've only just got here!'

'I know. But a golden opportunity has just arisen, and we must grasp it *now*, or the whole voyage will have been a complete waste of time and effort. Do you understand me?'

'But provisions – we're low on food – we'll need water – we can't sail all the way back to Jo'ami on the little we've got left.'

'I am High Sorcerer. I will take care of it. Do as I say, little man, or I shall insist that you return every last chip of my payment, with interest – and I shall also ensure that you are never allowed to enter Jo'ami Haven again.'

Helplessly, Beygan stared at her grim and implacable face. Then, with what sounded like a sob of despair, he turned and shouted to his men.

Sé Mo-Tarmé smiled. 'I knew he would see sense,' she remarked to her cousin. 'The man is little more than an idiot, but one must make use of the tools to hand, however unsuitable they may be, if they are all that one has to work with. Are you ready?'

Slowly, pale with apprehension or excitement, her companions nodded.

'Good,' said the High Sorcerer. 'And remember our plan – remember our reasons and our purpose. On our success, or failure, depends not only the fate of Jo'ami, but the fate of the world. The boat is ready? Then let us go ashore.'

*

'Back again? We can't keep you away!' One of the Penyan refugees, a big muscular man with whipcord arms and a ready grin, staggered past Mallaso with his back bent almost double under a huge bundle of grey canvas, presumably some of the tents. He tipped them over the quayside into a waiting barge, straightened with a grunt, and stopped on his way back to smile at Kiyu. 'How's my pretty girl today? How many teeth have you got now, little one?'

'Eight,' Mallaso said, with a loving glance at her daughter. 'Four at the top, and four on the bottom.'

'A year old and eight teeth already! My little boy only had six when he was your age, sweetheart.' The man gently poked Kiyu's fat round tummy under the soft blue cotton of her tunic, and the baby giggled and wriggled, delighted. 'Who's a pretty girl, then? Lovely as your mother, you are.' He winked at Mallaso. 'If I wasn't married already, I'd be after you myself.'

'Tumay? Tumay! We haven't got all day!'

'Sorry,' said the big man, and with a last gentle tickle under Kiyu's chin, he hurried away to finish unloading the tents.

Mallaso strolled on, keeping out of the way of the bustling line of volunteer labourers. In a few days' time, the fleet would sail. The largest ships were already fully laden, and only the smaller craft remained to be filled with the less essential supplies: food, water and weapons were already on board.

She wondered whether the Emperor knew what was being planned. If the new Spymaster was even half as efficient as his predecessor, then he certainly did. Officially, Kerenth did not tolerate the presence of Imperial agents snooping within her borders, but everyone knew that one or two at least must be operating in the city, perhaps even now hanging round the docks, or preparing a report to be sent back to Toktel'yi tied round a pigeon's leg. Preparations on this scale could not be hidden. But Essyan and his son had, so far, managed to keep the exact date of the invasion a secret, known only to themselves and to a few of their most trusted comrades. Mallaso, although she worked with them every day, had not been told. But, like everyone else in Kerenth City, she could guess.

And only Essyan and Gemain and their Council knew, too, exactly where their army would land on Penya.

But most people thought that it wouldn't matter if Olkanno was sent every detail of the plans in hand-high letters of scarlet ink, because the Emperor no longer had any realistic hope of keeping Penya within the Empire. The mainland provinces, and Tulyet with its vital iron mines, were his first priority. The fact that he had denuded the island's garrison in the attempt to crush the Tatht rebellion proved the point. And Mallaso hoped that this pragmatic and logical reasoning was not flawed, that Penya really was almost defenceless, and that Olkanno did not harbour some deep and devious ulterior motive that his withdrawal of the troops had cunningly disguised.

But unless he had five thousand heavily armed soldiers somehow already hidden away on the island, she did not think that Essyan and his amateur invasion force would be walking into a trap.

'Hallo, Mallaso.'

It was Essyan's son. He had a sheaf of papers in his hand, and the usual lines of tension and anxiety marring his handsome face. Mallaso smiled, and greeted him in return. She liked Gemain, who was far less forbidding and remote than his grim father: it was even possible to exchange a joke with him, or make a witty remark that was not greeted with a disapproving glance. He was very good-looking, with the black skin and proud features of many Penyans, and Mallaso was well aware that he admired her. If she had been ambitious, she might have encouraged him: marriage to such a man, even in Penya's egalitarian society, would bring status and prestige. But Gemain had always lived in his formidable father's shadow, and the thought of waking up to that worried face every morning was not appealing. He was a man who had to be pushed to make up his mind, and Mallaso, strengthened by experience, knew that she needed someone who was as tough as she was.

'A lovely afternoon, isn't it?' he said, pausing to smile at Kiyu. The baby smiled back, revealing all her small, gleaming teeth, and uttered a string of unintelligible babble.

'I think she's saying hallo,' Mallaso told him.

'I expect so. Still hankering after sailing with us?'

She nodded, with a rueful smile. 'Yes, I am. But I know I have to stay behind with Kiyu. Send us word, Gemain, and as soon as it's safe, we'll be on the first boat to a free Penya.'

'As will thousands of others in your position. Did you know that a year or so back, my father organized a census of all the Penyans in Kerenth? There were nearly seven thousand children who had been born in exile, and four thousand more who had fled the island when they were very young – some only babies, younger than Kiyu.' He made a speech very similar to this almost every day, and Mallaso's attention was beginning to wander. 'They are our future, and freedom is their inheritance. One day, your daughter and others like her will be adult, and they will rule Penya. For their sake, the sooner we take our land back, the better.'

'I know.' Mallaso's gaze drifted over the crowded harbour, ships at rest, ships sailing out with the tide, barges ferrying goods to and fro, and the small triangular sails of passenger boats skimming like water-bound birds through the complicated tangle of anchor chains, buoys, and other obstacles. 'Although her father was not Penyan, she belongs to us, rather than to his people.'

Gemain looked politely curious. Mallaso had always been reticent about the identity of Kiyu's father, and although in Kerenth, and to a certain degree in Penya as well, the mother's lineage was the most important, he had obviously been wondering about the unknown man who had once been Mallaso's lover.

But she had no intention of giving him any intimate details of her past life. He knew that she'd been a slave in Toktel'yi, then a dancer. Except for Ammenna and Vanaina, and Al'Kalyek of course, she had told no one about Bron, or about their flight to Jo'ami, or about Kiyu's possible inheritance. Her history was her own business, and hers alone. At moments like this, though, she yearned for the company of an old friend, especially Sargenay, with whom she needed no concealment or pretence.

One of the passenger boats was flying over the water towards them, so swiftly that she must be driven by sorcery. Kiyu gazed at it, her face alight with pleasure, and shouted in her incomprehensible private language.

There was something familiar about the grey-haired woman standing in the bow of the boat. She was small and sturdy, and wearing long garments of a dull muddy green colour, in gloomy contrast to the bright robes of the men and women behind her. Mallaso was certain that she had seen her before, a long time ago, but for an instant she could not place her.

And then, with a sickening, terrified jolt of the heart, she remembered.

Sé Mo-Tarmé, the High Sorcerer of Jo'ami. Wise, sometimes: kindly, when it suited her: sweeping all obstacles from her path when she wanted her own way: and so convinced of the justice of her cause that she had tried to detain Mallaso on Jo'ami against her will, so that Bron's child could be brought up under her personal supervision.

With Bron's help, she had managed to escape. And now, it seemed that Sé Mo-Tarmé had caught up with her, here in Kerenth.

There could only be one reason why the High Sorcerer and more than half her acolytes would have voyaged so many hundreds of miles from their beloved island. And that reason was held, warm and soft and blazingly alive, within the loving and protective circle of her mother's arms.

'Oh, no,' Mallaso whispered. 'Oh, no.' Her grip on Kiyu tightened, and the baby's happy grin changed to a frown of disquiet.

'What is it?' Gemain demanded. 'Mallaso, what's wrong?'

It was too late to run, even if she had thought it possible to hide Kiyu from the most powerful sorcerers in the known world. Only one person had ever been able to outwit them, and he was dead. He and his powers were forever beyond their reach: but Mallaso and her child were not.

Even so, she turned to flee, knowing that it was futile. At her first step, the sound of her name seemed to reverberate inside her head, although nothing had been spoken aloud. And then she found that she could not move another muscle.

This was how Bron had rescued her from Ba'alekkt's Palace on Tekkt, after she had tried to kill him. This was what he had done to the soldiers, and the courtiers, and the Emperor himself, so that she could escape. Her frantic brain sent a stream of signals to her paralysed limbs, and they would not respond. Nothing obeyed her, despite all her efforts. It was as if she had been turned to stone. But Kiyu, struggling within her tight and rigid grasp, seemed to be unaffected.

She could not see Gemain, who must be standing behind her, out of her sight, but he was surely also frozen by sorcery. But the people streaming past did not seem to have noticed their plight.

The voice of the High Sorcerer, brisk and impervious, spoke again inside her skull. *Mallaso, we have come for the child. She will be well cared for – she will come to no harm.*

But how can you take her away from me and not harm her? Despite the spell, it seemed that she was able to answer. Desperately, she tried to struggle free. *I am her mother – she needs me – please, Sé Mo-Tarmé, take me too, do not leave me behind!*

You will have other children. This one is ours, to rear on Jo'ami. We will guard her well, and train her to use her power. Your presence would interfere with that – you fear and distrust sorcery.

No, I don't! Mallaso cried in horror to that implacable voice. *I fear and distrust YOU! How can you take her – how can you possibly justify taking her away from me!*

For the good of the world, said Sé Mo-Tarmé. *Power such as hers, untrained and unchecked, is lethally dangerous.*

But what if she HASN'T any power? Al'Kalyek couldn't tell!

There was a tiny pause. *She has power*, said Sé Mo-Tarmé. *Let her go, Mallaso, to the glorious future awaiting her. One day, she, and you, will thank us for this.*

Never, never, NEVER, until the day I die, you evil selfish old crone! Mallaso cried, with desperate fury. *Please don't take her – I love her so much, oh, please, please don't take her—*

Sé Mo-Tarmé stood in front of her. In the flesh, she seemed much smaller than Mallaso remembered, but the pale blue eyes were as hard as pebbles, and less compassionate. With quick, relentless hands, she prised the baby from Mallaso's rigid grasp, finger by finger.

Oh, Kiyu, little bird – don't take her – no, Sé Mo-Tarmé, this isn't right, this isn't good, however good your reasons are – this is so cruel, to take her away from me – at least take me too, for pity's sake, I am her MOTHER!

'For the good of the world, I do this,' said the High Sorcerer, aloud, but very quietly. 'And for Jo'ami. Do not try to follow us, Mallaso of Penya. A wall of sorcery will surround and protect Kiyu always, and you will never be allowed to enter it. Her father understood the meaning of sacrifice for the greater good. Now you too must give up your most precious possession. We will treat her as well as you do, if not better – do not fear for her, she will be safe.'

But you will not LOVE her! Mallaso screamed inside her head. *You don't know the meaning of the word!*

Accept her fate, said Sé Mo-Tarmé silently. Kiyu's dark eyes were distended with shock and bewilderment, and suddenly her mouth opened in a howl of horror and fury. The High Sorcerer turned away, and Mallaso could not move to see, but she could hear Kiyu's frantic screams echoing all round the waterfront, until they ended very abruptly, as if a hand had been placed over her mouth.

Do not follow. The order boomed in her mind, eclipsing all independent thought. *Do not follow. Do not follow. Do not follow. Do not follow . . .*

'Mallaso! Sweet mother, what happened? Are you all right? Where's Kiyu?'

Gemain was kneeling beside her, urgently and ineffectively patting her hands. Mallaso became aware that she was lying on the cobbled stones of the quayside, with a considerable crowd around her. Her head ached as if someone had struck it with a hammer. And sunk like a stone in her heart was the terrible knowledge that Kiyu, her beloved child, the light of her life, the reason for her existence, had been wrenched from her arms and taken away by ruthless strangers.

She pushed Gemain aside, scrambled to her feet and ran to the edge of the quay. There were a score of small sails out there, a hundred anchored ships. If Kiyu was near or far, she could not tell: her mind reached frantically forward into a dark and formless void, bereft of life, of love, of hope.

'Get a boat!' she cried. 'They've taken Kiyu – get a boat!'

Even as she spoke, the furthest ship from the shore raised her anchor and hoisted two patched and shabby sails, and turned away from Kerenth.

'Who's taken her? Why have they taken her?' Gemain was saying helplessly. 'Mallaso, I don't understand – what's happened to her?'

And for the last time, the voice of Sé Mo-Tarmé spoke inside her head.

It is too late. We have gone. Do not follow. Do you not realize, Mallaso of Penya? If you try to pursue us, you will surely deserve your fate – and whatever you may try to do, Kiyu is ours now. You will never see her again.

As the *Lady Inrai'a* cleared the mole and set her course for Jo'ami, Mallaso understood at last that her daughter was gone for ever. Defeated by the terrible loss, overwhelmed by grief and despair, she sank down at the water's edge, and wept, for her heart was truly broken.

As the horned moon of Sarraliss rose above the city, Gemain, after much searching, finally managed to hire a donkey-sled to take them back to Essyan's house. There, Mallaso was tended with great care and kindness, given words of comfort that meant nothing, and a potion that could not make her sleep.

All night she lay, cold and alone, feeling the absence of Kiyu's warm, loving presence, as if she had lost the greater part of herself. And when the sun rose on her first day without her child, she had faced the dreadful truth, and made her decision.

Kiyu had been taken. She knew enough about the sorcerers of Jo'ami to be sure that she would never be able to reach her, no matter how hard she tried. Sé Mo-Tarmé was proof against all feelings of compassion or warmth. Kiyu was gone for ever. She would never see her again. Her daughter was as lost to her as if she had died.

She rose dry-eyed, and went to Essyan's study. He was already at his desk, poring over charts of Penya: Gemain had told her, with pride, that he needed only a couple of hours' sleep each night.

She told him, quietly and simply, what had happened to Kiyu, and why. He listened in silence, asking no questions, not even when she explained about Bron, and his extraordinary powers. And when her tale was ended, she received the answer she wanted.

Six days later, when the invasion fleet sailed at last out of Kerenth Bay, Mallaso, a sword at her side, stood on the deck of Essyan's flagship, gazing across the blue ocean to the distant smudge on the horizon that marked the island of her birth.

CHAPTER
FOURTEEN

'There's a storm coming.'

'Really, weather-worker?' Kazhian gestured with a lavish hand at the absolute and unsullied sapphire sky above them. 'Where? Over there, perhaps?'

'No,' said Sargenay, who had long been inured to his Captain's cheerful teasing. 'Off the south coast of Tulyet, actually.'

'Then it shouldn't affect us, should it?' Kazhian leaned over the stern rail and gazed down at the white foaming track of the *Sea Serpent*, slithering through the sleek waters of the Southern Sea. Nothing marred the hazy circumference of the horizon, but the gaggle of squawking gulls, swooping hopefully in their wake, was a sure sign that land lay beyond their sight. To the north was Annatal, and eastwards lurked Onnak's Tail, a long scattering of rocky islets. But in all this expanse of ocean, there was not a single sail to be seen.

The shores of Balki had become too hot for them: they'd been chased by a couple of Navy galleys, and nearly caught. Traders were warier now, less eager to sail too close to an unknown ship. The chest of gold they'd taken from Arkun's agent had long since run out, spent on wine, women and a refit for the *Sea Serpent*, before the perils of the rainy season, in an isolated and friendly fishing village on one of the larger Scatterlings. Now, her hull cleaned of barnacles, her leaks plugged, her sails repainted in bright red and yellow vertical stripes and her rudder-gear renewed, Kazhian's ship sailed sweetly and swiftly through the water, ready and hungry for prey. But it seemed as if the sailors of Annatal, Onnak and all the Scatterlings between had somehow got wind of their arrival, for they'd seen nothing except a few distant fishing boats in nearly half a month of cruising up and down the empty sea south of Annatal.

'We shouldn't have come here,' Kazhian said, still gazing down at the water. 'All the main ports of Onnak and Annatal are on their northern coasts, not the south. We'd have done better to stay in the Scatterlings.'

'Or raiding the rainy-season traffic between Toktel'yi and Tekkt,' said Sargenay, grinning.

'I can't think of a better way to ensure we get strung up from a Navy masthead. And I don't fancy being shark-bait just yet. How far away is that storm, weather-worker?'

'Three or four hundred miles. It's moving north-east, heading for the gap between Jo'ami and Tulyet – in other words, straight for us. And it's the biggest one this year, by the look of it. Too big for me to cope with.'

A subtle change in his voice made Kazhian glance up. After a pause, he said, 'You're worried, aren't you? And when you're worried, weather-worker, you scare the shit out of me. How long have you known about this? Storms don't just appear overnight.'

'This one did. And in answer to your question, about half an hour.' At his Captain's look, Sargenay added defensively, 'I needed to be sure where it was going. Most storms at this time of year begin far in the south, and track north-east, between Annatal and Onnak, before battering the southern coast of Penya. This one isn't an exception. The only unusual thing about it is its size and strength.'

'How fast is it moving?'

'If it was possible to stay in this exact spot, it would be on us before sunrise tomorrow. On this course, we're heading straight towards it. If we put about, and run before it, it should catch up with us some time tomorrow morning.'

'And be driven on to some gods-forsaken rock,' said Kazhian. 'Well, we've survived all the others – so far. What are our chances of surviving this one?'

'Good, I'd say – as long as we can keep to the open sea. If we're thrown on to a lee shore, we're lost.'

'I know that – the perils of a lee shore are set out on the first page of my manual of seamanship.' Kazhian narrowed his eyes, staring forward to the distant horizon beyond the *Sea Serpent*'s prow. 'Strange, isn't it? If I didn't have you on board, I'd have no idea of what's coming. Not even a prickle on the skin. Sky blue, sea calm, wind gentle. Not a hint of trouble.'

'It proves,' said Sargenay pointedly, 'that a competent weather-worker is an invaluable member of the crew.'

'It does indeed. It doesn't explain why you've only just detected this one.'

'I told you, it appeared very suddenly. Are you complaining?'

'No, just curious. I thought you could see for hundreds of miles in that scrying bowl of yours.'

'I can – when it lets me. Scrying is the most difficult and inexact branch of my Art. If the bowl does not chose to reveal all its secrets, I am powerless.'

'It's all right, weather-worker.' Kazhian gave him a friendly clap on the shoulder. 'I'm teasing you, or hadn't you noticed? And those storms move bloody fast. At least we've been warned of this one in time. Let's go below and consult the chart – we can work out where to find shelter.'

Sargenay waited in the familiar stuffy darkness while his Captain tripped over a pile of books, swore, found steel and stone, struck a light, and eventually, after much muttering and cursing, located the map underneath a pile of dirty clothes. He unfolded it and laid it on the mattress, and they peered down at it in the flickering light.

'Why was I fumbling round in the dark when you can produce witchfire with a snap of your fingers?' Kazhian grumbled, with a sly glance at his sorcerer. 'You're pretty useless, weather-worker – I don't know why I ever took you on.'

'Because no one else was fool enough to risk sailing with a lunatic,' Sargenay pointed out. He was so close to his Captain that their clothes were touching. Once, such proximity to the man he loved would have caused him acute anguish. The two years on Kazhian's ship had not diminished his feelings, but at least they had taught him to become accustomed to them. He could shut off his senses: ignore the warmth of the other man's body; refuse to look at the strong sinewy arms and surprisingly fine hands, calloused with work on rope and tiller, the long curling strands of black hair falling over his narrow face, and the green eyes, sometimes dark with despair, more often, as at present, glinting with wicked laughter.

One of the younger members of the crew, a pleasant and handsome Balkian, now shared Sargenay's bed, and the edge of his physical hunger had been blunted. But still, hopeless and helpless, he was in love, and could see no remedy. Another man might have slept with him once or twice, out of misplaced kindness. Kazhian had made it clear where he stood, and what he did not want. Friendship was offered, warmly, but no more than that. And since it was a greater gift than Sargenay knew he had a right to expect, he had accepted it, even though it would not ever be enough.

Kazhian never referred to his sorcerer's devotion, never teased him about it and never made sly digs in front of the crew. Sargenay was grateful, for it was humiliating enough to know his love was hopelessly unrequited. To be the subject of sniggering gossip amongst the other sailors would have dealt his pride and self-esteem a mortal blow.

He had the measure of Kazhian now. For a man trained to kill, brought up in the merciless, utterly ruthless mould of Eska'anen, he could be astonishingly gentle, astonishingly considerate. That, and his hidden vulnerability, his wicked sense of humour, his dagger-sharp intelligence, was why Sargenay loved him. The dark moods, and above all the wild recklessness which had prompted him, so many times, to flirt with disaster as he would with a lover, were less favourable traits. And if he wanted to plunge into the heart of the storm, as he had after rescuing Megren, then Sargenay intended to tell him exactly what he thought of such irresponsible audacity.

The chart was drawn on Tekktish goatskin, which was less susceptible than paper to the ravages of salt water. Even so, the ink was blotched and faded in several places, and part of the south-western coast of Tulyet had almost disappeared. Kazhian stabbed a finger at the empty space between Annatal and the islands trailing out to the west of Onnak, known as the Tail. 'We're somewhere here. Where's that storm?'

'Here – between Tulyet and Jo'ami, if that's where Jo'ami is.'

'An old sailor told me once that it was carried about the Southern Sea on the backs of a dozen giant whales. It's more likely to be inaccurately marked. This is the best chart I could lay my hands on in Balki, but it's not exactly a cartographer's dream – more of a sailor's nightmare.'

The unknown map-maker had certainly been more interested in depicting an imaginative selection of sea-monsters on any available blank area of sea, than in drawing an accurate representation of the Archipelago. Even to Sargenay, whose knowledge of the islands was scanty, the distance between Tekkt and Balki was too small, the Scatterlings were too scattered, and Penya was shown as being much further from the coast of Kerenth than it was in reality. He said doubtfully, 'Is it right?'

'Is Olyak Lord of Life? Of course it's not bloody right, but it's the best we can do – unless you can persuade your scrying bowl to be a bit more helpful.' Kazhian studied the chart, frowning. 'Unless we make for the south of Onnak, we'll be blown ashore somewhere. And even if we do, we risk being driven onto the rocks around the Tail. Or we could try to run up the channel between Annatal and Tulyet – but I don't think we've got enough time.' He paused, his eyes flicking from island to island. 'Onnak it'll have to be. And who knows, if we find shelter somewhere on the southern coast, there might be rich pickings.' He grinned wolfishly. 'Spice ships. Wine ships. Annatal for you – you must be getting low. And khlar.'

'Admit it,' said the sorcerer, attempting to match the other man's apparent cheerfulness. 'It's the only reason you want to go to Onnak.'

'Oh, it is.' Kazhian uncoiled his body with the smooth grace of a leopard, and stretched up his hands, bracing himself against the low, beamed ceiling of the cabin. 'After all, I haven't tasted a pipe for over a year. Any other considerations, such as our survival, are of course trivial by comparison.' His eyes glinted mischief as he blew out the lamp. 'Let's go tell Hadjiken and the rest what's in store.'

The *Sea Serpent* continued south-west on her old course, towards the storm. As the sun plunged down towards the rim of the sea, its bright clear disc became blurred and red, and the wind began to rise. Sargenay, glancing astern, saw that the pursuing gulls had vanished, presumably to seek the shelter of land. In all the vastness of the Southern Sea, they were quite alone. And on his own limited powers of sorcery, on Kazhian's seamanship and the dubious accuracy of a primitive chart, all their lives now depended.

As night fell with tropical swiftness, dark clouds, harbingers of the storm, were stretching ominous fingers towards them from the west. Her lamps lit, the *Sea Serpent* ploughed on through the rising swell, while Kazhian crouched on deck, poring over the map by lantern light, and occasionally glancing up at the sky. Overhead and to the north, as yet out of reach of the storm, the stars were still bright. Sargenay had consulted his bowl again, but it told him nothing that he did not already know. Weather-workers could control small winds and small waves, but against the fierce might of this hurricane, his puny powers were useless.

For what seemed like hours, they beat against the wind. The *Sea Serpent* pitched and tossed in the heaving sea, her sharp bow almost burying itself in each huge wave, then shaking itself free on the crest with a shower of white spray before plummetting down to the next trough. Sargenay began to feel sick, and used all his powers of Healing to fight the nausea. And Kazhian, dark, silent, intent, would not give the word for which they were all waiting.

As the first rain fell, drumming on the deck in huge fat stinging drops, the *Sea Serpent*'s Captain shouted the order. Hadjiken, the steersman, pushed the tiller hard over. For an instant, the ship lay wallowing helplessly, broadside to the waves. Sargenay closed his eyes, and with an effort of concentration so great that it brought the sweat bubbling up on his brow, forced her bow around. The sails, close-hauled, flapped loudly and then filled, and the *Sea Serpent* gathered way with increasing speed, propelled by wind and wave. For the moment, the danger was past.

Kazhian showed him where they were heading. The new course would take them out of the storm's path, and into the comparatively sheltered waters south of Onnak. If the gods smiled, if the storm followed the track which Sargenay had predicted, if the ship did not spring a leak, if the chart was more or less accurate, and Kazhian's calculations were correct, then they would reach safety sometime during the following day.

None of the *Sea Serpent*'s crew managed any sleep that night. Kazhian, responsible for his ship and all aboard her, kept his station by the steersman, relieving him at regular intervals. There were no stars left now to steer by, no moon to guide them: only the chart, and the wild fickle vacillations of the lodestone, and the roar of wind and water and weather.

Dawn came long after Sargenay had been hoping for it, a feeble improvement from impenetrable darkness to grey gloom. If they had altered course too soon, they would shortly run on to the Tail. And if Kazhian had left it too late, they would be sailing at full speed into the endless, empty waters south of the Archipelago, unknown and uncharted, with no hope of landfall ahead.

Hadjiken kept the tiller steady, with a couple of shipmates to help him. Sargenay uncovered his scrying bowl, but the sea was too rough to use it. He felt sick, cold, stiff, ancient and unbelievably tired. And still the storm showed no sign of abating.

'Come with me?'

Kazhian's shout, right in his ear, jerked Sargenay out of his numb exhaustion. He stared at his Captain in bewilderment.

'Up there. Someone's got to take a look, now it's lighter. And the wind's beginning to drop.'

The sorcerer had never grown accustomed to heights. He shook his head. 'No, I can't. I'd fall. You take care.'

'Don't I always?' said Kazhian, grinning as if he had had many hours of dreamless sleep, instead of none at all. 'I'll be back soon. Be good.'

Sargenay watched as he swung up the rigging, with that lithe, enviable strength and agility. The wild tossing of the mainmast seemed like the furious movements of some untamed creature, intent on hurling its burden into the sea. Kazhian, his long hair streaming, clung ape-like to the ropes, and would not be dislodged. The masthead platform, known as the stork's nest, was a precarious perch in the calmest waters. Now, it was less secure than a bareback seat on an unbroken horse.

Kazhian had been a sailor since boyhood. He wrapped his arms round the mast-rigging, tucked his feet into the storm-straps, and peered through the murk. Being flung so violently up and down and from side to side was no help to his concentration, the wind had pulled his hair loose so that it whipped across his face, and his vision was constantly blurred by the driving rain. But there, on the port bow, was what he had been seeking: a dim, hunched shape, just visible above the waves, a couple of miles away. They had done it. Unless the wind went round to the south, which was very unlikely, they were safe. All they had to do now was to sail up the coast until the storm blew itself out, or until they found a convenient cove or bay where they could shelter.

Was that another sail, much closer inshore? He shielded his eyes with one hand and stared intently. No, it was not a plume of spray, but definitely the sail of a sizeable ship. And if she was not already on the rocks, she would strike very soon.

There was nothing he could do. If the wind continued to drop, the *Sea Serpent* might be able to stand in and search for survivors. If not, she would be swept on past, helpless to render assistance. And though he was a pirate, a ruthless plunderer of other men's property, Kazhian had never, yet, failed to aid another ship in trouble.

But the storm was dying. It was not his imagination. He turned and saw, far on the western horizon, a thin line of clear sky. The black heart of the hurricane was racing on up the broad channel between Annatal and Onnak: here, with the Tail between them and the worst weather, the wind was growing less relentless, the waves less fierce.

The sail was still there. It was difficult to tell what she was, but the most likely vessel in these waters would be a trader of some kind, from Onnak or even Kerenth.

As he watched, she struck. He saw the sail jerk as the ship beneath hit the unseen rocks, and then collapse with appalling speed. The height of the waves and the clouds of spray obscured her hull: if he had not spotted her sail, he would never have known she was there.

Crouched soaked and frozen at the masthead, Kazhian made certain calculations, involving the force of the wind, the power of the waves, and the state of the tide, which by now should be falling fast. He had sailed up this coast a couple of times before, in his Navy days, but he didn't know it very well. It would help to be sure of where the *Sea Serpent* was. The tall, rocky cliffs of the Tail's islands concealed several secluded, deep-water coves – and some, also, that were known as ship-snares, shallow and ridged with invisible, lethal rocks. Make the wrong choice, and they'd all drown – and so would everyone aboard that other vessel.

Back down on the streaming, heaving deck, it was almost possible to hear himself think. He glanced up at the ship's pennant, flying brave but tattered from the mizzen-mast. The wind had changed direction, slightly but significantly: it was now blowing from the west, according to the lodestone. The rain had almost stopped, and that line of clear sky behind them, a lemon-pale slash beneath the clouds, was closer and much larger than before.

'It's almost over,' said Sargenay. The sorcerer looked exhausted, his cheeks hollow and deep lines graved round his mouth. 'I can help you now, if you need it, Captain.'

'There's a ship wrecked, off that land there.' Kazhian gestured at the port bow. Down here, so close to the waves, there was nothing visible save the hump of the island, a little closer than before. 'I think that's the first of the Tail – the Spike, it's called. If I'm right, the ship has struck on a chain of rocks guarding the entrance to one of the coves along its southern shore.'

'And you want us to stand in and take a look?' Sargenay glanced up at the mast above them. It was moving less vehemently than before, and the pennant was beginning to flap instead of streaming.

'If it's safe. And yes, you will need to go up there.' Kazhian indicated the stork's nest. 'I'll send Vanna up with you – he's got keen eyes and he knows what he's doing.'

Rather sooner than he would have liked, after a terrifying climb which had convinced him that each heave of the ship would fling him off into the vicious grey and white ocean, the sorcerer found himself securely roped to the mast. He felt more than a little nauseous, he was soaked and cold and lamenting the loss of a fingernail to a slippery shroud, but at least he was still alive. Beside him crouched the sturdy figure of Vanna, a Tulyettan of few words who treated the effete landlubber with exaggerated and patronizing care, as if he'd never touched a rope before. It irritated Sargenay, and he had spent most of the climb wondering, when he wasn't terrified of falling off, just how he could have his revenge.

But at least up here he could assess the situation at once. Across a rushing, white-topped sea, bursts of spray marked the reef, trailing out from a cliff spur for a distance of perhaps half a mile. Almost at the end of the rocks, tragically close to safety, he could see the mastless hull of the wrecked ship, waves breaking over its deck. And beyond, the sheltered water that Kazhian had mentioned, choppy but unbroken by black rocks or white surf, and therefore probably deep enough for the *Sea Serpent* to anchor in safety. He only had to guide her in, and try to avoid whatever mistake had driven that other unfortunate vessel to its doom.

The men, of course, thought that Kazhian's motive for this hazardous operation was plunder. Sargenay suspected that he was the only man on board who knew that his Captain was actually intent on rescuing any survivors. Salvaging the cargo was a secondary consideration. and as he peered through the tired morning light, spray salt on his lips and his eyes aching with effort, Sargenay wondered whether, by doing this, Kazhian felt that he was in some way atoning for all the lives his father's ruthlessness had taken.

They were close enough now to see the black shapes of the other ship's crew, clinging to the remains of the rigging. Even as Sargenay watched, a huge wave overwhelmed the wreck. When the water had receded, at least half the survivors had vanished into the surf.

'Don't go no closer than this!' Vanna bellowed down, through cupped hands. Sargenay saw Kazhian's wave of acknowledgement from the tiller, where he had taken charge. The Tulyettan turned to Sargenay, his sullen dark face displaying the mild contempt of all true mariners for the weather-workers who tried to manipulate wind and tide. 'See that ship there? Give it a wide berth – three or four shiplengths at least. There's rocks under those white waves for certain. Then when she's past, Captain will put us round and into shore.'

That, thought Sargenay as he began the inner chant of concentrated power, definitely came under the heading of 'easier said than done'. He had only been a weather-worker for two years: until he stepped on board Kazhian's ship, his knowledge of the subject had been limited to a couple of months' study of charts and theory at the Terebis School of Wizards, followed by four days of extremely chaotic and haphazard practice at sea. He'd picked up a lot from his Captain, and learned the rest by trial and error. Up until now, it had seemed to work well enough. But apart from that storm to the north of Balki, which had proved too strong for his limited skills, he'd never before tried to control such a powerful combination of wind and wave.

There was a tide running with them, and the wind was pushing them along at what seemed like reckless speed. He altered its direction slightly, and the *Sea Serpent* settled more easily into her course, which was designed to miss those rocks by about a quarter of a mile. Sargenay relaxed slightly. This was less difficult than he'd feared. The forces of nature were doing most of the work, and he only needed to fine-tune it slightly . . .

'Rocks!' Vanna bellowed. 'Rocks dead ahead!'

And Sargenay suddenly saw, shockingly, hideously close, the rearing jagged line of an unsuspected reef, hardly a ship's length in front. Down below, Kazhian had swung the tiller hard over, with all his strength, but the *Sea Serpent*, carried by the inexorable flow of the tide, was being swept broadside towards her doom.

Magic burst from Sargenay in a frantic flood of power. A magewind filled the ship's shuddering sails, her bow bit into the waves. Slowly, agonizingly slowly, she began to claw her way round the lurking rocks. He wondered desperately how long he could keep up a level of sorcery that needed all his skill and all his strength. The smallest lapse in concentration, and they would be lost.

He couldn't hold it for much longer. The *Sea Serpent* plunged through the waves, pushed by the unnatural wind. The tide was too strong for him, though, dragging the ship ever closer to her doom. He clenched his jaw, his face fierce with effort. *Just a bit more – sweet Lord of Life, help me – just a few moments more!*

He was losing it. Lightning seemed to sear his mind. He gave a great cry of anguish, and sagged forward.

The western wind beat at the sails. The *Sea Serpent*, helpless in the grip of the tide, was flung sideways in a vast wall of water.

Flung sideways, over the rocks eager to tear out her heart, and into the safety of the sheltered bay beyond.

For a few moments, dazed and bewildered, they did not believe it. Then a ragged cheer of relief struggled from the men's hoarse throats, as they realized that, for the moment, they had cheated death.

Sargenay woke to find Vanna shaking him brusquely. 'You all right, weather-worker? You did a good job there – though you could have tried to keep it going for a bit longer, we bloody nearly didn't make it.'

'Really?' The sorcerer's head hurt, and he was in no mood for banter. 'You have a go next time, then, if you think you can do any better.'

A loud rattle and splash from below announced that the *Sea Serpent* had dropped anchor. Men came scrambling up the ratlines to furl the mainsail. Numb, shaking, too exhausted to care, Sargenay sat and stared at the wreck, by now hardly visible amidst the waves shattering on the rocks around her, and sent his weary spirit in search of survivors.

There were still lives there: despairing, terrified, dragged to the limits of their endurance. And one, so vivid, so strong, that the sorcerer gasped in astonishment.

'Come on, weather-worker,' Vanna said, not unkindly. 'Let's get you down on deck.'

Several willing pairs of hands guided him to safety. His knees gave way at the bottom, and he fell in an undignified sprawl by the gunwhale. Kazhian crouched beside him, his hair plastered wet to his skull and his eyes gleaming with wild joy. 'Hey, get up, it's not over yet! Are you coming in the boat?'

A few moments ago, Sargenay would have rather cut off his own hand than be lowered into the *Sea Serpent*'s skiff. Amazingly, it seemed to have survived the storm more or less intact, but it must have received a tremendous battering – he wouldn't be surprised if it sank as soon as it touched the water.

But now, that imperative, frantic call filled his mind. There were people out there on the point of death, and it lay in his power to save them. 'Of course I am,' said Sargenay, and struggled to his feet. 'But hurry – there isn't much time left.'

The boat didn't sink, which was just as well, because he hadn't the energy to keep it afloat with sorcery, and he was certainly too exhausted to swim. The sailors, far stronger and fitter and used to hardship, rowed with urgent precision, obeying Kazhian's chant to keep the rhythm. The little craft danced through the choppy, treacherous water, towards the reef.

They couldn't risk getting in too close. Four of the crew kept the boat steady, well away from danger. Kazhian had tied one end of a rope around his waist, and the other to the stem-post. He swung himself neatly into the water, and struck out strongly for the rocks. The rest of the sailors, and Sargenay, followed him.

He was insane, he must be. The water wasn't cold, but his trailing robes hampered every stroke, and he was making very slow progress. But that summons kept beating in his head, overpowering all rational thought, lending strength to his weary limbs. *Help me, save me – come quickly, or I am lost!*

'Sargenay!'

It was Kazhian's voice. He saw his Captain standing balanced on a streaming, slippery ridge of rock, his hand outstretched. 'What are you doing down there, weather-worker? It's much drier out here!'

Spluttering, Sargenay struggled out of the water. The rocks were much broader and more substantial than they had appeared from out at sea, and at low tide would look more like an island than a reef. A wave smacked into the seaward side, battering them both with spray. Wiping his dripping face, the sorcerer glanced around. The wreck was only a score of paces to his right, but she seemed to be breaking up fast as the breakers pounded her. Already, two of the *Sea Serpent*'s crew were standing beside her shattered bow, and one threw up a rope to a man balanced precariously above them on her deck.

'There's someone there,' Sargenay said urgently. His legs felt as if they were made of lint, and he knew that he'd never be able to clamber along the treacherous rocks to the ship. 'A sorcerer, someone of power – I don't know who – calling for help.'

'Don't worry,' Kazhian said, and smiled brilliantly. 'Stay there, weather-worker – unless a really big wave strikes, you'll be safe enough, and the tide's falling. I'll find your sorcerer for you.'

By the time Kazhian had made his way along the reef to the hull, he had been knocked over twice and lost his footing several times on slimy strands of seaweed. Fortunately, he'd earned no worse than grazed legs and a badly cut finger. The first of the survivors were scrambling towards him, some on their hands and knees, helped by a couple of his crew. With surprise, and interest, he saw that there were women amongst them, so their ship must be Kerentan. He wondered what had brought her too close to this treacherous coast. Well, he'd find out soon enough, once they were all back on board the *Sea Serpent*.

'Any more?' he asked Vanna, who was helping to lower an injured Kerentan man down from the wreck.

'No, sir – apart from the Captain up there, that's the lot.'

'Eight left,' Kazhian said softly. 'Not many – but better than nothing.' He paused, and in a momentary lull, he heard a faint cry.

It might have been a seagull, but somehow he knew it was not. He raised his hand for silence, and listened intently. No birds were soaring above them, and anyway the sound had come from the reef beyond the ship, not from the sky.

Vanna was helping the groaning sailor to safety. The Captain of the wrecked ship climbed laboriously down the rope. He was a balding, ugly man, haggard and soaked. He said hoarsely, in bad Toktel'yan, 'Thank you – oh, thank you – you've saved our lives!'

'You would do the same for us, I hope,' Kazhian said briefly. Naked and overwhelming gratitude always disturbed him. 'Are you the last one?'

'Yes – everyone else was washed away – and we had five passengers, but they took the boat and rowed for it before we struck,' said the Captain bitterly. 'Left us to the mercy of the sea – if they'd stayed, we'd have weathered the storm – bloody, thrice-cursed, stinking sorcerers! That's the last time I ever give Jo'amians passage, I can tell you – ungrateful, stinking wizards! Oh, my poor, poor ship!' And he began to sob incoherently, tears and spray streaming down his face.

'Sorcerers? In a boat? Did they reach land?' Kazhian demanded. He could no longer hear that faint cry above the Captain's lamentations, but he was beginning to feel, insistent, desperate, the same force that had drawn Sargenay. And it must be extraordinarily strong, for he had never before been susceptible to sorcery.

'I don't know and I don't care – I hope they all drowned!' the Captain wailed, knuckling his eyes like a child.

'Well, I think at least one of them is still alive,' Kazhian told him. 'Follow the others – I'll go and look.'

He left the bereaved Captain, and began to clamber round the wreck's prow. She had struck at a point where the reef rose quite high out of the water, and he had to negotiate a jumble of black, treacherous rocks before he could see beyond.

The summons was fainter now, dying fast, but still desperate. Whatever was out there couldn't last much longer. Kazhian clung to the rocks and stared along the jagged line of the reef, to a place where it vanished for a short distance beneath the boiling sea.

There was something there, wedged between two slabs of barnacled stone, about twenty paces away. With more speed than was wise, he scrambled towards it, slipping and stumbling over the rocks. The tide was ebbing, but waves were still regularly breaking over the exposed reef. Once he was nearly washed into the sea, but managed to haul himself out of the swirling water. His legs were leaden with exhaustion, and he was bleeding profusely from encounters with the sharp rocks and shells, but he had no thought of going back.

It was not a body, but a wooden box of some sort, jammed just clear of the waves. And even as he stared at it in surprise, a feeble but unmistakable wail straggled out of it.

A baby. A soaked, terrified, desperate baby, too far gone to fight much more against the inexorable approach of death. And as he bent to pull it out of the box that might once have been a cradle, and was now almost a coffin, Kazhian knew that, astonishingly, *this* was the source of the summons.

The child was heavy, but he tucked the sodden, inert bundle under his right arm, and began the long trek back. In contrast to his outward toil, something now seemed to guide his feet, avoiding slips and falls with unerring agility and skill, and the burden he carried did not hinder him at all, even during the tricky climb around the remains of the wreck. His rational mind put it down to the falling tide, to the diminishing wind and waves, to his own intense desire to save this one small life. But an older, deeper instinct told him that none of these reasons were valid.

Vanna and another sailor were waiting for him. The skiff, laden with survivors and crew, was dangerously close to the rocks, the oarsmen frantically keeping the boat still in the heaving, sucking water.

'What you got there, sir?' the other sailor demanded eagerly. 'Crock of gold?'

'No,' Kazhian said, grinning stupidly. He didn't know whether the child was alive or dead, it hadn't moved at all since he'd picked it up, but at least he had given it a chance of survival. And they had saved eight other lives, too. The risk had been justified: a good morning's work.

Once in the boat, of course, reaction set in with a vengeance. His task completed, he became catastrophically aware of the fact that he was drenched, cold to his bones' marrow, and utterly exhausted. The salt water stung the cuts on his legs and hands, and he saw, looking down, that the rocks and barnacles had slashed his stout leather sandals to shreds, and his feet were bleeding copiously.

He had given the baby to Sargenay, who was no drier or warmer than anyone else, but who at least possessed the power of Healing. Kazhian wiped his hair out of his eyes, his hand leaving a smear of blood across his forehead, and addressed his sorcerer. 'Is it still alive?'

Nothing could be seen of the child but a lump beneath Sargenay's robes: he had unwrapped its sodden tunic and thrust it under his clothes, next to his skin, so that it would at least have some chance of regaining vital warmth.

'Yes,' said the sorcerer briefly, his eyes closed. Kazhian knew that he was concentrating his mind on the infant, and did not press him for details. The time for that would come later, in private.

'Sir?' It was the Kerentan Captain, his voice urgent. As the skiff began to draw away from the reef, he leaned past the midships rowers and added, 'That baby – that's the one the sorcerers had.'

Kazhian stared at him, stupid with fatigue. 'What sorcerers?'

'My passengers, like I told you. They were sorcerers from Jo'ami. They took the baby with them when they left us. If that's the one you've rescued, then their boat must have gone down.'

It didn't make sense. None of it made sense. Why were sorcerers from Jo'ami on a Kerentan ship? Why hadn't they stayed to help save her? And if they were sorcerers, and presumably very powerful ones, why had they failed to save their own boat? And what about the baby? What on earth were a bunch of Jo'amian wizards doing with a *baby*?

'Well, I'm not going to look for them now,' Kazhian said. 'If they're still alive, they can swim for it. And if they want the child that badly, they'll have to come and ask us nicely to give it back.'

A small but emphatic whimper escaped from beneath Sargenay's robe, somewhere in the region of his chest. The sorcerer smiled suddenly with relief, and one of the Kerentan women gave a faint cheer.

The infant wailed louder. Sargenay's expression changed rapidly from delight to dismay. He said with exaggerated indignation, 'Would you believe it – she's hungry!'

'She?' said Kazhian. He'd assumed, of course, that the child was male. Apart from anything else, if it *had* been the source of that summons, it was surely impossible for girls to possess powers of sorcery.

'She,' said the Kerentan woman firmly. 'Her name is Kiyu. It's Jo'amian. I think someone on Kerenth abducted her, and they were taking her back.'

Well, that explained some of the puzzle. But still, various inconsistencies kept nagging at his brain. *Later*, Kazhian told himself. *Later, when we're all dry and warm and fed.*

The *Sea Serpent* loomed above them, her rail crowded with those who had stayed on board. The skiff touched her side, and the bow and stern were made fast to ropes lowered from the davits. The first survivors crawled up the rope ladder, to an excited, cheering welcome. Even the injured man, who had a broken arm and heavily bruised ribs, found the strength to climb unaided. Once on deck, there were dry blankets awaiting them, and the cook had lit the galley fire and was passing round bowls of hot salt meat and lentil broth.

Kazhian, shivering and dripping by the rail, found Sezen, his Fabrizi mate, standing beside him solicitously. 'Why don't you go below, sir? Everything's organized. And you look as though you could do with a Healer's services.'

'So could he.' Kazhian gestured at the injured survivor. 'Get Sargenay to look at him first. I'll stay on deck.'

He sat down by the pinioned tiller, glad of a little space in which to collect his erring thoughts. The bowl of broth sat warm and comforting in his hands, and beneath the thick woollen blanket which Sezen had draped over his shoulders, he was no longer shivering quite so violently. Even so, he wondered if he'd ever be truly warm again. And all those survivors, and the men who had rescued them, would be feeling just the same. He was no different: just because he was their acknowledged leader, he did not need privileged treatment.

The hot, thick liquid settled comfortingly in his belly. He began to plan the rest of the day. It was not yet noon, and the storm had almost blown itself out. He could order all but a handful of men below to sleep. The *Sea Serpent* was securely anchored with a couple of fathoms beneath her keel, and they could stay here for a day or two to rest and recuperate, perhaps salvage what they could from the wreck, and search for bodies. And then what?

'Captain.' Sargenay stood in front of him. The baby was cuddled in his arms, wrapped in a thick cocoon of blankets. Her eyes, dark and solemn, stared out from a small, amber-skinned face, and she was sucking her thumb.

'She seems well on the way to recovery,' said Kazhian, smiling at the infant.

She gave a whimper, and hid her head in Sargenay's shoulder. The sorcerer sat down beside his Captain, and said softly, 'There are matters we should discuss. About this.'

'I know. When I can bludgeon my brain into action. At the moment, my mind's still frozen solid. Didn't you say she was hungry? What in Kaylo's name do babies eat? We haven't any goat or cow to give us milk.'

'Try her with some bread soaked in broth. Just a little.' Sargenay produced a piece of loaf and dunked it into Kazhian's bowl. 'Here, little one. Food.'

But the child, evidently still gripped by shyness, would not even look round. Sargenay shrugged, and put the bread in his own mouth. 'At least she's warm now, and alert,' he said. 'Once we've gained her trust, she'll eat. Do you know anything about babies?'

'Nothing whatsoever – except that they're wet at both ends and tend to yell a lot. There were several women amongst the survivors – surely one of them will look after her.'

'In Kereneth, it's often the men who take care of the children.'

'Well, one of the men, then – I don't mind as long as I don't have to do it.' Kazhian grinned. 'A true Toktel'yan.' He drained his bowl, swallowed, and stared with sudden seriousness at his weather-worker. 'That call you felt – the sorcery – I felt it too.'

'I thought you had.'

'And I think it came from her. From the baby. *Is* that possible?'

Sargenay glanced down at the black curly hair of the child he held, and shook his head. 'No. No, it shouldn't be. Sorcerers aren't born, they're made. According to the theory, a child this young can't take Annatal, or wield power. You are right, though, that summons came from her. I know it shouldn't be possible, but it is.'

'Though if she *is* Jo'amian – well, who knows what they get up to there? Perhaps they've managed to breed a race of natural sorcerers. Or perhaps this one is unique. She certainly must be pretty valuable to them if they went all the way to Kerenth to get her back.'

'Or to get her.' Sargenay's expression was totally devoid of his usual arch flippancy. 'I don't know for sure. I don't *know* at all. But I've been thinking, and guessing. I've had a quick word with the Kerentan Captain. Despite what that woman told us, he's pretty sure that the Jo'amians took the child from her mother, in Kerenth. So she doesn't belong with them – they abducted her, presumably because they wanted to exploit the power she carries. This child, this *female* child, is a fledgling sorcerer, without benefit of Annatal or training. And although that goes against everything that every mage in the Empire has ever been taught, it's true. She has power – power strong enough at least to call us to her aid. And that's not so unlikely, after all. Normal sorcerers often find their magic is enhanced by strong emotions, such as anger or fear. She must have been terrified, so she cried for help – with her voice, and with her mind. And you heard them both.'

Kazhian looked at the child. Small, plump, vulnerable, she seemed as innocent and unknowing as any year-old baby. He said slowly, 'So what has happened to the sorcerers? If you're right, they would never let her go willingly.'

Sargenay shrugged. 'Who knows? My guess, like yours, is that they're dead. Perhaps the gods were angry with them for stealing the child, so they drowned them all but made sure that the baby was safe.'

'It's as good an explanation as any. And since she's too young to tell us, it's the only explanation we're likely to get,' Kazhian pointed out. 'Well, what do we do now? Take them all back to Kerenth, I suppose.'

'Why not? We have nothing better to do. And perhaps we'll run up alongside a fine fat trader on the way – one who won't suspect a thing until it's too late.'

'Kerenth it is,' said Kazhian. 'Land of women. The men will be delighted. Let's just hope we can find the child's mother there. Having a baby on board will certainly cramp our style.'

'Don't worry,' said Sargenay. 'I think we'll locate her easily enough. And in any case, I suspect I know who she is.'

CHAPTER
FIFTEEN

Mallaso had not seen Penya since the day when she had been herded with all the other sobbing and bewildered children into a transport ship, to be sold as slaves in Toktel'yi. She had thought that the image of her homeland had been burnt into her mind for ever, as cruel and sharp as a Ma'alkwen knife. And now the reality did not match with her memory at all, and she was distressed and disturbed by it.

She had found it hard enough to accept the loss of Kiyu: she had achieved a temporary mastery over her grief only by seizing on the only other reason for her existence, the recovery of Penya. After the death of her elder daughter, Grayna, she had channelled all her desperate, obsessive sorrow into her attempted assassination of Ba'alekkt. For a time, she had hovered on the borders of insanity, but Bron had rescued her from the consequences of her actions, and had restored her desire to live.

It was different now. After all, Kiyu was still alive. She was in the hands of strangers, but at least Mallaso knew she would not be harmed. That did not lessen her grief, or make it any easier to bear, but she still possessed some grains of hope, despite Sé Mo-Tarmé's hostile words. And she could try to convince herself that her emptiness, her sense of loss and desolation, were hers alone. Kiyu was only a year old, used to being in the care of others, and a happy-natured, sociable child. She would give them that enchanting, dimpled smile, and make her delightful, chuckling laugh, and the sorcerers of Jo'ami would be her slaves. They would never adore her as Mallaso did, but Kiyu's own charm would ensure that she earned their loving affection.

She could convince herself of all this, she could spend her daylight hours in frantic activity, denying her bereavement with cool, rational logic. But every night she fell asleep longing for her lost child, and every morning, when she woke, her pillow was drenched with tears.

Everyone treated her with careful sympathy, but she could see the bewilderment in their faces when they looked at her. They couldn't understand why she had made no attempt to pursue her child's abductors, and they certainly had no idea why the sorcerers had wanted

Kiyu. How could she possibly explain about the powers that the little girl might, or might not, possess, or convince her friends that it would be utterly futile to defy the ruthless and implacable High Sorcerer of Jo'ami? Bron had successfully outwitted her, on more than one occasion, but his magic had far exceeded Sé Mo-Tarmé's. She, Mallaso, was powerless. Kiyu had gone for ever and it was pointless, and also dangerous, to attempt to get her back.

So she had signed on with the invasion fleet, because Penya needed her even if Kiyu did not, and now she stood by the rail of Essyan's flagship, a round-hulled Kerentan trader, and watched the south coast of the island draw gently closer. They had rounded the huge eastern outcrop of towering cliffs, known as the Hammer from its shape on the maps, and were now approaching Penya Harbour, the chief port and largest town.

She had lived there once, with her father and mother and her two older brothers, in a white house on the hillside. Her father had grown vines and peaches and pomegranates, and owned a fishing-boat in which he had often taken his children sailing. Her mother, Tipeya, had been quiet and gentle, with a soft laugh and a warm, generous nature. If Kiyu had inherited anything from her natural grandmother, it was her gift for happiness.

Mallaso thrust the baby's image from her mind, and gazed at Matamenya, the small island guarding the entrance to the harbour. It was dedicated to Sarraliss, the Mother Goddess, and in the wooded groves at its heart, adolescent girls had once been initiated by their mothers into the mysteries of Her worship. Mallaso had been too young to make the solemn lamplit voyage across the dark water, and her mother had been slain by the Toktel'yan invaders. If Essyan succeeded, perhaps there were enough women left to restore the island to its former place as the centre of the island's spiritual life. And he had vowed to rebuild the Meeting House, the big stately building on the quayside, where the elected Council that governed Penya had once met.

She remembered Matamenya's lush forest, but there were now huge ugly scars on its gentle slopes, where the sacred trees had been hacked down for their timber, or simply burned where they stood. The turquoise waters of the harbour, deep and sheltered, were not blue today, but reflected the sullen grey of the winter sky. The tall peaks of the interior were shrouded in a lowering mist. And few remained of the host of white and colourwashed houses set against the lavish and verdant green of the hillside above the harbour.

The Penya buried in Mallaso's heart and soul was dead. But there was hope. Despite all the destruction, the land had not forgotten its fertility. And the Penya-to-come would be rebuilt by the energy and vision of the people around her, more lovely and more blessed than ever before.

There were a couple of ships anchored in the bay, both traders, but there was no one waiting for them, no hostile army drawn up on the quayside, ready to repulse invasion. A prickle of unease tingled down Mallaso's back, and she clenched her hand on her sword. Where were the garrison who were supposed to hold Penya for the Empire? Were they lying in ambush? Or perhaps they had realized how heavily they were outnumbered, and hidden themselves in the mountainous heavily forested interior of the island, planning to harry the invaders as the Penyan resistance fighters had once harried them.

No such doubts, obviously, troubled Essyan. His flagship, the *Sacred Moon*, glided purposefully past the moored traders. From her mainmast flew the banner of Penya, a yellow crescent moon against the deep blue of an evening sky, accompanied by one brave star of hope. Her sails furled, her anchor dropped, and she came to a gentle stop about two ships' lengths from the quay. With similarly smooth grace and efficiency, the other members of Essyan's fleet, some twenty vessels, moored around her.

In the dull afternoon air, thick and still and humid, no sound came from the land. There were certainly several thousand people still living in Penya, soldiers, Toktel'yan settlers, and a handful of the original population. But although everyone scanned the hills near and far, the slopes of Matamenya, the deserted quayside, the wrecked and derelict buildings, not a trace of movement was visible except for a couple of sea eagles, drifting lazily on the air currents above the cliffs to the east of the bay.

At last, Essyan gave the orders, and half-a-dozen small boats, laden with his heavily armed bodyguard, were lowered from the *Sacred Moon* and set out for the shore. With thumping hearts, the rest of the Penyans watched as they reached the sandy beach at the end of the stone quay. Their leader was first ashore, and they all saw him kneel in thanksgiving on their native land.

As he did so, a shaft of golden sunlight slid through the heavy clouds, and laid a bright finger on his helm and armour.

Sarraliss had given Her blessing. A wild, spontaneous cheer erupted from all the ships, and Mallaso felt tears of emotion gather in her eyes. This, this was her home: not Toktel'yi, not Tekkt, not Kerenth. Penya was where she belonged: and whether it happened within the next few hours, or after many, many years, death would come to her here.

The Penyan flag was raised on the quay, the signal which ordered all the rest of the force to land. Boat after boat put off from the anchored fleet, and rowed with fervent speed towards the shore. Soon the white crescent of sand to the east of the quay was full of beached skiffs, and by the time every man and woman of Essyan's army stood on Penyan soil, the little boats were packed so close that the latecomers had to climb over them to come ashore.

And still there was no one, hostile or welcoming, to greet them.

By nightfall, they had ascertained that the town was empty. Those few houses that had been inhabited all contained eloquent evidence of hasty departure: food left on tables, overturned storage jars, abandoned possessions. There were several nervous, bewildered dogs roaming around, and a quantity of cats and poultry who had presumably been too difficult to catch. But there were no people, anywhere.

One of the houses that was still relatively intact had once belonged to Mallaso's family. Staring round at the shabby, peeling walls, the inexpertly patched roof, the dilapidated outbuildings, she could not believe that this was the neat, beautiful home in which she had spent the ten happy years of her childhood. But here, sadly neglected, was the old and twisted lemon tree under which her mother had taught her to read and write. There, almost lost under the tangle of fallen beams, was the store-room in which her eldest brother had been discovered with a girl. And, most persuasive of all, when she turned she could see that marvellous sweep of the great bay, the island of Matamenya guarding the entrance, the cliffs to the left, the gentler, terraced slopes to her right: and below, the harbour, studded with bare-poled ships riding at anchor, in waters so deep, so sheltered and so safe that no vessel had ever sunk beneath them, no matter how fierce the storm.

She closed her eyes, summoning the shades of her family. But there was no answer: no ghosts lingered here, save within her mind.

Someone had taken her house, but they could keep it. She did not wish to displace anyone, even if they were Toktel'yan. And so many had died, in the years of conquest, that there would be plenty of space for everyone, settlers, natives and returning exiles. She could not bear the thought of scratching a living in a corner of this sad house, a wrecked travesty of the happy, lively and beautiful home that she remembered. If she had still had Kiyu, she would have felt differently. But there were too many memories, too much bitter grief, for her to confront here alone.

With a silent prayer for their souls, and another for Kiyu, wherever she might be, Mallaso turned and left the house where she had been born, and went back down to the quayside.

The invasion force spent a rather uneasy night in the ruins of the Meeting House, the only place large enough to house all the four thousand exiles. It was not very comfortable: the floors were strewn with rubble, and large areas were open to the sky. In the middle of the night, it rained heavily, and the wind rose. Mallaso, huddled under her cloak with her head pillowed on her kitbag, slept very little, and to judge from the yawns and groans and heavy eyes of her comrades the next morning, neither had anyone else.

But they had landed on Penya, there had been no resistance, and they were now in possession of the harbour and the town. And despite their weariness, there was a spring in everyone's step, a joy in their faces, that fatigue could not erase.

Essyan gathered them all together in the Central Hall. It was still largely intact, though the high roof leaked and there were puddles everywhere on the newly cleared stone floor. These men and women formed only half his invasion force: the rest, led by his second-in-command, Rassienna, had landed at Farli'enn, the largest port on the northern coast. If all went according to plan, the two halves of the army would march into the centre of the island, eliminating resistance on the way, and meet in the Vale of Clouds, a great fertile bowl in the heart of Penya.

'Of course, a small rearguard will stay here, just as Rassienna will leave some soldiers to guard Farli'enn,' Essyan said. 'But we did not expect to walk into an empty town. And as our quarrel is not with the settlers, but with the Toktel'yan garrison, no civilian is to be harmed unless it is absolutely necessary for self-defence. Even if they offer violence, we must avoid more slaughter, if we possibly can. The Mother abhors the shedding of blood on her sacred soil. The rape and destruction of Penya has surely caused her great grief. Despite our own quite natural desire for revenge, we must not vent our anger on those who are innocent. There is more than enough land for everyone. The settlers must be persuaded that we mean them no harm, and that they can return to their homes and live in peace and freedom alongside us, if they wish. I know that several of you have found your old homes and lands occupied. I know that you wish to take back what was once yours. But I must emphasize – there is plenty for all. You must let the settlers stay. I myself have found that my property here is being farmed by Toktel'yans. But I am willing, for the sake of future peace, to forgo my rights to it. Do I make myself clear? There will be no expulsions. When the whole island is secure, we will begin the business of allotting land and houses. Penya is nearly two hundred miles across, and more than a hundred from south to north. There are less than twenty thousand families planning to return here. Once, this island supported ten times that number of households. It does not require much thought to calculate that, for a long time to come, large tracts of good land must lie fallow, until the population increases. So, I repeat – there is no need to drive the settlers out. This island has been steeped in blood. Let us not anger the Mother by adding to the sorrows of Penya. She has given us Her Blessing, and we must not risk Her displeasure, for we are here by Her will.'

Mallaso, looking round at her companions, saw that some of them seemed less than enthusiastic. She could understand their feelings: no one liked the thought of the Toktel'yans being able to seize their land with impunity. But she knew that Essyan was right. Embarking on a campaign of wholesale violence, intimidation and eviction would make the exiles no better than the loathed and despicable Imperial Army.

There was bound to be trouble, though, despite their leader's stern warnings. It was impossible to exert absolute control over such a large force, and feelings were running high and furious. If the hotheads were denied the chance to have their revenge on the Toktel'yan garrison, they'd almost certainly turn on the settlers.

That afternoon, scouts left the town and began to search the hills above Penya Harbour. They nailed notices, written in Toktel'yan, Kerentan and Penyan, to trees and fence-posts and gates, announcing the arrival of the invasion force and promising safety and freedom to those who returned peacefully to their homes. Then on the following day, leaving behind some five hundred troops to secure the town, Essyan and the rest of the army moved north, into the island's interior.

Mallaso, trudging along muddy, pot-holed roads with her comrades, began to realize, for the first time, the immensity of the struggle they all faced. The island was the largest in the Archipelago, and bigger than several Toktel'yan provinces. To attempt to rebuild houses, reorganize the social structure, restore the old system of government, and bring ruined farms and neglected vineyards and orchards back into cultivation, was a task far beyond one man, and probably beyond even the thousands of returning exiles. The land was so broad, the people so few. Even under the most favourable circumstances, it would surely be half a century or more before the island could once more approach her former glory. And if Olkanno decided that he wanted Penya after all, it would be impossible to do any of the work that Essyan and his Council had planned so carefully.

They began to see people, peering at them from hillsides, or cowering in barns and houses. United under Essyan's firm leadership, they ignored them, but put up the reassuring notices along the road. And six days after their landing on Penya, the army tramped wearily down the long straight highway that led to Hegril, the town in the centre of the Vale of Clouds, where they were supposed to meet up with the other half of the invasion force.

They were there. With cheers and laughter, the two armies embraced. Rassienna had a very similar tale to tell, of an unopposed landing, deserted houses, and a complete lack of resistance throughout their march. But they had been greeted in Hegril by a small and tattered band of native Penyans, almost mad with joy and relief. And these people had told them that the remaining five hundred men of the Toktel'yan garrison had fled into the mountains to the west of the Vale of Clouds, where they would almost certainly prove very difficult, if not impossible, to dislodge. But crack Imperial troops did not usually run away, however great the odds against them, so their morale was obviously low. Essyan could tackle them at his leisure, once the rest of the island was secure.

For nearly a month, the exiles remained in Hegril. It had suffered less than Penya Harbour, or Farli'enn, and most of the buildings were more or less intact, though dilapidated and neglected. There was no time to rest, however. Columns of troops were sent out in the town and into the countryside around, to forage for food, to make lists and records of what was left, to begin the register of land, to scout and explore. Others started to rebuild the town's Meeting House, far larger and more spacious than before, for Essyan had decided to make Hegril, which lay almost in the centre of the island, his capital. Gemain had already moved into a deserted farm on the outskirts of the town, with an overgrown but potentially very productive vineyard on a south-facing slope. And, much to her alarm and embarrassment, he had asked Mallaso to join him.

Ever since the day that Kiyu had been stolen, he had been hovering protectively around her, treating her with overpowering sympathy. He had irritated Mallaso so much that she had made a point of emphasizing her strength and resilience in his presence. She had done it before, of course: running an eating-house in Toktel'yi was impossible for a woman unless she could cultivate a tough and unshakeable air of invulnerability. Grayna's death, Bron's affection and Kiyu's love had set cracks in her carapace. Now, bereft of them all, she had tried to reconstruct her shell, to keep out Gemain.

He was bewildered and disappointed at her refusal. She ruthlessly ignored his hurt expression, bid him a cool farewell, and went straight to Essyan, to ask him permission to return to Penya Harbour.

Gemain's father obviously knew a lot more about the situation than she had realized: perhaps his son had unwisely spoken of his hopes. He said, in his clipped, curt voice, 'So you do not wish to stay here?'

'No. I was born in Penya Harbour. I would like to help rebuild it. And I miss the sea.'

'I understand,' Essyan said. He rose from his desk and held out his hand. 'I thank you, Mallaso. Your help has been invaluable to us.'

'It hasn't ended yet,' she pointed out drily. 'I shall be working for Penya for the rest of my life.'

'And so shall I, and my son, and all the other exiles. Well – good luck.' Essyan coughed. 'There are several messages which I would like taken back – will you carry them for me?'

'Of course.'

'Can you ride?'

Mallaso looked at him doubtfully. 'Only on donkeys.'

'A donkey is all I'm offering,' said Essyan, with an expression on his face that was the closest she'd ever seen to a smile. 'We've only managed to find one horse so far. Well, once more my thanks to you, Mallaso – goodbye, and may the Mother hold you always in Her heart and in Her hand.'

The sun was shining as she rode away from Hegril, and the orchards were coming into blossom. A new year, a new spring, a new life. And despite the dreadful, never-ending ache of loss still gnawing at her soul, she could not help but take pleasure in the sights and sounds and scents around her. Like Kerenth, Penya was blessed with a delightful climate. Most rain fell in winter, though there were always a few refreshing showers during the summer months. The constant sea breezes ensured that even with the sun at its zenith, the weather was never uncomfortably hot: and the cooler part of the year was still pleasantly mild, while the winds quickly dispersed any sea fogs or mountain mists. All sorts of plants flourished under such kind conditions, and the woods and fields and orchards, even in neglect, were lush with vegetation, teeming with animals and insect life, and blazing bright with flowers.

Penya the Great: Penya the Beautiful: and once more, surely, Penya the Blessed. A small black fox, of the kind her father used to curse for stealing their chickens, trotted across the road in front of her, giving her a cursory glance. Overhead, summer swifts swooped and circled, and a brilliance of butterflies skipped amongst the flowers lining the verge.

She came to the last ridge late in the afternoon, two days after leaving Hegril. The sun had almost sunk behind the hills to the west of the harbour, but Matamenya was still flushed with golden light, and the Southern Sea, for the first time since she had landed on Penya, was coloured in the breathtaking pure turquoise that she remembered so clearly from her childhood. Up here, in the still, mild air, it was possible to believe that the last twenty years of slaughter and destruction had never happened. Surely, if she rode on down the hill, she would come to a villa with a door painted red, and she would walk inside, and be welcomed by her parents as if she had just returned from visiting her best friend Mai'ar.

There were tears, slippery and cold, on her cheeks. She wiped them away and rode on, down the steep and twisting road to Penya Harbour.

She could not help glancing at her old house as she passed. There was smoke, threading almost invisibly from the kitchen chimney. On an impulse, she slid off the donkey's back, tied the animal to a tree, and knocked on the faded red door.

After a long pause, a woman's voice said in Toktel'yan, 'Who's there?'

She answered in the same language. 'My name is Mallaso. I am alone, and I mean you no harm. May I speak with you in friendship?'

Eventually the door creaked open about a finger's length. The woman was still young, but she had a sullen defeated look, as if her life had broken all its promises. 'What do you want?'

'I just wanted to tell you that I have no intention of claiming this house. My family lived here once, but they are all dead save for me, and I do not want it – there are too many sad memories for me here. You are welcome to stay.'

The woman stared at her suspiciously. 'So you say. But what if you change your mind?'

'Even if I did, you would still have the right to live here. Haven't you seen the notices Essyan has put up? No one is to be evicted. We only want peace, and there is plenty of room for everyone.'

Within the house, a baby started to wail fretfully. 'Lying claptrap,' said the woman wearily. 'Now sod off and leave us alone.' And she shut the door in Mallaso's face.

Well, she had tried. But it was with some sadness that she untied the donkey and walked beside it down the road. If such attitudes prevailed amongst the settlers, then there was small hope of friendly coexistence, let alone cooperation. And it would only need one unfortunate incident, one rash Penyan eager to assert himself, one defensive settler trying to hang on to his land, and the Toktel'yans would never trust Essyan again.

It was dusk when she arrived at the Meeting House. Someone had hung up a couple of lanterns above the main entrance, and she smelt smoke, and cooking. She tied up the donkey outside, and went in.

In the month of her absence, a great many people had obviously worked extremely hard. The roof had been patched, and the rubble cleared away. There were still gaping holes in the exterior walls, where iron window-grilles had been wrenched out, but some enterprising person had woven very adequate substitutes from marsh-grass. And the great welcoming fresco of Sarraliss amidst a field of flowers, damaged and defaced by the Toktel'yans, had been carefully and lovingly restored.

Everyone was in the main Hall, eating at long, makeshift trestle tables made of salvaged wood. Mallaso was greeted with a warmth that surprised her. She gave them all the latest news, passed on Essyan's messages, and devoured two bowls of chicken soup, mopped up with a lump of coarse dark bread. She looked round with pleasure at the familiar faces of the men and women who were her comrades, and now, it seemed, also her friends. Tomorrow, she would join them in her work of restoration, and once more try to lose her grief in ceaseless and useful activity.

Over the next few days, she found she had no time for thought, for all her waking hours were spent clearing rubble and rebuilding walls. When she needed a less strenuous job, she joined a man called Ka'avan, who had been given the task of making a detailed plan of the town and its surroundings. Essyan's insistence on all this paperwork was almost Toktel'yan in its thoroughness, but she could understand his reasons. Land and property had to be redistributed fairly and impartially, and that could not be done without at least some record of what already existed.

A month and a half after the exiles' return, several Kerentan ships entered the Harbour, carrying many of their families. Amongst them were Ammenna and her daughter. It was good to see her friends again, but Mallaso could not help being reminded of Kiyu whenever she saw S'raya's face. When they took over a deserted, half-ruined house at the eastern end of the quay, and asked Mallaso to join them, she declined. There would be too many painful memories there, too much sympathy, and the inevitable awkwardness might sour their friendship. She wanted to stay with the independent exiles, within their cheerful community in the Meeting House. At least when she was in their company, she could sometimes forget that she had ever been a mother.

A few days after Ammenna's arrival, another fleet arrived from Kerenth. Mallaso did not bother to watch yet more women and children step on to Penyan soil with tears of thankfulness and joy. Instead, she went with Ka'avan up to a village on the headland to the east of the town, to record the farms and houses there. It was a bleak and windswept place, utterly deserted. There were no animals or crops in the salty fields, and most of the dwellings had been reduced to overgrown heaps of wood and stone. It would be a very long time before this settlement was inhabited again.

It was dark when they came back to the Meeting House. There was a quarter-moon rising over Metamenya, laying a slender ribbon of silver on the dark waters of the harbour. Mallaso and Ka'avan fed and watered their donkeys, and then walked inside.

'Message for you, Mallaso,' said Tegerno, whom Essyan had appointed leader of the Penya Harbour exiles, until proper elections could be held. 'From Ammenna – you know her? She wanted you to go round to her house as soon as you got back.'

'Before or after I've eaten?' The smell from the makeshift outside kitchen was delicious, and she'd had nothing but bread and cheese all day.

Tegerno shrugged. 'I don't know, she didn't say. But I think it was urgent. Perhaps her daughter's ill.'

It wasn't far to Ammenna's house. Mallaso ignored the protests from her empty stomach, and hurried along the quayside. Lantern oil was in short supply, so it was very dark, and the shadows were impenetrable despite the moonlight. But she felt no fear for her safety. The town was patrolled at night by half-a-dozen guards, but there was no real need: it was more to reassure those few settlers who had returned, and to guard against the remote possibility of Toktel'yan attack, than to deter non-existent criminals.

There was a light in Ammenna's house, though her door was shadowed by a crumbling, creeper-clad wall. Mallaso knocked on it. Voices within ceased abruptly, and she heard running footsteps. The bolts drew back, and Ammenna, breathing hard, stood on the step. She was a serious woman, but tonight her smile almost reached her ears. She drew Mallaso inside. 'Come in, my dear, come in – we have visitors.'

So S'raya could not be ill. And indeed, here she was, her face similarly illuminated by joy. 'Oh, Mallaso, Mallaso, come and see.'

They led her across the courtyard, and into the largest of the three rooms which Ammenna had managed to make habitable. It was simply furnished, with a few cushions and rugs on the floor, and a low table made from salvaged wood roughly nailed together. The single lamp threw a warm but limited light on the two men sitting there. At her entrance, one of them stood, smiling, and held out the two hands of friendship to her.

She stared at him in bewildered astonishment.

'Don't you recognize me, dearest Mallaso?' said the light, affected voice of her tame sorcerer. 'Sargenay, remember?'

In wondering, delighted disbelief, Mallaso whispered, 'I thought you were dead.'

'It takes a lot more than one mad vindictive Emperor to kill me,' Sargenay said. 'Well, aren't you glad to see me?'

'Oh, Sargenay, of course I am,' Mallaso cried, and flung herself joyfully into his embrace.

It was more than two years since she had seen him last, and then she had still been the old Mallaso, keeper of the Golden Djarlek, successful woman of business, assured and capable and in complete control of her life. And since then she had briefly acquired a lover, lost one child and borne another, and lost her too. A vast gulf separated then from now, but somehow Sargenay, almost her oldest and certainly her dearest friend, seemed to have bridged it merely with his presence.

'Don't weep,' said the sorcerer softly. 'That isn't the Mallaso I knew. And this is an occasion for joy, not sorrow. I have come here to return something of yours that was lost, and we found. Look.'

The other man came forward. Mallaso saw that he was carrying a heavy bundle in his arms, as tenderly as if it had been a baby. Then he turned back a fold of cloth, and she saw that it was a baby, sleeping with the absolute abandonment of the very young.

It was Kiyu.

Mallaso gave a cry, or a gasp. She reached out her hand, and then stopped, terrified that the child was an Illusion, to fade away at her touch.

'She is real,' Sargenay said softly. 'She is yours, isn't she? Then take her.'

She had never thought she would ever feel this warmth, this weight, this joy in her hands again. The baby stirred as she was handed over, and then snuggled deep into her mother's arms, as if she had never been lost. Then Mallaso sank down to her knees, her tears pouring on to Kiyu's dark curls, and the rest of the room, the people, even Sargenay, shrank away from her mind, leaving only herself and her daughter.

CHAPTER
SIXTEEN

A long time later, when Kiyu had woken, and seen her mother's face, and smiled, and had been fed and laid down at last to sleep in S'raya's bed, Mallaso sat cross-legged on Ammenna's blue and red Kerentan rug, and wondered how there could ever be time for all the questions fermenting inside her head.

She chose the most obvious, and said to Sargenay, sitting opposite, 'How did you find her, and me?'

'It's a long story,' said the sorcerer. He glanced at the man beside him. 'And my Captain here bears a considerable responsibility for it.'

Mallaso gave his companion her full attention for the first time. Since taking her daughter from his arms, she had barely noticed him. Now she wondered why she hadn't, for his appearance was hardly ordinary, and full of unlikely contrasts. He had almost as many earrings as a Fabrizi pirate, and his black hair was just as wild and even longer, but his high-boned, brown-skinned face was pure and aristocratic Toktel'yan. He was dressed, though, in a short, roughly woven linen tunic, with a gold-hafted dagger at his belt, and his strong hands and muscular arms and legs indicated a life of hard work, not pampered idleness. And she had seen him before, she was certain of it. Somewhere in her old life, she had encountered this man.

A picture rose up in her mind, of the central hall of the Blue Hyacinth, the brothel where she had spent a miserable year just after she had been freed from slavery. A group of young Toktel'yans, loud, wealthy, drinking and smoking khlar, were fondling some of the girls. Amongst them, had been Sargenay's Captain. His hair had been much shorter, his garments more conventional, but she was sure it was him. And a friend had leant across with a pipe, saying. 'Try this, Lord Kazhian.'

Kazhian. Eldest son of the last Emperor, Eska'anen. He had occasionally patronized the Blue Hyacinth, but he had never chosen her. At the time, she hadn't cared one way or the other: a customer was a customer, and as long as he treated her with respect, she hadn't minded who he was. Now, though, she felt considerable relief. If he was a friend of Sargenay's, he would undoubtedly become her friend too. He had rescued Kiyu from the Jo'amians, so she would be grateful to him for the rest of her days. And, finally and most cogently, he was extremely attractive.

She hadn't been interested in any man since Bron. She saw him looking at her: his eyes were unexpectedly green, sharp and intelligent. Then suddenly he grinned, and said, 'I've seen you before, have I not?'

'You have,' said Mallaso, hiding her unwonted embarrassment with an answering smile. 'In the Blue Hyacinth.'

That surprised him. His eyes widened, and then he laughed. 'Really? You did well to get out of there.'

Ammenna was looking bewildered. Mallaso gave her a brief and expurgated explanation. Brothels were unknown in Penya, or in Kerenth, where the Priestesses of Sarraliss lay with any men who paid them enough, in coin and honour and pleasure, and the Mother granted them long life and good luck in return. Toktel'yan attitudes to women were incomprehensible, even blasphemous, to those who worshipped Her.

Something else occurred to her. She said, 'Aren't you supposed to be dead?'

'He is,' said Sargenay, with an arch glance at his Captain. 'But as you can see, he has successfully cheated Olyak, many times.'

Mallaso knew that look, and felt a pang of sympathy for her friend. He was obviously in love with Kazhian, and equally obviously, his feelings were unrequited. She remembered some of the stories about this particular Vessel of the Blood Imperial, who was now, astonishingly, sitting in this half-ruined house on Free Penya, and so close that she could have reached out and touched him. He had always enjoyed a reputation for wildness and excess, but, unlike so many of his family, no one had ever described him as cruel or vicious. And gossip had asserted that Eska'anen had loathed him, so he couldn't be all bad.

'One day,' said Kazhian drily, 'Olyak is sure to have the last laugh. Until he does, I intend to go on enjoying my life to the full. Please continue, weather-worker – the lady asked you how you found her baby. And if you don't hurry up and start now, we'll be here all night.'

No, Kazhian didn't return Sargenay's feelings: his tone was teasing and affectionate, but contained no more than friendship. She remembered that his favourite girl at the Blue Hyacinth, a supple and slender acrobat from Jaiya with dyed yellow hair, had boasted with irritating frequency to the others about her high-born customer's skill and virility.

'Very well,' Sargenay said. He settled himself more comfortably on the cushions, took a sip of his wine, and began.

As his Captain had warned, it did take a very long time. He began with the events leading up to the *Wind of Morning*'s wreck on Balki, Megren's tragic death, and Kazhian's fateful decision to turn pirate. Mallaso listened as the sorcerer described the storm that had driven the Kerentan ship on the rocks of the Tail, and the good luck that had brought the *Sea Serpent* to the same place at the same time. At his account of Kiyu's discovery and rescue, she felt tears seep from her eyes, and the hair rose on her arms. So nearly, nearly had her beloved died. And Kiyu's power, the power that Mallaso had hoped she did not possess, had saved her, by summoning Sargenay and Kazhian to her aid.

The rest of the story was almost an anti-climax. They had sailed back to Kerenth, with the survivors of the *Lady Inrai'a* on board, and had begun to search for the child's mother. Since many people in Kerenth City had known of her, and of Kiyu's abduction, they had soon been directed on to Penya. 'And everyone here knows you too, dear friend,' Sargenay said. 'They said, "Take her to Ammenna's house, and S'raya will look after her until Mallaso comes home." And Ammenna very kindly took us in – so here we are.'

'Thank you both,' Mallaso said softly. 'To the end of my days, I can never repay either of you for what you have done. When they stole her from me, I was certain that I would never see her again. Sé Mo-Tarmé is a very formidable and ruthless woman. She ordered me not to follow – she made terrible threats.' The memory of that dreadful, implacable voice echoing in her mind made her shiver with fear. She added uneasily, 'Is she dead?'

'Yes, she is,' Kazhian told her. 'The Kerentan Captain told us that the Jo'mians had left his ship in the small boat, taking the child. They apparently thought they'd be safer, but they were wrong. When the sea had calmed, we sent out the skiff to look for more survivors. There were only pieces of wreckage, and corpses washed up on the rocks. We found five bodies, so there were none unaccounted for, and the Captain identified the High Sorcerer as one of them.'

'Her robes are a dull green colour,' Mallaso said.

'Yes, that was her. There's a lot I don't understand, though. Why was the High Sorcerer of Jo'ami so keen to abduct your baby? Why did they leave the ship? And why, with all that power, did they not survive the storm? The child did – and yet Sargenay tells me that it should be impossible for anyone so young to possess raw, untrained sorcery, let alone use it. Was that why the Jo'amians wanted her so much?'

'Yes,' Mallaso said. She knew that she must give him some explanation, but it was difficult, even now, to tell them all the events of the past two years. She described briefly her relationship with Bron, her failed attempt to kill Ba'alekkt, and their flight to Jo'ami, where Kiyu had been conceived against the wishes of the High Sorcerer, who had been convinced that a child of Bron's would one day destroy the island.

Sargenay drew in his breath. 'So the man who called himself Hanno of Minassa—'

'Was really Bron, son of the King of Zithirian. And Kiyu is his daughter.'

The sorcerer whistled softly. 'Well, that certainly explains a great deal. That man possessed enormous power, *terrifying* power. Certainly he terrified me. The face of one of Kaylo's boys of Paradise, and the soul of a demon.'

'No,' Mallaso said sharply. 'That is wrong. The Wolf within him was under his control.'

'If it was, why did he nearly boil that loudmouthed fool Bereth in his own blood?'

'He fought the Wolf,' Mallaso told him. 'He drove it out, on Jo'ami. No demon would have done that.'

'And now that child – *your* child – seems to have inherited at least some of his power.' Sargenay's face was full of fascinated but troubled curiosity. 'No wonder she summoned us. But since we rescued her, I have felt no sorcery in her at all. I knew she was his – I don't know how, perhaps the baby herself put it into my mind. And I guessed that she might therefore also be yours. But I still find it very difficult to believe something so small and so young could command any sorcery at all.'

'I do too,' said Mallaso. 'Al'Kalyek never knew for certain whether she had power. He must be back on Onnak now, and I'm glad he didn't find out. He wanted to train her, teach her—'

'And you don't?' enquired Kazhian his eyebrows raised.

'His power was never less than a terrible burden to Bron. He was bred for it, like a horse or a dog, and all his life people wanted to use his sorcery for their own purposes. In the end, it killed him. Do you think I want that for Kiyu? It was why I left Jo'ami. It was why Sé Mo-Tarmé stole her. I don't *want* my daughter to be exploited, trained, moulded to someone else's design. I want her to be happy, and loving, and *ordinary*. Can you understand that?'

There was a strange look on Kazhian's face. He said quietly, 'Yes. I am Eska'anen's son. I understand very well.'

There was an uneasy pause that continued too long. Ammenna

stifled a yawn. 'It's very late. Time for more talk in the morning. Will you stay with us, all of you? The rugs and cushions in here will make a couple of beds for the men. Mallaso, you and Kiyu can sleep on the spare mattress in S'raya's room.'

The baby stirred and sighed happily as Mallaso crept under the blanket beside her. Tomorrow, she would have to plan the future which, until a few hours ago, had seemed so grey and bleak, and which was now as bright and rich and joyful as the yellow and scarlet flowers on Ammenna's courtyard wall. But for the moment, it was more than enough to have Kiyu in her arms, to feel her soft breathing, her blissful warmth, her love. She did indeed possess power, the power that her mother had feared so much, but Bron's awesome inheritance had saved her from death, and brought her home.

Mallaso fell asleep smiling, and dreamed of him.

This time, he was not standing in empty grassland: he sat instead under a tall, stately tree. It had low, sweeping branches and a myriad of prickly dark green needles instead of leaves. The place looked so lovely in the sunlight and dappled shadow that she could not believe that it lay in Olyak's Halls. Or perhaps this was another part of some northern afterworld, alien to her eyes but familiar to him.

'You have her back,' Bron said, and smiled. After Kazhian's dark, vivid face, he seemed pallid and almost ethereal. And yet in that smile she could see the likeness to Kiyu, bright with joy.

'They found her because she summoned them,' Mallaso said.

'I know.' He had always 'known', seeming to absorb information with the air he breathed. 'And Sé Mo-Tarmé is dead, slain by her own arrogance and selfishness, and most of her acolytes with her. Even now, the fire-mountain of Jo'ami is waking from its sleep. So few sorcerers are left, and they will not be able to contain it for very long.'

'So the prophecy was right,' Mallaso whispered in horror. Because of your legacy, because of Kiyu, Jo'ami will be destroyed.' And despite her hatred of the High Sorcerer, she felt a terrible surge of grief, for what would be lost.

'Don't weep for them. Their time has gone. And when the island finally erupts, they will have had enough warning. No one will perish, and most of their ancient lore and learning will be saved. But their influence will fade away to nothing, for many centuries to come.'

'How do you know all this? You said the future was closed to you.'

'Then, it was. Now, things are different. I have changed, I am not the Bron you once knew. You are not the Mallaso I knew, for your life has moved on. I know I promised you once that I would come to find you, but that is not possible now. You have Kiyu back, and new doors are opening. Your future lies on Penya, as it was always meant to. And do not refuse anything for my sake, Mallaso – do not deny what will be offered, because of me.'

'What do you mean?' she demanded. But his voice was fading, his image wavering.

'You will know, when it comes. Remember me, when you hold Kiyu. Remember me, when the sun turns the sea to turquoise, and the birds sing in the summer sky, and the west wind blows through the grass. But memories cannot feed the heart for long. I will watch over you and Kiyu for always, Mallaso of Penya – but you are mine no longer.'

He was gone. She opened her eyes to darkness, and the soft regular sound of S'raya's breathing. Beside her, Kiyu stirred, and snuggled closer with a sigh as happy and peaceful as if she had never been stolen. And Mallaso silently gave thanks to Sarraliss the Mother, and to Kazhian and Sargenay, for the return of her child, and the restoration of hope and joy.

'It's very beautiful,' said Sargenay, with surprise in his voice.

They were standing on Beacon Hill, which rose above the western arm of Penya Harbour. Behind them, their donkeys grazed peacefully in the scrub, their ears and tails constantly working to keep insects at bay. Ka'avan was down in the village clustered round the cove to their right, making his endless notes and lists, and Mallaso had brought her friends up here, ostensibly to survey the fields and farms, but really to admire the view, and to talk in private, away from the Penyan's inquisitive ears.

'Of course it's beautiful,' Mallaso said. 'It's Penya. But then I am biased.'

'I know,' Sargenay said fondly. 'You have two hearts now, dearest Mallaso. One has always been Penya's. And the other belongs to Kiyu, does it not?'

'Yes.' She sat down in the thick tufted grass, and hugged her knees. On this hot, breezy day she had chosen her simplest garment, a calf-length Kerentan dress of thin, pale blue cotton, belted at the waist. Her hair had grown out of the severe crop which she had worn in Toktel'yi, and stood in a ruffled dark nimbus round her head. She looked elegant, confident, and yet far more relaxed and happy than she had ever done in the old days at the Golden Djarlek.

'I don't understand how you could bear to leave her behind

today,' Sargenay went on curiously. 'You have only had her back for a few days. I'd have thought you wouldn't want to let her out of your sight.'

'I know. I thought so too. But S'raya was so desperate to look after her again that I couldn't refuse. And Kiyu adores her, she thinks of her as a big sister. I shall be glad to get home, all the same, just to make sure she's all right, and not missing me too much.'

'I have absolutely no experience of babies,' Sargenay said. 'But Kiyu seems to me to be remarkably good-natured and placid.'

'Oh, no, she isn't! She has a fierce temper – if you take a toy away from her, she screams and screams. But she isn't a nervous or fretful child. And even – even after what has happened to her, when you'd expect her to cry and cling, she's still her usual sunny self.'

'Perhaps she knows she's safe,' the sorcerer suggested. 'When Kazhian rescued her, she was almost dead. But we brought her back to the *Sea Serpent*, and warmed her up and fed her, and she recovered very quickly. She behaved as if she'd known us all her life, as if she *knew* we could be trusted. And yet Beygan, the Kerentan Captain, told us that she'd been very difficult for the Jo'amians – screaming all the time, refusing to eat. She even bit the High Sorcerer once.'

Mallaso gave a gasp of laughter. 'Oh, Kiyu, how naughty – but I can't blame her.'

'She does have power,' Sargenay said softly. 'It lies there within her, dormant until she needs to use it. Perhaps she doesn't even know she possesses it – or she uses it unthinkingly, as she uses her eyes and ears. But soon, like it or not, you will have to explain to her what she is. And someone will have to teach her the basics of sorcery, as soon as she is old enough to understand them.'

'But I don't *want* her to become a sorcerer!'

'I know you don't. But she *is* one, even now, and she is alive because of it. Your mind has accepted that fact, although your heart is resisting for a little longer. In the end, you know you must acknowledge what she is, to yourself and to Kiyu herself, or she will be very dangerous.' He paused, and then added softly, 'If you like, if you want – I will help you to teach her.'

Mallaso looked round at him in surprise. 'You mean – you will stay here? But what about Kazhian?'

The sorcerer's hooded eyes closed briefly, hiding his pain. 'He will just have to find another weather-worker. I was never much good at it, anyway. I signed on from necessity, with Olkanno's men hunting for me after your little exploit on Tekkt. I suspect he only took me on as a gesture of defiance. Always the rebel, is Kazhian. And I can't imagine why I stayed so long.'

'Because you love him, of course.'

'Oh dear.' Sargenay spread his hands in mock despair, his tattered robes swirling in the breeze. 'Can nothing be hidden from your eagle eyes?'

'I've known you very well for years, remember. I've seen you in love before. Does he know?'

'Yes, though we've never discussed it. He isn't interested in men, though, so I shall just have to pine in vain.' Despite his casual tone, she could recognize his genuine sorrow. He added, smiling bravely, 'He's noticed you, by the way, so be careful. Kazhian gets through women like a tiger working his way down a line of tethered goats. He'll eat you up and spit you out and never remember he's had you.'

'I think I can remember how to look after myself,' Mallaso said firmly. 'And in any case, is it really true?'

Sargenay dropped his gaze. After a while, he said, 'I may have exaggerated slightly. Kazhian makes his own rules. He's not like the rest of his kind. For instance, he has no ambition to be Emperor. To hear him talk, he's never looked beyond the next woman, the next bottle of wine, the next pipe of khlar. But that's only part of him. In all our time together, I've only come close to him once or twice, and that was when he was drunk enough to let his guard down. He hides a great deal behind that careless mask, and most of it is connected with his father. Did you know that Eska'anen murdered his mother?'

'No, but it doesn't surprise me.'

'And it was Eska'anen who paid the steersman to wreck Kazhian's galley, five years ago. I suppose he hoped his son would drown. As it was, his career in the Navy was ruined. But the Blood Imperial has been changed in him. He is not vicious, or cowardly, or cruel. He is clever and resourceful and courageous, and he is the most remarkable man I have ever met. I will love him until I die. And that, dearest Mallaso, is why I want to stay here on Penya. For I don't think I can bear to have just his friendship, when there is nothing more on offer, and never will be.'

'Oh, Sargenay.' Mallaso took his hands and then, seeing the tears in his eyes, embraced him. 'You will find someone else. There must be someone else. And I would love you to stay on Penya. Ammenna has asked me to share her house, and now that I have Kiyu back I have accepted. If you employ some of your famous sorcerer's charm on her, perhaps she won't mind if you move in too. And one day you'll meet a man who will return your love.'

'Really? On Penya?'

'There are some things that will never be tolerated here. Cruelty. Injustice. Waste. Poverty. But never love, no matter what guise it takes. My uncle had a male lover, and no one disapproved, or even thought it unusual. On Penya, there are few rules. And the most important is to treat others as you'd like to be treated yourself.'

'It sounds idyllic,' said Sargenay, his voice restored to its usual lightness. He smiled at her, and indicated the view, sea, sky, sun, island, spread around them. 'It *is* idyllic. I thought that Ba'alekkt had laid it all to waste.'

'So he did. But the land is very fertile, and very strong. Most of the buildings are in ruins, but Sarraliss has done Her best to hide the destruction. It will take many years, though, to mend the damage, and probably I will not live to see it – though Kiyu might. She and S'raya and the other children are the island's future. That's why the exiles in Kerenth took such pains to pass on their knowledge, and to keep the old customs and traditions alive.'

'If Olkanno lets it happen.'

'I think – I pray – that he'll have no choice but to leave us alone.' Mallaso rose to her feet and brushed the grass-seeds off her dress. 'Time to move on – I can't let poor Ka'avan do all the work. By all accounts the eastern provinces of the Empire are in chaos. Our invasion was only possible because Olkanno withdrew most of the garrison to help subdue the rebellion in Tatht.' She glanced at Sargenay, who was a native of that province. 'And from what I've heard, he'll need every soldier he can get, if he's not to lose Tatht and Terebis as well as Djebb.'

Sargenay stood beside her, gazing as she did at the great hazy, empty arch of blue sky. 'In Kerenth, they were talking about the Flamebearer, who is supposed to be leading the people of the Empire to freedom. No one knows who he is, or where he comes from. No one has ever seen him, save as a shadow in their dreams. And yet he has inspired millions of people to rise up and demand their freedom. No wonder Olkanno has put a price of a hundred thousand gold Imperials on his head. If he ever appears in reality, he will either be killed out of hand, or lead the whole Empire out of Olkanno's grasp.'

'We are free,' Mallaso said. 'But no Penyan has ever seen him, inside or outside their dreams.'

'Perhaps those in Tatht and Djebb required more help than you did. But whoever or whatever he is – god, demon, human – many may one day have reason to thank him.'

'Or to curse his name, as they are dragged back into slavery,'

Mallaso said. She turned away from the glorious sea, and began to walk back to her donkey. 'That is what frightens me most of all – that all this is not for ever. That Olkanno will eventually crush the rebellions, and then send his armies to destroy us, to rob us of our freedom again, before we have had the chance to enjoy it. And there are still some soldiers here. There are five hundred men of the Toktel'yan garrison, hiding somewhere in the mountains. Essyan has been trying to catch them, but so far he hasn't succeeded. They could stay there for ever, living off the country, raiding farms, always a threat to our peace.' She shivered. 'We will never feel truly secure here until every hostile Toktel'yan is driven from the land, and the Empire destroyed.'

'Until the sun sets in the east, dear Mallaso,' said the sorcerer, with gentle derision. 'No one is ever truly secure. We must learn to make the best of what we already have.' He laughed. 'How wise I've become in my old age. We'd better find Ka'avan before I inflict any more gems of philosophy on you.'

Ka'avan was still diligently compiling his lists, and they helped him to finish his task before riding home along the coast road to Penya Harbour, some five or six miles away on the eastern side of the bay.

Kiyu hadn't missed her mother at all, S'raya told them, beaming. 'And Essyan is coming tomorrow, and there's to be a welcome feast, and Tegerno asked Mother if you'd dance. She said she didn't know if you would, but perhaps now that Kiyu's back . . .'

Now that she had her daughter again, she would dance. She had a costume, Penyan traditional dress, that she had bought in Kerenth, and a few items of jewellery. Sargenay would see no comparison with the splendidly attired woman who had danced in Toktel'yi – but oh, how different and how glorious now would be her spirit.

Everyone living in and around Penya Harbour was invited to the feast, the Toktel'yan settlers as well as the returned exiles. And also Sargenay, who was still occupying a temporary bed in Ammenna's house: and Kazhian and his crew.

After their first night on Penya, the *Sea Serpent*'s Captain had returned to his ship. Ammenna had urged him to stay, and there was enough room for him, but he had politely and charmingly declined. Now, remembering Sargenay's comments earlier, Mallaso wondered if he had deliberately withdrawn himself from the warmth and friendliness of the household. And of course, he might also be wary of sharing a room with the man who was so hopelessly in love with him. She had regretted his departure: she liked Kazhian, and his air of mystery intrigued her. Even after Sargenay's disparaging remarks about tethered goats, she felt very strongly the attractiveness of his personality and the force of his charm. The sorcerer had always before fallen in love with men more notable for their beauty than for their good nature, and some of them had led him a merry dance. But it seemed that in Kazhian he had found someone whom he could admire without reservation or restraint. And since Sargenay was a man of experience and sophistication, Kazhian was surely worth her own attention.

Was *that* what Bron meant, when he had urged her to move on, to take what was offered? Had he been thinking of Kazhian?

If he had, Mallaso decided, he was counting a remarkable number of Imperials before they'd been earned. As yet, Eska'anen's son had done no more than glance at her. She only had Sargenay's word that he was interested at all. She resolved to take each day as it came, and refuse to indulge in fruitless anticipation or speculation. And if he and his ship left Penya Harbour tomorrow, she would surely experience only the mildest feeling of regret.

CHAPTER
SEVENTEEN

Essyan rode into the town on a white horse, which had been shipped over with several others from Kerenth, at the head of a hundred well-armed men and women, with the moon and star of Penya borne proudly before them. He had come, so Tegerno had said, to check on the progress of the rebuilding, and to tell them about his future plans. Despite these mundane reasons for his visit, a splendid festival was planned, for no Penyan had ever needed much excuse for a celebration. And although the island had been in their possession for nearly two months now, so far there had been no commemoration of their joyful and triumphant return from exile.

So the Meeting House was garlanded with leaves and flowers, hiding the raw scars of damage and destruction, and a huge fire had been built in the courtyard behind it, over which a couple of goats would be roasted. One of the Kerentan ships had brought a cargo of wine, so there was plenty to drink. And during the meal, there would be entertainers: musicians, a troupe of tumblers, a display of Magical Illusion (Mallaso had worked hard to persuade Sargenay to show off his talent), and, of course, traditional dancing.

Mallaso dressed with care in her Penyan costume, which consisted of two huge rectangles of soft, flame-coloured silk, clasped at the shoulder and belted at the waist. Ammenna had lent her a pair of very old garnet earrings, that had belonged to her great-grandmother, and she had borrowed from other friends the jewelled clasps, the ring-bracelets, and the necklace. She looked magnificent, and knew it. Kiyu laughed to see her mother all pretty and sparkly, and tried to grab the long, swinging earrings. Mallaso kissed her, and with the child in her arms and her flimsy finery covered by an old grey cloak, walked alongside Ammenna and S'raya to the Meeting House.

One of the small offices had been set aside for the babies and younger children, with mattresses laid out on the floor, and several women taking it in turns to watch over them. Mallaso settled Kiyu with some difficulty, for the baby wanted to share in the excitement.

Eventually, she sang to her until the little girl's eyes closed in sleep, and then crept quietly out of the room.

By now, the celebrations were in full spate. The wide space of the main Hall was hot and crowded with men, women and older children, eating, drinking, talking, or watching the tumblers leaping and somersaulting in the centre of the floor. Sargenay came up to her. He wore deep crimson robes, with various arcane symbols embroidered in silver around the hem and along the edges of his flowing, extravagantly impractical sleeves. His normally handsome face was shiny with sweat and anxiety, and his hands fussed nervously with his belt. 'Oh, there you are, dear Mallaso – I've been looking for you everywhere! I can't do it, my dear, I just *can't*! You'll have to tell your hatchet-faced leader that I'm indisposed.'

'You mean Essyan?' said Mallaso, trying not to smile. Sargenay had performed some Illusions for her at the Golden Djarlek, and she knew that this exhibition of stage-fright was the essential prologue to his show. She added briskly, 'No, I won't. You'll go on next, after the acrobats, exactly as we arranged with Tegerno this morning, and you'll astonish them. You can't fail – these are Penyans, remember, and most of them won't have seen Toktel'yan sorcery. It's a shame you won't be on last – everything else will seem tame after your display.'

Some of the anxiety left Sargenay's face. 'Are you sure?'

'Of course I'm sure. Have a cup of wine to calm your nerves. After all, you've performed in public before, and the audience at the Golden Djarlek were tigers compared to this lot. One Illusion, and they'll be spellbound. Give them your best, and they'll be eating out of your hand.'

'*They* haven't seen it before. But *he* has.'

Mallaso followed his gaze. Kazhian was standing on the other side of the room, wine-cup in hand, talking to a very beautiful Penyan girl who couldn't be much older than S'raya. She said firmly, 'Don't think about him. Think about your show. If you impress Tegerno, she might make you the official Penya Harbour Sorcerer – a plum job for life!'

'I'm not sure I want it,' said Sargenay, but his mood was already changing. Mallaso could sense his concentration growing, pulling the tattered rags of his self-esteem back into its usual splendour.

The tumblers finished, to loud applause, and ran off. Tegerno stepped forward, her sturdy figure magnificently draped in a gown of amber silk. 'Thank you very much, Erekay and friends. I feel quite exhausted after watching you! Now, we have a less energetic entertainment for your delight, one which has never before been seen here on Penya. Please welcome, my friends and comrades, Sargenay of Tatht, Sorcerer Extraordinary!'

Mallaso gave him a little push. He looked round with arch indignation, and then swept through the crowd and into the central space.

As soon as he began speaking, she knew he would be all right. She watched him for a while, entranced, although she had seen him make his Illusions many times in Toktel'yi.

'He's good, isn't he?'

The deep voice startled her. She turned and saw Kazhian standing very close to her. He had put on a long, formal Toktel'yan gown in a muted shade of sea-green, with a little restrained embroidery round the square neck. His hair was loose, and dressed with scented oils, but he hadn't removed any of his earrings, and he looked interestingly and splendidly barbaric.

'Very good,' Mallaso said. 'But I've see him do this before, at the Golden Djarlek.'

'I never went there,' Kazhian said regretfully.

'I know. It was probably much too respectable for you.'

His green eyes were assessing her wickedly. 'I can be very respectable, when I choose. What could be more boringly conventional than this gown?'

'In Toktel'yi, yes. In Penya, it certainly isn't – as I suspect you know very well.' Mallaso gave him a challenging smile. She was enjoying this, although his extreme proximity was disturbing her equilibrium. Hoping he hadn't noticed it, she turned her attention back to Sargenay. He had produced a pair of comically exaggerated donkeys, who were trying to avoid being ridden by a very fat man with a huge bundle of sticks. Most of the Penyans, lubricated by good food and wine, were rocking with laughter.

'I do,' Kazhian said. He was just a little taller than she was, and his face was very close, the surprising green eyes intent. 'But in private, as I'm sure you can guess, I cast restraint to the winds.'

He was definitely drunk. She could smell the aroma of good Kerentan wine on his breath, dark and potent. In a moment, he would touch her. An image of tethered goats rose in her mind, and she grinned. 'What a pity I shan't take the opportunity to find out. I think I am to dance very shortly. Pray excuse me, Lord Kazhian.'

At least Sargenay was showing some restraint: in Toktel'yi, she'd seen him create Illusions of astonishing obscenity. Fortunately, he seemed to have realized that Penyans weren't quite so uninhibited about sex, preferring a certain amount of dignity and privacy. The donkeys had gone, and in their place he had made a miniature tree of glorious delicacy, placing on its branches a score of different flowers in every colour of the rainbow, attended by bright butterflies and a small hovering bird like a feathered jewel.

The image faded at last, and Sargenay dropped his arms and bowed his head. There was a rapt, reverent pause, and then the cheering began.

It continued for a long time, but the sorcerer, obviously exhausted, would do no more. Eventually, they allowed him to leave the floor, and he stumbled to Mallaso's side like an old man. While the musicians played, she found him a drink and some food, and somewhere quiet to sit until he had recovered a little. Then, hearing her name above the noise, she made her way over to Tegerno, who was the organizer of the evening's entertainment.

'Your wizard was excellent,' she said to Mallaso, smiling. She was in her fifties, a strong, sensible and down-to-earth woman who had fought the Toktel'yans for some years after the invasion, before fleeing to Kerenth. 'Is he going to stay with us?'

'I was going to ask you if he could. He wants to. He's Toktel'yan, I know, but he's from Tatht, and he has no love for the Empire. If you're doubtful, I'll stand surety for him.'

'No need. He's your friend, and he brought Kiyu back – that's assurance enough. And what about the other one, Lord Kazhian? I don't think he's quite so harmless, unfortunately.'

Mallaso glanced round, but couldn't see him. All the same, she lowered her voice. 'So you know who he is?'

'I do, along with everyone else in Penya Harbour. Dressed like that, he hardly passes for one of us, after all. So is the disgraced and outlawed pirate son of the late Emperor trustworthy, do you think?'

'I honestly don't know. He saved Kiyu, so naturally I'm biased in his favour. I like him, and Sargenay admires him greatly. But I expect he'll go back to piracy.'

'That might be his loss, and ours, you know.' Tegerno was looking very thoughtful. '*If* he is trustworthy, *if* he could be persuaded to stay with us, he and his ship could be extremely useful. I know one vessel doesn't make a fleet, but it's a start, and he has naval experience, hasn't he? So he could help train more men for the ships we must build in the future. Our shores need to be patrolled and guarded against any future invasion from the Empire. If Toktel'yi has outlawed him, then he might take the opportunity to do something worthwhile here. It depends on his loyalty to his homeland. If he is prepared to renounce the Empire, and throw in his lot with us, he will be welcome. But if he has some idea of trying to use Penya as a base from which to claim the Onyx Throne—'

'Sargenay told me that he has no desire to be Emperor. From what I've seen of Kazhian – and that's very little – I think he's right.'

'I'll talk to Essyan,' said Tegerno. 'Perhaps he can have a private word with your pirate tomorrow. Ah, the music is ending – your turn now, Mallaso. Good luck!'

She had danced in Kerenth, to mark the beginning of hope. Now, before many, many more people, she danced to celebrate its triumph, and her own, more personal joy. The players wove their ancient, familiar patterns, and she gave them the Flame Dance, eloquent of love, and then the Harvest Revel, adapted for a solo performer. Finally, after whispered instructions to the musicians, she created her own steps and leaps, wild and exultant and spectacular, to the rousing tune called 'The Homecoming'. This was for Kiyu, for Sargenay, and for all the exiles, and the sense of glory in her heart elevated her dancing to a level she had never attained before, so marvellous that she felt as if Sarraliss Herself had laid Her blessing upon her.

Breathless, exhilarated, she stood gracefully still at the end, accepting their wild applause with a smile of thanks. Then Essyan escorted her from the floor, pressed wine and food into her hot hands, and engaged her in conversation. He even forgot his severity, and smiled at her. She smiled back, although, as always, she had left the emotional peak of the performance, and now longed only for peace, and quiet, and a little privacy.

At last she managed to slip away from the noisy, stifling Hall. Rather to her relief, there was no sign of Sargenay or Kazhian, although she had seen them both earlier, watching her dance. She looked in on Kiyu, found her sleeping curled up against another little girl, and tiptoed out with a nod to the woman in charge, yawning on her cushions. She stood for a moment in the empty entrance lobby, looking at the fresco of Sarraliss, gracious and smiling, her hands full of grapes and flowers and ears of ripe corn. Silently, she uttered a prayer of thanks: then, seeking coolness and quiet, she went outside.

The quayside was deserted. The moon rode high over Matamenya, and crickets called endlessly. A soft breeze stirred against her hot skin. Beset by memories, by old regrets and a new, aching, almost melancholy joy, she walked along the waterfront, barefoot, until she came to the place where steps led down to the long strip of white sand, curving round the western side of the bay, where the smaller fishing-boats were drawn up.

As she descended the steps, she thought she heard something. She turned, but there was no one behind her. Reassured, she reached the sand and began to walk down to the sea. A swim, she thought, with sudden eagerness. A swim in soft, warm water would wash away the sweat of exertion, and perhaps restore her calm.

Once more she glanced over her shoulder, but there was no movement anywhere on the beach. She unclasped her belt, and slipped the thin silk dress over her head. Clad only in her borrowed jewellery, she slid into the welcoming water.

She did not swim for long, but it was time enough to relax, to float in the gentle, almost imperceptible swell, to gaze up at the profusion of brilliant stars in the silken black sky. Then she waded back to the shore, sluiced the surplus water from her body with her hands, and put her dress back on, ignoring the sticky and salty dampness of her skin. The swim had soothed her vivid emotions, and she felt ready now to enjoy the rest of the night.

As she walked back to the steps, she saw that someone was there, watching her. Her heart began to thud: she paused, and then walked firmly on.

'Hallo, Mallaso,' said Kazhian softly. His back was against the harbour wall, and his legs stretched out along the middle step, so that she would have to walk over him to get past. He was holding some kind of flask, and as she halted below him, he drank from it and wiped his mouth with the back of his hand.

'Good evening, Lord Kazhian,' Mallaso said, with deliberate formality, and in Toktel'yan.

'You can leave out the "Lord". I renounced any claim to that title years ago.' There was more than a trace of bitterness in his voice. 'Will you sit with me for a while?'

'Were you following me earlier?' she demanded indignantly.

'No. Yes. Possibly.' Kazhian laughed, and took another drink from the flask. 'Want some ral? It's Balkian.'

'That's hardly a recommendation. No, thank you.'

'It isn't, is it? Balki, home of the sour wine and sour earth and sour women. Very different from Penya, blessed by Sarraliss above all other islands in the world . . . and therefore a target for wanton destruction. Why don't you speak Penyan? This language seems like a blasphemy here.'

Mallaso stared at him, her anger evaporated. She thought of what Sargenay had told her about this man, the contradictions, the mysteries, the hidden vulnerability. But even so, his unexpected perception caught at her heart. She said softly, in her own tongue. 'Do you know Penyan?'

'I'm fluent in Kerentan, but the two are nearly the same, aren't they? One is a dialect of the other, and Penya and Kerenth have been arguing since time began as to which is which.' He looked down at her, still standing on the bottom step, and she saw the white gleam of a smile. 'Sit with me, Mallaso of Penya. I promise I won't rape you.'

Startled into laughter, she said, 'That wasn't what I was afraid of.'

'Wasn't it? But you're alone at night with a notorious Vessel of the Blood Imperial. A beautiful woman like you should be afraid.'

'After what your people have done to me, I have little left to fear,' Mallaso pointed out drily.

'I know. I am sorry. Sargenay has told me about you,' said Kazhian. 'And all I can say is . . . I am not the same as most of my kind.'

'You wouldn't be here if you were. You'd be in some brothel like the Blue Hyacinth, out of your mind on khlar—'

'No, I wouldn't. I'd be dead. D'you think Olkanno would have let me live? Apart from Kekaylo, and he's a priest and so it's unlucky to kill him, I'm the last one left. Olkanno even had my uncle Kadjak murdered, and his two grandchildren, Gorek's little son and daughter – did you know that? A sick old man exiled on a rock, and two small children hardly older than Kiyu. And yet he saw them as a threat, so he killed them.' Kazhian took another gulp of the ral, and said harshly, 'I hate the Empire. I hated my father, my brother, and most of my cousins – except for Megren. I despised them and all they represented, and I'm glad they're dead. I have no country now – I have cut myself free of them. I will never betray you, or your people. Whatever happens, you are safe from me.'

'I know,' Mallaso whispered, astonished and appalled by the sudden savagery in his voice. 'And if you want to stay with us—'

'I don't know. I don't know what I want. But at this precise moment, I need company.' He took a deep, ragged breath. 'I'm sorry. I'm too drunk to think straight. Go on back to your friends. They'll be wondering where you are.'

'I doubt it. They're enjoying themselves too much.' She climbed the steps and sat down beside him, wondering what she was letting herself in for, even as she did so. 'What did you say was in the flask?'

He laughed suddenly. 'Balkian ral. It's a spirit – very strong. Are you sure?'

'I'll try almost anything once,' said Mallaso. She took a sip, and coughed at the rasp of the fiery liquid in her throat. 'Sweet mother, what does that do to your gut? You can have it back, with my blessing.'

'There's not much left, anyway,' said Kazhian regretfully. He drained the rest and tossed the flask lightly on to the sand. 'You dance very well.'

'It was my living, in Toktel'yi. But tonight I performed for the joy of it.'

'I could see that. It was beautiful. *You* were – are – beautiful.' Kazhian leaned his head back against the wall. The moonlight illuminated, with pure and desperate clarity, the long line of throat and jaw, the tangle of curling hair. 'I'm not making much sense, am I?' he added, with a sudden and disarming grin.

'No – but I'll forgive you. With all that ral inside you, it's no wonder your wits are snarled up.'

'I'll regret it later. I always do.'

'Then why do it?'

There was an unexpectedly long pause. Then Kazhian said, very quietly, 'Because I want to let go. Be ordinary. Forget who I am and what I am. You understand that, don't you? I know you do, because of what you said when we brought Kiyu back.'

'Yes.' Mallaso stared at him in the eerie moonlight, seeing not an enemy, not a threat, nor a potential lover, but a man who, like her but in different ways, had been formed and moulded and twisted in the savage heat of Toktel'yi, and suffered from it. A man who, unlike her, had not yet discovered happiness: a human being in sore need of comfort. Obeying a sudden, uncharacteristic impulse, she reached up and took his hand. 'Why did you hate your father?'

'He hated me – I suppose, because I wasn't like him. All through my childhood, I craved his approval, I would have done anything to earn his praise. And instead, he gave it all to Suken, my half-brother. He was six years younger than me, and he was always Eska'anen's favourite. And oh, how he flaunted it, even when he was small. I hit him once, because of what he said, and my father thrashed me in person, until I bled. He said I was no better than a Tulyettan bandit – that if I misbehaved again he'd send me to the iron mines. He meant it. I was eleven years old, and a year before that he'd had my mother murdered.'

'My mother was killed when I was ten,' Mallaso said. 'So was my father, and my brothers. Most of the people here have a similar tragedy in their past. Beside what happened to us, you have no special claim on anyone's sympathy.'

For a moment, she thought she had lost him. Then Kazhian gave a bark of bitter laughter. 'I'm sorry. I forgot. Too wound up in my own self-pity . . . What did I suffer? Not rape, or slavery. And most of the misfortunes have been of my own making. If I had been more like Suken—'

'Well, you are not – and be glad that you aren't. I certainly am. Suken would have left Kiyu to die.' She took a deep breath, feeling his hand, lax and warm in hers, knowing that somehow, though they were almost strangers, she could help him. 'You are yourself. You are what your father's hatred has made you – that is true. But if his love produced a snake like Suken, I should be grateful that he did not love you.'

There was a long silence. At last, Kazhian said, 'Perhaps you are right. Are you always so wise, Mallaso the beautiful, Mallaso the dancer?'

'No. But I wanted you to stand back a little, to see things differently. Do you?'

'I don't know.' This time, his laughter was softer, with genuine amusement. 'Possibly. Trouble is, will I remember all this in the morning?'

'I will. I'll tell you again then, if you like.'

'It wouldn't work. I can't talk like this if I'm sober.'

'You should try. Anyway, Essyan might want to see you. He may have an interesting proposition to put to you.'

'Let me guess. He wants me and my ship to keep stray Toktel'yans at bay. Don't look so surprised – it's obvious when you think about it. Perhaps I will. I never made a very good pirate – I left too many people alive to tell the tale.'

'So Sargenay said.'

'Sargenay's image of me is altogether too shiny bright for comfort. You know he's in love with me?'

'He's one of my oldest and dearest friends. Of course I know.'

'I've never had a man in love with me before,' Kazhian said reflectively. 'I wish he wasn't – he is my friend too, and I don't want to hurt him. But I've never been interested in sleeping with him. Women are more my style.' He smiled suddenly. 'Especially women like you.'

'Like a tethered goat, you mean?' Mallaso enquired sweetly.

'Like what?'

'Sargenay compared your appetite for women to a tiger working his way along a line of tethered goats.'

'I'll kill him, the miserable lying little weather-wizard!'

'Then he was right.'

There was a short pause. 'Yes,' said Kazhian, laughing ruefully. 'Yes, he was right.'

'Then I give you notice, here and now, that I do not think of myself in any way as a tethered goat.'

'That's a relief. I don't either. Think of you as a goat, I mean – your horns are very unobtrusive, and I can't see your beard in this light. Lord of Life, my head's spinning. Tomorrow,' said Kazhian forcefully, 'I am either going to remember nothing of this conversation, or regret every word of it . . . will you do something for me?'

'It depends on what it is.'

'Take me back to your friend's house – if there's still a spare bed.'

'Of course – though it's right the other end of the quay.'

'I'll manage it – I'm not falling-down drunk, not yet. And will you do something else for me, beautiful Mallaso?'

Warned by the sudden deepening of his voice, she knew what to expect. When he added, almost in a whisper, 'Kiss me?', she rose, and obediently planted her lips demurely on his cheek.

'Not like that,' Kazhian said, laughing, and pulled her into his embrace. 'Like this.'

His mouth found hers, and suddenly she was struck by sensations at once old and new. The warm wine taste of him, the gentleness that was somehow not unexpected, an exploration of potential passion.

'Very definitely not a tethered goat,' he murmured at last.

'They're all supposed to be sheep-shaggers on Balki, aren't they?'

'Don't be so rude, woman. Anyway, I'm not from Balki.'

'Then how can you tell the difference?' Mallaso enquired, and bleated softly.

'Oh, take me home, or I'll want much more than a kiss – I *do* want more than a kiss, but I want to sleep this off first.' Kazhian stood up, reeled, and managed to brace himself against the wall. 'Come on, let's go, before I'm tempted to pass out here.'

It was a long walk to Ammenna's house, but Mallaso wasn't tired. Kazhian had draped an affectionate arm around her, and they progressed together, rather unsteadily and haphazardly, along the quayside. After a while, he asked, 'What's the Penyan for "goat"?'

'It's not quite the same as in Kerentan. And it depends on what sort of goat. "Sashen" is a billy-goat. An "ur-sashen" is a sort of supreme billy-goat, well-horned and hung.'

'A female?'

'That's a "sashalla". A young female is a "sashir".'

'Sashen. Sashalla. Sashir.' Kazhian stopped and turned, drawing her close. 'Beautiful Sashir, will you come to my bed tomorrow night?'

'I don't think Sargenay would want to watch!'

'Not at your friend's house – on the *Sea Serpent*.'

'I don't know. Kiyu—'

'It's all right. If you don't want to, just tell me. As I said, rape is not required.' He pulled her against him suddenly, and she felt the hasty beat of his heart, and the strength of him, warm and waiting. 'I'm sorry. I shouldn't have asked. Forget it. Did you love him very much?'

'Bron?' She was startled by the question, but not angry. 'I don't know. He saved me, he healed me, he gave me Kiyu – I owe him my life and my sanity and my happiness, but love . . . I just don't know.'

'Love is for fools and children. My father said that to me once. Was he right?'

'No,' Mallaso told him fiercely. 'Love is for everyone who knows how to give it, and take it, and make it. And those who think otherwise are to be pitied indeed.'

'Wise Mallaso.' Kazhian released her, though he kept hold of her hand as they walked on. 'But nothing on earth will make me pity my father. He and Suken deserved their fates, and the Empire, and all the known world, is a better place without them. It would be even better without Olkanno, too.'

Mallaso said nothing, her heart cold. Killing Emperors was a lethal business. Bron had died alongside Ba'alekkt: Suken had survived Eska'anen only by a few heartbeats. And suddenly, she could not bear the thought that Kazhian might be tempted to risk a similar fate.

'Don't worry,' he added, grinning. 'I'll leave such heroics to others. Anyway, kill one Emperor and the next is invariably worse. I don't want the Onyx Throne. I never want to set foot on Toktel'yan soil again. Lord Kazhian, Vessel of the Blood Imperial, died years ago. You see before you, Sashir, only Kazhian the notorious pirate, and bane of all tethered goats!'

They had reached Ammenna's house at last. It was dark and silent. Mallasso pushed open the door, finding her way to Sargenay's room by touch and memory. Behind her Kazhian stumbled, knocked into obstacles, and swore with drunken hilarity at every collision. She found a lamp, lit it, and indicated the further mattress. 'There you are. I'll find Sargenay and warn him.'

'Tell him not to take advantage of my temporary incapacity, will you?'

'Don't joke about it,' Mallasso said softly. 'I don't want him laughed at. He saved Kiyu's life, remember? He's worth more than our mockery.'

'I know. I'm sorry. He saved my life too, once,' said Kazhian.

He was standing just inside the door, his face hazy with weariness. She walked back to him, and smiled. 'Thank you. I enjoyed this evening, very much.'

His sudden delighted grin was reward in itself. 'Did you really, Sashir? That does surprise me. I did, too. Not many women can make me laugh.'

'Baa-a,' said Mallaso. She kissed him affectionately on the mouth, and went out.

It was true, she reflected, walking back to the Meeting House, where the festivities were obviously still in full swing. She had delighted in his company, for despite his past, Kazhian still possessed a wicked and mischievous sense of humour, and a willingness to laugh at himself that was extraordinarily attractive.

And it would be very easy to be attracted, but Mallaso was naturally cautious. She had always guarded herself against hurt: she had adored her children utterly and unreservedly, but she had deliberately kept her lovers at a distance. Even Bron, whom she had known so briefly: even Bron, she realized now, had not truly possessed her heart.

But she had never laughed with Bron as she had with Kazhian tonight. There had always been too much seriousness, too many threats looming over their future. His sorcery had frightened her, though she had successfully hidden her fear from him. In Kazhian, though, despite his faults, there was a generous warmth that invited intimacy, a sense of a common past, a united spirit, and the chance of a shared future.

Do not deny what is offered because of me, Bron had told her in her dream. And she understood now what he meant.

Sashir. If Ammenna heard Kazhian call her that, she'd never hear the end of it.

Smiling to herself, Mallaso made a noise like a goat, and walked into the loud brightness of the Meeting House, in search of Sargenay.

CHAPTER
EIGHTEEN

Kazhian woke with a revolting taste in his mouth, and his head pounding like an Onnak woodsman's axe. It was almost light, and the birds were singing, and he could hear a peculiar, rhythmic noise that he identified eventually as Sargenay's snores.

He lay very still, trying to remember. Confused snatches of conversation drifted through his mind. He'd said a great deal, very little of which had made sense to him, even at the time. And he had probably revealed far more of himself than he should, to a woman who was almost a stranger.

Sashir. Goatling. The thought made him smile with sudden delight, and her image leapt into his mind. Mallaso, Mallaso, dancing like a flame in scarlet silk, beautiful, graceful, wild as fire, transfigured by joy, for both her child and her homeland had been restored to her.

He rolled over and sat up. It was a mistake: his head felt as if it would split apart at any moment. Why had he drunk so much? Ral always had the same effect on him. Khlar was a little more gentle, but he hadn't been able to get hold of any for months – not since that Annatal trader.

He waited until the pain and nausea had receded, and then opened his eyes. The light, filtered through the window-grille, showed him the slumbering hump of Sargenay on the other mattress, his splendid robes crumpled on the floor beside him. Kazhian's own sea-green gown was for some reason stuffed under his pillow. He hoped he'd taken it off after Mallaso had left.

His ordinary clothes were on the *Sea Serpent*, and he didn't fancy wearing Toktel'yan dress again – it was too formal, and much too eloquent of the nation that must be loathed here above all others. He had renounced the land and people of his birth, and he didn't want to remind the Penyans of who and what he was. Tact wasn't normally his strong point, but intuition told him that it was worth making an effort.

There was a crude wooden chest in the corner. He opened the lid and found an old tunic of soft, undyed linen, probably Sargenay's. He put it on, buckled up the embossed leather belt he'd worn last night, and left the room as silently as a prowling cat.

Outside, Ammenna's small courtyard was still in shadow, so it must be very early. Even so, the light seemed painfully harsh, and he screwed up his eyes. Through the pounding in his head, he heard a clank and a splash. Someone was standing by the central well, and at that moment he would have given all the gold in the *Sea Serpent*'s secret store for a long cold drink of water. Still adjusting to the brightness, he walked carefully forward.

It was Mallaso, hauling a brimming bucket up to the top. She heaved it off the hook and set it gently down on the ground beside her. 'Good morning,' she said coolly, in the Penyan dialect he was beginning to understand much better than before.

'Good morning,' he answered, and indicated the bucket. 'May I have some? I'll draw some more for you afterwards.'

'Is your thirst for water the equal of your thirst for ral?' enquired Mallaso, an astringent note in her voice.

Kazhian gave her a wry grin. She was just as beautiful as he remembered, although this morning her lithe dancer's body was concealed by the same blue, belted dress she had worn when he had given Kiyu back to her. There was little trace, however, of the warm friendliness and laughter he remembered, somewhat hazily, from last night. Instead, she was eyeing him as warily as if he were an Onnak panther, sleek, secretive, and deadly. Which wasn't really surprising: he was Toktel'yan, after all, and therefore her enemy, however much he protested that his allegiance had changed. And he'd seen her at the Blue Hyacinth, so perhaps she feared that he might still think of her as a whore, available to any man, whether she wanted him or not, whether he paid her or not. But he didn't know how to tell her the truth without laying open the wounds that scarred them both.

'Are you going to drink it, or shall I pour it over your head?' Mallaso demanded caustically, and he realized that he'd been standing witlessly staring at her for fully twenty heartbeats.

'Both,' he said, grinning, and picked up the bucket. Several deep gulps satisfied his thirst, for the moment, and he offered it back to her. 'Go on. It might help my headache, and it'll certainly improve your mood.'

For the first time that morning, Mallaso smiled. 'With pleasure,' she said, took the bucket from his outstretched hands, and hurled the contents full in his face.

Gasping, dripping, Kazhian let out a yell of delighted laughter. '*That* wasn't what I meant, Sashir!'

'Wasn't it? I bet it's sobered you up, though.' Mallaso hooked the bucket back on to the rope and began to lower it down into the well. 'More? I can oblige—'

'No, thank you.' Kazhian wiped a hand across his face, and glanced ruefully down at the sodden front of his tunic. 'Have I offended you, Sashir?'

'Of course not.' The bucket hit the water with an echoing splash, and Mallaso waited for it to fill before hauling it up again.

'Let me do that,' Kazhian said, and took over the rope.

Mallaso watched the swift, efficient movements of his muscular body, and tried not to make her appreciation too obvious. If he realized that she was interested, very interested, he would immediately assume that she was his for the taking. It had been stupid to let him kiss her, last night: to a Toktel'yan, that was tantamount to giving him complete licence over her body.

Ironically, she knew that in Toktel'yi, she'd have leapt eagerly into his bed at the first opportunity. But she was Penyan now, with a child, and her own life, her own future, to consider. She didn't feel ready for a lover, not yet: only a few days ago, she had turned down Gemain's offer. But here was Kazhian, so completely different, outwardly at any rate, from any Toktel'yan she had ever met. Just looking at him made her knees knock, she wanted him so much. But she wanted also to *know* him, to be his friend and companion, to share more than a common lust, easily satisfied, easily quenched. And that would take time.

'There you are,' Kazhian said, putting down the second bucketful. 'Don't drink it all at once – and please don't tip it over my head, I'm not used to such treatment first thing in the morning.'

'Aren't you? Don't worry, I wasn't intending to. Ammenna likes a cup or two of kuldi with her breakfast, and so do I, so I'm going to boil it up. Do you want some too? The fire's lit, it won't take long.'

He followed her into one of the roofless rooms on the ruined side of the courtyard. A young tree grew up through a crack in a corner of the tiled floor, but the rest of the debris had been cleared, and in the centre a neat ring of stones contained a cheerfully blazing fire, with a small black pan standing on an iron trivet over the flames. Kazhian carefully emptied the water into the pot. It sizzled and spat as it touched the hot metal, and then settled down to simmer.

'Was all the house like this?' asked Kazhian, looking round at the weather-stained walls, the missing plaster, the damaged floor, the empty doorway.

'No. Three of the rooms still had a roof, more or less, though some of the tiles had fallen off. Ammenna has been repairing the worst damage as best she can, and at least now we'll be dry when the rains come. There are more important things to do than rebuild a couple of rooms. The whole of Penya needs rebuilding.'

'I know it does. Why did she choose this house? Is it the one where she used to live?'

'No – she's from Hegril, originally. And the house where I lived as a child is much further up the hill. Anyway, a family of settlers have it now, and I told them they could keep it. Essyan has confirmed their right to it, and in any case I don't want to live there again. The memories are too painful.'

The fire crackled, and the water, approaching boiling point, hissed softly against the side of the pot. Kazhian said at last, 'What we did to you can never be forgiven, can it?'

'Don't worry,' Mallaso said. 'You must have been far too young to be responsible for it.'

'About the same age as you, at a guess.' Kazhian glanced at her. 'When were you born?'

'2290. A Fire Year, according to Penyan belief. Fire, sky, gold, earth, iron, water, silver, stone, copper, rain, wind, lightning. When were you born?'

'The year before you.'

'A Lightning Year. People born then are supposed to be stormy, passionate and dangerous.'

'Ah.' Kazhian's eyes gleamed suddenly, green and wicked. 'An accurate description of me, don't you think?'

'Since this is only the third or fourth time we've talked together, how can I judge? The water's boiling – pass me that box, can you?'

She emptied a handful of dried leaves into the water, and at once the aromatic, refreshing fragrance of kuldi filled the air. With a pair of tongs, Mallaso removed the pot from the fire and set it down on the floor. 'Give it a little while to infuse, then it'll be ready.'

'Good. I was never very fond of kuldi, but at this moment I could down the whole pot.'

'I shouldn't try until it's cooled a bit, or you'll never eat or drink again.'

Kazhian laughed. 'Are you always so literal, Sashir?'

'Not always. And if you persist in calling me Sashir, I shall have to adopt a suitable name for you. La'aren, perhaps.'

'I don't know it. What does it mean?'

'I'm not going to tell you. Not yet.'

'Then this isn't going to be our last encounter?'

'Well, if Essyan does want you to organize the Penyan Navy, it probably isn't. Tegerno, who's his deputy here, was asking me about you last night, at the feast.'

'Oh? And what did you tell him?'

Mallaso surveyed him thoughtfully. 'Well, I didn't tell *him* anything. Tegerno, in common with many important and influential people on Penya, is a woman.'

'I'm sorry,' said Kazhian.

'I hope you manage to shed the whole of your Toktel'yan skin – manner, attitudes, prejudices, even your clothes. Because until you do, you will never entirely be trusted or accepted. Once a renegade, always a renegade, they'll say, and watch you for the least sign that your true loyalty is still to the Empire, rather than to Penya. That is, if you *want* to be loyal to Penya.'

For the first time that morning, his vivid green eyes were entirely serious. At last he said, 'I cut myself off from the Empire to save my own skin. It was pure self-interest, and I admit it. But then I began to realize that there were other, and much better reasons for deserting Toktel'yi. While there is still so much oppression, injustice and cruelty all around the Onyx Throne, I will have no part of it. I *am* different, Sashir – I don't know why, my father tried hard enough to beat it out of me. Perhaps my mother's blood was stronger – certainly I seem to have more in common with a Tulyettan bandit than with those I used to call friends. I want to help you, and all your people. If that means fighting against my native country, so be it. Penya will be my country now. If Essyan wants me and the *Sea Serpent*, then I will swear any oath of loyalty he specifies.'

Mallaso studied him. She was certain that he was speaking the truth, but would Essyan be able to see it? And if he accepted the offer of Kazhian's services, would the other Penyans be able to trust him too? She knew them, she knew that many still nourished a deep, obsessive and entirely understandable hatred of all Toktel'yans. '*A wolf never casts his fangs*', as the proverb said. There were no wolves on Penya now, unless in the remotest parts of the central mountains, but some of Essyan's comrades might still believe that Kazhian's Toktel'yan fangs were ready to tear out Penya's throat . . .

'Do that,' she said. 'Be careful, though. Essyan seems stern, but he is a just man, and very fair. Not everyone will be as tolerant, or as unprejudiced.'

'And you?'

'You know that I will always be your friend – for Kiyu's sake, and Sargenay's.'

'But for my sake?'

'Perhaps,' Mallaso said. She avoided his intense gaze, and began to pour the kuldi into the row of waiting cups. She added, 'If you are going to stay on Penya – will you do something for us, if you have the time?'

'Of course – as long as it's within my power, you understand.'

'I should imagine it is, though you might consider it demeaning for a Vessel of the Blood Imperial.'

'The blood in my body is no more or less significant than anyone else's,' Kazhian said passionately. 'Haven't you understood that yet, Sashir?'

'I have – but old habits notoriously die hard.'

'Not in this case. Well? What do you want me to do?'

'Will you help me and Ammenna to rebuild the rest of this house?'

There was a small pause. She looked up, and saw Kazhian's eyes flicking round the derelict room. He said drily, 'Is that all? I thought you'd want some unattainable marvel – a ship made of amethyst and crystal, or a tame firebird, or a talking monkey.'

'I'll leave that sort of thing to Sargenay. Will you? It'll be hard work.'

'I can see that. I'm not afraid of hard work, but neither am I a builder, or a carpenter. I only know about ships.'

'You'll learn. You can get Bannil to give you a few tips. He's done most of the work on the Meeting House. And don't look so doubtful – you should have seen the state of it when we first landed.'

'I'm sure he's very competent,' Kazhian said, grinning. 'I just want you to understand that I'm not – so please don't blame me if all the angles are out of true, or the floor isn't level.'

'I won't, I promise. But will you do it?'

'Of course I'll do it, Sashir,' said Kazhian. 'But before I commit myself to any more impossibilities, can I please have some of that kuldi?'

He had agreed. Astonishingly, he had agreed. And yet, when she added up all that she knew or guessed of him, it was not so surprising.

Once he had eaten, and gone off to see Essyan, she told Ammenna.

Her friend listened with raised eyebrows, and at the end gave her distinctive crow of laughter. 'Does he *know*?'

'The significance of it? No, he doesn't. And please, 'Menna, don't tell him. I want this to take time. And if it doesn't come to anything, then neither of us will be embarrassed.'

'I can't imagine that young man has ever been embarrassed in his entire life,' said Ammenna. 'But don't worry, I won't say anything, and I'll tell S'raya not to say anything either.' She studied Mallaso. 'You don't *look* like a woman in love.'

'I don't think I am – not yet. I want to be sure. I want *him* to be sure. And this gives us a chance to become friends, if nothing else.'

'But he is Toktel'yan.'

'I know he's Toktel'yan! But he's told me he has abandoned the Empire for good.'

'And you believe him?'

'Yes, I do believe him. And if Essyan does too, he and his ship will be the foundation for the Penyan Navy.' Mallaso smiled suddenly. 'Remember, he brought Kiyu back. He is Sargenay's friend. He can't be all bad.'

'Oh, Sargenay,' Ammenna said, and her face filled with maternal affection. 'I wish we could find a nice boy for him – it would stop him pining over Kazhian.'

'I don't think the most beautiful boy in the world would stop him doing that. But, Ammenna – do you agree? Will you let Kazhian rebuild those rooms?'

'If he does it,' said her friend, 'then I will be his devoted admirer for ever more. I have my doubts, though. Aristocratic Toktel'yans don't get their hands dirty.'

'This one does. You don't grow muscles like that lifting a wine-cup to your mouth.'

Ammenna laughed. 'Of course you have my blessing. I'm sorry to be so cynical, but I've ten years more on my shoulders than you do. Will you forgive a crabbed and pernickety old woman?'

'Of course,' Mallaso said, and they joined hands smiling, in friendship.

Essyan had brought his map of Penya with him from Hegril. It hung on the wall behind his temporary office at the Meeting House, the heavy parchment weighted by a pole slung through loops sewn along the bottom edge. Kazhian, with his far-sighted, sailor's eyes, could make out most of it. The names of the towns and villages had been written in the cursive Toktel'yan script, and the physical features – mountains, rivers, forests, roads – were clearly and carefully depicted in variously coloured inks. A host of tiny labels clustered around Penya Harbour, on the south coast, and Hegril, in the centre, with a further scattering along the northern shore.

'That shows all the places at present occupied, either by returned exiles or by existing settlers from Toktel'yi,' Essyan said. 'There are many areas we haven't yet managed to record, of course – mainly on the west coast, and in the mountains.'

'Where five hundred Toktel'yan soldiers are presently in hiding, so I believe,' said Kazhian.

'You speak our language very well. Has Mallaso been teaching you?'

'A little, yes. But I speak Kerentan fluently, and that is very similar. One of my crew is half Penyan – I picked up quite a lot from him. Sailors tend to be linguists, from necessity.'

'Of course.' Essyan was sitting behind a large trestle table, which was covered with neat and orderly stacks of paper. 'Well, I do not intend to waste any time on small-talk. I have an offer to make you – has Mallaso told you of this?'

'She did give me some indication of it, yes.'

'Good. Briefly, I need – Penya needs – a reliable and trustworthy mariner to patrol our coastline. There is always the danger that we may be invaded again – although at present the Emperor seems to have his hands full in the eastern provinces, the situation there may change. We have no ships of our own – we came here in hired Kerentan traders, and although I intend to keep some of them on long-term contracts, and to build our own ships eventually, I need a man who can organize and lead them. He will have to be reliable – and he will have to obey orders. I don't want some reckless hot-head bringing the Empire's wrath down on us because he couldn't resist attacking some tempting Imperial galley. Do you understand me, Lord Kazhian?'

'I understand you perfectly well. And please do not call me "Lord" – I have discarded all that. I have renounced Toktel'yi.'

'So is your loyalty for hire?'

'No, it is not.'

'But I was given to understand—'

'I am not in the business of *selling* my allegiance,' Kazhian said softly. 'I will *give* it, yes, gladly and freely and absolutely – but I will not *sell* it. You need not fear being outbid by the Emperor, Essyan. If Penya wants my services, you may have them, but not for hire.'

'No?' The Penyan's dark face was frankly sceptical. He leaned back in his chair, and surveyed the younger man curiously. 'You have a ship to maintain, and a crew to pay, not to mention your own personal needs.'

'I didn't say I would give you my personal services for nothing,' Kazhian said, without rancour. 'Of course I shall have expenses, and I shall expect some remuneration – doubtless we shall haggle over the exact sum in due course. It is my *loyalty* that comes free, Essyan. Even if you sack me after a couple of months, I intend to stay on Penya. I want to make my home here.'

There was a small, significant pause. Essyan said at last, 'Is that because of Mallaso?'

'I don't think that's any of your business, do you? Besides, I hardly know her. If gossip says we are old friends, or anything more, gossip is wrong. My weather-worker, Sargenay of Tatht, knew her in Toktel'yi.'

'I see.' Essyan picked up a reed-pen, dipped it into a small earthenware ink-pot, and began to write on the piece of paper nearest to him. Kazhian waited, wondering if he was going to regret this decision. At the very least, he could find himself fighting old comrades, old friends . . .

Who meant nothing to him now. After two years of shared danger and hardship and success, the crew of the *Sea Serpent* were his comrades. Sargenay was his friend, and so, perhaps, was Mallaso. And if he did not choose Penya, where else could he go? He would be doomed to pursue the uncomfortable and not especially lucrative trade of piracy, until retribution inevitably caught up with him, in the guise of a ferocious storm, an uncharted rock, or a Toktel'yan naval galley. At least fighting for Penya was well worth the risk.

And Mallaso? Friendship, probably. He suspected that he'd have to earn anything more, but after what Toktel'yi had done to her, he could hardly blame her for being so cautious. Perhaps that was why she had asked him to rebuild Ammenna's house. He was glad, for it gave him an excuse to stay, and the chance to know her better. Sargenay would be hurt, but that, unfortunately, was inevitable. He'd have to find his weather-worker some handsome boy. Perhaps Essyan would know one.

At the thought, he almost laughed aloud. He must have made some sound, for the Penyan leader glanced up with a frown. He wrote a few more words, then laid the pen down, blew on the wet ink, and handed the paper over to Kazhian. 'I have set down the terms and conditions of your hire. Please read them through, and sign if you agree.'

The document, like Essyan himself, was extremely plain and straightforward. For ten gold Imperials a month, Kazhian would be in charge of the embryonic Penyan Navy. He had to make two public renunciations of any former loyalty to Toktel'yi, once in Penya Harbour and once in Hegril, and vow allegiance to Essyan and to Penya. The same would be required of every member of his crew. And in return, the responsibility for guarding the island against attack or invasion rested solely on his shoulders.

It was a great burden. It was a huge and daunting challenge. But Kazhian, aware of a rising, intoxicating feeling of excitement, knew that here at last was the chance to prove, once and for all, that he was worth far more than his father had ever imagined.

He took up the reed-pen, and set his name down with a flourish beside Essyan's, at the foot of the paper.

The Meeting House was packed to suffocating with every inhabitant of Penya Harbour, come to witness the renegade son of the last Emperor swear allegiance instead to them and their leader. Most of them had already seen Kazhian at the Feast, two days previously. Already, gossip had vastly exaggerated his capacity for drink, his attraction for women, and the nature of his friendship with Sargenay, and also with Mallaso. Nor did his appearance disappoint them: he wore almost as much jewellery as a woman, his hair was exotically long, and his face excitingly handsome. And his deep voice, resonating round the Hall as he spoke the oath of loyalty, sent more than one woman into paroxysms of delight.

Mallaso was well aware that at this moment she was probably the most envied person on Penya. Other people's opinions, however, had never worried her. The years of slavery and degradation in Toktel'yi had wiped out any possible embarrassment she might feel. If they believed that Kazhian was a past lover, or that he shared a bed with her and Sargenay in some wild bisexual orgy, then good luck to them. Those who really mattered to her knew the truth.

'And if I prove false to my vow,' Kazhian said, 'may the sea eagle rip out my eyes, and the lightning sear my heart, and the denizens of the deep shred the flesh from my bones: and so in the name of Sarraliss, Mother of us all, I pledge my faith unto death, to the island of Penya and her people.'

There was an instant of silence when his last words had died away, and then a spontaneous eruption of cheering, so loud that Mallaso involuntarily glanced up at Bannil's new plasterwork. Even Kazhian looked astonished by this outpouring of genuine good will, as yet unearned. Essyan gave his tight, reluctant smile, and offered his newest and most unlikely recruit the hands of friendship. And to further applause, Kazhian took them, and the two men embraced.

He was Penyan now. He had renounced Toktel'yi, and its greedy, bloodthirsty Emperors, its cruelty and its injustice. This man, brought up in a luxury most of them could hardly imagine, trained for the possibility of wielding absolute power over nine-tenths of civilization, had instead chosen Penya, and was prepared for the sake of his conscience to rough it along with everyone else. And already Bannil had spread the news that their Imperial ally had offered to rebuild Ammenna's house for her. The Penyans, a hard-working and practical people, could understand and appreciate the gesture.

So they had accepted Kazhian, and apparently taken him to their hearts. Mallaso, listening to the comments around her, looking at the faces, knew that their approval was genuine. But one mistake, one misunderstanding, one error of judgement, and they might turn against him. A wolf can never shed his fangs, nor a panther change the colour of his skin. And it would not be so easy for Kazhian to cast off the hated mantle of Toktel'yi.

But if he could in some way prove his loyalty, as obviously and spectacularly as possible, then his future on Penya would surely be secure.

CHAPTER
NINETEEN

A few hours after Kazhian and his crew had made their dramatic public vows in the Meeting House, a pigeon flew into the Penya Harbour loft, bearing an urgent message from Essyan's son Gemain, who was still in Hegril.

Completely unexpectedly, the Toktel'yan soldiers had emerged from their mountain refuge and launched an attack on the town. Fighting was still fierce, and several Penyans had already been killed. If Hegril was not to fall, Essyan must return at once to the rescue.

Even marching all night, they would not reach the town until the afternoon of the following day, for it was nearly fifty miles away. But this was the first real challenge to the exiles, and all their hopes, and their future here, depended on the outcome. If they could not inflict a decisive defeat on the Toktel'yans, they faced years of grim warfare, grinding down all their efforts to restore and rebuild the island, destroying their peace and security.

So when the rescue force formed up on the quay outside the Meeting House, most of the adult inhabitants of Penya Harbour had joined it. Ammenna was not amongst them, nor was S'raya, who at twelve was much too young. But Mallaso had offered her services: and to her surprise, Essyan had not turned her away, despite the fact that she had a young child dependent on her.

If the worst happened, Ammenna had already promised to rear Kiyu as her own: her daughter would never lack for love or care. And the imminent conflict was so vital to the future of free Penya that Mallaso did not feel that she could evade it, even though she would have been quite justified in using Kiyu as a legitimate excuse to stay behind. She was young, fit and strong: she had a borrowed sword, and she knew how to use it. And there were many more who shared her sense of purpose: so many that when Essyan led his makeshift army up the hill out of Penya Harbour, the hundred men and women who had escorted him here had been joined by eight times that number. And as well as Mallaso, Tegerno, Ka'avan, Bannil and many other friends and comrades, they included Sargenay, gingerly handling the alien weapon at his belt, and Kazhian and the rest of his crew, better armed, better equipped and more competent than almost anyone else, save for Essyan and his bodyguard.

Mallaso had said goodbye to Kiyu earlier. If the child's hidden power had given her any understanding of what was happening, or what might happen, the deep brown eyes gave no indication of it. She smiled in S'raya's arms, and waved just as she did every time her mother went to the Meeting House, or off on her donkey with Ka'avan. 'Be good, little one – and see you soon,' Mallaso had said to her daughter, and wondered, in terror, whether Kiyu would ever set eyes on her mother again.

But she had chosen to put her life in danger, for the best of reasons, and although she dreaded death, she would not back out now. And all her friends were marching alongside her. As they began the long tramp up the hill, people all around were singing the tune which she had heard Bron play in Toktel'yi, with its haunting refrain:

> My heart still longs for Penya,
> The mountains and the valleys
> And the pure and golden wine.

That song was too sad: if they defeated the Toktel'yans, someone would have to write another, happier and more hopeful. If Bron had still been alive, she would have asked him to do it. But Bron had drowned in the Kefirinn, nearly two years ago, and all his music had died with him.

Kazhian was singing too: he had a pleasant voice, despite his obvious ignorance of the words. Mallaso, walking just in front of him, could hear Sargenay too, although the sorcerer's many talents didn't extend to keeping in tune. And suddenly it all seemed so easy. There were nearly a thousand of them, and twice that number in Hegril. Why shouldn't they beat off those five hundred Toktel'yans, and chase them out of Penya for ever?

At midnight, they stopped to rest at a deserted village. They had been marching for eight hours, and they were still less than half-way to Hegril. Mallaso and Tegerno discovered a ruined barn, and managed to gather enough old, musty hay to make a comfortable bed. Sleep was more difficult to find, but in the end, Mallaso must have succeeded, for she dreamed of Bron.

His image was not as vivid on this occasion: his face was in shadow, and his voice seemed to come from a great distance. Afterwards, she could remember very little of what he had said, save only that he had told her to take care.

She woke when Tegerno shook her shoulder. 'Time to be going.' And in the hurry of getting up, of snatching a few mouthfuls of bread and cold meat, the dream faded from her mind, overpowered by grim, frightening reality. The eastern sky was just beginning to lighten. And before darkness cast its soft, concealing cloak once more over Penya, she and many of her friends might be dead.

They had received no further messages from Gemain, but Essyan had already sent him a pigeon from Penya Harbour, telling his beleaguered son that help was coming. And now, in the first brilliant rays of sunrise, a second bird was released, the precious scrap of paper tied to its leg, giving news of hope to Hegril. Mallaso watched it circle above them, flushed with new rosy light, as it fixed its bearings. Then suddenly, as fierce and straight as an arrow, it shot off to the north-west, in the direction of the distant town, somewhere hidden in the misty blue bowl of the Vale of Clouds. And with determination, and excitement, and apprehension, Essyan's army followed it.

They were about five miles from Hegril when two messengers brought word from Gemain. The news, passed down the line of waiting people, was grim but not hopeless. The Toktel'yans, their numbers swollen by two or three hundred resentful settlers, had secured the eastern half of the town, up to the main street and market-place in the centre of Hegril. Gemain still held the Meeting House and the western part. He had lost about fifty of his troops, but Toktel'yan casualties had also been heavy. Both sides had been fighting sporadically for much of the night, and there was at present a lull, as the exhausted combatants rested and regrouped during the heat of midday. If Essyan attacked the enemy now, in the rear, while they were least expecting it, victory was almost certain. But there was no time to be lost. In a couple of hours, the chance would disappear.

The sun burned fiercely down on Mallaso, although she had wrapped a white scarf round her head to protect it. At least everyone around her was accustomed to such heat, although not marching or fighting in these conditions. They had walked over forty miles in twenty hours, and they were tired, hungry and thirsty. But more than water, or food, or rest, they wanted to beat the Toktel'yans.

Kazhian appeared beside her, and offered her a flask. She looked at him doubtfully, and he grinned. 'It's just water, I promise you. Have a few sips. You can't tell me you don't need it.'

She drank gratefully. The water was warm, but relieved her dry mouth and throat. She handed it back to him with a smile. 'Thank you. And good luck.'

'The Lord of Life, for some reason, always seems to favour me. Sargenay thinks I'm immortal.'

Mallaso shivered, despite the heat. 'Please don't say that. Olyak might be tempted to snatch you out of his brother's grasp.'

'I hope not,' he said, and smiled briefly. 'And good luck to you too. Can you use that thing?'

She glanced down at the old notched sword hanging from her belt. 'Yes, if I have to.' She didn't add that after trying to kill the Emperor Ba'alekkt with the pin from a shoulder-clasp, any weapon seemed more than adequate.

'Let's hope you don't,' Kazhian said. 'Let's hope they all run away. The sight of my crew should be enough to scare them out of their wits.'

Mallaso laughed, but she knew, as well as he did, that the Toktel'yans were desperate men, with nothing to lose. If they were cornered, they would fight to the death.

Genedek, harassed leader of the Toktel'yan garrison of Penya, had experienced six miserable months since Year-turn. First, he had been forced to comply as three-quarters of his men had been ordered to Tatht to contain the rebellion there. He had protested that their departure dangerously weakened the island's defences, and put the lives of the few settlers at risk. The Commander of the transport fleet had privately sympathized with him, but had pointed out that orders were orders. And Tatht, wealthy and populous, was far more valuable to the Empire than Penya, still poverty-stricken and sparsely inhabited after the years of slaughter and destruction.

So Genedek had been left to hold the entire island with five hundred troops, plus roughly the same number of male settlers. In common with everyone else, he had heard the rumours about the exiles' preparations in Kerenth, but found it easier and more comforting to dismiss them as scaremongering lies. The whole world knew that Penyans were a soft and idle bunch of farmers, all talk and no action. They would probably sit safely in Kerenth for years to come, boasting about all the heroic deeds they'd perform to get their island back.

So when the trader from the Scatterlings sailed into Penya Harbour with the appalling news that the Penyan invasion fleet was actually at sea, Genedek had panicked. Someone who had seen the preparations in Kerenth had spoken of two hundred ships. He'd dismissed that as a gross exaggeration, but the Scatterling Captain repeated the figure.

'Sails as far as I could see,' he had told Genedek. 'Thousands of soldiers, I reckon.'

Genedek had led his men up into the mountains. He had served two years on Penya, so he knew a little of the island's geography, and its bloodstained recent history. If the returning exiles wanted vengeance – as Toktel'yans would – for the slaughter of their families and friends, then he had no intention of presenting them with easy prey.

The settlers were mostly poor and previously landless people from the eastern mainland provinces, lured to Penya by the false dream of an easy life and wealth for the taking. They had abandoned their homes in terror. Genedek preferred to see his precipitate flight as a tactical withdrawal. He and his men could live in the mountains indefinitely: the Penyan resistance fighters had lurked there for years, until Ba'alekkt had exterminated them, so he could surely do the same.

But the Penyans knew their island intimately. Genedek did not. The mountains were beautiful, but harsh. He lost ten men in a landslide, and several more down a cliff. Ba'alekkt obviously hadn't got rid of all the bandits, because soldiers kept disappearing. After two months, he and his troops were exhausted, demoralized and hungry. Their weapons were rusting, and the younger ones had begun to talk longingly of home. And there were now only four hundred and fifty of them. If he kept losing men at this rate, they'd all be dead in a year's time.

So Genedek decided to stake his life and his reputation on one last gamble. If it worked, a glorious future beckoned to the man who had forced Penya back into the Empire. And if it didn't, he preferred to die a hero's death in battle, rather than skulk ignominiously in the mountains until disease, hunger or a well-aimed arrow finished him off.

Much to his relief, over two hundred settlers had found their way to his camp. Others stayed in their homes, but kept him informed of the Penyans' movements. Lack of resistance to their invasion had made the returning exiles temptingly over-confident. There were no attacks on the settlers, no efforts made to expel them from the island, and no real attempt to track down Genedek and his men. The Toktel'yan waited with increasing hope and anticipation.

The news which he had been hoping for came at last. The Penyan leader had taken a considerable force down to Penya Harbour, leaving his headquarters at Hegril, at the feet of the mountains, dangerously exposed. If Genedek could take the town and slaughter its garrison before Essyan returned, there was an excellent chance that he could destroy the entire invasion force, piece by piece. Together, their numbers were too great to attack. But with the main force split, and many exiles now scattered to their new homes, surely the superior fighting skills, training and equipment of the Imperial Army would prevail against the amateur Penyan soldiers.

Once down at Hegril, fighting the men, and women, whom he had previously despised, Genedek could not acknowledge, even to himself, that he had made an error of judgement which might possibly be fatal. The soft, idle Penyans refused to run away: even when taken by surprise, they fought with desperate and furious courage, giving ground only as a last resort, and inflicting heavy casualties. When morning came at last, Genedek had nearly half of Hegril in his possession, but he had lost nearly forty men, including several key officers, and the remainder of his troops were exhausted and in desperate need of rest. As the sun reached its zenith, the Toktel'yan commander ordered his most reliable soldiers to hold the front line along the eastern side of the town's main street. The others were told to slake their hunger and thirst from the food and water supplied by sympathetic settlers.

On the other side of the broad street, empty save for a cluster of corpses and the carrion birds already at work on them, the enemy appeared to be doing likewise. A spurious peace settled over Hegril in the suffocating, airless heat of midday, and Genedek, gulping water with relief, felt able to relax just a little. No one would be mad enough to try anything until this furnace had cooled, later in the afternoon.

Once more, he had underestimated the Penyans. As he discussed their immediate strategy with his senior officers, he became aware of a confused noise of shouting in the distance. Even as his brain registered the fact, it grew louder and more insistent. Was that the clash of metal?

With a sudden and dreadful premonition of disaster, Genedek broke off his briefing and ran out of the courtyard. At the gate, which led into a side alley running parallel with the main street, he almost bumped into one of the armed settlers, wild-eyed and shouting in panic. It took several precious moments to calm the man, and to understand what he was saying in his thick Mynakkan dialect: and when he realized, Genedek's heart clenched in despair. Somehow, a force of several hundred Penyans had appeared out of nowhere and fallen upon the unsuspecting Toktel'yans in the rear. And now they were being hunted from house to house through the maze of Hegril's alleys and lanes, while on the other side of the main street, the town's defenders would certainly attack in strength as soon as they realized what was happening.

He was the commander of the Imperial Garrison of Penya. The six hundred surviving soldiers and settlers looked to him for leadership.

They were trapped, but he would not surrender to the unknown and probably limited mercy of the Penyan leader. At least if they died fighting bravely, Olyak would be kind to their shades, and their families would be honoured: a pension for life was granted to the children of Toktel'yan heroes.

'Let's drive these Penyan dogs into the sea!' Genedek cried, and unsheathed his sword with a flourish. 'Drive them back, and kill them all!'

'But if we turn and attack these ones,' his deputy objected, 'what is to prevent those who hold the western half of the town from taking us in the rear?'

'If we hurry, they might not realize what is happening,' Genedek told him, with more conviction than he actually felt. 'What are you waiting for, Sabran? Order the charge!'

The fighting in the cruel heat of Hegril that afternoon was noisy, savage and confused. Only the kites and carrion crows, alerted by the stench of blood and death, could view the whole course of the chaotic struggle as they circled overhead. On the ground, in lanes and alleys and courtyards, the combatants were unable to see further than the next wall, or the next turn in a backstreet. Death might come from above, from a thrown spear or a Penyan arrow or, in desperation, a hail of roof-tiles or blocks of stone. Each door or gateway might conceal a friend, or an enemy: every window-grille might hide a Penyan archer or a Toktel'yan spearcaster, lurking ready to pick off some unlucky or unwary foe.

Essyan, who knew Hegril far better than Genedek, had given his troops precise orders, and had issued them with a concise repertoire of whistled signals. Even so, confusion and error, often fatal, was unavoidable. But they were winning. Slowly, inexorably, they were beginning to drive the Toktel'yans back towards the centre of Hegril. And Gemain's revived and invigorated force poured out of the barricaded Meeting House and ran across the market square and main street to close the second jaw of the trap.

Inevitably, given the terrain, Essyan's army had split into many bands, clearing each house and street in turn. Mallaso, her borrowed sword in her hand and the sweat of fear cold on her face, had stayed with Kazhian and his sailors, suspecting that they were more proficient fighters than most of her other comrades. There were nearly forty of them, with her and Sargenay and a few other prudent Penyans, and under Kazhian's leadership they had swiftly evolved a highly effective method of checking for enemy presence in each house they came to, making expert use of the available cover of walls, corners and doorways. The outer door would be kicked in, the house searched with the maximum speed and the minimum noise, rooms nearest the alley or lane first so that snipers couldn't pick off those on watch outside. They took no prisoners, for the Toktel'yans fought to the death. And Mallaso, remembering the brutality with which soldiers like these had slaughtered the unarmed men, women and children of Penya, could feel no pity for them.

But her sword was still clean. Unless she was directly attacked, she did not want to use it. Kazhian and his men were highly effective killers, and she and Sargenay and the other Penyans were happy to let them prove, to themselves and to everyone else, that Toktel'yi was their enemy now.

Mallaso had lost count of the men they had slain, but five of the *Sea Serpent*'s crew were dead, and Kazhian himself had a long slash across his right arm where a thrown spear had almost found its mark. It didn't affect his ability to fight, though, and she realized for the first time that he used his left hand. It made him a formidable opponent in close combat, for almost everyone was right-handed, and soldiers didn't expect him to be any different, until too late.

They were now in a thoroughfare broader than the narrow, twisting alleys they had so far encountered. One of the Penyans, a young woman who was familiar with Hegril, told them that this was only two blocks away from the main street. Over to the right, a chorus of whistles, followed by the clash of conflict, announced the presence of Toktel'yans. Pressed into the doorway of the house which they'd just found to be unoccupied, Mallaso glanced up and down. The road was empty. And by the sound of it, their comrades needed help.

Sargenay stood beside her, muttering something. Already, his own special skills had been put to good use. Now, another, counterfeit Penyan, so solid that he cast a shadow, appeared just in front of her. He seemed amazingly real, but she knew better than to touch him. Sargenay, frowning in concentration, moved his Illusion boldly out into the middle of the street.

A movement up on the flat roof of the house opposite caught Mallaso's eye. At the same instant, a cast spear hissed with lethal accuracy through suddenly empty air. An arrow shot upwards almost before the weapon had hit the ground, and the Toktel'yan, with a despairing cry, clutched at his chest and toppled backwards out of sight.

'Never fails,' said the sorcerer, with satisfaction. 'All clear.'

From the next doorway along, Kazhian and half a dozen of his men began to run down the street, swords at the ready. In the big two-storey house at the end, where the road bent round it and out of sight, serious fighting seemed to be taking place.

'Come on,' Sargenay said. His taut, clever face was showing obvious signs of fear and fatigue, just as hers must. 'Let's follow them before I lose my nerve.'

They sprinted along in Kazhian's footsteps, staying close to the rough-cast walls. Mallaso hoped that the houses were empty: it was all too easy to imagine some well-armoured Toktel'yan stepping out of a dark doorway to spear her in the back. But they reached the big house unscathed, to join the rest of the pirates in the gateway. Above them, a faded sign announced that this was a tavern called the Blue Olive.

It had obviously been a wealthy establishment, and its tall, arched gate led into a spacious courtyard. The quadrangle was filled with fifty or more Toktel'yans, desperately fighting off a similar number of poorly armed Penyans, Essyan and Tegerno amongst them.

'Ready?' Kazhian's voice cut through the ringing sound of sword on sword, the shouts of the combatants and the moans and screams of the injured and the dying. 'Charge!' And with a wild yell, he ran straight into the mêlée.

The rest followed him. Mallaso, bringing up the rear with Sargenay, saw Essyan look round, his face full of relief. The nearest Toktel'yan, a big man with a red plume in his conical helmet, raised his sword to take advantage of the Penyan leader's temporary distraction. Without appearing to aim at all, Kazhian whipped his jewelled dagger from its scabbard, and hurled it at the Toktel'yan. It struck him full in the throat, the most exposed and vulnerable part of an Imperial soldier's body, and the man staggered back. A swift slash from a huge Fabrizi pirate ended his struggles, and then the crew of the *Sea Serpent* engaged the enemy with gleeful enthusiasm.

Mallaso felt quite superfluous. They certainly didn't need her. The Toktel'yans were outnumbered now, and fighting with increasing desperation. She saw a young Penyan trying to crawl out of the way, and ran to him. He had a wound in the belly that made her feel sick, but she forced herself to ignore it, and helped him up. With her support, he staggered a few paces to the edge of the courtyard, under the colonnade, and collapsed moaning against the wall.

Sargenay arrived, and she turned to him gratefully. 'Can you do anything for him?'

The sorcerer's lean mouth compressed suddenly. 'I'll get something to staunch the blood,' he said, and disappeared into the ransacked room behind them. He came back with a ripped cushion which was leaking feathers copiously, and Mallaso pushed it against the young man's stomach. He seemed too far gone to understand what she was doing, and tried feebly to fight her off, screaming in pain.

At last, she realized that she couldn't help him, and looked round for Sargenay. To her horror, she saw him trying to fight off two Toktel'yan settlers, only a few paces away.

Mallaso forgot her weariness, her fear, and her desire to save the dying Penyan. She snatched up her sword and ran to his aid. The smaller of his opponents gave a gasp of surprise as he realized that she was female, and lowered his blade. With the strength and courage of desperation, Mallaso swung her own weapon double-handed across his, knocking it out of his grasp, and followed it up with a savage thrust at his unprotected chest. The settler went down with a howl of pain, and she turned to attack the other man just as Sargenay, his face distorted as if in agony, delivered the decisive and fatal blow.

'Thanks,' said the sorcerer, breathing hard. 'Those bastards came at me from nowhere. I don't know about you, but I've got the taste now for Toktel'yan blood. Want to go and kill a few more?'

And insanely, Mallaso followed him.

It was difficult to relate this chaotic, lethal scrimmage to the all-too-brief hours of her training in Kerenth, when the recruits had been taught to wield their swords in patterns, like dancers: up, across, back, *thrust*! She had lost her fear, lost the tremor in her hand and the nausea in her throat: she concentrated only on staying with Sargenay, and staying alive. Together, shoulder to shoulder like heroes in a traditional tale, they stood a good chance of survival, even against Imperial troops. Separated, neither of them would last ten heartbeats.

Kazhian's shout tore through the clamour. She hacked at the Toktel'yan who had tried to cut her down, and Sargenay finished him off with a viciously lethal blow to the head that even a bronze helmet couldn't deflect. As he fell, she glanced over to her left. Somehow, Essyan had become separated from the other Penyans. He was fighting off two of the enemy at once, and giving ground before their onslaught. Then Kazhian ran in from the side, his sword slicing low. One of the Toktel'yans fell, while the other attacked Essyan with renewed urgency. Mallaso screamed a futile warning as a third man lunged at the Penyan leader.

Kazhian flung himself through the net of blades, and his sword took the assailant in the chest. Suddenly, every combatant in the courtyard seemed to swarm around them, and Mallaso couldn't see him any more.

The strength of her fear for Kazhian astonished her: even as she ran, she knew that this time, Olyak must have had the last laugh.

Then, with shouts and war-cries, more Penyans poured through the gateway. Mallaso was knocked to the ground as Gemain pushed past her, waving his sword, and the defenders of Hegril flooded the courtyard. The remaining Toktel'yans, trapped and vastly outnumbered, turned at bay.

The screaming and the clashing of metal seemed to last for ever, but in reality it was all over very quickly. Dazed, bruised and winded, Mallaso picked herself up from the dusty stone paving, and realized suddenly that she could hear only the moans of the wounded.

There were bodies everywhere. Most, but not all, were Toktel'yan. All around her, men and women embraced, crying and laughing. Someone began to sing 'My Heart Belongs to Penya', in a cracked, raucous voice. Gemain shouted something, and a ragged, exhausted cheer rasped from two hundred throats. Incredibly, it seemed that they had won. They had defeated the mighty Toktel'yan Army. And she had survived: she would see Kiyu again.

But what of her friends? What had happened to Kazhian, Sargenay, Essyan? She stumbled through the crowd, and saw the sorcerer kneeling on the bloodstained stones, his face cast in sorrow. *Oh, sweet Mother*, she cried in her heart, in anguish – *not yet, not before* –

It was Essyan lying there, his eyes decently closed, his tunic drenched with blood. He had died at the moment of victory, and his formerly stern face wore a peaceful, almost contented expression, as if he had realized, at the last beat of his heart, that Penya was saved.

'Sashir—'

She turned and saw Kazhian. He looked like a participant in the notorious rites of D'yardek, a fire mountain in the Scatterlings which was tamed and propitiated by drunken sacrifice. His hair curled like a nest of black snakes over his shoulders, his face was smeared with dirt and blood, his tunic was spattered red and soaked with sweat, but he was undeniably, gloriously alive. And with a sob of utter relief, Mallaso dropped her sword and embraced him.

His arms circled her, close and strong. She could feel his ragged breathing, smell the fear and pain and effort he had expended in the fighting. She didn't care. They had both survived, and at this moment of victory, it was all that mattered.

CHAPTER TWENTY

Night came to Penya with its usual tropical swiftness. The moon, a broken circle of silver low in the west, cast mercifully little light on the murky alleys and lanes of Hegril, where four hundred and fifty Imperial soldiers, over fifty settlers and a hundred and twenty Penyans lay dead. Tomorrow, they would collect the bodies: the Toktel'yans to be burned on a huge single pyre, the Penyans to be interred in the soft, dark, forgiving earth, returned to the Mother. The most seriously hurt, over seventy of them, had been carried to the Meeting House, where Sargenay and other Healers laboured to staunch blood and clean wounds and repair the damage wrought by spear and sword and dagger. Despite their efforts, some would inevitably die. Everyone had lost a friend, a comrade, and some had lost wife or husband or lover. They had all lost Essyan. And yet amidst their grief, a wondering, disbelieving joy was beginning to creep into their faces, for now they were truly free of Toktel'yi.

Their leader's body had been placed on a bier and laid, with sorrow and regret, in a side-room of the Meeting House, so that all his followers could pay their last respects. His stern personality had not inspired love, or even affection. But his determination, his organizing skills and his powers of leadership had made the recovery of Penya possible. No one else could have done it, a fact of which everyone, especially his son Gemain, was well aware. They owed him their island and their future, and in return he had given his life. And for that, he would be honoured evermore in the annals of Penya.

Gemain kept vigil at the head of the bier. He wore a plain armoured tunic, and held his sword point down, to symbolize his grief. He had always looked rather young for his age, but now, after the stress of the last few days, his face showed every one of his thirty years, and more. Mallaso felt very sorry for him: not only had he lost his father, but he must probably blame himself for the circumstances of Essyan's death. And now, inevitably, many of the exiles would look to him to provide leadership, and Gemain surely knew in his heart that he wasn't equal to the task.

Mallaso wondered who was. Of those she knew best, Tegerno was the obvious candidate. But she didn't know whether she, or Essyan's chosen deputy Rassienna, possessed the energy, skills and ability needed to set Penya firmly on the long hard road back to prosperity. Someone must be chosen to lead them, though, and soon, before Olkanno was tempted to take advantage of their indecision.

She went with Tegerno to see Essyan. That transitory expression of peace had vanished, and the old man's face, exposed above the plain cotton shroud, seemed somehow shrunken into insignificance, bereft of the spirit behind it. Tomorrow, he would be laid to rest with his fallen comrades. Tonight, the small room was packed with mourners standing quietly, bidding a silent farewell in the manner of Penya. And at next Year-turn, there would be many more lights to launch on the dark sea, in loving and sorrowful memory of the dead.

It seemed cold, despite the numbers of people, and Mallaso shivered suddenly. She felt uncomfortable and uneasy, as if there were more spirits in this unnaturally silent place than there were bodies to house them.

The door opened again, and Kazhian entered. He was still wearing the bloodstained tunic, and there was a makeshift and filthy bandage round his gashed arm. He looked, and smelt, like the grim reality of war: blood, sweat, dirt. Sargenay was with him, his face still haggard. Mallaso hoped that someone had told them about Penyan mourning customs. She hadn't had the chance to speak to either of them since that moment of extreme emotion in the courtyard of the Blue Olive.

But of course Kazhian was a highly intelligent and perceptive man. She saw him glance quickly and unobtrusively round, to see what everyone else was doing, and then he moved quietly forward to stand at the foot of the bier, quite close to her and Tegerno. His head was bowed, and he had tied his hair back with a strip of red cloth. She could see the fine dark short hairs on the nape of his neck, the intricate cluster of rings in his ear, the braced tension in the muscles beneath his tunic, and her need for him suddenly engulfed her senses. Her head swam, and she held on to the side of the bier, both for support and to stop her hand reaching out to touch him.

'What are you doing here?'

The harsh, angry voice was shockingly loud. Astonished, Mallaso looked round and saw Gemain, at the other end of the bier. His hand was pointing straight at Kazhian, dark and self-contained, standing opposite him with the shrouded length of Essyan's body between them.

Tegerno muttered something angrily, and began to push her way through the intervening crowd towards the Penyan. His voice rang out again. 'How dare you come here, Toktel'yan traitor, to gloat over the corpse of your victim!'

A gasp of appalled disbelief hissed into the air. Mallaso stared at Kazhian. He was shaking his head: then he spoke, his deep voice, calm and reasonable, contrasting sharply with the hysterical edge to Gemain's. 'What do you mean, my "*victim*"? Are you suggesting that I killed your father?'

'Don't be ridiculous!' Tegerno had reached Gemain's side, and Mallaso hoped that her brisk air of common sense would alleviate some of the sudden tension thrumming around them. 'I was there, remember. Kazhian tried to save your father. It was a Toktel'yan who killed him.'

'Yes,' said Gemain. '*That* Toktel'yan.'

A murmur of anger rose from the mourners. To her horror, Mallaso realized that some of them seemed to believe the accusation. And if Gemain could direct their grief and desire for vengeance towards Kazhian, then he would be in mortal danger.

'I did not kill Essyan,' Kazhian said, softly and vehemently. 'I will swear it by any god or goddess you choose. A Toktel'yan soldier killed him. I vowed my loyalty to Essyan and to Penya, only two days ago. And I do not break my vows.'

'Traitor! Murderer!' Gemain cried, his hand shaking. 'I demand your death – to avenge my father, I demand it!'

'Wait,' said Tegerno sharply. 'Did you see this, Gemain?'

'It's obvious, isn't it? He's a spy, a traitor, planted by the Emperor!'

'But did you *see* him kill Essyan?'

There was a sullen pause. 'No,' said Gemain, at last.

'You couldn't have done,' Tegerno pointed out. 'You didn't come into the courtyard until after he went down. So why are you saying this, Gemain? Where is your proof?'

'Someone said something to me, afterwards.'

'Who?'

He shook his head angrily. 'I don't know – I didn't recognize him.'

'Is he here now?'

Essyan's son stared round the crowded room. 'I can't see him. I don't think so.'

'So on the basis of one accusation from someone else, feeding your own prejudices, you would have Kazhian done to death?'

Someone at the back shouted, 'Kill *all* the bastards! Penya won't be free until we do!' And there was more than one mutter of agreement.

'Silence!' Tegerno said, and the room fell quiet. But Mallaso, looking round at all the faces, hostile or disbelieving, could feel the ugliness of the emotions simmering in the air.

'Tell me, Gemain,' Kazhian said mildly. 'What weapon did I use to kill Essyan?'

'So you admit it, murderer!'

'I'm not admitting anything. What weapon am I supposed to have used?'

'A sword,' Gemain answered, without hesitation.

'But I saw him killed by a man with a stabbing-spear.'

'Liar!' the Penyan screamed suddenly, his face distorted with rage and hatred and grief. 'Liar! Traitor! Murderer!'

In the face of his hysteria, Kazhian stayed calm, his green eyes steady and thoughtful. He said quietly, 'Why are you accusing me, Gemain? Are you jealous of the influence I might have? Do you fear I'll turn traitor eventually, so you'll have me killed now before I get the chance to do some real damage? Or do you just want someone to blame for your own failings?'

There was a terrible pause. Gemain's eyes bulged with fury. Tegerno laid a warning hand on his arm, and he shook it off and began to push his way round the bier towards Kazhian. Who was unarmed, with not even the jewelled dagger at his belt: whereas Gemain had his sword, still crusted and dulled with Toktel'yan blood.

Fortunately, Mallaso was not the only one to have realized it. Before he had gone two steps, Gemain's arms had been pinioned, and despite his shouts and struggles, someone had wrenched his weapon out of his hand. Tegerno's loud, vigorous voice flattened the rising commotion. 'In the name of the Mother, remember where you are! Let us all go outside, so that we can discuss this matter in more appropriate surroundings.'

By the time they reached the square in front of the Meeting House, the news had spread, and several hundred people were waiting for them. Gemain, led along by two of his biggest comrades, was no longer struggling, but his eyes were still wild. Mallaso, bewildered, wondered why he had suddenly turned on Kazhian. Was it, as the Toktel'yan had suggested, a mixture of jealousy, guilt, and the need to blame someone else for his own mistakes? Or a genuine error?

Or had Kazhian really slain his father?

She could not believe it. Although she had only known him for a short while, she was certain that Kazhian had neither the desire nor the motive to murder the Penyan leader. But she could see, all too clearly, why others would readily think the worst. Like Gemain, they must assume that he was one of Olkanno's agents, sent to Penya to sow discord and hatred amongst the exiles. And rescuing Kiyu was an excellent way of gaining their trust.

It was so convincing that she might have believed it herself. But her heart knew differently, because she had been given that brief glimpse of the real Kazhian, released by ral and desperation.

Or had that episode been a carefully planned pretence, cunningly designed to win her over?

Tegerno picked up a piece of wood from the heap of timber waiting to be used in the rebuilding work, and banged it smartly on a bronze bucket. Even that didn't entirely dispel the noise, so she clambered up on to the pile, and surveyed her massed comrades in the light of the moon and the flickering torches outside the Meeting House. 'For those of you who don't know what's happened – Gemain son of Essyan has accused Kazhian son of Eska'anen of murdering his father in the courtyard of the Blue Olive this afternoon. I was there. I know what I saw. Raise your hand if you were also a witness. And I don't want lies or hearsay or guesswork or prejudice – I want the truth.'

Several arms shot into the air. Tegerno pointed at one, 'Tugil! Tell everyone what you saw.'

The man glanced around at the expectant faces. 'I didn't see a lot – there was too much going on, and I was fighting for my life. I saw some Imperial soldier thrust at Essyan, and then the pirate came in from the side and killed the Toktel'yan. Just afterwards, the Hegril lot arrived.'

'And Gemain was amongst them.'

'Yes!' several voices cried.

'So according to this witness, and my own recollection, you weren't even in the courtyard when your father was killed. You are not a *witness*, Gemain. You *saw* nothing.'

'I *know* Kazhian killed him,' the Penyan repeated, as if only those words held any reality. 'He murdered him.'

'No, he didn't.' Mallaso spoke loudly and clearly, her heart thudding. 'I saw it too. Kazhian tried to save him, but he came too late.'

'She's lying!' Gemain cried. 'She's his whore – she's lying to save his skin!'

Fury suddenly took hold of Mallaso, blasting her usual caution to shreds. 'How dare you call me that, when you yourself asked me to share your bed? I go with whom I please, and it's none of your business, or anyone else's. I know what I saw, and *I* am not lying, Gemain – you are!'

The shouts of approval almost obliterated the yells from those who took Gemain's side. Tegerno, frowning, raised her hands for quiet. 'Who else saw? *Saw*, as opposed to *believes*?'

Several had, but their accounts added little to what had already been said, and a few, taking their mood from Gemain, were shouting for vengeance. Mallaso listened in horror. This was *Penya* – these were her friends, her comrades, people who had always prided themselves on their tolerance, their restraint and their sense of fairness. Yet many of them were baying for blood, just like the Toktel'yan mobs they professed to loathe and despise.

Tegerno had bent down to listen to someone speaking close to her. She straightened, and clapped her hands. 'Quiet! I said, be *quiet*! This is not a riot, and I don't intend to let anything get out of hand. We are not barbarians, and I will not allow the sort of brutality that some of you, who should know better, have been proposing. Do you understand me?'

In Kerenth, Tegerno had been in charge of a school. Like a bunch of unruly adolescents, the more outspoken elements shuffled their feet and muttered resentfully. Tegerno put her hands on her hips, and smiled grimly. 'That's better. Let's keep things calm, shall we? No one is going to be flogged, or tortured, or strung up. This is *Penya*, remember? And today, despite our tragic losses, we defeated the Toktel'yans. We have won the war, friends and comrades – and there is no need now to fight amongst ourselves. I do not want it, most of you do not want it, and emphatically Essyan, *whoever* killed him, would not want it either. So let's keep it civilized. An accusation has been made. It has been refuted. I myself saw what happened, and I saw the Imperial soldier kill Essyan with a stabbing-spear. Then he was slain in his turn by Kazhian, with a sword. As I remember, that sword was an edged, not a pointed weapon, made for slashing rather than thrusting. Am I right, Kazhian?'

He was standing in front of her, his face thoughtful. At her use of his name, he glanced up and nodded. 'Yes.'

'But I myself helped to wash Essyan's body, and place it on the bier.' It was Rassienna speaking, in her low, rather rasping voice. 'The wound that slew him was a thrust to the heart. I have seen many like it before, all caused by a Toktel'yan stabbing-spear.' She looked round at the other Penyans, her arms folded and a belligerent expression on her face. 'I was in the courtyard too. Kazhian did not have a spear, he had a sword. How then could he have killed Essyan?'

'I *know* he did!' Gemain cried despairingly.

'You do *not* know,' Tegerno told him, her voice as stern and unforgiving as Essyan's once had been. 'You have made this accusation without proof, without seeing anything of what really happened, and in the face of all other accounts and also the incontrovertible evidence of Essyan's death-wound. Are you calling *me* a liar? Or Tugil? Or Rassienna? We were there. We saw. You did not. So why did you accuse Kazhian, Gemain? Did you want a Toktel'yan to blame, and he was the only one available? Or, even more despicably, were you jealous because you thought Mallaso had chosen him in preference to you? What happened to truth, Gemain, to fairness and justice? Will you do the honourable thing, and withdraw your accusation?'

Shamed, biting his lip, Essyan's son at last nodded assent, and then buried his face in his hands.

'On behalf of us all, Kazhian,' Tegerno said, her voice set in the formal cadences with which justice was dispensed, 'will you accept my apology on behalf of all the people of free Penya, for this entirely undeserved allegation? You risked your own life in the attempt to save Essyan, so you deserve our thanks, our heartfelt gratitude. Instead, you have met with unjust calumny from one who, however distraught at his father's death, should have known better. I would not blame you if you now wanted nothing more to do with Penya or its people. But we want you to stay, because we like you and value you, and also, to be honest, because we need you.' She smiled suddenly, guessing his response. 'Will you stay with us?'

'Of course I will,' Kazhian said. His deep, pleasant voice carried to the furthest parts of the market square, and there was now absolute quiet. 'I swore my allegiance to Essyan, but I will do the same for whoever we shall choose to be his successor. I am Penyan now – you are my people, and Penya is my home, and Toktel'yi is my enemy. And I hope that in spite of what has been said this evening, you will welcome me and my crew. Will you?'

The fervent roar of assent was almost deafening, but Mallaso, looking round from her position close to Tegerno, could see a significant number of faces displaying disagreement, suspicion, wariness or open hostility. It was plain that Kazhian would have to earn their approval. And some of them, those who had suffered most at Toktel'yan hands, might never be able to forgive this renegade for the horrors perpetrated by his countrymen.

She could. But she had lived almost all her adult life in Toktel'yi, not in bitter exile in Kereneth, and so she was unable to see the citizens of the Empire as a homogeneous mass of brutes and murderers. Some were, of course, but many were not. And though Kazhian came of a corrupt, tainted and evil dynasty, for some strange reason his blood ran true to the older, deeper ideals of honesty, fairness, and friendship. He was not like his father. And so there was hope, not only for him, but for Toktel'yi too.

'So you have your answer, Kazhian son of Eska'anen,' Tegerno said, when the shouting had diminished at last. 'We welcome you with gladness to our island and our community. You and your men have given us invaluable help today, and without you our victory might not have been so easy, or so complete. Once more, my thanks. I have already appointed guards, to patrol the town in case there are still Toktel'yans who have escaped us. Tomorrow, we have the sad task of burying our friends. Tonight, let us remember them in our silent hearts, even as we rejoice in our triumph. And I have resolved to place a monument in the centre of this square, to be carved in stone with all the names of those who have died today in the defence of Penya, so that they may live with everlasting fame in our memory, and our children's. Does that meet with your approval?'

This time, there were no dissenting faces. With a satisfied smile, Tegerno went on to describe her plans for the next few days, and Mallaso's attention wandered. She glanced round to where Kazhian had been standing, and saw that he had gone.

And so had Gemain.

Suddenly, fear gripped her. Essyan's son had just been publicly humiliated, and in his present distraught and vengeful mood, he would be quite capable of murder.

And Kazhian was quite capable of killing him in self-defence, with consequences almost as dire.

Mallaso turned and began to fight her way out of the crowd, using her hands and elbows and feet with ruthless urgency. As if she was caught in some dreadful nightmare, she couldn't push through those who were too intent on what Tegerno was saying to notice her, those who were feeling uncooperative, and those friends who were eager to relive events of the day and congratulate her on her survival. But at long last she managed to struggle free of the crush, grateful for the chance to breathe adequately again.

Tegerno was still standing in front of the columned portico of the Meeting Hall, with several hundred Penyans clustered around her. The rest of the market square, which was about fifty paces in each direction, seemed empty of life in the moonlight, although there were bodies strewn about here and there, like a child's discarded toys.

She saw movement, and followed it, only to discover a scavenging dog, drawn out of hiding by the stench of death. The corpse was Toktel'yan, and she hoped that his spirit would not mind what was happening to its former housing. The afterlife in Olyak's many Halls was their most important belief, but no one could enter until their bodies had been cleansed of the impurities of the world with fire. The ghosts of the drowned were supposed to wander in an eternal limbo, wailing in the wind for the comforts and companionship of their lost afterlife. She shivered suddenly, realizing for the first time that it was an act of real courage for a Toktel'yan to take to the sea.

Behind her, Tegerno was still speaking, and everyone else was giving her their rapt attention. Nothing else stirred in these further corners of the square, but her senses prickled with the portent of danger.

'Mallaso?'

Unmistakably, it was Kazhian's voice. Joy overwhelmed her. She turned towards the sound and saw him standing by the dark entrance to one of the side-streets, no more than a shadow against the wall behind him.

Before she could speak, another shadow emerged from the gloom of the alley, and flung itself upon him. Mallaso began to run, knowing she would be too late. She saw the two figures struggling frantically, an arm raised to strike, a grunt of pain. One of the combatants collapsed, and the other stood over him menacingly. With a sob of despair, Mallaso hurled herself at him, her dagger in her hand.

It was wrested from her with brisk speed and efficiency. 'I never knew you hated me so much,' said Kazhian, his voice rich with amusement.

Astonished and delighted, Mallaso let relief turn her fear to anger. 'Next time you want rescuing in a hurry, call someone else!'

'Like me.' Sargenay stepped forward from the shadows, his tone deceptively light and sardonic. 'Handy, don't you think, having a tame sorcerer to protect you?'

Mallaso stared helplessly at the two men standing in front of her. Then she gestured at the prone figure lying at their feet. 'Is that Gemain?'

'I'm afraid it is.' Kazhian sounded mildly regretful. 'How did a man like Essyan ever come to breed such a half-wit?'

'You'd do some pretty stupid things too, in his shoes,' Mallaso retorted, and then stopped, suddenly aware of the implications of what she'd said.

'Don't worry, he isn't dead,' said Sargenay, smoothly filling the awkward pause. 'Sorcery can fell a man just as effectively as an ironwood club. If we leave him here, he'll wake up in an hour or so with a splitting headache, and absolutely no idea of what happened to him – which will probably be good for his self-esteem, if he's got any left. And now, if you will both excuse me, I have my duties as a Healer to consider.'

'Thank you,' Mallaso said. She was shaking, from reaction if nothing else, and felt glad of the dim light.

'It was nothing,' Sargenay said, with a smile. 'A trifle, no more.' He touched her lightly on the shoulder. It was a gesture familiar from the old days at the Golden Djarlek, expressing a wish for luck or a hope for success. And so she did not offer to go back to the Meeting House with him, but stayed, facing Kazhian's shadowy shape over the prone body of the other man who wanted her.

'I'm sorry.'

They had both spoken at once, and laughed, though the tension seemed to vibrate in the air between them. 'We'll have to stop meeting like this,' Kazhian added, the amusement still rich in his voice. 'Not very appropriate, is it?'

'For what?'

'I'm sorry I laughed at you. It wasn't very fair.'

'Considering I thought it was you lying on the ground, and that you were dead, no, it wasn't.'

'Does it matter so much to you, then, whether I am dead or not?'

Goaded out of her usual caution, for at least the third time that day, Mallaso cried passionately, 'Of course it bloody matters, you fool!'

'Why?'

'Oh, use some of that intelligence everyone else seems to think you possess,' Mallaso said in exasperation. 'I'm in love with you, that's why.'

There was a short pause. 'Good,' Kazhian said softly. 'I thought so. I just wanted to hear you admit it.'

'As if it's a crime? You choose a very round-about way of doing it, then!'

'I know. But I also know you – a little. And myself, rather better. You see, I feel the same. I am in love with you. But I couldn't bring myself to say it aloud, until I heard you tell me.'

Shaken, shaking, Mallaso said wonderingly, 'Why? We hardly know each other.'

'But we do, don't we? I showed you my heart on the steps at Penya Harbour, though it took three flasks full of ral to work up the courage to do it. You showed me yours today, in the courtyard of the Blue Olive. I saw it in your face, when you found I was alive.'

What have I done? Mallaso cried inwardly in panic. *I want this so much – and yet I am afraid, so afraid—*

Of what?

It seemed to be Bron's voice, gentle in her mind. *What are you afraid of?*

Of being hurt – I don't know if I can trust him—

You can trust him. Remember me, but I have told you already – do not spurn what is offered, for my sake. Your life has changed – do not run away from it – that isn't the woman I loved.

'Mallaso? What's wrong?'

'I – I don't know.' She found that she had put her hands over her ears – to shut Kazhian out, or Bron? How could he speak to her, if he was dead? How could he know what was happening to her? Was he watching over her like some omnipotent, all-seeing, all-pervading deity?

She gave a sob of fear, or horror, at the thought. Swiftly, Kazhian stepped round Gemain's supine body and pulled her into his arms. And, wrenched out of her carapace of calm control by grief, confusion and weariness, she wept on his shoulder as his hands held her close to his heart.

Mallaso never knew when the nature of that embrace changed from friendly comfort to something rather more. But longing began to seep slowly along her veins, drying her tears, quickening the beat of her heart. She lifted her head from his shoulder. Like Bron, he was not a tall man, and their faces were almost level. She could not see the expression in his shadowed eyes, but she could sense the tension within him, the passion, the urgency winding his nerves as tight as a djarlek string. And because she loved him too much to reject him, and because her own desire had surged out of her control, she set her lips on his.

A while later, when her mouth felt bruised, and her breathing was disrupted, and every pore of her skin seemed desperate to absorb the essence of him, he said urgently, 'Is there somewhere we could go, Sashir? Lord of Life, I want you so much—'

She thought of the mattress awaiting her in some crowded communal room in the Meeting House. 'No – I don't think so – I don't know.'

'Somewhere in this town there must be an empty room with a bed and a roof and a door.' Kazhian's own breathing was noticeably wild, and his hand was caressing her breasts inside her unlaced tunic while his mouth nuzzled at hers. 'Can you wait any longer? I know I can't.'

The thought of stumbling over the unseen corpses in the streets behind them was peculiarly horrible. But only half of Hegril had been a battleground. She shivered at his touch, and pressed her body against his. 'No. But there must be somewhere, behind the Meeting House. Come on, follow me!'

She slid out of his arms, and turned, catching his hand. Together, breathless with passion and longing, they ran across the square. Tegerno had gone, and most of the crowd had dispersed, but the soldiers on guard under the portico waved at them, and one of them whistled with appreciation. Suddenly exploding with laughter and joy, she led Kazhian round the high side of the building and into the tangle of streets and alleys beyond. They were identical to those in which they had fought today, but here there would be no bodies, no horror, no terrible reminders of how close she and Kazhian had come to death.

She bumped into a half-open door down a twisting alley. She had no idea where they were, or whose house, if anyone's, it might be. But it wasn't derelict: the courtyard, visible in the moonlight, was clear of debris, and the roof seemed intact.

'Sashir!' Kazhian pulled her hungrily into his arms again, his mouth searching for hers. 'Oh, sweet Mother, hurry!'

'I will if you just let me go,' she said, laughing, and twisted mischievously out of his embrace. 'La'aren—'

'What does that mean?' He followed her, his hand on her arm as if he could not keep from touching her. 'You never told me.'

'You have to guess. Not another kiss until you've got it right. Ow – what was that?'

In the darkness of the room they were exploring, something rolled clattering away from her stubbed toe.

'A cooking-pot, probably. This must be the kitchen.'

'Really? I'd never have guessed.' She slid adroitly past him, and went back out into the courtyard. 'Let's hope no one's here.'

'They'd have heard us by now if there was. Try this door.'

This room contained a sleeping-mattress. She found it by feeling around with her foot in the darkness. It was lumpy and coarse, but at least it was unoccupied. She grinned at Kazhian, who was blocking the doorway. 'Tell me what La'aren means.'

He came up to her. 'Dog.'

Mallaso gasped at the unerring accuracy of his hands. 'Try again.'

'Mouse.'

'No. Oh, don't stop!'

'Er – lion?'

'You do know – you're teasing me!'

'You're the one doing the teasing, darling Sashir – and I am ready to devour you with love.' He pulled her so close that she could feel all the hard contours of his body, pressed passionately against hers. 'La'aren the tiger. *Now* will you kiss me?'

It had been two years and more since she had lain with Bron, on the sorcerer's isle of Jo'ami. In all the time since, absorbed with Kiyu and with Penya, she had never felt the lack of a man in her bed. Now, overwhelmed by the power of the feelings that Kazhian had roused, she let their shared desire sweep them both away from reality, away from death and fear and pain, and into an enchanted realm of sensual delight, full of laughter, and tenderness, and love.

When they lay quiet at last, still linked in the darkness, their arms around each other and the memory of passion pulsing within them, she said, her mouth against his, 'When did you fall in love with me?'

'When you danced, that night in Penya Harbour. You looked as if all the joy in the world had been poured into your heart. When did you fall in love with me?'

She thought for a moment, smiling at the memory. 'On the steps at Penya Harbour, I think. But I couldn't acknowledge it until today, when I thought you were dead, and found you were not.'

'In the Blue Olive?'

'Yes, in the Blue Olive.' She lay still, feeling his slowing breaths, his hair tickling her arm, the warmth and strength of his body, and wishing she could see him. 'Do you remember what I asked you to do, in Ammenna's house?'

'Yes. You wanted me to rebuild it. Well, I've got other things on my mind at the moment, Sashir, but if I ever get this very luscious and wanton woman out of my heart, I'll be glad to do as you ask.'

'Aren't you *ever* serious?'

'Not when it really matters, no. Well, what about Ammenna's house? Are you going to let me off?'

'Of course not. But there was something I didn't tell you.'

'I thought it seemed too straightforward. What is it? Do I have to do it all between two full moons? Or pave the floors with sapphires and emeralds? Or roof it with tiles of beaten gold, and get Sargenay to weave a spell of happiness over it?'

'I don't need that now. I don't want any of them. But in Penya, once, it was the custom for a woman to request the man of her heart to prove his love for her by performing some task. If she was sure of him, the task would be easy. If she was not, it would be difficult, or arduous, or time-consuming.'

'Like rebuilding Ammenna's house?'

'Exactly. But I wasn't sure even of my own feelings then, let alone of yours.'

'And only two days later, you are?'

'Yes,' Mallaso said, softly, vehemently. 'Yes, I am sure. I want you. I want you not just for one night, but for many nights to come. I want to discover you, and I want you to discover me. In time, if you wish it too, and if the Mother blesses us, I would like your children. Does that frighten you?'

There was a pause, too long for her liking. Then Kazhian said quietly, 'If I am honest, yes, it does. I am a pirate, a sailor, a man of the sea. I have never even kept a concubine, let alone a wife. My responsibility, such as it is, has only been to my crew and to my ship.'

'I'm not asking you to be responsible for me,' Mallaso said with some asperity. 'I don't want you to set me up in some luxurious empty villa to twiddle my thumbs all day while you provide for me and Kiyu. This isn't Toktel'yi, this is Penya. And in Penya, the word for "wife" or "husband" is *tiarnen* – the same as the word for "partner". Does that give you any clues? You don't have to be responsible for me, or protect me, or look after me. I can do that for myself.'

'I know you can,' Kazhian said drily. 'But if that isn't what you want – what *do* you want, beloved?'

'I told you, didn't I? I want a *lover*. I don't want you to agree to something you might later regret, I don't want you to tie yourself to me unless you want it too.'

'That wasn't ever my particular perversion, but if it's yours, darling Sashir—'

'Be serious!' She kissed him with loving exasperation. 'For twenty heartbeats, at least.'

'I'll try.' Her face felt him smile. 'I am a restless soul, Sashir – I always have been. But perhaps I have found now what I have been seeking. And if it is, then demons and fire-monsters could not tear me away from you. Do you understand? Here on Penya there are people worth friendship, and a task worth doing, and above all a woman worth loving.' His hands, sure and gentle, caressed her with entrancing tenderness. 'Perhaps I am ready for this, Sashir. Perhaps I am not. But I will always be honest with you – and that is a promise I will never break. I love you, and I will do everything in my power to keep you from hurt. But I don't want to make any more vows, not yet. At this moment I would promise you the world, the sun and the stars to keep you in my arms and myself in your heart for ever, but I am too changeable to be trusted. So I will not commit myself now for all time.'

'That doesn't matter,' Mallaso whispered. 'Just tonight will do – and tomorrow night, and the next night after that, and the next—'

Laughing, he kissed her, and for a long time she forgot everything except the exquisite sensations of touch, and pleasure, and utter fulfilment. But later, lying wakeful on the uncomfortable mattress, as he slept with his head on her shoulder, she pondered his words. He had promised as much of himself to her as he could, and that was more than she had ever dreamed he would do. The man she loved lay sleeping in her arms, for this night and for many to come. And for the moment it was enough that he, and she, and Kiyu, would be together, beginning to build a shared life and a shared love that would carry them all into the future, for as far as she could see.

PART FOUR

FINAL SACRIFICE

CHAPTER
TWENTY-ONE

'I have news, Imperial Majesty.'

Olkanno raised his head from contemplation of the heaped documents on his desk, and stared with cold hostility at his Spymaster. 'Indeed? Then I desire you to share it with me, Arkun.'

The younger man's fierce face was, as usual, totally devoid of expression. Whether he was announcing the end of the world or, alternatively, the Second Coming of Kaylo and the Golden Age of pleasure and bliss, his eyes would probably look exactly the same. Olkanno had never liked him – liking, or loving, or any of the softer human emotions had long since been completely expunged from his brain, if indeed they had ever existed there at all. But he had come to appreciate his protégé's ruthlessness, his attention to detail, his efficiency, his energy, and above all his devious subtlety: all qualities essential in a good agent, or a good Spymaster.

Unfortunately, ruthless, subtle and devious men did not usually inspire trust. And although Olkanno had never trusted anyone in his life, once seated on the Onyx Throne he had swiftly realized that an Emperor, far more even than a Spymaster, needed a cohort of Ministers and assistants on whom he could rely. The amount of business involved merely in the routine daily trivia of administering such a vast Empire kept thousands of greater and lesser bureaucrats gainfully employed, both in the city itself and in the provinces. In times of crisis, their numbers seemed to multiply like a colony of sand-rats. No single man could ever hope to keep track of everything – indeed, the Emperor Tenkul the Obsessive had been driven mad in the attempt. And so although he had spies watching the Spymaster, as he had in every other Ministry, Olkanno was forced to take a great deal on trust, while loathing the need for it.

And although Arkun had never given him any cause for suspicion or complaint – apart from that uncharacteristic and unrepeated mistake in Ukkan – Olkanno knew that one day his loyal and invaluable servant would turn against him. He could not see it, nor could he hear it, but he sensed his Spymaster's hidden hostility. Such treachery, however, was not inevitable. Judge the right man, judge the moment, and he could act first, and Arkun, no longer faithful, no longer indispensable, would suffer a slow death under Olkanno's own hands.

So far, it had not been necessary. Other Ministers, however, had felt the full force of Olkanno's retribution. Governors of rebellious provinces, those who had not been lynched by their unruly subjects, had suffered the full penalty for their failings. In the three years since he had seized the Onyx Throne, Olkanno had become the first Emperor for several centuries to see his dominions contract. A pragmatist, he had swallowed his bitter humiliation, and concentrated on saving those regions which were most valuable, either to the Empire as a whole, or in terms of prestige.

He had been forced to relinquish Djebb, always volatile and economically backward, and its people had promptly and gleefully proclaimed independence under some ridiculous but well-born nonentity who called himself King. By all accounts, he was having almost as much trouble controlling his turbulent subjects as their last Imperial Governor, a situation not helped by the fact that all the remaining provinces of the Empire had been forbidden to trade with Djebb. True, the northern cities were attempting to fill the gap, but their wealth could not compare with that of Toktel'yi, and there were many essential commodities – cotton, oil, paper, iron, spices – which could only be obtained from the Empire. Importing them through Minassa doubled their price, and apparently there had already been rioting against profiteers and shortages. Freedom, as the Djebbans were only now discovering, often had a very large price-tag attached. Olkanno gave them five years, at the most, before they came crawling back to the Empire, begging to be readmitted to the fold.

Djebb had been comparatively easy to give up, not least because doing so freed thousands of troops for service elsewhere. But Tatht was another matter. Its silk and cotton, its fertile farmland, its productive coastline and wealthy, sophisticated towns and cities, not to mention its shared border with Kerenth, gave it a vital strategic and economic importance. When news came that rebellion had spread to the province, Olkanno knew that he could not afford to lose Tatht as well. He occupied the Onyx Throne because he had eliminated all the alternatives. As yet, no one had dared to challenge him. But if the Empire began to disintegrate in earnest . . .

So he had thrown every spare soldier, every coin, every effort, into the subjugation of his easternmost province. Even the troops holding Penya were despatched to put down the rebellion. The island didn't matter to him: it had been Djamal's trophy, and Ba'alekkt's toy, and between them they had made it a wasteland, little more than a dumping ground for surplus Toktel'yan peasants. The Penyans were welcome to it. Tatht was vital.

But the flames of revolt had proved surprisingly persistent. No matter how vigorously his soldiers stamped them out, more would spring up, as if by sorcery, in another town, another city. Olkanno did not want to repeat Ba'alekkt's mistakes: he knew that devastating the province would be counter-productive, for its wealth was too valuable to lose. But now, he realized that such a drastic course might be the only way to keep Tatht within his dominions. The Empire's need for the region's wealth was not, in the end, more essential than the Empire's need for unity. And Olkanno had never shrunk from grim necessity. Indeed, he would enjoy directing the programme of mass slaughter and destruction himself. Very soon, his patience would expire, and then the province would feel the full might and terror of his hoarded fury. For Olkanno, vengeance was all the more sweet for being delayed.

If Tatht and Djebb had been the only regions in revolt, he would have been less anxious. But Tulyet was also aflame. In itself, this was nothing new: the peninsula's mountainous terrain and sparse soil lent itself to banditry, and its people were a fierce and lawless breed, scornful of authority. Instead of welcoming the death of the unpopular Prince Skallyan, however, they had used it as an excuse to rebel yet again. Nearly three years later, much of the interior, and almost all of the iron mines, were in enemy hands. Olkanno had sent many thousands of prisoners to the Tulyet mines, for it was a useful and convenient way of eliminating subversives and undesirables, and the six months they usually lasted were said to be more horrible than any torture. But the bandits had liberated them, destroyed as much of the workings as they could, and disappeared back into the mountains, their numbers now swollen by the five thousand Toktel'yan men, women and children whom they had rescued from hideous slavery and certain death.

Olkanno had sent as many soldiers as he dared: the garrisons of Tekkt, Balki, Jaiya and Lai'is had all been drastically reduced. At the same time, he issued an Imperial Decree. All those now engaged in their compulsory Army service were now forced to stay on for an extra two years, making a total of seven. It was a deeply unpopular measure, and Enmek, the General-in-Chief, a competent soldier without any of his predecessor Sekkenet's shrewdness and political acumen, complained strongly to the Emperor about the drastic effect on morale. Few were surprised when, a few days later, he suddenly fell ill and died.

Fewer still marvelled at the identity of his replacement, a Fifty Thousand Commander called K'yar, who was notorious for his ferocity towards both the enemy and the unfortunate troops under his command. Those who objected were summarily executed, and morale thereafter apparently ceased to be a problem.

But Tulyet remained unsubdued: Tatht was still stubbornly resisting, and Djebb was a humiliating and insolent reminder of his failure. The first three years of his reign had been conspicuously disastrous. Olkanno, as grim and patient as a spider, had no intention of letting matters get any further out of hand. Now that the rainy season was over, and before the summer's heat, he planned to visit Tatht for the fifth time. On each previous occasion, there had been a parade of freshly mutilated corpses in every town and city, and a noticeable improvement thereafter in the attitudes and loyalty of his subjects. It seemed as if only the menace of his actual presence was effective. On this visit, he intended to make a terrible example of the province, and ensure that no other part of the Empire ever dared to contemplate rebellion again.

He had spent, in fact, more months in Tatht and Tulyet than he had in Toktel'yi. He had taken his Councillors with him, to keep them under control and in reach. But on every occasion, he had left his wife behind.

After Djeneb had nearly died miscarrying his child, that insolent Healer had warned him – threatened him – that he must never treat her so cruelly again. The man's outrageous impudence had moved Olkanno only to cold anger, and he regretted that the Healer had escaped his vengeance by some devious means – it was almost as if he had vanished into thin air. But although he had outwardly scorned the threat, he was forced reluctantly to face the fact that he still needed Djeneb. He had married her to improve his claim to the throne, and while she remained his wife, an important section of Toktel'yan aristocracy would stay loyal to him. And besides, he had not given up hope of founding a dynasty. He was too old to be sure of living long enough to mould his sons in his own image, but some deep part of his soul longed for the satisfaction of knowing that his line would continue after him. Djeneb might have other children. And while he was too busy to arrange the betrothal of a second wife, he would continue to visit her in her lonely splendour in the Women's Quarters, and force her to copulate with him in the variously perverted ways which were necessary to arouse him.

Arkun's agents spied on her, as did her Chief Eunuch, who was in her husband's pay. She was his wife, his property. If she bore him a son, he would take the boy away from her, to be reared in his likeness. A daughter would be smothered at birth. And he had made sure that she knew of his plans for their children.

But since that night when he tortured her in front of Arkun, he had refrained from using such naked brutality again. He still needed to hurt her, to see fear, rather than contempt or hatred, in her hazel eyes. Sometimes, she obliged. Sometimes, she lay like a dead woman beneath his labouring body. But despite all his efforts she had failed to conceive another child, in three years of marriage. He needed another wife, a lovely young girl who would shake with terror at his touch, and bear his sons. And for those who, like Djeneb, had lost their usefulness, Olkanno had only one remedy. He had told her that, too, as she lay on the bed with that blank look on her face, as if her mind had deserted her body. He had told her that if she did not conceive, he would kill her. But since her illness, her wits seemed to have left her: she had stared at him with bovine dullness, and he had no way of knowing if she had understood.

He had summoned Healers to examine her. None could find any reason why there had been no more children. For the first time, the Emperor regretted that he had not yet appointed his own Sorcerer. His predecessor had chosen some fawning nonentity, whom Olkanno had removed as soon as he won the throne. Since then, he had ruled without the aid of magic, preferring the lesser but more certain methods of bribery, spying and terror. But as the troubles in the Empire grew greater, his mind had changed. Six months ago, after listening to reports from all over his dominions, he had sent out an Imperial Summons to a small town on the extreme western borders of the province of Lai'is, close to the steppes. And a month later, the Black Mage known as I'amel had arrived in Toktel'yi.

Sorcery was generally an admired and respected profession. Men like Al'Kalyek were famous for their wisdom as well as their power. The Schools of Wizards taught their pupils the Four Rules of Ai-Mayak, over a thousand years old, and ensured that the apprentices adhered to them. True, a few sorcerers were incompetent, foolish or even wicked. But such men were usually ejected from the Schools long before they had completed their training. Only those who had studied for the full seven years, and obtained their qualifications, could obtain a licence to practise.

I'amel had no licence. Out in the remoter hills of western Lai'is, even the inevitability of Imperial bureaucracy quailed before the grim realities of life, and death, on the edge of the wilderness. But his reputation had long interested Olkanno. In its place, conventional sorcery was a useful tool. Its effectiveness was limited, however, Ba'alekkt had relied on it to protect him, and instead it had killed him. Olkanno had no intention of entrusting his life or his schemes to the tender conscience of an ordinary wizard. But I'amel and his kind, operating on the fringes of the Empire, had smashed the boundaries of orthodox practice, and greatly enhanced their power as a result. And Olkanno had no qualms about the methods which his chosen sorcerer used to obtain his impressive results. Indeed, he was sorry that he had not appointed the Black Mage at the very beginning of his reign.

As a result of I'amel's skills, Arkun's news was not news to the Emperor.

'Imperial Majesty, it distresses me to inform you that fighting has broken out in the province of Jaiya.'

'So I understand.' Olkanno's black eyes were fixed unwaveringly upon his Spymaster. 'You are not my only source of information, Arkun. So – when did this occur?'

The red-haired man's face was still expressionless, despite the jibe. 'Yesterday, Imperial Majesty. The pigeon has just arrived.'

'And what else have you learned?'

'That so far the city of Jaiya itself is quiet. Only the town called Endeyel is affected, so far. According to the Governor's report the rioting will be put down in a few days. Minor only.'

'He would not have bothered to inform you of minor rioting. Did he mention a reason for this disturbance?'

'No, Imperial Majesty. There probably wasn't room on the paper.'

'Indeed.' Olkanno's gaze became, if anything, even more unfriendly. 'No mention of the Flamebearer?'

'Certainly not, Imperial Majesty. Why? Is there—'

'Enough. I pay you to answer questions, not to ask them. What agents do you have operating in Jaiya at present?'

'Nearly two dozen, Imperial Majesty, including one at the heart of the Governor's household, and another in the town you mentioned.'

'Can you contact them quickly?'

'There is a courier ship at present in port, Imperial Majesty, so it will take a couple of days at most.'

'Good. I want up-to-date and comprehensive reports – and discreet. If that Governor is right, and it all blows over in a few days, then there will be no harm done. And if not . . . well, I shall be ready. And the town of Endeyel and all its inhabitants shall be taught a lesson that the rest of Jaiya will never forget. Do not fail me, Arkun.'

'I will not, Imperial Majesty.' The Spymaster made his obeisance, and withdrew.

Olkanno pondered for a while. Then he sent a slave to fetch his tame sorcerer.

The man who entered in answer to his summons was, like all sorcerers of mature years, at once aged and ageless. He had no hair on his head, and the yellowish skin was stretched so tightly over the bones of his skull that it looked as if it would split. His eyes were deeply set, slanting like those of the steppe tribes, and indeed I'amel made no secret of the fact that his grandmother had been a Ska'i, one of that fearsome and now exterminated people who had worshipped Olyak in his most terrible aspect, Ayak, the Wolf-God of Death.

'You called me, Imperial Majesty?'

'I did.' Olkanno closed his nostrils against the stench of decay wafting from the sorcerer's black robes and surreptitiously began to breathe through his mouth.

'This trouble in Jaiya,' he continued. 'How serious is it?'

'It is at present in its infancy, Imperial Majesty, so I cannot yet say. The bowl tells me, though, that it is more serious and significant than it seems.'

The sorcerer's sibilant Lai'issian accent was hard to understand, but Olkanno concealed his irritation. It was useless to blame the man for his provincialism when that very quality was what made him useful. He said softly, 'Is there any trace of him whom we have discussed before?'

'The Flamebearer?' I'amel, unlike his employer, had no hesitation in mentioning the name. 'I sense him. He has succeeded in Djebb – he is struggling in Tatht, and Terebis has turned away from him in the fear of vengeance. Now he is sowing his perfidious seed in fresh soil. May it wither and die in the blast of your Imperial Majesty's wrath!'

'You sense him. What is he, I'amel? Who is he? Where does he come from?'

The Black Mage shook his head. 'He keeps himself well hidden. I can catch no more than a fleeting glimpse of him, or of his spirit. But one fact is abundantly clear – he is a sorcerer. A sorcerer with the power to influence men's hearts and minds, and also with the power to hide himself from those who would seek him out. But he is a man, Imperial Majesty – a man, not a god. And men can be captured, and killed. All we have to do is find him.'

Olkanno stared at him, frowning. I'amel was not a prepossessing figure. Short, shrivelled, clad in black rags, at first sight he seemed to be some dim-witted village wizard, barely able to locate a lost goat. But even the Emperor, at whose name grown men had been known to weep, had felt the menace emanating from those opaque, slanting eyes, and shivered inwardly with fear. It would be fatally easy to underestimate I'amel or his powers. But if he could find the Flamebearer, and put a permanent end to his activities, then Olkanno would happily do anything, pay any price, to keep his Empire intact.

And what more would I'amel want? Summoned from deep obscurity, he had already been showered with wealth, power and status far beyond the most hectic dreams of any provincial wizard. And he had a master who was happy, indeed eager, to supply him with all the necessary raw materials for his particular kind of sorcery. Olkanno had chosen to ignore his Court Sorcerer's activities, both because the use of corpses was the foundation of I'amel's power, and because it gave him a weapon to be used in case of need. Necromancy was a crime punishable by death, in all parts of the Empire.

'Can you find him?'

The Black Mage smiled, showing a mouthful of teeth as pointed as fangs: following tribal custom, they had been sharpened long ago, in his adolescence. 'Give me time, Imperial Majesty, and I will find him. He is not in Jaiya. He is not in Toktel'yi. His influence comes from somewhere in the east. Give me the means, and I will locate him for you.'

'How many?'

'A dozen. I shall return to my courtyard now. As soon as I have received them, I shall begin.'

'How soon will you know?'

'It depends, Imperial Majesty . . . it depends on many things. A day, at least – perhaps several days. But if I do not find him for you, may the Wolf tear out my heart!'

Despite his sophistication, his pragmatism and his urbane intelligence, the skin tingled on the back of Olkanno's neck. He wondered briefly why he had ever considered employing such an uncouth barbarian. It was certainly considered extremely ominous to tempt Olyak in such dramatic terms. And this bloodthirsty Wolf seemed to be a god who was infinitely darker and more terrible than the almost kindly Lord of Death worshipped by the Toktel'yans.

'I trust that will not be necessary,' he said, with his bland smile. 'You may have all the prisoners you require, I'amel. They will be brought to your courtyard after dark. And remember – find him, find this man, and my generosity will be considerable.'

'You have already been more than generous to my humble and unworthy self, Imperial Majesty.'

Once I'amel had gone, Olkanno let out his breath in a long sigh of triumph. At last, his careful encouragement of the Black Mage was about to bear fruit. If he could track down the Flamebearer, he would be worth ten times his weight in gold Imperials. And the Emperor had great confidence in his servant. Like Arkun, I'amel owed everything to Olkanno's favour. But unlike the Spymaster, he would never betray his master.

He thought of the prisoners, who would soon be screaming in pain and terror under I'amel's knife. Then another image slunk into his mind. He rose, summoned his bodyslaves, and told them to prepare him for a visit to the Women's Quarters.

The Lady Djeneb was playing Kal-Gan with her favourite slave, Tezna, and Kedrain, the Chief Eunuch, and for once she was winning. Usually she could never make any regular shape from her pieces, no matter how many she collected. But today she already had two rectangles and a triangle, and if Tezna hadn't spotted it yet, there was a piece in the pool that would join with the three she still had in her hand, and make up a square. And that would give her the game.

Then Vagak put his head round the door and said in his high-pitched voice, 'Lady, your husband is coming.' And all her carefully hoarded, trivial store of contentment trickled away through her fingers, leaving her clutching three small flat pieces of wood.

He hadn't been near her for half a month. Something must have happened. Djeneb felt sick, and for a moment blind panic threatened to choke her.

'Lady?' There was a warm, comforting touch on her hand. 'Lady, you must make ready.'

'Thank you, Tezna. Of course.' Djeneb put her three pieces back into the pool, and rose to her feet. 'You may robe me.'

'Of course, lady,' said the girl, and escorted Djeneb to her private chamber.

Everyone in the Women's Quarters knew that Tezna was in the pay of the Spymaster, just as they knew that Kedrain reported to Olkanno. It was inevitable that there would be informers amongst them, and at least the Fabrizi slave seemed genuinely fond of her mistress. But Tezna had told no one that Djeneb knew that she was Arkun's spy.

Three years ago, she had pledged her heart in friendship to the

Emperor's wife, as Djeneb hovered at Olyak's door. She took Arkun's money, hoarding it to buy her freedom, and fed him harmless information. In truth, there was little to tell. Djeneb was not indulging in conspiracy, or drink, or gambling, or wild perverted orgies with animals or slave-girls, or any of the other peculiar diversions with which the abused or neglected wives of past Emperors had passed the endless days of seclusion. If she had a vice, or a perversion, Tezna did not know of it. In fact, there were only two details about Djeneb's tedious and miserable life that would be of interest to the Spymaster, and of even more interest to the Emperor himself. And Tezna had no intention of telling either of them.

Duty compelled any wife to array herself as splendidly as possible when her husband visited her apartments. Some women looked forward eagerly to such occasions, and gladly put on their finest clothes, and had themselves anointed with expensive aphrodisiac oils, intended to keep the man at her side for as long as possible. But not Djeneb. She had no wish to inflame his lust or to prolong her ordeal. All she wanted was the courage to endure everything he inflicted upon her. And Tezna had found her the answer.

The taste of the potion, even after all this time, still reminded her sharply and bitterly of Kazhian. He was officially dead, but she had never believed it. No mere tempest could have extinguished the brilliant vitality of her cousin. And Tezna had told her all the stories circulating in Toktel'yi. He was on Penya, apparently. She would never see him again, but at least he was alive.

As the drug seeped through her body, she stood motionless, allowing the slave to dress her in a gown of semi-transparent silk, to sprinkle her with musk-water and other exotic fragrances from Onnak and Annatal, and to brush her heavy fall of black hair. And all the while the khlar-induced feeling of remoteness increased, until she reached the point where she could step aside from her self, leaving a gorgeous painted wooden doll that resembled those she had had as a child, unthinking, unfeeling, unresponding: an effigy in the likeness of Djeneb, but not Djeneb at all.

Scores of times, now, she had submitted to Olkanno's brutal demands while under the influence of khlar. Since he treated her as an object, never speaking to her or requiring any normal response, he had not realized it. He would tie her up, hit her, hurt her, and although the drugged Djeneb might flinch or whimper, the real woman, the secret stubborn heart of her, stood aside and laughed at him, for he had not the wit to understand that she kept her soul safe from his evil.

And she would never bear the child he wanted: Tezna had ensured that too. No infant monster of cruelty would inherit its father's tainted blood. And knowing that, Djeneb had found the strength and courage to endure the unendurable. She lay beneath him, unmoving and uncaring, while he vented his rage and frustration on someone else. Dimly, through the fog, she heard a distant commotion. Then, incredibly, the door to her bedchamber opened.

Olkanno wrenched himself out of her, leaving her lying bleeding on the bed, and turned in fury on the intruder.

It was Kedrain, the Chief Eunuch, his smooth face twisted with fear and distress. And beside him stood the Spymaster Arkun.

The shock drove the fumes of the drug from her mind. Astonished at this unprecedented interruption, Djeneb sat up, forgetting her half-naked body, and the obvious signs of her husband's vicious cruelty.

She saw, as if in a dream, a wilderness of answering emotions on Arkun's usually impassive face. Disgust, contempt, anger: and unmistakable even as it fled from his eyes, the flare of physical desire.

And then, as Olkanno knocked her back against the pillows with a casually spiteful blow to the side of her head, she saw how she might, at long last, have her revenge.

'How dare you enter here!' the Emperor demanded savagely. 'You'd better have good reason, my friend, or I'll have you gutted alive and your bowels burnt before your eyes.'

'I crave your pardon, Imperial Majesty – the news is most urgent, and I knew that you would wish to be informed immediately—'

'*What* news?'

'Balki has risen up in revolt, Imperial Majesty. The rebels have slain the Governor and all loyal members of the garrison, and declared their independence. The island is entirely in their hands.'

And as Olkanno flung himself out of the room, calling for his slaves, calling for I'amel, he did not see the bitter satisfaction on his wife's bruised and bleeding face.

CHAPTER
TWENTY-TWO

'You cannot do it, lady! It will mean death if you are discovered! A horrible, lingering, agonizing death—'

'Enough, Tezna.' Djeneb, her head cleared by several steamingly fragrant cups of kuldi, touched her slave's lips with her fingers. 'My mind is made up. What could possibly be worse than what I now endure? Death would be a release. I do not fear it. Olyak is always kindest to those who have suffered greatly in life – and he will know that I have been driven to do this. And how will Olkanno find out? I am not going to tell him. Neither will you. Nor will Arkun, for it will be death for him, too. Kedrain is easy to outwit. And no one else will know.'

'*I* don't want to die,' Tezna said stubbornly. 'Not like that, anyway. And you know as well as I do, lady, that the Emperor will kill every one of us if he learns what you have done.'

'Or send you to the mines in Tulyet, if there are any left.' Djeneb closed her eyes, seeing again the lust in Arkun's face. He was a good-looking man, despite that fierce nose and stern mouth. And he had wanted her, she was certain of it.

She did not want him. Olkanno had purged her of all desire, and she could not imagine ever enjoying the presence of a man in her bed. But he would be an instrument of her vengeance, and the means of her salvation.

She had never seduced anyone in her life, but she knew what to do. All wealthy Toktel'yan girls were instructed in the erotic arts, usually by their mother, or by their father's chief concubine. And if she could persuade Arkun to have sex with her, she would be revenged for all the pain she had suffered at Olkanno's hands. Without Tezna's secret potion, she might even become pregnant. Her husband would think that the child was his, and he would no longer be tempted to murder her.

And one day, Arkun's son, the grandchild of a Fabrizi slave, might sit upon the Onyx Throne. It was the perfect deception, the perfect vengeance.

She began to laugh, and found it difficult to stop. Tezna watched her anxiously, her dark blue eyes round with concern. 'Oh, lady – please, lady, stop – you'll make yourself ill!'

Djeneb forced her wild emotions back under control. She wiped her streaming eyes, and said on a gasp, 'Don't worry Tezna – I'm not mad.'

'I do hope you are not, lady.'

'But I want to do this. I *will* do this. And if you do not help me, I will do it alone.'

'You need my help, lady, you know you do. If you want it kept a secret, you must rely on me – you can't do it without me.'

'Exactly.' Djeneb drew a long shaky breath. Perhaps it was the influence of the khlar, still lingering in her blood, or perhaps it was the intoxicating lure of a purpose, a reason to continue, after all the aimless, pointless years of boredom and misery and fear within the Women's Quarters. But at this moment, the enormity of her decision had not struck her, nor any real awareness of the possible consequences. She said softly, 'You go to his rooms, don't you – to make your report and receive your money. If I pretend to be you, it's easy. We're both tall, and I've become almost as thin as you. Have you and he ever been lovers?'

Tezna shook her head. 'No, he's never laid a finger on me. But he's not uninterested in women – he used to keep a concubine, apparently. Oh, lady, do think of what might go wrong! What if he doesn't want you? What if – if he tells the Emperor?'

No doubt entered Djeneb's mind. She remembered Arkun's face when he had seen Olkanno torture her. And she knew that however loyal he seemed to be, in his heart he hated his master.

'No,' she said. 'He will not tell.'

'But how can you be so sure?'

'Because I *know*,' said Djeneb softly. 'Oh, Tezna, please, trust me – do as I say, and help me?'

The Fabrizi girl was close to tears now, but at last she nodded. 'Very well, lady. I will help you, if you really are determined to – to do this. But can you promise me one thing, lady?'

'Of course,' said Djeneb, smiling in relief.

'If – if it is discovered, will you make sure that I am dead before *he* can hurt me – please, lady?'

'Oh, Tezna,' Djeneb whispered, her resolve faltering suddenly. 'It will never happen – of *course* we will never be found out.'

But deep in her soul, she knew that they might, and that this was the most dangerous, reckless, insane idea that she had ever had, far more foolhardy than her precipitate flight from Skallyan, nearly five years ago.

Perhaps she *was* mad. If so, then Olkanno's cruelty and her desperation to escape had driven her into the abyss. But even if it went horribly wrong, she would have rebelled at last against the unbearable agony of her life. She would have dealt Olkanno's self-esteem a terrible blow. And she would have forced him to acknowledge that she was not an object to be manipulated, but a woman with her own thoughts, feelings and desires.

The slave-girl was late. The water-clock told Arkun that it was nine hours after midday, and she was usually here by eight. He put his name at the bottom of yet another piece of paper, authorizing the arrest and interrogation of yet another probable dissident, and stretched wearily. His bodyslaves were all in bed, and his apartments were silent. He himself had usually retired by this time, preferring to rise at dawn rather than fashionably late in the morning. It was impossible to think clearly or work effectively in the fierce noon heat, and his mind was always at its best early in the day.

Ever since the news about Balki had arrived, several days ago, the Emperor's moods had been more than usually vicious. Arkun counted himself fortunate, in the circumstances, not to have been one of the many who had been summarily executed for some trifling misdemeanour or oversight. But he was still more useful alive than dead. Even in the midst of his fury, the Emperor had kept his urge to kill the Spymaster under control – just. Arkun had seen the hatred in his master's eyes, and knew that it must be reflected in his own.

And nor could he forget his brief glimpse of the Emperor's wife, her full, voluptuous body damaged and bleeding, her face blank with suffering. He remembered her fierce courage, on Kazhian's ship, and the degradation and torture which Olkanno had forced her to endure in his presence. For the brutal treatment of his wife alone, the Emperor deserved Arkun's undying enmity.

But instead, for the sake of his obsessive ambition, he had long ago sworn undying loyalty. Arkun knew, though, that one day he would turn upon the man who ruled him, who owned him, who had raised him up from ignominious obscurity to one of the most powerful positions in the Empire. Olkanno had given him the power of life and death over millions. And perhaps he had also given him, unwittingly, the power of life and death over his master?

If Olkanno died, then the Empire's disintegration would acquire an unstoppable momentum. And Arkun, looking at the prospect with his usual clear and ruthless logic, knew that he would shed no tears for its passing.

The sound of footsteps in the courtyard outside roused him from thought. The slave-girl was here. When she had gone, he could go to bed at last.

There was a soft scratch on the door, and his chief slave entered. 'The girl, sir,' he said, and stood aside to let her past.

Despite her heavy veil, Arkun knew at once it was not Tezna. With the slave present, he gave no indication that he had realized, but waited until the man had shut the door and returned to his post at the entrance to his apartments. Then he said softly, 'Have you anything to report?'

The thick dark red folds of her veil trembled as she breathed. 'No, sir.'

'The Lady Djeneb leads a singularly uninteresting life,' Arkun observed. He rose to his feet and picked up the little pile of coins by his hand, before walking round his desk to face her. Suddenly, without warning, he reached out and pulled off her veil.

It was not Tezna, whose naked face he had never seen. It was the Lady Djeneb, wife of the Emperor.

As at that other unveiling, long ago on the *Wind of Morning*, she did not flinch. Her hazel eyes gazed steadily into his, and she smiled. 'Was it so very obvious?'

'I knew you were not the slave. I did not know it was you. Lady, what are you doing here?'

She did not answer him, but glanced down at the coins in his hand. 'You don't pay her very much.'

'I pay her what she is worth. She has never complained. I did not know that you were aware of the situation.' He studied the young woman in front of him. Her face and eyes had been painted with great skill, but no cosmetic could disguise the marks on her skin.

'Tezna has no secrets from me, nor I from her.'

'I see. Are you lovers?'

'No,' she said, still smiling.

'Well, I repeat, lady – why are you here? Is Tezna ill?'

'No. I came to see you.'

She was wearing some warm, exotic perfume. He remembered, as clearly as if she was half-naked now, how she had sat on her bed, her eyes dark with despair: and how, despite all his efforts, he had desired her.

And she had known that he did.

Even as the truth burst into his mind, she came closer, so that they were nearly touching. 'To see you, Arkun,' she said softly, and her hand reached out to his.

Every fibre in his body begged him to respond. And every nerve in his brain screamed at him to withdraw. She was the Emperor's wife, and the Emperor's property. Even to be discovered alone with her would invite disaster. And the penalty for adultery was branding, castration, mutilation and death.

But why should anyone know? The veil, symbol of the subjection of Toktel'yan women, also guaranteed anonymity to those who wore it. His visitor had come at Tezna's appointed time, wearing Tezna's clothes. She was the same height as the slave-girl, although her figure was fuller. And if no one save Tezna knew that she had come here, none of his slumbering slaves need know either. Even if the unthinkable happened, and someone found them together, she would not be recognized. In all the Empire, apart from the eunuchs and slaves of her household, only three people knew for certain what Djeneb looked like. Olkanno; Kazhian; and Arkun.

'Why?' It was becoming increasingly difficult to control his breathing. He had once thought her ugly and unfeminine, but she was not. And he knew that the body hidden by the ample folds of her dress was firm, voluptuous and inviting, defying the dangers of touching it.

'Why? Because I want you.' Her voice was low, husky, enticing. Her hands stroked his arm, and at her touch his skin tingled as if she had used sorcery.

'Or because you want to trap me.' With a tremendous effort, he stepped back, out of her reach. 'I thought Olkanno had more imagination than that – and I also thought you had more intelligence.'

'I am not trying to trap you. Olkanno does not know I am here. No one knows I am here, except Tezna.'

'Do you expect me to believe that, lady? I did not reach my present position by being so gullible. I suggest you leave now, and quickly, before I accuse you in front of all my household of trying to seduce me. And I am sure you know the consequences of that.'

There was silence. He looked down at Djeneb, conscious that few men in Toktel'yi could do likewise. She seemed taken aback, as if this was an answer she had never expected. And Arkun was suddenly, acutely conscious that there was a person behind that face: a person who could feel, as a man could feel, desire, need, pain and humiliation.

He said quietly and more gently, 'You had better go.'

She took a deep breath, and drew herself up proudly. 'Yes,' she said coolly. 'I am sorry for troubling you, Spymaster. I was acting under a serious misapprehension. Do you intend to tell my husband? If you do, he might take his anger out on you, as well as me.'

'Oh, lady.' Arkun stopped, astonished by the strength of his sympathy and admiration for her. 'Do you really think I would?'

'Why not? You are his creature, his servant. I have betrayed him, in my intention if not in fact. It is your duty to denounce traitors.'

'You are not a traitor, lady.'

'But I *want* to betray him.' Her own control was beginning to slip: he could see her trembling, and her voice shook suddenly. 'I want to pay him back for what he has done to me, and to so many others.'

'So I am no more than tool – a means to an end? And what an end it is, lady, for you cannot let Olkanno know of your vengeance without ensuring your own death, and mine, and probably the execution of your entire household as well. And surely the point of avenging yourself on your enemy is that they should realize what you have done?'

'I know. I am sorry. I have been very stupid. I will go now. Forgive me for troubling you, Lord Arkun.' She turned, and made for the door.

'Lady, stop. Wait!' Arkun grabbed her arm. Djeneb gave a gasp and struggled for a moment against his hold. Then quite suddenly she collapsed against him, sobbing as if her heart and spirit alike were utterly broken.

Which they were, he realized, for he and Olkanno had crushed her between them. He was beginning dimly to understand the horrible realities of her existence, married to a man who had killed his first wife, and who would undoubtedly kill her too, as callously as a cat might exterminate its prey, when he no longer had any use for her. Women in Toktel'yi had no status and no rights, but at least most men treated their wives with consideration, sometimes even with affection. It was not much to ask, and not much to give. And Djeneb had never even had that. In all the known world, her only friend was the Fabrizi slave he paid to spy on her.

Slowly, her desperate weeping grew quieter. He said softly, 'I am still holding your veil, lady. That is why I asked you to wait.'

'Thank you. May I have it?'

He handed it to her. Averting her gaze, she wiped her eyes. Drowned in misery, she was even less beautiful, but there was a despairing courage in her face which would have melted the stone heart of a statue.

He had succumbed to compassion before. Once, he had given water to an injured man, and that man, moments later, had slain the Emperor Ba'alekkt. Once, too, he had failed to kill Kazhian, and thus allowed his cousin to escape. Both acts had had immeasurable consequences. He had thought himself cured of such foolishness, but it seemed he was not. He said gently, 'If you wish to – to talk to me, lady, I will not deny you. And I will keep what you have to say a secret between us alone, for all time to come.'

Djeneb looked up at him. Her eyes were smudged with tears and cosmetics, but she was no longer weeping. She said, 'You are the Spymaster. How can I believe you?'

'You were ready to trust your body to me, lady. A conversation does not carry the same penalty.'

'If Olkanno discovered I came to see you, alone and at night, I would suffer the same punishment for a conversation or a game of Kal-Gan, as for a night of passion. You know that.'

'He will not discover it. You are married, lady, to a man who is a monster of cruelty. Ba'alekkt and Eska'anen were kindly men, compared to him. At least they could feel normal human emotions. Olkanno cannot. Everyone exists only to be used, then thrown away. Myself included. I have given him loyal service, but he does not deserve it. He deserves only death.'

'But what will happen if he dies? There is no one else.'

'Between them, Eska'anen and Olkanno have eliminated almost all the Vessels of the Blood Imperial. But Kazhian is not dead. And Megren's son, if he is still alive, will one day grow up.'

'Kazhian told me that he did not want the Onyx Throne. Tezna said that he is on Penya now, and has renounced the Empire.'

'That is true, lady. But I shall have to speak to Tezna. You are not supposed to hear such things. Olkanno remembers how you escaped from the Palace, five years ago, and he has given orders that you be kept confined as close as possible. The Chief Eunuch is supposed to be responsible for that.'

'Kedrain? He only sees what's put under his nose,' Djeneb said scornfully. 'He doesn't know I'm here. He thinks I'm fast asleep in my bed. And he also thinks I'm too stupid and feeble to try anything like this. I'm sure Olkanno does the same.'

'But they both know of your previous escapade.'

'Olkanno does, but Kedrain doesn't. He just thinks all women are the same.'

'You undervalue yourself,' said Arkun.

'I said that to Kazhian, once.' She paused, remembering. 'I used to wish that he was not estranged from Eska'anen – then he and I would probably have been married.' She smiled ruefully. 'What a fool I was!

But when you are young, you have stupid dreams. Or did you not, Spymaster?'

'I did, once. Kazhian shared them with me. But I gave them to Olkanno to destroy. Did he kill yours, too?'

'Yes. Do you hate him as much as I do?'

Arkun's brown eyes were bleak. 'Yes, I do – perhaps more. Unlike you, I have not directly suffered his cruelty, yet, but I have witnessed it inflicted on others, countless times. That is why he must kill me, eventually – I know too much, and I have seen too much. And if certain people were to discover what I know, Olkanno's life would be worthless. The Emperor is not all-powerful or all-knowing, whatever he might like to think. He can't be. The Empire is too vast for one man to govern alone. There will always be those who escape, those who refuse to be cowed, those who vow vengeance. He rules by fear, but he knows how precarious his position is. Only by killing everyone opposed to him can he survive. And long before that point, someone will have killed him.'

'And then?'

'Then, with any luck, the Empire will die. It is dying already. Djamal and Ba'alekkt sowed the seeds in Penya, and now their successor is reaping the cost. Djebb is gone, Penya is gone, Balki is gone, Tulyet has almost left, and Tatht and Jaiya will follow. He can't stop it. The Army is overstretched, and morale is very low. There is a shortage of equipment, and the General-in-Chief is an incompetent brute. If Olkanno can't rely on the Army, he is well and truly lost. Probably the heartland provinces, the ones that have been part of the Empire for hundreds and thousands of years, will stay loyal, for they have no memory or culture of freedom. The rest will break away. And if it was left to me, I would not raise a hand to prevent it.'

'But you will do Olkanno's bidding,' said Djeneb acidly.

'Yes, because I want to stay alive. Don't you?'

'I don't know.' Her voice was very bleak. 'Sometimes I think that anything, even death, would be preferable to what I endure. And then I see the sky, or the full moon reflected in the pool in the centre of the Women's Quarters, or hear a Nightsinger, or win at Kal-Gan, and I realize that life can still be sweet. Perhaps I am stupid and shallow, to receive so much pleasure from things so small. But they are all I possess.' She smiled wryly. 'I am sorry, Spymaster. I do not usually indulge in maudlin self-pity. I will go now.'

'No don't go yet,' he said, on impulse. As she stared at him in surprise, he added, 'I welcome the opportunity to talk to someone of intelligence, without the need to watch every word I say. Don't you?'

She nodded. 'Yes. Tezna is my friend, but she is still also my slave. There will always be a gulf between us, however much we may try to bridge it.'

'But I am the son of a slave.'

'I never think of it,' Djeneb said, with perfect truth. 'I saw your face, that night Olkanno . . .' She paused, swallowed, and went on. 'I suspected then that you might be a friend – because you knew who I was, and you were so disgusted by what he did to me. And when you burst in on us the other day – but I thought he would kill you for that. Or ask you to join in.'

'I would have found some excuse to refuse,' he said softly.

'Then you did not want . . .'

She let the words trickle into silence. Looking down, he saw that she was biting her lip. And for many reasons, not the least of which was that it was the truth, he said, 'Yes, I did. I wanted to then, and I want to now.'

'So why did you tell me to go?' she whispered, her face averted, her hands clenched.

'Because I am no longer anyone's slave, lady.'

'You are Olkanno's.'

'No, I am not.'

'Then prove it.' Djeneb turned suddenly, her face fierce. 'I don't want a slave – I want a lover. I want you.' She took his hand and placed it on her breast, and drew him close.

And then he could resist her no longer. He bent to kiss her, and felt the tension stiffening every sinew of her body. Of course, she only knew the brutality of Olkanno: sex and pleasure had never before been combined in her. He had a small inner room beyond his office, with a cushioned couch on which he sometimes rested when working hard or late. He guided her there, and laid her down, and began to teach her, with growing affection and burgeoning tenderness, some of the delights that a man and a woman could make between them.

By Toktel'yan standards, he was not an experienced lover, but he had always been discriminating and considerate. And if his own feelings, newly aroused, were surprising, her wakening ardour astonished him. Starved of affection, starved of pleasure, she clung to him desperately, and soon he forget that she was the Emperor's wife, Vessel of the Blood Imperial, and knew only that he wanted more, and more, and more, of this wild and frantic passion.

And when it was over, he knew that, in the scant space of an hour, the course of his life had irrevocably changed. He could stand by no longer. Now, whatever it cost him, he must work against the Emperor, not with him. And if he were to see many more days, he must do it subtly, carefully, deviously, so that neither Olkanno nor that foul Black Mage realized what was happening.

This reckless affair with the Emperor's wife would hardly help him. And the more frequently they met, the more likely they would be discovered eventually. So he must rebuild a little of that self-control he had lost tonight, and try to resist the temptation she offered. And he was certain that although Djeneb had tonight abandoned herself utterly to the needs of her body, in the morning she would acknowledge the vital importance of secrecy, care and discretion. She had a good brain, for a woman, and it was a shame that she had not been born a man.

She was studying him thoughtfully, although the look of wondering disbelief had not yet faded from her eyes. 'I must go,' she said. 'If I am missed—'

'Yes, go.' He kissed her briefly. 'I do not need to tell you to be careful, do I?'

'You do not.' Djeneb sat up, unashamed now of her nakedness. Her eyes, the same greenish-hazel as Ba'alekkt's, smiled suddenly and gloriously. 'Whatever happens to us – *whatever* the consequences – I shall remember this night until I die.'

'And I too, lady.'

'Djeneb. I am *Djeneb*. And Arkun . . . thank you.'

'You have no need to thank me. Not all the pleasure was yours, after all. And I, too, will not forget.' He kissed her again. 'Now go. And take care.'

She put on Tezna's gown, and Tezna's veil. Her face and figure once more concealed, she left him, with the coins he had intended for his informer clutched in her hand. The chief slave obviously guessed what they had been doing all this time, and there was a gleam in his eye as he ushered her out of the Spymaster's apartments.

So late at night, the great sprawling Palace around her was almost deserted, and Djeneb passed only a couple of incurious slaves, replenishing lamp oil. There was no sign on her back proclaiming that she, the Emperor's wife, was now Arkun's lover. No one knew, and no one would know. Even if someone snatched off her veil, her face, outside the Women's Quarters, was unknown. She took on Tezna's servile ways along with her clothes, and scuttled along with her head down, the picture of a meek and submissive woman.

The same young eunuch who had let her out was still on duty at the side-entrance. She slipped him one of her coins, as Tezna had told her to do, and muttered something in response to his bored comment about the noise of the crickets. Then she made her way through the intricate corridors and courtyards until she reached Tezna's room, in the heart of the Women's Quarters.

The slave leaped to her feet as Djeneb entered. 'Did it – did you – what happened, lady? You've been gone so long, I was worried.'

Her mistress pulled off her veil, and smiled. The Fabrizi girl's face blenched in shock, and Djeneb realized that Tezna had never really imagined that she would actually seduce the Spymaster. She whispered in horror, 'Oh, no, lady – you did!'

'I did, and it was the most wonderful thing that has ever happened to me.' Djeneb pulled her slave's gown over her head and stretched like a cat, glorying in the memory of sensual satisfaction. 'Oh, Tezna, don't look so appalled! I am so happy. I never knew, never suspected how marvellous it could be.'

'Oh, Lord of Life preserve us.' The girl made the sign against evil. 'You haven't fallen in love with him?'

'No.' Djeneb picked up her night-robe, lying ready on Tezna's bed, and slipped it on. Now, if Kedrain came in, he would see nothing more than his mistress and her favourite slave having a cosy midnight gossip. 'No. Not yet. Tezna, why did you never try to seduce him?'

'He frightens me,' the girl whispered. 'I never dared – he looks so fierce.'

And of course the gulf between the slave and Spymaster, even if he himself was the son of a slave, would be too great for her to cross. Whereas Djeneb, Vessel of the Blood Imperial, acutely conscious of her exalted status, had managed to find the courage to offer herself.

And he had accepted her. She lay on her soft bed in the dim light, unable to sleep, her blood fizzing with excitement and wonder and fear. Had she really risked her life and gone to the Spymaster's apartments in disguise to proposition him? Had they really made love? And had her abused body responded to his caresses with such astonishing and unexpected ardour?

Her senses, sated and yet still hungry for him, knew the truth. Whatever the consequences of this, she could not regret it. For the first time, she felt absolutely, truly, gloriously alive. And nothing Olkanno could do would ever taint or remove the memory of it from her mind.

Tomorrow, she would have to pretend to be her former self, dull, miserable and cowed. If her husband came to her bed, she would have to behave as if she knew of nothing more than the horrible travesty of love that he would inflict on her.

It might be impossible to prevent her joy shining through, arousing suspicion in all those around her. Perhaps she would never again be able to risk visiting Arkun. Looking back now, the chance she had taken seemed insane. So much could have gone wrong. Nothing had, of course, but good fortune would not always smile on her.

And she wanted his child, to buy her freedom from Olkanno's demands. It might also eventually buy her death, once he had his heir, but she did not dare to look so far ahead. And in any case, Arkun had seemed to believe that sooner or later, the Emperor would be assassinated.

Tomorrow, she thought, *I will go the Palace Temple, and pray to the Lord of Life.* For Kaylo, lover of pleasure in all its many forms, and bringer of luck, would surely look kindly on her. She had a necklace of sapphires from Onnak, of which she was particularly fond. It was very beautiful, and old, and valuable, and she did not want to part with it, but that would make her sacrifice even more acceptable to the god.

She fell asleep at last, smiling, and for the first time since her marriage to Olkanno, the dreadful Horses of the Night did not disturb her rest.

CHAPTER
TWENTY-THREE

The prisoners had all been sacrificed. They had been brought to I'amel's apartments at the darkest hour of the night, drugged, bound and blindfolded. As they were due to be executed anyway, this different, more gruesome but in some ways kinder fate did not disturb their guards. In any case, the Black Mage's reputation was so sinister, and the stench of death lay so strongly in his courtyard, that the gaolers were desperately eager to leave before the necromancer could decide that they, too, might be useful to him.

The foul smells did not trouble I'amel: indeed, he relished the stink. After all, slaughter and decay were the weapons of his trade. The prisoners were killed by slitting their throats, and their blood collected in silver urns. Before or after death, various significant parts of their bodies could be removed. He had a collection of lovingly sharpened instruments for the purpose, their silver handles intricately engraved with the arcane symbols of Ayak, Wolf of Death, and woven about with ancient spells of power. Finally, the unwanted remains of the carcasses were boiled up in a huge iron cauldron kept permanently simmering in what had once been the Governor of Djebb's kitchen. He had been killed by his rebellious subjects, and his family had fled into exile, so Olkanno had given his unoccupied apartments, well away from the busier parts of the Palace, to the Black Mage.

I'amel lived there alone. He had no assistants, no acolytes, no slaves, and wanted none. The work of a Black Mage was repugnant and forbidden even to the Toktel'yans, who only enjoyed the lighter, more frivolous aspects of sorcery. The necromancer regarded them with complete contempt. The creation of Illusions, the mixing of love potions, the manipulation of the weather or the difficult, ambiguous skills necessary to be a successful scryer, were all trivial, futile exercises. Even the Healing of minor illnesses and injuries did not interest him. For he and his kind alone could command real power: the power to Coerce, the power to influence minds, and above all the power to destroy. And of all the Black Mages scattered balefully along the remote western fringes of Jaiya and Lai'is, I'amel unquestionably reigned supreme in skill, and strength, and evil.

The blood lay in the bowl, mixed with a potion of his own recipe to keep it liquid. All around the small, hot room, its window shuttered and its door closed, lights flickered from candles made of rendered human fat, and clenched in the severed hands of dead men. The incantations were over: now the Discovery could begin.

Although I'amel's particular methods gave him great power, there were many times when the bowl failed to show him what he wished to see, or indeed refused to show him anything at all. The sorcerer had learned long ago that he must never give way to his anger. The bowl worked best when unclouded by mortal human emotions. Fear, rage, frustration or impatience, all obscured or distorted the picture. And so his face was quite still, his hands calm, as he gazed down at the gleaming red surface of the prisoners' blood.

At first he saw only the same reflections that would look back at him from a humble puddle of dirty water. Then slowly the image of his face and the lights behind him darkened and disappeared and in its place grew the picture of a wild and alien landscape. I'amel stared at the place in bewilderment. The high bare hills, the distant ranks of mountains, the groves of dark green trees and the broad river flooding through them, were all utterly unfamiliar. Where in all the known world was this?

Too soon, the scene wavered and began to fade. I'amel forced down his annoyance and focused his mind anew. Somewhere out there, inside the Empire or outside it, was a sorcerer who possessed the power to enter men's dreams. It was a skill that he himself had spent long years struggling to attain, and even now it required intense concentration. The thought of a mage strong enough to affect whole populations was at once astonishing and supremely infuriating. It should not be possible, but apparently it was. And I'amel, who had long been accustomed to think of himself as the mightiest sorcerer in all the known world, found it very difficult to accept that there might be one who was greater than he was.

Of course, it was most likely to be a group of wizards, acting together to concentrate their power. Until recently, the sorcerers of Jo'ami would have been the obvious suspects. But since the destruction of the island in a cataclysmic eruption, their legendary School had ceased to exist. In his bowl, I'amel had seen the smoking, ash-covered remnants of Jo'ami, a huge sea-filled gulf separating the two jagged, shredded lumps of rock that was all that remained of it. No one knew why the slumbering demon beneath the island had suddenly broken free of the sorcery which had bound it in harmless impotence for so long. I'amel guessed that the mages of Jo'ami had become too weak, decadent and ignorant to control the monster. It only reaffirmed his high opinion of his powers, and made the appearance of the Flamebearer even more galling.

Another picture appeared in the blood. A man stood on a quayside, looking at the broad brown river that lay in front of him. He was black-skinned, his robes were of richly embroidered silk, and his staff was tipped with silver. I'amel stared down at the scene intently. Was this man a sorcerer, as seemed likely from his garments? And was it the present, or the past?

Another man, magnificent in full armour, came to join the first. Behind him, I'amel could see other soldiers, holding back crowds of civilians waving their arms. Plainly the man in armour was very important: the people of the Empire usually reserved such enthusiasm for their rulers. But which Emperor was this?

I'amel felt his concentration deepen. The image widened a little. He saw a beautifully ornamented and gilded barge, tied up at the quayside. There were other people whom he recognized. Olkanno was there, fat and unmistakable in a long green gown, and another man, wearing dusty riding-clothes. It was Arkun, the Spymaster, but obviously he had not yet achieved his present high rank.

Then the Emperor turned, and I'amel knew his features from the coins still in circulation in the more remote parts of the Empire. This was Ba'alekkt, about to cross the Kefirinn. With a feeling of pleasurable anticipation, the necromancer watched the ninety-ninth Emperor board the boat, the black sorcerer following him. They had to step over something lying in the bottom of the barge, but from this vantage point I'amel couldn't see what it was. A phalanx of trumpeters blew a silent fanfare, the oarsmen pushed away from the quayside, and the glorious conquest of the northern cities had begun.

It lasted for precisely thirty-four strokes of the oars. The river Kefirinn was wide, deep and fast-flowing, but even so there was no apparent reason why the boat should suddenly rock violently in mid-stream. Then, so abruptly that it took the necromancer by surprise, although he knew what would happen, the barge flipped over, tipping all its occupants into the water.

Ba'alekkt, weighed down by his marvellous steel armour, sank like a stone. Only the heads of the rowers and the black sorcerer remained above the surface, swimming for safety.

So who had been responsible for the disaster? The sorcerer, undoubtedly. I'amel watched until the man staggered ashore on the Minassan, enemy bank. The rescue boat came to pick him up, but the old man turned away and began to trudge northwards, forsaking the Empire.

Al'Kalyek, Court Sorcerer to Ba'alekkt, and to his father before him. He was certainly a renegade, and probably an assassin. If he had slain the Emperor, he would not scruple to incite rebellion in the aftermath of murder. True, I'amel had heard no indication that his predecessor was unusually powerful, nor, until now, that Al'Kalyek had been responsible for Ba'alekkt's death. But he had been in the right place at the right time, and the necromancer had no hesitation in blaming the old man.

Al'Kalyek, it seemed, was the Flamebearer, or so the bowl implied. I'amel was no green novice, to trust everything his scrying revealed, but intuition told him that he was right. He had asked to see the Flamebearer, and he had been shown Al'Kalyek.

So where did the old sorcerer now live? In that bare bleak landscape? But it could lie anywhere in the steppe lands north of the Empire, in Gulkesh or Zithirian or around the Kerentan Sea. He must ask the bowl again, to locate Al'Kalyek more precisely.

This time, he spent much longer preparing his mind for the task. It was by now deepest night outside, and the candles had burned down half their length, but paltry afflictions like tiredness had never troubled I'amel, and besides, he had taken three times his normal dose of Annatal to help him find the Flamebearer. The feelings of elation and omnipotence lay within him still. He chanted the spell of finding to the bowl, over and over again. *Find him. Find Al'Kalyek. Show him to me. Tell me where he is.* Then, as he felt the familiar tingling surge of power through his fingers, he drew his flat hands away from the surface of the blood.

And the picture was there immediately. Hardly daring to move, I'amel cautiously leaned forward, the better to see.

The image was so bright that he blinked. It depicted a tropical shoreline, fringed by dazzling white sand, and shaded by leaning palms. Children ran and played in the surf, while a group of dark-skinned men launched a small boat from the beach. I'amel frowned. This was emphatically not the chilly north.

A tiny child ran down to the water's edge. Walking slowly behind, leaning on a stick, came an old man. He wore the flowing loose robes affected by most sorcerers, but in plain dark cotton. He bent, picked up a stone, and skimmed it across the water. Either there was magic involved, or he was uncommonly skilful, for it bounced more than ten times over the waves before sinking.

The child laughed, and clapped its hands. The old man, smiling, lifted up his staff. A spherical object appeared on the sand. Without a touch, it began to bounce by itself. The child chased it along the edge of the shore, joined by the other children. But all the time, the ball remained tantalizingly just out of their reach.

It was, unquestionably, Al'Kalyek, though he was much slower and older than in the earlier image. I'amel's lip curled in contempt. Children's games! Surely this man was not the Flamebearer.

The scrying bowl grew dark, as if offended by its master's anger. With a curse, I'amel swept it off the table. The silver clanged on the stones, and the crimson blood splattered across the floor and walls in great congealing gobbets.

As so often when his rage briefly overmastered him, the Black Mage regretted the impulse as soon as it was past. But there was more blood, and he could try again. And at least he knew now that Al'Kalyek was living on one of the islands of the Archipelago – Annatal, perhaps, or Onnak. Somewhere in the Spymaster's offices in the Old Palace there would be files on him, bulging with information on the former Court Sorcerer, the important alongside the trivial. Olkanno might even know where he was. And I'amel intended to make sure that his master realized the folly of keeping such a dangerous enemy alive, in his own dominions, for so long.

He began to blow out the candles, one by one. Outside, dawn must already be slipping into the sky, and I'amel was a creature of darkness. He left the room, shading his eyes against the light outside, and made his way to his resting-chamber, on the other side of the courtyard. Tonight, he would tell Olkanno what he had learned. The Emperor would be overjoyed to be told that the Flamebearer had been found so easily. And now, with I'amel's information and assistance, they could locate Al'Kalyek, and kill him.

'Are you certain?'

'It was his image in the bowl, Imperial Majesty.'

'But you have never met him. How can you be so sure? Tell me exactly what you saw.'

'I saw a wharf, Imperial Majesty, by a broad brown river. On the quayside stood a young man in steel armour, with a garland of crimson flowers round his neck.'

Olkanno's eyes narrowed. 'Yes?'

'I saw a much older man, black-skinned, with white hair. His robes were dark blue, with a little silver embroidery. That is the man I took to be Al'Kalyek.'

The Emperor's face was intent. 'Continue.'

'I also saw the Spymaster, Arkun, though he was dressed in garments more humble than those he wears now. And I saw you, Imperial Majesty. You stood with Arkun and watched as the Emperor and his sorcerer embarked in the royal barge to cross the river. And I saw the boat overturned, and Ba'alekkt lost within the water. That was undeniably the work of sorcery, Imperial Majesty, and since Al'Kalyek was on the barge, and immediately afterwards deserted the Empire in favour of its enemies, he must be guilty of the Emperor Ba'alekkt's murder – and must also be the Flamebearer.'

'But he was not the only sorcerer present,' Olkanno said softly. 'Tell me, I'amel – who was on the boat before it sank?'

'The rowers, Imperial Majesty. Al'Kalyek. And the Emperor.'

'No one else?'

The necromancer turned his inward eye upon the image he had seen in the bowl. He said at last, 'No, Imperial Majesty.'

'You are wrong. There was also a prisoner in the boat. I advised the Emperor not to carry him over, but he insisted – and paid for his folly with his life. And that prisoner was a very powerful sorcerer indeed – the son of Ansaryon, King of Zithirian.'

'I have heard of him,' I'amel said. 'But I did not know that he was drowned with the Emperor. Was it his magic that overturned the boat? If he was bound, he must have known that he would die as well.'

'Certainly the man was bound and helpless. Perhaps it was Al'Kalyek, then. I do not remember him objecting to the prisoner's presence in the barge. I would guess that Al'Kalyek saw the opportunity to get rid of a dangerous rival, and kill Ba'alekkt at the same time. That was why he deserted the Empire.'

'And where is he now? I saw him in the bowl, walking along a beach of white sand, fringed with palm trees.'

'Did you?' Olkanno smiled. 'Your bowl is exceptionally accurate, I'amel. He returned to the Empire about three years ago. One of Arkun's agents heard that he was living quite openly with his brother on the southern side of the island of Onnak. I suppose the old fool thinks we're no longer interested in him.'

'But he is wrong,' said the Black Mage, smiling, and his pointed teeth gleamed in the lamplight. 'The bowl revealed him to me. He is the

Flamebearer. He is responsible for the rebellions in Djebb and Tatht and Lai'is. Kill him, and your problems end with his life.'

'Are you sure?' Olkanno rose to his feet, and stared intently at I'amel. 'I know little of your arts, my friend, but I have learned enough to be certain that it is most unwise to take what the bowl reveals at face value. Al'Kalyek was never famous for his power. He had an undeserved reputation for wisdom and honesty, he was experienced and skilful, but was his sorcery strong enough to enter the dreams of an entire province full of people? Is yours?'

'I have never attempted such a feat, Majesty,' I'amel said, rather defensively. 'But I am certain that it would be within my power. My sorcery, however, is without doubt superior to any other's.'

'Including Al'Kalyek's?'

'Of course, Imperial Majesty.'

'Then he may not be powerful enough to be the Flamebearer.'

'But, Imperial Majesty, as I have already told you – I asked the bowl to show me the Flamebearer, and I was shown Al'Kalyek. You yourself have testified to the accuracy of what I saw. I then asked it to show me where he is now, and once more the bowl showed the truth, although I had no idea at the time that he was on Onnak.' A note of annoyance had entered the necromancer's sibilant voice. 'And if Al'Kalyek is not the Flamebearer, then who is? The wizards of Jo'ami are destroyed. The son of the King of Zithirian is dead. In all the known world, I have heard of no one else. The power comes from the east, and is Onnak not in the east?'

'Your geography is faulty. The island lies *south*-east.'

'A minor detail, Imperial Majesty. It *must* be Al'Kalyek. Seize him, kill him, and the Flamebearer will be extinguished for ever, and the Empire will be saved.'

'But how?' Olkanno demanded. 'How shall I seize him? He is a sorcerer, after all. If he has the power you claim, then he must also be able to evade capture.'

'But if he does not suspect capture, Imperial Majesty, then he will not be able to evade it until too late. And then,' said I'amel, with his wolfish smile, 'I shall take the greatest pleasure in destroying him.'

Olkanno's face was suddenly hostile. 'No. I want him brought back to Toktel'yi.'

I'amel stared at him, his unnaturally smooth brow distorted by a frown. 'Imperial Majesty, that is lunacy! If he escapes, or tries to harm you—'

'If he is truly your inferior in power, then you will be able to protect me,' Olkanno pointed out coldly. 'And if you have over-estimated your own abilities, my friend, then you will not be able to capture him, let alone kill him. I do not believe that he alone is the Flamebearer. But I suspect that he may be acting together with other sorcerers. If you kill him out of hand, the others will merely continue without him. And I do not have the time, or the patience, to sit by while you and your precious bowl search for a dozen sorcerers who may be scattered through all the provinces of the Empire and beyond. I want you to find him, and seize him, and bring him here to me. And do not glower at me, necromancer. I can break you as easily as I made you. I will tolerate you and your kind only for so long as you can be useful to me, and no further. Do you understand me? Sorcerers are not invulnerable. They are not immune to capture, or torture, or death. I expect your Wolf is looking forward to devouring you.'

I'amel's eyes seemed to glow red in their sockets. He hissed softly, and lifted his staff. Olkanno clapped his hands, and at once the door behind the Black Mage burst open, and four soldiers stood on the threshold, spears pointed menacingly.

Either the necromancer's power was not so great as he pretended, or he realized the folly of harming the man who had raised him from obscurity and given him such power. He let his staff drop, and bowed to the floor in the humblest obeisance, that of slave to master. 'I am forever yours to command, Imperial Majesty.'

Olkanno smiled, and gestured to his guard. With a clashing salute, they left the room. When the door had shut behind him, he looked down at I'amel, still spread-eagled on the floor, his black robes spread about him like a puddle of night. 'Good. You have seen sense. You understand what I want you to do?'

'Yes, Imperial Majesty.'

'Even so, I shall make my wishes absolutely clear, so that there can be no mistake. I want Al'Kalyek brought back to Toktel'yi, alive, and unharmed, and harmless. One I have him confined here, it will be easy to extract any information of value from him. I believe that withholding his supply of Annatal will be the easiest method?'

'That is indeed so, Imperial Majesty. But he will inevitably die.'

'I know that. I want him dead. But not before he has told me everything I could ever wish to know about the Flamebearer. You will help me, I'amel. I do not imagine you will flinch from the task. And then you may, if you wish, take his body. Will it be useful to you?'

The necromancer's eyes gleamed greedily. 'Indeed it will, Imperial Majesty. I have never had the opportunity to use the flesh and blood of a sorcerer before.'

'Excellent. You will leave on tomorrow's morning tide. There is a fast courier ship ready to take you and Arkun to Onnak.'

'Arkun? The Spymaster?'

'Yes, I will order him to go with you. He has the skill and cunning necessary to arrange the capture. It was he who seized the Zithiriani sorcerer, before Ba'alekkt's death. After that feat, securing Al'Kalyek should present no problems. He will not like working with you, but he will carry out my orders with unquestioning efficiency. He will make a full report to me on his return. And I expect him to return, I'amel – Arkun, and Al'Kalyek, and you. Do you understand me?'

'I understand you very well, Imperial Majesty,' said the necromancer, and smiled. 'Have no fear. Before the month is out, I will bring him to you.'

'Good.' Olkanno smiled in return. 'And remember – the rewards for success will be very great. But so will the penalty for failure. Now you may leave, and make ready. A litter will come for you at midnight, to take you to the ship. And I need hardly emphasize the need for extreme secrecy. No one must know of this enterprise, least of all our quarry. Arkun will bring you near enough to seize him. I shall enjoy meeting him again – and I look forward to watching him suffer.'

'So shall I, Imperial Majesty,' said I'amel. 'But still more shall I look forward to his death.'

The courier ship *Flying Fish* slunk after dark into the great bay on the southern coast of the main island of Onnak. She carried no lights, but her Captain, one of the best in the Toktel'yan Navy, knew these waters well, and was skilled in night navigation. She dropped anchor two miles off shore, on the eastern side of the bay, and waited.

During the ten days of the voyage, threading through the thousand crowded islands of the Scatterlings, Arkun had been forced to share I'amel's company, a situation he found barely endurable. The man's appearance alone was enough to set worms crawling over his skin, and the very thought of the necromancer's horrible practices revolted him. The man stank of rotting flesh and old blood. He had brought three heavy wooden chests on board with him, each one hung about with a cloud of hopeful flies, and his cabin looked and smelt like a charnel-house. He claimed such foul things gave him power, but Arkun was sceptical. The most powerful sorcerer he had ever encountered had had no need of these horrors. And the thought of the wise and gentle Al'Kalyek in the clutches of the Black Mage turned his stomach.

If he had been given the choice, he would never have come on this mission. But Olkanno had ordered him to accompany the necromancer, making it clear to his Spymaster that he did not trust I'amel. And Arkun hoped that he could somehow warn Al'Kalyek, or otherwise save him from the terrible fate awaiting him in Toktel'yi. He knew, though, that the Emperor did not trust him either, and had probably told I'amel to watch him. That was worrying, for the Black Mage was quite capable of making some malicious false accusation of disobedience or treachery. In the end, Olkanno might have to choose which of his minions to believe. And Arkun knew that the survivor would be the one most useful to him, not necessarily the one who spoke the truth.

Even though he loathed I'amel, he was glad to leave Toktel'yi for a while. Djeneb had now visited his apartments three times, and he knew that the risk of discovery was increasing. Away from her, he found it easy to deny to himself that the affair had any importance. Each time she appeared, disguised in Tezna's clothes, he vowed to send her away: and each time his rebellious desires overruled his innate and extreme sense of caution. Sooner or later, if they continued this madness, they would undoubtedly be found out. But he could not resist the temptation she offered so readily.

And besides, he liked her, he admired her courage and her endurance, and he felt sorry for her. He did not know if her feelings for him had progressed beyond mere lust, or whether she still viewed him as a weapon of vengeance against her husband. Their meetings were almost silent, for nothing else mattered but the urgent satisfaction of their mutual need. He did not want to look any deeper, or to answer the inconvenient questions that sometimes haunted his mind. Soon, he must end the affair. Not now, but when they next met. And perhaps by the time he returned from Onnak, they would both have come to their senses.

Since the mere thought of her was enough to fill his thoughts with lust, it would not be easy. For many years, he had ignored or suppressed his natural desires in his single-minded climb to the top of his profession. He had kept a concubine for a while, until he had found her rifling his papers. The greedy, self-indulgent decadence of so many other men was an example to be deplored, not emulated. He lived alone, save for his slaves, and occasionally visited a brothel where he was not known. The encounters there were anonymous and impersonal. He knew the techniques, but had little experience of intense, emotional sex. And Djeneb, confused, desperate, astonished by her own capacity for pleasure, had shown him a glimpse of what lay behind the door he had always kept bolted and barred.

Arkun prayed that I'amel would never turn his scrying and spying in his direction. If any sorcerer managed to enter his head, his guilt would be obvious. But the Black Mage's attention was concentrated on the imminent capture of Al'Kalyek.

In the warm night, under a myriad brilliance of stars, he leaned on the rail of the *Flying Fish* and gazed at the low black shape of Onnak, stretched across his vision. The moon was in its dark phase, so no light would betray the courier ship as it rode at anchor. He had planned this very carefully, with the aid of Al'Kalyek's file, taken from the document stores in his offices in the Old Palace. Within the worn and bulging leather folder lay all the papers charting the sorcerer's long life. The record of his birth on Onnak, seventy-five years ago; the details of his diploma from the prestigious Toktel'yi School of Wizards, with especial commendations for Healing and Illusions; notes of his first post, as resident sorcerer to one of the wealthiest families in the Empire; the invitation to return to his old School to teach; his rise to Chief Healer, then Deputy Principal, and finally the Headship; his appointment as Court Sorcerer by the Emperor Djamal, at the age of forty-six, the youngest incumbent for over a century; confirmation of his position by Djamal's son Ba'alekkt; and last of all, a terse note of his defection. There were also several confidential investigations, carried out by agents at various stages of his career, and, most recently, the details of his present location on his native island, Onnak.

Arkun had studied these very closely, in conjunction with the most accurate map he could find. Al'Kalyek now resided with his brother, a fisherman a few years his junior, and his wife and family. As was common on the island, the household contained several generations and numbered nearly thirty people. Since his return, the old sorcerer had lived quietly, doing no more than a little Healing. The village wizard, however, was an elderly and bitter man who thought the interloper threatened his livelihood, and he had been only too pleased to give Arkun's agent every detail of his exalted rival that might be damaging.

So Arkun knew, though he had never set foot on the island before, that the lights flickering straight ahead of him were those of Pekken, Al'Kalyek's village: that the houses were made of wood and reeds, and scattered haphazardly above the beach: that they were built on stilts to raise them above the high tides and storm waters that regularly surged up this coast: and that the one in which his quarry lived was close to the beach, and on the eastern edge of the village.

He had also noted that Al'Kalyek's brother had spent many years breeding his own strain of Onnak hounds, famous for their hunting ability, and also for their ferocity. When the last report had been made, two years previously, no fewer than seven dogs of various ages had shared, and guarded, the household.

I'amel knew it too, and had, so he assured Arkun, the ideal solution. Deliberately, the Spymaster had not asked for details. He was not squeamish, but something about the necromancer's manner informed him that the answer would not be pleasant.

And besides, if I'amel was wrong, and the dogs gave the warning that might save Al'Kalyek, then that would solve Arkun's ethical dilemma very neatly.

Below him, the ship's skiff had been lowered. Four sailors climbed down the ladder, and began to tie muffling-cloths to the rowlocks. Arkun looked round for the sorcerer. A dark amorphous shape and a suffocating waft of decay announced his arrival.

'You're late,' the Spymaster said, making no secret of his dislike. 'If we are to be gone by daybreak, we must hurry.'

'No need. They are all asleep, and ready for us,' said the Black Mage, and pushed past him to the head of the ladder. Grimly suppressing his sense of sick anger and dread, Arkun followed him down. The skiff cast off, and the oarsmen began to row softly through the calmly slumbering sea towards Onnak.

Under orders, no one spoke. There was no noise save for the tiny, burbling ripple of water against the skiff's hull, and the gentle surf against the distant shore. In the village, nothing stirred: no voices, no barks. Save for the faint lambent light of the lanterns, there was no indication that the place even existed. Stupidly, Arkun found himself wishing that Al'Kalyek had gone away, even that he was dead.

The Black Mage hissed softly, and raised his head. The rowers stopped, and quietly shipped their oars. The boat lay on the surface of the sea, rising and falling gently as the long deep swells passed rhythmically beneath her. Arkun peered at the shore, wondering what I'amel was planning.

He opened his mouth to ask why they had paused, and felt the sorcery prickle the bare skin of his arms. I'amel had neither moved nor spoken, but something had passed from his mind to the shore. The hairs rose on the back of Arkun's neck, and he arranged the fingers of the hand which the sorcerer could not see into the universal sign against evil. He had never been superstitious, but he had never felt the full force of magic before, stirring the air as sharp and deadly and accurate as an arrow.

His eyes had adjusted to the darkness now. Something moved on the pale strip of beach, which must still be two or three hundred paces away. He couldn't tell if it were man or animal: all he could see was the movement.

Over the sea came a new sound. Something had entered the water. But he could still make out shapes crossing the sand. And the Black Mage's power continued to tingle against his cringing skin.

The thing in the water was coming closer. He could hear regular splashes, and heavy panting breaths. I'amel turned to him and smiled. 'See? I said I would deal with the dogs.'

The first of the Onnak hounds, black or brown like most of its kind, was swimming towards the skiff. Arkun could make out the white water around its flailing paws, and the gleam of its fangs, no sharper than the sorcerer's. He whispered in alarm. 'What in Olyak's name are you doing?'

'No need for concern, Spymaster,' said I'amel, sibilantly menacing. 'Watch.'

The animal made no attempt to approach the boat: indeed, it did not even appear to notice that it was there. It swam laboriously past, so close that Arkun could have reached out and grasped its studded collar, and on, towards the open sea. After it came another, and another, and another.

'They will swim on until they become exhausted and drown,' said the necromancer with pride. 'No other sorcerer in the Empire can command animals. I alone possess the skill and the power to do this.'

There were eight dogs, all following a trail, or an order, that only they could understand. Arkun had imagined a method of disposal far more dramatic and gruesome. Yet there was something very terrible about the spellbound animals, swimming so strenuously and with such determination to their doom.

'And now,' said I'amel triumphantly, 'for the man.'

At his signal, the sailors began to row once more towards the shore. The tingle of sorcery still flowed from the necromancer, but Arkun could sense that it was now travelling out to sea, laying the trail for the hounds to follow. A blinding flash of lethal magic would have been a kinder method of destruction, but kindness was not a feeling that had ever entered I'amel's head. And at least this method ensured secrecy.

But sorcerers could detect when power had been used. Surely the summoning of his brother's dogs would have woken Al'Kalyek?

Even as the thought occurred to him, I'amel hissed again. Once more, the rowers laid down their oars, and an eerie silence descended.

Arkun stared intently at the shore, his heart pounding and the sweat cold on this brow.

I'amel lifted his arms and stretched them towards Onnak. The skiff lay much closer now, just clear of the waves breaking gently on to the beach, and any movement across the empty, glimmering strip of sand would have been instantly visible. But there was no sign or sound of any disturbance at all.

The surge of power from the man beside him caught Arkun by surprise. He gasped involuntarily, and crossed his hands over his head, while the air around him seemed to vibrate with the overwhelming strength of I'amel's sorcery. Only a brush of wind had served to lure the hounds to their doom. This was the command for Al'Kalyek.

The Black Mage began to chant in a whisper, his voice rising and falling like the keening of some strange wild animal. Arkun felt sick with horror, sick with dread. The sensations of power filled his ears and swamped his mind, yet he was only an onlooker. What must be happening to the recipient?

Eventually, he found the strength and courage to raise his head. The rowers were still crouched over their oars. Briefly, he wondered how they would be able to return to the *Flying Fish* if the sailors were immobilized by terror, and I'amel was fully occupied in keeping his captive under control.

Someone was coming down the beach, moving with the dazed, shambling gait of a sleepwalker. I'amel's chant rose louder. Despite the desperate urge to hide his face, his eyes, his mind, Arkun made himself watch as the Black Mage's prey waded through the gentle waves, his night-robe trailing in the water, and came right up to the boat.

The necromancer hissed in triumph. He barked an order, and two of the sailors, wrenched from their fear, balanced the boat while the others dragged Al'Kalyek, unresisting, on board. The chanting did not resume, and the sorcery had suddenly diminished to a level that was almost bearable. I'amel crouched over the man lying in the bottom of the boat, placed a hand on each side of his head, and muttered something. Arkun felt a last flare of power, and then nothing.

'He will sleep for as long as I wish,' said the Black Mage. He gave a gleeful cackle of laughter. 'That was even easier than I expected. He is a weak man, old and tired, and no match for my overwhelmingly superior power. With a combination of drugs and sorcery, I can keep him docile until we reach Toktel'yi.' He grinned evilly at Arkun. 'Well, Spymaster? Are you prepared to recognize a power greater than your own?'

'With such an example before me,' Arkun said, his voice giving no indication of his loathing for the man beside him, 'how can I ever think otherwise?'

And he knew that I'amel's vainglorious crow of triumph would haunt his dreams for all the life that was left to him.

CHAPTER
TWENTY-FOUR

Al'Kalyek, once sorcerer to two Emperors and now a humble citizen of Onnak, woke to darkness. For a few moments he had no idea where he was. In his room in his brother's house, perhaps? But he could not hear the soft, rhythmic hush of the sea. In his apartment in the Imperial Palace? But he had long ago left Toktel'yi, and besides, there were always lights and lanterns showing through the window-grilles: no place within that vast complex of buildings was ever completely dark.

Then certain unpleasant external sensations began to infiltrate his consciousness. He was bound hand and foot to a hard surface, probably a table, and a most unpleasant smell of decay filled his nostrils.

Memory washed back. The summons, breaking into his sleep, overpowering all independent thought, destroying his will. The long walk in obedience to that awful command, when he had been aware of what was happening to him, but utterly unable to fight it. And then the sensation of absolute, hideous evil enveloping him as he lay in the boat, blotting out the last despairing vestiges of conscious thought.

Now he was no longer under Coercion, but his body would not obey his will, and his powers of sorcery seemed lost. He could not even prevent himself from breathing the foul air around him. He was forced to lie helpless amidst his own ordure, and pray to Kaylo, Lord of Life, that this nightmare, worse than nightmare, would soon be ended: and then to Olyak, the Dark God, for an easy death.

It was futile, for he knew now where he was, and who must have power over him. But still there was a chance that one of the Twin Gods would listen, and take pity on him.

Eventually he slept, and was woken by loud, confident voices. Al'Kalyek lay still, listening for a clue to his fate.

'The effects of the drugs should be wearing off a little, Imperial Majesty.' The voice was harsh, sibilant and provincial, and he did not recognize it, but the cruelty of evil, barely concealed, froze his heart.

'Excellent,' said Olkanno, once Spymaster, now Emperor, a man whom Al'Kalyek had always loathed and mistrusted. He had achieved the Onyx Throne by stepping on the corpses of his victims, and the old man knew that he could expect no pity or kindness from his former adversary.

But why? Why had they captured him now? Olkanno would never waste time and effort dragging Al'Kalyek to Toktel'yi purely for revenge, or as a punishment for his defection. The Emperor must want something from him: and from the sound of it, he would very soon discover what it was.

The light came from a half-shuttered lantern, but after so long in the dark it was still bright enough to hurt his eyes. He screwed them tight shut, and heard Olkanno laughing. 'By the time we have finished with you, old man, you'll have been hurt by a lot worse than a light.'

Al'Kalyek hoped that he would have the strength to endure the agony, and the courage to deny Olkanno whatever he sought. But he knew himself too well. He was an old man, and for most of his life he had been accustomed to luxury, comfort and respect. Nothing like this had ever happened to him before, and he was not prepared for it.

'Now, my friend Al'Kalyek – *now* we can begin.'

Reluctantly, he opened his eyes once more. Olkanno had not altered very much in five years, although his formal gown, in Imperial turquoise and scarlet, was considerably more splendid than any he had worn as Spymaster, and the jewelled hawk pectoral of the Empire lay across his chest. No splendour, however, could diminish his corpulence, or add hair to his balding scalp, or remove the black greedy glitter of cruelty in his eyes.

'Let me introduce you,' said the Emperor softly, 'to your successor, I'amel of Lai'is. Have you heard of him?'

Al'Kalyek tried to move his head, failed, and managed a whisper. 'No.'

'You should,' said the sibilant voice he had heard outside. 'You will remember me now for the rest of your life, brief and agonizing though it will be.'

'It was I'amel who summoned you from your bed,' said Olkanno. 'I'amel's power and I'amel's drugs have kept you helpless. I am surprised that you do not know of him, old man, for his sorcery is certainly far superior to yours.'

A head moved into Al'Kalyek's limited vision. Eerily lit by the single lantern, it was sharply shadowed, and the skin was stretched so tightly over the bone beneath that it seemed more skull than face. But the eyes gleamed redly, deep within their sockets, and the mouth opened, revealing yellowing, pointed teeth.

'Beside me,' it said, 'you are no more than an untalented apprentice. So tell me, before you die – are you the Flamebearer?'

Al'Kalyek stared at him. His chest move raggedly, and a peculiar sound issued from his half-paralysed throat.

'Answer me!' the other sorcerer hissed, thrusting his face closer to his prisoner.

'He is laughing,' Olkanno observed. 'Interesting. I wonder what he finds so amusing about his situation. Could it be the certain inconsistency in your reasoning, I'amel? After all, if he is truly the weak and feeble old man you claim, how can he possibly be the Flamebearer?'

The Black Mage banged his staff on the floor of the cell. 'I will *not* be ridiculed! Those who mock me live to regret it!'

'And those who cross me, do not live,' said Olkanno gently. He bent over Al'Kalyek, and picked up his hand. 'Such a useful part of ourselves, is it not? What would we do without it? And of course each finger is invaluable. If the thumb were to be lost, for example . . . or even the smallest digit – or more.' His fingers stroked the black, wrinkled skin with lingering, hideous tenderness. 'Are you the Flamebearer, old man?'

'No,' Al'Kalyek said.

'Quite sure, old man? After all, why lose a finger to no purpose? I have my instruments here with me, and they have been freshly honed especially for you. Tell me the truth now, and I will not use them – yet. You have heard of the Flamebearer?'

'Yes.'

'Of course you have. The whole world has. Some have seen him, too, in their dreams. Have you?'

'No.'

'Beware, old man. Tell me the truth. You were always famous for it – although as I recall, the honesty you proclaimed so self-righteously was only a mask to hide your cunning. Through your incompetence, or ignorance, or more likely your own devious plotting, the Emperor Ba'alekkt was killed. Am I right?'

'Yes.'

'Do not look so anxious. I bear no grudge for that. After all, I might not now occupy the Onyx Throne – without you, I would have been forced to kill Ba'alekkt myself. And he was a far more difficult quarry than the idle, debauched fools I actually did despatch once he was out of the way. Who knows what might have happened? He could even have realized my stratagem, and made sure that I was killed before I could kill him. So I am grateful to you, old man, and to that strange young sorcerer too. Did he tip up the boat, or was it you?'

'No,' Al'Kalyek whispered. 'Him.'

'Really? That is not what I'amel thought, when he looked in his bowl. I'amel is more powerful than you, old man. Do you acknowledge his superiority?'

'Yes.'

'Do you also know why he is superior?'

Almost imperceptibly, the old man nodded.

'Yes, he is a Black Mage. He has sold himself to the Wolf of Death, whom those uncouth provincials on our western borders seem to prefer to our more civilized Olyak. I have employed him for six months, and in that time he has nearly emptied every prison in Toktel'yi. Indeed, the people are growing resentful because there are so few public executions these days. I'amel likes to use fresh blood, fresh meat, fresh and supple skin. Like a peasant's pig, no part is wasted – save only the screams.' Olkanno chuckled softly. 'He is very much looking forward to using you – perhaps even before your death. That should be interesting, old man. And remember – you will certainly die. Very soon, your life will end here, on this table. Whether your death is quick or slow, easy or hard, peaceful or agonizing, depends on you. Do you understand me?'

'Yes.'

The Emperor smiled. 'Good. The drugs have rendered you helpless. You have not been given any Annatal since your arrival here, so already your power will be failing. Have you discovered that already?'

Al'Kalyek made no answer. Olkanno's fingers found the pressure point on the inside of his wrist, and squeezed hard. The pain was so severe that he gasped, and flinched.

'Is your power dying, old man?' Olkanno put his face down very close to Al'Kalyek's. 'Tell me, before I begin on your fingers.'

He could have answered, and saved himself, and them, much trouble. But the old sorcerer had come to a decision. He knew he would regret it: he knew it would inevitably lead him to a prolonged and dreadful death. But he was not this man's helpless victim, not yet.

Deliberately, with as much strength as he could muster within his enfeebled mind and body, he spat in the Emperor's face.

Arkun had never visited I'amel's rooms in the Palace, and had absolutely no wish to do so. But an Imperial summons was impossible to ignore, so he left his own courtyard and made his way, with extreme and apprehensive reluctance, to the necromancer's lair on the outer fringes of the Palace. He had hoped that he would be able to avoid taking any part in the destruction of Al'Kalyek, but it seemed that his master wanted him to be present. With luck, the reason for this peremptory command was no more than that. But if Olkanno had somehow discovered that he and Djeneb were lovers . . .

Since his return from Onnak, two days previously, she had not visited him. His rational self was glad that she might at last have come to her senses. But his body yearned for her, as it had never longed for anyone before.

He cast her voluptuous image from his mind, and entered the necromancer's courtyard to find out, although he did not wish to know, what Olkanno and I'amel were doing to Al'Kalyek.

The shuddering, moaning, blood-soaked huddle of rags on the table in the sorcerer's shuttered room bore no relation to the dignified Court Sorcerer, nor to the comatose old man he had brought from Onnak. Arkun felt the bile rise in his throat, and swallowed it grimly down. Let either of those two monsters of cruelty know that he found them and their activities so grossly repulsive, and his own life would be worth less than Al'Kalyek's.

'What progress?' he enquired, when Olkanno had finished cutting.

I'amel turned and studied the Spymaster. Though it took all his self-control, Arkun did not avoid his gaze. He felt unseen fingers touch his mind, and instinctively erected a defensive bulwark of hostility.

The Black Mage was quite accustomed to hatred and revulsion, but the red gleam in his hooded eyes was a warning. He said in his hissing whisper, 'Not long now. He is not the Flamebearer, that is certain, but he knows who it is, and he is still trying to protect him, the fool! Why bother? Death is inevitable – we have given him no Annatal for two days now.'

'Then you had better hurry up,' Arkun pointed out. 'Even if he's stronger than you think, you've only got a day or two more before he dies, surely.'

'We are very close,' Olkanno said. His bare arms were red to the elbows, and his brown, plump, sweating face was streaked with blood. Next to his victim lay his instruments, many of the gleaming blades blunt and crusted. 'He is a stubborn old fool, but he will tell us soon. And if he proves still so intransigent, he will surely reveal everything once the delirium of Annatal starvation affects him. Then I'amel will be able to enter his mind. So far, he has managed to defend it.' There was a note of reluctant admiration in his voice. 'Who would have thought that the old man would prefer *this* to confession?'

'Let me try, Imperial Majesty,' said Arkun. 'Perhaps a change of method . . .'

Olkanno studied him thoughtfully. 'Are you becoming squeamish suddenly, Spymaster? That is not why I pay you so handsomely, for a slave's bastard.'

The insult no longer affected Arkun, save to increase his secret contempt for the Emperor. 'No,' he said quietly. 'But sometimes the change to an apparently kinder and more sympathetic face may persuade the most obstinate mind to crack.'

'Perhaps.' Olkanno frowned, and glanced down at the quivering wreckage beneath his hands. 'But not in this case. I intend to be the means of his destruction – he will *not* defeat me! You may watch, and listen, and see how it should be done.'

For what seemed like a lifetime of horror, Arkun was forced to witness the lovingly crafted torture and mutilation of a man whom he had always respected. He watched as a Healer was brought in to restore a little strength and consciousness to the prisoner, so that he might survive the next agonies. And he prayed so desperately that Olyak might take Al'Kalyek away from this unspeakable torment, that he felt the bloodstained walls must surely give tongue to his entreaties.

At last the man on the table shuddered convulsively, and then lay still and silent. Arkun stared at him, hoping that his pleas had been answered. Olkanno, a look of fury on his face, flung his knife down on the floor. 'No! No, I will not have it! Bring him back, I'amel – you're the Wolf's creature, you bring him back!'

The Black Mage swept forward, chanting, his arms raised and his sleeves spreading out like two monstrous dark wings. Arkun, his gorge rising, took several steps back, and nearly slipped on the congealing blood puddled sullenly over the floor. *Keep him, Olyak*, he urged silently. *Keep him free from pain now in your halls, and treat him kindly.*

I'amel gave a wild screech of triumph. 'I have him! I have his spirit! Who is he? Who is the Flamebearer? *Answer me!*'

No sound came from Al'Kalyek's distorted and bleeding mouth. The necromancer hung over him like a hovering falcon ready for the kill. Arkun felt something stir the thick reeking around him, and then at last it was gone.

I'amel sank down on the floor, his breath coming in harsh gasps. Olkanno strode round the table and stood over his sorcerer. 'Well?' he demanded.

'He is dead.' I'amel began to cackle with insane glee. 'Dead, dead, dead!'

As Arkun thanked Olyak for his mercy, the Emperor reached down, grabbed a fistful of the Black Mage's filthy robes, and hauled him roughly to his feet. 'Answer me, you stinking, verminous wizard, or I'll carve you up myself. *What did he tell you?*'

I'amel shook himself free and the scarlet menace in his eyes made Arkun shiver suddenly. 'You cannot control *me* so easily, Imperial Majesty,' he said. 'You would do well to remember my power, and the reason for it.'

'And *you* would do well to remember that I am Emperor of all Toktel'yi!'

'But not for much longer, if the Flamebearer has his way.' I'amel straightened his tattered garments, and glared at Olkanno. 'Unless you find him, your days are numbered – and the number of them is not very great.'

'Who *is* he?'

'Al'Kalyek did not know.'

The Emperor gave a great howl of fury. 'I don't believe you! Tell me what he told you!'

I'amel stared at his master, and the look of contemptuous malevolence on his face made even Olkanno recoil. 'He *told* me nothing. But I entered his mind as it fled from his body, and found certain . . . thoughts of interest. He did not *know* who the Flamebearer is, but he had guessed.'

'Who? Who? Tell me now!' Olkanno was almost incandescent with fury and frustration.

'He thought that the Flamebearer was the man who killed Ba'alekkt. The son of the King of Zithirian.'

There was a stunned silence. Then the Emperor said hoarsely, 'That is not possible. The man is dead. I saw him die myself.'

'Did you find his body?'

'No, we did not – but neither did we find Ba'alekkt's, and no one has ever suggested that he survived. The Kefirinn likes to keep hold of its victims.'

'That means nothing. And I see now that the bowl did not lie. I asked it to show me the Flamebearer, and it obliged. Unfortunately, I assumed that Al'Kalyek was the culprit. Now I know better, and it all fits. That man was a sorcerer of enormous power. He must have killed Ba'alekket and escaped, using sorcery to make it appear as if he had drowned along with his victim. Al'Kalyek did not understand why or how he had managed to survive, but he could see no other possible candidate. He has the power, and the motive – he loathes you for what you did to him, and he wants to see the end of the Empire because it threatens his father's kingdom.'

'He is dead,' Olkanno repeated, as if that fact could be ensured merely by reciting it. 'How can he have survived? The beating Ba'alekkt gave him had all but killed him before he ever went into the river.'

'If he possessed as much power as you have credited to him, then he could certainly still be alive.'

'Then where is he now? Where can I find him?'

'The old man did not know. He was not protecting the Flamebearer, but his woman and his child.'

There was a short silence. Arkun, standing unnoticed against the wall, tried to accept what I'amel had said. So that sick, unconscious fugitive, the man he had captured and brought back to Tamat, the man to whom, in a moment of compassion, he had given water, the man who had killed Ba'alekkt – that man had survived drowning to become the Flamebearer, curse of Olkanno's reign, catalyst for the disintegration of the Empire.

If he could believe that astonishing fact, then it made sense. I'amel had said all along that the Flamebearer must possess enormous power. Many other people loathed Olkanno, and desired the collapse of the Empire, but who else in all the known world had ever been a sorcerer great enough to enter so many men's dreams?

'He had a woman, you say? And a child? So where are they now?'

'They were in Kereneth. They are now, I think, on Penya. The woman's name is Mallaso.'

Olkanno drew in his breath sharply. 'Mallaso! That was the name of the Penyan woman who tried to kill Ba'alekkt on Tekkt.'

'The one who escaped,' Arkun said. 'Sorcery was involved then too, was it not?'

Olkanno stared at him. 'Yes. The same man was involved. Bron, or Bronnayak, the son of the King of Zithirian. It all fits!'

'*What* was the man's name?' I'amel demanded urgently.

'Bron, or Bronnayak. It is not a Zithiriani name.'

'No. It is Ska'i. In the language of my grandmother, it means "slave of death". So this sorcerer is dedicated to the Wolf, and uses the same methods as I do!' I'amel's taut, sinister face was alight with interest.

Arkun was sure that the man whom he had hunted down would loathe and abhor necromancy and all the other filthy habits and rituals which gave the Black Mage his power. But he had no intention of informing I'amel. If some battle of sorcerers was foreshadowed here, the less the necromancer knew of his opponent, the better.

'If this Bronnayak has a woman and a child on Penya, then he may be there too.' Olkanno was frowning in thought, his fingers drumming a rhythm of impatience on the table-top. 'You said the source of the power came from the east, after all – and Penya is almost due east of Toktel'yi.'

'Does Penya possess mountains, or pine trees like those of Gulkesh? The first picture in my bowl showed me such a place.'

'It has a few central hills and mountains, I believe, but I know nothing about its trees. Arkun?'

'Penya has some pines, but they are tall and spread out at the top, like parasols.'

'In the bowl, the trees were broad at the base and tapered to a point.'

'Trees in the northern lands look like that. Perhaps the Flamebearer is in the far hills of Kerenth, or beyond.' Olkanno smiled at his necromancer. 'But you will seek him out for me, will you not, I'amel? Now that you know who and what he is, he should be easy to find. And besides, we will have his woman and his child in our hands. Once you send him their screams, he will come.'

Arkun closed his eyes for a moment. He saw the endless torture, the infinity of blood, running like a river through the tunnel of eternity. He said, swallowing his horror, 'Penya is large, but thinly populated, and I have agents there amongst the settlers who have stayed on after the invasion. I can be there and back within half a month.'

Olkanno gave him a long, considering look and Arkun's gut clenched suddenly. 'You are very eager, my friend,' the Emperor observed suspiciously.

'If my eagerness can ensure the future stability of the Empire, Imperial Majesty, then yes, I am eager to bring the Flamebearer to justice.'

'Very praiseworthy,' Olkanno said. 'But it is not a task I mean to entrust to you. Remember that the renegade Kazhian is now based on Penya. You and he are mortal enemies, are you not? He knows you, and if you are seen it will mean failure at the least. And I will not tolerate failure, as you well know, Spymaster. Your one lapse was caused by Kazhian. I will not risk another. Who is your best agent?'

'Tebret, Imperial Majesty.'

'Really? Is Ga'alek no longer available? If he is, then send him. He is extremely efficient. Tebret can be rash and impatient, and caution and secrecy are vital. Send Ga'alek, with a galley. He speaks Penyan, and he has relatives settled on the island. If they're still there, he can find out where the woman Mallaso is living, and then lead a raid to seize her and the child. I shall want them whole and unharmed, do you understand? Ga'alek and his raiding party can do as much damage as they want to other Penyans, but the woman and the child must not be hurt. They are the bait to lure the Flamebearer to his doom. To save their lives, he will put himself in our power.'

'Will he?' I'amel said disbelievingly. 'If I had a woman and a child, I would not lift a finger to save them if it would endanger myself or my power.'

'No, you would not,' said Olkanno. 'But you are a creature of stronger metal. Remember, this Bronnayak rescued the woman from Tekkt, though he risked death or capture. I am sure he will come. And you must bind him, I'amel, bind him and slay him once he is helpless, with no mercy and no delay. Ba'alekkt let him live a little too long, and paid for it with his own life. Do you understand me, my trusted servants? The fate of the Empire depends on the Flamebearer's death. There is no room for mercy, or stupidity, or failure. You are both my loyal subjects. If you do not succeed, you and you alone will be responsible for the consequences – and I shall be merciless in punishing you.'

'I understand, Imperial Majesty.'

'And you, Spymaster?'

Arkun looked at the man who had raised him from obscurity, fed his ambition, and given him one of the most powerful and lucrative posts in all the Empire. 'Of course,' he said, his face as usual giving no indication of his true feelings.

'The news from Jaiya is bad, and Lai'is may be next. You will have already received the report from the Governor of Tamat, indicating his concern, and mentioning that the Flamebearer is active there too. If we do not hurry, there will be no Empire left to save. I'amel?'

'Yes, Imperial Majesty?'

'If the Flamebearer has put ideas of rebellion into men's dreams, will it not also be possible for a loyal sorcerer or similar power to persuade the people to obey their Emperor?'

'It should, Imperial Majesty. But it will take a great deal of . . . raw material. The Flamebearer must have given the Devourer many, many souls to gain so much power.' He glanced down at the butchered body of Al'Kalyek, stiffening and congealing in its bonds on the table. 'The blood and flesh of a sorcerer is especially valuable. He can be rendered down and concentrated to make a very powerful potion. With its help, I can slay the Flamebearer. And his flesh will transmit his own strength to me, so that I may begin to undo the damage he has done.'

'Excellent.' Olkanno laughed, and the soft, menacing sound seemed to echo round the ghastly, splattered walls of the room. 'It was a good day for both of us, I'amel, when I summoned you to Toktel'yi. Where would you be now without me, eh? Still making mischief and stealing corpses in that scrubby little frontier town. And now you have power you never envisaged, and treasure piled at your feet. If you can rid me of the Flamebearer, I'll give you a province all of your own – a toy for you to play with as you please. Lai'is, if you like, or Tatht, or Tamat – anywhere that has dared to defy my rule. I am sure you will enjoy punishing them at your leisure, even more than I will enjoy hearing about it.'

'Your Imperial Majesty is kind beyond words to your humble servant.' I'amel threw himself on the ground in a gesture of grovelling gratitude.

But Arkun had seen the flash of red in his deep-set hooded eyes, and heard the falsely obsequious note in his sibilant voice. Suddenly he realized what I'amel really wanted, and where his ambition was leading him. And then all the Empire, not just one province, would be his plaything: and Toktel'yi would enter a nightmare of horror beside which the reign of Olkanno would seem a sunlit golden age of peace and happiness.

CHAPTER
TWENTY-FIVE

'Mama, Kazhian's back!'

Mallaso put down the basket of peaches and turned to greet her daughter. Kiyu came skipping through the orchard, as light and fleet and graceful as the little bird after which she had been named. In the dappled shadows cast by the young trees, her dress gleamed sun-yellow and dull ochre, and her long, tangled hair bounced on her shoulders. And as always when she beheld her child, Mallaso's heart clenched for love of her, and fear for her. Kiyu was nearly five years old now, almost the age at which her other daughter Grayna had died, and her mother could not rid herself of the belief that this child, too, would not see her seventh birthday.

Kiyu was slight and slender, but her apparent fragility disguised robust health and a hearty appetite, and her pretty face, with long-lashed dark eyes and golden-brown skin, masked an obstinate will and a volatile temper. There were no half-measures with Kiyu: she was either utterly delightful or totally obnoxious. Fortunately, her tantrums were now becoming rarer, and Mallaso hpoed that she would soon grow out of them. But despite her faults – and no child could be perfect – she was loving, intelligent and beautiful.

'Kazhian's back,' she repeated, and danced around her mother. 'Mama, can I have a peach?'

'You've had four already today. Wait until supper. Has he anchored yet?'

'Not yet, he's not in the bay, but he's coming. *Please* can I have a peach?'

To a casual observer, Kiyu was a perfectly normal little girl, but every so often she would say or do something that reminded Mallaso, sharply and painfully, of what her father had been: and of the decision that she had been afraid to make for too long.

She loathed the idea that her beloved child, her baby, possessed powers of sorcery. She had seen the burden that Bron had carried, the awesome responsibility, the dreadful desire of unscrupulous or malevolent people to manipulate or exploit his unique abilities to their own advantage. All his life, people had tried to control him, and he had died because of it. She did not want, and had never wanted, that fate for Kiyu: she would almost rather that the child was crippled, or lacking in her wits.

But she had also to accept that the power which had tempted the wizards of Jo'ami to abduct Kiyu had also saved her life. And if her daughter had not been stolen, she would never have met Kazhian. She could not imagine, now, how much poorer her days, and Kiyu's, would have been without him.

It was now more than three years since Kazhian had erupted into her life, changing it for ever. She had never before kept a lover for so long, but then she had never had a lover like Kazhian. And daily, hourly, she gave silent thanks to the Mother, for the man who shared her bed.

He had rebuilt Ammenna's house with much laughter and grumbling and at considerable cost to his dignity and the skin of knuckles, arms and knees. He had fallen off ladders, hit his thumbs with hammers, grazed legs and trapped fingers. But through it all he had laughed at himself, and resolved a variety of setbacks – plaster sliding from the walls, roof-beams cut too short, and a particularly unfortunate mishap while digging a drain – with resourcefulness and cheerful good humour. When finished, Ammenna's house was obviously not the work of a professional, but it was dry, watertight and clean, and Mallaso's friend was so astonished and delighted at its completion (and in less than six months, in between voyages) that she held a huge party to celebrate, at Year-turn, and invited everyone in Penya Harbour.

Kazhian, for the first time since he and Mallaso had become lovers, got very drunk: and after making love to her on the beach (which was not as much fun as she had imagined, for the sand got *everywhere*), had held her in his arms and whispered, with slurred and loving desperation, 'Well, Sashir, I've built Ammenna's house for you, I've completed your labour of love, and now I know what I want – will you marry me?'

It was far more than she had ever expected, and she could not turn away this unique and astonishing gift. So, a few days later, at a quiet formal cermony presided over by Tegerno, now elected Leader of Penya, Kazhian, son of the Emperor Eska'anen and Vessel of the Blood Imperial, became her husband.

Their marriage had not been unalloyed delight, of course, for they were both too strong-willed for perfect peace, and Kazhian's laughter was balanced by darker moods and a quick temper. But their love was strong enough to survive these brief and usually minor storms, and their shared sense of the absurd disarmed many conflicts. In addition, Kazhian's many absences, patrolling in the *Sea Serpent* or supervising the construction of two new ships at Farli'enn on the other side of the island, or training Penyans to crew them, seemed paradoxically to reinforce the bond between them. Mallaso knew that his voyages gave his restless nature the temporary freedom he craved, and that he would always come back to her.

Two years ago, she had become pregnant, but their son had been still-born. The intensity of his grief had surprised her, even though she had known already how different he was from most Toktel'yan men. Up until now, she had not conceived again – although, as Kazhian pointed out, it was certainly fun trying – but she watched her body's signs closely, and knew that this time they had succeeded. They had made love the night before his departure, nearly a month ago, and now she was sure. She wanted to swim out to the ship and announce the glorious news in front of all his crew, but she was afraid that after the previous tragedy, he would urge her to spend the next eight months resting.

Kiyu's giggles interrupted her thoughts. Mallaso realized that her daughter had filched a peach from the basket, and had already eaten half of it, the juice streaming down her chin. She saw her mother's accusing look and said, 'You didn't say I *couldn't*. You just said I'd had four already.'

'That's definitely the last one, then, until supper.' Mallaso touched the little girl's wild hair affectionately. 'You're a monkey, you are, with an answer for everything. You'll lead poor Ennas a merry dance when you go to school. Shall we walk back now? I've picked all I want.'

Kiyu nodded, her mouth full of peach. Mallaso lifted the two baskets and made for the track leading down to the harbour. This piece of land, like all the others allotted to the returning exiles, contained a mixture of poor and fertile soil, mostly terraced, on the south-facing slopes above the town. She and Ammenna had decided to grow fruit, vines and olives on the best section, and vegetables for their own use on the rest. There was also a fenced-off area for the chickens, in which Kiyu had a special interest, and they had ten goats in the herd which grazed the rough scrubland at the top of the hill. Like everyone else on Penya, they had worked very hard since their return to the island, and at last all the effort and all the hope were beginning to make a difference. By the time Kiyu was grown, Penya would no longer be just a ruined shadow of its former glory.

Beyond their own land lay an unclaimed swathe of shaggy grass, into which Kiyu disappeared with shrieks of delight, popping up every so often to surprise her mother. On any other island but this, Mallaso would have forbidden her to go anywhere near such a place, for fear of snakes, but Penya, blessed long ago by the Mother, was completely free of them, and also of other dangerous creatures such as scorpions or poisonous spiders.

She ignored Kiyu's shouts and glanced back at the orchard. The peaches were doing well. Next year, they might have enough to start producing the sweet, aromatic distilled spirit so popular on Penya and beyond. Next year, if the Mother smiled. Kazhian had jokingly told her that he could hardly wait.

She looked the other way, down the steep sloping hill, crowded with newly patched roofs, to the achingly lovely turquoise blue of the harbour. And there, just nosing round the western channel between Matamenya and the mainland, came the familiar gracefully curvaceous shape of the *Sea Serpent*, her sails almost slack in the still afternoon air.

'Look!' she called to Kiyu. 'There's the *Sea Serpent*!'

'I know, Mama – I told you.' Kiyu emerged from the long grass, seeds sticking to her short cotton tunic and bristling in her hair. 'Shall we go down and meet him on the quayside?'

They walked down the steep, zig-zagging track which connected the town with the fields above it, several hundred houses strung along it like beads on a cord. They passed Mallaso's birthplace, where the settler family still lived: they had become a little more friendly now that they realized that they would be left in peace. She was glad that she had not taken the house, for the ghosts of her past might have played havoc with the delightful present. And the line of her life, despite the horrors and the grief, led inexorably to the happiness she now enjoyed. She could not even regret being sold into slavery, when it had eventually brought her Kiyu, and Kazhian.

Kiyu was humming a strange tune, part chant, part song, that sounded vaguely familiar. Mallaso asked curiously, 'What's that?'

But the little girl was already skipping on ahead, and her voice came only in breathless snatches. Smiling, Mallaso followed her down into the town, and along the quayside to Ammenna's house.

S'raya, now sixteen, was giggling over gossip and cups of kuldi with her friend Nara'amis, and Ammenna was sitting at her loom in the shade of the overhanging roof, weaving the fine patterned cotton that was her special skill. Kiyu ran over to her. 'Kazhian's back, 'Menna, Kazhian's back.'

'Good,' said Mallaso's friend, deftly threading the shuttle through the taut strands of the warp. 'Fish for supper, then.'

On his last return, Kazhian had brought back a huge meaty spearfish, and half the town had dined on it. Mallaso laughed. 'I hope he caught it today, or it'll be stinking in this heat. We're going out to greet him.' She put the baskets down by the loom. 'I'll do these later. Don't eat too many, girls, or there'll be none left to keep.'

'We won't!' S'raya called as they left, and their mischievous giggles followed Mallaso and Kiyu along the quayside.

The *Sea Serpent* had now anchored in her usual place, her sails furled and her crew bustling on the deck. Kiyu's hand in hers, Mallaso walked along the harbour wall and sat down on a convenient bollard. Several other people were waiting too, and she saw Sargenay's lover, a dark and merry young man called Bidran, leaning against the wall of the Wine Cask. Most of the staff of the tavern were looking out expectantly, for the *Sea Serpent*'s crew were their best customers.

Kiyu, impatient and soon bored, went down the far steps to play on the sand. Mallaso remained on her bollard, her heart thumping and her palms damp. Mixed with her longing to see him again was her perennial dread that one day he would not come back. A sailor's life was hazardous even on the calmest of seas, and she knew Kazhian's reckless nature and foolhardy courage often led him to take serious risks. A year ago, he had broken his wrist and several ribs falling from the rigging in a gale. Next time, he might not be so lucky.

At last the skiff was lowered, and began to weave its way between the host of smaller moored craft between the deep outer anchorage and the quay. Mallaso rose to call Kiyu, and saw the child running back up the steps, her hands full of shells. 'He's nearly here, Mama – look, there he is in the front!'

The boat was too far away even to distinguish the sex of the small figure in the bows, but Mallaso knew that she was right. And the moment when she would no longer to able to ignore the truth about Kiyu crept a little nearer.

The skiff, rowed by a dozen eager sailors, swept up to the quayside. The man in the bow tied the boat to one of the rings set in the stone, climbed effortlessly up the iron ladder and ran into Mallaso's arms.

As in the very first embrace, she felt enfolded by his warmth and his strength, and his kiss, lingering and exploring, was at once an affirmation of his love and a promise of shared delight in the near future. Ignoring the cheerful teasing of his crew as they passed by on their way to the Wine Cask, Mallaso let herself be swept into their enchanted private world, full of sensual pleasure and joyous laughter.

'Oh, I've missed you, Sashir,' he whispered at last. 'Have you missed me?'

'Missed you? You've been gone less than a month, I haven't had time to miss you!'

'Mama's joking,' said Kiyu solemnly. 'She's missed you lots really.'

'And I'm glad to hear it,' Kazhian told her. 'How are you, then, little bird? Have you been good while I've been away?'

'Sometimes,' Kiyu said. She giggled as he swept her up and planted a brisk paternal kiss on the end of her small turned-up nose. 'But I can't be good *all* the time, can I? *You* aren't.'

'What have you been telling her?' Kazhian demanded of his wife, in apparent horror.

'I don't need to tell her. She can see for herself.' Mallaso kissed her affectionately, and put her arms around her beloved and her child. 'No fish, then?'

'*Fish?* It wasn't a fish, it was a monster – the width of the ship, at least, and pulling so hard I thought it'd have us over.' He launched into one of his fantastic stories, a kernel of truth embedded somewhere in the edifice of astonishing incident and vividly unlikely description. Kiyu listened avidly, fascinated into silence all the way back to Ammenna's house, while Mallaso's sides and face ached with laughter.

He told it again, over a supper of spiced chicken and vegetables in the courtyard, and even Ammenna, usually a serious woman, laughed until the tears ran down her cheeks. Sargenay had joined them, with his lover, and S'raya and her friend were also present, and afterwards Bidran produced his djarlek and played several favourite tunes, while Nara'amis, who had a lovely voice, sang as sweetly as a Nightsinger. Sargenay, who'd drunk quite a lote of wine, wept unashamedly, and even Mallaso felt the tears welling up with a joy so intense and overflowing that it was almost painful. Her daughter sat beside S'raya, her eyes shining, joining in with the songs she knew, and her lover, her husband, her beloved, lay with his head in her lap, while her hand gently stroked the loose, exuberant curls of his hair.

Bidran finished at last, flexing his fingers. 'Any requests?'

Ammenna was pouring more wine, and S'raya replenished the lamp. It was long past dusk now, and above them the stars of Penya blazed as brilliant as flames in an infinity of darkness.

'Can you play this, please, Bidran?' Kiyu asked, and began to hum the same tune that she had sung coming down the hill that afternoon.

'Sorry, little one, I don't know it,' he said, shaking his head apologetically. 'Do you know it, Mallaso?'

'I'm sure I've heard it somewhere, a long time ago – but where, or what it is, I can't remember.' She looked at Kiyu's disappointed face. 'Where did you hear it, sweetheart?'

'The Singing Man taught it to me,' said her daughter. 'And he said you'd know it.'

Mallaso stared at her, puzzled. 'The Singing Man? Who's he?' There were several men and women who wandered around Penya making music – indeed, Bidran had been one of them until he met Sargenay. But none had visited the town since Year-turn.

'He's my friend,' Kiyu said. 'He knows lots and lots of songs, and he plays the djarlek even – *almost* as well as you do, Bidran.'

'Where does he live?' Mallaso asked. 'Do I know him?'

'He says you used to, very well. But I don't know where he lives. There are lots of funny trees there, like arrowheads pointing up, very dark green.'

Deep within her, Mallaso felt something, some tingle of premonition, shiver into life. She said softly, gently, 'When do you meet him, sweetheart?'

And Kiyu, perfectly matter-of-fact, said, 'When I'm asleep.'

Kazhian abruptly sat up. Sargenay said, 'Oh, Lord of Life – do you see him, little one? What does he look like?'

The child stared round in bewilderment at the intent adult faces. Then, her eyes wide, she turned to her mother. 'He *isn't* nasty, he *isn't*! He's my friend!'

'No one said he was nasty, sweetheart,' Mallaso told her gently. 'And there's nothing wrong. We're just surprised, that's all, and we'd like to know more about him. What does he look like? Is he young or old?'

Kiyu frowned. 'He's got white hair like an old person, but his face is young, it's almost white too, but his eyes are dark, and he wears funny clothes – a tunic like Kazhian's but things round his legs like sleeves. And I call him the Singing Man because he sings to me in my sleep.'

'So you *dream* of him?' Sargenay asked.

Kiyu nodded. 'Not every night. He came to me last night, though. That's when he played me the song I wanted you to play, Bidran.'

'It's called, "The Woodcutter",' Mallaso said. 'It's from Onnak. Bron sang it in Toktel'yi.' She had begun to tremble, and felt Kazhian's arm go round her. 'I remember it now. He beat the rhythm with his foot.'

'No, he didn't,' said Kiyu. 'He used his hand on the strings.'

'Bron . . .' Sargenay's voice lingered over the brief syllable, making Bidran frown. 'But he's dead. He's been dead for five years. How can he come to Kiyu in dreams?'

'He came to my dreams,' Mallaso told him. 'Not for a long while now, but when I was in Kerenth, and when I first came to Penya, I dreamed of him once or twice.' Her mind was seething with questions, she wanted to see inside Kiyu's head, see the man who sang to her, the man who was her father . . . who, it seemed, was not dead after all.

And she could not, yet, confront the implications of that. Instead she said to Kiyu, 'How long has he been coming to you, sweetheart?'

The child screwed up her face with the effort of remembering. 'I don't know,' she said at last. 'Sometime before Year-turn, I think, because I was only three then. And I'm four now,' she added, looking round at the gathering with pride. 'I'll be five soon, before next Year-turn.'

'So if this Singing Man has been visiting your dreams for at least eight or nine months – why didn't you tell me?'

'Well, you don't tell me *your* dreams,' Kiyu pointed out. 'Anyway, he asked me not to. He said it was a secret just between the two of us. He said you'd be upset if you knew.' She gazed at Mallaso with anxious concern. '*Are* you upset, Mama?'

'No, I'm not,' Mallaso said calmly, though it took a supreme effort not to reveal her distress. 'I – just wish you'd told me, sweetheart, that's all.'

'But he told me not to,' Kiyu repeated, her own eyes, huge and dark, filling with tears. She looked round at the serious adults, and added, her voice rising to a wail, 'I didn't *mean* to be naughty!'

'It's all right,' Mallaso said, and the little girl scrambled on to her lap and clung to her, sobbing noisily. With a quick glance of apology at her friends, she struggled to her feet, Kiyu in her arms, and carried her off to bed.

It took a long while to calm her daughter, for the child had been tired and over-excited by Kazhian's return, even before the relevations about the Singing Man. But when at last she lay quiet in her bed, tucked up under one of Ammenna's bright striped blankets, her face washed clean of tears and her hair neatly plaited for the night, she looked up and said, 'Mama, are you cross with me?'

Smiling, Mallaso shook her head. 'No, I'm not cross at all. If he wanted it to be a secret, then I quite understand why you didn't tell me. Do – do you know what his name is, sweetheart?'

Kiyu nodded. 'Yes. He said to call him *djada*.'

Bewildered, Mallaso stared at her. '*Djada?*' If this was not Bron after all, but some evil counterfeit—

And then she remembered that in Zithiriani, his own language, and one which she knew a little, it meant, 'father'.

'*Do* you know him, Mama? He said you used to know him very well. Was he your friend?'

'Yes, he was. Tell me about him – tell me again what he looks like, and where you see him.'

She listened as Kiyu's sleepy voice described the Singing Man, and his unfamiliar home. She saw him through the child's eyes, with a child's matter-of-fact opinions. Kiyu liked his music and she liked his stories, full of strange beasts and wonderful happenings. She could not remember every detail, but she said that they were the most marvellous stories she had ever heard.

'And the place where he lives?' Mallaso asked her. 'You said it was full of funny trees.'

Kiyu nodded, yawning. 'Yes, and mountains, and rivers. But it isn't hot like it is here. He said there was snow every Year-turn. He showed me some, on the mountains. High, huge, *giant* mountains, far taller than ours. And a great big river town, a city he said it was, all full of towers, with a river rushing past.'

Zithirian. It had to be Zithirian. But there was another man in her life now, a man whom she loved as she had never loved any other, even Bron: a man whose warmth and laughter and outrageous brilliance had finally drawn her out of the darkness of her past, and into the sunlight, just as she had done for him.

Two men, two very different men, who loved her. And which of them, in the name of the Mother, would she choose? The father of the child beside her, who bore some of his strangeness and some of his burden? Or the father of the baby, scarcely begun, who nestled deep within her?

'Don't worry, Mama.' Kiyu's eyes were closing, and her voice hovered drowsily on the verge of sleep. 'He knows, and he doesn't mind.'

'Knows what?' Mallaso asked, but her daughter's soft regular breathing was the only answer.

She sat for a while longer beside the sleeping child, trying to think, and then rose to her feet and crept softly out, leaving the oil-lamp lit in the corner.

The courtyard was empty, save for Ammenna gathering up the rugs and cushions. She smiled at Mallaso. 'All well? Everyone else has gone to bed.'

'She's asleep. She was very tired – it's not often she stays up so late.'

'No.' Ammenna stood in the starlit courtyard, rugs laid over one arm and cushions grasped in the other hand. 'Who is this man she's been seeing in her sleep?'

'Her father,' Mallaso said. Her friend knew, of course, the bare bones of her past, but she had never confided the detailed truth.

'The sorcerer? Ah,' said Ammenna. 'That explains it.' She added, with a nod at the closed door to her left, 'He's waiting for you.'

Kazhian. Suddenly her tired, confused mind focused on her husband. What must he be thinking? Did he imagine that she would desert him now that Bron seemed to be alive after all? She knew of his deep-rooted vulnerability and insecurity. Was he still sure of her love?

She had made her choice three years ago, in the bloodstained, corpse-strewn courtyard of the Blue Olive in Hegril. She had put her past to one side, with sadness but with acceptance, and she had gladly embraced the warm, living, loving present. *Do not refuse what is offered*, Bron had told her, from the place that she had assumed, then, to be the northern land of the dead. And she had not.

And just now, before she fell asleep, Kiyu had told her, 'He knows, and he doesn't mind.' That must surely mean that he was aware of her relationship with Kazhian. But did he not mind because he was so far away, and time had faded his passion, or was he generous enough to acknowledge the depth of her feelings for her new love?

Or did he not mind because he was a creature of the spirit only, a ghost on the wind, visible only in dreams?

She shivered suddenly. She was not, and would never be afraid of him, only of his power: but if he had become a wraith wandering homeless through the world, she felt only a terrible pity and sorrow.

But not love. She loved Kazhian, who was emphatically not a dream, or a wraith. She must make him realize what really mattered to her now. And she must tell him about the baby.

With a sense of purpose, and also of apprehension, Mallaso bade Ammenna good night, and opened the door of the room she shared with Kazhian.

He was lying on the sleeping-mattress, his face buried in the pillow. He was still fully clothed, as if he had flung himself down too tired, or disturbed, to undress. Mallaso paused, wondering if he was asleep. She shut the door, and as the latch made a soft click, he rolled over and sat up.

In the lamplight, his face was hard to read. He said, his voice rough and abrupt, 'Is she asleep?'

'Yes, at last.' Mallaso walked over and sat down beside him. She longed to take him in her arms, but she could sense the savage tension within him, and knew that this could not be healed merely by a loving embrace. She prayed silently that she would be able to find the right words, to explain the truth burning in her heart.

'So the Singing Man is Bron. Kiyu's father. And he is probably alive after all.' Kazhian's face was averted, and his fingers were twisting the loose fabric at the corner of the pillow. 'If – if you want to go to him, Sashir, I will understand.'

'No,' Mallaso said, with passionate intensity. As his head jerked round in astonishment, she added vehemently, 'No, no, *no*. He is Kiyu's father, and once he was dear to me, but that was in the past, beloved, before I met you. If he's alive, it makes no difference to us. It is *you* I love, *you* I want, now and for ever.'

His eyes, dark with pain, stared into hers. 'Do you?'

'Of course I do, you stupid man! Even if I didn't love you to distraction, even if I wasn't hungry for you every night, even if I didn't think you were the most marvellous lover who ever breathed – do you really think I'd go traipsing off into the wilderness in pursuit of an old flame who might or might not be still alive, and leave all this behind? I may be soft in the head, beloved, but I'm not utterly mad. I love you. I love Kiyu. I love Penya. And here with you all I intend to stay.' She took up his hand, and placed it on belly. 'Besides, travel isn't supposed to be good for pregnant women.'

Kazhian drew in his breath sharply. 'You're *pregnant*? When? How long? When will it be born?'

'Next spring, if the Mother wills. We must have made him, or her, the night before you left for Farli'enn.'

'And what a night it was.' His eyes were glowing with joy, and the delight in his face lit an answer in hers. 'Oh, Sashir, Sashir, how I love you – and this time, nothing will go wrong.'

'It's in the Mother's hands,' she reminded him quietly. 'All children are in Her gift. Do you want a son?'

'I don't mind – I'll settle for a baby.' His hands caught hers, and he smiled at her. 'Are you sure?'

'Of course I'm sure. This isn't the first time I've been pregnant.'

'No, I don't mean that. Are you sure about – about staying?'

'Oh, beloved.' At last she embraced him, pulling him close, feeling the anguished tautness of his body. 'I have never been more sure about anything in my life. You are my dearest love – I would never leave you. And Bron knows that. Before she slept, Kiyu told me that he doesn't mind.'

'Generous of him,' said Kazhian drily, his lips against her cheek, and one hand beginning to wander pleasurably towards her breast. 'And do you really hunger for me every night?'

'Not *every* night – I was exaggerating a little.'

'I see. How about this night?'

She pressed herself closer, eager for his touch. 'Perhaps. I might have to be persuaded.'

'You don't seem to need much persuading to me,' murmured Kazhian, his voice rough with desire. 'But perhaps this will settle it.' He kissed her, and she gave herself up to the sensations that even now, after three years together, seemed as glorious and overwhelming as on the first night they had shared, in the abandoned house in Hegril. And then they made love with passionate fluency, so attuned to the rhythms and pleasures of each other's bodies that arousal and fulfilment arrived with joyous and spectacular ease.

Later, she said drowsily, 'Kiyu. We must decide what to do about Kiyu.'

'What about Kiyu?' Kazhian's eyes were closed, and his face wore an uncharacteristic look of peace and relaxation.

'Her power. Beloved, she doesn't even *know* she has power. She saw you coming today before the *Sea Serpent* was even in sight round the headland. She probably thinks that every child has a Singing Man who visits their dreams. Perhaps if we'd told her before, she wouldn't have been so bewildered and frightened tonight.'

'Her dreams didn't upset her – it was our reaction to them,' Kazhian pointed out. 'But I thought you didn't want to do anything about her power yet.'

'I don't – but if Bron is in contact with her, we haven't any choice, have we?' Mallaso heard the note of bitterness in her voice, and hated it. 'I don't want her to be frightened any more. I want her to be *told*, and taught. I'll have a word with Sargenay in the morning.'

'He'll be glad.'

'I know. I know I've delayed too long. You understand why, don't you? But I can see now that we can't deny the inevitable any longer.' Mallaso sighed, and rested her head on his shoulder. 'I love her so much – I never wanted this for her.'

'If we are careful, it surely need never be the terrible burden it was for Bron.'

'I hope not. I pray not. And yet I am so afraid for her.' She shivered suddenly. 'I can't bear to think of her innocence and joy, spoilt and corrupted.'

'Now who's being foolish?' Kazhian rolled over and took her in his arms. 'The wizards of Jo'ami are dead. And who else knows of her existence? Only Bron, and he would never harm her, surely.'

'And Al'Kalyek. And he adored her. Perhaps he would come over for a few months, and give us some advice.'

'I don't see why not.' Kazhian yawned, and snuggled down under the blanket. 'There should be a trader leaving soon. But make him the only sorcerer you invite here, otherwise I shall soon feel outnumbered!'

And with a smile on her face, her worries eased a little, Mallaso finally fell asleep in his arms.

The men scrambling up on to the quayside from the small open boat bobbing below on the high tide had never visited Penya Harbour before, but their instructions were exact and detailed. There were twenty of them, clad in the lightweight bronze armour of Toktel'yan marine soldiers, and they ran swiftly and silently along the deserted wharf, in and out of the few pools of light cast by the lamps: past the Meeting House, with the Penyan flag hanging lifeless from its pole in the still night air: past the Wine Cask, long since shuttered and barred after is last customers had staggered home: and up to the small house almost at the end of the docks, conspicuously festooned with flowering vines and creepers.

No one in the town now bothered much with locks or bolts. The door yielded to two well-judged blows with an axe. Even as the first sounds of alarm rose from outside, the soldiers poured over the threshold and into Ammenna's courtyard.

One of them had a smouldering torch. He flung it at the loom, and the light dry cotton flared up instantly, illuminating the scene with a brilliant orange glare. The other soldiers, obeying orders, wrenched open the doors, seeking amongst the dazed and bewildered sleepers the woman and the child they had been told to find.

Mallaso woke to screams and shouts. The door crashed open, and dark shapes filled the room, outlined by the violent flicker of fire. Beside her, Kazhian leaped to his feet, naked and unarmed, and she saw a sword's evil thrust and shrieked a frantic warning. Then rough hands grasped her and yanked her up and out into the courtyard. Someone peered into her face, and nodded. 'Yes, that's her. Get her out now – and find the child!'

Screaming and hysterical with rage and terror, Mallaso struggled wildly, trying to escape. One of them punched her on the side of the head, and lights exploded agonizingly inside her brain. Then her legs gave way beneath her, and dazed and half-stunned, she was dragged out on to the quayside.

Through the foggy pain in her head, she heard shouts and a howl of pain. *Oh, Kiyu, run, hide, RUN!* she cried in desperate silence to her child. One of the soldiers picked her up and slung her roughly over his shoulder, so that her face banged painfully against the hard ridged metal of his back armour as he ran along the quayside. She opened her eyes, saw the wild flames leaping up from Ammenna's house, and began to shout and hit and struggle in a frantic attempt to get free.

'Shut up, you bitch,' said the man in Toktel'yan, and his grip tightened so much that she could hardly move or breathe. Nausea and dizziness overwhelmed her. She had no strength left to resist as other hands dragged her off him, and dumped her unceremoniously into the bottom of a large open boat. The Toktel'yans clambered down after her, cast off, and began to row with huge clumsy strokes, away from the harbour wall.

Everything hurt: her head, her face, her arms, her knees, her ribs, her elbow where it had banged against a thwart. Sick with panic, she struggled painfully into a sitting position, and was promptly kicked back.

'Easy, Hennlek! You know she's not to be damaged!'

'The bloody Penyan bitch hit me, so I'll do as I want! And Ga'alek's not here to see, is he?'

'No, but I am,' said a different, aristocratic voice from the bows. 'Touch her again, and I'll report you. Stop! This is far enough.'

The rowing ceased. Mallaso made another despairing effort, and managed to haul herself up.

There were five men in the boat with her, two aft and three forward. Probably one of these was the vindictive Hennlek. She wasn't interested in them, though: she twisted round, trying to see what was happening on the quayside, now perhaps some twenty or thirty paces away across the water.

The people living along the waterfront had obviously been roused from their beds, and had run out to confront the Toktel'yan raiders, some perhaps in their night-clothes, and armed only with makeshift weapons. She stared at the confused, struggling mass of combatants, and thought with despair of her friends, Ammenna and S'raya,

Sargenay and Bidran, and above all of Kazhian, so recklessly courageous, and of Kiyu. *Oh, Mother, I beg you, keep them all safe . . .*

Kiyu had been dreaming, but not this night of the Singing Man: instead, she was helping her Mother to gather peaches, and eating as many as she could while Mama wasn't looking. And then Mama *had* seen, and shouted at her, and her shouts seemed to go on and on so that Kiyu was frightened and began to cry.

Then she woke up, and realized that the shouts were real. And even as she sat up in alarm, her mother's voice echoed frantically inside her head, as it had never done before. *Oh, Kiyu, run, hide, RUN!*

Wild with fear, the little girl leaped up from her mattress. At the same instant, the door burst open and several huge armed men poured into the room.

Quick as a shadow, her wits and her powers sharpened by terror, Kiyu dodged the clutching hands and flung herself out into the courtyard. The loom was well alight, and the wooden pillars of the colonnade were beginning to burn. She saw Sargenay wielding a broken table-leg, and Bidran cracking a storage jar over a soldier's head, while several others were dragging Mallaso outside.

She screamed for her mother, and ran after them. Someone grabbed her from behind, and snatched her up. She threshed and struggled and scratched his face, but with a yell of triumph he turned for the door.

Hysterical with fear and rage, Kiyu felt something tingle in her arms and legs, and strength far beyond her years surged within her. She burst out of the man's grip and fell to the ground amidst a forest of trampling legs. It was painful, but there was no time for tears. She scuttled on hands and knees between the combatants, evaded a hostile grab with a quick twist to one side, saw the open doorway, and sprinted for freedom.

Outside, there was more shouting, more fighting. Soldiers thronged the quayside, and the people of Penya Harbour, in their night-clothes or with no clothes at all, were battling with swords or any possible weapon that had come to their hands: firewood, oars, cooking-pots, axes, hammers.

Small and light and fleet-footed, Kiyu dodged between them. She could see a soldier running away, with a heavy burden on his back, and she knew that he was carrying her mother.

Someone shouted her name. It was Kazhian's voice, but she ignored it, running desperately on in pursuit.

'Kiyu! No, *Stop!*'

His urgency at last penetrated her panic. She turned, and saw him swerving past a couple of soldiers, who were then engaged by Sellano, landlady of the Wine Cask, screeching abuse and wielding a large clay jug in each hand. Kazhian was here. Kazhian would rescue Mama. She began to sob with relief. 'They're taking her away, oh save her, please save her!'

Kazhian, still several strides away, shouted suddenly, but too late. Someone grabbed her arm from behind, twisting it painfully. She struggled, and felt something hard and very sharp jab at her neck. 'Keep still,' said her captor, in harshly accented Penyan. 'Keep still, you little fiend, or I'll slit your throat.'

He meant it – she could hear the menace in his voice. Whimpering in fear, she stood rigid in his grasp, and saw Kazhian, naked, unprotected, unarmed save for his eating-knife, rooted to the stones in front of her, just out of reach.

'You too,' the Toktel'yan added brutally. 'One move and I'll kill the child.' He started to walk backwards, dragging Kiyu with him, his knife, lethal and sharp, scratching menacingly at her slender brown throat. Kazhian watched helplessly as he hauled her to the edge of the dock, and jumped in, still holding her.

She reached the surface spluttering and coughing, and her captor began to swim vigorously, towing her with him. Sobbing, she was dragged through the sea, hauled up over the side of a boat by several rough hands, and flung dripping on top of someone else.

Kiyu knew, without having to look, that it was her mother, and burst into hysterical tears.

She was making far too much noise to be badly hurt. Mallaso held the little girl tightly and thanked the Mother that at least her beloved daughter was safe, even if she was a captive too.

'Row, damn you!' the man who had seized Kiyu yelled, in Toktel'yan.

'But what about the rest of them?' objected the aristocrat in the bows.

'They don't matter. We've got the woman and the child, and that's what we came here for. Their widows will get good pensions. Now *row*!'

'Wait!' said the man in the bow. 'For Kaylo's sake, man, they're jumping into the water! Wait for them!'

'No. I'm under orders to take these two back to Toktel'yi *whatever* the cost. We've got them, and that's the end of it.'

'I said *no*! They're *my* boat, and *my* crew, and *my* soldiers. They take their orders from me, and I am responsible for them. You're only one of Olyak's messengers, and as far as I'm concerned you're just a couple of rungs further up the ladder than a jellyfish.'

'You'll regret this,' said the agent.

'No, I won't. There's some poor sod swimming for his life only twenty paces away, and the least we can do is pick him up. The Penyans are still fully occupied on the quay, there's no risk to us.'

Mallaso peered past the men in the stern of the boat, trying to see what was happening ashore. Sounds of battle were diminishing, and she heard the high ululation of Penyan triumph. A last soldier jumped, or fell, into the sea, and the roar of victory redoubled.

'He's almost up with us – Urlan and Karmelek, help him in.'

The swimmer was very close now, his arms flashing through the water in the fast Toktel'yan style. The aft rowers moved to the rearmost thwart and leaned over, shouting encouragement. *He's quick for a man in a bronze tunic*, Mallaso thought. And then, even as the truth burst on her, the swimmer was hauled on board.

It was Kazhian, a knife in his hand. He used it on the nearest rower as the other one yelled in alarm, 'It's a Penyan, sir!'

The rower, dead or dying, toppled into the water. The boat rocked violently as the other oarsman grappled wildly for possession of the dagger. Kiyu screamed as they struggled. 'Kazhian, Kazhian, look out!'

The Spymaster's agent had pulled the nearest oar from its rowlock. He lifted it dripping in his hands. Kiyu leaped up and grabbed his arm. The wet wood hit Kazhian across the shoulder. He gave a cry of pain and dropped the knife. Another sailor hauled the screaming child away as the agent raised the oar again. This time, it struck the back of Kazhian's head, knocking him down against the gunwale. He lay quite still, his head and arms hanging over the side of the boat.

'Heave him overboard,' said the agent, dropping the oar back into its rowlock. 'And get a move on, before someone else tries the same thing.'

'No!' Mallaso could not see the Toktel'yan Captain, behind her in the bow, but she could sense his anger. 'We'll keep him.'

'You're mad,' the agent said furiously. 'He's probably dead, and if he isn't he's worth nothing. All I want is the woman and the child. I don't need him.'

'Didn't you hear what the child called him?' The boat rocked as the Captain came aft, stepping over thwarts and legs with a sailor's instinctive balance. Mallaso saw that he was short and stocky, with a fringe of dark hair round a balding head. 'Kazhian, he said. We know he's on Penya. And this is just the sort of thing he'd do – he always was a bloody lunatic. Well, Urlan, has Ga'alek knocked his brains out?'

Kiyu, once more crouched beside Mallaso, touched her hand and shook her head slightly.

'No, sir, he's breathing. Is that really him, sir? Really Lord Kazhian?' There was a note of awe and wonder in his voice as he looked down at the dripping and unconscious man sprawled over the side of the boat.

'Of course it's him – I'd know him anywhere. And he's a Vessel of the Blood Imperial, you ape, so treat him gently. The woman and the child too, the Emperor wants them unharmed.'

'Captain Eslen. May I remind you that His Imperial Majesty wants to receive his prisoners in person, not a report that we had them in our possession and then they were rescued?' demanded the agent with barely concealed rage.

'Of course, Ga'alek. But please remember that the Emperor will surely be delighted to have Lord Kazhian in his power at last. And if we'd rowed on as you wanted, we wouldn't have caught him. I shall make a full report.'

'And so shall I – and it will *not* be flattering.'

Kazhian was laid in the bottom of the boat, and the rowers settled down to their work. The vessel began to push through the water, while the Captain and the agent continued to argue. Mallaso did not care. Their future was bleak and uncertain, but at least Kazhian was still alive. And his presence gave her enormous comfort. During the long voyage, and through the horrors that must surely lie ahead, she and Kiyu would not after all be alone.

CHAPTER
TWENTY-SIX

Captain Eslen, of His Imperial Majesty's war galley *Battlecry*, put down his reed-pen and stretched wearily. He had spent the rest of the night writing his report, leaving out no derogatory reference to Ga'alek, Imperial Agent and currently the bane of his life, and he needed some sleep. His sailing master was quite capable of guiding the ship through the dangerous waters south of Penya without any assistance from him, but he should still check on their progress before he turned in.

He climbed the ladder on to the deck. The rising sun cast long slanting blue shadows across the smooth white wood of the poop deck, and illuminated the scarred, burnt and aching backs of the galley-slaves, labouring at their oars to the ceaseless thump of the row-master's drum. The steersmen stood at their posts, keeping the great vessel steady with the huge steering oars, one to each side and manipulated by a complex arrangement of levers and ropes. Eslen looked around at the azure morning sea. Penya still lay to starboard, half-a-dozen miles away, her cliffs and mountains hazy and featureless with distance. There was no sign of pursuit, but he did not expect it. After all, the leader of the tiny Penyan Navy lay imprisoned below, in the forward cabin.

'The weather-worker says it's set fair,' said his sailing master. 'We'll clear the island well before nightfall, and then there's fifty miles of open water till we come to the Scatterlings.'

'Excellent. Keep her steady. I'm going to check on the prisoners.'

The rowers did not look up as he walked along the narrow plank running down the centre of the ship, above their heads. A galley this size carried two hundred slaves, chained to the thwarts and to each other, whipped for the slightest misdemeanour and given only enough food, water and rest to keep them alive. It did not matter much, though, if they died: there was always a plentiful supply of prisoners, criminals or dissidents or rebels, to take their place. Few lasted more than a year before succumbing to disease, exhaustion or sunstroke. Eslen wondered with interest whether Kazhian would end his life on the galleys. He, and the Emperor, would appreciate the irony.

He climbed the ladder to the tiny forward deck, opened the hatch and looked down. The dark hot space below was often used to carry passengers on official business, so it was furnished with mattresses, a chest, a bucket, and a couple of tiny unglazed portholes high up in the bow. To turn it into a prison, he had only needed to have the ladder removed.

Two faces, one dark, one small and golden, stared up at him. The woman said, in fluent and perfect Toktel'yan, 'Get us some water. It's too hot in here.'

'Of course, my lady,' Eslen said mockingly. He turned his attention to the man lying on the mattress behind them, his nakedness decently covered with a thin cotton sheet. By the look of him, he was still unconscious, which was hardly surprising after that crack on the head, and the child was bathing his face with a damp cloth.

The *Battlecry*'s Captain had come across his prisoner frequently in the past, but the two men had never been friendly. Eslen, more than fifteen years Kazhian's senior, had deeply resented the speed with which the young Vessel of the Blood Imperial had risen through the naval hierarchy, and had been extremely jealous of the fact that he had attained a Captaincy before his twenty-fifth birthday, whereas Eslen had not been given such responsibility until he was almost forty. So the news of the spectacular end to Kazhian's career had caused him great satisfaction, tempered only by the news that the young idiot had subsequently been given command of a courier ship. His defection, and ensuing turn to piracy, had only confirmed Eslen's view that he was just another arrogant, corrupt and decadent sprig of the Imperial tree, promoted far beyond his competence and resorting to treachery when found out.

And now he was a prisoner on Eslen's own ship. He smiled with delight. The only pity was that in the cramped confines of the war galley, there was nowhere else to put him – he would have to stay with the woman and the child. And since they were to be treated kindly, under orders from the Emperor himself, Kazhian couldn't be singled out for punishment. It was a great shame. Eslen would have enjoyed starving him, or chaining him up. And he couldn't risk putting him in with the slaves – if he keeled over and died, Olkanno might not be very pleased.

'How is he?' he enquired, using the politest inflections of the language.

The woman was certainly aware of the irony. She said angrily, 'He may still die. Can we have some water?'

'Dear me,' Eslen said. 'Such a lack of courtesy in a lady causes me real grief.'

The woman looked as if she would have liked to throw something at him. Instead, obviously hating it, she lowered her eyes and said in conciliatory tones, 'I beg of you, honoured Captain – please may we have some more water?'

'I'll see to it,' Eslen said. 'You can have food, too – and some clothes,' he added, with a significant leer at her ripped dress. 'You're not for punishment – yet.' He let the hatch down with an ominous thud, and returned to the poop.

Alone in the dim light, Mallaso and Kiyu looked at each other. 'Horrible man!' said the little girl, covering her fear with anger. 'I *hate* him!'

'He saved Kazhian's life – he realized who he was. Otherwise, he'd have been thrown overboard.' For the fiftieth time, Mallaso found her husband's slack wrist and felt for the pulse. Was it stronger, or weaker? She had no idea. She only knew that she was utterly helpless, powerless to save him if he was dying, powerless to bring him back to life, powerless to escape . . .

But she could not give way to panic and hysteria, not with Kiyu beside her. She added cheerfully, 'It could be a lot worse, sweetheart. He's alive, and I'm sure he'll come to himself soon. And we're together, and they'll bring us food and more water. The Emperor has told them to be nice to us.'

'Well, *I* don't think this is very nice,' Kiyu said. She stared at her mother anxiously. 'Mama, why did they take us?'

'I don't know, sweetheart.'

'The Emperor wants us. But he's a bad man, isn't he?'

'He may just want to ask us something, and then let us go.' And that's about as probable, Mallaso thought grimly, as Kiyu sprouting wings.

'I shall tell him I don't like his Captain,' her daughter announced. 'Or his soldiers . . .' Her voice trembled, and her hand crept out to her mother's. 'Why do they want us? What have we done? We haven't hurt anyone, and *we're* not bad, so why have they put us in prison?'

'I don't know,' Mallaso repeated. She could sense Kiyu's rising distress, and cast around in her mind for a distraction. 'Let's sing something, shall we? A cheerful, happy song. What would you like?'

Kiyu brightened at once. 'Oh, the woodcutter song, the one the Singing Man taught me.'

Together, rather hesitantly, they stumbled through a couple of verses. Then Mallaso launched into a series of children's rhymes and stories. Kiyu knew them all by heart, but their familiarity was very comforting in the hot, dark cabin.

> Ten yellow lizards, sitting in a line,
> One crawled away, and then there nine!
>
> Nine yellow lizards, sitting on a gate,
> One fell off, and then there were eight!
>
> Eight yellow lizards, less than eleven,
> One was eaten by a bird, and then there were seven!
>
> Seven yellow lizards, crawling up a stick,
> One stayed behind and then there were six!
>
> Six yellow lizards, barely alive,
> One turned up its toes and then there were five!
>
> Five yellow lizards, lying on the floor,
> One got trodden on and then there were four.
>
> Four yellow lizards, climbing up a tree,
> One fell off and then there were three.
>
> Three yellow lizards with nothing much to do,
> One was bitten by a snake and then there were two.
>
> Two yellow lizards, sitting in the sun,
> One got frazzled up and then there was one!
>
> One yellow lizard, wishing for some fun,
> Went away to find some more, and then there were none!

Under her fingers, Mallaso felt the slightest movement of Kazhian's hand. She shushed Kiyu, who was beginning another rhyme. 'I think he's waking up.'

'Where in Olyak's Halls is this?'

Her husband's voice was barely above a whisper, but it was unmistakably his. Suddenly awash with relief, Mallaso brushed tears from her eyes. 'We're on a ship.'

'Mallaso?' He peered up at her, trying to focus in the limited light. 'Oh, Sashir, is that you?'

'And I'm here too,' Kiyu announced, walking on her knees over to his mattress and flopping down beside her mother. 'You've had a bang on the head because a horrible man hit you with an oar, but you're better now.'

'Am I?' Kazhian's free hand explored his scalp gingerly. 'Lord of Life, that hurts. I'm surprised my skull's not cracked.'

'You must have a very hard head,' Kiyu informed him earnestly. 'Is it *very* painful? There isn't any more water, though the horrible Captain said he'd get us some more, but I can touch it better if you like.' And before Mallaso could stop her, she leaned forward and put her brown paw across her stepfather's forehead.

'Kiyu—' Mallaso began, and then saw Kazhian's face. Something prickled on her skin, and goosebumps broke out on her arms.

'Better now,' said the child, removing her hand. And it was not a question, but a statement of fact.

'Thank you,' Kazhian said. 'I feel almost normal.' His eyes caught Mallaso's briefly and significantly. 'Can you help me sit up?'

The woman took his hands and pulled him gently upright, while the little girl collected cushions and pillows from the chest and piled them between his back and the side of the ship. As he leaned against them with a sigh, the hatch above opened, and a man's face peered down.

'Captain said to give you this,' he said, with a suspicious glance at Kazhian. 'Stay well away from the rope, or I'll pull it up again and you'll go hungry. Let the child untie it.'

Obediently, they watched as a basket was lowered, full of food, with a couple of long Toktel'yan gowns folded on the top. Kiyu scuttled forward and undid the knots. At once the thin rope snaked up again, to return a few moments later with a large wooden bucket, half full of water, on the end of it. Only as Kiyu wrestled with the wet cord did Mallaso realize, with a sense of shock, that the sailor had spoken in Toktel'yan. And although both she and Kazhian were of course fluent in that language, at home the child had only ever heard them talk in Penyan.

But the sight of the food and, more importantly, the water, drove those unsettling thoughts from her head. They could wipe hands and faces clean of dirt and blood, and there was still enough left to drink now or later. The basket contained two flat loaves of bread, some fruit, dried meat, raisins and a jar of honey. Mallaso distributed it all, making sure that Kiyu had plenty. Despite the Emperor's orders, she did not trust the Captain.

The contentment of a full stomach, combined with her exhaustion after the terrors and disturbances of the previous night, soon made Kiyu drowsy. Mallaso settled her down on a mattress in the darkest corner, and watched as her daughter fell asleep, her thumb in her mouth, as peacefully and innocently as if she occupied her own bed in Ammenna's house. Then she went back to Kazhian. His arms opened, and she clung to him, shivering, soaking up his strength and comfort, lending him her own.

'You shouldn't have come after us,' she said at last, when there was no longer any risk of her weeping. 'They didn't want you. The agent nearly threw you overboard, but Captain Eslen persuaded him not to.'

'Eslen? That surprises me. He was never a friend of mine. Old, a plodder, jealous of my connections and absolutely overjoyed when I piled the *Spear of Vengeance* on that rock. Did he gloat?'

'I'm afraid he did.'

'Well, I suppose it's justified,' said Kazhian, and she could tell from his voice that he was grinning. 'It's probably his first successful mission – and a bonus prisoner as well! I expect he's hoping to be made Shipmaster on the strength of it.'

Mallaso drew back a little to study him. The green eyes were alight with mischief and his mouth was trying in vain to be serious. He looked as if he was enjoying a relaxing evening at home. And instead he, and she, and Kiyu, were incarcerated on an Imperial galley, and being carried inexorably towards a destiny that was almost certain to be so hideous and so frightening that her mind shrank from it. She remembered her mother, forced to watch the cruel execution of her husband and her children before her own protracted death. Was her own fate to be the same?

'Oh, Sashir,' he said, seeing her fear in her face. 'I know. I feel it too. But at the moment we are completely powerless. Eslen would die rather than let us escape – all the gold in Penya would not buy him. And for Kiyu's sake, we must keep our spirits up, however much we may despair.'

'She's asleep.'

'Perhaps. But how much does she understand? At a guess, a lot more than we imagined. Sargenay was right – she has power. She Healed my headache, just now – and she's never been taught. She doesn't even *know* she's a sorcerer.'

'And if I hadn't been so frightened of her gift,' Mallaso said bitterly, 'Sargenay would have taught her to use it, and perhaps she would have been able to help us escape.'

'Perhaps she still could.'

'I don't think so. Her power seems to be quite instinctive. Bron's was like that when he was a child – he told me that he used it unconsciously, without thought. And strong emotion always enhanced it. I suspect that if we sat her down and told her to set us free, nothing would happen – and she would be very distressed and upset.'

'I think you're right.' Kazhian's hand stroked her face with loving gentleness. 'There's no use lamenting what can't be changed – that is one of the lessons you taught me, Sashir. And remember this – whatever happens to us, *whatever*, I shall have no regrets.'

'Nor shall I,' she whispered. 'But . . . but I keep remembering my mother. If I was alone, I think I could find the courage to face it. But when I think of watching you, or Kiyu . . .'

'Don't,' he said fiercely. '*Don't* think of it, Sashir. We are alive, and together. And we may be making a very large mountain out of a small rock. We don't know why they want us, after all.'

'I don't think Olkanno has gone to all this trouble just for the pleasure of our company at his supper-table, do you?'

'Perhaps not. But I can guess why he wants me. I'm the last Vessel of the Blood Imperial left alive, remember.'

'Yes, but the galley wasn't sent for you. It was sent for *us*, for me and Kiyu, by special order of the Emperor. Why does he want us?'

'There can only be three reasons,' Kazhian said. 'First, that you were intended as bait to lure me into Olkanno's clutches.'

'I don't think so. If that's the case, why not get rid of me and Kiyu once they'd realized who you were? No, it was *us* they had orders to fetch. You were just a bonus.'

'I'm flattered,' Kazhian said drily. 'So, perhaps not that. Second reason, that it's something to do with your attempt to kill Ba'alekkt on Tekkt.'

Mallaso said in bewilderment, 'Why would Olkanno have a grudge against me because I tried to kill Ba'alekkt?'

'Olyak alone knows. That one is so deep and devious even my father couldn't see to the bottom of him. But you know the saying, of course. "*Vengeance is like good wine – worth hoarding.*" And from what I know of Olkanno, he'd agree wholeheartedly.'

'Even though *he* wanted to kill Ba'alekkt too? I doubt it, somehow.'

'So do I, on reflection. Which leaves us with the third reason – that it's something to do with Bron.'

'How could he know that Bron and I . . .'

'Were once lovers? Or that Kiyu is his child? I don't know, but it doesn't surprise me that Olkanno might have found it out. He has a tame sorcerer, after all – a very nasty piece of work, by all accounts. But I don't think he wants you for your past, or Kiyu for any power she might have. Last night – was it only last night? – I did some thinking, while you were settling her. We know that, wherever Bron is, he has the power to enter her dreams as the Singing Man. And he's entered yours, too. What if he has the power to visit everyone else in their sleep as well?'

Mallaso felt her throat constrict. 'You mean – he is the Flamebearer?'

'Why not? Once we accept that he's alive, he's the most likely candidate. Look at it from Olkanno's point of view, if you can bear to. The Flamebearer is responsible for all the unrest in the provinces, and the secession of Djebb. Olkanno must loathe him. And now, by some means, he has discovered that Bron didn't drown in the Kefirinn after all – he is the Flamebearer. He knows that if Bron isn't stopped, the disintegration of the Empire will gather momentum. Already he's lost Djebb, Penya and Balki. Tatht and Tulyet will probably soon follow. The latest news is that Jaiya and Lai'is are in revolt too. If he's going to rule more than Toktel'yi itself before the year's out, he needs to act, and act fast. And if there *are* any other members of my family left, he'll imagine that they'll be ready to murder him and seize the throne in order to save the Empire. Olkanno must be a frightened man. Terrified of the Flamebearer and scared shitless of losing the Empire. So he's given orders to capture you and Kiyu, either to try and find out where he is, or to lure him to Toktel'yi to save you. And as for me—'

'He'll kill you out of hand,' Mallaso said, and her voice cracked suddenly. 'Oh beloved, why did you come after us?'

'Would you rather I stayed on the quay, and watched all I love being stolen from me? You know me better than that.'

'I know that I love you, and that I can't bear the thought of what is going to happen.' Mallaso swept her tears away with a fierce gesture. 'There must be some way to escape.'

'But we're in the middle of the Southern Sea. And even I can't swim twenty miles, not forgetting that the water is full of sharks. No, our only hope of escape is in Toktel'yi. And we'll probably dock in two or three days' time, if the weather holds.' He smiled. 'Plenty of time to think of something. Trust me, Sashir.'

'Yes,' she said at last.

'Liar.' He kissed her gently. 'I love you so much . . . and I cannot believe that such evil will be allowed to triumph. The gods will surely not permit it.'

'Why not? Penya was destroyed.'

'Yes, but not for ever. You came back, you defeated them. Penya is free now, and Djebb is free. Olkanno can't always win, Sashir. Sooner or later he will fall, whether it is Bron's doing or someone else's. He *must* fall, or what point is there to the world?'

She knew that he was trying to hearten her, but he must know as well as she did that his words were empty. This was not some ancient tale, full of impossible heroism. This was the present and dreadful reality. And unless some astonishing miracle happened, evil would gloatingly triumph after all.

Once the *Battlecry* had drawn clear of the Penyan coast and set her course through the Scatterlings for Toktel'yi, Captain Eslen had sent a message back to the city, borne by a pair of white Imperial pigeons. They both carried the same message, to ensure that even if mishap befell one of them, the news would still reach the Emperor. The birds would fly as straight as a spear-cast for the Imperial pigeon-house, within the grounds of the Palace, and long before the galley reached home waters, Olkanno would know that the mission had been even more successful than originally planned.

Eslen did not know that the agent Ga'alek, acting under orders from the Spymaster, had already secretly sent his own pigeon. This bird, however, had not been bred for the use of Emperors. A dove-grey hen with a bright eye and a swift and unerring flight, she flew over the Scatterlings, across the expanse of open sea between the sprinkled islands and the smooth sweeping curve of the mainland. She drifted down to Toktel'yi on graceful wings, and landed on one of the outer perches of Arkun's pigeon-house, in the overgrown garden of the Old Palace, in the heart of the city.

Arkun's bodyslave brought him the small square of much-folded paper, still sealed. When he was alone again, the Spymaster opened it, and stared down at the neat and tiny writing of his senior agent.

When he had absorbed the details of the message, he lit a lamp and burned it to ashes, rubbing the charred remnants between his hands to ensure that no trace of it remained. Then he blew out the flame, sat down at his desk, and put his head in his hands, trying to think clearly.

So they had the woman and the child. Many soldiers had been lost, but Arkun did not care about that. He closed his eyes, and let Ga'alek's terse words march again through his mind.

We have also captured Lord Kazhian, who tried and failed to rescue them. He will be kept safe to await the Emperor's punishment.

And Arkun knew, only too well, what form that punishment would take. A very public example would be made of the renegade Kazhian. And in the eyes of most loyal Toktel'yans, he would deserve it.

No, Arkun said to himself, beating his fist softly, urgently against his forehead. *No, no, no. He shall not end like that – not if I can help it.*

And the woman and the child too – what had they done to offend Olkanno? They were only tools, to be used, broken, and thrown away. He knew, deep in his soul, that he had reached the point of crisis. He could not continue to pretend to himself that he liked or approved of what Olkanno did, or planned. Even for the greater good of the Empire, the price was too high for him to pay.

But *he* would not pay it. If he did nothing, the woman Mallaso, and her child, and Kazhian, would suffer.

He remembered, with bitter clarity, his cousin's words long ago in his cabin on the *Wind of Morning*, in the days after Ba'alekkt's death. 'Whatever else I've done to be ashamed of, at least I haven't betrayed that dream – *your* dream, Arkun, the hypocrite!'

And, even longer ago, two boys sitting on a wall near a villa on the coast of Tulyet, talking of how they would one day change the world for the better. Once, he had regarded Kazhian with contempt. Now, he saw that his cousin had remained faithful to his ideals, even though he had betrayed his own country by doing so. But he, Arkun, had stayed loyal to the Emperor, and thereby stained his hands indelibly with blood.

He thought of all the people Olkanno had caused to be killed, the squirming bodies on which he had gloatingly and lovingly practised his hideous torture: and of his wife, Djeneb, abused beyond reason.

His final decision made, he felt only relief. At long last the nightmare would soon be ended, one way or the other. And Ga'alek's message had given him the means to do it.

The *Battlecry* sailed into Toktel'yi on the evening tide, her sails furled, her slaves labouring to the beat of the drum. She slid neatly into one of the berths reserved for naval ships, and at once a crowd of well-drilled dockers made her fast at bow and stern.

Eslen, standing on the poop as his sailing master gave the orders, noticed a small boat approaching. It had eight rowers fore and aft, and a closed leather-curtained cabin occupied the space amidships. It came swiftly and discreetly up to the galley's riverward side, and a small, black-clad man climbed up the boarding ladder with impressive agility. 'Captain Eslen? I'm here to take charge of your prisoners.'

The Captain stared at him doubtfully. 'Have you a warrant?'

'Of course, sir. Here.' The man pulled a long, folded piece of paper from his tunic.

Eslen saw the Imperial seal, and nodded. 'Fine. I'll have them brought up now.'

In a few moments, the three dishevelled, blinking captives were escorted aft by Ga'alek. The little girl clutched her mother's skirts, and looked round fearfully, her eyes wide. The man, his hands tightly bound, lifted his unshaven jaw and stared with contemptuous arrogance at the soldiers and sailors who crowded round him. They were loyal subjects of the Empire, and a renegade and traitor, even one who was a Vessel of the Blood Imperial, was repugnant to them. By the time the prisoners reached the side of the ship, Kazhian had been kicked, spat upon and punched in the face.

Eslen, grinning, made no attempt to stop it, despite Mallaso's furious protests. Kazhian himself, with his mouth pouring blood, a burgeoning black eye and a sprinkling of new bruises on arms and legs, had not uttered a word: nor had he shed that infuriating expression of haughty disdain. In all their years together, Mallaso had never seen him display more clearly his two thousand years of Imperial ancestry. And the whisper spread along the docks. 'Lord Kazhian!' 'I'd know him anywhere!' 'Lord Kazhian's been taken!'

Followed by Ga'alek, they climbed down the ladder, and stepped into the boat. The black-clad agent hustled them into the little cabin, and the curtains were laced tightly around them. The sailors lining the galley's sides yelled and jeered, and Kiyu put her hands over her ears.

'It's all right, sweetheart,' Mallaso said, fighting her own overwhelming sense of impotent range. 'Don't listen to them. They're stupid men, they don't understand.'

The boat rocked as the rowers pushed away from the *Battlecry*. Kazhian wiped his bleeding mouth with the back of his hand, and grinned ruefully at his wife. 'You're too kind. Scum of the earth, that lot. Eslen should be flogged and demoted for allowing it.'

'Are you hurt?'

'Nothing that won't mend, given time.' Kazhian paused, as if remembering that they might not have much time left. 'Are *you* all right? And Kiyu?'

The little girl nodded. Kazhian reached across, lifted up Mallaso's hand, and kissed it gently. 'I don't think they have any intention of letting us escape,' he said softly. 'I'm sorry.'

'I'm not. I don't want to see you killed in some futile bid for freedom – and by the look of them, they wouldn't have needed much excuse.' Mallaso swallowed hard, her free hand stroking Kiyu's tangled hair. 'Where do you think they're taking us?'

'I don't know. The Palace, perhaps?'

Mallaso shook her head. 'Then the ship would have tied up at the Imperial Dock, rather than at the Navy berths. Shall I look? There's a gap in the curtain.'

'Be careful,' Kazhian warned.

'Don't worry. They're under orders not to damage me, remember?' She twisted round, pulled the two halves of the curtain apart between the laces, and peered cautiously out. The sunlight, even at this late hour, seemed dazzling, and for a moment all she could see were the heads and shoulders of the rowers, intent on their work. Then Ga'alek, sitting in the bow, spotted her, and shouted angrily. 'You! Get back inside!'

The rhythm of the oarsmen faltered. Mallaso stared defiantly at the agent who had captured them. He was tall, for a Toktel'yan, and he possessed an air of menacing ruthlessness. Refusing to be cowed, she said clearly, 'No, I will not. Not until you've told me where you're taking us.'

'You'll find out soon enough,' Ga'alek said, 'Now get inside, or I'll use this!' He touched the knife at his belt.

'I'm sure the Emperor would not approve,' Mallaso told him calmly. 'You said yourself he had ordered that we be well treated. If I appear before him with a knife wound, he'll blame you.'

'Then I'll make sure Lord Kazhian gets hurt instead,' said the agent. 'Back inside, bitch.'

For a few heartbeats longer, Mallaso stared him out. Then, with cool and contemptuous dignity, she withdrew her head and turned to face her husband. She said softly, 'We're going upstream, towards the Old City.'

'Certainly not the Palace, then.'

'The New Palace, no. But what about the old one?'

'That's the Spymaster's domain. Ga'alek is the Spymaster's agent. So is the man who was sent to pick us up.' He smiled suddenly. 'And the Spymaster is, as far as I know, still Arkun. Who is also my cousin.'

Mallaso stared at him in surprise. 'Your *cousin*? But I thought he was supposed to be a freed slave—'

'He is the son of a Fabrizi slave, who was the concubine of my mother's brother in Tulyet. As boys, we were friends. My mother was very kind to him, and perhaps he's remembered that – although the last time we met, he did his best to kill me.' Kazhian paused, thinking back. 'In fact, he could have done, easily. We fought, and he knocked me out cold. He had ample opportunity to knife me then and there. But when I woke up, he'd gone – so I fled before he could change his mind.' He glanced down at Kiyu, sitting beside her mother, and added very softly, 'So there may, just, be a reason for hope. If Arkun has us, and Olkanno does not know . . .'

It seemed very unlikely to Mallaso. To rely on the compassionate intentions of one of the most notoriously ruthless men in the Empire seemed extremely foolhardy. But anything was better than despair: and for Kiyu's sake, she was determined not to break again beneath the burden of hopelessness and dread.

CHAPTER
TWENTY-SEVEN

The Old Palace had not been inhabited by the Emperors of Toktel'yi for over two hundred years. They had fled the foul waterways and foetid air and disease-ridden streets of the city's heart, and built themselves a splendid new residence of white Annako stone, studded with gardens and courtyards like green jewels, down by the shore, where the sea breezes blew cooling and healthy over the over-heated land.

The home they had abandoned became the official centre of the Empire's huge and obsessive bureaucracy, and was popularly known as the Imperial Heart. Most Ministers had offices and archives here, and it was said that every subject of the Empire, if he looked long and hard enough, could find his name written on at least one of the millions of pieces of charsh paper filed away in tens of thousands of boxes on thousands of shelves in hundreds of tiny, windowless rooms, somewhere in that vast building.

The Spymaster, by far the most powerful of the many officials working in the Old Palace, occupied the two lowest of its five floors. One, at ground level, was reserved for files and archives, presided over by fifty clerks, all hoping one day to be promoted to the far more exciting and prestigious position of agent. The basement, partly dug into the soggy damp marsh beneath, and inadequately lined with stone, housed the cells and interrogation rooms reserved for the Spymaster's personal use.

Under Olkanno, these dark, stinking holes had been full to overflowing, and the Spymaster and his deputies had subjected thousands of unfortunates to rigorous questioning under torture. Many had died in agony, or had succumbed to hunger, disease or neglect. And even more had been taken from these cells to be publicly executed in the great square outside.

Unfortunately, the new Spymaster seemed to have little of Olkanno's relish for cruelty. All the equipment was still lovingly cleaned and oiled by the Chief Keeper, Turgek, but Arkun had seldom ordered its use, preferring his gentler techniques of persuasion, and claiming, to the disgust of the gaolers, that they achieved results just as good as Olkanno's torture and mutilation.

There were still some prisoners in the cells, though, and Turgek took considerable delight in making their lives as miserable as possible before execution. And if they perished from hunger, disease or ill-treatment, their bodies were pushed into murky depths of the Kefirinn.

He had received with pleasure the news that a fresh batch of very important prisoners was expected. As usual, he had no idea who they were, but it did not matter. All who entered the Water Gate of the Old Palace, whether slave or aristocrat, became equal before long, for Turgek, like the Lord of Death, bestowed no favours on the undeserving.

The iron grille clanked slowly upwards, and the boat glided beneath the dripping gate. It was lowered behind them with much creaking of antiquated machinery. Within the curtains, Mallaso heard the booming echoes, and the eerily loud splash of water drops, and knew that they had entered the Old Palace. Once, Emperors had been rowed in state into this dank hall. Now, the only people to be brought here were the condemned.

Abruptly, the curtains were unlaced, and Ga'alek peered inside. 'Come on, you,' he said brusquely. 'Out.'

One by one, the three prisoners emerged reluctantly from inside the small cabin. The air within had been hot and stuffy, but in the Water Hall of the Old Palace, the cold struck so deep that it made Mallaso shiver. Kiyu whimpered, and hung back. Ga'alek picked her up and dumped her on to the wet, slippery stones beside the boat. He laughed at Mallaso's indignant protest, and watched with a sneer as she scrambled out and took the sobbing child in her arms. Kazhian came next, his hands still bound, and as he stepped over the side one of the rowers slid his oar out through the rowlock, knocking his legs from under him. Unable to break his fall, he crashed to the ground, and the oarsman sniggered.

'That's enough.'

The new voice, hard as adamant, took Mallaso by surprise. Still furious, she turned and saw a tall, red-haired man standing by the huge door which presumably led to the cells. He wore a long black gown, plain and unadorned, and his mouth was no more than a thin line.

'Enough,' he repeated. 'We are not barbarians. Help him up.'

'I don't need it,' Kazhian said. Stubbornly, he shook off the nearest rower's reluctant hand, and struggled to his feet. Despite the blood and dirt and bruises, the sneer was still insultingly explicit on his face. He stared contemptuously at the tall man, and added softly, 'Come to gloat, *cousin*?'

The other man walked forward until he was standing directly in front of Kazhian. There was no resemblance at all between then, but even if Kazhian had not addressed him as 'cousin', Mallaso would still have known that he was the Spymaster.

'I am no kin of yours, traitor,' said Arkun. 'Take him to his cell.'

The shadows behind him moved. Two men in the black, hooded garments that all agents wore came swiftly forward. They grabbed Kazhian's pinioned hands and dragged him unceremoniously away. He glanced back over his shoulder as they hustled him through the doorway, and Mallaso heard his voice calling her name.

'Please let us stay together!' she cried in distress.

'He will not be far away,' said the Spymaster. 'You will hear him, I promise you.' His voice was full of menace. 'Now your turn, lady.'

Two more agents came up to her. She picked up Kiyu, who was still weeping, and stared at them defiantly. 'Keep your hands away from us. I will come with you quietly.'

'Good,' Arkun said. 'I'm glad you at least seem to have some sense. I will see you later, lady.'

Her head high, she walked slowly between the two black-clad men to the door. Kiyu was heavy, but she had no intention of putting her down. It looked as though the Spymaster was not, despite Kazhian's hopes, inclined to be merciful, and she would not give him any pretext to take the child away from her.

As she reached the doorway, several more minions ran past. Puzzled, she turned round. The rowers, together with Ga'alek and the other agent, were still in the boat. Arkun said something curtly, and the new arrivals paused on the quayside. She saw their arms move in a curious, low, slicing pattern. The air hummed. Ga'alek clutched his face and collapsed backwards on to one of the oarsmen. The other agent, bewildered, struggled to his feet, only to drop without a sound into the bottom of the boat. Within a few heartbeats, the vessel contained only a tangled heap of twitching corpses, where there had been, just a moment before, ten living men.

'Come on,' said one of the agents sharply. And suddenly sick with horror, Mallaso turned away from the carnage and hurried through the doorway.

A long corridor stretched before her, lined with barred cells. The stink of filth and damp and decay was appalling, but she had lived for fifteen years in Toktel'yi, and this was not very much worse than Cormorant Channel in summer. Doubtless tonight ten more corpses, stripped and anonymous, would be pushed into the foul water of the

Kefirinn, to be washed out to sea by the cleansing tide, or collected days later by the scavengers and burnt on the public pyre.

Her heart was full of dread, but she walked steadily on up the long central corridor. She noticed that many of the cells were empty, and those that were occupied were furnished only with heaps of dirty rushes. Rats scuttled everywhere, and most of the unfortunate prisoners appeared to be ill, or even dying. Kazhian was not amongst them.

Half-way down the passage, there was a crossroads, and waiting there, arms folded, was a man with a huge bunch of keys at his belt, who must be the gaoler. He was big, for a Toktel'yan, and his vast belly strained his sweaty, stained cotton gown. As Mallaso approached, his face broke into a beaming smile. 'Ah, another guest! *Two* guests! Welcome to my humble establishment, lady. Will you come this way? My Lord Spymaster has instructed me to look out the most luxurious and spacious accommodation in these lodgings, and I must spare no effort to make sure that you are comfortable. There you are, lady – just round the corner from my own room. If you need anything, you only have to ask – and you might receive it. Dinner will be served at sunset.' And with a gleeful smile, he pulled the iron grille shut behind her. 'Delighted to have you with us, lady. I do hope you enjoy your stay, brief though it may be. Goodbye!'

It was better than the cells she had just seen. There was actually a mattress, though it was torn and filthy, with a couple of ragged blankets flung across it. Clean, shredded rushes had been scattered over the floor, and there was a wooden bucket in the corner.

Kiyu raised her tear-streaked face from Mallaso's shoulder and stared round in weary bewilderment. 'Mama, where is this?'

'Prison, sweetheart,' Mallaso said. At least there appeared to be no rats, though a positive thicket of spiders' webs clustered in the corners above them, and anything might be lurking in the deep cracks between the ancient and crumbling stones.

'How long are we going to stay here?' the little girl asked. 'Mama, I don't like it here, I *don't*.'

'I don't like it here either, but until they let us go there's nothing we can do.' Mallaso sat down on the mattress, her arms and back aching with the effort of holding Kiyu for so long. 'Are you tired?'

'I'm hungry,' her daughter announced firmly. 'When did that nastily nice man say dinner would be?'

'At sunset.' In other circumstances, the 'nastily nice man' would have made Mallaso smile. Now, she was too tired and full of dread to gain any amusement at all from their terrible situation. Kazhian would have done: but Kazhian had been taken from them, and she did not know if she would ever see him again.

Tears prickled her eyes, and she almost gave way to despair, but Kiyu was asking urgently when sunset would be, and for the child's sake she had to hide her fear. 'About an hour, or so – not long,' she told her, and surreptitiously wiped her eyes.

'Good,' said Kiyu. She looked round again, frowning, her composure nearly restored in the almost miraculous way of small children. 'Where's Kazhian?'

'I don't know, sweetheart. The tall man said he'd be close.' She shivered at the horrible implications of Arkun's words.

'I'll call him, then.' Kiyu jumped up from the mattress and went to the iron grille that separated the cell from the passage outside. 'Kazhian? KAZHIA – A – A – N!'

Her raucous, childish voice echoed down the long corridors. Distantly, someone cried out in reply, but it was not her stepfather. Kiyu shouted several times more, but there was no further response. Mallaso squeezed her hands together until they hurt. Was he already dead?

'Stop,' she said sharply to her daughter, who was inflating her chest for another yell. 'Please stop. He isn't answering.'

'But why not, Mama?'

'I don't know. Come and sit by me. Please.'

Kiyu surveyed her. Then she said quietly, 'It's all right, Mama. I don't mind if you cry.'

And that, as perhaps she had intended, broke down even Mallaso's desperate self-control.

Captain Eslen, having got rid of his prisoners and successfully discharged his mission, was pleased to see a detachment of the Imperial Guard march up to the wharf beside his ship, shortly before sunset. Smiling in expectation of the fat reward he had been promised, he walked down the gangplank to greet them.

The officer-in-charge saluted with a clash of arms. 'His Imperial Majesty requests custody of the captives brought from Penya, Captain.'

Eslen stared at him in bewilderment. 'But I have already handed them over. A boat took them away just after we docked – about an hour ago.'

The Hundred-Commander's face changed abruptly, as if an iron shutter had slammed down across it. 'Then they are no longer in your possession?'

'They are not.' Eslen was beginning to feel alarmed. Something had evidently gone wrong, and he did not need to be a soothsayer to know where the blame would be placed. A cold sweat broke out on his brow. 'I handed them over in good faith – the man had the Emperor's own warrant—'

'Indeed, Captain. Well, perhaps you had better explain all this to His Imperial Majesty. He has been waiting with extreme eagerness for these prisoners, and as I am sure you will appreciate, if they have somehow gone astray he will be grievously disappointed. Now, will you come with me, sir?'

His tone was courteous and polite, but he had twenty heavily armed troops behind him, and Eslen knew there was no choice. He swallowed hard, trying to conceal his fear, and nodded. 'Of course.'

A litter had been brought, presumably for the prisoners: it resembled a curtained cage on poles. Thankfully, Eslen was not offered the chance to ride in it. He walked alongside the officer, hoping he looked as nonchalant as if he was in fact going to collect his due reward for good service.

And instead, he knew that he would be very lucky to escape with his life.

He had set foot in the Palace before, on various official occasions, but never, in his worst dreams, had he expected to enter it as a virtual prisoner. Still with that ominously chilly courtesy, he was ushered through a succession of outer courtyards, and tried to work out where, in this huge labyrinth of a building, he was being taken. Surely the Imperial suite lay in the other direction?

They came to a courtyard that was shabby and neglected compared to those through which they had just passed. Eslen looked round in bewilderment at the weeds and broken flagstones and peeling plaster. There was an evil stench in the air, as if this were some squalid slum off one of the back channels of the Kefirinn. The officer laughed at his expression of distaste. 'Don't you know who lives here? Go on in, he's waiting for you.'

Eslen was neither clever nor quick: it took a few heartbeats for the awful truth to penetrate his confusion. Then he blenched, and shook his head vehemently. 'No. Oh, no. I'm not going in there. No – you can't make me – no!'

'You are a servant of His Imperial Majesty,' said the officer contemptuously. 'You have no choice. Are you a man, or a cowardly rat? In!'

Still Eslen hesitated. With an expression of disgust, the officer unsheathed his sword and pointed it at the other man's belly. 'In!'

At last, the Captain turned, his bowels loosening in the extremity of his terror, and stumbled through the dark entrance to the foul room beyond. The door slammed shut behind him, and someone sniggered softly, expectantly.

'Captain Eslen?'

It was the Emperor's voice, as soft and slippery as silk. At once Eslen flung himself to the floor in a gesture of grovelling apology. 'Imperial Majesty – forgive me – I didn't know – I suspected nothing – oh, please forgive me!'

There was a brief silence, full of unspeakable menace. Olkanno said softly, 'Am I to understand, Captain, that you bring no prisoners with you?'

'N-no, Imperial Majesty.'

'But your message stated unequivocally that you had captured them, and would deliver them to me here. Where are they, then, Captain Eslen? Do tell me. I look forward to hearing your explanation.'

By the sound of his voice, the Emperor was standing right over him. Crushed by terror, Eslen whimpered like a baby.

'I have been awaiting these people day and night for half a month. My future plans – indeed, the future of the whole Empire – may depend on their safe arrival. And now Captain Eslen seems to have mislaid them. A little careless of him, don't you think, I'amel?'

The Court Sorcerer's serpentine voice, eerily sibilant, was even more sinister than his master's. 'I do indeed, Imperial Majesty.'

'My good friend here agrees with me. Well, Eslen, where did you lose them? Did they fall overboard? Did a sea monster rise up out of the waves and seize them in its tentacles? You can tell me everything,' said Olkanno, as softly and kindly as a Priest of Kaylo. 'Tell me the truth.'

'Imperial Majesty, I swear on my life I do not know!'

'Know what? Tell me, Eslen, or I shall grow impatient. And that might prove very unpleasant for you.'

'I-Imperial M-M-Majesty, they were t-taken when we docked!'

'*Taken?* By whom?'

'A boat, Imperial Majesty. The agent Ga'alek seemed to know the man in charge. And he showed me his warrant. Everything was in order, so I allowed him to take the prisoners away.'

'How closely did you examine this man's credentials?'

'I – I gave them a glance, Imperial Majesty, and they seemed in order. Your seal was on the paper—'

'No, it was not. That paper was a forgery. The only warrant I signed was given to K'net, the Hundred-Commander who brought you here.' A toe nudged his arm sharply. 'Get up, Eslen. I said, *get up*!'

Hastily the Captain scrambled to his feet. He was taller than Olkanno, but felt at no advantage. The Emperor's face was plump and smooth in the flickering light of the candles around the walls of the room, and his smile was at once gentle, and full of terrible cruelty. 'Your eyesight must be poor indeed, Eslen, to have overlooked such an obvious counterfeit. Much too poor for you to keep your present command. However, my friend here has a remedy for that. I'amel?'

'Your Imperial Majesty wishes?'

'His eyes are useless. Remove them.'

Eslen screamed in horror, and turned to run. The necromancer hissed something, and coils of sorcery froze his limbs. The last thing he saw, as he waited helplessly for his fate, was the Black Mage's skull-like face, and the smile on his thin lips as he raised the knife.

Much later, when Eslen's agonies had ended at last, Olkanno watched as I'amel carefully drained the Captain's blood into his silver scrying bowl. 'I want to know where they are, and who has taken them.'

'Certainly, Imperial Majesty.' I'amel carried the vessel over to his table, which was heaped with bones and pieces of flesh, and crusted with gobbets of dried blood. He set it down with infinite care. 'The bowl shall give me the answers you seek, Imperial Majesty. And as you know, it has not failed me yet.'

Olkanno waited. The room stank hideously of rotting corpses, fresh blood and excrement, but he had long since grown used to the reek of torture and death. He watched as the necromancer cradled the wide bowl in his hands, and crooned to it in the harsh language of the Ska'i, almost like a mother soothing her fractious infant. Then the chant died away, and I'amel passed his hands three times over the dark murky surface of Eslen's blood. He uttered a high, keening wail that would have chilled any other soul but Olkanno's. The Emperor stared with interest at the liquid, but it remained obstinately clear of any image, for only sorcerers could see within the bowl.

'A-a-ah!' I'amel breathed a soft sigh of exultation. 'I see the woman. She is tall and black-skinned. A child is with her.'

'Yes?' Olkanno prompted, with carefully harnessed impatience.

'The image is wavering. I cannot hold it – no, it is gone.' I'amel's fangs sank in his lip. 'A curse on that man's foul blood. It has spoilt the scrying.'

'Tell me *exactly* what you saw, my friend.'

'The woman and the child. They were weeping together. They seemed to be imprisoned.'

'Where?'

'I do not know, Imperial Majesty. The bowl does not speak – it only shows. And the scene I saw may be the past, or the present. But the walls were of stone, so they are not now on the ship.'

'Stone walls.' Olkanno's hand smacked down on the table. 'I knew it! The worm has finally turned traitor!'

'What do you mean, Imperial Majesty?'

'The Imperial gaol has walls of mud brick, my friend. The only prison in Toktel'yi with walls of stone is, as you will remember, under the Old Palace. And controlled by—'

'Arkun, the Spymaster. Ai-ee!' The Black Mage's skinny arms stretched up as he screeched in triumph. 'At last we have him! For months now I have feared that he is disloyal in his heart. And if we find the woman Mallaso in his custody, that will be all the proof we need of his treachery.'

'Yes,' said the Emperor. 'I knew he would one day turn against me, the ungrateful slave-born cur! I raised him from the gutter, and made him one of the greatest powers in the Empire. And this is how he repays me!'

'The woman is handsome, Imperial Majesty. So is the child. Perhaps he wants to use them for his own purposes.'

'No. Arkun is not a womanizer or a pervert. He has been as celibate as a Priest of Olyak in recent years. No, there is some other reason. The renegade Kazhian is his cousin – perhaps he still feels some obligation of kinship.'

'Imperial Majesty, you are making excuses for his inexcusable treachery and disloyalty.'

Olkanno stared at his sorcerer coldly. 'I shall be the judge of that. Do not presume to question me, or my motives, or my actions, I'amel. Like Arkun, I have raised you far above your lowly origins – and like his, your fall will be very great.'

'I am Your Imperial Majesty's most humble servant.'

'I advise you not to overdo the grovelling servility, I'amel. Well, since we now know the location of our prisoners, I suggest that we pay a surprise visit to the Spymaster's lair.'

*

There was little light in the prison beneath the Old Palace. It filtered through the small, high, barred windows, and crept miserly into those cells which faced the outer walls. Mallaso, huddled with Kiyu on the mattress, knew that it must now be later than sunset, for darkness was spreading out from the dim corners which it inhabited all day. But there was no food for them yet, and no water either. How long would it take to die of thirst?

Alone, she could have endured it, withdrawing into the stone core of her heart that had sustained her during the long, terrible years of slavery. But Kiyu shared her captivity, making the horror a thousand times worse. She knew that she should try to smile and sing songs to keep the demons at bay. But when she saw her daughter's wan, frightened face, and thought of what fate might soon bring to Kiyu, her resolution faltered. As the little girl slept, exhausted, beside her, she prayed desperately to Sarraliss, the Mother who above all other deities would understand and wish to help. *Keep her safe. Let her not see, or feel, or experience the horror that awaits us. I do not care what happens to me, so long as she does not suffer!*

And her heart ached, too, for Kazhian, who might already be dead: for the happiness of the past, and the joyful future which had now been wrenched so brutally away from them. She grieved for their unborn child, who would die with her: but at least it would never know the fear and horror that would surely destroy Kiyu's sanity and any hope of happiness, even if by some miracle she survived.

She heard footsteps approaching along the stone corridor. From the heavy tread and the flat jangle of keys, it must be the gaoler. She got up very carefully, trying not to wake Kiyu, and took the five brief steps to the grille which formed the front wall of their cell.

The man was carrying a tray. He set it down on the slimy stone floor and selected a key. Mallaso watched as he turned it in a lock near the bottom of the grille, lifted up a sliding panel of iron bars, and pushed the tray through into the cell. 'There you are, lady. Dinner as promised – a little late, but better late than never, eh? Enjoy your meal!'

'Wait!' Mallaso said urgently. 'A light – can we have a light?'

The gaoler looked at her, his falsely jovial smile still creasing his fat face. 'A light, lady? No one in here has a light.'

'The Emperor has ordered that we be well treated,' Mallaso said, trying to sound authoritative rather than desperate. 'My child is afraid of the dark. His Imperial Majesty will not be pleased if she is made ill with fear.'

The keeper roared with laughter, so loudly that Kiyu whimpered and sat up. 'The *Emperor*? You are not here at the *Emperor's* command, lady. This is the *Spymaster's* domain. And he has said—'

'Let her have a light.'

One of the growing, lurking shadows had become human. Mallaso's hands clenched on the bars as she watched Arkun approach. In his black garments, with his pale skin and red hair, he was a sinister and frightening figure. She could not imagine this man ever being friendly with Kazhian, or harbouring any feelings of compassion or humanity whatsoever. And they were in his power, not the Emperor's. Why? Did the Spymaster plan to use them as weapons or bargaining counters in some conspiracy of his own against Olkanno?

Grudgingly, the gaoler handed his lantern to his master. Arkun took it. 'Open the cell, then leave us.'

The gaoler thrust his key into the grille's central lock, and turned it. The door creaked wide with a groan of rusty metal. With a last, reproachful look at the Spymaster, he turned and lumbered away.

Arkun stood holding the lantern until the fat man had turned the corner. Then he nodded at the tray of food. 'Eat. The child looks hungry, and it will not poison you.'

Mallaso stared at him with loathing. Finally, she said, 'How can I possibly be sure of that?'

'You can't. But if it helps, ask yourself why I would want to kill you now, having gone to so much trouble to bring you here.'

She knew it made sense, but she still could not trust him. She picked up the tray and carried it over to Kiyu. There was a bowl of soggy brown rice, another of overcooked vegetables swimming miserably in a pool of greasy yellow water, and several shrivelled starfruits. She sampled the rice and stew, found both dishes tasteless but safe, and pushed them over to her daughter. As the little girl began to eat hungrily, she turned back to Arkun. 'Where is Kazhian?'

'Elsewhere. You need not worry. He is unharmed.'

'I would prefer to see that for myself.'

'Don't you trust me?' Arkun asked. His brown eyes surveyed her thoughtfully. 'Are you his woman?'

Mallaso drew herself up proudly. 'I am his wife.'

'His *wife*?' For the first time, Arkun's chilly composure was cracked. 'He *married* you?'

'Don't look so surprised,' Mallaso said with hostility. 'Is it so unlikely?'

'Given his past history, yes.' Arkun smiled suddenly, and the transformation was astonishing. 'May I sit down?'

Mallaso looked round at the barely furnished cell. 'If you must.'

With care, he folded himself on to the free end of the mattress. Kiyu, still shovelling rice and vegetables into her mouth, barely glanced up from the bowls. At home, Mallaso would have scolded her for lack of manners: here, when this meal might be their last, she could not bring herself to be angry with the child.

'Listen to me, Mallaso of Penya. I know you do not trust me. I know you fear and hate me and all I represent, and you have every right to do so.' His voice had dropped almost to a whisper, quiet but urgent. 'But I did not have you brought to Toktel'yi. That was Olkanno's doing. I managed to intercept you. You were intended to be the bait in his trap, and now you are the bait in mine. But I have no desire to harm you. Do you believe me?'

'Perhaps,' said Mallaso, studying him. Like all of his kind, he seemed so expert at deception and concealment that sincerity, however genuine, could not ring true. She wanted desperately to cling to the hope he offered, like a drowning sailor to a spar. But she could not. Kazhian and Sargenay were the only Toktel'yans she had ever fully trusted. Why make an exception for Olkanno's Spymaster, loathed and feared throughout the Empire?

'I don't blame you,' he said, and smiled again. 'Do you know why you have been brought here? Why Olkanno wants you and the child?'

She glanced at Kiyu, whose frantic feeding had now slowed to a more decorous pace. 'No. I have no idea.' She had no intention of revealing how much she and Kazhian had suspected until she was certain that Arkun did indeed mean them no harm.

'No?' He stared at her thoughtfully. 'If what I have heard of you is true, then you must at least have guessed.'

'I told you – I don't know.'

'As you wish.' Arkun looked down at his hands. 'A long time ago, five years ago, when Ba'alekkt lived and Olkanno was still the Spymaster, I was his most trusted agent, sent on missions of utmost secrecy. Of course, I was with my master as the Imperial Army gathered at Tamat. And the night before Ba'alekkt was due to begin the attack on Minassa and Zithirian, Olkanno called me to him, and ordered me to search in secret for an escaped prisoner, who had already tried, and failed, to kill the Emperor. He was supposed to be an extremely powerful and dangerous sorcerer, but my master suspected that he would be hurt, because of the beating he had received at his capture, and later from the Emperor himself.'

Mallaso drew a deep, shivering breath. The present Spymaster glanced at her, and then continued.

'As it happened, much to my relief, Olkanno was right. The sorcerer had tried to reach the western border, which was so inadequately guarded that it would have been easy for him to cross. But he never got there. The dogs found him ten miles short of safety. He was unconscious and feverish. I ordered him to be loaded into a cart, and taken back to Tamat. Olkanno planned to use him to gain the Emperor's favour, and also to turn Ba'alekkt against Al'Kalyek, whom he suspected of assisting the sorcerer's escape.

'I presented the assassin to the Emperor. He was delighted – and, as Olkanno had hoped, furious with Al'Kalyek, particularly as the old man had refused, until forced, to confirm that the sorcerer was indeed the bastard son of the King of Zithirian. Ba'alekkt rashly decided to take the prisoner with him, and ordered him to be put in the Imperial barge. Olkanno protested, but the Emperor insisted. And that was his undoing – for the sorcerer was not so helpless as he appeared. Half-way over the Kefirinn, he sent the boat to the bottom, and Ba'alekkt and himself with it. But Al'Kalyek survived, although he abandoned the Empire and disappeared for almost a year – before turning up at Onnak. Olkanno sent me to bring him to Toktel'yi, and now he is dead.'

'Al'Kalyek is dead? But how—'

'I will spare you the details. He refused to reveal anything until the very end, when his spirit was finally deserting his body. That is how Olkanno knew about you and your child. A child who is apparently the daughter of that assassin whom I captured outside Tamat. How old is she?'

'She will be five just before this coming Year-turn,' said Mallaso. 'If she lives that long.'

'I intend to ensure that she does – and that you and Kazhian celebrate her birthday with her.' Arkun glanced at the child. 'So he cannot even have known of her existence.'

'He did.' Mallaso remembered, with poignant clarity, the night of Kiyu's conception, and the words that Bron had sent to her, just before he went into the river.

Arkun gave her a considering look. 'Then you admit the child is his.'

'There is a chance that she is Ba'alekkt's.'

Kiyu raised her head, and stared at her mother and the black-clad stranger. To a casual observer, she bore no resemblance to the fair-haired, pale-skinned man who had fathered her. But Arkun nodded suddenly. 'His eyes were very dark, like hers are. And I remember something else. His powers were all the more extraordinary because they owed nothing to Annatal or to any other drug – they were natural, inborn. So if she has inherited his eyes, has she also inherited his sorcery? Is *that* why I'amel wants her? Not as bait to catch the Flamebearer, but as a prize in her own right?'

Mallaso felt sick. She said, 'Kiyu is not a sorceress. She's only four years old, for the Mother's sake! And I've never seen the slightest indication that she possesses any power whatsoever.'

'Well, I hope you never have to convince I'amel. He is a Black Mage, a necromancer. Do you know what they are?'

Her nausea increased. She nodded not trusting herself to speak.

'Such creatures have a vile reputation, and I'amel is worse than vile. But with all his ghastly rites, he is still less powerful than he claims. It was not his magic that defeated Al-Kalyek, but the kindness of Olyak.' He shuddered, his eyes shadowed with the memory. 'Neither he nor Olkanno can claim any knowledge or understanding of decency, or kindness, or compassion, or even humanity – though no animal takes delight in inflicting pain for its own sake. For too long I have locked away my own disgust and revulsion. The manner of Al'Kalyek's death turned the key in my heart – and you and your daughter have opened the door.'

'I'm not interested in your motives,' said Mallaso, wondering uneasily how much of this intense, whispered conversation Kiyu had heard, or understood. 'But I want to know why you think Bron – her father – is not dead.'

'He is the Flamebearer. I'amel saw it in his scrying bowl, or so he claimed. At first he thought it was Al'Kalyek – that is why they sent me to take him. But I'amel soon realized that Al'Kalyek could not have been the Flamebearer. Only Bron possessed enough power – and so Bron must still be alive. Do you know where he is?'

Mallaso shook her head. 'No I do not. So do Olkanno and I'amel think they can lure him here to save us? Is *that* why we've been brought here, as the bait in a trap?'

Arkun nodded. 'Yes. But I snatched you first. Neither of them, whatever they may like to think, is omnipotent, or infallible. And their continued absence from Olyak's nethermost Halls of torment is an affront to all the known world. You and Bron and Kazhian will help me to send them there. And when their foul excrescence has been obliterated, all of you may go in peace.'

She could not say when she had begun to believe him. Perhaps it was when she had realized, reluctantly, that he had no need to tell her all this, save to confide the truth that had long been eating away at his soul. She whispered, 'Thank you.'

He smiled at her, and at the child. Kiyu regarded him thoughtfully, her dark eyes, Bron's eyes, watchful and opaque. Mallaso, who had always been sensitive to the use of sorcery, felt a faint and subtle tingling on her skin.

'You are our friend,' said the little girl suddenly. 'Will you really let us go?'

'I will, I swear it – but not yet. I'm afraid that you must stay here for the moment.'

'Why?'

'It won't be long, sweetheart,' Mallaso told her. 'And at least he is our friend.'

'A good one,' Arkun said. He rose to his feet and stood looking down at them. 'I gave him water, when he was lying in the boat. And I have often wondered since then, if I thereby gave him the strength to kill Ba'alekkt – and the strength to survive. If so, then I am glad that I did.'

'So am I,' Mallaso said. She got up, and gave him the two hands of friendship. 'Thank you, Spymaster, for all your kindness.'

'My name is Arkun. And you should thank me when this is over, one way or the other – for nothing is certain yet. I must go – I have much to do. Turgek, the gaoler, will be given strict orders to be kind to you, and supply you with anything you need. I will return later. And remember – *whatever* happens, *whatever* appearance I may give, *whatever* I may say or do – I am your friend, and Kazhian's, now and always. Do you believe me, lady?'

And it was Kiyu, her dark eyes serious and steady, who said, 'Yes.'

CHAPTER
TWENTY-EIGHT

Foul deeds in Toktel'yi were usually committed under cover of darkness. Even in a city so corrupt and decadent, murderers, rapists, arsonists, and thieves felt safest within the comforting shroud of night. And despite their terrifying and apparently absolute authority, Emperors still conducted their most horrible crimes well out of the public gaze – particularly if, like Olkanno, they felt their power to be under threat.

So the detachment of the Imperial Guard did not leave the Palace until an hour after the sun had set. They had been split into two groups. The smaller contingent would be ferried from the Palace dock, over the Kefirinn's main channel, which had no bridge, to the large swampy island on which the Old City was built. They would then march up through the narrow, squalid streets until they reached the Old Palace at the northern tip. Meanwhile, the remainder, perhaps fifty men, would be rowed upstream in a flotilla of boats, and surround the building by water. If Arkun, learning of imminent disaster, attempted to smuggle himself and his valuable prisoners out through the Water Gate, he would be seized immediately.

Olkanno, who remembered with disturbing clarity the unfortunate end of Ba'alekkt, accompanied the smaller force, in a plain curtained litter, his sorcerer following in a similar conveyance. If anyone dared to look out from the houses they passed, there would be no sign that the Emperor himself was present. But the sight and sound of the soldiers had already sent all the dubious denizens of the night scuttling back to their lairs.

The Old Palace showed no lights. Most respectable workers were home by sunset, and the rest had long since joined those in search of entertainment in the Old City's brothels, eating-houses, taverns, music-rooms or kuldi-houses. Olkanno knew that even if any over-enthusiastic bureaucrat did still linger over his papers, he would make himself scarce at the first sign of trouble. It was always safer not to see too much, in Toktel'yi.

He waited outside the Prison Gate, on the eastern side of the building, while K'net, the Hundred-Commander who had arrested

Captain Eslen earlier that day, beat on the door with the hilt of his sword, and demanded entry in the Spymaster's name, for an important prisoner and his escort. He smiled as he heard the sounds of the gaoler's surprise, followed by the opening of the door.

And once inside Arkun's domain, it would be easy for thirty men of the Imperial Guard, the best soldiers in the finest army in the known world, to overcome Arkun's agents and assassins.

The litter was set down. Olkanno waited until K'net pulled back the curtains and then emerged.

The expression on the gaoler's face was an amusing blend of horror and astonishment. He tried to shout something, perhaps a warning to his comrades, but I'amel was standing next to the Emperor, and his outstretched hand withered the words in Turgek's throat. Mute, helpless, the fat warder stared at them, his eyes bulging.

'Bind him securely, and take him to the larger interrogation room,' said Olkanno. I'amel had informed him earlier, when they had discussed their strategy, that he would need the man for his rites. The Emperor had long since ceased to feel any frisson of excitement at the prospect of torturing and mutilating a mere gaoler. However, the thought of what he planned to do to Kazhian, and to the woman and the child, had been quickening his heart all evening.

After her conversation with Arkun, Mallaso had found herself hungry enough, and hopeful enough, to eat the food that Kiyu had left. It was cold and unappetizing, but she devoured it all. Then, with the small valiant flame of the lantern glowing in a corner of their cell, she lay down on the mattress with her daughter snuggled beside her, and tried in vain to find sleep.

Snatches of Arkun's words kept returning to reverberate in her mind with new significance. *'You were intended to be the bait in his trap. Now you are the bait in mine.' 'Is that why I'amel wants her. . . as a prize in her own right?' 'You and your daughter and Kazhian may go in peace.'*

Kiyu trusted him. And Kiyu, perhaps without even realizing what she was doing, had used her power to see inside his head. But what could a four-year-old child, whose life up until now had been almost entirely filled with happiness and love and peace, know of treachery or deceit?

She tried to work out Arkun's plan. From what he had told her, she could guess that he hoped Olkanno and his sorcerer would come to seize the prisoners. But what would happen then? Would Arkun kill the Emperor? And how did he intend to dispose of the terrifying Black Mage? I'amel seemed to be as foul a sorcerer as the witch D'thliss, who had left appalling scars on Bron's mind.

But in the end, Bron had proved stronger than D'thliss, stronger even than the Devourer. He was surely more powerful than the necromancer. She suspected that Arkun knew it, and wanted to use Bron to destroy I'amel.

But in the process, she and Kiyu and Kazhian might be hurt or killed. And she suspected, with cold and bitter clarity, that despite his comforting words earlier, the Spymaster thought that all three of them were expendable. The destruction of Olkanno and his sorcerer was the only thing that really mattered. And beside the threat they posed to all the civilized world, the lives of a man and a woman and a child meant nothing.

She lay in the dim, kindly glow of the lantern, her eyes tightly shut, and prayed over and over again to Sarraliss, to save them. For Olkanno would dismember Kiyu piece by piece, if he thought it would bring the Flamebearer into his power.

Suddenly, she heard voices, and the tramp of many marching feet. It was pointless to try and hide, so she sat up on the mattress, and gathered the sleeping child into her arms hoping that she would not be woken by the horrible sounds of fighting and slaughter outside their cell.

In a few moments, it was all over. She could see the glow from several torches, flickering along the wall outside the cell. Then, horribly close, she heard the soft, unmistakable voice of Olkanno, and her bones seemed to crumble in terror.

The last time that sound had assaulted her mind, she had also been a captive, just after her failure to assassinate Ba'alekkt. And still, in her nightmares, she could remember Olkanno's gloating face as he described in loving detail exactly what he would do to her before she died.

Sick with dread, she held Kiyu tightly, and waited. The tramping feet came closer. She heard doors being unlocked, and the sounds of search. At last a tall soldier of the Imperial Guard, a flaming torch held high in his hand, strode up to the barred door of their cell. He turned and shouted. 'Here, Imperial Majesty! They're here!'

'Excellent.' Olkanno walked along the passage and stood on the other side of the grille, looking in. His monstrous moving shadow stretched right across the stone floor, and up the far wall behind her. 'Secure them, and take them to the interrogation room.'

The soldier unlocked the door and the two others stepped in. Mallaso was pulled to her feet and her hands tied in front of her with rope. Kiyu, she was relieved to see, was left unbound, but one of the soldiers picked her up, despite her cries and struggles, and carried her out of the cell. As Mallaso was pulled after her, Olkanno smiled. 'Yes, I remember you very clearly. Do you remember me, Penyan bitch?'

She stared at him contemptuously, hiding her overwhelming fear and did not answer.

'You would do well to cooperate, Mallaso of Penya. It would certainly make your death more pleasant – and your child's death too, when we have finished with you both. I am very much looking forward to this night, and so is I'amel. Have you heard of my friend from Lai'is?'

Reluctantly, she nodded.

'Good. Then you know what his favourite practices are. Perhaps you will even come to regard me as a friend, in preference to him. He is very keen to meet you, and your daughter. He has plans for you both. As I have plans for Lord Kazhian, who has evaded justice for so long. Take her away!'

Unkind hands pushed her out of the cell, that now seemed like a refuge. The corridor was full of soldiers, and she could hear more shouting in the distance. Fear filled her. How could Arkun possibly prevail against this overwhelming force?

She was hustled along past other cells, all dark and apparently empty. The black-clad bodies of several agents lay where they had fallen. At the end of the long passage lay an open door, made of solid wood instead of iron bars. Several soldiers stood on guard outside. Mallaso stumbled past them, and into the room beyond.

It was large, and well lit by several torches thrust into brackets on the walls. High up, near the ceiling, there were several long, narrow barred openings, but no other windows. The air within was smoky, and very hot. A brazier burned with sullen portent, casting an evil red glare at the knives and instruments laid out ready on the central table.

The soldiers pushed Mallaso roughly into a corner, and dumped Kiyu beside her. The little girl, sobbing, cowered against her mother. She could not hold her, but at least they were together, and could take comfort in touch.

The fat gaoler, chained to the wall opposite, was not so fortunate. His face was scarlet and pouring sweat, his eyes distended with terror. It did not demand much intelligence, or a particularly lurid imagination, to guess what a necromancer might wish to do to him.

Kiyu suddenly shuddered, and buried her face in her mother's shoulder. Mallaso saw the soldiers step back from the door. One furtively made the sign against evil, and a shadow darkened the entrance.

The child had felt it first: now Mallaso sensed the malevolence pausing outside, gathering its power in readiness. She wanted to hide her eyes too, but some last remnant of defiance made her watch steadfastly as the Black Mage entered the room.

Seen without the burden of knowledge and fear, he would not be particularly impressive. He was small and thin, clad in ragged and filthy black robes, and he carried a silver-tipped staff. But Mallaso looked at the skull-like head, the yellowish skin stretched taut over the sharp bones, the small, deep-set eyes that seemed to hold a red glow, and terror washed over her. She turned her face away, afraid to meet the necromancer's malignant, baleful gaze, but she was aware of his soft approach.

'Look up, woman,' said a sibilant voice, like a whisper of evil. She felt the pull of his mind, and resisted for as long as she could. But at last, unwillingly, she lifted her head.

He was standing so close to her that his foul, reeking garments were almost touching her shrinking skin. He saw her terror and smiled, the rictus pulling his lips back to display his sharpened yellow fangs. 'Good,' he said softly. 'I like it when people show me the proper respect. So you are the Flamebearer's woman? And that is your child? And his, I understand. The Emperor is certain that he will be foolish enough to try and rescue you. I hope he is right, for then I will have him in my power. And once he is slain, you and your daughter will have served that purpose – but I will still have other uses for you, especially the child.' He smiled again, relishing her horror. 'Young flesh has particularly valuable qualities. Enjoy your last hours of life, woman. We must begin soon – this business will be finished by dawn.'

He turned away, laughing softly, and the stink from his robes filled her nostrils. Overcome by nausea, she desperately struggled not to vomit. Beside the Black Mage, Olkanno seemed as harmless as a kitten. What hope did Bron have, *if* he was alive, *if* he came to rescue them, of defeating this nightmare of evil?

There were voices raised outside the room. The Hundred-Commander entered, saluting with a clash of bronze. 'Imperial Majesty, we have found the Spymaster.'

'Have you indeed?' Olkanno glanced at his sorcerer, and smiled with satisfaction. 'Bring him in.'

'He was with Lord Kazhian, Imperial Majesty. Shall we fetch him too?'

'Of course,' said the Emperor, and licked his lips like a hungry jackal. 'There is plenty of room in here for everyone.'

Taller and more imposing by far than the fat, diminutive Olkanno, Arkun walked coolly through the door. He stood facing his master, his face quite expressionless, showing neither fear nor alarm. 'Ah, Imperial Majesty. I am glad to see you here.'

'Are you?' Olkanno stared at him malevolently. 'Tell me why you have stolen my prisoners, Spymaster. Tell me why you and your agents forged the Imperial Seal – a capital offence in itself – and duped Captain Eslen. Your explanation had better be extremely good. I am waiting, and so is my friend I'amel.'

'I had word of a plot, Imperial Majesty,' Arkun said softly. He glanced round at the soldiers filling the doorway. ' A plot against your life.'

Olkanno laughed contemptuously, but the sound seemed a little forced. 'What nonsense is this? *You* are the plotter, Arkun, and for your treachery you will die tonight – slowly, and agonizingly. And I shall enjoy inflicting pain on you even more than I enjoyed torturing Al'Kalyek.'

'I beg you, Imperial Majesty, please listen to me. If you do not, you may regret it.' Arkun's voice was beginning to sound strained and urgent. 'I am Your Imperial Majesty's most loyal subject. I am no conspirator. Indeed, by taking the prisoners from Captain Eslen, I may have saved your life.'

'Really?' Olkanno's gaze was suddenly sharp. 'Explain.'

'My agent, Ga'alek, warned me by pigeon that Captain Eslen was planning to release Lord Kazhian. Once free, he and the Captain would have staged a coup, with the help of certain officers in the Army and also in the Fleet, with the object of killing you and placing Lord Kazhian on the Onyx Throne. I therefore thought it wise to remove the prisoners from the *Battlecry* as soon as she docked, and bring them here, where they would be secure.'

'This is not the story Captain Eslen told me.'

'Well, he would hardly confess his treachery voluntarily,' Arkun pointed out, as calmly as if he were debating some obscure philosophical point in an intellectual gathering. 'Where is he now?'

Olkanno glanced at his necromancer. 'Unfortunately, the Captain is no longer able to confirm or deny your accusations.'

'But Lord Kazhian is. I was interrogating him with considerable success, Imperial Majesty, before we were so abruptly disturbed by your soldiers. He has told me a great deal.'

'*Kazhian?*' Olkanno's face was frankly incredulous. 'What methods have you used?'

'They are bringing him in now, Imperial Majesty, so you may see for yourself. I know him well, after all, I am his cousin. I know his weaknesses and his strengths. He is a stubborn and courageous man, he would laugh at pain. So I decided to try a different approach, and it worked.'

Two soldiers entered, dragging a third man between them. They released him, and he fell in a heap on to the stone floor. Arkun walked over, took a fistful of long black hair, and yanked his head up. His eyes were hugely dilated, and his face was slack and vacant.

As Mallaso stared in horror, Arkun laughed, and let him sag forward. 'The famous pirate and renegade Lord Kazhian! He doesn't look so formidable now, does he? But of course he was always too fond of drink and drugs. All I had to do was offer him a pipeful of khlar and a cup or two of spiked wine. His own degeneracy did the rest. In that state, he will tell you anything you want to know, just as he told me.'

'No!' Mallaso cried despairingly. 'No – no, he wouldn't!'

'Wouldn't he?' Arkun smiled with chilling cruelty. 'But he did. He trusted me – just as you were foolish enough to trust me earlier, Mallaso of Penya. Did you think I was somehow going to rescue you? I must have given a remarkably convincing performance. Unfortunately for you, I was lying. I am His Imperial Majesty's most loyal servant. Why should I endanger my present position of power and wealth for the sake of a dissolute turncoat and his whore?' His foot prodded Kazhian in the ribs and the drugged man moved sluggishly. 'Get up traitor. I said, *get up!*'

Dimly, the words must have eventually penetrated the clouded haze of Kazhian's mind. He tried to rise, but his legs buckled beneath him, and he sat down again, laughing softly.

'Tell him to get up, Mallaso,' Olkanno said. 'Perhaps he will listen to you.'

She knew that the Spymaster had indeed lied to her, and that there was no hope, no hope at all. But she would not play their dreadful game with Kazhian. She shook her head defiantly.

'Tell him to get up,' the Emperor repeated. His voice had still not wavered from its gently persuasive tone, but the sound was far more terrifying and sinister than shouts or threats would have been. She tried to obey, but her throat was dry with fright and despair. Kazhian was still laughing, a quiet, mindless, terrible noise that seemed to amplify the horror she felt.

'Up,' Arkun said, and kicked him. The laughter stopped, and Kazhian looked round with vague indignation. Contempt printed sneeringly on his face, the Spymaster bent and hauled his cousin upright.

'What'd you do that for?' Kazhian said, his voice slurred. 'I told you what you wanted, didn't I?' He shook off Arkun's hand and peered with unfocused eyes round the room. 'Mall'so? Mall'so, what you doing here?'

'Oh, sweet Mother,' she whispered, and struggled to her feet. She had seen him drunk several times, but this dreadful simple-minded travesty of the quick, clever man she loved appalled her.

'Don' look so offended,' he said, and lurched towards her, clinging to the table to keep himself upright. 'Good stuff he's got, my cousin Arkun. You should try some. Get you going, eh, darling? C'mon, give us a kiss, you stuck-up bitch.'

Pressed into the corner, Kiyu clinging to her skirt, she could not avoid him. He reeled against her, his clothes and breath stinking of khlar, his lips nuzzling against her averted cheek and his hand fumbling for her breast.

And she felt something small and cold and sharp slide between her bound wrists.

Even as she realized what he had done and what it meant, Arkun strode over and wrenched him away. For an instant his eyes met hers, no more than a green ring around the black pits of his dilated pupils, and then the Spymaster flung him contemptuously back against the table. 'You can't even keep your hands off her here! You disgust me, *cousin*, did you know that? You had all the advantages I was never given, and you squandered them in a morass of drink and drugs and women. Whatever happens to you tonight, you will richly deserve – and I shall enjoy every minute of it.'

'Not as much as he will,' Kazhian said, turning blearily to look at Olkanno. 'Nasty repellent little pervert – should've drowned with Ba'alekkt. And your slimy snake of a sorcerer's no better.' He sniggered stupidly. 'Probably can't even make a decent Illusion – or an indecent one. 'S your wife I feel sorry for, though – I bet you can't even get it up without carving her up first.'

'Shut him up,' said Olkanno, his eyes narrowed. 'Or I'll do it myself.'

'With pleasure.' Arkun stepped forward and gripped the shoulders of Kazhian's torn tunic. His cousin smiled. ''S good stuff you gave me – got any more?'

'No,' said Arkun viciously, and hurled him back against the wall.

Kazhian's head hit the stone with a crack, and he collapsed in an undignified sprawl at Arkun's feet. Mallaso swallowed a gasp of fear, wondering if this, too, was pretence – and, if it was, whether Arkun's earlier promise to her could, after all, be trusted.

'Good,' said the Emperor, staring down at the last, and potentially most dangerous, Vessel of the Blood Imperial. 'Leave him there. I have plans for him later.'

'So have I,' said I'amel. He indicated the tall figure of the Spymaster. 'Imperial Majesty, surely you do not believe him? Lord Kazhian is undoubtedly a traitor, condemned out of his own mouth, and Arkun is too.'

'I am your Imperial Majesty's loyal and devoted servant,' Arkun said, breathing hard. His fierce face was very pale, and a few incongruous freckles stood out like the marks of a plague on his nose. 'As for I'amel, it is obvious that he would swear red was green and night day to cling on to power. If you are not careful, Imperial Majesty, he may decide that Court Sorcerer is not a position exalted enough to satisfy his ambitions.'

'Silence!' I'amel hissed, and lifted his staff threateningly.

'Put it down, necromancer,' Olkanno said, and for the first time there was real menace in his voice. 'For the moment, we have other important matters demanding our attention, and the night is drawing on. I will decide what to do with you later, Spymaster. If you are telling the truth, then your initiative will be handsomely rewarded. And if you are not . . . well, I am sure I'amel will be very glad to make use of you. For now, you may watch the evening's entertainment.'

Someone hammered urgently on the door. Olkanno glanced round impatiently. 'Yes? What is it?'

The Hundred-Commander entered the room hesitantly. 'Imperial Majesty, Serlen has just arrived from the Palace. When he was searching the Spymaster's apartments on your orders, he found an intruder in his office. He has brought her here. Do you wish to interrogate her?'

'A *woman*?' Olkanno said in disbelief. 'There was a *woman* in his rooms? But you do not keep a concubine, do you, Arkun?'

The Spymaster was looking bewildered. 'No, Imperial Majesty, I do not.'

'Who is this women, K'net?'

'I do not know for certain, Imperial Majesty, but she is probably one of the slaves from the Women's Quarters. Serlen has her outside. Do you want her brought in?'

I'amel opened his mouth to protest, but Olkanno silenced him with an angry gesture. 'Yes, K'net. I would like to see this spy.'

The tall, heavily built young woman now escorted into the interrogation room was unveiled: her dark hair was loose down her back, and she was wearing a plain red gown. She stood proudly and unflinching before the curious eyes of the soldiers, and her manner was not that of a subservient slave.

Olkanno was staring at her in astonishment. Then he turned and waved a hand at K'net and the other soldiers. 'You have done well. Now get out – and shut the door behind you.'

The Hundred-Commander frowned. 'But, Imperial Majesty, if you should be in need of protection—'

'With I'amel beside me, I fear nothing and no one. Out, and keep your distance. If I find you listening at the door, I'll hand you over to the Black Mage. Understand?'

'Yes, Imperial Majesty,' K'net said. He saluted, and retreated from the interrogation room with a look of considerable relief on his face.

When the sound of the soldiers' footsteps had dwindled away, Olkanno addressed the tall woman, his voice deceptively gentle. 'Would you like to tell me, wife, what you were doing in the Spymaster's apartments? Do please explain.'

Wife. So this was the Lady Djeneb, sister of Ba'alekkt. Rumour was right, she was not beautiful, and Mallaso could now see, in her prominent nose and large hazel eyes, a considerable resemblance to her brother. Her face, though, unlike his, was not marked by malevolence or cruelty, but carried instead a fierce and stubborn pride.

Djeneb glanced round at the occupants of the room. She said calmly, 'I had gone to the Spymaster's courtyard to plead for a life.'

'At midnight? You are lying. Admit it – you were intending to commit adultery with him.'

The woman looked astonished. 'No, of course not!'

I'amel sniggered suggestively. Djeneb gave him a cold stare. 'I had only just learned that Lord Kazhian was a prisoner. I have been fond of him since childhood, Imperial Majesty. I wished to ask the Spymaster for mercy.'

'How touching. Your childhood sweetheart, was he?'

'I am your loyal and faithful wife, Imperial Majesty. It was for the sake of past friendship, that is all.'

The smile on Olkanno's plump face became a sneer. 'Really? Or was it to beg for his release so that you could conspire with him to seize the throne?'

Djeneb stared at him indignantly. 'That is not true, husband! In any case, he told me once that he had no desire to be Emperor.'

'Nonsense. He is a Vessel of the Blood Imperial. Of course he covets the Onyx Throne.'

'He does not,' Mallaso said.

Djeneb swung round to look at her. Their eyes met, and for a brief, astonishing moment Mallaso perceived the intelligence behind the unlovely face, the acuteness of the mind busily at work. Then she turned back to her husband. 'Is this his woman, then?'

'She is the Flamebearer's woman too,' said Olkanno. 'The whore has no discrimination, obviously.'

'Obviously,' Djeneb said, and smiled. 'The Flamebearer. Have you found him yet, then?'

'Not yet, but we will have him soon,' the Emperor said. 'The woman and the child will bring him here to save them.'

'And Lord Kazhian? Is that him over there? Is he dead?'

'No, lady,' Arkun said. 'He is merely suffering from the effects of too much khlar, and a surfeit of insolence. When the time comes, he will know what is happening to him, I assure you.'

'Then he will die.' Djeneb's face was a cold mask, displaying no emotion.

'Of course he will,' Olkanno said, with some impatience. 'Such filth cannot be allowed to live. I will work on him myself, and then he will be given to the public executioner so that all Toktel'yi may watch his end. So may you, wife. His death will be a very powerful reminder to potential traitors.'

'I am not a traitor, husband.'

'Are you not?' Olkanno walked forward. She stood almost a head taller than he did, and somehow her expression as she stared down at him was more contemptuous that any number of spoken insults. 'I do not believe you, wife. The links in the chain of treachery and conspiracy are much too obvious. The Flamebearer has been identified by I'amel as Bronnayak, bastard son of the King of Zithirian. The woman Mallaso here was once his lover, and the child is his. When they parted, she became the concubine of Kazhian, who helped to defend Penya against the Empire and who doubtless also helped the Flamebearer.'

'I am not his concubine, or his whore,' Mallaso said angrily. 'I am his wife.'

'Silence, woman, unless you want I'amel's mind inside yours. As for you, wife, by your own admission you regard Kazhian as your friend – indeed, your *liking* is so strong that you felt the urge to visit the Spymaster's rooms at midnight in order to beg for his life! Fortunately, I had ordered my soldiers to search his apartments for incriminating evidence. And of course, you would hardly have compromised your honour so dangerously had you thought – perhaps with good reason – that your pleas would fall on deaf ears. You knew Arkun would listen, because for some strange reason he still felt some kinship with Kazhian.'

'Be assured, Imperial Majesty, I feel no sympathy whatsoever for him now.'

'Enough, Arkun. Perhaps, wife, you also know of this alleged conspiracy to place Kazhian on the Onyx Throne?'

'I have already told you – he does not want it.'

'I am afraid I do not believe you.'

'He does not want to be Emperor,' Djeneb repeated, quietly and vehemently. 'And I am guilty, husband, of nothing more than a certain impulsive folly. I knew Arkun would turn me away, but I was desperate. I would not expect you, though, to understand feelings of mercy, or of friendly affection.' Her voice was suddenly full of venom. 'That is what makes you an Emperor feared and loathed throughout your remaining dominions, and beyond.'

There was a stunned silence. Mallaso glanced at the crumpled figure of Kazhian, but he had not moved. No one was looking at her: carefully, with infinite caution, her thumbs rubbed the blade he had given her against the rope binding her wrists.

'You have no need of her,' I'amel said greedily. 'She is a traitor, a conspirator. She can die with the others.'

'Who are you, little wizard, to propose my death?' Djeneb demanded. Her face showed no fear, only haughty disdain. 'I am the daughter, the sister, and the wife of Emperors. And soon I will be the mother of one, too.'

Her words sank slowly into silence. Olkanno stared at her, astounded. 'Are you—'

'Yes, husband, I am pregnant. Your son will be born, if you and the Lord of Life and the Mother allow it, at the end of the rainy season. If you think back, Imperial Majesty, to a night a month or so before High Summer, you will remember his conception.'

'I do remember.' The Emperor stared at her as if he had just been given a mountain of treasure. 'You – you are sure of this, wife?'

'I have been sure for some time now, Imperial Majesty. I was waiting for the right moment to tell you, but you have been rather . . .

busy of late.' Djeneb's voice sharpened. 'Am I to take it, then, that you will at least endeavour to keep me out of I'amel's clutches until your son is born?'

Something made Mallaso glance at Arkun. He, too, was staring at Djeneb as if struck by lightning. And suddenly a wild suspicion, an astonishing but plausible explanation for Djeneb's behaviour, burst over her. Casually, she turned her attention back to the Emperor, praying that no one had noticed her understanding in her face.

'Imperial Majesty,' said I'amel, with a glare at Djeneb that would have powdered the bones of anyone less splendidly self-assured. 'Imperial Majesty, you can deal with these people later. If you wish me to destroy the Flamebearer, I must act now. Once the sun is up, my powers will be considerably weakened.'

'Yes – yes, of course. You may proceed,' said Olkanno. He gave Djeneb one last lingering glance, and gestured to the long bench against one wall. 'You and the Spymaster may sit there, wife and watch. The experience should be very interesting. I am only sorry that my unborn son is not in a position to witness the destruction of my greatest enemies.'

Mallaso looked round at those whose fates, one way or another, would be sealed before daylight. I'amel, black-robed, sinister, evil. Olkanno, his master, who perhaps exerted less control over his sorcerer than he would like. Arkun, pale and calm. Djeneb, whose proud and disdainful confidence must surely hide her quivering terror. The gaoler, whose name she could not remember, hanging spell-fast and helpless in his chains. Kazhian, lying like an untidy heap of rubbish against the wall a few strides away. And herself and Kiyu, huddled together in their corner.

I'amel's hooded eyes swept round the room, and he smiled. 'Good. All is ready. Let the rite begin.'

CHAPTER
TWENTY-NINE

The silver bowl lay on the table in the centre of the room. Fortunately for the gaoler, I'amel's need for haste had spared him the usual preliminaries of torture and mutilation. The man's huge corpse hung lifeless in its chains, and the hot stuffy chamber reeked of the blood that soaked his clothes and lay puddled on the floor around him. But the bowl was full, and the necromancer gazed at it intently. He muttered a long, crooning incantation, and passed his hands over the surface of the blood.

Mallaso felt as sick and exhausted as if the liquid in the bowl had been drained from her own body, but she could not look away. If this foul, evil man were to summon Bron, she wanted to watch everything that happened. For some stubborn part of her still could not believe, even in this extremity, that such absolute and terrible darkness could triumph so completely over the light.

Kiyu still lay huddled against her, her hands clinging to her mother's dress. Mallaso might almost have thought that she was asleep, save for the long, shuddering tremors that shook her body. She prayed that the child had understood little of what had happened, but she knew in her heart that Kiyu, whose gift must make her abnormally sensitive to the thoughts and feelings of others, was well aware of the dreadful presence of evil, only a few paces away.

'Ai-ee! I see him!' I'amel's sibilant voice suddenly intruded on the tense silence. 'He is there – the Flamebearer – he is there.' And he began chanting in a high, eerie wail, his hands weaving an intricate pattern over the bowl. 'He hears – he knows – he will come!'

Mallaso felt a sudden surge of hope. Perhaps Bron would have the power to overcome the Black Mage. He was their best chance of escaping this nightmare, for Arkun might prove a false friend, and Kazhian was still lying on the floor. She could see him breathing, but he had not moved, and she knew that she could not rely on his help. He had given her the knife, though: its work done, it lay hidden between her fingers. And if necessary, if she could, she would use it to kill Kiyu, rather than let her suffer I'amel's sorcery and Olkanno's torture.

She remembered the techniques of meditation and concentration that Bron had always used, and sent him a silent, desperate message. *Wait until you are ready. There is great danger here – do not come in haste, or unprepared.*

I'amel gave a sudden exclamation of anger. 'What is happening? The bowl has gone dark! Where is he?'

'How should I know?' demanded the Emperor, his rising tension betrayed by the unusual anger in his tone. 'This was your idea, I'amel, and if it doesn't work I am hardly the one to blame.'

'Silence!' the mage hissed. 'I will try again. He is aware – I know it – but some other influence has made the image disappear. If the blood congeals before I can finish the rite, I shall have to use a fresh source.' His eyes rested, with malevolence, on his enemy Arkun.

'*I* will decide who your next victim is to be,' said Olkanno. 'Proceed.'

With a glare at his master, the necromancer bent once more over the bowl, muttering. Mallaso felt his power as a stirring on her skin, a menace in her blood. Beside her, Kiyu gave a compulsive sob, and her grip tightened in fear.

I'amel's chant went on and on, while the onlookers, silenced by expectation or dread, waited for something to happen. Mallaso glanced up and met Djeneb's speculative gaze. She gave her a quick smile, but the Emperor's wife was looking now at something beside her. Her eyes widened for an instant, and then she turned to watch her husband, who was standing next to I'amel, all his attention fixed on the sorcerer.

Mallaso did not dare to look round, but suddenly Kiyu stirred, and raised her face. It was grimy and streaked with tears, but her dark eyes shone suddenly with hope. Unseen by anyone else, she smiled at her mother, and touched a finger to her lips.

And then the voice, once so dear and familiar, spoke inside her head. *I am here. I'amel does not know it yet. Do not move or speak.*

Once before, he had entered her mind. It had angered and frightened her, and she had asked him not to do it again. But he had sent her words of love just before his supposed death, and later he had entered her dreams. And now, she had never felt anything more wonderful in her life than the touch of his spirit, and the hope it brought in this abyss of despair.

I'amel broke off his chant with a screech of fury, and hurled the bowl to the floor. Blood sprayed everywhere, and the sickly stench of it filled the air. As the vessel rolled clanging away across the stones, a voice spoke aloud, quietly but emphatically.

'Perhaps that was a little unwise, I'amel. Whose blood will you use now?'

The Black Mage stiffened and jerked upright. His lips drew back from his teeth, and he gestured savagely with his staff. Red fire streamed from its tip and flashed across the room to explode against the wall beside Mallaso, showering her and Kiyu with stinging dust and grit.

'Missed,' said Bron, with some satisfaction. She turned and saw him, kneeling beside Kazhian. Briefly, their eyes met. He had not changed at all, save that his hair was now perfectly white. Then he smiled at her, and rose to his feet. Sorcery shimmered around him like a transparent shield. I'amel's lance of witchfire slashed again through the air, and pierced the space he had occupied a heartbeat after he had stepped aside.

'Kill him!' Olkanno shouted furiously. 'Kill him, you fool!'

'He will if he can,' Bron said. 'But I think he's finding it rather more difficult than he anticipated.' He smiled at the necromancer, a cold smile full of contempt. 'Why don't you try again?'

With a howl of rage, I'amel raised his staff. Suddenly, Mallaso felt the power rise to a new and awesome level. The buzzing in the air around her seemed to be scrambling her brain, preventing all rational thought, and she pressed her hands to her ears.

I'amel launched his third attack. Sorcery, like a ball of lightning, smashed against Bron. He staggered and almost fell. For a moment, his slight figure, clad in the tunic and trousers of the northern people, was all outlined in flickering red fire. I'amel screamed in triumph, and raised his staff for the final, lethal strike.

Without warning, Arkun leaped to his feet and grabbed the necromancer's arms. I'amel seemed to explode in crimson flames. There was a roar and a blinding flash. It hurled the Spymaster to the ground with terrible force. His limbs jerked and twitched convulsively, and then he lay still and lifeless. A hideous reek of burnt meat filled the room.

'I told you he was a traitor!' I'amel cried gleefully.

Feeling sick, Mallaso glanced at Djeneb. Her expression had not changed, but all the colour had drained away from beneath her olive skin.

'Where is he?' Olkanno demanded, staring round the room. 'He's gone, you fool! Get him back!'

I'amel lowered his staff cautiously. The air still tingled with power, and smoke was rising from Arkun's charred chest. The necromancer glanced at the dead, and the living. 'I cannot force him to return. But remember, we still have our bait.'

With an exclamation, Olkanno stepped across Arkun's body and hurried over to Mallaso and Kiyu, still crouched in the corner furthest from the door. His hands were shaking, and his forehead was awash with sweat. 'Give me the child!'

She had the knife in her hand, and the ropes that bound her were severed. As he bent over, she leaped up at him, striking for his face. The blade slashed deep across one plump cheek, and the Emperor screamed and staggered back, his hands raised to protect himself. 'I'amel – I'amel, do something!'

From the floor close by, Kazhian moved. As Mallaso felt the necromancer's coercive spell freeze her limbs, her beloved staggered to his feet. There was a knife in his hand too, one of Olkanno's dreadful implements, sharp and deadly. With all his strength, he hurled it at the Emperor.

His aim was not accurate, and it struck Olkanno in the belly. He gave a howl of agony and doubled over the blade, his fingers plucking at the handle. Coolly, Djeneb walked over to him and wrenched it out, giving the weapon a vicious twist. Olkanno screamed then, and screamed again as she plunged it into his heart. He fell at her feet, his blood splattering her red dress, and died before the last echoes of his cries had ended.

I'amel had made no further move to save his master. Instead, he had snatched Kiyu up, and held her arm tightly in his grasp.

The spell left Mallaso so suddenly that she staggered and almost fell. She gave a wild howl of terror. 'Kiyu – Kiyu, don't hurt her!'

'You heard – you harm her at your peril,' Bron said. He had appeared like a wraith, just in front of Mallaso. He added, inside her head, *Get away from me. Get back into the corner, and get down.*

Frantic with terror for Kiyu, she hesitated, and he repeated the command more sharply. *You're in the line of his fire! For Hegeden's sake, MOVE!*

Slowly, she backed away. Kazhian was reeling unsteadily in the opposite direction, towards Djeneb. Bron stood quite calm and still, facing I'amel, who held the child's arm clenched in one claw, his staff in the other.

'Don't harm her,' Bron repeated softly. 'If you do, you'll regret it.'

'I will not if you submit,' I'amel said, his eyes glowing red. 'Submit, Flamebearer, and I will let her and the woman go free.'

'Something tells me that you are lying.' Bron's voice was suddenly contemptuous. 'Your foul kind knows no morality, and owns no other lord but the Devourer. If you kill me now, the Onyx Throne will be yours – and the Empire will descend into the abyss.'

'I told you,' I'amel hissed. 'Submit, or the child dies – slowly.'

Kiyu, her face a weeping mask of terror, hung in his grip. Mallaso could not look away: her eyes fixed on her child, she crouched close to the wall.

'Let her go,' Bron repeated. 'Or it will be the worse for you.'

I'amel laughed, a cackle of unbearable evil. 'What can you do against me, puny Northerner? My power comes from the Devourer – and the Lord of Death reigns supreme over the world.'

'No.' Bron's voice was filled with a menace she had never heard from him before, and the hairs rose on her arms. 'No. *I* am stronger. The Devourer lived in my heart, and I cast him out. *I* am stronger, I'amel. Let her go. Or are you afraid to lose?'

The Black Mage picked up one of the wickedly shaped instruments on the table. 'Very well, Northerner. Since you are so stubborn, I will persuade you to see sense. This blade is sharp. The child's arm is very slender – and her fingers even more fragile. She won't be so pretty if she loses them.'

Mallaso watched in horror as the shining silver knife began to move towards Kiyu's helpless hand. *Do something!* She screamed in her mind to Bron. *DO something – don't just stand there—*

The child saw the knife descending. Her eyes widened in horror, and she began to struggle wildly. For an instant her thin arm seemed to bend as she writhed frantically against the necromancer's grip. Then the little girl's figure shimmered briefly. He opened his hand with a sudden screech of pain, and she dropped to the floor.

I'amel made a grab for her, but Kiyu was quick, agile, and propelled by terror. She scuttled underneath the table, and the sorcerer lunged after her, too late. As he ran round to the other side, the little girl shot out from her hiding place and fell into Mallaso's arms.

Bron said softly, 'You have less power than that child, I'amel. *Now* will you submit?'

The necromancer's face resembled the skull masks worn by Olyak's priests. Only the eyes, deep in their bony sockets, still held the flicker of life. For a moment he seemed to be faltering on the edge of surrender. And then his lipless mouth opened, his arms lifted, and red lightning crackled madly. 'Prepare to die, Northerner!'

A lance of silver flame streaked from Bron's outstretched fingers, at the same instant that a crimson blaze burst from the tip of I'amel's staff.

A sheet of fire leaped up between them, so bright that Mallaso hid her face with her hands. She felt the heat, and heard the necromancer screeching his spells. If Bron had faith in his own power, he could defeat the Black Mage. And he must win, for the alternative was too terrible to imagine.

Desperate to see what was happening, she parted her fingers. Two huge flames, one red, the other white, seemed to be struggling above the table. Each in turn roared higher, until she could no longer see I'amel behind the curtain of brilliant witchfire. Bron stood, a slight black shape delineated by the brightness, his arms raised in front of him. She remembered how the High Sorcerer had tested him on Jo'ami, using the Illusion of D'thliss to sap his confidence, and how in the end he had found the strength, with her help, to overcome it. But compared to this inferno, that blaze had been as harmless as a lantern light.

The red flame was growing now, licking at the ceiling of the room, sending wicked bloody tongues of fire towards Bron. I'amel's voice rose to a wild howl of triumph. His opponent seemed to sag back before the necromancer's attack. Power seethed in the air, so overwhelmingly that Mallaso could hardly think. She tried desperately to send her support to him, but her mind could not obey. She gave a sob of despair, and saw Bron fall to his knees before the devastating onslaught of evil.

Suddenly, Kiyu wrenched herself out of her mother's arms and ran to him. She linked her hands with his, and a new fire, the deep glowing yellow of ripe corn, sprang up to join the faltering white. The two flames twisted together in a rope of silver and gold, the colours of happiness and hope.

The necromancer's voice wavered. And like a snare of light, the combined power of the man and the child engulfed I'amel's fire and seized him in a deadly embrace.

The Black Mage staggered back, enveloped in a roaring cloak of flame, his eyes and mouth dark pits of soundless agony as the witchfire devoured him.

'Enough,' Bron said at last. His hands dropped, carrying Kiyu's with him. For an instant longer, the white flame seared into I'amel's flesh and bones, and then died. The gold lingered for a few heartbeats more, before it also faded away.

The necromancer lay dead, blackened and contorted like a piece of charred wood on the stone floor.

Mallaso realized that she was shaking. For a moment, there was utter silence within the room. Then she heard the sound of retching, and saw Kazhian bent over in the corner, with Djeneb crouched beside him.

'It's over,' Bron said. He was still holding his daughter's hands. With his white hair and his thin face sunken with exhaustion, he looked like an old man, but his eyes were smiling. 'It's over. He is dead, and so is Olkanno.'

Mallaso struggled painfully to her feet, wondering if her legs would support her. The room stank of blood and burnt flesh and death, and the floor and ceiling and central table had been scorched and blackened in the searing heat of the witchfire. She said hesitantly, 'Kiyu?'

Her beloved daughter looked round. Beneath the grime and tear-tracks, her face held an expression of awed wonder, and also, most disturbingly, a fierce trace of triumph. 'Mama,' she said, her eyes glowing, 'Mama, this is the Singing Man.'

'I know he is, sweetheart.' Mallaso felt a terrible, rending pity for her child, thrust so abruptly and so brutally into the knowledge of her power, her innocence burned to ashes, just as Bron's had been, in the furnace of her own sorcery.

'Is Kazhian all right?' the little girl said, her face suddenly wrinkled with concern. 'He doesn't look very well.'

'He'll live,' Djeneb said. Her strong features contained an expression that was almost maternal as she looked down at her cousin. 'Too much khlar always has that effect.'

Kazhian lifted his head. Under his tan, his skin was greyish-green, but he was smiling. 'Hallo, Sashir. I'm sorry for the things I said to you. Will you forgive me?'

'Perhaps,' Mallaso said, smiling back. 'It wasn't all pretence, though, was it?'

'No. It was Arkun's idea, may Olyak be kind to his soul. He remembered how I had rescued Megren and his family by pretending to be doped stupid, so he would think it was safe to leave me alone on my ship and take the Lady Djeneb here ashore. He thought I could do it again, and convince Olkanno and I'amel that I was harmless.'

'Nothing about you is harmless,' Mallaso said. 'But you certainly fooled me, until you put the knife into my hands.'

'As you said, though, it wasn't all acting. I took quite a lot – overdid it again.' He wiped his mouth with his hand, and rose shakily to his feet. Djeneb, Mallaso noted, was still standing very close to him, lending him unobtrusive support.

'Are they really all dead?' he added, looking round at the corpses strewn across the floor. 'I can't believe – I can't believe it's over at last.'

'It is,' Bron said. 'Olkanno and I'amel are now with Olyak – and I do not feel somehow that the Lord of Death will be very merciful towards them.'

'But perhaps he will be sympathetic to Arkun.' Kazhian made his way round the table and stood, his hands gripping the charred wood, looking down at the body of his cousin. 'He was our friend at the last, when it mattered – and he paid for his change of heart with his life. I wish he had not died – I wish he could have lived to share in our hope.' He glanced round at Djeneb, standing tall and stately beside him. '*Were* you lovers?'

The daughter, sister and wife of Emperors smiled suddenly and sadly. 'Yes, we were. And the child in my womb is his, not Olkanno's.'

'A pity Olkanno never knew of your betrayal,' Kazhian observed grimly. 'Instead, he died thinking that his spawn would inherit the Empire.'

'He will not,' Djeneb said. 'Surely, the Onyx Throne is now yours.'

'When will people understand that I want nothing to do with the Empire!' Kazhian said vehemently. 'Never, ever, ever again. If I had my way, it would end here and now, with Olkanno's death.'

Djeneb stared at him. 'I know you told me that before, but surely now, when it is yours for the taking—'

'I do not want it! I want to go back to Penya with Mallaso and Kiyu, and forget I ever was a Toktel'yan. I know I am the last adult male Vessel of the Blood Imperial left alive, but I wish with all my heart that I were not, for then the Empire would be truly dead. Don't you want it to die? Don't you think that two and half thousand years is enough oppression and injustice and torture for any nation to endure, or inflict? Surely you can see that, lady?'

Djeneb's large hazel eyes, so disconcertingly like Ba'alekkt's, gazed into his. At last she said softly, 'Perhaps I can. But what can we do? How can we end something that has lasted so long?'

'Only because it has been glued together with blood and chained up with slavery,' Mallaso said. 'Give the provinces and the islands the choice, to stay or to leave. And then rule the city of Toktel'yi in your son's name, and bring him up to respect law and life and freedom, for men and for women too. Do what you can, and if you fail, at least you will have tried. And if you smash the Empire, many millions will live to thank you.'

'I don't know,' Djeneb said, looking suddenly and uncharacteristically afraid, and very young. 'I don't know if it's possible.'

'I'm certain it won't be easy,' Mallaso said. 'Freedom is hard work, on Penya, but we continue for the love of it, and for our children. Can you do the same, for yours?'

The younger woman's face was still irresolute and unsure. Then suddenly she smiled. 'I will try,' she said. 'You told me once, Kazhian, that I should have been born a man, and taken the Onyx Throne. I thought you were mocking me.'

'No,' Kazhian told her softly. 'No, lady, I was not. And in your son's name you will rule Toktel'yi better and more wisely than any who have come before you. You will not be an Emperor, but you will be greater than all your predecessors.'

And Mallaso, looking at the strength and courage shining in Djeneb's face, knew that he spoke the truth.

'Kazhian?' Kiyu had appeared beside her mother. 'Kazhian, *are* you all right?'

Her stepfather turned slowly, and smiled down at her. 'Yes, yes, I am, little bird. I was sick, but I'm better now. And you?'

She gave him one of her mischievous smiles, as though she was still the enchanting, innocent child that Mallaso had always prayed for her to be. 'Now *they're* dead, I'm better too. Kazhian, come and see the Singing Man.'

Bron was still on the floor, but he had moved so that his back was leaning against the far wall. Mallaso knelt beside him, and he opened his eyes and smiled at her. 'Thank you. Thank you all. I could not have defeated him without your help.' He glanced up at his daughter. 'And especially not you, little bird.'

'What have you done to her?' Mallaso whispered. So many questions seethed in her mind, but as usual her concern for her child overcame every other consideration.

'I did nothing,' Bron said. 'She did it herself, of her own free will. She has so much power within her, and she cannot now hide it, nor can you deny it any longer. Sargenay can teach her how to control it, and when she is ready, she can come to me.'

Mallaso stared at him. 'Come to you? When? Where? In Zithirian?'

'No. Did you think I would claim you, or her? Did you think I would force you to choose between me and Kazhian? You know me better than that, Mallaso of Penya. Your choice was made long ago, and so was mine.'

'I don't understand,' she said flatly. 'I thought you were dead, but you survived – how? And you promised me before I left Jo'ami that you would find me, in Kerenth. Why did you never come?'

Behind her, she heard Kazhian's sharp intake of breath. Bron's gaze dropped for a moment, and he studied his hands, lying quiet and harmless now in his lap. He said at last, 'It is a long story, and my memory of some parts is a little imperfect. But I know that I broke my promise – I let you believe that I was dead, and I let you rear Kiyu without a father.'

'Wrong.' Kazhian said softly. 'In all the ways that matter most, *I* am her father.'

'Yes, I know that – I am sorry.' Bron looked up at the man who had married his lover, and his eyes were dark with remembered pain. 'You have no reason for jealousy, Kazhian. I know that you love her, and Kiyu, and I know that they love you. I will never seek to interfere with the bond that binds you all together. I was Mallaso's lover once, but no longer. I loved her, and I love her still, but I have no claim on her, or on Kiyu. By my own choice I gave them up. After – after what happened in Tamat, I knew that I could never go back to my old life.'

'What did happen in Tamat?' Mallaso asked.

'I went into the river with Ba'alekkt. He died, but I did not. I don't know why – perhaps my need for life was too strong. The current bore me away, and I used the little power I had left to keep myself alive until the Kefirinn spat me out on the northern bank, several miles downstream.' He paused, his eyes bleak. 'I was all but dead. A child found me, and her mother nursed me back to health. It took almost half a year, and at the end my hair was white. And the long months of illness had given me a new sense of purpose. I knew that if I tried to find you, I would . . . lose myself. I can't express it any more clearly than that. But I have been given power greater than anyone in all the known world before – and with that power comes the burden of responsibility. I knew that I should use it to change the world, as the prophet of Jo'ami foretold that I should. And in Kerenth, where my magic is alien and forbidden, I would be unable to practise sorcery.'

'And Inrai'a might remember you,' Mallaso said drily.

'To be honest, I never thought about Inrai'a.' He smiled reminiscently. 'She would be mortified. But I thought endlessly about you, and about our child. And I realized that our lives had not been destined to coincide for more than those brief months.'

'So you came to my dreams and told me . . . you told me that it was never meant to be for ever.'

'Yes. But I still watched over you – I guarded you. I led Al'Kalyek to you – and I also led Kazhian to Kiyu, on the rocks of Onnak.'

'Did you?' said her husband. 'I always thought it was her power, summoning me and Sargenay.'

'It was. But I helped you to decide which course to set – the course that led you to her. I did not destroy the wizards of Jo'ami, though. Sé

Mo-Tarmé's own arrogance and selfishness led them to disaster. But I made sure that Kiyu was saved. And I could see that you and Mallaso needed each other.'

'I'm not at all certain,' said Kazhian grimly, 'that I like the idea of you manipulating our lives from afar. I'm quite capable of making my own mistakes, thank you.'

Bron grinned suddenly. 'So am I. I promise you, I won't interfere again. Your dreams are safe from me now.'

'And Kiyu?' Mallaso asked.

'I think that eventually you will find the courage to let her go – to let her be herself. It may take three years, or five, or ten, before she is ready. But when she feels the time is right, she will come to me to learn what she truly is, and what she can do.'

'How will she know?'

'She will know. She will know where to find me. And she will not be alone, either. She is not the only child in the world with power, although she may be one of the most gifted. And that is my duty, now that the Flamebearer's role is almost ended – to guide the children, and teach, and learn from what we can do together. Jo'ami has gone, just as the seer predicted, and now a new kind of sorcery is rising up to replace the old. Can you give her to such a future?'

Not trusting herself to speak, Mallaso nodded at last.

'Thank you.' His dark eyes considered them in turn, the child, the two women, the man. 'Do you remember me, Lady Djeneb?'

'I remember your voice,' Djeneb said softly and wonderingly. 'You called yourself Galken, didn't you, when you came and Healed me?'

'Yes,' Bron said. 'I found that there were some things that were impossible to stand and watch. I did what I could for you – I am sorry that I did not do more.'

'You saved my life,' Djeneb told him. 'I thought you were dead – I wanted so much to thank you.'

'You can thank me by being even more strong and courageous in the future than you were then. The fate of the world is in your hands now.'

'Wait!' Djeneb said sharply. 'Are you leaving us? You can't – we need you.'

'No, you don't,' Bron told her. 'You are the daughter, sister, wife and mother of Emperors, remember? Think carefully, Lady Djeneb, and remember Kazhian's words. Because of me, the world has changed. Because of what you do, it will change for the better – or for the worse. I'm not going to stand behind your shoulder and wield my power through you. You have to manage by yourself, and teach your son to do the same. And although he is not Olkanno's child, the world will think that he is. He may be the Emperor, or King, or Governor – but whatever he is, make him wise, Lady Djeneb, make him strong and gentle and compassionate, for if you do not, then all this slaughter and grief will have been for nothing. And perhaps by the time he is grown, Toktel'yi will have come to accept its lesser place in the world. It is up to you now. But I think that you will succeed, even without my help.'

'I will do my best,' she said, her voice faltering suddenly. 'For my son's sake, and yours, and Arkun's.'

'I'm glad. Good luck to you, lady – you deserve it.' He smiled at her, and at Mallaso and Kiyu, kneeling beside him. 'The soldiers have gone. They all fled when I'amel and I did battle, even those who were watching from the river. There is no one alive here now except the four of you, and me. You are free to go. And so am I.'

In between one heartbeat and the next, his hand, warm and substantial, seemed to slide through her fingers and out of the air. Bewildered, Mallaso stared at the place where he had been, the absence he had left, still vaguely shimmering.

'It's all right, Mama.' Kiyu said. 'He was very tired, and he wanted to go home. We'll see him again one day.'

Mallaso felt an odd sense of anger, mixed with sadness and disappointment. Why had he deserted them now, when they needed him so much?

'Mama!' Kiyu was pulling at her dress. 'Look, Mama, there's a door over there, and it's open. He opened it for us. Please let's go, I don't want to stay here any longer.'

Her hand took her mother's and pulled. Mallaso scrambled to her feet, and saw that there was indeed an opening in the far corner of the room, leading straight into the Water Hall, echoing and empty. She could see a boat tied up waiting, and the iron gate was raised. And beyond it lay the Kefirinn, running dark and free and powerful to the sea.

'Come on,' Kiyu said. 'Hurry! The soldiers might come back.'

'Where shall we go?' Mallaso asked, staring at the boat, her mind still dazed by the cataclysmic events of the night.

'To the Palace,' Djeneb said behind her. 'I rule in this city now, remember.' She strode confidently towards the opening. 'But I would like the chance to assert my authority before my husband's Guard suffers an outbreak of delayed loyalty. And besides, I am sick of death and slaughter. Shall we go?'

They stepped into the boat, and Kazhian took up the oars. Mallaso untied the rope and then sat down in the stern, Kiyu beside her. The little craft, propelled by his slow, rather ragged strokes, slid under the gate and out into the empty river beyond. Kazhian glanced behind him, and turned her south, towards the Palace and the sea.

'Wait!' Kiyu said suddenly. She jumped up, and the boat rocked. 'No, Mama, don't touch me – please, leave me alone.'

Mallaso, bewildered and uneasy, watched as her daughter stared up at the looming shape of the Old Palace above them. Within those dark windows lay the bureaucratic heart of the Empire, the means by which all its lands and peoples were governed. And below all those floors and racks and shelves of documents, lay the last Emperor, murdered by his wife, together with the bodies of his Spymaster and his Sorcerer, who had both, but in different ways, betrayed him at the last.

Kiyu stretched out her hand towards the great edifice. Twin streaks of golden flame flashed from her fingertips. They arced across the darkness, and vanished. For a moment Mallaso, her eyes straining, could see nothing. Then, within one of the ranks of windows, fire leaped into vivid life, and the little girl crowed triumphantly.

'Kaylo's bones!' Kazhian said, and began to laugh, the wildness of it betraying the khlar still thick in his blood. 'What made you think of that, little bird?'

'He told me to do it, before he went home,' Kiyu said. She sat down again beside Mallaso, grinning as the blaze took greedy hold. 'He said paper burns very well – and the Emperor and his friends need a pyre.'

'Well, don't do the same to the Lady Djeneb's Palace,' Kazhian said. 'Or at least try and wait until we're not inside it.' He dipped the oars into the water and began to row with renewed vigour. And Mallaso put her arm around her astonishing, perilous daughter, and watched her beloved's firelit, unshaven and disreputable face as he propelled them towards safety, and freedom.

And behind them, the heart of the Empire, finally destroyed, poured smoke and flames and ash into the blackness of the night sky.

EPILOGUE

These were once known as the Empty Lands, home only to wild animals and birds. In winter, even now, no travellers brave the high bleak hills, where the wind howls like a troop of Olyak's demons, and snow splatters against your face with the force of slingshot. The moors are left to those creatures hardy enough, and desperate enough, to endure such cold and privation.

But after the first thaws of spring, the wilderness is cloaked not with snow and ice but with a different, gentler garment of rich green grass and a profusion of brilliant flowers. Steppe poppies, all the hues of fire from the sharp yellow of new flame to the dull, glowing crimson of old embers, spread their glorious colours in vast drifts across the hillsides. Young deer and antelope gambol through the meadows, and every valley is graced by a narrow rushing stream of pure, sparkling water, that fell as snow a few months ago. And the wolves of winter retreat to the mountains, to become just an unpleasant memory to those animals lucky enough to escape their savagery.

In the summer, the people come, following the ancient roads. Now that the Empire is ended, there is no one to prevent the steady, determined trickle of those who have been summoned. In the first few years after the fall of Toktel'yi, the numbers making the long, perilous journey could be counted in ones and tens. Now, there are hundreds. Enterprising inhabitants of Kerenth, and the newly independent lands of Djebb and Tatht, have explored the routes north, and have set up way-stations in the ruins of places which once performed the same function five hundred years ago. Inns, lodging-houses and supply stalls have begun to flourish. And some people, liking life in the Empty Lands, where there are no laws, no restrictions and no taxes, have staked out fields, built houses, and begun to farm. So these are not truly the Empty Lands any more, and the journey has now lost much of its hardship and peril.

It is seven hundred miles, as the eagle flies, from Kerenth City to the place where ancient roads end, and just as far from Toktel'yi. So the people set out in spring, as soon as the warmer air breathes up from the hot lands around the Southern Sea, to melt the steppe snow and clear away the grim grey clouds. Even if they dawdle, there is plenty of time to reach their destination before winter returns. And everyone travels with hope, for the future is bright, and those who have returned from this enchanted place amid the forests and mountains, or who have visited it in their dreams, speak of wonders and marvels so beautiful and fantastic that everyone longs to go there, even if they have no better reason than curiosity.

They have come from all over the known world, these intrepid travellers – men, women and children, particularly children. They have come from Toktel'yi itself, where the Lady Djeneb, daughter, sister and wife, but not mother, of Emperors, reigns on behalf of her seven-year-old-son, K'sa'an, which in Toktel'yan means *youth,* or *beginning.* There are pilgrims from the heartland of Mynak and Sabrek, which, along with the island of Tekkt, still form part of Djeneb's domain. And there are also people from those provinces which have taken the opportunity to escape from the Empire that is now no longer an Empire, but a Kingdom. Djebb is also a Kingdom, and so are Jaiya and Lai'is. Tulyet has descended into chaos. Ukkan is controlled by a group of wealthy aristocrats, and Terebis and Tatht, along with the rest of the Archipelago, have followed the example of Penya, now entering a new Golden Age, and are governed by elected representatives.

All the lands are different, and glorying in their disparity and in their freedom from Imperial rule, although everywhere there is a tiny minority of people who regret the passing of old certainties, old orders. For almost everyone, though, there is a new mood of hope, and a sense of vast and wonderful possibilities opening up in the future. And those people travelling north to the ancient city of Tyr, reborn with sorcery like a firebird from its own ruins, are partly the symptom, partly the cause, of the optimism bubbling within the boundaries of the lands that, less than ten years ago, formed the Empire of Toktel'yi.

And women, in particular, see the Lady Djeneb walking with her face uncovered in the streets of the city, or riding in her barge, or playing with her son on the shores of the Southern Sea, and wish to follow where she has so courageously led. The men, especially older men, grumble and protest, but they know in their hearts that the spirit of freedom, once released, is impossible to recapture, or to return to its cage. The world has changed, and there can be no going back to the injustice and oppression of the past.

Liberty is not easy, and there will be many dangers and uncertainties ahead for those who have never before tasted its delights, but they have a touching and perhaps naïve faith in their own power to transform these newly independent lands into places where everyone can live in peace and prosperity. And some whose minds were first opened by the Flamebearer still find him in their dreams, speaking now of Tyr, and what can be found there. Many discover that their children have also encountered him in their sleep – although they call him the Singing Man, the Harper of the West all made of twilight and of hope, who takes their dreams and with his harp spins them into a rope.

And so, urged by their sons and daughters, parents begin to travel north, to see for themselves the future that this new generation will share with them.

This particular family is at first glance quite ordinary. They have come through Kerenth after Year-turn, making the traditional pilgrimage to Skathak, the Birthplace of the Goddess, before striking due north along one of the old roads, still running straight and clear along the valleys, across broken bridges and over the hills for five hundred miles between Sarquaina and Tyr. Other, larger groups are going the same way, but this family prefers to travel alone, although there are only two men, a woman, and three children.

The woman is plainly from the Archipelago: she is tall, elegant and dark-skinned, and although she wears the calf-length dress of Kerentan women, she has wound a brightly coloured scarf around her head in the manner of women all over the islands, from Annatal to Penya. Beside her is a man from a different mould: his features are aristocratic Toktel'yan, but his face, with its high-bridged nose and smiling mouth, is tanned like a sailor's and the laughter lines around his sharp green eyes speak of a quick and merry nature. He rides restlessly, often galloping his horse up to the next ridge as if he is impatient to see what lies beyond, but always he comes back to her, and with a smile and a touch of his hand communicates his love and affection.

The other man watches them a little wistfully. By his robes, he is a Toktel'yan-trained mage, and certainly the summer rain-showers and thunderstorms which afflict many travellers have never troubled this particular group.

But conventional mages, harnessed like oxen to Annatal, have been loud to condemn the new brand of magic being peddled, so they say, by the charlatan residing in Tyr. They have spread terrible tales about him – that he is a thief of children, a lunatic, a pervert. In vain, however: for new students at the School of Wizardry have dwindled almost to nothing in the last seven years, and the future of all such institutions looks bleak. After all, why should anyone take an addictive drug that will age them before their time, when they can, with care and training, become a mage using only the natural gifts that lie within them? Those who still wish to follow the old route to sorcery are invariably the most unsuitable applicants, with no aptitude or ability. Small wonder, then, that the wizards of Toktel'yi denounce the Singing Man so furiously. They are a dying breed, and they know it.

So this sorcerer, his lean, handsome, bearded face already showing signs of premature ageing, must have other reasons to travel to Tyr. Perhaps one of them is the eldest of the children. The younger two, a boy and a girl perhaps seven and four years of age, ride with their parents, or on a fat brown mule laden with packs. But their sister is older, at least eleven or twelve, and has her own mount, a spirited bay mare which she rides with a great deal of dash and bravado, often galloping in her father's dust at a speed which makes her mother, at once laughing and anxious, bite back her pleas for her daughter to be careful. It is obvious that this girl, with the wild tangle of hair and deep dark eyes, has the innate power that the Singing Man has promised to nurture in all who possess it, for sometimes the air shimmers around her. But she has taught the horse not to be afraid of her, and at night she speaks softly to it, and tends it with loving affection.

The winds are beginning to back round to the north, and there is a taste of frost in the air, when at last the family come to the foothills of the great rampart of mountains rising like a vast wall from the steppe. The road leaps over a broad, rushing river, a tributary of the Estris, and vanishes amid wide, sloping green meadows, sprinkled with tall pines. The woman notices that many of the stones in the five-arched bridge look new, although there is no sign of trampled ground or building work. And her daughter smiles, and points to the trees, the same as those she has seen in her dreams, but never in reality until now.

They cross the bridge and ride on. At the crest of the next hill, the two riders are waiting to greet them. They are young, in their very early twenties, and dressed in the practical tunic and trousers of the north. The boy has red hair and freckles, and tells them that his name is Homan. The girl's pale hair is braided into half-a-dozen plaits, in the manner of the western nomad tribes, and she is called Zathti. The dark-skinned woman smiles in recognition, for she remembers the stories of her lively, unquenchable spirit. It is a spirit which burns brightly, too, in her daughter Kiyu, who is Zathti's niece.

They all ride on together, through the pines. The sun is beginning to sink towards the west. Over there, through three hundred miles of trackless, unmapped forest, lies the city of Lelyent: and further still, at the feet of the mountains, the Silver City, Zithirian, where the sorcerer King Ansaryon, who is Homan and Zathti's father, rules with his barbarian Queen Halthris. They are due to visit Tyr in the spring, says Homan, and they will bring their youngest child Charnak, now thirteen years old, and showing great promise as a sorcerer. And Kiyu smiles with delight, and tells him that it will be wonderful to meet her grandparents at last.

So they are a merry company until the final hill. On its summit, Homan and Zathti pause, and so do the others, staring in wonder at what lies in the broad valley below.

For five hundred years, since the earthquake that destroyed it, the city of Tyr has lain desolate, inhabited only by birds, and wild animals, and the fifty thousand ghosts of the people slain in that final cataclysm. Until a man called Bron chanced upon it in his wanderings, and was caught and entranced by its devastated beauty, and a vision of its resurrection. To Tyr he had fled once he had recovered a little from his sickness after the death of Ba'alekkt: and the pure air, the peace, the utter loneliness, had finally healed him. And, returned to health, he had begun to build, using his powers to the limit to place stone on stone, to lift beams and fix tiles and restore, house by house, tower by tower, the lost city of Tyr to its age-old glory.

Now, its stones glow the colour of honey in the last rays of the sun, and it lies on its island at the union of the rivers like a hoard of gold, a treasure beyond compare: and Mallaso feels her eyes fill with tears at the sight.

'Someone is coming to meet us,' says Kazhian beside her. And although he is smiling, she senses that he, too, is overwhelmed by the beauty and wonder of what Bron has created. But although Kazhian used only his bare hands when he laboured to rebuild Ammenna's house for her, more than ten years ago, he is no less beloved because he cannot command such wonders as these. Love and warmth and above all laughter and happiness are the gifts he has brought to her, and beside such delights, all the sorcery in the world seems of little importance.

'Who is it?' she asks, shading her eyes, although the slight, bareheaded figure walking up the hill towards them is suddenly and sharply familiar.

Kiyu gives the answer. With a whoop of joy she urges her horse down the hill at break-neck speed, as the rest of the party watches with a mixture of admiration and concern. She pulls the mare up in a flurry of dust, her hair flying, leaps from the saddle and flings herself into her father's arms.

Smiling, her family and friends stand watching for a little while longer. Then they, too, ride down to the golden city, the city of dreams, the city of Tyr.

All Pan Books are available at your local bookshop or newsagent, or can be ordered direct from the publisher. Indicate the number of copies required and fill in the form below.

Send to: Macmillan General Books C.S.
           Book Service By Post
           PO Box 29, Douglas I-O-M
           IM99 1BQ

or phone: 01624 675137, quoting title, author and credit card number.

or fax: 01624 670923, quoting title, author, and credit card number.

or Internet: http://www.bookpost.co.uk

Please enclose a remittance* to the value of the cover price plus 75 pence per book for post and packing. Overseas customers please allow £1.00 per copy for post and packing.

*Payment may be made in sterling by UK personal cheque, Eurocheque, postal order, sterling draft or international money order, made payable to Book Service By Post.

Alternatively by Access/Visa/MasterCard

Card No.

Expiry Date

Signature _____

Applicable only in the UK and BFPO addresses.

While every effort is made to keep prices low, it is sometimes necessary to increase prices at short notice. Pan Books reserve the right to show on covers and charge new retail prices which may differ from those advertised in the text or elsewhere.

NAME AND ADDRESS IN BLOCK CAPITAL LETTERS PLEASE

Name _____

Address _____

_____

_____

_____

8/95

Please allow 28 days for delivery.
Please tick box if you do not wish to receive any additional information. ☐